D1107482

A TREASURY OF GREAT SCIENCE FICTION

A Treasury of GREAT SCIENCE FICTION

VOLUME TWO

Edited by Anthony Boucher

DOUBLEDAY & COMPANY, INC.
Garden City, New York

This book is for
PHYLLIS
as what is not?

All of the characters in this book are fictitious, and any resemblance to actual persons, living or dead, is purely coincidental.

CONTENTS

Volume Two

BRAIN WAVE
by Poul Anderson

CHAPTER ONE

THE TRAP HAD CLOSED at sundown. In the last red light, the rabbit had battered himself against its walls until fear and numbness ached home and he crouched shaken by the flutterings of his own heart. Otherwise there was no motion in him as night and the stars came. But when the moon rose, its light was caught icily in his great eyes, and he looked through shadows to the forest.

His vision was not made to focus closely, but after a while it fell on the entrance to the trap. It had snapped down on him when he entered, and then there had been only the flat bruising beat of himself against the wood. Now slowly, straining through the white unreal haze of moonlight, he recalled a memory of the gate falling, and he squeaked ever so faintly with terror. For the gate was there now, solid and sullen against the breathing forest, and yet it *had* been up and *had* come thunking down, and this now-then doubleness was something the rabbit had never known before.

The moon rose higher, swinging through a sky full of stars. An owl hooted, and the rabbit froze into movelessness as its wings ghosted overhead. There was fear and bewilderment and a new kind of pain in the owl's voice, too. Presently it was gone, and only the many little murmurs and smells of night were around him. And he sat for a long time looking at the gate and remembering how it had fallen.

The moon began to fall too, into a paling western heaven. Perhaps the rabbit wept a little, in his own way. A dawn which was as yet only a mist in the dark limned the bars of the trap against gray trees. And there was a crossbar low on the gate.

Slowly, very slowly, the rabbit inched across until he was at the entrance. He shrank from the thing which had clamped him in. It smelled of man. Then he nosed it, feeling dew cold and wet on his muzzle. It did not stir. But it had fallen down.

The rabbit crouched, bracing his shoulders against the crossbar. He strained then, heaving upward, and the wood shivered. The rabbit's breath came fast and sharp, whistling between his teeth, and he tried again. The gate moved upward in its grooves, and the rabbit bolted free.

For an instant he poised wildly. The sinking moon was a blind dazzle in his eyes. The gate smacked back into place, and he turned and fled.

Archie Brock had been out late grubbing stumps in the north forty. Mr. Rossman wanted them all pulled by Wednesday so he could get the plowing started in his new field, and promised Brock extra pay if he would see to it. So Brock took some dinner out with him and worked till it got too dark to see. Then he started walking the three miles home, because they didn't let him use the jeep or a truck.

He was tired without thinking of it, aching a little and wishing he had a nice tall beer. But mostly he didn't think at all, just picked them up and laid them down, and the road slid away behind him. There were dark woods on either side, throwing long shadows across the moon-whitened dust, and he heard the noise of crickets chirring and once there was an owl. Have to take a gun and get that owl before he swiped some chickens. Mr. Rossman didn't mind if Brock hunted.

It was funny the way he kept thinking things tonight. Usually he just went along, especially when he was as tired as now, but—maybe it was the moon—he kept remembering bits of things, and words sort of formed themselves in his head like someone was talking. He thought about his bed and how nice it would have been to drive home from work; only of course he got sort of mixed up when driving, and there'd been a couple of smashups. Funny he should have done that, because all at once it didn't seem so hard: just a few signals to learn, and you kept your eyes open, and that was all.

The sound of his feet was hollow on the road. He breathed deeply, drawing a cool night into his lungs, and looked upward, away from the moon. The stars were sure big and bright tonight.

Another memory came back to him, somebody had said the stars were like the sun only further away. It hadn't made much sense then. But maybe it was so, like a light was a small thing till you got up close and then maybe it was very big. Only if the stars were as big as the sun, they'd have to be awful far away.

He stopped dead, feeling a sudden cold run through him. Jesus God! How far *up* the stars were!

The earth seemed to fall away underfoot, he was hanging on to a tiny rock that spun crazily through an everlasting darkness, and the great stars burned and roared around him, so far up that he whimpered with knowing it.

He began to run.

The boy rose early, even if it was summer and no school and breakfast wouldn't be for a while yet. The street and the town outside his windows looked very clean and bright in the young sunshine. A single truck clattered down the road and a man in blue denim walked toward the creamery carrying a lunch pail, otherwise it was as if he had the whole world to himself. His father was already off to work, and Mom liked to go back to bed for an hour after fixing his breakfast, and Sis was still asleep, so the boy was all alone in the house.

His friend was coming over and they'd go fishing, but first he wanted to get some more done on his model plane. He washed as thoroughly as you could ask a ten-year-old to, snatched a roll from the pantry, and went back to his room and the littered table there. The plane was going to be a real beauty, a Shooting Star with a CO_2 cartridge to make a jet. Only somehow, this morning it didn't look as good as it had last night. He wished he could make a real jet motor for it.

He sighed, pushing the work away, and took a sheet of paper. He'd always liked to doodle around with numbers, and one of the teachers had taught him a little about algebra. Some of the fellows had called him teacher's pet for that, till he licked them, but it was real interesting, not just like learning multiplication tables. Here you made the numbers and letters do something. The teacher said that if he really wanted to build spaceships when he grew up, he'd have to learn lots of math.

He started drawing some graphs. The different kinds of equations made different pictures. It was fun to see how $x=ky+c$ made a straight line while $x^2+y_2=c$ was always a circle. Only how if you changed one of the x's, made it equal 3 instead of 2? What would happen to the y in the meantime? He'd never thought of that before!

He grasped the pencil tightly, his tongue sticking out of the corner of his mouth. You had to kind of sneak up on the x and the y, change one of them just a weeny little bit, and then——

He was well on the way to inventing differential calculus when his mother called him down to breakfast.

CHAPTER TWO

PETER CORINTH CAME OUT of the shower, still singing vigorously, to find Sheila busy frying bacon and eggs. He ruffled her soft brown hair up, kissing her on the neck, and she turned to smile at him.

"She looks like an angel and cooks like an angel," he said.

"Why, Pete," she answered, "you never——"

"Never could find words," he agreed. "But it's gospel truth, me love." He bent over the pan, inhaling the crisp odor with a contented sigh. "I have a hunch this is one of those days when everything will go right," he said. "A bit of *Hubris* for which the gods will doubtless visit a *Nemesis* on me. Ate: Gertie, the slut, will burn out a tube. But you'll amend it all."

"Hubris, Nemesis, Ate." A tiny frown creased her broad clear forehead. "You've used those words before, Pete. What do they mean?"

He blinked at her. Two years after marriage, he was still far gone in love with his wife, and as she stood there his heart turned over within him. She was kind and merry and beautiful and she could cook—but she was nothing of an intellectual, and when his friends came over she sat quietly back, taking no part in the conversation. "What do you care?" he asked.

"I was just wondering," she said.

He went into the bedroom and began dressing, leaving the door open so he could explain the basis of Greek tragedy. It was much too bright a morning to dwell on so somber a theme, but she listened closely, with an occasional question. When he came out, she smiled and went over to him.

"You dear clumsy physicist," she said. "You're the only man I ever knew who could put on a suit straight from the cleaners and make it look like you've been fixing a car in it." She adjusted his tie and pulled down the rumpled coat. He ran a hand through his black hair, immediately reducing it to unkemptness, and followed her to the kitchenette table. A whiff of steam from the coffeepot fogged his horn-rimmed glasses, and he took them off and polished them on his necktie. His lean, broken-nosed face looked different without them—younger, perhaps only the thirty-three years which was his actual age.

"It came to me just when I woke up," he said as he buttered his toast. "I must have a well-trained subconscious after all."

"You mean the solution to your problem?" asked Sheila.

He nodded, too absorbed to consider what her query meant. She usually just let him run on, saying "yes" and "no" in the right places but not really listening. To her, his work was altogether mysterious. He had sometimes thought she lived in a child's world, with nothing very well known but all of it bright and strange.

"I've been trying to build a phase analyzer for intermolecular resonance bonds in crystal structure," he said. "Well, no matter. The thing is, I've been plugging along for the past few weeks, trying to design a circuit which would do what I wanted, and was baffled. Then I woke up just this morning with an idea that might work. Let's see——" His eyes looked beyond her and he ate without tasting. Sheila laughed, very softly.

"I may be late tonight," he said at the door. "If this new idea of mine pans out, I may not want to break off work till—Lord knows when. I'll call you."

"Okay, honey. Good hunting."

When he was gone, Sheila stood for a moment smiling after him. Pete was a—well, she was just lucky, that was all. She'd never really appreciated how lucky, but this morning seemed different, somehow. Everything stood out sharp and clear, as if she were up in the Western mountains her husband loved so well.

She hummed to herself as she washed the dishes and straightened up the apartment. Memory slid through her, the small-town Pennsylvania girlhood, the business college, her coming to New York four years ago to take a clerical job at the office of a family acquaintance. Dear God, but she had been unsuited for that kind of life! One party and boy friend after another, everybody fast-talking, jerky-moving, carefully hard-boiled and knowing, the expensive and market-wise crowd where she always had to be on her guard—— All right, she'd married Pete on the rebound, after Bill walked out calling her a stupid——never mind. But she'd always liked the shy, quiet man, and she had been on the rebound from a whole concept of living.

So I'm stodgy now, she told herself, *and glad of it, too.*

An ordinary housewifely existence, nothing more spectacular than a few friends in for beer and talk, going to church now and then while Pete, the agnostic, slept late; vacation trips in New England or the Rocky Mountains; plans of having a kid soon—who wanted more? Her friends before had always been ready for a good laugh at the shibboleth-ridden boredom which was bourgeois existence; but when you got right down to it, they had only traded one routine and one set of catchwords for another, and seemed to have lost something of reality into the bargain.

Sheila shook her head, puzzled. It wasn't like her to go daydreaming this way. Her thoughts even sounded different, somehow.

She finished the housework and looked about her. Normally she relaxed for a while before lunch with one of the pocket mysteries which were her prime vice; afterward there was some shopping to do, maybe a stroll in the park, maybe a visit to or from some woman friend, and then supper to fix and Pete to expect. But today——

She picked up the detective story she had planned to read. For a moment the bright cover rested between uncertain fingers, and she almost sat down with it. Then, shaking her head, she laid it back and went over to the crowded bookshelf, took out Pete's worn copy of *Lord Jim,* and returned to the armchair. Midafternoon came before she realized that she had forgotten all about lunch.

Corinth met Felix Mandelbaum in the elevator going down. They were that rare combination, neighbors in a New York apartment building who had become close friends. Sheila, with her small-town background, had insisted on getting to know everyone on their own floor at least, and Corinth had been glad of it in the case of the Mandelbaums. Sarah was a plump, quiet, retiring *Hausfrau* sort, pleasant but not colorful; her husband was a horse of quite another shade.

Felix Mandelbaum had been born fifty years ago in the noise and dirt and sweatshops of the lower East Side, and life had been kicking him around ever since; but he kicked back, with a huge enjoyment. He'd been everything from itinerant fruit picker to skilled machinist and O.S.S. operative overseas during the war—where his talent for languages and people must have come in handy. His career as a labor organizer ran parallel, from the old Wobblies to the comparative respectability of his present job: officially executive secretary of a local union, actually a roving trouble shooter with considerable voice in national councils. Not that he had been a radical since his twenties; he said he'd seen radicalism from the inside, and that was enough for any sane man. Indeed, he claimed to be one of the last true conservatives—only, to conserve, you had to prune and graft and adjust. He was self-educated, but widely read, with more capacity for life than anyone else of Corinth's circle except possibly Nat Lewis. Fun to know.

"Hello," said the physicist. "You're late today."

"Not exactly." Mandelbaum's voice was a harsh New York tone, fast and clipped. He was a small, wiry, gray-haired man, with a gnarled beaky face and intense dark eyes. "I woke up with an idea. A reorganization plan. Amazing nobody's thought of it yet. It'd halve the paper work. So I've been outlining a chart."

Corinth shook his head dolefully. "By now, Felix, you should know that Americans are too fond of paper work to give up one sheet," he said.

"You haven't seen Europeans," grunted Mandelbaum.

"You know," said Corinth, "it's funny you should've had your idea just today. (Remind me to get the details from you later, it sounds interesting.) I woke up with the solution to a problem that's been bedeviling me for the past month."

"Hm?" Mandelbaum pounced on the fact, you could almost see him turning it over in his hands, sniffing it, and laying it aside. "Odd." It was a dismissal.

The elevator stopped and they parted company. Corinth took the subway as usual. He was currently between cars; in this town, it just didn't pay to own one. He noticed vaguely that the train was quieter than ordinarily. People were less hurried and unmannerly, they seemed thoughtful. He glanced at the newspapers, wondering with a gulf if *it* had started, but there was nothing really sensational—except maybe for that local bit about a dog, kept overnight in a basement, which had somehow opened the deep freeze, dragged out the meat to thaw, and been found happily gorged. Otherwise: fighting here and there throughout the world, a strike, a Communist demonstration in Rome, four killed in an auto crash—words, as if rotary presses squeezed the blood from everything that went through them.

Emerging in lower Manhattan, he walked three blocks to the Rossman Institute, limping a trifle. The same accident which had broken his nose years ago had injured his right knee and kept him out of military service; though being yanked directly from his youthful college graduation into the Manhattan Project might have had something to do with that.

He winced at the trailing memory. Hiroshima and Nagasaki still lay heavily on his conscience. He had quit immediately after the war, and it was not only to resume his studies or to escape the red tape and probing and petty intrigue of government research for the underpaid sanity of academic life; it had been a flight from guilt. So had his later activities, he supposed—The Atomic Scientists, the United World Federalists, the Progressive Party. When he thought how those had withered away or been betrayed, and recalled the brave clichés which had stood like a shield between him and the Soviet snarl—there for any to see who had eyes—he wondered how sane the professors were after all.

Only, was his present retreat into pure research and political passivity—voting a discouraged Democratic ticket and doing nothing else—any more balanced? Nathan Lewis, frankly labeling himself a reactionary, was a local

Republican committeeman, an utter and cheerful pessimist who still tried to salvage something; and Felix Mandelbaum, no less realistic than his chess and bull-session opponent Lewis, had more hope and energy, even looked forward to the ultimate creation of a geniune American Labor Party. Between them, Corinth felt rather pallid.

And I'm younger than either one!

He sighed. What was the matter with him? Thoughts kept boiling up out of nowhere, forgotten things, linking themselves into new chains that rattled in his skull. And just when he had the answer to his problem, too.

That reflection drove all others out. Again, it was unusual: ordinarily he was slow to change any train of thought. He stepped forward with a renewed briskness.

The Rossman Institute was a bulk of stone and glass, filling half a block and looking almost shiny among its older neighbors. It was known as a scientist's heaven. Able men from all places and all disciplines were drawn there, less by the good pay than by the chance to do unhampered research of their own choosing, with first-rate equipment and none of the projectitis which was strangling pure science in government, in industry, and in too many universities. It had the inevitable politicking and backbiting, but in lesser degree than the average college; it was the Institute for Advanced Study—less abstruse and more energetic, perhaps, and certainly with much more room. Lewis had once cited it to Mandelbaum as proof of the cultural necessity for a privileged class. "D'you think any government would ever endow such a thing and then, what's more, have the sense to leave it to itself?"

"Brookhaven does all right," Mandelbaum had said, but for him it was a feeble answer.

Corinth nodded to the girl at the newsstand in the lobby, hailed a couple of acquaintances, and fumed at the slowness of the elevator. "Seventh," he said automatically when it arrived.

"I should know that, Dr. Corinth," grinned the operator. "You've been here—let's see—almost six years now, isn't it?"

The physicist blinked. The attendant had always been part of the machinery to him; they had exchanged the usual pleasantries, but it hadn't meant a thing. Suddenly Corinth saw him as a human being, a living and unique organism, part of an enormous impersonal web which ultimately became the entire universe, and yet bearing his own heart within him. *Now why,* he asked himself amazedly, *should I think that?*

"You know, sir," said the attendant, "I been wondering. I woke up this morning and wondered what I was doing this for and if I really wanted more out of it than just my job and my pension and——" He paused awkwardly as they stopped to let off a third-floor passenger. "I envy you. You're going somewhere."

The elevator reached the seventh floor. "You could—well, you could take a night course if you wanted," said Corinth.

"I think maybe I will, sir. If you'd be so kind as to recommend—— Well, later. I got to go now." The doors slid smoothly across the cage, and Corinth went down hard marble ways to his laboratory.

He had a permanent staff of two, Johansson and Grunewald, intense young men who probably dreamed of having labs of their own someday. They were already there when he entered and took off his coat.

"Good morning . . . 'Morning . . . 'Morning."

"I've been thinking, Pete," said Grunewald suddenly, as the chief went over to his desk. "I've got an idea for a circuit that may work——"

"*Et tu, Brute*," murmured Corinth. He sat down on a stool, doubling his long legs under him. "Let's have it."

Grunewald's gimmick seemed remarkably parallel to his own. Johansson, usually silent and competent and no more, chimed in eagerly as thoughts occurred to him. Corinth took over leadership in the discussion, and within half an hour they were covering paper with the esoteric symbols of electronics.

Rossman might not have been entirely disinterested in establishing the Institute, though a man with his bank account could afford altruism. Pure research helped industry. He had made his fortune in light metals, all the way from raw ores to finished products, with cross-connections to a dozen other businesses; officially semi-retired, he kept his fine thin hands on the strings. Even bacteriology could turn out to be useful—not very long ago, work had been done on bacteria extraction of oil from shales—and Corinth's study of crystal bonds could mean a good deal to metallurgy. Grunewald fairly gloated over the prospect of what success would do to their professional reputations. Before noon, they had set up a series of partial differential equations which would go to the computer at their regular scheduled time to use it, and were drawing up elements of the circuit they wanted.

The phone rang. It was Lewis, suggesting lunch together. "I'm on a hot trail today," said Corinth. "I thought maybe I'd just have some sandwiches sent up."

"Well, either I am too, or else I'm up you know what creek with no paddle," said Lewis. "I'm not sure which, and it might help me straighten out my ideas if I could bounce them off you."

"Oh, all right. Commissary do?"

"If you merely want to fill your belly, I suppose so." Lewis went in for three-hour lunches complete with wine and violins, a habit he had picked up during his years in pre-Anschluss Vienna. "One o'clock suit you? The peasantry will have gorged by then."

"Okay," Corinth hung up and lost himself again in the cool ecstasy of his work. It was one-thirty before he noticed the time, and he hurried off swearing.

Lewis was just seating himself at a table when Corinth brought his tray over. "I figured from your way of talk you'd be late," he said. "What'd you get? The usual cafeteria menu, I suppose: mice drowned in skim milk, fillet of sea urchin, baked chef's special, baked chef—well, no matter." He sipped his coffee and winced.

He didn't look delicate: a short square man of forty-eight, getting a little plump and bald, sharp eyes behind thick, rimless glasses. He was, indeed, a hearty soul at table or saloon. But eight years in Europe did change tastes, and he insisted that his postwar visits had been purely gastronomical.

"What you need," said Corinth with the smugness of a convert, "is to get married."

"I used to think so, when I began leaving my libertine days behind. But, well, never mind. Too late now." Lewis attacked a minute steak, which he always pronounced as if the adjective were synonymous with "tiny," and scowled through a mouthful. "I'm more interested in the histological aspect of biology just now."

"You said you were having trouble——"

"That's mostly with my assistants. Everybody seems jumpy today, and young Roberts is coming up with even wilder ideas than usual. But it's my work. I've told you, haven't I? I'm studying nerve cells—neurones. Trying to keep them alive in different artificial media, and seeing how their electrical properties vary with conditions. I have them in excised sections of tissue—Lindbergh-Carrel technique, with modifications. It was coming along pretty good—and then today, when we ran a routine check, the results came out different. So I tested them all—— Every one is changed!"

"Hm?" Corinth raised his eyebrows and chewed quietly for a minute. "Something wrong with your apparatus?"

"Not that I can find. Nothing different—except the cells themselves. A small but significant shift." Lewis' tones came faster, with a hint of rising excitement. "You know how a neurone works? Like a digital computer. It's stimulated by a—a stimulus, fires a signal, and is thereafter inactive for a short time. The next neurone in the nerve gets the signal, and is thereafter inactive for a short time. The next neurone in the nerve gets the signal, fires, and is also briefly inactivated. Well, it turns out that everything is screwy today. The inactivation time is a good many microseconds less, the—well, let's just say the whole system reacts significantly faster than normally. And the signals are also more intense."

Corinth digested the information briefly, then, slowly: "Looks like you may have stumbled onto something big."

"Well, where's the cause? The medium, the apparatus, it's all the same as yesterday, I tell you. I'm going nuts trying to find out if I've got a potential Nobel Prize or just sloppy technique!"

Very slowly, as if his mind were shying away from a dimly seen realization, Corinth said: "It's odd this should have happened today."

"Hm?" Lewis glanced sharply up, and Corinth related his own encounters.

"Very odd," agreed the biologist. "And no big thunderstorms lately—ozone stimulates the mind—but my cultures are sealed in glass anyway——" Something flashed in his eyes.

Corinth looked around. "Hullo, there's Helga. Wonder what made her so late? Hi, there!" He stood up, waving across the room, and Helga Arnulfsen bore her tray over to their table and sat down.

She was a tall, rangy, handsome woman, her long blonde hair drawn tightly around the poised head, but something in her manner—an impersonal energy, an aloofness, perhaps only the unfeminine crispness of speech and dress—made her less attractive than she could have been. She'd changed since the old days, right after the war, thought Corinth. He'd been taking his doctorate at Minnesota, where she was studying journalism, and they'd had fun together; though he'd been too much and too hopelessly in love with his work and another girl to think seriously about her. Afterward they had corresponded, and he had gotten her a secretarial post at the Institute, two years before. She was chief administrative assistant now, and did a good job of it.

"Whew! What a day!" She ran a strong slim hand across her hair, sleeking it down, and smiled wearily at them. "Everybody and his Uncle Oscar is having trouble, and all of them are wishing it on me. Gertie threw a tantrum——"

"Huh?" Corinth regarded her in some dismay. He'd been counting on the big computer to solve his equations that day. "What's wrong?"

"Only God and Gertie know, and neither one is telling. Allanbee ran a routine test this morning, and it came out wrong. Not much, but enough to throw off anybody that needed precise answers. He's been digging into her ever since, trying to find the trouble, so far without luck. And I have to reschedule everybody!"

"Very strange," murmured Lewis.

"Then different instruments, especially in the physics and chemistry sections, are a little crazy. Murchison's polarimeter has an error of—oh, something horrible like one tenth of one per cent, I don't know."

"Izzat so?" Lewis leaned forward, thrusting his jaw out above the dishes. "Maybe it's not my neurones but my instruments that're off whack—— No, can't be. Not that much. It must be something in the cells themselves—but how can I measure that if the gadgets are all awry?" He broke into vigorous German profanity, though his eyes remained alight.

"Lots of the boys have come up with brave new projects all at once, too," went on Helga. "They want immediate use of things like the big centrifuge, and blow their tops when I tell them to wait their turn."

"All today, eh?" Corinth pushed his dessert aside and took out a cigarette. "'Curiouser and curiouser,' said Alice." His eyes widened, and the hand that struck a match shook ever so faintly. "Nat, I wonder——"

"A general phenomenon?" Lewis nodded, holding excitement in check with an effort. "Could be, could be. We'd certainly better find out."

"What're you talking about?" asked Helga.

"Things." Corinth explained while she finished eating. Lewis sat quietly back, blowing cigar fumes and withdrawn into himself.

"Hm." Helga tapped the table with a long, unpainted fingernail. "Sounds—interesting. Are all nerve cells, including those in our own brains, suddenly being speeded up?"

"It's more basic than that," said Corinth. "Something may have happened to—what? Electrochemical phenomena? How should I know? Let's not go off the deep end till we've investigated this."

"Yeah. I'll leave it to you." Helga took out a cigarette for herself and inhaled deeply. "I can think of a few obvious things to check up on—but it's your child." She turned again to smile at Corinth, the gentle smile she saved for a very few. "Apropos, how's Sheila?"

"Oh, fine, fine. How's yourself?"

"I'm okay." There was a listlessness in her answer.

"You must come over to our place sometime for dinner." It was a small strain to carry on polite conversation, when his mind was yelling to be at this new problem. "We haven't seen you in quite a while. Bring the new boy friend if you want, whoever he is."

"Jim? Oh, him. I gave him the sack last week. But I'll come over, sure." She got up. "Back to the oars, mates. See you."

Corinth regarded her as she strode toward the cashier's desk. Almost in spite of himself—his thoughts were shooting off in all directions today—he murmured: "I wonder why she can't keep a man. She's good-looking and intelligent enough."

"She doesn't want to," said Lewis shortly.

"No, I suppose not. She's turned cold since I knew her in Minneapolis. Why?"

Lewis shrugged.

"I think you know," said Corinth. "You've always understood women better than you had any right to. And she likes you better than anyone else around here, I think."

"We both go for music," said Lewis. It was his opinion that none had been written since 1900. "And we both know how to keep our mouths shut."

"Okay, okay," laughed Corinth. He got up. "I'm for the lab again. Hate to scrap the phase analyzer, but this new business——" Pausing: "Look, let's get hold of the others and divide up the labor, huh? Everybody check something. It won't take long then."

Lewis nodded curtly and followed him out.

By evening the results were in. As Corinth looked at the figures, his interest lost way to a coldness rising within him. He felt suddenly how small and helpless a thing he was.

Electromagnetic phenomena were changed.

It wasn't much, but the very fact that the supposedly eternal constants of nature had shifted was enough to crash a hundred philosophies into dust. The subtlety of the problem held something elemental. How do you remeasure the basic factors when your measuring devices have themselves changed?

Well, there were ways. There are no absolutes in this universe, everything exists in relation to everything else, and it was the fact that certain data had altered relatively to others which was significant.

Corinth had been working on the determination of electrical constants. For the metals they were the same, or nearly the same, as before, but the resistivity and permittivity of insulators had changed measurably—they had become slightly better conductors.

Except in the precision apparatus, such as Gertie the computer, the change in electromagnetic characteristics was not enough to make any noticeable difference. But the most complex and delicately balanced mechanism known to man is the living cell; and the neurone is the most highly evolved and specialized of all cells—particularly that variety of neurones found in the human cerebral cortex. And here the change was felt. The minute electrical impulses which represented neural functioning—sense awareness, motor reaction, thought itself—were flowing more rapidly, more intensely.

And the change might just have begun.

Helga shivered. "I need a drink," she said. "Bad."

"I know a bar," said Lewis. "I'll join you in one before coming back to work some more. How about you, Pete?"

"I'm going home," said the physicist. "Have fun." His words were flat.

He walked out, hardly aware of the darkened lobby and the late hour. To the others, this was still something bright and new and wonderful; but he couldn't keep from thinking that perhaps, in one huge careless swipe, the universe was about to snuff out all the race of man. What would the effect be on a living body——?

Well, they'd done about all they could for now. They'd checked as much as possible. Helga had gotten in touch with the Bureau of Standards in Washington and notified them. She gathered, from what the man there said, that a few laboratories, spotted throughout the country, had also reported anomalies. *Tomorrow*, thought Corinth, *they'll really start hearing about it.*

Outside—the scene was still New York at evening—hardly changed, perhaps just a little quieter than it should be. He bought a newspaper at the corner and glanced at it as he stood there. Was he wrong, or had a subtle difference crept in, a more literate phrasing, something individual that broke through the copyreader's barriers because the copyreader himself had changed without knowing it? But there was no mention of the great cause, that was too big and too new yet, nor had the old story altered—war, unrest, suspicion, fear and hate and greed, a sick world crumbling.

He was suddenly aware that he had read through the *Times'* crowded page in about ten minutes. He shoved the newspaper into a pocket and hastened toward the subway.

CHAPTER THREE

THERE WAS TROUBLE EVERYWHERE. An indignant yell in the morning brought Archie Brock running to the chicken house, where Stan Wilmer had set down a bucket of feed to shake his fist at the world.

"Look a' that!" he cried. "Just look!"

Brock craned his neck through the door and whistled. The place was a mess. A couple of bloody-feathered corpses were sprawled on the straw, a few other hens cackled nervously on the roosts, and that was all. The rest were gone.

"Looks like foxes got in when somebody left the door open," said Brock.

"Yeah." Wilmer swallowed his rage in a noisy gulp. "Some stinking son of a——"

Brock remembered that Wilmer was in charge of the hen house, but decided not to mention it. The other man recalled it himself and paused, scowling.

"I don't know," he said slowly. "I checked the place last night as usual, before going to bed, and I'll swear the door was closed and hooked like it always is. Five years I been here and never had any trouble."

"So maybe somebody opened the door later on, after dark, huh?"

"Yeah. A chicken thief. Though it's funny the dogs didn't bark—I never heard of any human being coming here without them yapping." Wilmer shrugged bitterly. "Well, anyway, somebody did open the door."

"And then later on foxes got in." Brock turned one of the dead hens over with his toe. "And maybe had to run for it when one of the dogs came sniffing around, and left these."

"And most of the birds wandered out into the woods. It'll take a week to catch 'em—all that live. Oh, Judas!" Wilmer stormed out of the chicken house, forgetting to close the door. Brock did it for him, vaguely surprised that he had remembered to do so.

He sighed and resumed his morning chores. The animals all seemed fidgety today. And damn if his own head didn't feel funny. He remembered his own panic of two nights before, and the odd way he'd been thinking ever since. Maybe there was some kind of fever going around.

Well—he'd ask somebody about it later. There was work to do today, plowing in the north forty that had just been cleared. All the tractors were busy cultivating, so he'd have to take a team of horses.

That was all right. Brock liked animals, he had always understood them and got along with them better than with people. Not that the people had been mean to him, anyway for a long while now. The kids used to tease him, back when he was a kid too, and then later there'd been some trouble with cars, and a couple of girls had got scared also and he'd been beaten up by the brother of one of them. But that was years back. Mr. Rossman had told him carefully what he could do and could not do, kind of taken him over, and things had been all right since then. Now he could walk into the tavern when he was in town and have a beer like anybody else, and the men said hello.

He stood for a minute, wondering why he should be thinking about this when he knew it so well, and why it should hurt him the way it did. *I'm all right,* he thought. *I'm not so smart, maybe, but I'm strong. Mr. Rossman says he ain't got a better farm hand nor me.*

He shrugged and entered the barn to get out the horses. He was a young man, of medium height but heavy-set and muscular, with coarse strong features and a round, crew-cut, red-haired head. His blue denim clothes were shabby but clean; Mrs. Bergen, the wife of the general superintendent in whose cottage he had a room, looked after such details for him.

The barn was big and gloomy, full of the strong rich smells of hay and horses. The brawny Percherons stamped and snorted, restless as he harnessed them. Funny—they were always so calm before. "So, so, steady, boy. Steady, Tom. Whoa, there, Jerry. Easy, easy." They quieted a little and he led them out and hitched them to a post while he went into the shed after the plow.

His dog Joe came frisking around him, a tall Irish setter whose coat was like gold and copper in the sun. Joe was really Mr. Rossman's, of course, but Brock had taken care of him since he was a pup and it was always Brock whom he followed and loved. "Down, boy, down. What the hell's got into yuh, anyway? Take it easy, will yuh?"

The estate lay green around him, the farm buildings on one side, the cottages of the help screened off by trees on another, the many acres of woods behind. There was a lot of lawn and orchard and garden between this farming part and the big white house of the owner, a house which had been mostly empty since Mr. Rossman's daughters had married and his wife had died. He was there now, though, spending a few weeks here in upper New York State with his flowers. Brock wondered why a millionaire like Mr. Rossman wanted to putter around growing roses, even if he was getting old.

The shed door creaked open and Brock went in and took the big plow and wheeled it out, grunting a little with the effort. Not many men could drag it out themselves, he thought with a flicker of pride. He chuckled as he saw how the horses stamped at the sight. Horses were lazy beasts, they'd never work if they could get out of it.

He shoved the plow around behind them, carried the tongue forward, and hitched it on. With a deft motion, he twirled the reins loose from the post, took his seat, and shook the lines across the broad rumps. "Giddap!"

They just stood, moving their feet.

"Giddap there, I say!"

Tom began backing. "Whoa! Whoa!" Brock took the loose ends of the reins and snapped it with whistling force. Tom grunted and put one huge hoof on the tongue. It broke across.

For a long moment, Brock sat there, finding no words. Then he shook his red head. "It's a ac-ci-dent," he said aloud. The morning seemed very quiet all of a sudden. "It's a ac-ci-dent."

There was a spare tongue in the shed. He fetched it and some tools, and began doggedly removing the broken one.

"Hi, there! Stop! Stop, I say!"

Brock looked up. The squealing and grunting were like a blow. He saw a black streak go by, and then another and another— The pigs were loose!

"Joe!" he yelled, even then wondering a little at how quickly he reacted. "Go get 'em, Joe! Round 'em up, boy!"

The dog was off like burnished lightning. He got ahead of the lead sow and snapped at her. She grunted, turning aside, and he darted after the next. Stan Wilmer came running from the direction of the pen. His face was white.

Brock ran to intercept another pig, turning it, but a fourth one slipped aside and was lost in the woods. It took several confused minutes to chase the majority back into the pen; a number were gone.

Wilmer stood gasping. His voice was raw. "I saw it," he groaned. "Oh, my God, I saw it. It ain't possible."

Brock blew out his cheeks and wiped his face.

"You hear me?" Wilmer grasped his arm. "I saw it, I tell you, I saw it with my own eyes. Those pigs opened the gate themselves."

"Naw!" Brock felt his mouth falling open.

"I tell you, I saw it! One of 'em stood up on her hind legs and nosed the latch up. She did it all by herself. And the others were crowding right behind her. Oh, no, no, no!"

Joe came out of the woods, driving a pig before him with sardonic barks. She seemed to give up after a minute and trotted quietly toward the pen. Wilmer turned like a machine and opened the gate again and let her go in.

"Good boy!" Brock patted the silken head that nuzzled against him. "Smart dog!"

"Too God damned smart." Wilmer narrowed his eyes. "Did a dog ever make like that before?"

"Sure," said Brock uncertainly.

Joe got off his haunches and went back into the woods.

"I'll bet he's going after another pig." There was a kind of horror in Wilmer's voice.

"Sure. He's a smart dog, he is."

"I'm going to see Bill Bergen about this." Wilmer turned on his heel. Brock looked after him, shrugged heavy shoulders, and went back to his own task. By the time he finished it, Joe had rounded up two more pigs and brought them back, and was mounting guard at the gate of the pen.

"Good fellow," said Brock. "I'll see yuh get a bone for this." He hitched Tom and Jerry, who had been standing at their ease. "All right, yuh bums, let's go. Giddap!"

Slowly, the horses backed. "Hey!" screamed Brock.

This time they didn't stop with the tongue. Very carefully, they walked onto the plow itself and bent its iron frame with their weight and broke off the coulter. Brock felt his throat dry.

"No," he mumbled.

Wilmer nearly had a fit when he learned about the horses. Bergen only stood there, whistling tunelessly. "I don't know." He scratched his sandy head. "Tell you what. We'll call off all work having to do with animals, except feeding and milking, of course. Padlock every gate and have somebody check all our fence lines. I'll see the old man about this."

"Me, I'm gonna carry a gun," said Wilmer.

"Well, it might not be a bad idea," said Bergen.

Archie Brock was assigned to look at one section, a four-mile line enclosing the woods. He took Joe, who gamboled merrily in his wake, and went off glad to be alone for a change.

How still the forest was! Sunlight slanted down through green unstirring leaves, throwing a dapple on the warm brown shadows. The sky was utterly blue overhead, no clouds, no wind. His feet scrunched dully on an occasional clod or stone, he brushed against a twig and it scratched faintly along his clothes, otherwise the land was altogether silent. The birds seemed to have quieted down all at once, no squirrels were in sight, even the sheep had withdrawn into the inner woods. He thought uneasily that somehow the whole green world had a waiting feel to it.

Like before a storm, maybe?

He could see how people would be scared if the animals started getting smarter. If they were really smart, would they keep on letting humans lock them up and work them and castrate them and kill and skin and eat them? Suppose Tom and Jerry, now—— But they were so gentle!

And—wait—weren't the people getting smarter too? It seemed like in the last couple of days they'd been talking more, and it wasn't all about the weather and the neighbors either, it was about things like who was going to win the next election and why a rear-engine drive was better in a car. They'd always talked like that now and then, sure, but not so much, and they hadn't had so much to say, either. Even Mrs. Bergen, he'd seen her reading a magazine, and all she ever did before in her spare time was watch TV.

I'm getting smarter too!

The knowledge was like a thunderclap. He stood there for a long while, not moving, and Joe came up and sniffed his hand in a puzzled way.

I'm getting smarter.

Sure—it had to be. The way he'd been wondering lately, and remembering things, and speaking out when he'd never said anything much before—what else could it be? All the world was getting smarter.

I can read, he told himself. *Not very good, but they did teach me the alpha-bet, and I can read a comic book. Maybe I can read a real book now.*

Books had the answers to what he was suddenly wondering about, things like the sun and moon and stars, why there was winter and summer, why they had wars and Presidents and who lived on the other side of the world and——

He shook his head, unable to grasp the wilderness that rose up inside him and spread till it covered creation further than he could see. He'd never wondered before. Things just happened, and were forgotten again. *But*— He looked at his hands, marveling. *Who am I? What am I doing here?*

There was a boiling in him. He leaned his head against the cool trunk of a tree, listening to the blood roar in his ears. *Please, God, let it be real. Please make me like other people.*

After a while he fought it down and went on, checking the fence as he had been told.

In the evening, after chores, he put on a clean suit and went up to the big house. Mr. Rossman was sitting on the porch, smoking a pipe and turning the pages of a book over in his thin fingers, not really seeing it. Brock paused timidly, cap in hand, till the owner looked up and spied him.

"Oh, hello, Archie," he said in his soft voice. "How are you tonight?"

"I'm all right, thank you." Brock twisted the cap between his stumpy hands and shifted from one foot to another. "Please, can I see you for a minute?"

"Why, of course. Come on in." Mr. Rossman laid his book aside and sat smoking while Brock opened the screen door and walked over to him. "Here, take a chair."

"That's all right, thanks. I——" Brock ran his tongue across dry lips. "I'd just like to ask you 'bout something."

"Ask away, Archie." Mr. Rossman leaned back. He was a tall spare man, his face thinly carved, proud under its kindness of the moment, his hair white. Brock's parents had been tenants of his, and when it became plain that their son would never amount to anything, he had taken charge of the boy. "Everything okay?"

"Well, it's about, uh, about this change here."

"Eh?" Rossman's gaze sharpened. "What change?"

"You know. The animals getting smart and uppity."

"Oh, yes. That." Rossman blew a cloud of smoke. "Tell me, Archie, have you noticed any change in yourself?"

"Yes, I, uh, well, I think maybe I have."

Rossman nodded. "You wouldn't have come here if you hadn't changed."

"What's happening, Mr. Rossman? What's gone wrong?"

"I don't know, Archie. Nobody knows." The old man looked out into a gathering blue twilight. "Are you so sure it's wrong, though? Maybe something is finally going right."

"You don't know——"

"No. Nobody knows." Rossman's pale blue-veined hand slapped the newspaper on the table beside him. "There are hints here. The knowledge is creeping out. I'm sure much more is known, but the government has suppressed the information for fear of a panic." He grinned with a certain viciousness. "As if a world-wide phenomenon could be kept secret! But they'll hang on to their stupidity to the very end in Washington."

"But, Mr. Rossman——" Brock lifted his hands and let them fall again. "What can we do?"

"Wait. Wait and see. I'm going to the city soon, to find out for myself—those pet brains of mine at the Institute should——"

"You're leaving?"

Rossman shook his head, smiling. "Poor Archie. There's a horror in being helpless, isn't there? I sometimes think that's why men fear death—not because of oblivion, but because it's foredoomed, there's nothing they can do to stop it. Even fatalism is a refuge from that, in a way—— But I digress, don't I?"

He sat smoking for a long while. The summer dusk chirred and murmured around them. "Yes," he said at last, "I feel it in myself too. And it's not altogether pleasant. Not just the nervousness and the nightmares—that's merely physiological, I suppose—but the thoughts. I've always imagined myself as a quick, capable, logical thinker. Now something is coming to life within me that I don't understand at all. Sometimes my whole life seems to have been a petty and meaningless scramble. And yet I thought I'd served my family and my country well." He smiled once more. "I do hope I'll see the end of this, though. It should be interesting!"

Tears stung Brock's eyes. "What can I do?"

"Do? Live. Live from day to day. What else can a man do?" Rossman got up and put his hand on Brock's shoulder. "But keep on thinking. Keep your thinking close to the ground, where it belongs. Don't ever trade your liberty for another man's offer to do your thinking and make your mistakes for you. I had to play the feudal lord with you, Archie, but it may be that that's no longer necessary."

Brock didn't understand most of it. But it seemed Mr. Rossman was telling him to be cheerful, that this wasn't such a bad thing after all. "I thought maybe I could borrow some books," he said humbly. "I'd like to see if I can read them now."

"Why, of course, Archie. Come on into the library. I'll see if I can find something suitable for you to begin on——"

CHAPTER FOUR

Selections from the New York *Times*, June 23:

PRESIDENT DENIES DANGER IN BRAIN SPEEDUP

'Keep Cool, Stay on Job,' Advises White House—No Harm To Humans in Change

U. S. Scientists Working On Problem—Expect Answer Soon

FALLING STOCK MARKET WORRIES WALL STREET

Declining Sales Bring Down Stock Market and Prices

U. S. In Danger of Recession, Says Economist

CHINESE TROOPS MUTINY

Communist Government Declares Emergency

NEW RELIGION FOUNDED IN LOS ANGELES

Sawyer Proclaims Self 'The Third Ba'al' —Thousands Attend Mass Meeting

FESSENDEN CALLS FOR WORLD GOVERNMENT

Iowa Isolationist Reverses Stand in Senate Speech

JOHNSON SAYS WORLD GOVERNMENT IMPRACTICAL AT PRESENT TIME

Oregon Senator Reverses Former Stand

REBELLION IN UPSTATE HOME FOR FEEBLE-MINDED

RIOT IN ALABAMA

Conference.

Everybody was working late, and it was ten o'clock before the meeting which Corinth had invited to his place was ready. Sheila had insisted on putting out her usual buffet of sandwiches and coffee; afterward she sat in a corner, talking quietly with Sarah Mandelbaum. Their eyes strayed occasionally to their husbands, who were playing chess, and there was a creeping fear in the gaze.

Corinth was playing better than he had ever done before. Usually he and Mandelbaum were pretty evenly matched, the physicist's slow careful strategy offsetting the unionist's nerve-racking bravura. But tonight the younger man was too distracted. He made schemes that would have delighted Capablanca, but Mandelbaum saw through them and slashed barbarically past his defenses. Corinth sighed at last and leaned back.

"I resign," he said. "It'd be mate in, uh, seven moves."

"Not so." Mandelbaum pointed a gnarled finger at king's bishop. "If you moved him over here, and then——"

"Oh, yes, you're right. No matter. I'm just not in the mood. What's keeping Nat?"

"He'll be along. Take it easy." Mandelbaum removed himself to an armchair and began stuffing a big-bowled pipe.

"I don't see how you can sit there like that when——"

"When a world's falling to pieces around my ears? Look, Pete, it's been falling apart as long as I can remember. So far, in this particular episode, no guns have come out."

"They may do so yet." Corinth got up and stood looking out the window, hands crossed behind his back and shoulders slumped. The restless glimmer of city light etched him against darkness. "Don't you see, Felix, this new factor—if we survive it at all—changes the whole basis of human life? Our society was built by and for one sort of man. Now man himself is becoming something else."

"I doubt it." The noise of a match, struck against Mandelbaum's shoe, was startlingly loud. "We're still the same old animal."

"What was your I.Q. before the change?"

"I don't know."

"Never took a test?"

"Oh, sure, they made me take one now and then, to get this or that job, but I never asked for the result. What's I.Q. except the score on an I.Q. test?"

"It's more than that. It measures the ability to handle data, grasp and create abstractions——"

"*If* you're a Caucasian of West European-American cultural background. That's who the test was designed for, Pete. A Kalahari bushman would laugh if he knew it omitted water-finding ability. That's more important to him than the ability to juggle numbers. Me, I don't underrate the logic and visualization aspect of personality, but I don't have your touching faith in it, either. There's more to a man than that, and a garage mechanic may be a better survivor type than a mathematician."

"Survivor—under what conditions?"

"Any conditions. Adaptability, toughness, quickness—those are the things that count most."

"I think kindness means a lot," said Sheila timidly.

"It's a luxury, I'm afraid, though of course it's such luxuries that make us human," said Mandelbaum. "Kindness to whom? Sometimes you just have to cut loose and get violent. Some wars are necessary."

"They wouldn't be, if people had more intelligence," said Corinth. "We needn't have fought World War II if Hitler had been stopped when he entered the Rhineland. One division could have bowled him over. But the politicians were too stupid to foresee——"

"No," said Mandelbaum. "It's just that there were reasons why it wasn't —convenient, shall we say?—to call up that division. And ninety-nine per cent of the human race, no matter how smart they are, will do the convenient thing instead of the wise thing, and kid themselves into thinking they can somehow escape the consequences. We're just built that way. And then, the world is so full of old hate and superstition, and so many people are nice and tolerant and practical about it, that it's a wonder hell hasn't boiled over more often throughout history." Bitterness edged his voice. "Maybe the practical people, the ones who adapt, are right after all. Maybe the most moral thing really is to put 'myself, my wife, and my little Hassan with the bandy legs' first. Like one of my sons has done. He's in Chicago now. Changed his name and had his nose bobbed. He's not ashamed of his parents, no, but he's saved himself and his family a lot of trouble and humiliation. And I honestly don't know whether to admire him for tough-minded adaptability, or call him a spineless whelp."

"We're getting rather far from the point," said Corinth, embarrassed. "What we want to do tonight is try and estimate what we, the whole world, are in for." He shook his head. "My I.Q. has gone from its former 160 to about 200 in a week. I'm thinking things that never occurred to me before. My former professional problems are becoming ridiculously easy. Only, everything else is confused. My mind keeps wandering off into the most fantastic trains of thought, some of them pretty wild and morbid. I'm nervous as a kitten, jump at shadows, afraid for no good reason at all. Now and then I get flashes where everything seems grotesque—like in a nightmare."

"You're not adjusted to your new brain yet, that's all," said Sarah.

"I feel the same sort of things Pete does," said Sheila. Her voice was thin and scared. "It isn't worth it."

The other woman shrugged, spreading her hands. "Me, I think it's kind of fun."

"Matter of basic personality—which has not changed," said Mandelbaum. "Sarah's always been a pretty down-to-earth sort. You just don't take your new mind seriously, Liebchen. To you, the power of abstract thought is a toy. It's got little to do with the serious matters of housework." He puffed, meshing his face into wrinkles as he squinted through the smoke. "And me, I get crazy spells like you do, Pete, but I don't let it bother me. It's only physiological, and I haven't time for such fumblydiddles. Not the way things are now. Everybody in the union seems to have come up with some crank notion of how we ought to run things. A guy in the electrical workers has a notion that the electricians ought to go on strike and take over the whole government! Somebody even fired a shotgun at me the other day."

"Huh?" They stared at him.

Mandelbaum shrugged. "He was a lousy shot. But some people are turning crank, and some are turning mean, and most are just plain scared. Those like me who're trying to ride out the storm and keep things as nearly normal as possible, are bound to make enemies. People think a lot more today, but they aren't thinking straight."

"Sure," said Corinth. "The average man——" He started as the doorbell rang. "That must be them now," he said. "Come in."

Helga Arnulfsen entered, her slim height briefly concealing Nathan Lewis' bulk. She looked as cool and smooth and hard as before, but there were shadows under her eyes. "Hullo," she said tonelessly.

"No fun, huh?" asked Sheila with sympathy.

Helga grimaced. "Nightmares."

"Me too." A shudder ran along Sheila's small form.

"How about the psych man you were going to bring, Nat?" asked Corinth.

"He refused at the last minute," said Lewis. "Had some kind of idea for a new intelligence test. And his partner was too busy putting rats through mazes. Never mind, we don't really need them." Alone of them all, he seemed without worry and foreboding, too busy reaching for the sudden new horizon to consider his own troubles. He wandered over to the buffet and picked up a sandwich and bit into it. "Mmmmm—*delikat*. Sheila, why don't you ditch this long drink of water and marry me?"

"Trade him for a long drink of beer?" she smiled tremulously.

"*Touché!* You've changed too, haven't you? But really, you ought to have done better by me. A long drink of Scotch, at the very least."

"After all," said Corinth gloomily, "it's not as if we were here for any special purpose. I just thought a general discussion would clarify the matter in all our minds and maybe give us some ideas."

Lewis settled himself at the table. "I see the government has finally admitted something is going on," he said, nodding at the newspaper which lay beside him. "They had to do it, I suppose, but the admission won't help the panics any. People are afraid, they don't know what to expect, and—well, coming over here, I saw a man run screaming down the street yelling that the end of the world had come. There was a monster-sized revival in Central Park. Three drunks were brawling outside a bar, and not a cop in sight to stop them. I heard fire sirens—big blaze somewhere out Queens way."

Helga lit a cigarette, sucking in her cheeks and half closing her eyes. "John Rossman's in Washington now," she said. After a moment she added to the Mandelbaums: "He came to the Institute a few days back, asked our bright boys to investigate this business but keep their findings confidential, and flew to the capital. With his pull, he'll get the whole story for us if anyone can."

"I don't think there is much of a story yet, to tell the truth," said Mandelbaum. "Just little things like we've all been experiencing, all over the world. They add up to a big upheaval, yes, but there's no over-all picture."

"Just you wait," said Lewis cheerfully. He took another sandwich and a cup of coffee. "I predict that within about one week, things are going to start going to hell in a handbasket."

"The fact is——" Corinth got out of the chair into which he had flopped and began pacing the room. "The fact is, that the change isn't over. It's still going on. As far as our best instruments can tell—though they're not too exact, what with our instruments being affected themselves—the change is even accelerating."

"Within the limits of error, I think I see a more or less hyperbolic advance," said Lewis. "We've just begun, brethren. The way we're going, we'll all have I.Q.'s in the neighborhood of 400 within another week."

They sat for a long while, not speaking. Corinth stood with his fists clenched, hanging loose at his sides, and Sheila gave a little wordless cry and ran over to him and hung on his arm. Mandelbaum blew clouds of smoke, scowling as he digested the information; one hand stole out to caress Sarah's, and she squeezed it gratefully. Lewis grinned around his sandwich and went on eating. Helga sat without motion, the long clean curves of her face gone utterly expressionless. The city banged faintly below them, around them.

"What's going to happen?" breathed Sheila at last. She trembled so they could see it. "What's going to happen to us?"

"Christ alone knows," said Lewis, not without gentleness.

"Will it go on building up forever?" asked Sarah.

"Nope," said Lewis. "Can't. It's a matter of neurone chains increasing their speed of reaction, and the intensity of the signals they carry. The physical structure of the cell can take only so much. If they're stimulated too far—insanity, followed by idiocy, followed by death."

"How high can we go?" asked Mandelbaum practically.

"Can't say. The mechanism of the change—and of the nerve cell itself—just isn't known well enough. Anyway, the I.Q. concept is only valid within a limited range; to speak of an I.Q. of 400 really doesn't make sense, intelligence on that level may not be intelligence at all as we know it now, but something else."

Corinth had been too busy with his own work of physical measurements to realize how much Lewis' department knew and theorized. The appalling knowledge was only beginning to grow in him.

"Forget the final results," said Helga sharply. "There's nothing we can do about that. What's important right now is: how do we keep organized civilization going? How do we eat?"

Corinth nodded, mastering the surge of his panic. "Sheer social inertia has carried us along so far," he agreed. "Most people continue in their daily rounds because there's nothing else available. But when things really start changing——"

"The janitor and the elevator man at the Institute quit yesterday," said Helga. "Said the work was too monotonous. What happens when all the janitors and garbage men and ditchdiggers and assembly-line workers decide to quit?"

"They won't all do it," said Mandelbaum. He knocked out his pipe and went over to get some coffee. "Some will be afraid, some will have the sense to see we've got to keep going, some—well, there's no simple answer to this. I agree we're in for a rough period of transition at the very least—people throwing up their jobs, people getting scared, people going crazy in one way or another. What we need is a local interim organization to see us through the next few months. I think the labor unions could be a nucleus—I'm working on that, and when I've got the boys talked and bullied into line, I'm going to approach City Hall with an offer to help."

After a silence, Helga glanced over at Lewis. "You still haven't any idea as to the cause of it all?"

"Oh, yes," said the biologist. "Any number of ideas, and no way of choosing between them. We'll just have to study and think some more, that's all."

"It's a physical phenomenon embracing at least the whole Solar System," declared Corinth. "The observatories have established that much through spectroscopic studies. It may be that the sun, in its orbit around the center of the galaxy, has entered some kind of force-field. But on theoretical grounds—dammit, I won't scrap general relativity till I have to!—on theoretical grounds, I'm inclined to think it's more likely a matter of our having *left* a force-field which slows down light and otherwise affects electromagnetic and electrochemical processes."

"In other words," said Mandelbaum slowly, "we're actually entering a normal state of affairs? All our past has been spent under abnormal conditions?"

"Maybe. Only, of course, those conditions are normal for us. We've evolved under them. We may be like deep-sea fish, which explode when they're brought up to ordinary pressures."

"Heh! Pleasant thought!"

"I don't think I'm afraid to die," said Sheila in a small voice, "but being changed like this——"

"Keep a tight rein on yourself," said Lewis sharply. "I suspect this unbalance is going to drive a lot of people actually insane. Don't be one of them."

He knocked the ash off his cigar. "We have found out some things at the lab," he went on in a dispassionate tone. "As Pete says, it's a physical thing, either a force-field or the lack of one, affecting electronic interactions. The effect is actually rather small, quantitatively. Ordinary chemical reactions go on pretty much as before, in fact I don't think any significant change in the speed of inorganic reactions has been detected. But the more complex and delicate a structure is, the more it feels that slight effect.

"You must have noticed that you're more energetic lately. We've tested basal metabolism rates, and they have increased, not much but some. Your motor reactions are faster too, though you may not have noticed that because your subjective time sense is also speeded up. In other words, not much change in muscular, glandular, vascular, and the other purely somatic functions, just enough to make you feel nervous; and you'll adjust to that pretty quick, if nothing else happens.

"On the other hand, the most highly organized cells—neurones, and above all the neurones of the cerebral cortex—are very much affected. Perception speeds are way up; they measured that over in psych. You've noticed, I'm sure, how much faster you read. Reaction time to all stimuli is less."

"I heard that from Jones," nodded Helga coolly, "and checked up on traffic accident statistics for the past week. Definitely lower. If people react faster, naturally they're better drivers."

"Uh-huh," said Lewis. "Till they start getting tired of poking along at sixty miles an hour and drive at a hundred. Then you may not have any more crack-ups, but those you do have—wham!"

"But if people are smarter," began Sheila, "they'll know enough to——"

"Sorry, no." Mandelbaum shook his head. "Basic personality does not change, right? And intelligent people have always done some pretty stupid or evil things from time to time, just like everybody else. A man might be a brilliant scientist, let's say, but that doesn't stop him from neglecting his health or from driving recklessly or patronizing spiritualists or——"

"Or voting Democrat," nodded Lewis, grinning. "That's correct, Felix. Eventually, no doubt, increased intelligence would affect the total personality, but right now you're not removing anyone's weaknesses, ignorances, prejudices, blind spots, or ambitions; you're just giving him more power, of energy and intelligence, to indulge them—which is one reason why civilization is cracking up."

His voice became dry and didactic: "Getting back to where we were, the most highly organized tissue in the world is, of course, the human cerebrum, the gray matter or seat of consciousness if you like. It feels the stimulus—or lack of inhibition, if Pete's theory is right—more than anything else on Earth. Its functioning increases out of all proportion to the rest of the organism. Maybe you don't know how complex a structure the human brain is. Believe me, it makes the sidereal universe look like a child's building set. There are many times more possible interneuronic connections than there are atoms in the entire cosmos—the factor is something like ten to the power of several million. It's not surprising that a slight change in electrochemistry—too slight to make any important difference to the body—will change the whole nature of the mind. Look what a little dope or alcohol will do, and then remember that this new factor works on the very basis of the cell's existence. The really interesting question is whether so finely balanced a function can survive such a change at all."

There was no fear in his tones, and the eyes behind their heavy lenses held a flash of impersonal excitement. To him this was sheer wonder; Corinth imagined him dying and taking clinical notes on himself as life faded.

"Well," said the physicist grayly, "we'll know pretty soon."

"How can you just sit there and talk about it that way?" cried Sheila. Horror shook her voice.

"My dear girl," said Helga, "do you imagine we can, at this stage, do anything else?"

CHAPTER FIVE

Selections from the New York *Times*, June 30:

CHANGE DECELERATING

Decline Noted, Effects Apparently Irreversible

Rhayader Theory May Hold Explanation

UNIFIED FIELD THEORY ANNOUNCED

Rhayader Announces Extension of Einstein Theories—Interstellar Travel a Theoretical Possibility

FEDERAL GOVERNMENT MAY RESIGN FUNCTIONS

President Asks Local Authorities to Exercise Discretion

N. Y. Labor Authority Under Mandelbaum Pledges Co-operation

REVOLUTION REPORTED IN SOVIETIZED COUNTRIES

News Blackout Declared—Organized Insurrection Spreading

Revolutionaries May Have Developed New Weapons and Military Concepts

WORLD ECONOMIC CRISIS WORSENING

Food Riots in Paris, Dublin, Rome, Hong Kong

Shipping Approaches Complete Standstill as Thousands of Workers Quit

THIRD BA'AL CULT REVOLTS IN LOS ANGELES

National Guard Demoralized Fanatics Seize Key Points— Street Fighting Continues

---

N. Y. City Hall Warns of Local Activities of Cultists

TIGER KILLS ATTENDANT, ESCAPES FROM BRONX ZOO

Police Issue Warning, Organize Hunt

Authorities Consider Shooting All Formidable Specimens

FRESH RIOTING FEARED IN HARLEM

Police Chief: 'Yesterday's Affair Only a Beginning'—Mounting Panic Seems Impossible to Halt

PSYCHIATRIST SAYS MAN CHANGED 'BEYOND COMPREHENSION'

Kearnes of Bellevue: 'Unpredictable Results of Neural Speed-up Make Old Data and Methods of Control Invalid—Impossible Even to Guess Ultimate Outcome'

They had no issue the following day; there was no newsprint to be had.

Brock thought it was strange to be left in charge of the estate. But a lot of funny things had been happening lately.

First Mr. Rossman had gone. Then, the very next day, Stan Wilmer had been attacked by the pigs when he went in to feed them. They charged him, grunting and squealing, stamping him down under their heavy bodies, and several had to be shot before they left him. Most had rushed the fence then, hitting it together and breaking through and disappearing into the woods.

Wilmer was pretty badly hurt and had to be taken to the hospital; he swore he'd never come back. Two of the hands had quit the same day.

Brock was in too much of a daze, too full of the change within himself, to care. He didn't have much to do, anyway, now that all work except the most essential was suspended. He looked after the animals, careful to treat them well and to wear a gun at his hip, and had little trouble. Joe was always beside him. The rest of the time he sat around reading, or just with his chin in his hand to think.

Bill Bergen called him in a couple of days after the pig episode. The overseer didn't seem to have changed much, not outwardly. He was still tall and sandy and slow-spoken, with the same toothpick worried between his lips, the same squinted pale eyes. But he spoke even more slowly and cautiously than he had done before to Brock—or did it only seem that way?

"Well, Archie," he said, "Smith just quit."

Brock shifted from one foot to another, looking at the floor.

"Said he wanted to go to college. I couldn't talk him out of it." Bergen's voice held a faintly amused contempt. "The idiot. There won't be any more colleges in another month. That leaves just you and my wife and Voss and me."

"Kind of short-handed," mumbled Brock, feeling he ought to say something.

"One man can do the bare essentials if he must," said Bergen. "Lucky it's summer. The horses and cows can stay out of doors, which saves barn cleaning."

"How about the crops?"

"Not much to do there yet. To hell with them, anyway."

Brock stared upward. In all his years on the place, Bergen had been the steadiest and hardest worker they had.

"You've gotten smart like the rest of us, haven't you, Archie?" asked Bergen. "I daresay you're about up to normal now—pre-change normal, I mean. And it isn't over. You'll get brighter yet."

Brock's face grew hot.

"Sorry, I didn't mean anything personal. You're a good man." He sat for a moment fiddling with the papers on his desk. Then: "Archie, you're in charge here now."

"Huh?"

"I'm leaving too."

"But, Bill—you can't——"

"Can and will, Archie." Bergen stood up. "You know, my wife always wanted to travel, and I have some things to think out. Never mind what they are, it's something I've puzzled over for many years and now I believe I see an answer. We're taking our car and heading west."

"But—but—Mr. Rossman—he's de-pen-ding on you, Bill——"

"I'm afraid that there are more important things in life than Mr. Rossman's country retreat," said Bergen evenly. "You can handle the place all right, even if Voss leaves too."

Fright and bewilderment lashed into scorn: "Scared of the animals, huh?"

"Why, no, Archie. Always remember that you're still brighter than they are, and what's more important, you have hands. A gun will stop anything." Bergen walked over to the window and looked out. It was a bright windy day with sunlight torn in the restless branches of trees. "As a matter of fact," he went on in the same gentle, remote tone, "a farm is safer than any other place I can think of. If the production and distribution systems break down, as they may, you'll still have something to eat. But my wife and I aren't getting any younger. I've been a steady, sober, conscientious man all my life. Now I wonder what all the fuss and the lost years were about."

He turned his back. "Good-by, Archie." It was a command.

Brock went out into the yard, shaking his head and muttering to himself. Joe whined uneasily and nuzzled his palm. He ruffled the golden fur and sat down on a bench and put his head in his hands.

The trouble is, he thought, *that while the animals and I got smarter, so did everybody else. God in Heaven—what sort of things are going on inside Bill Bergen's skull?*

It was a terrifying concept. The speed and scope and sharpness of his own mind were suddenly cruel. He dared not think what a normal human might be like by now.

Only it was hard to realize. Bergen hadn't become a god. His eyes didn't blaze, his voice was not vibrant and resolute, he didn't start building great engines that flamed and roared. He was still a tall stoop-shouldered man with a weary face, a patient drawl, nothing else. The trees were still green, a bird chattered behind a rosebush, a fly rested cobalt-blue on the arm of the bench.

Brock remembered, vaguely, sermons from the few times he had been in church. The end of the world—was the sky going to open up, would the angels pour down the vials of wrath on a shaking land, and would God appear to judge the sons of man? He listened for the noise of great galloping hoofs, but there was only the wind in the trees.

That was the worst of it. The sky didn't care. The Earth went on turning through an endlessness of dark and silence, and what happened in the thin scum seething over its crust didn't matter.

Nobody cared. It wasn't important.

Brock looked at his scuffed shoes and then at the strong hairy hands between his knees. They seemed impossibly alien, the hands of a stranger. *Sweet Jesus,* he thought, *is this really happening to me?*

He grabbed Joe by the ruffed neck and held him close. Suddenly he had a wild need for a woman, someone to hold him and talk to him and block out the loneliness of the sky.

He got up, sweat cold on his body, and walked over to the Bergens' cottage. It was his now, he supposed.

Voss was a young fellow, a kid from town who wasn't very bright and hadn't been able to find any other employment. He looked moodily up from a book as the other man entered the small living room.

"Well," said Brock, "Bill just quit."

"I know. What're we gonna do?" Voss was scared and weak and willing to surrender leadership. Bergen must have foreseen that. The sense of responsibility was strengthening.

"We'll be all right if we stay here," said Brock. "Just wait it out, keep going, that's all."

"The animals——"

"You got a gun, don't you? Anyway, they'll know when they're well off. Just be careful, always lock the gates behind you, treat 'em good——"

"I'm not gonna wait on any damn animals," said Voss sullenly.

"That you are, though." Brock went over to the icebox and took out two cans of beer and opened them.

"Look here, I'm smarter than you are, and——"

"And I'm stronger'n you. If you don't like it, you can quit. I'm staying." Brock gave Voss one can and tilted the other to his mouth.

"Look," he said after a moment, "I know those animals. They're mostly habit. They'll stick around because they don't know any better and because we feed 'em and because—uh—respect for man has been drilled into 'em. There ain't no bears or wolves in the woods, nothing that can give us trouble except maybe the pigs. Me, I'd be more scared to be in a city."

"How come?" Despite himself, Voss was overmastered. He laid down the book and took up his beer. Brock glanced at the title: *Night of Passion*, in a two-bit edition. Voss might have gained a better mind, but that didn't change him otherwise. He just didn't want to think.

"The people," said Brock. "Christ knows what they'll do." He went over to the radio and turned it on and presently got a newscast. It didn't mean much to him; mostly it was about the new brain power, but the words were strung together in a way that didn't make a lot of sense. The voice sounded frightened, though.

After lunch, Brock decided to take a scout through the woods and see if he couldn't locate the pigs and find out what they were up to. They worried him more than he would admit. Pigs had always been smarter than most people knew. They might also get to thinking about the stores of feed kept on a farm watched by only two men.

Voss wasn't even asked to come; he'd have refused, and in any event it was wise to keep one man on guard at home. Brock and Joe went over the fence and into the six hundred acres of forest alone.

It was green and shadowy and full of rustling in there. Brock went quietly, a rifle under one arm, parting the underbrush before him with habitual ease. He saw no squirrels, though they were ordinarily plentiful. Well—they must have thought it out, the way crows had done long ago, and seen that a man with a gun was something to stay away from. He wondered how many eyes were watching him, and what was going on behind the eyes. Joe stuck close to his heels, not bounding on all sides as he normally did.

An overlooked branch slapped viciously at the man's face. He stood for an instant of creeping fear. Were the trees thinking too, now? Was the whole world going to rise in revolt?

No— After a moment he got control of himself and went stolidly on along the sheep trail. To be changed by this—whatever-it-was—a thing had to be able to think in the first place. Trees had no brains. He seemed to recall hearing once that insects didn't either, and made a note to check up on this. Good thing that Mr. Rossman had a big library.

And a good thing, Brock realized, that he himself was steady. He had never gotten too excited about anything, and was taking the new order more calmly than seemed possible. One step at a time, that was it. Just go along from day to day, doing as much as he could to stay alive.

The thicket parted before him and a pig looked out. It was an old black boar, a big mean-looking creature which stood immovably in his path. The snouted face was a mask, but Brock had never seen anything so cold as its eyes. Joe bristled, growling, and Brock lifted the rifle. They stood that way for a long time, not moving. Then the boar grunted—it seemed contemptuous—and turned and slipped into the shadows. Brock realized that his body was wet.

He forced himself to go on for a couple of hours, ranging the woods but seeing little. When he came back, he was sunk in thought. The animals had changed, all right, but he had no way of telling how much, or what they would do next. Maybe nothing.

"I been thinking," said Voss when he entered the cottage. "Maybe we should move in with another farmer. Ralph Martinson needs extra help, now his hired man has quit."

"I'm staying."

Voss gave him a cool glance. "Because you don't want to go back to being a moron, huh?"

Brock winced, but made his answer flat. "Call it what you like."

"I'm not going to stay here forever."

"Nobody asked you to. Come on, it's about time for the milking."

"Judas, what'll we do with the milk from thirty cows? The creamery truck ain't come around for three days."

"Mmmmm—yeah— Well, I'll figger out something. Right now, we can't let 'em bust their teats."

"Can't we just?" muttered Voss, but followed him out to the barn. Milking thirty cows was a big job, even with a couple of machines to help. Brock decided to dry up most of them, but that would take some time, you had to taper them off gradually. Meanwhile they were restless and hard to control.

He came out and took a pitchfork and began throwing hay over the fence to the sheep, which had flocked in from the woods as usual. Halfway through the job, he was roused by Joe's wild yammer. He turned and saw the farm's enormous Holstein bull approaching.

He's loose! Brock's hand went to the pistol at his belt, then back to his fork. A popgun wasn't much use against such a monster. The bull snorted, pawing the ground and shaking his horn-cropped head.

"Okay, fella." Brock went slowly toward him, wiping sandy lips with his tongue. The noise of his heart was loud in his ears. "Okay, easy, back to the pen with yuh."

Joe snarled, stiff-legged beside his master. The bull lowered his head and charged.

Brock braced himself. The giant before him seemed to fill the sky.

Brock stabbed under the jaw. It was a mistake, he realized wildly, he should have gone for the eyes. The fork ripped out of his hands and he felt a blow which knocked him to the ground. The bull ground his head against Brock's chest, trying to gore with horns that weren't there.

Suddenly he bellowed, a horror of pain in his voice. Joe had come behind him and fastened jaws in the right place. The bull turned, one hoof grating along Brock's ribs. The man got his gun out and fired from the ground. The bull began to run. Brock rolled over, scrambled to his feet, and sprang alongside the great head. He put the pistol behind one ear and fired. The bull stumbled, falling to his knees. Brock emptied the gun into his skull.

After that he collapsed on the body, whirling toward darkness.

He came to as Voss shook him.

"Are yuh hurt, Archie?" The words gibbered meaninglessly in his ears. "Are you hurt?"

Brock let Voss lead him into the cottage. After a stiff drink he felt better and inspected himself. "I'm all right," he muttered. "Bruises and cuts, no bones broke. I'm okay."

"That settles it." Voss was shaking worse than Brock. "We're leaving here."

The red head shook. "No."

"Are you crazy? Alone here, all the animals running wild, everything gone to hell—are you crazy?"

"I'm staying."

"I'm not! I got half a mind to make you come along."

Joe growled. "Don't," said Brock. He felt, suddenly, nothing but an immense weariness. "You go if you want to, but leave me. I'll be all right."

"Well——"

"I'll herd some of the stock over to Martinson's tomorrow, if he'll take 'em. I can handle the rest myself."

Voss argued for a while longer, then gave up and took the jeep and drove away. Brock smiled without quite knowing why he did.

He checked the bull's pen. The gate had been broken down by a determined push. Half the power of fences had always lain in the fact that animals didn't know enough to keep shoving at them. Well, now they did, it seemed.

"I'll have to bury that fellow with a bulldozer," said Brock. It was becoming more and more natural for him to speak aloud to Joe. "Do it tomorrow. Let's have supper, boy, and then we'll read and play some music. We're alone from here on, I guess."

CHAPTER SIX

A CITY WAS AN ORGANISM, but Corinth had never appreciated its intricate and precarious equilibrium before. Now, with the balance gone, New York was sliding swiftly toward disruption and death.

Only a few subways were running, an emergency system manned by those devoted enough to stay by a job which had become altogether flat and distasteful. The stations were hollow and dark, filthy with unswept litter, and the shrieking of wheels held a tormented loneliness. Corinth walked to work, along dirty streets whose traffic had fallen to a reckless fragment of the old steady river.

Memory, five days old: *the roads jammed, a steel barricade ten miles long, honking and yelling till the high windows shivered, filling the air with exhaust fumes till men choked—blind panic, a mob fleeing a city they had decided was finished, flying from it at an estimated average speed of five miles an hour. Two cars had locked bumpers and the drivers got out and fought till their faces were bloody masks. Police helicopters had buzzed impotently overhead, like monster flies. It was saddening to know that multiplied intelligence had not quenched such an animal stampede.*

Those who remained—probably three-fourths of the city's dwellers—were still scraping along. Severely rationed gas, water, and electricity were being supplied. Food still trickled in from the country, though you had to take what you could get and pay exorbitantly. But it was like a pot, rumbling and seething and gathering itself to boil over.

Memory, three days old: *the second Harlem riot, when fear of the unknown and rage at ancient injustice had stood up to fight, for no reason except that untrained minds could not control their own new powers. The huge roar of burning tenements, giant red flames flapping against a windy night sky. The restless luminance like blood on a thousand dark faces, a thousand ill-clad bodies that stamped and swayed and struggled in the streets. A knife gleaming high and slaking itself in a human throat. A broken howling under the noise of fire. A scream as some woman went down and was stamped shapeless beneath a hundred running feet. The helicopters tossing and twisting in the storm of superheated air rushing up from the flames. And in the morning, empty streets, a haze of bitter smoke, a dim sobbing behind shuttered windows.*

Yes, still a thin tight-held semblance of order. Only—how long could it endure?

A tattered man with a ragged, new-looking beard was ranting on a street corner. Some dozen people stood around him, listening with a strange intensity. Corinth heard the words loud and harsh in the quiet: "—because we forgot the eternal principles of life, because we let the scientists betray us, because we all followed the eggheads. I tell you, it is life only that matters before the great Oneness in whom all are one and one are all. Behold, I bring you the word of the returned——"

His skin crawled, and he made a swift detour around that corner. Was it a missionary of the Third Ba'al cultists? He didn't know, and didn't feel like stopping to find out. Not a cop in sight to report it to. There was going to be real trouble if the new religion got many followers here in town. It gave him some comfort to see a woman entering the Catholic church nearby.

A taxi rounded a corner on two wheels, sideswiped a parked car, and was gone in a burst of noise. Another automobile crept slowly down the street, the driver tightfaced, his passenger holding a shotgun. Fear. The shops were boarded up on either side; one small grocery remained open, and its proprietor carried a pistol at his belt. In the dingy entrance to an apartment house, an old man sat reading Kant's *Critique* with a strange and frantic hunger which ignored the world around him.

"Mister, I haven't eaten for two days."

Corinth looked at the shape which had slunk out of an alley. "Sorry," he answered. "I've only got ten bucks on me. Barely enough for a meal at present prices."

"Christ, I can't find work——"

"Go to City Hall, friend. They'll give you a job and see that you're fed. They need men badly."

Scorn: "That outfit? Sweeping streets, hauling garbage, trucking in food—I'd starve first!"

"Starve, then," spat Corinth, and went on more swiftly. The weight of the revolver dragging down his coat pocket was cheering. He had little sympathy for that type, after what he had seen.

Though could you expect anything different? You take a typical human, a worker in factory or office, his mind dulled to a collection of verbal reflexes, his future a day-to-day plodding which offered him no more than a chance to fill his belly and be anesthesized by a movie or his television—more and bigger automobiles, more and brighter plastics, onward and upward with the American Way of Life. Even before the change, there had been an inward hollowness in Western civilization, an unconscious realization that there ought to be more in life than one's own ephemeral self—and the ideal had not been forthcoming.

Then suddenly, almost overnight, human intelligence had exploded toward fantastic heights. An entire new cosmos opened before this man, visions, realizations, thought boiling unbidden within him. He saw the miserable inadequacy of his life, the triviality of his work, the narrow and meaningless limits of his beliefs and conventions—and he resigned.

Not everyone left, of course—not even the majority. But enough people did to throw the whole structure of technological civilization out of gear. If no more coal was being mined, then the makers of steel and of machines could not stay by their jobs even if they wanted to. Add to that the disturbances caused by emotions gone awry, and——

A naked woman walked down the street, carrying a market basket. She had set out to think for herself, Corinth imagined, and had decided that clothes in summer were ridiculous, and had taken advantage of the fact that the police had other worries to shed hers. No harm in that per se, but as a symptom it made him shiver. Any society was necessarily founded on certain more or less arbitrary rules and restrictions. Too many people had suddenly realized that the laws were arbitrary, without intrinsic significance, and had proceeded to violate whichever ones they didn't like.

A young man sat on a doorstep, his arms clasped about knees drawn up under his chin, rocking to and fro and whimpering softly. Corinth stopped. "What's wrong?" he asked.

"Fear." The eyes were bright and glazed. "I suddenly realized it. I am alone."

Corinth's mind leaped ahead to what he was going to say, but he heard out the panic-blurred words: "All I know, all I am, is here, in my head. Everything exists for me only as I know it. And someday I'm going to die." A line of spittle ran from one corner of his mouth. "Someday the great darkness will come, I will not be—nothing will be! You may still exist, for you—though how can I tell that you aren't just a dream of mine?—but for me there will be nothing, nothing, nothing. I will never even have been." The weak tears dribbled out of his eyes, and Corinth went on.

Insanity—yes, that had a lot to do with the collapse. There must be millions who had not been able to stand that sudden range and sharpness of comprehension. They hadn't been able to handle their new power, and it had driven them mad.

He shuddered in the hot still air.

The Institute was like a haven. When he walked in, a man sat on guard: submachine gun lying beside his chair, chemistry text on his lap. The face that lifted to Corinth's was serene. "Hullo."

"Had any trouble, Jim?"

"Not yet. But you never can tell, with all the prowlers and fanatics."

Corinth nodded, feeling some of the clamminess leave him. There were still rational men who did not go kiting off after suddenly perceived stars, but stuck quietly to the immediate work.

The elevator attendant was a seven-year-old boy, son of a man in the Institute; schools were closed. "Hi, sir," he said cheerily. "I been waiting for you. How on earth did Maxwell work out his equations?"

"Huh?" Corinth's eyes fell on a book lying on the seat. "Oh, you've been studying radio, have you? Cadogan is pretty stiff to start out on, you should try reading——"

"I seen circuit diagrams, Mr. Corinth. I wanna know why they work, only Cadogan here just gives the equations.

Corinth referred him to a text on vector calculus. "When you've been through that, come see me again." He was smiling when he got off on the seventh floor, but his smile faded as he walked down the corridor.

Lewis was in his laboratory, waiting for him. "Late," he grunted.

"Sheila," replied Corinth.

The conversation here was rapidly becoming a new language. When your mind was of quadrupled capability, a single word, a gesture of hand, a flicker of expression, could convey more to one who knew you and your mannerisms than whole paragraphs of grammatical English.

"You're late this morning," Lewis had meant. "Have any trouble?"

"I got started late because of Sheila," Corinth had told him. "She's not taking this well at all, Nat, frankly, I'm worried about her. Only what can I do? I don't understand human psychology any more, it's changing too much and too fast. Nobody does. We're all becoming strangers to each other—to ourselves—and it's frightening."

Lewis' heavy body moved forward. "Come on. Rossman's here and wants a confab with us."

They went down the corridor, leaving Johansson and Grunewald immersed in their work: measuring the changed constants of nature, recalibrating instruments, performing all the enormous basic labor of science again from the ground up.

Throughout the building the other departments mapped out the altered faces of their own disciplines. Cybernetics, chemistry, biology, above all psychology—men grudged the time for sleep, there was so much to do.

The department heads were gathered around a long table in the main conference room. Rossman sat at its end, tall and thin and white-haired, no movement in his austere features. Helga Arnulfsen was at his right and Felix Mandelbaum at his left. For an instant Corinth wondered what the labor organizer was doing here, then realized that he must be representing the emergency city government.

"Good day, gentlemen." Rossman went through the forms of Edwardian courtesy with a punctilio that would have been laughable if it were not so obviously a desperate effort to cling to something real and known. "Please be seated."

Everyone seemed to be here now, for Rossman got directly to business: "I have just returned from Washington. I have called you together because I feel that an exchange of ideas and information is urgently needed. You will feel better for knowing what I can give you of the over-all picture, and I will certainly be happier for what scientific explanation you have found. Together we may be able to plan intelligently."

"As for the explanation," said Lewis, "we've pretty well agreed here at the Institute that Dr. Corinth's theory is the right one. This postulates a force-field of partly electromagnetic character, generated by gyromagnetic action within atomic nuclei near the center of the galaxy. It radiates outward in a cone which, by the time it has reached our section of space, is many light-years across. Its effect has been to inhibit certain electromagnetic and electrochemical processes, among which the functioning of certain types of neurones is prominent. We suppose that the Solar System, in its orbit around galactic center, entered this force-field many millions of years ago—hardly later than the Cretaceous. Doubtless many species of that time died out. However, life as a whole survived—adapted nervous systems compensated for the inhibiting force by becoming that much more efficient. In short, all life forms today are—or were, immediately before the change—about as intelligent as they would have been anyway."

"I see," nodded Rossman. "And then the sun and its planets moved out of the force-field."

"Yes. The field must have a rather sharp boundary, as such things go in astronomy, for the change took place within a few days. The fringe of the field—from the region of full intensity to the region of no effect at all—is perhaps only ten million miles wide. We're definitely out of it now; physical constants have remained stable for several days."

"But our minds haven't," said Mandelbaum bleakly.

"I know," cut in Lewis. "We'll come to that in a minute. The general effect of Earth's coming out of the inhibitor field was, of course, a sudden zooming of intelligence in every life form possessing a brain. Suddenly the damping force to which every living organism was adjusted, was gone.

"Naturally, the lack of that force has produced an enormous unbalance. Nervous systems have tended to run wild, trying to stabilize and function on a new level; that's why everybody felt so jumpy and frightened to begin with. The physical layout of the brain is adapted to one speed—one set of speeds, rather—of neurone signals; now suddenly the speed is increased while the physical structure remains the same. In plain language, it'll take us a while to get used to this."

"Why aren't we dead?" asked Grahovitch, the chemist. "I should think our hearts and so on would start working like mad."

"The autonomic nervous system has been relatively little affected," said Lewis. "It seems to be a matter of cellular type; there are many different kinds of nerve cells, you know, and apparently only those in the cerebral cortex have reacted much to the change. Even there, the rate of functioning has not really gone up much—the factor is small—but apparently the processes involved in consciousness are so sensitive that it has made an enormous difference to what we call thought."

"But we will survive?"

"Oh, yes, I'm sure no physiological damage will result—to most people, anyway. Some have gone insane, to be sure, but that's probably more for psychological than histological reasons."

"And—will we enter another such force-field?" queried Rossman.

"Hardly," said Corinth. "On the basis of theory, I'm pretty sure there can only be one such, at most, in any galaxy. With the sun requiring some two hundred million years for its orbit around galactic center—well, we should have more than half that period before we have to start worrying about getting stupid again."

"M-hm. I see, gentlemen. Thank you very much." Rossman leaned forward, clasping his thin fingers before him. "Now as to what I have been able to find out, I fear it is not much, and that little is bad news. Washington is a madhouse. Many key men have already left their posts; it seems that there are more important things in life than administering Public Law Number Such and such——"

"Well, I'm afraid they're right," grinned Lewis sardonically.

"No doubt. But let us face it, gentlemen; however little we may like the present system we cannot scrap it overnight."

"What's the word from overseas?" asked Weller, the mathematician. "How about Russia?"

"We'd be helpless against an armed attack," said Rossman, "but what military intelligence we have left indicates that the Soviet dictatorship is having troubles of its own."

He sighed. "First things first, gentlemen. We have to worry about our own breakdown. Washington grows more helpless every day: fewer and fewer people listen to the President's commands and appeals, less and less force is at his disposal. In many areas martial law has already been declared, but any attempt to enforce it would only mean civil war. Reorganization is going to have to be on a local basis. That is essentially the news I bring to you."

"We've been working on it, here in New York," said Mandelbaum. He looked tired, burned out by days and nights of unresting effort. "I've got the unions pretty well into line by now. Arrangements will be made to bring in and distribute food, and we hope to get a volunteer militia to maintain some kind of order."

He turned to Rossman. "You're an able organizer. Your other interests, your businesses and your factories, are going down the drain, and here's a job which has to be done. Will you help us?"

"Of course," nodded the old man. "And the Institute——"

"Will have to keep going. We've got to understand just what's happened and what we can expect in the near future. We've got to have a thousand things developed immediately if not sooner."

The talk turned to organizational details. Corinth had little to say. He was too worried about Sheila. Last night she had woken up screaming.

CHAPTER SEVEN

WATO THE WITCH DOCTOR was tracing figures in the dust outside his thatch hut and muttering to himself. M'Wanzi heard him through the clank of weapons and the thick voices of the drums, as tall warriors passed back and forth: "——the law of similarity, that like causes like, may be expressed in the form *ya* or not-*ya*, thus showing that this form of magic obeys the rule of universal causality. But how to fit in the law of contagion——?"

M'Wanzi threw him an amused look as he strode by. Let the old man build his dusty dreams as he wished. The rifle on his shoulder was solid reality and enough for him. And it would be guns and not magic which fulfilled an ancient wish.

Free the black man! Drive the white oppressors back beyond the sea! Since his youth and the days of horror on the plantation, it had been his life. But only now——

Well, he had not been frightened by that which was happening within his soul, as the others were. He had seized this power to think with a swift fierce gladness, and his will had dominated whole tribes driven half-crazy with fear, ready to turn anywhere for the comfort of leadership. Over thousands of miles, from Congo jungles to the veldts of the south, men tormented and enslaved and spat upon had lifted weary faces to a message blown down the wind. Now was the time to strike, before the white man also rallied—the scheme was ready, lying in the soul of M'Wanzi the Elephant, the campaign was planned in a few flashing days, the subtle tongue won over leaders of a hundred conflicting groups, the army was stirring to life, now was the time to be free!

The drums talked around him as he went toward the edge of the jungle. He stepped through a wall of canebrake into the thick hot shadows of the forest. Another shadow moved down, flitted across the earth and waited grotesquely before him. Wise brown eyes regarded him with an inborn sadness.

"Have you gathered the brethren of the forest?" asked M'Wanzi.

"They come soon," said the ape.

That had been M'Wanzi's great realization. All the rest, the organization, the planned campaign, that was nothing beside this: that if the souls of men had suddenly grown immensely bigger, so also the souls of animals must have grown. His guess had been confirmed by terrified stories of raids on farms made by elephants of demoniac cunning, but when those reports came he was already working out a common language of clicks and grunts with a captured chimpanzee. The apes had never been much less intelligent than man, M'Wanzi suspected. Today he could offer them much in exchange for their help; and were they not Africans too?

"My brother of the forest, go tell your people to make ready."

"Not all of them wish this thing, brother of the fields. They must be beaten before they wish it. That takes time."

"Time we have little of. Use the drums as I taught you. Send word throughout the land and let the hosts gather at the appointed places."

"It shall be as you wish. When next the moon rises full, the children of the forest shall be there, and they shall be armed with knives and blowguns and assagais as you showed me."

"Brother of the forest, you have gladdened my heart. Go with fortune and carry that word."

The ape turned and swung lithely up a tree. A stray sunbeam gleamed off the rifle slung at his back.

Corinth sighed, yawned, and got up from his desk, shoving the papers away. He did not say anything aloud, but to his assistants, hunched over some testing apparatus, the meaning was clear: (To hell with it. I'm too tired to think straight any more. Going home.)

Johansson gestured with his hand, conveying as well as if he had spoken: (Think I'll stay here for a while, chief. This gimmick is shaping up nicely.) Grunewald added a curt nod.

Corinth fumbled automatically for a cigarette, but his pocket was empty. Smokes just weren't to be had these days. He hoped the world would get back on an operating basis soon, but it seemed less likely every day. What was happening outside the city? A few radio stations, professional and amateur, were maintaining a tenuous web of communications across western Europe, the Americas, and the Pacific, but the rest of the planet seemed to be swallowed by darkness—an occasional report of violence, like lightning in the night, and then nothing.

Mandelbaum had warned him yesterday to be on his guard. Missionaries of the Third Ba'al were definitely known to have entered the city despite all precautions and were making converts right and left. The new religion seemed to be wholly orgiastic, with a murderous hatred for logic and science and rationality of all kinds—you could expect trouble.

Corinth went down hallways that were tunnels of dusk. Electricity must be conserved; only a few power stations were still operating, manned and guarded by volunteers. Elevator service ended at sunset, and he walked down seven flights to ground level. Loneliness oppressed him, and when he saw a light in Helga's office he paused, startled, and then knocked.

"Come in."

He opened the door. She sat behind a littered desk, writing up some kind of manifest. The symbols she used were strange to him, probably her own invention and more efficient than the conventional ones. She still looked as severely handsome, but there was a deep weariness that paled her eyes.

"Hullo, Pete," she said. The smile that twitched her mouth was tired, but it had warmth. "How've you been?"

Corinth spoke two words and made three gestures; she filled in his intention from logic and her knowledge of his old speech habits: (Oh—all right. But you—I thought you'd been co-opted by Felix to help whip his new government into shape.)

(I have,) she implied. (But I feel more at home here, and it's just as good a place to do some of my work. Who've you got on my old job, by the way?)

(Billy Saunders—ten years of age, but a sharp kid. Maybe we should get a moron, though. The physical strain may be too much for a child.)

(I doubt it. There isn't much to do now, really. You boys co-operate pretty smoothly since the change—unlike the rest of the world!)

"I don't know if it's safe for you to come so far from where you live." Corinth shifted awkwardly on his feet. "Look, let me take you home."

"Not necessary." She spoke with a certain bite in her tones, and Corinth realized dully that she loved him.

And all our feelings have intensified. I never knew before how much of man's emotional life is bound up with his brain, how much more keenly he feels than any other animal.

"Sit down," she invited, leaning back in her seat. "Rest for a minute."

He smiled wearily, lowering himself into a chair. "Wish we had some beer," he murmured. (It'd be like the old days.)

"The old days—the lost innocence. We'll always regret them, won't we? We'll always look back on our blindness with a wistful longing that the new generation simply won't understand." She beat a clenched fist against the desk top, very softly. The light gleamed gold in her hair.

"How's your work coming along?" she asked after a moment. The silence hummed around them.

"Good enough. I've been in touch with Rhayader in England, over the short wave. They're having a tough time, but keeping alive. Some of their biochemists are working on yeasts, getting good results. By the end of the year they hope to be able to feed themselves adequately, if not very palatably as yet—food synthesis plants being built. He gave me some information that just about clinched the theory of the inhibitor field—how it's created. I've got Johansson and Grunewald at work on an apparatus to generate a similar field on a small scale; if they succeed, we'll know that our hypothesis is probably right. Then Nat can use the apparatus to study biological effects in detail. As for me, I'm going into the development of Rhayader's general relativity-cum-quantum mechanics—applying a new variation of communications theory, of all things, to help me out."

"What's your purpose, other than curiosity?"

"Quite practical, I assure you. We may find a way to generate atomic energy from any material whatsoever, by direct nucleonic disintegration: no more fuel problems. We may even find a way to travel faster than light. The stars—well——"

"New worlds. Or we might return to the inhibitor field, out in space—why not? Go back to being stupid. Maybe we'll be happier that way. No, no, I realize you can't go home again." Helga opened a drawer and took out a crumpled packet. "Smoke?"

"Angel! How on earth did you manage that?"

"I have my ways." She struck a match for him and lit her own cigarette with it. "Efficient—yeah."

They smoked in silence for a while, but the knowledge of each other's thoughts was like a pale flickering between them.

"You'd better let me see you home," said Corinth. "It's not safe out there. The prophet's mobs——"

"All right," she said. "Though I've got a car and you haven't."

"It's only a few blocks from your place to mine, in a safe district." Since it was not possible as yet to patrol the entire sprawling city, the government had concentrated on certain key streets and areas.

Corinth took off his glasses and rubbed his eyes. "I don't really understand it," he said. "Human relationships were never my long suit, and even now I can't quite—— Well, why should this sudden upsurge of intelligence throw so many back to the animal stage? Why can't they see——?"

"They don't want to." Helga drew hard on her cigarette. "Quite apart from those who've gone insane, and they're an important factor, there remains the necessity of not only having something to think with, but something to think about. You've taken millions—hundreds of millions—of people who've never had an original thought in their lives and suddenly thrown their brains into high gear. They start thinking—but what basis have they got? They still retain the old superstitions, prejudices, hates and fears and greeds, and most of their new mental energy goes to elaborate rationalization of these. Then someone like this Third Ba'al comes along and offers an anodyne to frightened and confused people; he tells them it's all right to throw off this terrible burden of thought and forget themselves in an emotional orgy. It won't last, Pete, but the transition is tough."

"Yeah—hm—I had to get an I.Q. of 500 or so—whatever that means—to appreciate how little brains count for, after all. Nice thought." Corinth grimaced and stubbed out his cigarette.

Helga shuffled her papers together and put them in a drawer. "Shall we go?"

"Might as well. It's close to midnight. Sheila'll be worried, I'm afraid."

They walked out through the deserted lobby, past the guards and into the street. A solitary lamp cast a dull puddle of luminance on Helga's car. She took the wheel and they purred quietly down an avenue of night.

"I wish——" Her voice out of darkness was thin. "I wish I were out of this. Off in the mountains somewhere."

He nodded, suddenly sick with his own need for open sky and the clean light of stars.

The mob was on them so fast that they had no time to escape. One moment they were driving down an empty way between blind walls, the next instant the ground seemed to vomit men. They came pouring from the side streets, quiet save for a murmur of voices and the shuffling of a thousand feet, and the few lamps gleamed off their eyes and teeth. Helga braked to a squealing halt as the surge went in front of them, cutting them off.

"Kill the scientists!" It hung like a riven cloud for a moment, one quavering scream which became a deep chanting. The living stream flowed around the car, veiled in shadow, and Corinth heard their breathing hot and hoarse in his ears.

Break their bones and burn their homes,
take their wimmin, the sons of sin,
wallow hollow an' open the door,
open an' let the Third Ba'al in!

A sheet of fire ran up behind the tall buildings, something was in flames. The light was like blood on the dripping head which someone lifted on a pole.

They must have broken the line of the patrols, thought Corinth wildly, they must have smashed into this guarded region and meant to lay it waste before reinforcements came.

A face dirty and bearded and stinking shoved in through the driver's window. "Uh woman! He got uh woman here!"

Corinth took the pistol from his coat pocket and fired. Briefly, he was aware of its kick and bark, the stinging of powder grains in his skin. The face hung there for an eternal time, dissolved into blood and smashed bone. Slowly it sagged, and the crowd screamed. The car rocked under their thrusts.

Corinth braced himself, shoving at his own door, jamming it open against the milling press of bodies. Someone clawed at his feet as he scrambled up on the hood. He kicked, feeling his shoe jar against teeth, and stood up. The firelight blazed in his face. He had taken off his glasses, without stopping to think why it was unsafe to be seen wearing them, and the fire and the crowd and the buildings were a shifting blur.

"Now hear me!" he shouted. "Hear me, people of Ba'al!"

A bullet whanged past him, he felt its hornet buzz, but there was no time to be afraid. "Hear the word of the Third Ba'al!"

"Let 'im talk!" It was a bawling somewhere out in that flowing, mumbling, unhuman river of shadows. "Hear his word."

"Lightning and thunder and rain of bombs!" yelled Corinth. "Eat, drink, and be merry, for the end of the world is at hand! Can't you hear the planet cracking under your feet? The scientists have fired the big atomic bomb. We're on our way to kill them before the world breaks open like rotten fruit. Are you with us?"

They halted, muttering, shuffling their feet, uncertain of what they had found. Corinth went on, raving, hardly aware of what he was saying. "—kill and loot and steal the women! Break open the bottle shops! Fire, clean fire, let it burn the scientists who fired the big atomic bomb. This way, brothers! I know where they're hiding. Follow me!"

"Kill them!" The cheering grew, huge and obscene between the cliff walls of Manhattan. The head on the pole bobbed insanely, and firelight wavered off its teeth.

"Down there!" Corinth danced on the hood, gesturing toward Brooklyn. "They're hiding there, people of Ba'al. I saw the big atomic bomb myself, with my own eyes I saw it, and I knew the end of the world was at hand. The Third Ba'al himself sent me to guide you. May his lightnings strike me dead if that ain't the truth!"

Helga blew her horn, an enormous echoing clamor that seemed to drive them into frenzy. Someone began capering, goatlike, and the others joined him, and the mob snake-danced down the street.

Corinth climbed to the ground, shaking uncontrollably. "Follow 'em," he gasped. "They'll get suspicious if we don't follow 'em."

"Sure thing, Pete." Helga helped him inside and trailed the throng. Her headlights glared off their backs. Now and then she blew the horn to urge them on.

There was a whirring high in heaven. Corinth's breath whistled between his teeth. "Let's go," he mumbled.

Helga nodded, made a U-turn, and shot back down the avenue. Behind them, the mob scattered as police helicopters sprayed them with tear gas.

After a silent while, Helga halted before Corinth's place. "Here we are," she said.

"But I was going to see you home," he said feebly.

"You did. Also you stopped those creatures from doing a lot of harm, to the district as well as us." The vague light glimmered off her smile, it was shaky and tears lay in her eyes. "That was wonderful, Pete. I didn't know you could do it."

"Neither did I," he said huskily.

"Maybe you missed your calling. More money in revivals, I'm told. Well—" She sat for a moment, then: "Well, good night."

"Good night," he said.

She leaned forward, lips parted as if she were about to say something more. Then she clamped them shut, shook her head. The slamming of the door was loud and empty as she drove off.

Corinth stood looking after the car till it was out of sight. Then he turned slowly and entered his building.

CHAPTER EIGHT

SUPPLIES WERE RUNNING LOW—food for himself, feed and salt for the animals left to him. There was no electricity, and he didn't like to use fuel in the gasoline lamp he had found. Brock decided that he would have to go to town.

"Stay here, Joe," he said. "I ought to be back soon."

The dog nodded, an uncannily human gesture. He was picking up English fast; Brock had a habit of talking to him and had lately begun a deliberate program of education. "Keep an eye on things, Joe," he said, looking uneasily to the edge of the woods.

He filled the tank of a battered green pickup from the estate's big drums, got in, and went down the driveway. It was a cool, hazy morning, the smell of rain was in the air and the horizon lay blurred. As he rattled down the county road, he thought that the countryside was utterly deserted. What was it—two months—since the change? Maybe there wouldn't be anyone in town at all.

Turning off on the paved state highway, he pushed the accelerator till the motor roared. He wasn't eager to visit normal humanity, and wanted to get it over with. His time alone had been peaceful—plenty of hard work, yes, to keep him busy; but when he wasn't too occupied or tired he was reading and thinking, exploring the possibilities of a mind which by now, he supposed, was that of a high-order genius by pre-change standards. He had settled down phlegmatically to an anchorite's life—there were worse fates—and didn't relish meeting the world again.

He had gone over to Martinson's, the neighbor's, a few days ago, but no one had been there, the place was boarded up and empty. It had given him such an eerie feeling that he hadn't tried anyone else.

A few outlying houses slid past, and then he was over the viaduct and into the town. There was no one in sight, but the houses looked occupied. The shops, though—most of them were closed, blind windows looked at him and he shivered.

He parked outside the A & P supermarket. It didn't look much like a store. The goods were there, but no price tags were shown and the man behind the counter did not have the air of a clerk. He was just sitting there, sitting and—thinking?

Brock went over to him, his feet curiously loud on the floor. "Uh—excuse me," he began, very softly.

The man looked up. Recognition flickered in his eyes and a brief smile crossed his face. "Oh, hello, Archie," he said, speaking with elaborate slowness. "How are you?"

"All right, thanks." Brock looked down at his shoes, unable to meet the quiet eyes. "I, well, I came to buy some stuff."

"Oh?" There was a coolness in the tone. "I'm sorry, but we aren't running things on a money basis any more."

"Well, I——" Brock squared his shoulders and forced himself to look up. "Yeah, I can see that, I guess. The national government's broken down, ain't—hasn't it?"

"Not exactly. It has just stopped mattering, that is all." The man shook his head. "We had our troubles here at the beginning, but we reorganized on a rational basis. Now things are going pretty smoothly. We still lack items we could get from outside, but we can keep going indefinitely as we are, if necessary."

"A—socialist economy?"

"Well, Archie," said the man, "that's hardly the right label for it, since socialism was still founded on the idea of property. But what does ownership of a thing actually mean? It means only that you may do just what you choose with the thing. By that definition, there was very little complete ownership anywhere in the world. It was more a question of symbolism. A man said to himself, 'This is my home, my land,' and got a feeling of strength and security; because the 'my' was a symbol for that state of being, he reacted to the symbol. Now—well—we have seen through that bit of self-deception. It served its purpose before, it made for self-respect and emotional balance, but we don't need it any more. There's no longer any reason for binding oneself to a particular bit of soil when the economic function it served can be carried out more efficiently in other ways. So most of the farmers hereabouts have moved into town, taking over houses which were deserted by those who chose to move away from the neighborhood altogether."

"And you work the land in common?"

"Hardly the correct way to phrase it. Some of the mechanically minded have been devising machines to do most of this for us. It's amazing what can be done with a tractor engine and some junk yard scrap if you have the brains to put it together in the right way.

"We've found our level, for the time being at least. Those who didn't like it have gone, for the most part, and the rest are busy evolving new social reforms to match our new personalities. It's a pretty well-balanced setup here."

"But what do you do?"

"I'm afraid," said the man gently, "that I couldn't explain it to you."

Brock looked away again. "Well," he said finally, his voice oddly husky,

"I'm all alone on the Rossman place and running short on supplies. Also, I'm gonna need help with the harvest and so on. How about it?"

"If you wish to enter our society, I'm sure a place can be found."

"No—I just want——"

"I would strongly advise you to throw in with us, Archie. You'll need the backing of a community. It isn't safe out there any more. There was a circus near here, about the time of the change, and the wild animals escaped and several of them are still running loose."

Brock felt a coldness within himself. "That must have been—exciting," he said slowly.

"It was." The man smiled thinly. "We didn't know at first, you see; we had too much of our own to worry about, and it didn't occur to us till too late that the animals were changing too. One of them must have nosed open his own cage and let out the others to cover his escape. There was a tiger hanging around town for weeks, it took a couple of children and we never did hunt it down—it just was gone one day. Where? What about the elephants and—— No, you aren't safe alone, Archie." He paused. "And then there's the sheer physical labor. You'd better take a place in our community."

"Place, hell!" There was a sudden anger in him, bleak and bitter. "All I want is a little help. You can take a share of the crop to pay for it. Wouldn't be any trouble to you if you have these fancy new machines."

"You can ask the others," said the man. "I'm not really in charge. The final decision would rest with the Council and the Societist. But I'm afraid it would be all or nothing for you, Archie. We won't bother you if you don't want us to, but you can't expect us to give you charity either. That's another outmoded symbol. If you want to fit yourself into the total economy—it's not tyrannical by any means, it's freer than any other the world has ever seen—we'll make a function for you."

"In short," said Brock thickly, "I can be a domestic animal and do what chores I'm given, or a wild one and ignored. For *my* sake—huh!" He turned on his heel. "Take it and stick it."

He was trembling as he walked out and got back into the truck. The worst of it, he thought savagely, the worst of it was that they were right. He couldn't long endure a half-in-half-out pariah status. It had been all right once, being feeble-minded; he didn't know enough then to realize what it meant. Now he did, and the dependent life would break him.

The gears screamed as he started. He'd make out without their help, damn if he wouldn't. If he couldn't be a half-tamed beggar, and wouldn't be a house pet, all right, he'd be a wild animal.

He drove back at a reckless speed. On the way, he noticed a machine out in a hayfield: a big enigmatic thing of flashing arms, doing the whole job with a single bored-looking man to guide it. They'd probably build a robot pilot as soon as they could get the materials. So what? He still had two hands.

Further alone, a patch of woods came down to the edge of the road. He thought he glimpsed something in there, a great gray shape which moved quietly back out of sight, but he couldn't be sure.

His calm temperament reasserted itself as he neared the estate, and he settled down to figuring. From the cows he could get milk and butter, maybe cheese. The few hens he had been able to recapture would furnish eggs. An occasional slaughtered sheep—no, wait, why not hunt down some of those damned pigs instead?—would give him meat for quite a while; there was a smokehouse on the place. He could harvest enough hay, grain and corn—Tom and Jerry would just have to work!—to keep going through the winter; if he improvised a quern, he could grind a coarse flour and bake his own bread. There were plenty of clothes, shoes, tools. Salt was his major problem—but there ought to be a lick somewhere within a hundred miles or so, he could try to look up where and make a trip to it—and he'd have to save on gasoline and cut a lot of wood for winter, but he thought he could pull through. One way or another, he would.

The magnitude of the task appalled him. One man! One pair of hands! But it had been done before, the whole human race had come up the hard way. If he took a cut in his standard of living and ate an unbalanced diet for a while, it wouldn't kill him.

And he had a brain which by pre-change measures was something extraordinary. Already, he had put that mind to work: first, devising a schedule of operations for the next year or so, and secondarily inventing gadgets to make survival easier. Sure—he could do it.

He squared his shoulders and pushed down the accelerator, anxious to get home and begin.

The noise as he entered the driveway was shattering. He heard the grunts and squeals and breaking of wood, and the truck lurched with his panicky jerk at the wheel. *The pigs!* he thought. *The pigs had been watching and had seen him go—*

And he had forgotten his gun.

He cursed and came roaring up the drive, past the house and into the farmyard. There was havoc. The pigs were like small black and white tanks, chuffing and grunting. The barn door was burst open and they were in the stored feed bags, ripping them open, wallowing in the floury stuff, some of them dragging whole sacks out into the woods. There was a bull too, he must have run wild, he snorted and bellowed as he saw the man, and the cows were bawling around, they had broken down their pasture fence and gone to him. Two dead sheep, trampled and ripped, lay in the yard, the rest must have fled in terror. And Joe——

"Joe," called Brock. "Where are yuh, boy?"

It was raining a little, a fine misty downpour which blurred the woods and mingled with the blood on the earth. The old boar looked shiny as iron in the wetness. He lifted his head when the truck came and squealed.

Brock drove straight for him. The truck was his only weapon now. The boar scampered aside and Brock pulled up in front of the barn. At once the pigs closed in, battering at the wheels and sides, grunting their hate of him. The bull lowered his head and pawed the ground.

Joe barked wildly from the top of a brooder house. He was bleeding, it had been a cruel fight, but he had somehow managed to scramble up there and save himself.

Brock backed the truck, swinging it around and driving into the flock. They scattered before him, he couldn't get up enough speed in this narrow place to hit them and they weren't yielding. The bull charged.

There wasn't time to be afraid, but Brock saw death. He swung the truck about, careening across the yard, and the bull met him head on. Brock felt a giant's hand throw him against the windshield.

Ragged darkness parted before his eyes. The bull was staggering, still on his feet, but the truck was dead. The pigs seemed to realize it and swarmed triumphantly to surround the man.

He fumbled, crouched in the cab and lifting the seat. A long-handled wrench was there, comfortingly heavy. "All right," he mumbled. "Come an' get me."

Something loomed out of the woods and mist. It was gray, enormous, reaching for the sky. The bull lifted his dazed head and snorted. The pigs stopped their battering attack and for a moment there was silence.

A shotgun blast ripped like thunder. The old boar was suddenly galloping in circles, wild with pain. Another explosion sent the bull crazy, turning on his heels and making for the woods.

An elephant, gibbered Brock's mind, *an elephant come to help—*

The big gray shape moved slowly in on the pigs. They milled uneasily, their eyes full of hate and terror. The boar fell to the ground and lay gasping out his life. The elephant curled up its trunk and broke into an oddly graceful run. And the pigs fled.

Brock was still for minutes, shaking too badly to move. When he finally climbed out, the wrench hanging loosely in one hand, the elephant had gone over to the haystack and was calmly stuffing its gullet. And two small hairy shapes squatted on the ground before the man.

Joe barked feebly and limped over to his master. "Quiet, boy," mumbled Brock. He stood on strengthless legs and looked into the wizened brown face of the chimpanzee who had the shotgun.

"Okay," he said at last. The fine cold rain was chilly on his sweating face. "Okay, you're the boss just now. What do you want?"

The chimpanzee regarded him for a long time. It was a male, he saw, the other was a female, and he remembered reading that the tropical apes couldn't stand a northern climate very well. These must be from the circus which the man in the store had spoken of, he thought, they must have stolen the gun and taken—or made a bargain with?—the elephant. Now——

The chimpanzee shuddered. Then, very slowly, always watching the human, he laid down the gun and went over and tugged at Brock's jacket.

"Do you understand me?" asked the man. He felt too tired to appreciate how fantastic a scene this was. "You know English?"

There was no answer, except that the ape kept pulling at his clothes, not hard, but with a kind of insistence. After a while, one long-fingered hand pointed from the jacket to himself and his mate.

"Well," said Brock softly, "I think I get it. You're afraid and you need human help, only you don't want to go back to sitting in a cage. Is that it?"

No answer. But something in the wild eyes pleaded with him.

"Well," said Brock, "you came along in time to do me a good turn, and you ain't killing me now when you could just as easy do it." He took a deep breath. "And God knows I could use some help on this place, you two and your elephant might make all the difference. And—and—okay. Sure."

He took off the jacket and gave it to the chimpanzee. The ape chattered softly and slipped it on. It didn't fit very well, and Brock had to laugh.

Then he straightened his bent shoulders. "All right. Fine. We'll all be wild animals together. Okay? Come along into the house and get something to eat."

CHAPTER NINE

VLADIMIR IVANOVITCH PANYUSHKIN stood under the trees, letting the rain drip onto his helmet and run off the shoulders of his coat. It was a good coat, he had taken it off a colonel after the last battle, it shed water like a very duck. The fact that his feet squelched in worn-out boots did not matter.

Vision swept down the hill, past the edge of forest and into the valley, and there the rain cut it off. Nothing stirred that he could see, nothing but the steady wash of rain, and he could hear nothing except its hollow sound. But the instrument said there was a Red Army unit in the neighborhood.

He looked at the instrument where it lay cradled in the priest's hands. Its needle was blurred with the rain that runneled across the glass dial, but he could see it dance. He did not understand the thing—the priest had made it, out of a captured radio—but it had given warning before.

"I would say they are some ten kilometers off, Vladimir Ivanovitch." The priest's beard waggled when he spoke. It was matted with rain and hung stiffly across his coarse robe. "They are circling about, not approaching us. Perhaps God is misleading them."

Panyushkin shrugged. He was a materialist himself. But if the man of God was willing to help him against the Soviet government, he was glad to accept that help. "And perhaps they have other plans," he answered. "I think we had best consult Fyodor Alexandrovitch."

"It is not good for him to be used so much, my son," said the priest. "He is very tired."

"So are we all, my friend." Panyushkin's words were toneless. "But this is a key operation. If we can cut across to Kirovograd, we can isolate the Ukraine from the rest of the country. Then the Ukrainian nationalists can rise with hope of success."

He whistled softly, a few notes with a large meaning. Music could be made a language. The whole uprising, throughout the Soviet empire, depended in part on secret languages made up overnight.

The Sensitive came out of the dripping brush which concealed Panyushkin's troops. He was small for his fourteen years, and there was a blankness behind his eyes. The priest noted the hectic flush in his cheeks and crossed himself, murmuring a prayer for the boy. It was saddening to use him so hard. But if the godless men were to be over-thrown at all, it would have to be soon, and the Sensitives were necessary. They were the untappable, unjammable, undetectable link which tied together angry men from Riga to Vladivostok; the best of them were spies such as no army had ever owned before. But there were still many who stood by the masters, for reasons of loyalty or fear or self-interest, and they had most of the weapons. Therefore a whole new concept of war had to be invented by the rebels.

A people may loathe their government, but endure it because they know those who protest will die. But if all the people can be joined together, to act at once—or, most of them, simply to disobey with a deadly kind of peacefulness—the government can only shoot a few. Cut off from its own strong roots, the land and the folk, a government is vulnerable and less than a million armed men may be sufficient to destroy it.

"There is a Red Star," said Panyushkin, pointing out into the rain. "Can you tell what they plan, Fyodor Alexandrovitch?"

The boy sat down on the running, sopping hillside and closed his eyes. Panyushkin watched him somberly. It was hard enough being a link with ten thousand other Sensitives across half a continent. Reaching for unlike minds would strain him close to the limit. But it had to be done.

"There is—they know us." The boy's voice seemed to come from very far away. "They—have—instruments. Their metal smells us. They—no, it is death! They send death!" He opened his eyes, sucked in a sharp gasp, and fainted. The priest knelt to take him up and cast Panyushkin a reproachful look.

"Guided missiles!" The leader whirled on his heel. "So they *do* have detectors like ours now. Good thing we checked, eh, priest? Now let us get away from here before the rockets come!"

He left enough metallic stuff behind to fool the instruments, and led his men along the ridge of hills. While the army was busy firing rockets on his camp, he would be readying an attack on their rear.

With or without the help of the priest's incomprehensible God, he felt quite sure that the attack would succeed.

Felix Mandelbaum had hardly settled into his chair when the annunciator spoke. "Gantry." The secretary's tone of voice said that it was important.

Gantry—he didn't know anybody of that name. He sighed and looked out the windows. Morning shadow still lay cool across the streets, but it was going to be a hot day.

There was a tank squatting on its treads down there, guns out to guard City Hall. The worst of the violence seemed to have passed: the Third Ba'al cult was falling apart rapidly after the prophet's ignominious capture last week, the criminal gangs were being dealt with as the militia grew in size and experience, a measure of calm was returning to the city. But there was no telling what still prowled the outer districts, and there were surely going to be other storms before everything was finally under control.

Mandelbaum sat back in his chair, forcing tensed muscles to relax. He always felt tired these days, under the thin hard-held surface of energy. Too much to do, too little time for sleep. He pushed the buzzer which signalled: Let him in.

Gantry was a tall rawboned man whose good clothes did not quite fit him. There was an upstate twang in the ill-tempered voice: "They tell me you're the dictator of the city now."

"Not exactly," said Mandelbaum, smiling. "I'm just a sort of general trouble shooter for the mayor and the council."

"Yeah. But when there's nothing but trouble, the trouble shooter gets to be boss." There was a truculence in the swift reply. Mandelbaum didn't try to deny the charge, it was true enough. The mayor had all he could do handling ordinary administrative machinery; Mandelbaum was the flexible man, the co-ordinator of a thousand quarreling elements, the maker of basic policy, and the newly created city council rarely failed to vote as he suggested.

"Sit down," he invited. "What's your trouble?" His racing mind already knew the answer, but he gained time by making the other spell it out for him.

"I represent the truck farmers of eight counties. I was sent here to ask what your people mean by robbing us."

"Robbing?" asked Mandelbaum innocently.

"You know as well as I do. When we wouldn't take dollars for our stuff they tried to give us city scrip. And when we wouldn't take that, they said they'd seize our crops."

"I know," said Mandelbaum. "Some of the boys are pretty tactless. I'm sorry."

Gantry's eyes narrowed. "Are you ready to say they won't pull guns on us? I hope so, because we got guns of our own."

"Have you got tanks and planes too?" asked Mandelbaum. He waited an instant for the meaning to sink in, then went on swiftly: "Look, Mr. Gantry, there are six or seven million people left in this city. If we can't assure them a regular food supply, they'll starve. Can your association stand by and let seven million innocent men, women, and children die of hunger while you sit on more food than you can eat? No. You're decent human beings. You couldn't."

"I don't know," said Gantry grimly. "After what that mob did when it came stampeding out of the city last month——"

"Believe me, the city government did everything it could to stop them. We failed in part, the panic was too big, but we did keep the whole city from moving out on you." Mandelbaum made a bridge of his fingers and said judicially: "Now if you really were monsters you'd let the rest of them stay here to die. Only they wouldn't. Sooner or later, they'd all swarm out on you, and then everything would go under."

"Sure. Sure." Gantry twisted his large red hands together. Somehow, he found himself on the defensive. "It ain't that we want to make trouble, out in the country. It's just—well, we raise food for you, but you ain't paying us. You're just taking it. Your scrip don't mean a thing. What can we buy with it?"

"Nothing, now," said Mandelbaum candidly. "But believe me, it's not our fault. The people here want to work. We just haven't got things organized enough yet. Once we do, our scrip will mean things like clothes and machinery for you. If you let us starve, though—where's your market then?"

"All that was said at the association meeting," replied Gantry. "The thing is, what guarantee have we got that you'll keep your end of the bargain?"

"Look, Mr. Gantry, we do want to co-operate. We want it so much that we're prepared to offer a representative of your people a seat on the city council. Then how can we double-cross you?"

"Hmmm—" Gantry's eyes narrowed shrewdly. "How many members on the council all told?"

They bargained for a while, and Gantry left with a city offer of four seats which would hold special veto powers on certain matters concerning rural policy. Mandelbaum was sure the farmers would accept it: it looked like a distinct victory for their side.

He grinned to himself. How do you define victory? The veto power wouldn't mean a thing, because rural policy was perfectly straightforward anyway. The city, the whole state and nation, would gain by the reunification of so large an area. Perhaps the piled-up debt to the farmers would never be paid—society was changing so rapidly that there might be no more cities in a few years—but that, however lamentable, was a small matter. What counted now was survival.

"North and Morgan," said the annunciator.

Mandelbaum braced himself. This was going to be tougher. The waterfront boss and the crazy political theorist had their own ambitions, and considerable followings—too large to be put down by force. He stood up politely to greet them.

North was a burly man, his face hard under its layers of fat; Morgan was slighter physically, but his eyes smoldered under the high bald forehead. They glared at each other as they came in, and looked accusingly at Mandelbaum. North growled their mutual question: "What's the idea bringing us in at the same time? I wanted to see you in private?"

"Sorry," said Mandelbaum insincerely. "There must have been a mix-up. Would you mind both just sitting down for a few minutes, though? Maybe we can work it out together somehow."

"There is no 'somehow' about it," snapped Morgan. "I and my followers are getting sick of seeing the obvious principles of Dynapsychism ignored in this government. I warn you, unless you reorganize soon along sensible lines——"

North brushed him aside and turned to Mandelbaum. "Look here, there're close to a hundred ships layin' idle in the port of New York while th' East Coast and Europe're yellin' for trade. My boys're gettin' fed up with havin' their voice go unheard."

"We haven't had much word from Europe lately," said Mandelbaum in apologetic tone. "And things are too mixed up yet for us even to try coastwise trading. What'd we trade with? Where'd we find fuel for those ships? I'm sorry, but——" His mind went on: *The real trouble is, your racket hasn't got any waterfront to live off now.*

"It all comes from blind stubbornness," declared Morgan. "As I have conclusively shown, a social integration along the psychological principles I have discovered would eliminate——"

And your trouble is, you want power, and too many people are still hunting a panacea, a final answer, thought Mandelbaum coldly. *You sound intellectual, so they think you are; a certain class still wants a man on a white horse, but prefers him with a textbook under one arm. You and Lenin!*

"Excuse me," he said aloud. "What do you propose to do, Mr. North?"

"New York started as a port an' it'll be a port again before long. This time we wanna see that the workers that make the port go, get their fair share in governin' it!"

In other words, you also want to be dictator. Aloud, thoughtfully: "There may be something in what you both say. But we can't do everything at once, you know. It seems to me, though, like you two gentlemen are thinking along pretty parallel lines. Why don't you get together and present a united front? Then I'd find it a lot easier to put your proposals before the council."

Morgan's pale cheeks flushed. "A band of sweaty human machines——"

North's big fists doubled. "Watch y'r langwidge, sonny boy."

"No, really," said Mandelbaum. "You both want a better integrated government, don't you? It seems to me——"

Hmmm. The same thought lit the two pairs of eyes. It had been shockingly easy to plant it. *Together, perhaps, we could . . . and then afterward I can get rid of him——*

There was more discussion, but it ended with North and Morgan going out together. Mandelbaum could almost read their contempt for him; hadn't he ever heard of divide and rule?

Briefly, there was sadness in him. So far, people hadn't really changed much. The wild-eyed dreamer simply built higher castles in the clouds; the hard-boiled racketeer had no vocabulary of ideas or concepts to rise above his own language of greed.

It wouldn't last. Within months, there would be no more Norths and no more Morgans. The change in themselves, and in all mankind, would destroy their littleness. But meanwhile, they were dangerous animals and had to be dealt with.

He reached for the phone and called over the web operated for him alone. "Hullo, Bowers? How're you doing? ——Look, I've got the Dynapsychist and the rackets boss together. They'll probably plan a sort of fake Popular Front, with the idea of getting seats on the council and then taking over the whole show by force—palace revolution, *coup d'état,* whatever you call it. ——Yeh. Alert our agents in both parties. I'll want complete reports. Then we want to use those agents to egg them on against each other. ——Yeah, the alliance is as unstable as any I ever heard of. A little careful pushing, and they'll bury the hatchet all right—in each other. Then when the militia has mopped up what's left of the tong war, we can start our propaganda campaign in favor of common sense. ——Sure, it'll take some tricky timing, but we can swing it.——"

For a moment, as he laid the phone down, his face sagged with an old grief. He had just condemned some scores of people, most of whom were merely bewildered and misled, to death. But it couldn't be helped. He had the life and freedom of several million human beings to save—the price was not exorbitant.

"Uneasy sits the butt that bears the boss," he muttered, and looked at his appointment list. There was an hour yet before the representative from Albany arrived. That was going to be a hot one to handle. The city was breaking state and national laws every day—it had to—and the governor was outraged. He wanted to bring the whole state back under his own authority. It wasn't an unreasonable wish, but the times weren't ripe; and when they eventually were, the old forms of government would be no more important than the difference between Homoousian and Homoiousian. But it was going to take a lot of argument to convince the Albany man of that.

Meanwhile, though, he had an hour free. He hesitated for a split second between working on the new rationing system and on the plans for extending law and order to outer Jersey. Then he laid both aside in favor of the latest report on the water situation.

CHAPTER TEN

THERE WAS A DIMNESS in the laboratory which made the pulsing light at the machine's heart stand out all the brighter, weirdly blue and restless between the coils and the impassive meter faces. Grunewald's face was corpse-colored as he bent over it.

"Well," he said unnecessarily, "that seems to be that."

He flicked the main switch, and the electric hum whined and the light died. For a moment he stood thoughtfully regarding the anesthesized rat within the coils. Hairlike wires ran from its shaven body to the meters over which Johansson and Lewis stood.

Lewis nodded. "Neural rate jumps up again." He touched the dials of the oscilloscope with finicking care. "And just about on the curve we predicted. You've generated an inhibitor field, all right." There would be other tests to make, detailed study, but that could be left to assistants. The main problem was solved.

Grunewald reached in with thick, oddly delicate hands and took out the rat and began extracting the probes. "Poor little guy," he murmured. "I wonder if we're doing him a favor."

Corinth, hunched moodily on a stool, looked up sharply.

"What use is intelligence to him?" pursued Grunewald. "It just makes him realize the horror of his own position. What use is it to any of us, in fact?"

"Would you go back, yourself?" asked Corinth.

"Yes." Grunewald's square blond face held a sudden defiance. "Yes, I would. It's not good to think too much or too clearly."

"Maybe," whispered Corinth, "maybe you've got something there. The new civilization—not merely its technology, but its whole value system, all its dreams and hopes—will have to be built afresh, and that will take many generations. We're savages now, with all the barrenness of the savage's existence. Science isn't the whole of life."

"No," said Lewis. "But scientists—like artists of all kinds, I suppose—have by and large kept their sanity through the change because they had a purpose in life to start with, something outside themselves to which they could give all they had." His plump face flashed with a tomcat grin. "Also, Pete, as an old sensualist I'm charmed with all the new possibilities. The art and music I used to swoon over have gone, yes, but I don't appreciate good wine and cuisine the less; in fact, my perception is heightened, there are nuances I never suspected before."

It had been a strange conversation, one of a few words and many gestures and facial expressions thrown into a simultaneous discussion of technical problems:

"Well," Johansson had said, "we've got our inhibitor field. Now it's up to you neurologists to study it in detail and find out just what we can expect to happen to life on Earth."

"Uh-huh," said Lewis. "I'm not working on that just now, though, except as a kibitzer. Bronzini and MacAndrews can handle it. I'm co-opting myself into the psychological department, which is not only more interesting but of more immediate practical importance. I'll handle the neurological-cybernetic aspect of their work."

"Our old psychology is almost useless," nodded Corinth. "We're changing too much to understand our own motivations any more. Why am I spending most of my time here, when maybe I should be home helping Sheila face her adjustment? I just can't help myself, I have to explore this new field, but—— To start afresh, on a rational basis, we'll have to know something about the dynamics of man—— As for me, I'm off this baby too, now that we've actually succeeded in generating a field. Rossman wants me to work on his spaceship project as soon as he can get it organized."

"Spaceship—faster-than-light travel, eh?"

"That's right. The principle uses an aspect of wave mechanics which wasn't suspected before the change. We'll generate a psi wave which—— Never mind, I'll explain it to you when you've gotten around to learning tensor analysis and matrix algebra. I'm collaborating with some others here in drawing up plans for the thing, while we wait for the men and materials to start building. We should be able to go anywhere in the galaxy once we've got the ship."

The two threads coalesced: "Running away from ourselves," said Grunewald. "Running into space itself to escape." For a moment the four men were silent, thinking.

Corinth got to his feet. "I'm going home," he said harshly.

His mind was a labyrinth of interweaving thought chains as he went down the stairs. Mostly he was thinking of Sheila, but something whispered of Helga too, and there was a flow of diagrams and equations, a vision of chill immensity through which the Earth spun like a bit of dust. An oddly detached part of himself was coolly studying that web of thought, so that he could learn how it worked and train himself to handle his own potentialities.

Language: The men of the Institute, who knew each other, were involuntarily developing a new set of communication symbols, a subtle and powerful thing in which every gesture had meaning and the speeding brain of the listener, without conscious effort, filled in the gaps and grasped the many-leveled meaning. It was almost too efficient, you gave your inmost self away. The man of the future would likely go naked in soul as well as in body, and Corinth wasn't sure he liked the prospect.

But then there was Sheila and himself; their mutual understanding made their talk unintelligible to an outsider. And there were a thousand, a million groups throughout the world, creating their own dialects on a basis of past experience which had not been shared with all humanity. Some arbitrary language for the whole world would have to be devised.

Telepathy? There could no longer be any doubt that it existed, in some people at least. Extrasensory perception would have to be investigated when things had quieted down. There was so much to do, and life was so terribly short!

Corinth shivered. Fear of personal extinction was supposed to be an adolescent reaction; but in a sense, all men were adolescents once more, on a new plane—no, children, babies.

Well, no doubt the biologists would within the next few years find some means of lengthening the lifespan, prolonging it for centuries perhaps. But was that ultimately desirable?

He came out on the street and located the automobile Rossman had provided for him. *At least,* he thought wryly as he entered it, *the parking problem has been solved. No more traffic like there once was.*

Eventually, no more New York. Big cities had no real economic justification. He came from a small town, and he had always loved mountains and forests and sea. Still, there was something about this brawling, frenetic, overcrowded, hard, inhuman, magnificent city whose absence would leave an empty spot in the world to come.

It was a hot night. His shirt stuck clammily to him, and the air seemed thick. Overhead, between the darkened buildings and the dead neon signs, heat lightning flickered palely and all the earth yearned for rain. His headlights cut a dull swath through the gummy blackness.

There were more cars abroad than there had been even a week ago. The city was just about tamed now; the gang war between Portmen and Dynapsychists, suppressed two weeks back, seemed to have been the last flare of violence. Rations were still short, but people were being put to work again and they'd all live.

Corinth pulled up in the parking lot behind his apartment and walked around to the front. The power ration authority had lately permitted this building to resume elevator service, which was a mercy. He hadn't enjoyed climbing fifteen flights when electricity was really short.

I hope—— He was thinking of Sheila, but he left the thought unfinished. She'd been getting thin, poor kid, and she didn't sleep well and sometimes she woke with a dry scream in her throat and groped blindly for him. He wished his work didn't take him away from her. She needed companionship badly. Maybe he could get her some kind of job to fill the hours.

When he came out on his floor, the hall was darkened save for a vague night light, but radiance streamed under his door. Glancing at his watch, he saw that it was later than her usual bedtime. So she couldn't sleep tonight, either.

He tried the door, but it was locked and he rapped. He thought he heard a smothered scream from within, and knocked harder. She opened the door so violently that he almost fell inside.

"Pete, Pete, Pete!" She pressed herself to him with a shudder. With his arms about her, he felt how close the delicate ribs lay to her skin. The lamplight was harsh, filling the room, and oddly lusterless on her hair. When she lifted her face, he saw that it was wet.

"What's the matter?" he asked. He spoke aloud, in the old manner, and his voice was suddenly wavering.

"Nerves." She drew him inside and closed the door. In a nightgown and bathrobe she looked pathetically young, but there was something ancient in her eyes.

"Hot night to be wearing a robe," he said, groping for expression.

"I feel cold." Her lips trembled.

His own mouth fell into a harsh line, and he sat down in an easy chair and pulled her to his lap. She laid arms about him, hugging him to her, and he felt the shiver in her body.

"This is not good," he said. "This is the worst attack you've had yet."

"I don't know what I'd have done if you'd been much longer about coming," she said tonelessly.

They began to talk then, in the new interweaving of word and gesture, tone and silence and shared remembering, which was peculiarly theirs.

"I've been thinking too much," she told him. "We all think too much these days." (Help me, my dearest! I am going down in darkness and only you can rescue me.)

"You'll have to get used to it," he answered dully. (How can I help? My hands reach for you and close on emptiness.)

"You have strength——" she cried. "Give it to me!" (Nightmares each time I try to sleep. Waking, I see the world and man as a flickering in cold and nothingness, empty out to the edge of forever. I can't endure that vision.)

Weariness, hopelessness: "I'm not strong," he said. "I just keep going somehow. So must you."

"Hold me close, Pete," *Father image*, "hold me close," she whimpered. Pressing to him as if he were a shield against the blackness outside and the darkness within and the things rising through it: "Don't ever let me go!"

"Sheila," he said. (Beloved: wife, mistress, comrade.) "Sheila, you've got to hang on. All this is just an increased power to think—to visualize, to handle data and the dreams you yourself have created. Nothing more."

"But it is changing *me!*" The horror of death was in her now. She fought it with something like wistfulness: "—and where has our world gone? Where are our hopes and plans and togetherness?"

"We can't bring them back," he replied. Emptiness, irrevocability: "We have to make out with what we have now."

"I know, I know—and I can't!" Tears gleamed along her cheeks. "Oh, Pete, I'm crying more for you now," (Maybe I won't even go on loving you.) "than for me."

He tried to stay cool. "Too far a retreat from reality is insanity. If you went mad——" Unthinkableness.

"I know, I know," she said. "All too well, Pete. Hold me close."

"And it doesn't help you to know——" he said, and wondered if the engineers would ever be able to find the breaking strength of the human spirit. He felt very near to giving way.

CHAPTER ELEVEN

SUMMER WANED as the planet turned toward winter. On a warm evening late in September, Mandelbaum sat by the window with Rossman, exchanging a few low-voiced words. The room was unlit, full of night. Far below them the city of Manhattan glowed with spots of radiance, not the frantic flash and glare of earlier days but the lights of a million homes. Overhead, there was a dull blue wash of luminance across the sky, flickering and glimmering on the edge of visibility. The Empire State Building was crowned with a burning sphere like a small sun come to rest, and the wandering air held a faint tingle of ozone. The two men sat quietly, resting, smoking the tobacco which had again become minutely available, Mandelbaum's pipe and Rossman's cigarette like two ruddy eyes in the twilit room. They were waiting for death.

"Wife," said Rossman with a note of gentle reproach. It could be rendered as: (I still don't see why you wouldn't tell your wife of this, and be with her tonight. It may be the last night of your lives.)

"Work, city, time," and the immemorial shrug and the wistful tone: (We both have our work to do, she at the relief center and I here at the defense hub. We haven't told the city either, you and I and the few others who know. It's best not to do so, eh?) *We couldn't have evacuated them, there would have been no place for them to go and the fact of our attempting it would've been a tip-off to the enemy, an invitation to send the rockets immediately. Either we can save the city or we can't; at the moment, there's nothing anyone can do but wait and see if the defense works.* (I wouldn't worry my Liebchen—she'd worry on my account and the kids' and grandchildren's. No, let it happen, one way or the other. Still I do wish we could be together now, Sarah and I, the whole family——) Mandelbaum tamped his pipe with a horny thumb.

(The Brookhaven men think the field will stop the blast and radiation), implied Rossman. *We've had them working secretly for the past month or more, anticipating an attack. The cities we think will be assailed are guarded now—we hope.* (But it's problematic. I wish we didn't have to do it this way.)

"What other way?" *We knew, from our spies and deductions, that the Soviets have developed their intercontinental atomic rockets, and that they're desperate. Revolution at home, arms and aid being smuggled in to the insurgents from America. They'll make a last-ditch attempt to wipe us out, and we believe the attack is due tonight. But if it fails, they've shot their bolt. It must have taken all their remaining resources to design and build those rockets.* "Let them exhaust themselves against us, while the rebels take over their country. Dictatorship is done for."

"But what will replace it?"

"I don't know. When the rockets come, it seems to me they'll be the last gasp of animal man. Didn't you once call the twentieth century the Era of Bad Manners? We were stupid before—incredibly stupid! Now all that's fading away."

"And leaving—nothing." Rossman lit a fresh cigarette and stubbed out the old one. The brief red light threw his gaunt, fine-boned face into high relief against darkness.

"Oh, yes," he went on, "the future is not going to look anything like the past. Presumably there will still be society—or societies—but they won't be the same kind as those we've known before. Maybe they'll be purely abstract, mental things, interchanges and interactions on the symbolic level. Nevertheless, there can be better or worse societies developed out of our new potentialities, and I think the worse ones will grow up."

"Hm." Mandelbaum drew hard on his pipe. "Aside from the fact that we have to start from scratch, and so are bound to make mistakes, why should that necessarily be so? You're a born pessimist, I'm afraid."

"No doubt. I was born into one age, and saw it die in blood and madness. Even before 1914, you could see the world crumbling. That would make a pessimist of anyone. But I think it's true what I say. Because man has, in effect, been thrown back into utter savagery. No, not that either; the savage does have his own systems of life. Man is back on the animal plane."

Mandelbaum's gesture swept over the huge arrogance of the city. "Is that animal?"

"Ants and beavers are good engineers." *Or were. I wonder what the beavers are doing now.* "Material artifacts don't count for much, really. They're only possible because of a social background of knowledge, tradition, desire—they're symptoms, not causes. And we have had all our background stripped from us.

"Oh, we haven't forgotten anything, no. But it's no longer of value to us, except as a tool for the purely animal business of survival and comfort. Think over your own life. What use do you see in it now? What are all your achievements of the past? Ridiculous!

"Can you read any of the great literature now with pleasure? Do the arts convey anything to you? The civilization of the past, with its science and art and beliefs and meanings, is so inadequate for us now that it might as well not exist. We have no civilization any longer. We have no goals, no dreams, no creative work—nothing!"

"Oh, I don't know about that," said Mandelbaum with a hint of amusement. "I've got enough to do—to help out with, at least—for the next several years. We've got to get things started on a worldwide basis, economics, politics, medical care, population control, conservation, it's a staggering job."

"But after that?" persisted Rossman. "What will we do then? What will the next generation do, and all generations to come?"

"They'll find something."

"I wonder. The assignment of building a stable world order is herculean, but you and I realize that for the new humanity it's possible—indeed, only a matter of years. But what then? At best, man may sit back and stagnate in an unchanging smugness. A horribly empty sort of life."

"Science——"

"Oh, yes, the scientists will have a field day for a while. But most of the physicists I've talked to lately suspect that the potential range of science is not unlimited. They think the variety of discoverable natural laws and phenomena must be finite, all to be summed up in one unified theory—and that we're not far from that theory today. It's not the sort of proposition which can ever be proved with certainty, but it looks probable.

"And in no case can we all be scientists."

Mandelbaum looked out into darkness. *How quiet the night is,* he thought. Wrenching his mind from the vision of Sarah and the children: "Well, how about the arts? We've got to develop a whole new painting, sculpture, music, literature, architecture—and forms that have never been imagined before!"

"If we get the right kind of society." (Art, throughout history, has had a terrible tendency to decay, or to petrify into sheer imitation of the past. It seems to take some challenge to wake it up again. And again, my friend, we can't all be artists either.)

"No?" (I wonder if every man won't be an artist and a scientist and a philosopher and——)

"You'll still need leaders, and stimulus, and a world symbol." (That's the basic emptiness in us today: we haven't found a symbol. We have no myth, no dream. 'Man is the measure of all things'—well, when the measure is bigger than everything else, what good is it?)

"We're still pretty small potatoes." Mandelbaum gestured at the window and the bluely glimmering sky. (There's a whole universe out there, waiting for us.)

"I think you have the start of an answer," said Rossman slowly. (Earth has grown too small, but astronomical space—it may hold the challenge and the dream we need. I don't know. All I know is that we had better find one.)

There was a thin buzz from the telephone unit beside Mandelbaum. He reached over and flipped the switch. There was a sudden feeling of weariness in him. He ought to be tense, jittering with excitement, but he only felt tired and hollow.

The machine clicked a few signals: "Space station robot reports flight of rockets from Urals. Four are due at New York in about ten minutes."

"Ten minutes!" Rossman whistled. "They must have an atomic drive."

"No doubt." Mandelbaum dialed for Shield Center in the Empire State Building. "Brace your machinery, boys," he said. "Ten minutes to go."

"How many?"

"Four. They must figure on our stopping at least three, so they'll be powerful brutes. Hydrogen-lithium warheads, I imagine."

"Four, eh? Okay, boss. Wish us luck."

"Wish *you* luck?" Mandelbaum grinned crookedly.

The city had been told that the project was an experiment in illumination. But when the blueness strengthened to a steady glow, like a roof of light, and the sirens began to hoot, everyone must have guessed the truth. Mandelbaum thought of husbands clutching wives and children to them and wondered what else might be happening. *Prayer? Not likely; if there was to be a religion in the future, it could not be the animism which had sufficed for the blind years. Exaltation in battle? No, that was another discarded myth. Wild panic? Maybe a little of that.*

Rossman had seen at least a good deal of truth, thought Mandelbaum. *There was nothing for man to do now, in the hour of judgment, except to scream with fear or to stoop over those he loved and try to shelter them with his pitiful flesh. No one could honestly feel that he was dying for something worthy. If he shook his fist at heaven, it was not in anger against evil, it was only a reflex.*

Emptiness— Yes, he thought, *I suppose we do need new symbols.*

Rossman got up and felt his way through the dusk to a cabinet where he opened a drawer and took out a bottle. "This is some '42 burgundy I've been saving," he said. (Will you drink with me?)

"Sure," said Mandelbaum. He didn't care for wine, but he had to help his friend. Rossman wasn't afraid, he was old and full of days, but there was something lost about him. To go out like a gentleman—well, that was a symbol of sorts.

Rossman poured into crystal goblets and handed one to Mandelbaum with grave courtesy. They clinked glasses and drank. Rossman sat down again, savoring the taste.

"We had burgundy on my wedding day," he said.

"Ah, well, no need to cry into it," answered Mandelbaum. "The screen will hold. It's the same kind of force that holds atomic nuclei together—nothing stronger in the universe."

"I was toasting animal man," said Rossman. (You are right, this is his last gasp. But he was in many ways a noble creature.)

"Yeah," said Mandelbaum. (He invented the most ingenious weapons.)

"Those rockets—" (They do represent something. They are beautiful things, you know, clean and shining, built with utter honesty. It took many patient centuries to reach the point where they could be forged. The fact that they carry death for us is incidental.)

(I don't agree.) Mandelbaum chuckled, a sad little sound in the great quiet around him.

There was a luminous-dialed clock in the room. Its sweep-second hand went in a long lazy circle, once around, twice around, three times around. The Empire State was a pylon of darkness against the dull blue arc of sky. Mandelbaum and Rossman sat drinking, lost in their own thoughts.

There was a glare like lightning all over heaven, the sky was a sudden incandescent bowl. Mandelbaum covered his dazzled eyes, letting the goblet fall shattering to the floor. He felt the radiance on his skin like sunshine, blinking on and off. The city roared with thunder.

—two, three, four.

Afterward there was another stillness, in which the echoes shuddered and boomed between high walls. A wind sighed down the empty streets, and the great buildings shivered slowly back toward rest.

"Good enough," said Mandelbaum. He didn't feel any particular emotion. The screen had worked, the city lived—all right, he could get on with his job. He dialed City Hall. "Hello, there. All okay? Look, we got to get busy, check any panic and——"

Out of the corner of one eye he saw Rossman sitting quietly, his unfinished drink on the arm of the chair.

CHAPTER TWELVE

Corinth sighed and pushed the work from him. The murmurs of the evening city drifted faintly up to him through a window left open to the October chill. He shivered a little, but fumbled out a cigarette and sat for a while smoking.

Spaceships, he thought dully. *Out at Brookhaven they're building the first star ship.*

His own end of the project was the calculation of intra-nuclear stresses under the action of the drive field, a task of some complexity but not of such overreaching importance that the workers couldn't go ahead on the actual construction before he finished. He had been out there just today, watching the hull take shape, and his professional self had found a cool sort of glory in its perfected loveliness. Every organ of the ship, engine and armor and doors and ports and controls, was a piece of precision engineering such as Earth had never seen before. It was good to be a part of such work.

Only——

He swore softly, grinding out the cigarette in an overloaded ashtray and rising to his feet. It was going to be one of his bad nights; he needed Helga.

The Institute hummed around him as he went down the familiar halls. They were working on a twenty-four hour schedule now, a thousand liberated minds spreading toward a horizon which had suddenly exploded beyond imagination. He envied the young technicians. They were the strong and purposeful and balanced, the future belonged to them and they knew it. At thirty-three, he felt exhausted with years.

Helga had come back to resume directorship here: on its new basis, it was a full-time job for a normal adult, and she had the experience and the desire to serve. He thought that she drove herself too hard, and realized with a muted guilt that it was largely his fault. She never left before he did, because sometimes he needed to talk to her. This was going to be one of those times.

He knocked. The crisp voice over the annunciator said, "Come in," and he did not miss the eagerness in her voice or the sudden lighting in her eyes as he entered.

"Come have dinner with me, won't you?" he invited.

She arched her brows, and he explained hastily: "Sheila's with Mrs. Mandelbaum tonight. She—Sarah—she's good for my wife, she's got a sort of plain woman sense a man can't have. I'm at loose ends——"

"Sure." Helga began arranging her papers and stacking them away. Her office was always neat and impersonal, a machine could have been its occupant. "Know a joint?"

"You know I don't get out much these days."

"Well, let's try Rogers'. A new night club for the new man." Her smile was a little sour. "At least they have decent food."

He stepped into the small adjoining bathroom, trying to adjust his untidy clothes and hair. When he came out, Helga was ready. For an instant he looked at her, perceiving every detail with a flashing completeness undreamed of in the lost years. They could not hide from each other and—she with characteristic honesty, he with a weary and grateful surrender—had quit trying. He needed someone who understood him and was stronger than he, someone to talk to, to draw strength from. He thought that she only gave and he only took, but it was not a relationship he could afford to give up.

She took his arm and they went out into the street. The air was thin and sharp in their lungs, it smelled of autumn and the sea. A few dead leaves swirled across the sidewalk before them, already frost had come.

"Let's walk," she said, knowing his preference. "It isn't far."

He nodded and they went down the long half-empty ways. The night loomed big above the street lamps, the cliffs of Manhattan were mountainously black around them and only a rare automobile or pedestrian went by. Corinth thought that the change in New York epitomized what had happened to the world.

"How's Sheila's work?" asked Helga. Corinth had obtained a job for his wife at the relief center, in the hope that it would improve her morale. He shrugged, not answering. It was better to lift his face into the wind that streamed thinly between the dark walls. She fell into his silence; when he felt the need for communication, she would be there.

A modest neon glow announced Rogers' Cafe. They turned in at the door, to find a blue twilight which was cool and luminous, as if the very air held a transmuted light. *Good trick*, thought Corinth, *wonder how they do it?*—and in a moment he had reasoned out the new principle of fluorescence on which it must be based. Maybe an engineer had suddenly decided he would prefer to be a restaurateur.

There were tables spaced somewhat farther apart than had been the custom in earlier times. Corinth noted idly that they were arranged in a spiral which, on the average, minimized the steps of waiters from dining room to kitchen and back. But it was a machine which rolled up to them on soft rubber wheels and extended a slate and stylus for them to write their orders on.

The menu listed few meat dishes—there was still a food shortage—but Helga insisted that the soya supreme was delicious and Corinth ordered it for both of them. There would be an aperitif too, of course.

He touched glasses with her over the white cloth. Her eyes were grave on his, waiting. "*Was hael.*"

"*Drinc hael*," she answered. Wistfully: "I'm afraid our descendants will not understand our ancestors at all. The whole magnificent barbarian heritage will be animal mouthings to them, won't it? When I think of the future I sometimes feel cold."

"You too," he murmured, and knew that she let down her reserve only because it made it easier for him to unburden himself.

A small orchestra came out. Corinth recognized three men among them who had been famous musicians before the change. They carried the old instruments, strings and a few woodwinds and one trumpet, but there were some new ones too. Well, until philharmonic associations came back, if they ever did, no doubt serious artists would be glad of a chance to play in a restaurant—at that, they'd have a more appreciative audience than usual in the past.

His eyes went around among the customers. They were ordinary-looking people, hornyhanded laborers side by side with thin stoop-shouldered clerks and balding professors. The new nakedness had obliterated old distinctions, everybody was starting from scratch. There was an easy informality of dress, open-necked shirts, slacks and jeans, an occasional flamboyant experiment. Physical externals were counting for less every day.

There was no conductor. The musicians seemed to play extemporaneously, weaving their melodies in and out around a subtle, tacit framework. It was a chill sort of music, ice and green northern seas, a complex, compelling rhythm underlying the sigh of strings. Corinth lost himself for a while, trying to analyze it. Now and then a chord would strike some obscure emotional note within him, and his fingers tightened on the wine glass. A few people danced to it, making up their own figures as they went. He supposed that in the old days this would have been called a jam session, but it was too remote and intellectual for that. Another experiment, he thought. All humanity was experimenting, striking out after paths in a suddenly horizonless world.

He turned back to Helga, surprising her eyes as they rested on him. The blood felt hot in his face, and he tried to talk of safe things. But there was too much understanding between them. They had worked and watched together, and now there was a language of their own, every look and gesture meant something, and the meanings flickered back and forth, interlocking and breaking and meeting again, until it was like talking with one's own self.

"Work?" he asked aloud, and it meant: (How has your task been the last few days?)

"All right," she said in a flat tone. (We're accomplishing something heroic, I think. The most supremely worthwhile job of all history, perhaps. But somehow I don't care very much——)

"Glad see you tonight," he said. (I need you. I need someone in the lightless hours.)

(I will always be waiting), said her eyes.

Dangerous subject. Hide from it.

He asked quickly: "What do you think of the music here? It seems as if they're already on the track of a form suited to . . . modern man."

"Maybe so," she shrugged. "But I can still find more in the old masters. They were more human."

"I wonder if we are still human, Helga."

"Yes," she replied. "We will always remain ourselves. We will still know love and hate, fear and bravery and laughter and grief."

"But of the same kind?" he mused. "I wonder."

"You may be right," she said. "It's become too hard to believe what I want to believe. There is that."

He nodded, she smiled a little: (Yes, we both know it, don't we? That and all the world besides.)

He sighed and clenched his fists briefly: "Sometimes I wish— No." *It's Sheila I love.*

(Too late, isn't it, Pete?) said her eyes. (Too late for both of us.)

"Dance?" he invited. (Come to forgetfulness.)

"Of course." (Oh, gladly, gladly!)

They got up and moved out on the floor. He felt the strength of her as he put his arm around her waist, and it was as if he drew of it. *Mother image?* jeered his mind. No matter. The music was entering him more fully now, he felt its curious beat in his blood. Helga's head was almost level with his, but her face was hidden from him. He was not a good dancer, he let her take the lead, but the pleasure of rhythmic physical movement was sharper for him now than it had been before the change. For a moment he wished he could be a savage and dance his sorrow out before the gods.

No, too late for him. He was a child of civilization—even now; he had been born too old. But what do you do, then, when you see your wife going mad?

Ah, Love, could thou and I with Fate conspire— What a childish thing that was! And yet he had liked it once.

The music ended, and they went back to their table. The hors d'oeuvres had arrived, borne by the machine. Corinth seated Helga and picked moodily at his dish. Presently she looked at him again.

"Sheila?" she asked: (She isn't well these days, is she?)

"No." (Thank you for asking.) Corinth grimaced. (Her work helps fill the time, but she's not good at it. She broods, and she's begun seeing things, and her dreams at night——)

Oh, my tormented dearest! "But why?" (You and I, most people, we're adjusted now, we aren't nervous any more; I always thought she was more stable than average.)

"Her subconscious mind . . ." (Running wild, and her consciousness can't control it, and worry over the symptoms only makes matters worse . . .) "She just isn't made for such power of mind, she can't handle it."

Their eyes met: *Something lost, of old innocence, all we once treasured stripped from us, and we stand naked before our own solitude.*

Helga lifted her head: (We have to face it out. Somehow we have to keep going.) *But the loneliness!*

(I'm coming to depend too much on you. Nat and Felix are wrapped up in their own work. Sheila has no strength left, she has been fighting herself too long. There's only you, and it's not good for you.)

(I don't mind.) *It's all I have, now when I can no longer hide from myself.*

Their hands clasped across the table. Then, slowly, Helga withdrew hers and shook her head.

"God!" Corinth's fists doubled. (If we could only learn more about ourselves! If we had a workable psychiatry!)

(Perhaps we will before long. It's being studied.) Soothingly: "And how is your own task coming?"

"Well enough, I suppose." (We'll have the stars within our grasp before spring. But what good is it? What use are the stars to us?) Corinth stared at his wine glass. "I'm a little drunk. I talk too much."

"No matter, darling."

He looked at her. "Why don't you get married, Helga? Find someone for yourself. You can't pull me out of my private hell."

Her face spoke negation.

"Better leave me out of your life," he urged in a whisper.

"Would you leave Sheila out of yours?" she asked.

The machine waiter came silently to remove their dishes and set the main course before them. Corinth thought vaguely that he ought to have no appetite. Didn't misery traditionally mean pining away? But the food tasted good. Eating—well, yes, a compensation of sorts, like drinking and daydreaming, work and anything else you cared to name.

(You have to endure) said Helga's eyes. (Whatever comes, you have to live through it, you and your sanity, because that is your heritage of humanness.)

After a while she spoke aloud, three clipped words which held an overwhelming meaning: "Pete, would you" (like to go out on the star ship?)

"Huh?" He stared at her so foolishly that she had to laugh. In a moment she spoke again, seriously and impersonally:

"It's being planned for two men." (Mostly robot-run, you know. Nat Lewis talked me into giving him one of the berths, as biologist. The problem of life elsewhere in the universe——)

His voice shook a little: "I didn't know you could control who went."

"Not officially." (In practice, since it's largely an Institute project, I can swing it for any qualified person. Nat wanted me along——) They traded a brief smile. *You could do worse, I could do better too.* "But of course a physicist is needed." (You know as much about the project, and have done as much for it, as anyone.)

"But——" He shook his head. "I'd like to——" (No, there isn't a strong enough word for it. I'd trade my chances of immortality for a berth like that. I used to lie on my back on summer nights, when I was a kid, and look at the moon rising and Mars like a red eye in heaven, and dream.) "But there's Sheila. Some other time, Helga."

"It wouldn't be a long trip," she said. (A couple of weeks' scouting around among the nearer stars, I imagine, to test out the drive and a number of astronomical theories. Nor do I think it's at all risky—would I let you go if I imagined that?) *As it is, I'll watch the sky every night and feel its great cold and clench my fists together.* (It's a chance I think you ought to have, for your own peace of mind. You're a lost soul now, Pete. You need to find something above your own problems, above this whole petty world of ours.) She smiled. "Maybe you need to find God."

"But I tell you, Sheila——"

"There's several months yet before the ship leaves." (Anything can happen in that time. I've kept in touch with the latest psychiatric research too, and there's a promising new line of treatment.) She reached over the table to touch his arm. "Think it over, Pete."

"I will," he said, a little thickly.

Part of him realized that she was holding out that tremendous prospect as an immediate diversion for him, something to break the circle of his worry and gloom. But it didn't matter. It was working anyway. When he came out again on the street with her, he looked up to the sky, saw a few suns dim through its haze, and felt a rush of excitement within him.

The stars! By Heaven, the stars!

CHAPTER THIRTEEN

SNOW FELL EARLY THAT YEAR. One morning Brock came out of the house and all the world was white.

He stood for a moment looking over the sweep of land, hills and fields and buried roads, to the steel-colored dawn horizon. It was as if he had never seen winter before, bare black trees against a sky of windless quiet, burdened roofs and frost-glazed windows, and a single crow sitting dark and disconsolate on a cold telephone pole. *And indeed,* he thought, *I never have—not really.*

The snowfall had warmed the air but his breath still misted from his nostrils and he felt a tingle in his face. He slapped his hands together, a startlingly loud crack in the stillness, and blew out his cheeks and said aloud: "Well, Joe, looks like we're settled down for the next half year. White Thanksgiving, and I wouldn't be surprised if we had a white Easter too."

The dog looked up at him, understanding most of it but with little means of replying. Then instinct got the better of him and he went romping and barking to wake the farm with his clamor.

A small stocky form, so bundled up that only the proportions of arm and leg indicated it was not human, came out of the house, shuddered, and bounded quickly over to stand by the man. "Cold," she chattered. "Cold, cold, cold."

"It'll get colder, I'm afraid, Mehitabel," said Brock, and laid a hand on the chimpanzee's fur-capped head. He still feared that the apes would not last out the winter. He had tried to do what he could for them—making clothes, and assigning most of their work in the house or barn where it was warm—but still their lungs were frail.

He hoped desperately that they would live. In spite of their natural flightiness and laziness, they had labored heroically with him; he could not have readied for winter alone. But more than that, they were friends—someone to talk to, once a pidgin dialect had been worked out between him and them. They didn't have much to say, and their grasshopper minds would not stay on one subject, but they broke the solitude for him. Just to sit watching their antics in the gymnasium he had rigged up for them was to laugh, and laughter had become a rare thing.

Curiously, Mehitabel had taken best to the farmyard chores while her mate, Jimmy, handled cooking and housekeeping. Not that it mattered. They were strong and clever helpers, whatever they did.

He trudged over the yard, his boots leaving a smudge in the virginal whiteness, and opened the barn door. A wave of animal heat struck him as he entered the dimness, and the strong odor was heady. Mehitabel went to get hay and ground corn for the livestock—fifteen cows, two horses, and the vast form of Jumbo the elephant—while Brock gave himself to milking.

What stock was left seemed to have fallen into a placid acceptance of the new order. Brock winced. They trusted him, he seemed to be a kind of informal god, and today he would have to violate their trust. No use putting it off any longer, that would only make it the more difficult.

The door creaked open again and Wuh-Wuh came lumbering in and found a milking stool and joined Brock. He said nothing, and his work went ahead mechanically, but that was not unusual. Brock imagined that Wuh-Wuh was incapable of speech, except the inarticulate stammerings and grunts which had earned him his name.

The imbecile had come tracking in one day a few weeks ago, ragged and filthy and starving. He must have escaped from some asylum—a small, knotty hunchback of uncertain age, his sloping head ugly to look on and a vacancy in his eyes. Wuh-Wuh's intelligence had, obviously, gone up like everyone else's, but that didn't change the fact that he was a defective, physically as well as mentally.

He had not been especially welcome. Most of the big tasks of harvest were done by then, and there was enough worry about supplies for winter without adding an extra mouth. "I kill him, boss," said Jimmy, reaching for a knife.

"No," said Brock. "We can't be that hard."

"I do it quick and easy," grinned Jimmy, testing the edge of the blade on one splay thumb. He had a charming jungle simplicity in him.

"No. Not yet, anyway." Brock smiled wearily. He was always tired, there was always something to do. *We're the lost sheep, and I seem to have been appointed bellwether. We all have to live in a world that don't want us.* After a moment he had added: "We need a lot of wood cut, too."

Wuh-Wuh had fitted in tolerably well, he was harmless enough once Jimmy—probably with the help of a stick—had broken him of some undesirable habits. And the business had made Brock realize with a new force that there must be many of his sort, struggling to live when civilization got too big to concern itself with them. Eventually, he supposed, the morons would have to get together somehow, establish a community and——

Well, why not admit it? He was lonely. Sometimes the depression of his loneliness was almost suicidally great. There were none of his kind to be found, not in all the wintry world, and he was working for nothing except his own unnecessary survival. He needed kinship.

He finished the milking and turned the animals out to get exercise. The water tank was frozen over, but Jumbo broke the thin crust with her trunk and they all clustered around to drink. Later in the day the elephant would have to be put to work getting more water from the emergency pump and carrying it to the tank. Jumbo looked quite shaggy now; Brock had never before realized how much hair could grow on an elephant when abrading jungle or the blowtorches of human owners didn't remove it.

He himself went over to the haystack outside the sheep fence. He had had to build a board wall around it to keep the flock from breaking through the wire and gorging themselves, but they respected his fences now. The whim of a god—— He wondered what sort of strange taboo-thoughts went on inside those narrow skulls.

Even before the change, sheep had been animals with personalities of their own, and he knew each of the forty as well as he could know any human. Bluff, quick-witted Georgina was pushing the timid Psyche away in her haste, fat old Marie Antoinette stood placidly and immovably chewing, Jo-girl did an exuberant dance all by herself in the snow—and there was the old ram, ring-horned Napoleon, magnificently regal, too conscious of supremacy to be arrogant. How could he kill one of them?

Yet there was no help for it. He and Joe and Wuh-Wuh couldn't live on hay, or even the clumsily ground flour and the apples and garden truck in the cellar; Jimmy and Mehitabel could use some broth too—and there were the hides and tallow, the very bones might be worth saving.

Only which one should it be?

He didn't like Georgina much, but she was too good to kill, he needed her blood in his future stock. Jo-girl the glad, Marie who came up and nuzzled his hand, coquettish Margy and shy Jerri and bravehearted Eleanor —which of his friends was he going to eat?

Oh, shut up, he told himself. *You made your mind up long ago.*

He whistled for Joe and opened the fence gate. The sheep looked curiously at him as they drifted from their completed meal to the shed where they nested. "Get Psyche over here, Joe," he said.

The dog was off at once, leaping the drifts like coppery fire. Mehitabel came out of the chicken house and waited quietly for what she had to do. There was a knife in her hand.

Joe nudged Psyche, and the ewe looked at him with a shy sort of wonder. The dog barked, a loud clear frosty noise, and nipped her gently on the flank. She came then, plowing through the snow and out the gate. There she stood, looking up at Brock.

"Come on, girl," he said. "This way."

He closed the gate and locked it. Joe was urging Psyche around the corner of the chicken house, out of sight of the flock.

The pigs had been tough and clever to start with, and had moreover seen many butcherings of their own kind in earlier days. The sheep didn't know. Brock thought that if a few of their number were led off during the winter and never came back, they would merely accept the fact without worrying about it. Eventually, of course, if man was to go on living off his animals, he would have to inculcate them with some—well, religion—which demanded sacrifices.

Brock shuddered at the thought. He wasn't cut out for the role of Moloch. The human race had been sinister enough without becoming a tribe of blood-drinking gods.

"Over here, Psyche," he said.

She stood quietly looking at him. He took off his gloves and she licked his palms, her tongue warm and wet against their sweatiness. When he scratched behind her ears, she bleated very softly and moved closer to him.

Suddenly he realized the tragedy of the animals. They had never evolved for this intelligence. Man, with his hands and his speech, must have grown up as a thinking creature, he was at home with his brain. Even this sudden crushing burden of knowledge was not too great for him, because intellect had always been potentially unlimited.

But the other beasts had lived in a harmony, driven by their instincts through the great rhythm of the world, with no more intelligence than was needed for survival. They were mute, but did not know it; no ghosts haunted them, of longing or loneliness or puzzled wonder. Only now they had been thrown into that abstract immensity for which they had never been intended, and it was overbalancing them. Instinct, stronger than in man, revolted at the strangeness, and a brain untuned to communication could not even express what was wrong.

The huge indifferent cruelty of it was a gorge of bitterness in the man's throat. His vision blurred a little, but he moved with savage speed, stepping behind the sheep and throwing her down and stretching her throat out for the knife. Psyche bleated once, and he saw the horror of foreknown death in her eyes. Then the ape struck, and she threshed briefly and was still.

"Take—take—" Brock stood up. "Take her yourself, Mehitabel, will you?" He found it oddly hard to speak. "Get Wuh-Wuh t' help you. I got other things to do."

He walked slowly away, stumbling a little, and Joe and Mehitabel traded a glance of unsureness. To them, this had only been a job; they didn't know why their leader should be crying.

CHAPTER FOURTEEN

WANG KAO WAS HARD AT WORK when the prophet came. It was winter, and the earth lay white and stiff about the village as far as a man could see, but there would be spring again and plowing to do, and all the oxen had run off. Men and women and children would have to drag the plows, and Wang Kao desired to ease their labor as much as could be. He was ripping apart the one fuelless tractor which was the only remnant of the Communists, in search of ball bearings, when the cry rose up that a stranger was approaching across the fields.

Wang Kao sighed and laid down his work. Fumbling through the gloom of the hut which was his smithy, he grasped his rifle and the few remaining cartridges and shrugged on a wadded blue coat. It had been a good friend, that gun, it had seen him through many hundred miles after the army broke up in mutiny and he walked home. There had still been Communist troopers loose then, to say nothing of starved folk turned bandit. Even now, one was never sure what a newcomer might be. The last stranger had come in a shining aircraft simply to bear word that there was a new government under which all men might be free; but that government was remote and feeble as yet, men had to defend themselves when the need arose.

His neighbors were waiting outside, shivering a little in the cold. Some of them had guns like his, the rest were armed only with knives and clubs and pitchforks. Their breath puffed pale from their noses. Behind their line, the women and children and old people stood in doorways, ready to dive for shelter.

Wang Kao squinted across the snow. "It is just one man," he said. "I see no weapons upon him."

"He rides a donkey, and leads another," replied his neighbor.

There was something strange here. Who had been able to manage a beast since the great change? Wang Kao felt a prickling along his neck.

It was an elderly man who neared them. He smiled kindly, and one by one the leveled guns sank. But it was odd how thinly he was clad, as if this were summer. He rode up to the line of men and greeted them in a friendly way. No one asked his errand, but the eyes that watched him were question enough.

"My name is Wu Hsi," he said, "and I have a message for you which may be of value."

"Come in, sir," invited Wang Kao, "and accept our poor hospitality. It must be bitterly cold for you."

"Why, no," said the stranger. "That is part of my message. Men need not freeze if they have no thick garments. It is all in knowing how not to freeze."

He crossed one leg over the donkey's shoulders and leaned forward. A small chill breeze ruffled his wispy gray beard. "I am one of many," he went on. "My master taught us, and now we go forth to teach others, and it is our hope that some of those we teach will themselves become prophets."

"Well, and what is it you teach, sir?" asked Wang Kao.

"It is only the proper use of the mind," replied Wu Hsi. "My master was a scholar in Fenchow, and when the great change came he saw that it was a change in men's way of thinking and set himself to search out the best ways of using his new powers. It is but a humble beginning which we have here, and yet we feel that it may be of service to the world."

"All of us can think more freely and strongly now, sir," said Wang Kao.

"Yes, I am clearly among worthy men, and yet it may be my poor words will have some newness. Think, people, how often the mind, the will, has mastered the body's weaknesses. Think how men have kept alive during sickness and famine and weariness, when no beast could do aught but die. Then think how much greater such powers must be now, if only a man can use them."

"Yes." Wang Kao bowed. "I see how you have triumphed over the chill of winter."

"There is not enough cold today to harm a man, if he but know how to keep his blood moving warmly. That is a little thing." Wu Hsi shrugged. "A heightened mind can do much with the body; I can, for instance, show you how to tell a wound to stop hurting and bleeding. But the ways of communicating with the beasts, and befriending them; the ways of remembering every tiniest thing one has ever seen or heard; the ways of having no feelings, no wishes, save those the mind says are good; the ways of talking soul to soul with another man, without ever opening the lips; the ways of thinking out how the real world must be, without blundering into vain fancies—these, I humbly feel, may be of more use to you in the long run."

"Indeed, honored sir, they would, and we are not worthy," declared Wang Kao in awe. "Will you not come in now and dine with us?"

It was a great day for the village, in spite of the news having come so quietly. Wang Kao thought that soon it would be a great day for the whole world. He wondered what the world would look like, ten years hence, and even his patient soul could hardly wait to see.

Outside the viewports, the sky was ice and darkness, a million frosty suns strewn across an elemental night. The Milky Way flowed as a river of radiance, Orion stood gigantic against infinity, and it was all cold and silence.

Space lay around the ship like an ocean. Earth's sun was dwindling as she ran outward toward endlessness, now there were only night and quiet and the titanic shining beauty of heaven. Looking at those stars, each a giant ablaze, and sensing their terrible isolation, Peter Corinth felt the soul within him quail. This was space, reaching out past imagination, worlds beyond worlds and each, in all its splendor, nothing against the mystery that held it.

"Maybe you need to find God."

Well—perhaps he had. He had at least found something more than himself.

Sighing, Corinth turned back to the metallic warmth of the cabin, grateful for finitude. Lewis sat watching the dials and chewing a dead cigar. There was nothing of awe in his round ruddy face, and he hummed a song to himself, but Corinth knew that the huge cold had reached in and touched him.

The biologist nodded ever so slightly. (Works like a charm. The psi-drive, the viewscreens, the gravity, ventilation, servomechanisms—a lovely boat we've got!)

Corinth found a chair and sat down, folding his lanky frame together and clasping his hands over one knee. Starward bound—it was a triumph, perhaps the greatest achievement of history. For it guaranteed that there would always be a history, an outwardness in man so that he could not stagnate forever on his one little planet. Only somehow he, as an individual, did not feel the exultation of conquest. This was too big for trumpets.

Oh, he had always known intellectually that the cosmos was vast beyond comprehension, but it had been a dead knowledge in him, colorless, ten to the umpteenth power quantities and nothing more. Now it was part of his self. He had lived it, and could never again be quite the same man.

Driven by a force more powerful than rockets, freed from Einsteinian speed limits, the ship reacted against the entire mass of the universe, and when traveling faster than light did not have a velocity in the strict sense at all. Her most probable position shifted in an enigmatic way which had required a whole new branch of mathematics to describe. She generated her own internal pseudogravity field, her fuel was mass itself—any mass, broken down into energy, nine times ten to the twentieth ergs per gram. Her viewscreens, compensating for Doppler effect and aberration, showed the naked blaze of space to eyes that would never look on it unaided. She carried and sheltered and fed her cargo of frail organic tissue, and they who rode like gods knew their own mortality with a stark and somehow heart-lifting clarity.

For all that, she had an unfinished look. In the haste to complete a thousand years of work in a few months, the builders had left out much they might have installed, computers and robots which could have made the ship altogether automatic. The men aboard could calculate with their changed minds as well and as swiftly as any machine yet built, solving partial differential equations of high order just to get the proper setting for a control.

There had been an almost desperate speed in the project, a vague realization that the new humanity had to find a frontier. The next ship would be different, much of the difference founded on data which the first one would bring back.

"Cosmic ray count holding pretty steady," said Lewis. The ship bristled with instruments mounted outside the hull and its protective warping fields. (I guess that kills off the solar-origin theory for good.)

Corinth nodded. The universe—at least out to the distance they had penetrated—seemed to hold a sleet of charged particles, storming through space from unknown origins to equally unknown destinations. Or did they have any definite points of departure? Maybe they were an integral part of the cosmos, like the stars and nebulae. The professional side of him wanted immensely to know.

"I think," he said, "that even the short trips we can make in this little segment of the galaxy are going to upset most of the past astrophysical theories." (We'll have to build a whole new cosmology.)

"And biology too, I'll bet," grunted Lewis. (I've been speculating on and off since the change, and now I'm inclined to think that life forms not based on carbon are possible.) "Well, we'll see."

We'll see—what a magical phrase!

Even the Solar System would need decades of exploration. The *Sheila*—man was beyond the animism of christening his works, but Corinth remained sentimental enough to think of the ship by his wife's name—had already visited the moon on a flight test; her real voyage had begun with a swing past Venus, ducking down to look at the windy, sandy hell of the poisonous surface, then a stop on Mars where Lewis went wild over some of the adaptations he found in the plant forms, and then outward. In one unbelievable week, two men had seen two planets and gone beyond them. The constellation Hercules lay astern: they meant to locate the fringes of the inhibitor field and gather data on it; then a dash to Alpha Centauri, to see if Sol's nearest neighbor had planets, and home again. All inside of a month!

It will be close to spring when I get back——

The late winter had still held Earth's northern hemisphere when they left. It had been a cold, dark morning. Low-flying clouds blew like ragged smoke under a sky of iron. The sprawling mass of Brookhaven had been almost hidden from them, blurred with snow and haze, and the city beyond was lost to sight.

There had not been many to see them off. The Mandelbaums had been there, of course, hunched into clothes gone old and shabby; Rossman's tall gaunt form was stiff on one side of them; a few friends, some professional acquaintances from the laboratories and workshops, that was all.

Helga had come, wearing an expensive fur coat, melted snow glistening like small diamonds in the tightly drawn blonde hair. Her jewel-hard coolness said much to Corinth, he wondered how long she would wait after the ship was gone to weep, but he had shaken hands with her and found no words. Thereafter she had talked with Lewis, and Corinth had led Sheila around behind the ship.

She looked small and fragile in her winter coat. Flesh had melted from her, the fine bones stood out under the skin and her eyes were enormous. She had become so quiet lately, she sat and looked past him and now and then she trembled a little. The hands that lay in his were terribly thin.

"I shouldn't be leaving you, honey," he said, using all the words in the old manner and making his voice a caress.

"It won't be for long," she answered tonelessly. She wore no make-up, and her lips were paler than they should be. "I think I'm getting better."

He nodded. The psychiatrist, Kearnes, was a good man, a plump fatherly sort with a brain like a razor. He admitted that his therapy was experimental, a groping into the unknown darknesses of the new human mind, but he had been getting results with some patients. Rejecting the barbarity of brain mutilation by surgery or shock, he felt that a period of isolation from familiarity gave the victim a chance to perform, under guidance, the re-evaluation that was necessary. . . .

("The change has been an unprecedented psychic shock to every organism possessed of a nervous system," Dr. Kearnes had said. "The fortunate ones —the strong-willed, the resolute, those whose interests have been by choice or necessity directed outward rather than introspectively, those to whom hard thinking has always been a natural and pleasurable process—they seem to have made the adjustment without too much damage; though I suppose we will all carry the scars of that shock to our graves. But those less fortunate have been thrown into a neurosis which has in many cases become deep psychosis. Your wife, Dr. Corinth—let me be blunt—is dangerously close to insanity. Her past life, essentially unintellectual and sheltered, has given her no preparation for a sudden radical change in her own being; and the fact that she has no children to worry about, and no problem of bare survival to occupy her, enabled the whole force of realization to turn on her own character. The old adjustments, compensations, protective forgetfulness and self-deception, which we all had, are no longer of use, and she hasn't been able to find new ones. Worry about the symptoms naturally increased them, a vicious circle. But I think I can help her; in time, when the whole business is better understood, it should be possible to effect a complete cure. . . . How long? How should I know? But hardly more than a few years, at the rate science can expand now; and meanwhile Mrs. Corinth should be able to compensate enough for happiness and balance.")

"Well——."

Sudden terror in her eyes: "Oh, Pete, darling, darling, be careful out there! Come back to me!"

"I will," he said, and bit his lip.

("Yes, it would be an excellent thing for her—I think—if you went on that expedition, Dr. Corinth. Worry about you is a healthier thing than brooding over the shadows her own runaway mind creates for her. It will help wrench her psychic orientation outward where it belongs. She's not a natural introvert. . . .")

A flurry of snow wrapped them for a moment, hiding them from the world. He kissed her, and knew that in all the years before him he would remember how cool her lips were and how they trembled under his.

There was a deep hollow ringing in the ground, as if the planet itself shuddered with cold. Overhead flared the transatlantic rocket, bound for Europe on some mission of the new-born world order. Corinth's eyes were on Sheila. He brushed the snow from her hair, feeling the softness of it and the childish inward curve of her nape under his fingers. A small sad laughter was in him.

With five words, and eyes and hands and lips, he said to her: "When I come home again—and what a homecoming that will be, honey!—I expect to find you well and inventing a robot housemaid so you'll be free for me. I don't want anything in all the universe to bother us then."

And what he meant was: *O most beloved, be there for me as You have always been, You who are all my world. Let there be no more darkness between us, child of light, let us be together as once we were, or else all time is empty forever.*

"I'll try, Pete," she whispered. Her hand reached up to touch his face. "Pete," she said wonderingly.

Lewis' voice sounded harsh around the flank of the ship, distorted by the wind: "All aboard that's going aboard!"

Corinth and Sheila took their time, and the others respected that need. When the physicist stood in the air lock waving good-by, he was well above ground, and Sheila's form was a very small shape against the muddy snow.

Sol was little more than the brightest star in their wake, almost lost in the thronging multitude of suns, out here as far as the orbit of Saturn. The constellations had not changed, for all the leagues that had fled behind them. The huge circle of the Milky Way and the far mysterious coils of the other galaxies glimmered as remotely as they had done for the first half-man who lifted his eyes skyward and wondered. There was no time, no distance, only a vastness transcending miles and years.

The *Sheila* probed cautiously ahead at well under light velocity. On the fringes of the inhibitor field Lewis and Corinth were preparing the telemetered missiles which would be shot into the region of denser flux.

Lewis chuckled with amiable diablerie at the caged rats he meant to send on one of the torpedoes. Their beady eyes watched him steadily, as if they knew. "Poor little bums," he said. "Sometimes I feel like a louse." He added with a grin, "The rest of the time I do too, but it's fun."

Corinth didn't answer. He was looking out at the stars.

"The trouble with you," said Lewis, settling his bulk into the adjoining chair, "is that you take life too seriously. You've always done so, and haven't broken the habit since the change. Now me—I am, of course, perfect by definition!—I always found things to swear about and cry over, but there was just as much which was outrageously funny. If there is a God of any kind—and since the change I'm beginning to think there may be, perhaps I've become more imaginative—then Chesterton was right in including a sense of humor among His attributes." He clicked his tongue. "Poor old G.K.C.!

It's too bad he didn't live to see the change. What paradoxes he would have dreamed up!"

The alarm bell broke off his monologue. Both men started, looking at the indicator light which blinked like a red eye, on and off, on and off. Simultaneously, a wave of dizziness swept through them. Corinth grabbed for the arms of his chair, retching.

"The field—we're approaching the zone——" Lewis punched a key on the elaborate control panel. His voice was thick. "Got to get outta here——"

Full reverse! But it wasn't that simple, not when you dealt with the potential field which modern science identified with ultimate reality. Corinth shook his head, fighting the nausea, and leaned over to help. *This switch —no, the other one——*

He looked helplessly at the board. A needle crept over a red mark, they had passed light speed and were still accelerating, the last thing he had wished. *What to do?*

Lewis shook his head. Sweat gleamed on the broad face. "Sidewide vector," he gasped. "Go out tangentially——"

There were no constants for the psi-drive. Everything was a variable, a function of many components depending on the potential gradients and on each other. The setting for "ahead" could become that for "reverse" under new conditions, and there was the uncertainty principle to reckon with, the uncaused chaos of individual electrons, flattened probability curves, the unimaginable complexity which had generated stars and planets and thinking humans. A train of equations gibbered through Corinth's brain.

The vertigo passed, and he looked at Lewis with a growing horror. "We were wrong," he mumbled. "The field builds up quicker than we thought."

"But—it took days for Earth to get out of it altogether, man, at a relative speed of——"

"We must have hit a different part of the cone, then, a more sharply defined one; or maybe the sharpness varies with time in some unsuspected manner——" Corinth grew aware that Lewis was staring at him, open-mouthed.

"Huh?" said the other man—how slowly!

"I said—what did I say?" Corinth's heart began thundering in his panic. He had spoken three or four words, made a few signs, but Lewis hadn't understood him.

Of course he hadn't! They weren't as bright as they had been, neither of them.

Corinth swallowed a tongue that seemed like a piece of wood. Slowly, in plain English, he repeated his meaning.

"Oh, yes, yes." Lewis nodded, too frozen to say more.

Corinth's brain felt gluey. There was no other word. He was spiraling down into darkness, he couldn't think, with every fleeting second he tumbled back toward animal man.

The knowledge was like a blow. They had plunged unawares into the field Earth had left, it was slowing them down, they were returning to what they had been before the change. Deeper and deeper the ship raced, into an ever stronger flux, and they no longer had the intelligence to control her.

The next ship will be built to guard against this, he thought in the chaos. *They'll guess what's happened—but what good will that do us?*

He looked out again; the stars wavered in his vision. *The field,* he thought wildly, *we don't know its shape or extent. I think we're going out tangentially, we may come out of the cone soon—or we may be trapped in here for the next hundred years.*

Sheila!

He bowed his head, too miserable with the physical torment of sudden cellular readjustment to think any more, and wept.

The ship went on into darkness.

CHAPTER FIFTEEN

THE HOUSE STOOD ON LONG ISLAND, above a wide strand sloping to the sea. It had once belonged to an estate, and there were trees and a high wall to screen it off from the world.

Roger Kearnes brought his car to a halt under the portico and stepped out. He shivered a little and jammed his hands into his pockets as the raw wet cold fell over him. There was no wind, no shadow, only the late fall of snow, thick sad snow that tumbled quietly from a low sky and clung to the windowpanes and melted on the ground like tears. He wondered despairingly if there would ever again be a springtime.

Well— He braced himself and rang the doorbell. There was work to do. He had to check up on his patient.

Sheila Corinth opened the door for him. She was still thin, her eyes dark and huge in the pale childlike face; but she wasn't trembling any more, and she had taken the trouble to comb her hair and put on a dress.

"Hello, there," he said, smiling. "How are you today?"

"Oh—all right." She didn't meet his eyes. "Won't you come in?"

She led the way down a corridor whose recent repainting had not quite succeeded in creating the cheerful atmosphere Kearnes wanted. But you couldn't have everything. Sheila could consider herself lucky to have an entire house and a pleasant elderly woman—a moron—for help and companionship. Even nowadays, it meant a lot if your husband was an important man.

They entered the living room. A fire crackled on the hearth, and there was a view of beach and restless ocean. "Sit down," invited Sheila listlessly. She threw herself into an armchair and sat unmoving, her eyes fixed on the window.

Kearnes' gaze followed hers. How heavily the sea rolled! Even indoors, he could hear it grinding against the shore, tumbling rocks, grinding away the world like the teeth of time. It was gray and white to the edge of the world, white-maned horses stamping and galloping, how terribly loud they neighed!

Pulling his mind loose, he opened his briefcase. "I have some more books for you," he said. "Psychological texts. You said you were interested."

"I am. Thank you." There was no tone in her voice.

"Hopelessly outdated now, of course," he went on. "But they may give you an insight into the basic principles. You have to see for yourself what your trouble is."

"I think I do," she said. "I can think more clearly now. I can see how cold the universe is and how little we are——" She looked at him with fright on her lips. "I wish I didn't think so well!"

"Once you've mastered your thoughts, you'll be glad of this power," he said gently.

"I wish they would bring back the old world," she said.

"It was a cruel world," he answered. "We're well off without it."

She nodded. He could barely hear her whisper: "O soldier, lying hollow on the rime, there is frost in your hair and darkness behind your eyes. Let there be darkness." Before he had time for a worried frown, she continued aloud, "But we loved and hoped then. There were the little cafes, do you remember, and people laughing in twilight, there were music and dancing, beer and cheese sandwiches at midnight, sailboats, leftover pies, worrying about income taxes, our own jokes, there were the two of us. Where is Pete now?"

"He'll be back soon," said Kearnes hastily. No use reminding her that the star ship was already two weeks overdue. "He's all right. It's you we have to think about."

"Yes." She knotted her brows together, earnestly. "They still come to me. The shadows, I mean. Words out of nowhere. Sometimes they almost make sense."

"Can you say them to me?" he asked.

"I don't know. This house is on Long Island, long island, longing island, island of longing, where is Pete?"

He relaxed a trifle. That was a more obvious association than she had sprung on him last time. What had it been? *But when the uttermost hollow-frozen and time so dark that lightlessness is a weight is, then tell me, what lies beneath it. . . .* Maybe she was healing herself in the quiet of her aloneness.

He couldn't be sure. Things had changed too much. A schizophrenic's mind went into lands where he could not follow, the new patterns had simply not been mapped yet. But he thought Sheila was acting a little more healthily.

"I shouldn't play with them, I know," she said abruptly. "That's dangerous. If you take them by the hand they'll let you guide them for a while, but they won't let go of your hand again."

"I'm glad you realize that," he said. "What you want to do is exercise your mind. Think of it as a tool or a muscle. Go through those drills I gave you on logical processes and general semantics."

"I have." She giggled. "The triumphant discovery of the obvious."

"Well," he laughed, "you're back on your feet enough to make snide remarks, at least."

"Oh, yes." She picked at a thread in the upholstery. "But where is Pete?"

He evaded the question and put her through some routine word-association tests. Their diagnostic value was almost nil—every time he tried them, the words seemed to have taken on different connotations—but he could add the results to his own data files. Eventually he would have enough material to find an underlying pattern. This new *n*-dimensional conformal-mapping technique looked promising, it might yield a consistent picture.

"I have to go," he said at last. He patted her arm. "You'll be all right. Remember, if you ever want help, or just company, in a hurry, all you have to do is call me."

She didn't get up, but sat there watching him till he was out of the door. Then she sighed. *I do not like you, Doctor Fell,* she thought. *You look like a bulldog that snapped at me once, many hundred years ago. But you're so easy to fool!*

An old song ran through her head:

"He is dead and gone, lady,
He is dead and gone;
At his head a grass green turf,
At his heels a stone."

No, she said to the other one who sang in her head. *Go away.*

The sea growled and grumbled, and snow fell thicker against the windows. She felt as if the world were closing in on her.

"Pete," she whispered. "Pete, honey, I need you so much. Please come back."

CHAPTER SIXTEEN

THEY FLASHED OUT OF THE FIELD, and the next few minutes were dreadful. Then:

"Where are we?"

The unknown constellations glittered around them, and the silence was so enormous that their own breathing was loud and harsh in their ears.

"I don't know," groaned Lewis. "And I don't care. Lemme sleep, will you?"

He stumbled across the narrow cabin and flopped into a bunk, shaking with wretchedness. Corinth watched him for a moment through the blur that was his own vision, and then turned back to the stars.

This is ridiculous, he told himself sharply. *You're free again. You have the full use of your brain once more. Then use it!*

His body shuddered with pain. Life wasn't meant for changes like this. A sudden return to the old dimness, numb days fading into weeks while the ship hurled herself uncontrollably outward, and then the instant emergence, clear space and the nervous system flaring up to full intensity—it should have killed them.

It will pass, it will pass, but meanwhile the ship is still outward bound, Earth lies farther behind with every fleeting second. Stop her!

He sat grasping the arms of his chair, fighting down the dry nausea. *Calmness,* he willed, *slowness, brake the racing heart, relax muscles that jerked against their bones, bank the fires of life and let them build up slowly as they should.*

He thought of Sheila waiting for him, and the image was a steadiness in his whirling universe. Gradually, he felt the strength spreading as he willed it. It was a conscious battle to halt the spasmodic gasps of his lungs, but when that was won the heart seemed to slow of itself. The retching passed away, the trembling stopped, the eyes cleared, and Peter Corinth grew fully aware of himself.

He stood up, smelling the sour reek of vomit in the cabin and activating the machine which cleaned the place up. Looking out the viewscreens, he gathered in the picture of the sky. The ship would have changed speed and direction many times in her blind race through heaven, they could be anywhere in this arm of the galaxy, but——

Yes, there were the Magellanic Clouds, ghosts against night, and that hole of blackness must be the Coal Sack, and then the great nebula in Andromeda—Sol must lie approximately in that direction. About three weeks' journey at their top pseudospeed; then, of course, they'd have to cast about through the local region to find that very ordinary yellow dwarf which was man's sun. Allow a few days, or even a couple of weeks, for that. Better than a month!

No help for it, however impatient he was. Emotion was, causally, a psychophysiological state, and as such ought to be controllable. Corinth willed the rage and grief out of himself, willed calmness and resolution. He went over to the controls and solved their mathematical problem as well as he could with the insufficient data available. A few swift movements of his hands brought the ship's flight to a halt, turned her about, and plunged her toward Sol.

Lewis was unconscious, and Corinth didn't wake him. Let him sleep off the shock of readjustment. The physicist wanted a little privacy for thinking anyway.

He thought back over the terrible weeks in the field. When they had been there, he and Lewis, their lives since Earth had left it had seemed dreamlike. They could hardly imagine what they had been doing; they could not think and feel as those other selves had done. The chains of reasoning which had made the reorganization of the world and the building of the ship possible within months, had been too subtle and ramified for animal man to follow. After a while, their talk and their desperate scheming had faded into an apathy of despair, and they waited numbly for chance to release them or kill them.

Well, thought Corinth on the edge of a mind that was dealing with a dozen things at once, *as it happened, we were released.*

He sat looking out at the stupendous glory of heaven, and the realization that he was bound home and still alive and sane was a pulse of gladness within him. But the new coolness which he had willed into himself overlay him like armor. He could throw it off at the proper time, and would, but the fact of it was overwhelming.

He should have foreseen that this would come. Doubtless many on Earth had already discovered it for themselves but, with communications still fragmentary, had not yet been able to spread the word. The history of man had, in one sense, represented an unending struggle between instinct and intelligence, the involuntary rhythm of organism and the self-created patterns of consciousness. Here, then, was the final triumph of mind.

For him it had come suddenly, the shock of re-emergence into full neural activity precipitating the change which had been latent in him. For all normal humanity, though, it must come soon—gradually, continuously, perhaps, but soon.

The change in human nature and human society which this would bring about was beyond even his imagination. A man would still have motivations, he would still want to do things, but he could select his own desires, consciously. His personality would be self-adjusted to the intellectually conceived requirements of his situation. He would not be a robot, no, but he would not resemble what he had been in the past. As the new techniques were fully worked out, psychosomatic diseases would vanish and even organic troubles ought to be controllable in high degree by the will; no more pain; every man could learn enough medicine to take care of the rest, and there would be no more doctors.

Eventually—no more death?

No, probably not that. Man was still a very finite thing. Even now, he had natural limitations, whatever they might be. A truly immortal man would eventually be smothered under the weight of his own experience, the potentialities of his nervous system would be exhausted.

Nevertheless, a life span of many centuries ought to be attainable; and the specter of age, the slow disintegration which was senility, could be abolished.

Protean man—intellectual man—infinity!

The star was not unlike Sol—a little bigger, a little redder, but it had planets and one of them was similar to Earth. Corinth sent the ship plunging into the atmosphere of the night side.

Detectors swept the area. No radiation above the normal background count, that meant no atomic energy; but there were cities in which the buildings themselves shone with a cool light, and machines and radio and a world-wide intercourse. The ship recorded the voices that talked through the night, later on the language could perhaps be analyzed.

The natives, seen and photographed in a fractional second as the ship went noiselessly overhead, were of the humanoid sort, mammalian bipeds, though they had greenish fur and six fingers to a hand and altogether unhuman heads. Thronging their cities, they were almost pathetically like the crowds in old New York. The form was alien, but the life and its humble desires were the same.

Intelligence, another race of minds, man is not alone in the hugeness of space-time—once it would have marked an epoch. Now it merely confirmed a hypothesis. Corinth rather liked the creatures that walked beneath him, he wished them well, but they were only another species of the local fauna. Animals.

"They seem to be a lot more sensible than we were in the old days," said Lewis as the ship spiraled over the continent. "I see no evidence of war or preparations for war; maybe they outgrew that even before they achieved machine technology."

"Or maybe this is the planet-wide universal state," answered Corinth. "One nation finally knocked out all the others and absorbed them. We'll have to study the place a bit to find out, and I, for one, am not going to stop now to do it."

Lewis shrugged. "I daresay you're justified. Let's go, then—a quick sweep around the day side, and we'll let it go at that."

Despite the self-command which had been growing in him, Corinth had to battle down a fury of impatience. Lewis was right in his insistence that they at least investigate the stars which lay near their homeward path. It wouldn't kill anyone on Earth to wait a few weeks more for their return, and the information would be valuable.

A few hours after entering the atmosphere, the *Sheila* left it again and turned starward. The planet fell rapidly behind her driving hull, the sun dwindled and was lost, a whole living world—life, evolution, ages of history, struggle and glory and doom, dreams, hates and fears, hope and love and longing, all the many-layered existence of a thousand million sentient beings—was swallowed by darkness.

Corinth looked out and let the shiver of dismay run free within him. The cosmos was too big. No matter how swiftly men fled through it, no matter how far they ranged in all ages to come and how mightily they wrought, it would be the briefest glimmer in one forgotten corner of the great silence. This single dust mote of a galaxy was so inconceivably huge that even now his mind could not encompass the knowledge; even in a million years, it could not be fully known; and beyond it and beyond it lay shining islands of stars, outwardness past imagination. Let man reach forth till the cosmos itself perished, he would still accomplish nothing against its unheeding immensity.

It was a healthy knowledge, bringing a humility which the coldness of his new mind lacked. And it was good to know that there would always be a frontier and a challenge; and the realization of that chill hugeness would draw men together, seeking each other for comfort, it might make them kinder to all life.

Lewis spoke slowly in the quiet of the ship: "This makes nineteen planets we've visited, fourteen of them with intelligent life."

Corinth's memory went back over what he had seen, the mountains and oceans and forests of whole worlds, the life which blossomed in splendor or struggled only to live, and the sentience which had arisen to take blind nature in hand. It had been a fantastic variety of shape and civilization. Leaping, tailed barbarians howled in their swamps; a frail and gentle race, gray like silver-dusted lead, grew their big flowers for some unknown symbolic reason; a world smoked and blazed with the fury of nations locked in an atomic death clutch, pulling down their whole culture in a voluptuous hysteria of hate; beings of centaur shape flew between the planets of their own sun and dreamed of reaching the stars; the hydrogen-breathing monsters dwelling on a frigid, poisonous giant of a planet had evolved three separate species, so vast were the distances between; the world-civilization of a biped folk who looked almost human had become so completely and inflexibly organized that individuality was lost, consciousness itself was dimming toward extinction as antlike routine took the place of thought; a small snouted race had developed specialized plants which furnished all their needs for the taking, and settled down into a tropical paradise of idleness; one nation, of the many on a ringed world, had scorned wealth and power as motivations and given themselves to a passionate artistry. Oh, they had been many and strange, there was no imagining what diversity the universe had evolved, but even now Corinth could see the pattern.

Lewis elaborated it for him: "Some of those races were much older than ours, I'm sure. And yet, Pete, none of them is appreciably more intelligent than man was before the change. You see what it indicates?"

"Well, nineteen planets—and the stars in this galaxy alone number on the order of a hundred billion, and theory says most of them have planets—What kind of a sample is that?"

"Use your head, man! It's a safe bet that under normal evolutionary conditions a race only gets so intelligent and then stops. None of those stars have been in the inhibitor field, you know.

"It ties in; it makes good sense. Modern man is not essentially different from the earliest Homo sapiens, either. The basic ability of an intelligent species is that of adapting environment to suit its own needs, rather than adapting itself to environment. Thus, in effect, the thinking race can maintain fairly constant conditions. It's as true for an Eskimo in his igloo as it is for a New Yorker in his air-conditioned apartment; but machine technology, once the race stumbles on to it, makes the physical surroundings still more constant. Agriculture and medicine stabilize the biological environment. In short—once a race reaches the intelligence formerly represented by an average I.Q. of 100 to, say, 150, it doesn't need to become smarter than it is."

Corinth nodded. "Eventually surrogate brains are developed, too, to handle problems the unaided mind couldn't deal with," he said. "Computers, for instance; though writing is really the same principle. I see your point, of course."

"Oh, there's more to it than that," added Lewis. "The physical structure of the nervous system imposes limitations, as you well know. A brain can only get so big, then the neural paths become unmanageably long. I'll work out the detailed theory when I get home, if somebody else hasn't beaten me to it.

"Earth, of course, is a peculiar case. The presence of the inhibitor field made terrestrial life change its basic biochemistry. We have our structural limitations too, but they're wider because of that difference in type. Therefore, we may very well be the smartest race in the universe now—in this galaxy, at least."

"Mmmmm, maybe so. Of course, there were many other stars in the field too."

"And still are. New ones must be entering it almost daily. Lord, how I pity the thinking races on those planets! They're thrown back to a submoronic level—a lot of them must simply die out, unable to survive without minds. Earth was lucky; it drifted into the field before intelligence had appeared."

"But there must be many planets in a similar case," urged Corinth.

"Well, possibly," conceded Lewis. "There may well be races which emerged, and shot up to our present level, thousands of years ago. If so, we'll meet them eventually, though the galaxy is so big that it may take a long time. And we'll adjust harmoniously to each other." He smiled wryly. "After all, pure logical mind is so protean, and the merely physical will become so unimportant to us, that we'll doubtless find those beings to be just like ourselves—whatever their bodies resemble. How'd you like to be a partner of a—a giant spider, maybe?"

Corinth shrugged. "I'd have no objections."

"No, of course not. Be fun to meet them. And we won't be alone in the universe any more——" Lewis sighed. "Still, Pete, let's face it. Only a very tiny minority of all the sentient species there must be in the galaxy can have been as fortunate as us. We may find a dozen kindred races, or a hundred—no large number. Our sort of mind is very lonely."

His eyes went out to the stars. "Nevertheless, it may be that that uniqueness has its compensations. I think I'm beginning to see an answer to the real problem: what is superbrained man going to do with his powers, what can he find worthy of his efforts? I still wonder if perhaps there hasn't been a reason—call it God—for all this to happen."

Corinth nodded absently. He was straining ahead, peering into the forward viewscreen as if his vision could leap light-years and find the planet called Earth.

CHAPTER SEVENTEEN

Spring had come late, but now there was warmth in the air and a mist of green on the trees. It was too nice a day to sit in an office, and Mandelbaum regretted his own eminence. It would be more fun to go out and shoot some golf, if the nearest course was dry enough yet. But as chief administrator of the area including roughly the old states of New York, New Jersey, and New England, he had his duties.

Well, when they had gotten the weather-turning force-screens into full production, he'd move his headquarters out in the country somewhere and sit in the open. Till then, he remained in the city. New York was dying, it had no more economic or social purpose and every day some hundreds of people left it, but the location was still convenient.

He entered the office, nodded at the staff, and went into his own sanctum. The usual stack of reports waited, but he had barely gotten started when the phone rang. He swore as he picked it up—must be rather urgent if his secretary had bucked it on to him. "Hello," he snapped.

"William Jerome." It was the voice of the superintendent of the Long Island food-factory project. He had been a civil engineer before the change and continued his old work on a higher level. "I need advice," he continued, "and you seem to be the best human-relations idea-man around."

He spoke a little awkwardly, as did Mandelbaum; both were practicing the recently developed Unitary language. It had a maximal logic and a minimal redundancy in its structure, there was a universe of precise meaning in a few words, and it would probably become the international tongue of business and science if not of poetry; but it had only been made public a week before.

Mandelbaum frowned. Jerome's work was perhaps the most important in the world today. Somehow two billion people must be fed, and the food synthesis plants would permit free distribution of an adequate if unexciting diet; but first they had to be built. "What is it this time?" he asked. "More trouble with Fort Knox?" Gold was an industrial metal now, valued for its conductivity and inertness, and Jerome wanted plenty of it for bus bars and reaction vats.

"No, they've finally begun delivering. It's the workmen. I've got a slowdown on my hands, and it may become a strike."

"What for? Higher wages?" Mandelbaum's tone was sardonic. The problem of money was still not quite solved, and wouldn't be until the new man-hour credit standard got world-wide acceptance; meanwhile he had established his own local system, payment in scrip which could be exchanged for goods and services. But there was only so much to go around: more money would be a valueless gesture.

"No, they've got over that. But the thing is, they don't want to work six hours a day. It's pretty dull, driving nails and mixing concrete. I've explained that it'll take time to build robots for that sort of work, but they want the leisure immediately. What am I going to do if everybody'd rather accept a minimum standard of living and sit around arguing philosophy in his off hours?"

Mandelbaum grinned. "Leisure time is part of the standard of living too. What you got to do, Bill, is make 'em want to stay on the job."

"Yeah—how?"

"Well, what's wrong with setting up loudspeakers giving lectures on this and that? Better yet, give every man a buttonhole receiver and let him tune in on what he wants to hear: talks, symphonies, or whatever. I'll call up Columbia and get 'em to arrange a series of beamcasts for you."

"You mean broadcasts, don't you?"

"No. Then they'd stay at home and listen. This series will run during working hours and be beamed exclusively at your construction site."

"Hmmm—" Jerome laughed. "It might work at that!"

"Sure. You find out what the boys want and let me know. I'll take care of the rest."

When the engineer had hung up, Mandelbaum stuffed his pipe and returned to his papers. He wished all his headaches could be fixed as easily as that. But this matter of relocation. Everybody and his dog, it seemed, wanted to live out in the country; transportation and communication were no longer isolating factors. That would involve a huge labor of transference and landscaping, to say nothing of clearing ownership titles. He couldn't resist so strong a demand, but he couldn't do it at once, either. Then there was the business of——

"O'Banion," said the annunciator.

"Hm? Oh, yes. He had an appointment, didn't he? Send him in."

Brian O'Banion had been an ordinary cop before the change; during the chaotic period he had worked with the civil police; now he was local chief of Observers. For all that, he was still a big red-faced Irishman, and it was incongruous to hear crisp Unitary coming from his mouth.

"I need some more men," he said. "The job's getting too large again."

Mandelbaum puffed smoke and considered. The Observers were his own creation, though the idea had spread far and would probably be adopted by the international government before long. The smooth operation of society required a steady flow of information, a fantastically huge amount to be correlated every day if developments were not to get out of hand. The Observers gathered it in various ways: one of the most effective was simply to wander around in the guise of an ordinary citizen, talking to people and using logic to fill in all the implications.

"Takes a while to recruit and train 'em, Brian," said Mandelbaum. "What exactly do you want them for?"

"Well, first, there's this business of the feeble-minded. I'd like to put a couple of extra men on it. Not an easy job; there are still a lot of 'em wandering around, you know, and they've got to be located and unobtrusively guided the right way, toward one of the little colonies that're springing up."

"And the colonies themselves ought to be watched more closely and guarded against interference—yeah. Sooner or later, we're going to have to decide just what to do about them. But that'll be part and parcel of what we decide to do about ourselves, which is still very much up in the air. Okay, anything else?"

"I've got a lead on—something. Don't know just what, but I think it's big and I think part of it is right here in New York."

Mandelbaum turned impassive. "What's that, Brian?" he asked quietly.

"I don't know. It may not even be criminal. But it's big. I have tips from half a dozen countries around the world. Scientific equipment and materials are going into devious channels and not being seen again—publicly."

"So? Why should every scientist give us a step-by-step account of his doings?"

"No reason. But for instance, the Swedish Observer corps tracked one thing. Somebody in Stockholm wanted a certain kind of vacuum tube, a very special kind. The manufacturer explained that his whole stock, which was very small because of the low demand, had been bought by someone else. The would-be purchaser looked up the someone else, who turned out to be an agent buying for a fourth party he'd never seen. That got the Observers interested, and they checked every lab in the country; none of them had bought the stuff, so it was probably sent out by private plane or the like. They asked the Observers in other countries to check. It turned out that our customs men had noted a caseful of these same tubes arriving at Idlewild. That put a bee in my bonnet, and I tried to find where those tubes had gone. No luck—the trail ended there.

"So I started asking Observers around the world myself, and found several similar instances. Spaceship parts vanishing in Australia, for example, or a load of uranium from the Belgian Congo. It may not mean anything at all, but, well, if it's a legitimate project, why all this secrecy? I want some more men to help me follow up on it. I don't like the smell of it."

Mandelbaum nodded. Something like a crazy, unsafe experiment in nucleonics—it could devastate his whole territory. Or there might be a more deliberate plan. No telling as yet.

"I'll see you get them," he said.

CHAPTER EIGHTEEN

EARLY SUMMER: the first shy green of leaves has become a fullness enchanted with sunlight, talking with wind; it has rained just an hour ago, and the light cool wind shakes down a fine sparkle of drops, like a ghostly kiss on your uplifted face; a few sparrows dance on the long, empty streets; the clean quiet mass of the buildings is sharp against a luminous blue sky, the thousand windows catch the morning sun and throw it back in one great dazzle.

The city had a sleeping look. A few men and women walked between the silent skyscrapers; they were casually dressed, some almost nude, and the driven feverish hurry of old days was gone. Now and then a truck or automobile purred down the otherwise bare avenue. They were all running off the new powercast system, and the smokeless, dustless air was almost cruelly brilliant. There was something of Sunday about this morning, though it was midweek.

Sheila's heels tapped loudly on the sidewalk. The staccato noise jarred at her in the stillness. But she could only muffle it by slowing her pace, and she didn't want to do that. She couldn't.

A troop of boys, about ten years old, came out of the deserted shop in which they had been playing and ran down the street ahead of her. Young muscles still had to exercise, but it was saddening to her that they weren't shouting. Sometimes she thought that the children were the hardest thing to endure. They weren't like children any more.

It was a long walk from the depot to the Institute, and she could have saved her energy—for what?—by taking the subway. But the thought of being caged in metal with the new men of Earth made her shiver. It was more open and free aboveground, almost like being in the country. The city had served its day, now it was dying, and the bare blind walls around her were as impersonal as mountains. She was alone.

A shadow ran along the street, as if cast by a cloud traveling swiftly overhead. Looking up, she saw the long metallic shape vanish noiselessly behind the skyscrapers. Perhaps they had mastered gravity. What of it?

She passed by two men who were sitting in a doorway, and their conversation floated to her through the quiet:

"—starvish esthetics-the change."

Swift flutter of hands.

"*Wiedersehen.*" Sigh.

"Negate: macrocosm, un-ego, entropy. Human-meaning."

She went on a little faster.

The Institute building looked shabbier than the Fifth Avenue giants. Perhaps that was because it was still intensely in use; it did not have their monumental dignity of death. Sheila walked into the lobby. There was no one around, but an enigmatic thing of blinking lights and glowing tubes murmured to itself in a corner. She went over to the elevator, hesitated, and turned off for the staircase. No telling what they had done to the elevator—maybe it was wholly automatic, maybe it responded directly to thought commands, maybe they had a dog running it.

On the seventh floor, breathing a little sharply, she went down the corridor. It hadn't changed, at least—the men here had had too much else to do. But the old fluorescent tubes were gone, not the air itself—or the walls, ceiling, floor?—held light. It was peculiarly hard to gauge distances in that shadowless radiance.

She paused before the entrance to Pete's old laboratory, swallowing a gulp of fear. *Stupid,* she told herself, *they're not going to eat you. But what have they done inside? What are they doing now?*

Squaring her shoulders, she knocked on the door. There was a barely perceptible hesitation, then: "Come in." She turned the knob and entered.

The place had hardly changed at all. That was perhaps the most difficult thing to understand. Some of the apparatus was standing in a corner, dusty with neglect, and she did not comprehend the thing which had grown up to cover three tables. But it had always been that way when she visited her husband in the old days, a clutter of gadgetry that simply didn't register on her ignorance. It was still the same big room, the windows opened on a heartlessly bright sky and a remote view of docks and warehouses, a shabby smock hung on the stained wall, and a faint smell of ozone and rubber was in the air. There were still the worn reference books on Pete's desk; his table-model cigarette lighter—she had given it to him for Christmas, oh, very long ago—was slowly tarnishing by an empty ashtray, the chair was shoved back a little as if he had only gone out for a minute and would return any time.

Grunewald looked up from the thing on which he worked, blinking in the nearsighted manner she recalled. He looked tired, his shoulders stooped more than they once did, but the square blond face was the same. A dark young man whom she didn't know was helping him.

He made a clumsy gesture. (Why, Mrs. Corinth! This is an unexpected pleasure. Do come in.)

The other man grunted and Grunewald waved at him. (This is) "Jim Manzelli," he said. (He's helping me out just now. Jim, this is) "Mrs. Corinth," (wife of my former boss.)

Manzelli nodded. Curtness: (Pleased to meet you.) He had the eyes of a fanatic.

Grunewald went over to her, wiping grimy hands. "Why" (are you here, Mrs. Corinth)?

She answered slowly, feeling her timidity harsh in her throat. (I only wanted to) "Look around." (I) "Won't bother" (you very) "long." Eyes, fingers twisting together: Plea for kindness.

Grunewald peered more closely at her, and she saw the expressions across his face. Shock: *You have grown so thin! There is something haunted about you, and your hands are never still.* Compassion: *Poor girl, it's been hard for you, hasn't it? We all miss him.* Conventional courtesy: (I hope you are over your) "Illness?"

Sheila nodded. (Where is) "Johansson?" she asked. (The lab doesn't seem the same without his long glum face—or without Pete.)

(He's gone to help out in) "Africa, I think." (A colossal job before us, too big, too sudden.)

(Too cruel!)

Nodding: (Yes.) Eyes to Manzelli: (Question.)

Manzelli's gaze rested on Sheila with probing intensity. She shivered, and Grunewald gave his partner a reproachful look.

(I came up) "From Long Island today." Bitterness in her smile, she has grown harder, and a nod: (Yes, they seem to think it's all right to let me loose now. At least, they had no way to compel me, and too much else to do to worry about me in any case.)

A grayness flitted through Grunewald's expression. (You came up to say good-by, didn't you?)

(I wanted to) "See" (the) "place" (once again, only for a little while. It holds so many of his days).

Sudden pleading in her: "He is dead, isn't he?"

Shrug, pity: (We can't say. But the ship is months overdue, and only a major disaster could have stopped her. She may have run into the) "Inhibitor field" (out in space, in spite of all precautions).

Sheila walked slowly past him. She went over to Pete's desk and stroked her fingers across the back of his chair.

Grunewald cleared his throat. (Are you) "Leaving civilization?"

She nodded mutely. *It is too big for me, too cold and strange.*

(There is still) "Work to do," he said.

She shook her head. (Not for me. It is not a work I want or understand.) Taking up the cigarette lighter, she dropped it into her purse, smiling a little.

Grunewald and Manzelli traded another look. This time Manzelli made a sign of agreement.

(We have been) "Doing work" (here which might—interest you), said Grunewald. *Give you hope. Give you back your tomorrows.*

The brown eyes that turned to him were almost unfocused. He thought that her face was like white paper, stretched across the bones; and some Chinese artist had penned the delicate blue tracery of veins across her temples and hands.

He tried awkwardly to explain. The nature of the inhibitor field had been more fully worked out since the star ship left. Even before that time, it had been possible to generate the field artificially and study its effects; now Grunewald and Manzelli had gotten together on a project of creating the same thing on a huge scale. It shouldn't take much apparatus—a few tons, perhaps; and once the field was set up, using a nuclear disintegrator to furnish the necessary power, solar energy should be enough to maintain it.

The project was highly unofficial: now that the first press of necessity was gone, those scientists who chose were free to work on whatever suited their own fancy, and materials weren't difficult to obtain. There was a small organization which helped get what was necessary; all that Grunewald and Manzelli were doing here at the Institute was testing, the actual construction went on elsewhere. Their labor seemed harmless to everyone else, a little dull compared to what was going on in other lines of endeavor. No one paid any attention to it, or reasoned below the surface of Grunewald's public explanation.

Sheila regarded him vaguely, and he wondered about the regions into which her inner self had gone. "Why?" she asked. "What is it you're really doing?"

Manzelli smiled, with a harshness over him. (Isn't it obvious? We mean to) "Build an orbital space station" (and set it going several thousand miles above the surface). "Full-scale field generators" (in it. We'll bring mankind back to the) "Old days."

She didn't cry out, or gasp, or even laugh. She only nodded, as if it were a blurred image of no meaning.

(Retreat from reality—how sane are you?) asked Grunewald's eyes.

(What reality?) she flashed at him.

Manzelli shrugged. He knew she wouldn't tell anyone, he could read that much in her, and that was what counted. If it didn't give her the excited joy Grunewald had hoped for, it was no concern of his.

Sheila wandered over to one side of the room. A collection of apparatus there looked peculiarly medical. She saw the table with its straps, the drawer with hypodermic needles and ampules, the machine which crouched blackly near the head of the table—— "What is this?" she asked. Her tone should have told them that she knew already, but they were too immersed in their own wishes.

"Modified electric-shock treatment," said Grunewald. He explained that in the first weeks of the change there had been an attempt to study the functional aspects of intelligence by systematic destruction of the cerebral cortex cells in animals, and measurement of the effects. But it had soon been abandoned as too inhumane and relatively useless. "I thought you knew" (about it), he finished. (It was) "In the biology and psych departments when Pete" (was still here. I remember he) "protested strongly" (against it. Didn't he gripe to) "you" (about it too)?

Sheila nodded dimly.

"The change" (made) "men cruel," said Manzelli. (And) "Now" (they) "aren't" (even that, any longer. They've become something other than man, and this world of rootless intellect has lost all its old dreams and loves. We want to restore humanness).

Sheila turned away from the ugly black machine. "Good-by," she said.

"I—well——" Grunewald looked at the floor. "Keep in touch, won't you?" (Let us know where you are, so if Pete comes back——)

Her smile was as remote as death. (He will never come back. But good-by, now.)

She went out the door and down the corridor. Near the staircase was a washroom door. It was not marked "Men" or "Women," even the Western world had gone beyond such prudery, and she went in and looked in a mirror. The face that regarded her was hollow, and the hair hung lank and dull to her shoulders. She made an effort with comb and water to spruce up, not knowing or caring why she did, and then went down the stairway to the first floor.

The door to the director's office stood open, letting a breeze find its way between the windows and the building entrance. There were quiet machines inside, probably doing the work of a large secretarial staff. Shelia went past the outer suite and knocked on the open door of the inner office.

Helga Arnulfsen glanced up from her desk. She'd grown a little thin too, Sheila realized, and there was a darkness in her eyes. But even if she was more informally dressed than had once been her habit, she was strong and smooth to look on. Her voice, which had always been husky, lifted a trifle in surprise: "Sheila!"

"How do you do?"

"Come in," (do come in, sit down. It's been a long time since I saw you). Helga was smiling as she came around the desk and took Sheila's hand, but her fingers were cold.

She pressed a button and the door closed. (Now we can have) "Privacy," she said. (This is the sign I'm not to be bothered.) She pulled up a chair across from Sheila's and sat down, crossing her long trim legs man-fashion. "Well, good" (to see you. I hope you're feeling well.) *You don't look well, poor kid.*

"I——" Sheila clasped her hands and unclasped them again and picked at the purse in her lap. "I——" (Why did I come?)

Eyes: (Because of Pete.)

Nod: (Yes. Yes, that must be it. Sometimes I don't know why—— But we both loved him, didn't we?)

"You," said Helga without tone, "are the only one he cared for." *And you hurt him. Your suffering was grief within him.*

I know. That's the worst of it. (And still) "He wasn't the same man," said Sheila. (He changed too much, like all the world. Even as I held him, he slipped by me, time itself carried him away.) "I lost him even before he died."

"No. You had him, it was always you." Helga shrugged. "Well, life goes on," (in an amputated fashion. We eat and breathe and sleep and work, because there is nothing else we can do.)

"You have strength," said Sheila. (You have endured where I couldn't.)

"Oh, I kept going," answered Helga.

"You still have tomorrow."

"Yes, I suppose so."

Sheila smiled, it trembled on her mouth. (I'm luckier than you are. I have yesterday.)

"They may come back," said Helga. (There's no telling what has happened to them. Have you the courage to wait?)

"No," said Sheila. "Their bodies may come back," (but not Pete. He has changed too much, and I can't change with him. Nor would I want to be a weight around his neck.)

Helga laid a hand on Sheila's arm. How thin it was! You could feel the bones underneath. "Wait," she said. "Therapy" (is progressing. You can be brought up to) "Normal" (in—well—a) "few years, at most."

"I don't think so."

There was a touch of contempt, thinly veiled, in the cool blue eyes. *Do you want to live up to the future? Down underneath, do you really desire to keep pace?* "What else" (can you do) "but wait? Unless suicide——"

"No, not that either." (There are still mountains, deep valleys, shining rivers, sun and moon and the high stars of winter.) "I'll find my—adjustment."

(I've kept in touch with) "Kearnes." (He) "Seemed (to) "think" (you were) "progressing."

"Oh, yes." *I've learned to hide it. There are too many eyes in this new world.* "But I didn't come to talk about myself, Helga." (I just came to say) "Good-by."

"Where" (are you going? I have to keep in touch with you, if he should come back.)

"I'll write" (and let you know).

"Or give a message to a Sensitive." (The postal system is obsolete.)

That too? I remember old Mr. Barneveldt, shuffling down the street in his blue uniform, when I was a little girl. He used to have a piece of candy for me.

"Look, I'm getting hungry," said Helga. (Why don't we go have) "Lunch?"

(No, thank you. I don't feel like it.) Sheila got up. "Good-by, Helga."

"Not good-by, Sheila. We'll see you again, and you'll be well then."

"Yes," said Sheila. "I'll be all right. But good-by."

She walked out of the office and the building. There were more people abroad now, and she mingled with them. A doorway across the street offered a hidden place.

She felt no sense of farewell. There was an emptiness in her, as if grief and loneliness and bewilderment had devoured themselves. Now and then one of the shadows flitted across her mind, but they weren't frightening any longer. Almost, she pitied them. Poor ghosts! They would die soon.

She saw Helga emerge and walk alone down the street, toward some place where she would swallow a solitary lunch before going back to work. Sheila smiled, shaking her head a little. *Poor efficient Helga!*

Presently Grunewald and Manzelli came out and went the same way, lost in conversation. Sheila's heart gave a small leap. The palms of her hands were cold and wet. She waited till the men were out of sight, then crossed the street again and re-entered the Institute.

The noise of her shoes was hard on the stairway. She breathed deeply, trying for steadiness. When she came out on the seventh floor, she stood for a minute waiting for the self-control she needed. Then she ran down the hall to the physical laboratory.

The door gaped ajar. She hesitated again, looking at the unfinished machine within. Hadn't Grunewald told her about some fantastic scheme to——? No matter. It couldn't work. He and Manzelli, that whole little band of recidivists, were insane.

Am I insane? she wondered. If so, there was an odd strength in her. She needed more resolution for what she was going to do than it took to put a gun barrel in her mouth and squeeze a trigger.

The shock machine lay like some armored animal beside the table. She worked swiftly, adjusting it. Memory of Pete's anger at its early use had, indeed, come back to her in the house of isolation; and Kearnes had been pleased to give her all the texts she asked for, glad that she was finding an objective interest. She smiled again. Poor Kearnes! How she had fooled him.

The machine hummed, warming up. She took a small bundle from her purse and unwrapped it. Syringe, needle, bottle of anesthetic, electrode paste, cord to tie to the switch so she could pull it with her teeth. And a timer for the switch, too. She had to estimate the safe time for what was necessary, she would be unconscious when the process must be stopped.

Maybe it wouldn't work. Quite likely her brain would simply fry in her skull. What of it?

She smiled out the window as she injected herself. Good-by, sun, good-by, blue heaven, clouds, rain, airy song of home-bound birds. Good-by and thank you.

Stripping off her clothes, she lay on the table and fastened the electrodes in place. They felt cold against her skin. Some of the straps were easy to buckle, but the right arm—well, she had come prepared, she had a long belt that went under the table, around her wrist, a padlock she could snap shut. Now she was immobile.

Her eyes darkened as the drug took hold. It was good to sleep.

Now—one quick jerk with her teeth.

THUNDER AND FIRE AND SHATTERING DARKNESS
RUIN AND HORROR AND LIGHTNING
PAIN PAIN PAIN

CHAPTER NINETEEN

"HELLO, EARTH. Peter Corinth calling Earth from Star Ship I, homeward bound."

Buzz and murmur of cosmic interference, the talking of the stars. Earth a swelling blue brilliance against night, her moon like a pearl hung on the galaxy's breast, the sun wreathed in flame.

"Hello, Earth. Come in, come in. Can you hear me, Earth?"

Click, click, zzzzz, mmmmmm, voices across the sky.

Hello, Sheila!

The planet grew before them. The ship's drive purred and rumbled, every plate in the hull trembled with thrusting energies, there was a wild fine singing in the crystals of the metal. Corinth realized that he was shaking too, but he didn't want to control himself, not now.

"Hello, Earth," he said monotonously into the radio. They were moving well under the speed of light and their signal probed blindly ahead of them, through the dark. "Hello, Earth, can you hear me? This is Star Ship I, calling from space, homeward bound."

Lewis growled something which meant: (Maybe they've given up radio since we left. All these months——)

Corinth shook his head: "They'd still have monitors of some kind, I'm sure." To the microphone: "Hello, Earth, come in, Earth. Anyone on Earth hear me?"

"If some ham—a five-year-old kid, I bet, in Russia or India or Africa—picks it up, he'll have to get the word to a transmitter which can reach us," said Lewis. "It takes time. Just relax, Pete."

"A matter of time!" Corinth turned from the seat. "You're right, I suppose. We'll make planetfall in hours, anyway. But I did want to have a real welcome prepared for us!"

"A dozen Limfjord oysters on the half shell, with lots of lemon juice," said Lewis dreamily, speaking all the words aloud. "Rhine wine, of course—

say a '37. Baby shrimp in fresh mayonnaise, on French bread with fresh-churned butter. Smoked eel with cold scrambled eggs on pumpernickel, don't forget the chives——"

Corinth grinned, though half his mind was lost with Sheila, off alone with her in some place of sunlight. It was good, it felt strangely warm, to sit and exchange commonplaces, even if those were overtly little more than a word and a shift of expression. All the long way home, they had argued like drunken gods, exploring their own intellects; but it had been a means of shutting out the stupendous dark quiet. Now they were back to man's hearth fire.

"Hello, Star Ship I."

They jerked wildly about to face the receiver. The voice that came was faint, blurred with the noise of sun and stars, but it was human. It was home.

"Why," whispered Lewis in awe, "why, he's even got a Brooklyn accent."

"Hello, Star Ship I. This is New York calling you. Can you hear me?"

"Yes," said Corinth, his throat dry, and waited for the signal to leap across millions of miles.

"Had a devil of a time getting you," said the voice conversationally, after the time lag had gone by in whining, crackling blankness. "Had to allow for Doppler effect—you must be coming in like a bat out of Chicago, are your pants on fire or something?" He mentioned nothing of the engineering genius which had made communication possible at all; it was a minor job now. "Congratulations, though! All okay?"

"Fine," said Lewis. "Had some trouble, but we're coming home in one piece and expect to be greeted properly." He hesitated for a moment. "How's Earth?"

"Good enough. Though I'll bet you won't recognize the place. Things are changing so fast it's a real relief to talk good old United States once again. Prolly the last time I'll ever do it. What the devil happened to you, anyway?"

"We'll explain later," said Corinth shortly. "How are our—associates?"

"Okay, I guess. I'm just a technician at Brookhaven, you know, I'm not acquainted. But I'll pass the word along. You'll land here, I suppose?"

"Yes, in about——" Corinth made a swift estimate involving the simultaneous solution of a number of differential equations. "Six hours."

"Okay, we'll——" The tone faded away. They caught one more word, "——band——" and then there was only the stillness.

"Hello, New York, you've lost the beam," said Corinth.

"Ah, forget it," said Lewis. "Turn it off, why don't you?"

"But——"

"We've waited so long that we can wait six hours more. Isn't worthwhile tinkering around that way."

"Ummmm—well——" Corinth yielded. "Hello, New York. Hello, Earth. This is Star Ship I signing off. Over and out."

"I did want to talk to Sheila," he added.

"You'll have plenty of time for that, laddy," answered Lewis. "I think right now we ought to be taking a few more observations on the drive. It's got a fluttery note that might mean something. Nobody's ever operated one continuously as long as we have, and there may be cumulative effects——"

"Crystal fatigue, perhaps," said Corinth. "Okay, you win." He gave himself to his instruments.

Earth grew before them. They, who had crossed light-years in hours, had to limp home now at mere hundreds of miles a second; even their new reactions weren't fast enough to handle translight speeds this near a planet. But theirs would probably be the last ship so limited, thought Corinth. At the fantastic rate of post-change technological advance, the next vessel should be a dream of perfection: as if the Wright brothers had built a transatlantic clipper for their second working model. He imagined that his own lifetime would see engineering carried to some kind of ultimate, reaching the bounds imposed by natural law. Thereafter man would have to find a new field of intellectual adventure, and he thought he knew what it would be. He looked at the swelling lovely planet with a kind of tenderness. *Ave atque vale!*

The crescent became a ragged, cloudy disc as they swung around toward the day side. Then, subtly, it was no longer before them but below them, and they heard the first thin shriek of cloven air. They swept over a vastness of moonlit Pacific, braking, and saw dawn above the Sierra Nevada. America fell beneath them, huge and green and beautiful, a strong-ribbed land, and the Mississippi was a silver thread across her. Then they slanted down, and the spires of Manhattan rose against the sea.

Corinth's heart slammed in the cage of his breast. *Be still,* he told it, *be still and wait. There is time now.* He guided the ship toward Brookhaven, where the spacefield was a slash of gray, and saw another bright spear cradled there. So they had already begun on the next ship.

There was a tiny shock as the hull found its berth. Lewis reached over to cut off the engines. When they died, Corinth's ears rang with the sudden quiet. He had not realized how much a part of him that ceaseless drumming was.

"Come on!" He was out of his seat and across the narrow cabin before Lewis had stirred. His fingers trembled as they wove across the intricate pattern of the electronic lock. The inner door swung smoothly open, and then the outer door was open too, and he caught a breath of salt air, blown in from the sea.

Sheila! Where is Sheila? He tumbled down the ladder in the cradle, his form dark against the metal of the hull. It was pocked and blistered, that metal, streaked with curious crystallization-patterns, the ship had traveled far and strangely. When he hit the ground he overbalanced, falling, but he was up again before anyone could help him.

"Sheila," he cried.

Felix Mandelbaum stepped forth, holding out his hands. He looked very old and tired, burned out by strain. He took Corinth's hands in his own but did not speak.

"Where's Sheila?" whispered Corinth. "Where is she?"

Mandelbaum shook his head. Lewis was climbing down now, more cautiously. Rossman went to meet him, looking away from Corinth. The others followed—they were all Brookhaven people, no close friends, but they looked away.

Corinth tried to swallow and couldn't. "Dead?" he asked. The wind murmured around him, ruffling his hair.

"No," said Mandelbaum. "Nor is she mad. But——" He shook his head, and the beaked face wrinkled up. "No."

Corinth drew a breath that shuddered in his lungs. Looking at him, they saw the blankness of will descend. He would not let himself weep.

"Go ahead," he said. "Tell me."

"It was about six weeks ago," Mandelbaum said. "She couldn't stand any more, I guess. She got hold of an electric-shock machine."

Corinth nodded, very slowly. "And destroyed her brain," he finished.

"No. Not that, though it was touch and go for a while." Mandelbaum took the physicist's arm. "Let's put it this way: she is the old Sheila, like before the change. Almost."

Corinth was dimly aware how fresh and live the sea wind felt in his nostrils.

"Come along, Pete," said Mandelbaum. "I'll take you to her."

Corinth followed him off the field.

The psychiatrist Kearnes met them at Bellevue. His face was like wood, but there was no feeling of shame in him and none of blame in Corinth. The man had done his best, with the inadequate knowledge at his disposal, and failed; that was a fact of reality, nothing more.

"She fooled me," he said. "I thought she was straightening out. I didn't realize how much control even an insane person would have with the changed nervous system. Nor, I suppose, did I realize how hard it was for her all along. None of us who endured the change will ever know what a nightmare it must have been for those who couldn't adapt."

Dark wings beating, and Sheila alone. Nightfall, and Sheila alone.

"She was quite insane when she did it?" asked Corinth. His voice was flat.

"What is sanity? Perhaps she did the wisest thing. Was the eventual prospect of being cured, when we learn how, worth that kind of existence?"

"What were the effects?"

"Well, it was a clumsy job, of course. Several bones were broken in the convulsions, and she'd have died if she hadn't been found in time." Kearnes laid a hand on Corinth's shoulder. "The actual volume of destroyed cerebral tissue was small, but of course it was in the most critical area of the brain."

"Felix told me she's—making a good recovery."

"Oh, yes." Kearnes smiled wryly, as if he had a sour taste in his mouth. "It isn't hard for us to understand prechange human psychology—now. I used the triple-pronged approach developed by Gravenstein and de la Garde since the change. Symbological re-evaluation, cybernetic neurology, and somatic co-ordination treatments. There was enough sound tissue to take over the functions of the damaged part, with proper guidance, once the psychosis had been lifted. I think she can be discharged from here in about three months."

He drew a deep breath. "She will be a normal, healthy pre-change human with an I.Q. of about 150."

"I see——" Corinth nodded. "Well—what are the chances of restoring her?"

"It will take years, at best, before we're able to recreate nervous tissue. It doesn't regenerate, you know, even with artificial stimulation. We'll have to create life itself synthetically, and telescope a billion years of evolution to develop the human brain cell, and duplicate the precise gene pattern of the patient, and even then—I wonder."

"I see."

"You can visit her for a short while. We have told her you were alive."

"What did she do?"

"Cried a good deal, of course. That's a healthy symptom. You can stay about half an hour if you don't excite her too much." Kearnes gave him the room number and went back into his office.

Corinth took the elevator and walked down a long quiet hallway that smelled of rain-wet roses. When he came to Sheila's room, the door stood ajar and he hesitated a little, glancing in. It was like a forest bower, ferns and trees and the faint twitter of nesting birds; a waterfall was running somewhere, and the air had the tingle of earth and greenness. Mostly illusion, he supposed, but if it gave her comfort——

He went in, over to the bed which rested beneath a sun-dappled willow. "Hello, darling," he said.

The strangest thing was that she hadn't changed. She looked as she had when they were first married, young and fair, her hair curled softly about a face which was still a little pale, her eyes full of luster as they turned to him. The white nightgown, a fluffy thing from her own wardrobe, made her seem only half grown.

"Pete," she said.

He stooped over and kissed her, very gently. Her response was somehow remote, almost like a stranger's. As her hands caressed his face, he noticed that the wedding ring was gone.

"You lived." She spoke it with a kind of wonder. "You came back."

"To you, Sheila," he said, and sat down beside her.

She shook her head. "No," she answered.

"I love you," he said in his helplessness.

"I loved you too." Her voice was still quiet, far away, and he saw the dreaminess in her eyes. "That's why I did this."

He sat holding himself in, fighting for calm. There were thunders in his head.

"I don't remember you too well, you know," she said. "I suppose my memory was damaged a little. It all seems many years ago, and you like a dream I loved." She smiled. "How thin you are, Pete! And hard, somehow. Everybody has grown so hard."

"No," he said. "They all care for you."

"It isn't the old kind of caring. Not the kind I knew. And you aren't Pete any more." She sat up, her voice rising a little. "Pete died in the change.

I watched you die. You're a nice man, and it hurts me to look at you, but you aren't Pete."

"Take it easy, darling," he said.

"I couldn't go ahead with you," she said, "and I wouldn't give you—or myself—that kind of burden. Now I've gone back. And you don't know how wonderful it is. Lonely but wonderful. There's peace in it."

"I still want you," he said.

"No. Don't lie to me. Don't you see, it isn't necessary." Sheila smiled across a thousand years. "You can sit there like that, your face all frozen—why, you aren't Pete. But I wish you well."

He knew then what she needed, and let himself go, surrendering will and understanding. He knelt by her bed and wept, and she comforted him as well as she could.

CHAPTER TWENTY

THERE IS AN ISLAND IN MID-PACIFIC, not far off the equator, which lies distant from the world of man. The old shipping routes and the later transoceanic airlines followed tracks beyond its horizon, and the atoll had been left to sun and wind and the crying of gulls.

For a brief while it had known humankind. The slow blind patience of coral polyps had built it up, and days and nights had ground its harsh wet face into soil, and the seeds of plants had been blown on a long journey to find it. A few coconuts washed up in the surf, and presently there were trees. They stood for hundreds of years, perhaps, until a canoe came over the world's rim.

Those were Polynesians, tall brown men whose race had wandered far in the search for Hawaiki the beautiful. There was sun and salt on them, and they thought little of crossing a thousand miles of emptiness, for they had the stars and the great sea currents to guide them and their own arms to paddle, *tohiha, hioha, itoki, itoki!* When they drew their boat ashore and had made sacrifice to shark-toothed Nan, they wound hibiscus blooms in their long hair and danced on the beach; for they had looked on the island and found it good.

Then they went away, but the next year—or the year after that, or the year after that, for the ocean was big and time was forever—they came back with others, bringing pigs and women, and that night fires burned tall on the beach. Afterward a village of thatch huts arose, and naked brown children tumbled in the surf, and fishermen went beyond the lagoon with much laughter. And this lasted for a hundred years, or two hundred, before the pale men came.

Their big white-winged canoes stopped only a few times at this island, which was not an important one, but nonetheless faithfully discharged their usual cargo of smallpox, measles, and tuberculosis, so that there were not many of the brown folk left. Afterward some resistance was built up, aided by Caucasian blood, and it was time for copra planters, religion, Mother Hubbards, and international conferences to determine whether this atoll, among others, belonged to London, Paris, Berlin, or Washington—large villages on the other side of the world.

A *modus vivendi* was finally reached, involving copra, Christianity, tobacco, and trading schooners. The island people, by this time a mixture of several races, were reasonably satisfied, though they did have many toothaches; and when one of their young men, who through a long chain of circumstances had studied in America, came back and sighed for the old days, the people laughed at him. They had only vague memories of that time, handed down through a series of interested missionaries.

Then someone in an office on the other side of the world decided that an island was needed. It may have been for a naval base, or perhaps an experimental station—the pale men had so many wars, and spent the rest of their time preparing for them. It does not matter any longer why the atoll was desired, for there are no men on it now and the gulls don't care. The natives were moved elsewhere, and spent some quiet years in a sick longing for home. Nobody paid any attention to this, for the island was needed to safeguard the freedom of man, and after a time the older generation died off and the younger generation forgot. Meanwhile the white men disturbed the gulls for a little, putting up buildings and filling the lagoon with ships.

Then, for some unimportant reason, the island was abandoned. It may have been through treaty, possibly through a defeat in war or an economic collapse. The wind and rain and creeping vines had never been defeated, only contained. Now they began the task of demolition.

For a few centuries, men had disturbed the timelessness of days and nights, rain and sun and stars and hurricanes, but now they were gone again. The surf rolled and chewed at the reef, the slow chill sliding of underwater currents gnawed at the foundations, but there were many polyps and they were still building. The island would endure for a goodly fraction of a million years, so there was no hurry about anything. By day fish leaped in the waters, and gulls hovered overhead, and the trees and bamboo grew with frantic haste; at night the moon was cold on tumbling surf and a phosphorescent track swirled behind the great shark who patrolled the outer waters. And there was peace.

The airjet whispered down out of darkness and the high bright stars. Invisible fingers of radar probed earthward, and a voice muttered over a beam. "Down—this way—okay, easy does it." The jet bounced to a halt in a clearing, and two men came out.

They were met by others, indistinct shadows in the moon-spattered night. One of them spoke with a dry Australian twang: "Dr. Grunewald, Dr. Manzelli, may I present Major Rosovsky—Sri Ramavashtar—Mr. Hwang Pu-Yi——" He went on down the list; there were about a score present, including the two Americans.

Not so long ago, it would have been a strange, even impossible group: a Russian officer, a Hindu mystic, a French philosopher and religious writer, an Irish politician, a Chinese commissar, an Australian engineer, a Swedish financier—it was as if all the earth had gathered for a quiet insurrection. But none of them were now what they had been, and the common denominator was a yearning for something lost.

"I've brought the control apparatus," said Grunewald briskly. "How about the heavy stuff?"

"It's all here. We can start anytime," said the Irishman.

Grunewald glanced at his watch. "It's a couple of hours to midnight," he said aloud. "Can we be ready by then?"

"I think so," said the Russian. "It is almost all assembled."

Walking down toward the beach, he gestured at the bulking shape which lay black and awkward on the moon-whitened lagoon. He and one comrade had gotten the tramp steamer months ago and outfitted her with machines such that they two could sail her around the world. That had been their part of the job: not too difficult for determined men in the confusion of a dying civilization. They had sailed through the Baltic, picking up some of their cargo in Sweden, and had also touched in France, Italy, Egypt, and India on their way to the agreed destination. For some days, now, the work of assembling the spaceship and her load had progressed rapidly.

The surf roared and rumbled, a deep full noise that shivered underfoot, and spouted whitely toward the constellations. Sand and coral scrunched beneath boots, the palms and bamboos rustled dryly with the small wind, and a disturbed parakeet racketed in the dark. Beyond this little beating of sound, there were only silence and sleep.

Further on, the ruin of an old barracks moldered in its shroud of vines. Grunewald smelled the flowers there, and the heavy dampness of rotting wood—it was a pungency which made his head swim. On the other side of the ruin stood some tents, recently put up, and above them towered the spaceship.

That was a clean and beautiful thing, like a pillar of gray ice under the moon, poised starward. Grunewald looked at her with a curious blend of feelings: taut fierce glory of conquest, heart-catching knowledge of her loveliness, wistfulness that soon he would not understand the transcendent logic which had made her swift designing and building possible.

He looked at Manzelli. "I envy you, my friend," he said simply.

Several men were to ride her up, jockey her into an orbit, and do the final work of assembling and starting the field generator she bore. Then they would die, for there had not been time to prepare a means for their return.

Grunewald felt time like a hound on his heels. Soon the next star ship would be ready, and they were building others everywhere. Then there would be no stopping the march of the race, and of time. Tonight the last hope of mankind—human mankind—was being readied; there could not be another, if this failed.

"I think," he said, "that all the world will cry with relief before sunrise."

"No," said the Australian practically. "They'll be madder'n a nest of hornets. You'll have to allow a while for them to realize they've been saved."

Well, there would be time, then. The spaceship was equipped with defenses beyond the capacity of pre-change man to overcome in less than a century. Her robots would destroy any other ships or missiles sent up from Earth. And man, the whole living race, would have a chance to catch his breath and remember his first loves, and after that he would not want to attack the spaceship.

The others had unloaded the jet from America and brought its delicate cargo to this place. Now they laid the crates on the ground, and Grunewald and Manzelli began opening them with care. Someone switched on a floodlight, and in its harsh white glare they forgot the moon and the sea around them.

Nor were they aware of the long noiseless form which slipped overhead and hung there like a shark swimming in the sky, watching. Only after it had spoken to them did they look up.

The amplified voice had been gentle, there was almost a note of regret in it. "Sorry to disappoint you, but you've done enough."

Staring wildly upward, Grunewald saw the steel shimmer above and his heart stumbled within him. The Russian yanked out a pistol and fired, the shots yammering futilely under the steady beat of surf. A gabble came from wakened birds, and their wings flapped loud among the soughing palms.

Manzelli cursed, whirled on his heel, and plunged into the spaceship. There were guns in it which could bring down that riding menace, and—Grunewald, diving for cover, saw a turret in the vessel's flank swing about and thrust a nose skyward. He threw himself on his belly. That cannon fired atomic shells!

From the hovering enemy sprang a beam of intense, eye-searing flame. The cannon muzzle slumped, glowed white. The thin finger wrote destruction down the flank of the ship until it reached the cones of her gravitic drive. There it played for minutes, and the heat of melting steel prickled men's faces.

A *giant atomic-hydrogen torch*—Grunewald's mind was dazed. *We can't take off now*——

Slowly, the very walls of the crippled spaceship began to glow red. The Swede screamed and pulled a ring off his finger. Manzelli stumbled out of the ship, crying. The force-field died, the machines began to cool again, but there was something broken in the men who stood waiting. Only the heavy sobs of Manzelli spoke.

The enemy craft—it was a star ship, they saw now—remained where it was, but a small antigravity raft floated out of her belly and drifted earthward. There were men standing on it, and one woman. None of the cabal moved as the raft grounded.

Grunewald took one step forward then, and stopped with his shoulders slumping. "Felix," he said in a dead voice. "Pete. Helga."

Mandelbaum nodded. The single floodlight threw a hard black shadow across his face. He waited on the raft while three quiet burly men, who had been detectives in the old world, went among the conspirators and collected the guns they had thrown away as too hot to hold. Then he joined the police on the ground. Corinth and Helga followed.

"Surely you didn't expect to get away with this," said Mandelbaum. His voice was not exultant but tired. He shook his head. "Why, the Observers had your pitiful little scheme watched almost from its beginning. Your very secrecy gave you away."

"Then why did you let it get so far?" asked the Australian. His tones were thick with anger.

"Partly to keep you out of worse mischief and partly so you'd draw in others of like mind and thus locate them for us," said Mandelbaum. "We waited till we knew you were all set to go, and then we came."

"That was vicious," said the Frenchman. "It was the sort of coldbloodedness that has grown up since the change. I suppose the intelligent, the expedient thing for you now is to shoot us down."

"Why, no," said Mandelbaum mildly. "As a matter of fact, we used a reaction damper along with the metal-heating field, just to keep your cartridges from going off and hurting you. After all, we'll have to find out from you who else has backed you. And then you all have good minds, lots of energy and courage—quite a big potential value. It's not your fault the change drove you insane."

"Insane!" The Russian spat, and recovered himself with a shaking effort. "Insane you call us!"

"Well," said Mandelbaum, "if the delusion that you few have the right to make decisions for all the race, and force them through, isn't megalomania, then what is? If you really had a case, you could have presented it to the world soon enough."

"The world has been blinded," said the Hindu with dignity. "It can no longer see the truth. I myself have lost the feeble glimpse of the ultimate I once had, though at least I know it was lost."

"What you mean," said Mandelbaum coldly, "is that your mind's become too strong for you to go into the kind of trance which was your particular fetalization, but you still feel the need for it."

The Hindu shrugged contemptuously.

Grunewald looked at Corinth. "I thought you were my friend, Pete," he whispered. "And after what the change did to your wife, I thought you could see——"

"He's had nothing to do with this," said Helga, stepping forward a little and taking Corinth's arm. "I'm the one who fingered you, Grunewald. Pete just came along with us tonight as a physicist, to look over your apparatus and salvage it for something useful." *Occupational therapy—O Pete, Pete, you have been hurt so much!*

Corinth shook his head and spoke harshly, with an anger new to his mildness. "Never mind finding excuses for me. I'd have done this alone, if I'd known what you planned. Because what would Sheila be like if the old world came back?"

"You'll be cured," said Mandelbaum. "Your cases aren't violent, I think the new psychiatric techniques can straighten you out pretty quick."

"I wish you'd kill me instead," said the Australian.

Manzelli was still crying. The sobs tore at him like claws.

"Why can you not see?" asked the Frenchman. "Are all the glories man has won in the past to go for nothing? Before he has even found God, will you turn God into a nursery tale? What have you given him in return for the splendors of his art, the creation in his hands, and the warm little pleasures when his day's work is done? You have turned him into a calculating machine, and the body and the soul can wither amidst his new equations."

Mandelbaum shrugged. "The change wasn't my idea," he said. "If you believe in God, then this looks rather like His handiwork, His way of taking the next step forward."

"It is forward from the intellectual's point of view," said the Frenchman. "To a nearsighted, soft-bellied, flatulent professor, this is no doubt progress."

"Do I look like a professor?" grunted Mandelbaum. "I was riveting steel when you were reading your first books about the beauties of nature. I was having my face kicked in by company goons when you were writing about the sin of pride and battle. You loved the working man, but you wouldn't invite him to your table, now would you? When little Jean-Pierre, he was a divinity student before the war, when he was caught spying for our side, he held out for twenty-four hours against everything the Germans could do to him and gave the rest of us a chance to escape. Meanwhile, as I recall, you were safe in the States writing propaganda. Judas priest, why don't you ever try those things you're so ready to theorize about?"

The dragging weariness lifted from him as he swung into the old joy of struggle. His voice raised itself in a hard fierce tone, like hammers on iron. "The trouble with all of you is that one way or another, you're all afraid to face life. Instead of trying to shape the future, you've been wanting a past which is already a million years behind us. You've lost your old illusions and you haven't got what it takes to make new and better ones for yourselves."

"Including the American delusion of 'Progress,'" snapped the Chinese.

"Who said anything about that? That's forgotten too, obsolete junk—another shibboleth born of stupidity and greed and smugness. Sure, all our past has been stripped from us. Sure, it's a terrible feeling, bare and lonely like this. But do you think man can't strike a new balance? Do you think we can't build a new culture, with its own beauty and delight and dreams, now that we've broken out of the old cocoon? And do you think that men —men with strength and hope in them, all races, all over the world—want to go back? I tell you they don't. The very fact you tried this secretly shows you knew the same thing.

"What did the old world offer to ninety per cent of the human race? Toil, ignorance, disease, war, oppression, want, fear, from the filthy birth to the miserable grave. If you were born into a lucky land, you might fill your belly and have a few shiny toys to play with, but there was no hope in you, no vision, no purpose. The fact that one civilization after another went down into ruin shows we weren't fitted for it; we were savages by nature. Now we have a chance to get off that wheel of history and go somewhere—nobody knows where, nobody can even guess, but our eyes have been opened and you wanted to close them again!"

Mandelbaum broke off, sighed, and turned to his detectives. "Take 'em away, boys," he said.

The cabal were urged onto the raft—gently, there was no need for roughness and no malice. Mandelbaum stood watching as the raft lifted slowly up into the star ship. Then he turned to the long metal form on the ground.

"What a heroic thing!" he muttered, shaking his head. "Futile, but heroic. Those are good men. I hope it won't take too long to salvage them."

Corinth's grin was crooked. "Of course, *we* are absolutely right," he said.

Mandelbaum chuckled. "Sorry for the lecture," he replied. "Old habit too strong—a fact has to have a moral tag on it—well, we, the human race, ought to get over that pretty soon."

The physicist sobered. "You have to have some kind of morality," he said.

"Sure. Like you have to have motives for doing anything at all. Still, I think we're beyond that smug sort of code which proclaimed crusades and burned heretics and threw dissenters into concentration camps. We need more personal and less public honor."

Mandelbaum yawned then, stretching his wiry frame till it seemed the bones must crack. "Long ride, and not even a proper gun battle at the end," he said. The raft was coming down again, automatically. "I'm for some sleep. We can look over this mess of junk in the morning. Coming?"

"Not just yet," said Corinth. "I'm too tired." (I want to think.) "I'll walk over toward the beach."

"Okay." Mandelbaum smiled, with a curious tenderness on his lips. "Good night."

"Good night." Corinth turned and walked from the clearing. Helga went wordlessly beside him.

They came out of the jungle and stood on sands that were like frost under the moon. Beyond the reef, the surf flamed and crashed, and the ocean was roiled and streaked with the cold flimmer of phosphorescence. The big stars were immensely high overhead, but the night sky was like crystal. Corinth felt the sea wind in his face, sharp and salt, damp with the thousand watery miles it had swept across. Behind him, the jungle rustled and whispered to itself, and the sand gritted tinily underfoot. He was aware of it all with an unnatural clarity, as if he had been drained of everything that was himself and was now only a vessel of images.

He looked at Helga, where she stood holding his arm. Her face was sharply outlined against the further darkness, and her hair—she had unbound it—fluttered loosely in the wind, white in the pouring unreal moonlight. Their two shadows were joined into one, long and blue across the glittering sand. He could feel the rhythm of her breathing where she stood against him.

They had no need to speak. Too much understanding had grown up between them, they had shared too much of work and watching, and now they stood for a while in silence. The sea talked to them, giant pulsing of waves, boom where they hit the reef, rush where they streamed back into the water. The wind hissed and murmured under the sky.

Gravitation (sun, moon, stars, the tremendous unity which is space-time)
+ Coriolis force (the planet turning, turning, on its way through miles and years)
+ Fluid friction (the oceans grinding, swirling, roaring between narrow straits, spuming and thundering over rock)
+ Temperature differential (sunlight like warm rain, ice and darkness, clouds, mists, wind and storm)
+ Vulcanism (fire deep in the belly of the planet, sliding of unimaginable rock masses, smoke and lava, the raising of new mountains with snow on their shoulders)
+ Chemical reaction (dark swelling soil, exhausted air made live again, rocks red and blue and ocher, life, dreams, death and rebirth and all bright hopes)

EQUALS

This our world, and behold, she is very fair.

Nevertheless there was a weariness and desolation in the man, and after a while he turned for comfort as if the woman had been his.

"Easy," he said, and the word and his tones meant: (It was too easy, for us and for them. They had a holy spirit, those men. It should have ended otherwise. Fire and fury, wrath, destruction, and the unconquerable pride of man against the gods.)

"No," she replied. "This way was better." Quietly, calmly: (Mercy and understanding. We're not wild animals any more, to bare our teeth at the fates.)

Yes. That is the future. Forget all red glories.

"But what is our tomorrow?" he asked. (We stand with the wreckage of a world about our feet, looking into a hollow universe, and we must fill it ourselves. There is no one to help us.)

"Unless there is a destiny," (God, fate, human courage) she said.

"Perhaps there is," he mused. "Consciously or not, a universe has been given into our hands."

She fled from the knowledge, knowing that to answer her he would have to summon up the bravery he needed. (Have we the right to take it? If we make ourselves guardians of planets, is that better than Grunewald—blindness of causality, senseless cruelty of chance, the querning in his poor mad head?)

"It would not be thus that we would enter on our destiny," he told her. "We would be unseen, unknown guides, guardians of freedom, not imposers of an arbitrary will. When our new civilization is built, that may be the only work worthy of its hands."

O most glorious destiny! Why should I feel sorrow on this night? And yet there are tears behind my eyes.

She said what had to be said: "Sheila was discharged a few days ago." *I weep for you, my darling in darkness.*

"Yes," he nodded. "I saw it." (She ran out like a little girl. She held her hands up to the sun and laughed.)

"She has found her own answer. You still have to find yours."

His mind worried the past like a dog with a bone. "She didn't know I was watching her." *It was a cold bright morning. A red maple leaf fluttered down and caught in her hair. She used to wear flowers in her hair for me.* "She has already begun to forget me."

"You told Kearnes to help her forget," she said. "That was the bravest thing you ever did. It takes courage to be kind. But are you now strong enough to be kind to yourself?"

"No," he answered. "I don't want to stop loving her. I'm sorry, Helga."

"Sheila will be watched over," she said. "She will not know it, but the Observers will guide her wandering. There is a promising moron colony——" *Anguish* "—north of the city. We have been helping it lately without its knowing. Its leader is a good man, a strong and gentle man. Sheila's blood will be a leaven in their race."

He said nothing.

"Pete," she challenged him, "now you must help yourself."

"No," he said. "But you can change too, Helga. You can will yourself away from me."

"Not when you need me, and know it, and still cling blind to a dead symbol," she replied. "Pete, it is you now who are afraid to face life."

There was a long stillness, only the sea and the wind had voice. The moon was sinking low, its radiance filled their eyes, and the man turned his face from it. Then he shuddered and straightened his shoulders.

"Help me!" he said, and took her hands. "I cannot do it alone. Help me, Helga."

There are no words. There can never be words for this.

The minds met, flowing together, succoring need, and in a way which was new to the world they shared their strength and fought free of what was past.

To love, honor, and cherish, until death do us part.

It was an old story, she thought among the thunders. It was the oldest and finest story on Earth, so it was entitled to an old language. Sea, and stars —why, there was even a full moon.

CHAPTER TWENTY-ONE

AUTUMN AGAIN, and winter in the air. The fallen leaves lay in heaps under the bare dark trees and hissed and rattled across the ground with every wind. Only a few splashes of color remained in the woods, yellow or bronze or scarlet against grayness.

Overhead the wild geese passed in great flocks, southward bound. There was more life in the sky this year—fewer hunters, Brock supposed. The remote honking drifted down to him, full of wandering and loneliness. It was a clear pale blue up there, the sun wheeled bright and heatless, spilling its coruscant light across a broad and empty land. The wind was strong, flowing around his cheeks and flapping his clothes, the trees were noisy with it.

He went slowly from the main house, scuffing the sere grass under his boots. Joe followed quietly at heel. From the shed came a hammering of sheet iron, Mehitabel and Mac were building their charcoal gas distillator: for them it was too much fun to let be, and the gasoline supplies were very low. Some of the people had gone to town, some were sleeping off their Sunday dinner. Brock was alone.

He thought he might stop in and chatter with Mehitabel. No, let her work undisturbed; her conversation was rather limited anyway. He decided to take a stroll through the woods; it was late afternoon already, and too nice a day to be indoors.

Ella Mae came out of one of the cottages and giggled at him. "Hello," she said.

"Uh, hello," he answered. "How're you?"

"I'm fine," she said. "Want to come inside? Nobody else in here now."

"No, thanks," he said. "I, well, I have to check a fence."

"I could come along?" she asked timidly.

"Better not," he said. "The pigs, you know. They might still be running around in there."

Ella Mae's watery blue eyes filled with tears, and she lowered her misshapen head. "You never stop by with me," she accused.

"I will when I get the chance," he said hastily. "It's just that I'm awful busy. You know how it goes." He made his retreat as fast as he could.

Have to get a husband for her, he reflected. *There must be a number of her kind wandering loose even now. I can't have her chasing after me this way, it's too hard on both of us.*

He grinned crookedly. Leadership seemed to be all burden and little reward. He was commander, planner, executive, teacher, doctor, father confessor—and now matchmaker!

He bent over and caressed Joe's head with a big rough hand. The dog licked his wrist and wagged a joyous tail. Sometimes a man could get damnably lonely. Even a friend like Joe couldn't fill all needs. On this day of wind and sharp light and blowing leaves, a day of farewell, when all the earth seemed to be breaking up its summer home and departing down some unknown road, he felt his own isolation like a pain within him.

Now, no more of such thoughts, he reproved himself. "Come on, Joe, let's take us a walk."

The dog poised, it was a lovely taut stance, and looked toward the sky. Brock's eyes followed. The flash of metal was so bright it hurt him to look.

An airship—some kind of airship. And it's landing!

He stood with his fists clenched at his sides, feeling the wind chill on his skin and hearing how it roared in the branches behind him. The heart in his breast seemed absurdly big, and he shivered under the heavy jacket and felt sweat on his palms.

Take it easy, he told himself. *Just take it easy. All right, so it is one of Them. He won't bite you. Nobody's harmed us, or interfered with us, yet.*

Quietly as a falling leaf, the vessel grounded nearby. It was a small ovoid, with a lilting grace in its clean lines and curves, and there was no means of propulsion that Brock could see. He began walking toward it, slowly and stiffly. The revolver sagging at his waist made him feel ridiculous, as if he had been caught in a child's playsuit.

He felt a sudden upsurge of bitterness. *Let Them take us as we are. Be damned if I'll put on company manners for some bloody Sunday tourist.*

The side of the aircraft shimmered and a man stepped through it. *Through it!* Brock's first reaction was almost disappointment. The man looked so utterly commonplace. He was of medium height, a stockiness turning plump, an undistinguished face, an ordinary tweed sports outfit. As Brock approached, the man smiled.

"How do you do?"

"How do." Brock stopped, shuffling his feet and looking at the ground. Joe sensed his master's unease and snarled, ever so faintly.

The stranger held out his hand. "My name is Lewis, Nat Lewis from New York. Hope you'll pardon this intrusion. John Rossman sent me up. He's not feeling very well or he'd have come himself."

Brock shook hands, a little reassured by Rossman's name. The old man had always been a decent sort, and Lewis' manner was ingratiating. Brock forced himself to meet the other man's eyes, and gave his own name.

"Yes, I recognize you from Rossman's description," said Lewis. "He's quite interested in how you people are making out up here. Don't worry, he has no intention of repossessing this property; it's just a friendly curiosity. I work at his Institute, and frankly, I was curious myself, so I've come to check up for him."

Brock decided that he liked Lewis. The man spoke rather slowly, it must be a slight effort for him to return to old ways of speech, but there was nothing patronizing about him.

"From what I hear, you've done a marvelous job," said Lewis.

"I didn't know that you—well—that we——" Brock halted, stammering.

"Oh, yes, a bit of an eye was kept on you as soon as we'd taken care of our own troubles. Which were plenty, believe me. Still are, for that matter. Here, may I offer you a cigar?"

"Hmmm—well——" Brock accepted but didn't smoke it. He had not formed the habit. But he could give the cigar to someone else. "Thanks."

"It's not a baby," Lewis grinned. "At least, I hope not!" He lit one for himself, using a trick lighter that worked even in the high, noisy wind. "You've doubtless noticed that the towns around here have all been evacuated," he said after taking a contented puff.

"Yes, for some months now," answered Brock. With defiance: "We've been taking what we needed and could find there."

"Oh, quite all right. That was the idea; in fact, you can move into any of them if you want. The colony committee just thought it was best to rid you of such, ah, overwhelming neighbors. The people didn't care; at the present stage of their development, one place is about as good as another to them." Wistfulness flitted across Lewis' face. "That's a loss of ours: the intimacy of giving our hearts to one small corner of the earth."

The confession of weakness relaxed Brock. He suspected that it was deliberate, but even so——

"And those who've strayed here to join you have often been unobtrusively guided," Lewis went on. "There will be others, if you want them. And I think you could use more help, and they could certainly use a home and security."

"It's—nice of you," said Brock slowly.

"Ah, it isn't much. Don't think you've been guarded against all danger, or that all your work was done for you. That was never true, and never will be. We've just—well, once in a while we've thrown a little opportunity your way. But it was up to you to use it."

"I see."

"We can't help you more than that. Too much for us to do, and too few of us to do it. And our ways are too different. Your kind and my kind have come to the parting of the roads, Brock, but we can at least say good-by and shake hands."

It was a warming speech, something thawed inside Brock and he smiled. He had not relished the prospect of being stamped out by a ruthless race of gods, and still less had he cared to spend his days as anyone's ward. Lewis made no bones about the fact of their difference, but he was not snobbish about it either: there was no connotation of superiority in what he said.

They had been strolling about the grounds as they talked. Lewis heard the clashing hammers inside the shed now, and glanced questioningly at Brock.

"I've got a chimpanzee and a moron in there, making a charcoal apparatus so we can fuel our engines," Brock explained. It didn't hurt to say "moron" —not any more. "It's our day off here, but they insisted on working anyway."

"How many have you got, all told?"

"Oh, well, ten men and six women, ages from around fifteen to—well, I'd guess sixty for the oldest. Mentally from imbecile to moron. Then a couple of kids have been born too. Of course, it's hard to say where the people leave off and the animals begin. The apes, or Joe here, are certainly more intelligent and useful than the imbeciles." Joe wagged his tail and looked pleased. "I draw no distinctions; everyone does what he's best fitted for, and we share alike."

"You're in command, then?"

"I suppose so. They always look to me for guidance. I'm not the brightest one of the lot, but our two intellectuals are—well—ineffectual."

Lewis nodded. "It's often that way. Sheer intelligence counts for less than personality, strength of character, or the simple ability to make decisions and stick by them." He looked sharply at his bigger companion. "You're a born leader, you know."

"I am? I've just muddled along as well as possible."

"Well," chuckled Lewis, "I'd say that was the essence of leadership."

He looked around the buildings and out to the wide horizon. "It's a happy little community you've built up," he said.

"No," answered Brock frankly. "It's not."

Lewis glanced at him, raising his eyebrows, but said nothing.

"We're too close to reality here for snugness," said Brock. "That may come later, when we're better adjusted, but right now it's still hard work keeping alive. We have to learn to live with some rather harsh facts of life—such as some of us being deformed, or the need for butchering those poor animals——" He paused, noticed that his fists were clenched, and tried to ease himself with a smile.

"Are you—married?" inquired Lewis. "Pardon my nosiness, but I have a reason for asking."

"No. I can't see taking what's available here. No matter, there's enough to do to keep me out of mischief."

"I see——"

Lewis was quiet for a while. They had wandered over by the corn crib, where a board across two barrels made a seat out of the wind. They sat down, wordlessly, and let the day bluster around them. Joe flopped at their feet, watching them with alert brown eyes.

Presently Lewis stubbed out his cigar and spoke again. He sat looking ahead of him, not facing Brock, and his voice sounded a little dreamy, as if he were talking to himself.

"You and your animals here are making the best of a new situation," he said. "So far it's not been a very good one. Would you want to return to the old days?"

"Not I, no," said Brock.

"I thought not. You're taking this reality which has been given to you, with all its infinite possibilities, and you're making it good. That's what my branch of the race is also trying to do, Brock, and maybe you'll succeed better than we. I don't know. I probably won't ever know—won't live that long.

"But I want to tell you something. I've been out in space—between the stars—and there have been other expeditions there too. We found that the galaxy is full of life, and all of it seems to be like the old life of Earth: many forms, many civilizations, but nowhere a creature like man. The average I.Q. of the whole universe may not be much over a hundred. It's too early to tell, but we have reasons to think that that is so.

"And what are we, the so-called normal humanity, to do with our strange powers? Where can we find something that will try and challenge us, something big enough to make us humble and offer us a task in which we can take pride? I think the stars are our answer. Oh, I don't mean we intend to establish a galactic empire. Conquest is a childishness we've laid aside, even now. Nor do I mean that we'll become ministering angels to all these uncounted worlds, guiding them and guarding them till their races get too flabby to stand on their own feet. No, nothing like that. We'll be creating our own new civilization, one which will spread between the stars, and it will have its own internal goals, creation, struggle, hope—the environment of man is still primarily man.

"But I think there will be a purpose in that civilization. For the first time, man will really be going somewhere; and I think that his new purpose will, over thousands and millions of years, embrace all life in the attainable universe. I think a final harmony will be achieved such as no one can now imagine.

"We will not be gods, or even guides. But we will—some of us—be givers of opportunity. We will see that evil does not flourish too strongly, and that hope and chance happen when they are most needed, to all those millions of sentient creatures who live and love and fight and laugh and weep and die, just as man once did. No, we will not be embodied Fate; but perhaps we can be Luck. And even, it may be, Love."

The man smiled then, a very human smile at himself and all his own pretences. "Never mind. I talk too much. Winelike autumn air, as the old cliché has it." He turned to Brock. "What's more to the point, we—our sort —are not going to remain here on Earth."

Brock nodded silently. The vision before him was too enormous for surprise.

"Your sort won't be bothered," said Lewis. "And then in a few years, when things are ready, we'll disappear into the sky. Earth will be left to your kind, and to the animals. And thereafter you will be altogether free. It will be up to you, as to the other kinds of life, to work out your own destiny. And if now and then a bit of luck comes to you—well, that has always been happening."

"Thank you." It was a whisper in Brock's throat.

"Don't thank me, or anyone else. This is merely the logic of events working itself out. But I wish you well, every one of you."

Lewis stood up and began walking back toward his aircraft. "I have to go now." He paused. "I wasn't quite honest with you when I came. It wasn't Rossman's curiosity that sent me; he could have satisfied that by asking the colony committee, or by dropping in himself. I wanted to check up here personally because—well, you'll be having a new member for your community soon."

Brock looked at him, wondering. Lewis stopped before his craft.

"She's an old friend," he said. "Her story is rather tragic, she'll tell you herself when she feels like it. But she's a good sort, a wonderful girl really, and we who know her want her to be happy."

The metal shimmered before him. He took Brock's hand. "Good-by," he said simply, and stepped inside. A moment later his vessel was high in heaven.

Brock stared after it till it had vanished.

When he turned back toward the house, the sun was sinking low and the chill bit at him. They'd have to light the fireplace tonight. Maybe they could break out some of the remaining ale if a new recruit was coming, and Jimmy could play the guitar while they all sang. The songs were rowdy, you couldn't expect more of a pioneer people, but there was warmth in them, steadfastness and comradeship.

He saw her then, walking up the driveway, and his heart stumbled within him. She was not tall, but her form was sweet and strong under the heavy clothing, and bronze-colored hair blew around a face that was young and gentle and good to look on. She carried a bundle on her back, and the suns of many days tramping down open roads had tinged her and dusted freckles across the large-eyed face. He stood for a moment without stirring, and then he ran; but when he came up and was before her, he could find no words.

"Hello," she said shyly.

He nodded awkwardly. It did not occur to him that he was a strong-looking man, not handsome, but with something about him that invoked trust.

"I heard talk this was a refuge," she said.

"Yes," he replied. "Have you come far?"

"From New York City." There was a small shiver in her, and he wondered what had happened there. Or maybe it was just the cold. The wind piped bitterly now. "My name is Sheila," she said.

"I'm Archie—Archie Brock." Her hand was firm within his. She did not act frightened, and he knew that while she might not be quite as smart as he, she had more than enough intelligence and will to meet this wintering planet. "You're welcome here. It's always a big event when someone new comes. But you'll find it strange, and we all have to work hard."

"I'm not afraid of either of those," she answered. "I don't think I can ever be afraid again."

He took her bundle and started back. The western sky was turning red and gold and a thin chill green. "I'm glad to know you, Miss—what did you say your last name was?"

"Sheila," she replied. "Just Sheila."

They walked up the driveway side by side, the dog and the wind at their heels, toward the house. In there was shelter.

BULLARD REFLECTS
by Malcolm Jameson

"WHEE! YIPPEE! YOW!"

The crowd went crazy. Staid, gold-braided captains and commanders jumped up and down on their seats and yelled themselves hoarse. Even the admirals present dropped their dignified hand clapping for unrestrained shouting. Spacemen of all ratings tossed their hats away, hugged whoever was next to them, and behaved generally like wild men. Alan MacKay had scored his tenth successive goal!

"Castor Beans, Castor Beans—waw! waw! waw!" went the *Pollux* bleachers derisively.

"Polliwogs, Polliwogs—yah, yah, yah!" came the prompt response from the space cruiser *Castor's* side of the arena. But it was a weak and disheartened chorus. 850 to 25 the wrong way at the end of the first half was not the sort of score to inspire a cheering section. The *Pollux's* Dazzle Dart team was mopping up—and how!

Captain Bullard of the *Pollux* was no exception to the rest. He flopped back into his seat red of face and utterly exhausted. His vocal cords had gone long since, and now he could only gasp and speak in weak whispers. Captain Ellington, commander of the mine division, leaned over and congratulated him.

"You've got the General Excellence Trophy in the bag," he said. "That is the third time in a row, isn't it? That means you keep it."

"Yes," said Bullard, feebly. "But, oh, boy, who would have dreamed of picking up a player like this MacKay! I asked for him on account of the way he handled that Jovian surrender, but I had no idea he was such a whiz at Dazzle Dart—"

Then Bullard's husky voice failed him altogether, and he turned to watch the parades between halves.

The interfleet athletic meet, held for the first time since the Jovian armistice, had been a howling success from his point of view from first to last. The hand-picked, well-trained skymen of the *Pollux* had taken every major sport. The meteor-ball contest had been a pushover; they earned over eight hundred of the possible thousand points at saltation—that grueling competition of leaping from a stand at all gravities from zero to two and a half. They had outswum, outrun and outplayed their competitors in practically every one of the events. And now, in the most critical test of all, they had a walkaway. He had expected it, of course, but not by such a tremendous margin.

In the meantime the crowd milled and whooped on the plain at the bottom of Luna's well-dome crater Ashtaroth which was the athletic field of the great Lunar Base. Captain Bullard regained his breath and sat watching. Good boys, his, he was thinking, all of them—whether at war or at play. Then there came another touch at his elbow and Lieutenant Commander Bissel was there, aide to the commandant.

"I hate to inject a serious note into the festivities," he apologized, "but there's something hot coming in over the transether. Remember Egon Ziffler, chief of secret police of the Jovian Empire—the Torturer, they called him?"

Bullard nodded.

"He's been located, and at Titania, of all places. He appeared in a Callistan cruiser and took the place by surprise. Apparently he massacred the entire garrison in the most fiendish manner; the admiral is talking now with the sole survivor who, somehow, manage to escape to Oberon. The worst of it is he is in possession of our experimental arsenal and proving grounds—"

"Yes?" said Bullard.

"Yes. It has not been released yet, but that deadly new electron gun worked perfectly and there are hundreds of them there. With those in their hands they will be almost invulnerable. Only the screens of a star-class cruiser can resist the hand-size model, and I doubt if those could stand up to the heavier Mark II we planned to build."

"That's bad," remarked Bullard, with a sigh. It seemed that no matter how much clean-up work they did, there was always trouble.

"Yes," agreed Bissel, soberly, "it is bad. But I'll toddle along and get the latest. By the time this is over maybe I can give you the full dope."

He slid out of the box, and Bullard turned his attention once more to the field, only now his thoughts were inside the *Pollux,* parked in her launching rack over at the sky yard. Swiftly he surveyed mentally every compartment in her, then he permitted himself to relax. He could find no fault. She was ready to soar. Just let them give the word.

By that time the playing field was empty. A whistle blew. The second half was about to begin. It seemed a useless waste of time, but the rules were unchangeable. A fleet championship game could not be conceded; it must be played out to the last second.

The Castoreans came onto the field in a somewhat more cheerful frame of mind. In this half they would have the advantage. They had the offensive. Then the Polliwogs tramped in, still jubilant. There was an enormous margin to their credit. They could hardly lose.

The game, essentially, was a simple one. But it called for the utmost a man could develop in alertness, agility and dexterity. Moreover, to get the best results, there must be instant teamwork, secured by long practice, for there was scant time to interpret and act upon the sharply barked code signals that demanded various degrees of co-operation.

The elements of it were these: it was played on a court not much different in layout from that required by basketball, football or jai-alai. There were two opposite goals, set high in backstops. The goals were six-inch black holes in which were selenium units. A semicircular wall, four feet high, guarded a forbidden area at the foot of each backstop. The quarterback of the offensive team had a flashlight—a superflashlight—which was loaded for each half with exactly one hundred ten-second flashes of light. The light was delivered in a thin pencil of one centimeter in diameter, and the inner mechanism of it was so designed that the operator could deliver it flash at a time by simply pointing it and pressing a button. But once the button was pressed, the light stayed on for a full ten seconds and then went out abruptly, counting as one serve. The idea was to cast the ray into the opposite goal hole. If the bell rang, the quarterback scored twenty-five points.

The defenders' aim was to intercept and deflect the light—into the other goal, if possible. Should they succeed, their score would be double. To effect this, they were equipped with as many slightly convex mirrors as they thought they could handle. The mirrors were not dissimilar from the type worn on the brow of a throat specialist. Players usually wore them strapped to their wrists, but stars could not only manage those, but also ones strapped at their waists and on the head as well. A good jumper was a distinct asset to a team, and the *Pollux's* five saltatory champs had been of invaluable assistance.

They took their positions. Weems, captain of the *Castor* team, had the torch. His twenty guards were ranged about him. The Polliwogs scattered out at the other end of the court, tense and waiting. Tackling, holding or slugging was barred, but a man could drop on all fours and make an onrushing opponent stumble over him. There was no more to the game than that.

Weems maneuvered for position, then leaped unexpectedly into the air, and it was a goodly leap, as they were playing on strictly Lunar gravity. At near the top of his flight his hand darted forth and he sent a beam of light at his goal. It struck the backstop not a foot from the goal, but before the eagle-eyed Weems could shift his hand, a Polliwog player was in the air and had caught it with one of his reflectors. A twist of the wrist sent it hurtling back to the other side, a narrow miss. The source of it—Weems—was falling now, and he jerked his arm, throwing the light sharply downward, where one of his own teammates caught it and shot it up at a steep angle under the hovering Polliwog guards. A bull's-eye! And not an instant too soon, for at that moment the light went out. Twenty-five points for the attackers.

So it went—so swiftly the eye could hardly follow. Despite the fact that it was customary to fill the arena dome with humid air and spray dust in it so as to illuminate the darting beam throughout its length, it took the glance of an eagle to keep pace with it. A battery of cameras, of course, recorded the play constantly, and the selenium-cell-operated bell bonged from time to time as the light ray hit it.

The second half was full of brilliant double and triple plays, where often the quarterback would turn and flash his light directly behind him to a confederate who relayed it across the court, who in his turn shot it into a momentarily undefended goal. The ultimate score, though, was against the Castoreans. Their defeat was so decisive as to admit no quibbling.

The cheering lasted for minutes, but hardly had the final goal bell rung before Bullard was aware that the grand admiral himself had entered his box and was sitting beside him.

"Congratulations," said he, then addressed himself to serious business. "You have already heard a little of what is going on on Titania? I sent Bissel. It is a scurvy trick to recall your crew and send you out on a desperate mission at an hour like this, but there is no other ship ready. Since the armistice it seems that there has been a letdown in discipline. Can you blast off in four hours?"

"I can blast off in one hour if you'll give me an all-Moon hookup on the public-address system," said Bullard, without batting an eye. He had not only been expecting the detail, but hoping for it. Ziffler was a creature he loathed from the bottom of his heart—treacherous, cruel and unprincipled, of a breed that extermination is the only cure for.

Within five minutes Bullard was making his appeal to his skymen.

"On the double!" were his last words, and he slammed down the transmitter.

The burned and looted fortress of Caliban lay directly under. Bullard pushed his navigator aside and took the controls himself. He set the antigravs at half strength and slowly lost altitude, constantly searching. At last he found them. There was a parked cruiser of the *Dernfug* class, and a horde of men camped outside alongside it. Phosphorescent flares burned, and he saw they were celebrating. Kegs of the type used as containers for the potent *snahger* liquor rolled all about, and the thickest of the rioting throng were gathered about others yet upright.

"The ship, first," said Bullard, grimly, and his gunnery officer—Fraser—said only, "Aye, aye, sir."

The searing, blinding beam of incredible power leaped downward, played a moment on the cruiser, then flickered out. On the ground there was left only a mass of running molten metal, sputtering a valedictory of brilliant sparks.

"Cease firing!" was Bullard's next crisp order. "The grand admiral wants them brought in alive, if possible." He reached for the antigrav control and pushed the deflectors on hard swing.

The *Pollux* came down a mile away to an easy landing on the dark plain. The people in her could plainly see the floodlamps of the rollicking bandits and the sharp reflections that glinted on the smooth terrain between. There was nothing to impede the progress of the landing force.

But by the time the landing force was ready for its trip, the lookout reported a new development. A party of men was approaching, and they were stretching their arms over their heads in gesture of surrender. A close scrutiny of them could discover no arms worth worrying about. The new electron projectors were said to be quite heavy, each requiring two men to carry and operate. Any less potent weapon the veterans of the *Pollux* could deal with, and deal with well.

"Find out who they are and what is their proposition," ordered Bullard. "If it sounds reasonable, let three in for a parley. No more. He is full of slimy tricks, that Ziffler. I wouldn't trust his words under any circumstances."

It was not Ziffler, but Skul Drosno, former vice premier of the Jovian regime, together with two high aides. They wanted to arrange terms of surrender, they said. Their story was that they had revolted against the atrocities of Ziffler and had him a prisoner in their camp. They would trade him—trussed up as he was—for personal immunity and a general pardon for their followers. They would willingly submit to trial, knowing now how they had been hoodwinked.

"Let them in," said Bullard, though he was still a trifle doubtful. "I will talk with them."

Skul Drosno began his appeal. Bullard recognized it at once as rank sophistry, but he continued to listen. Then, to his astonishment, Drosno suddenly slumped in his chair. His eyes were crossed to a painful degree, and his hands wavered uncertainly in the air. The next moment he pitched forward onto the deck and sprawled, apparently unconscious. One of his aides looked sick, and staggered to his feet, weaving about ridiculously.

"What an act!" thought Bullard, and sprang to his own feet, alert. He shot a glance to his side and saw that his executive, Moore, who had been with him, was an inert heap. And at that moment things began to blur before his own eyes. His knees wobbled, and he heard a harsh, metallic ringing in his ears. He fought for air, then choked. The floor plates rushed upward and struck him squarely in the face. After that Bullard remembered no more.

The next voice he heard was the high-pitched cackling of the unspeakable Ziffler.

"Can such things be!" crowed the vile Callistan. "A great personage, no less. I find as my prisoner the inimitable, the invincible, the incorruptible Bullard—hero of the nine planets!"

Bullard opened his eyes, ignoring the pounding in the back of his head. He was seated in a chair, strapped hand and foot, and the swaggering ex-police chief who had terrorized the Jovian satellites was standing before him, exulting.

"Perhaps he is not so invincible," pursued his tormentor, calmly lighting a cigarette and seating himself. "We have never seen him outside his formidable *Pollux*. But now that he is in our hands, I am curious to see how good he is. Hagstund! Come here!"

A big brute of a former convict strode forward.

"What do you say? Shall we have a little sport? Why not put these men in spacesuits and turn them loose for twenty-four hours? Then we can have a hunt. This man, in particular, has a gr-r-reat reputation for cleverness. Let's see what he can do on a barren and resourceless planet. We have counted them, so we know their numbers. I will give a prize, prizes. Ten thousand sols for this one, to whoever brings him down. Another ten thousand for the last man of the lot and another five for the next to the last. It'll be good fun, eh?"

Ziffler took a swig of *snahger* and delivered himself of an elaborate wink. Bullard did not believe for a moment he was drunk. Ziffler was too clever a scoundrel for that. It was a gesture meant to raise false hopes. Bullard knew all too well what the wastes of Titania were. He had been there before. Except for the port of Caliban, the arsenal and a few scattered stations which no doubt had been plundered by now, there was nothing but bleak, frozen plains, broken by rugged meteor craters.

"Swell, chief," agreed the henchman. "What about the ship?"

"Leave her lie as she is. They'll not send another for days. I don't want you baboons monkeying around inside her. Let's give these guys a run, then we'll get down to business. There's plenty of time."

Rough hands pulled Bullard to his feet, and at the point of one of the new and deadly electron guns they made him put on an ordinary spacesuit. As the mists cleared away in his throbbing head, he saw that he was in a large hall, and that other men and officers of his crew were being similarly treated.

"Oh, by the way," remarked Ziffler, offhandedly. "They say I am unkind. I'll save you one bit of mental torture. What got you down was our new hypnotic dust. It's very clever, really. Powder a coat with it, for example, then expose it to air. It vaporizes and puts everyone to sleep. My emissaries went out, too—naturally. All but one, that is, who had been heavily doped with an antidote beforehand. He survived long enough to open the door for us, then, unfortunately, died. It was regrettable, but in my business I find it necessary to do such things."

Bullard said not a word. He was ready. The outlook was black, but he had seen other outlooks that were quite as black.

"I'll be seeing you, Ziffler," he said, and hoped it was not mere braggadocio. Ziffler had a reputation for sadism, but not for courage. There was the bare chance that the single psychological shot in the dark might in time be digested and unsettle him. "Let's go. I prefer anything to your presence."

"Yeah?" said Ziffler, but he beckoned to his strong-arm squad.

The entire crew of the *Pollux* was there. They were pushed out through the portal of the dome in squads of four and told to get going. Bullard was let out last of all. Their captors promised tauntingly that they had a full Earth day before pursuit.

"Stay together, men," called Bullard into his helmet microphone, the moment the portal closed behind him. "All officers come up close to me."

The light on Titania is dim, even in full daytime. But it was good enough for his officers to read the swift manipulations of his fingers. Their skipper was using the sign language all trained Space Guards men used when they feared their words might be overheard.

"Poleward from here," Bullard told them, "some thirty miles, is a meteorite crater. For several years we have maintained a secret laboratory there and it is possible that these ruffians have not discovered it. That will be our destination. Under this gravity we should reach it within a few hours, though I am uncertain of its exact direction. Have the men spread out and hunt. There should be flares there, and the first man in should light one. The last time I visited the place it had a staff of eight or ten scientists, and an excellent interplanetary radio. They may have weapons, but at least we can flash an alarm."

Rapidly waved arms acknowledged, and the Polliwogs dispersed in the semidarkness.

It was Lieutenant Alan MacKay who reached the spot first. He had trouble in finding a flare, but eventually he found one and lit it. The laboratory was a shambles. The vandals had found the place, despite his captain's hopes to the contrary, and turned it upside down. The bodies of the physicists and chemists lay all about, and the unhappy director's corpse was discovered nailed to the wall, crucifix style. Torn papers, broken glass and tangled wire littered the floor. The radio had been smashed almost out of recognition. MacKay, a newcomer to the service, shuddered, but he carried out his orders.

Bullard arrived shortly after, and his face was not pretty to see as he viewed the wreckage. Now he regretted the flare. *They* undoubtedly had seen it, too. He had hoped to warn these people, send a message to the System in general, then have his forces scatter. A few of them might have hoped to survive the ruthless man hunt that was to follow.

But the situation was changed, and since any alternative seemed as hopeless as any other, he let the flare continue to burn. By keeping together, some resistance might be improvised. While he was waiting for the stragglers to come up, he busied himself with reassembling the torn pages of the notebooks and journals strewn about the floor.

Much of them dealt with routine analysis, but on a page written in red ink and numbered "97" he found a fragment that brought him to eager attention.

Unlike most meteorites, the one that made this crater failed to disintegrate upon impact—or rather, not all of it disintegrated. We have discovered a number of fragments, slightly curved, that indicate it was stratified, and that the stratum of radius, of about thirty meters and of one and a fraction inches in thickness, simply broke into bits instead of molecules. In the storehouse in the crater bottom there are more than a hundred of these fragments, running up to as high as twenty centimeters across. They are of a jadelike substance, subject to abrasion by ordinary methods and can be drilled by steel drills, and are not hard and ultradense as might have been expected. The curious thing about these fragments is that they defy X-ray analysis. For some odd reason they wreck every tube that is brought to bear upon them. They backfire, so to speak. Can it be that—

The page was at an end. Bullard sought frantically for page 98, but he could not find it. He called the trusty Benton.

"Take a gang of men and go down and search the crater. You ought to find a storehouse and in it a bunch of junky-looking rock fragments that look like jade. If you do, bring a flock of them up here. Quick!"

To the others standing around, he said:

"Clear out the wreckage in the workshop and see if those breast drills can be made to work. Strip the boots off of those dead men and cut them up into straps. As soon as you have done that, take off your own and cut them up, too. We haven't got time to lose."

Presently Lieutenant Benton came back, and a number of men were with him. They all bore armfuls of slightly curved pieces of a moss-colored, glass-like substance. Each was fairly large, but all had irregular and jagged edges. Bullard examined one hurriedly, hefting it critically.

"Get MacKay up here—quickly," he barked, suddenly. Then he wheeled on Benton. "Take all of these and drill two pairs of holes through each—here and here"—and he showed him. "Then affix straps, just as you would to those mirrors you use in the Dazzle Dart game."

Benton looked at him wonderingly, but he had learned a long time before to put his trust in his remarkable commander. He piled the shiny fragments of meteor stuff together and went out to call in his men.

Bullard felt better. What he was about to attempt was a wild gamble, but it was immeasurably better than waiting like a sheep for the slaughter or fleeing hopelessly across the cold wastes of Titania. He was very thankful, too, that on the occasion of his last visit to that satellite he had cut the governor general's party and ball and visited this secluded laboratory instead. For the day he had been there was shortly after the experiments described on the isolated page he now held in his hand. At that time nothing had been definitely determined as to the structure of the mysterious crystalline substance salvaged from the crater, but he recalled the speculations of the now dead scientists concerning it.

Lieutenant MacKay reported.

"Yes, sir?"

"Tell Commander Moore to have all the members of the Dazzle Dart team report to you here at once, and that means the men on the second team and the scrubs as well. Tell him to have everyone else find pits in the crater bottom and take shelter there until further orders. Clear?"

The ruffians of the Ziffler gang did not play entirely fair, as was to be expected. They beat the gun by several hours. It was Benton, in charge of the lookout, who sighted the mob advancing across the plain. They were in fairly close formation, as if by direction finders or some other means they already knew that the *Pollux* men were not scattered, but together at that so-called "Mystery Crater."

"Take stations," ordered Bullard, crisply. He was standing in the semi-darkness on the crater rim, some distance away from the damaged laboratory. To the right and left of him his victorious Dazzle Dart team were lying behind the irregular parapet made by the crater wall.

"Benton!" he called. "Scatter your squad both ways from me. When that gang of hoodlums is halfway up the hill, let 'em have your flame-gun blast. Then duck and beat it for the bottom of the crater and hide out until I call 'all clear.' "

Benton had found eight old flame guns in a work shed. They had been obsolete as fighting weapons for many years, but could deliver a nasty burn.

Captain Bullard had another look at the advancing hunting party. He saw that they had brought along a number of the new electron guns and were beginning to struggle up to the talus with them. The yelling mob reached a sort of ledge and waited for the guns to be brought up. A jeering voice, louder than the rest, called up:

"Will you come down and take it, you lice, or do we have to come up there and get you?"

"Now!" said Bullard softly into his microphone.

Eight feeble heat machines spat their ruddy blasts, then went out with a jerk as their operators let go of them and slid down the inner wall to safety. It was well that Bullard had foreseen the reply they would get, for the counterblast came almost instantaneously. A score of bright stars flamed out downhill and from them thin streams of almost invisible violet fire lashed upward and played along the crater rim. The rock sprang into incandescence and inches of it melted and flowed as bubbling, sparkling slag down the slope, where it quickly dulled to red and congealed.

"Now?" asked MacKay, anxiously. He was crouched beside the skipper.

"Not yet. Wait until they are closer."

The assault went on for a moment, then stopped. Bullard took a cautious peep and saw the Callistans had resumed their climb.

"What's the dirtiest thing you can call a Callistan?" whispered Bullard, grinning unseen in the dark. "You know the lingo."

"*Froahbortlen,*" replied MacKay without hesitation. The Callistan language was rich in epithets, but that one was the most comprehensive and unequivocal ever coined in any language. Even a depraved criminal of the lowest grade would resent it.

"Invite them up," said Bullard, grimly. "When they answer, do your stuff."

"On your toes, men," MacKay warned his teammates. Then he opened his mike wide and issued his sizzling, triple-barreled, insulting invitation.

Bullard involuntarily caught his breath. The die was cast. For an instant one of the qualms of uncertainty that rarely came to him held him in its grip. Was he right, or would they fail? Which side would be the victims of the massacre about to begin? Well, in a couple of seconds he would know.

The properties of the strange meteor substance was still unknown. It stopped Gamma and other hard rays. It wrecked the X-ray tubes focused upon it. How could that be, unless it also possessed that long-hunted, but never found, property of being able to deflect and reflect the high-pressure beams?

MacKay's helmet still vibrated with the last vile words of his superb taunt when the answering salvo of electric fire came. But that time there was more than inert rock to receive it. A row of alert young men stood on the crest, and a weird-looking crew they were. Glistening bits of rock were strapped to their wrists, to their foreheads, their belts, and even their ankles. In an instant they were leaping, dancing and twisting like mad dervishes, deftly parrying every violet pencil that struck above the rock at their feet. The devastating power was being hurled back whence it came.

The ruffians must have been amazed at the swift return of fire from men they thought to be totally disarmed, but they hung on doggedly for a few seconds more. Then their fire ceased altogether, and all that the observers on the rim could see were a few scared survivors scrambling down the way they had come.

"Too bad we haven't a weapon," sighed Bullard. "We could make a clean sweep."

He whipped out a flashlight and strode down to the ledge. There were many of the abandoned electron guns standing about on tripods, or overturned by the fleeing gangsters. Something soft gave under Bullard's boot. He played his light along the ground and saw a sight that under other circumstances would have been revolting. Loose hands and feet, attached to charred stumps of arm or leg, were strewn widely. Other and less readily indentifiable fragments of disintegrated humanity lay among them. Ziffler's strong-arm squad, once the terror of the outer planets, had been dispersed in the fullest sense of the word.

Bullard turned on his amplifier.

"O.K., Moore. Round up the men and bring them down. We're going back."

The trek back across the icy waste seemed infinitely shorter and easier than it had on the outward journey. Men's hearts were light now, and not leaden as before. To the Polliwogs, the knowledge they had lost their ship had been as dispiriting as the seeming certainty of their impending doom. Now all that was changed. A mile ahead of them lay the *Pollux*, just as they had left her.

The search for Ziffler and the stragglers took some time, but they found them, cowering and whimpering behind a boulder.

"Iron them well and thrown them into the brig," snapped Bullard, and went into his ship.

He grabbed a signal pad and wrote a brief report.

A little later the grand admiral at Lunar Base stretched out his hand for the flimsy bit of yellow paper his orderly had brought him. He read it, then read it again. He frowned a little and scratched his head.

"Has Bullard gone highbrow on us, or what the hell?" he asked, tossing the message over to Bissel. Bissel picked it up and read:

After reflection, the enemy succumbed.

BULLARD.

THE LOST YEARS
by Oscar Lewis

Had the assassin's mind dwelt on the enormity of the crime he was contemplating, had his resolution failed, or his hand wavered, the Nation might happily have been spared this overwhelming calamity. . . .

DR. JONATHAN BAUERMANN
APRIL 26, 1865

1865

Last evening while attending the theater, the President was attacked in his box by an unknown assailant, who then leaped to the stage, shouted some unintelligible words, and escaped in the confusion that followed. The wounded man was carried across the street to a lodging house and put to bed. His condition is said to be grave.

The Globe, *Philadelphia, Pa.*, April 15

Shortly after two o'clock this afternoon, the physicians who have been in constant attendance at the President's bedside issued this bulletin: "No marked change has occurred during the past 24 hours. The patient slept three hours this morning. At 12 o'clock noon his pulse and temperature remained high, his respiration was somewhat easier."

The Times-Journal, *Cincinnati, Ohio*, April 17

The President's physicians, while they continue to manifest deep concern, were noticeably less pessimistic this morning. For the first time in seven days the crowd before the roped-off area on Tenth Street was small. No bulletin was issued from the sickroom today.

The Star, *Albany, N.Y.*, April 22

Alonzo Hammond, M.D., stated today that, weather permitting, the President would be moved tomorrow morning to the Executive Mansion, where rooms have been made ready for him and for the nurses who will attend him during his convalescence.

The Daily Advertiser, *St. Louis, Mo.*, April 26

Now that the uncertainty and suspense of the last fortnight are past, and each day brings added assurance that the fanatical plot against the President's life has failed, every citizen, whatever his political faith, will breathe a sigh of relief. But our jubilation at this happy outcome must not blind us to the fact that the nation faces numerous problems of the utmost urgency that call for prompt action by the executive branch of the government. The Gazette, therefore, warmly endorses the proposal made by the Hon. Thaddeus Stevens during his address at Baltimore on Tuesday last: that pending the Chief Executive's recovery to a point where he can, with safety to himself and the union, reassume the duties of his office, the reins of authority be delegated to the cabinet, with full power to make decisions on such critical issues as cannot prudently be postponed until Congress reconvenes.

Editorial in The Gazette, *Boston, Mass.*, April 30

FROM MEMORIES OF A WARTIME NURSE
BY ELIZABETH PALMER BANKE
PUBLISHED BY TICKNOR & FIELDS
BOSTON, MASSACHUSETTS, 1867

ONE morning in late April [1865] an orderly came into the ward and told me I was wanted in the superintendent's office. As soon as I was able to leave I went downstairs and across the courtyard, trying to guess the reason for this summons. When I entered, Doctor Wilmot picked up a paper from his desk and handed it to me. I glanced through it hastily. It was a letter from the Surgeon General of the Army directing the superintendent to select a female nurse from the hospital staff and have her report to him at once for special duty.

To my look of inquiry, Doctor Wilmot replied that he knew nothing of the nature of this assignment, but that judging from the channels through which it had come it must be of considerable importance. He then wrote a brief note, addressed it to the Surgeon General, and asked me to deliver it in person. I returned to the ward, where I spoke briefly with the nurse who was to take over my duties, then hurried to the dormitory, stopping there only long enough to change into my street clothes and to gather up a few belongings. Five minutes later, seated in Doctor Wilmot's own carriage, which he had put at my disposal, I was hurrying across the city, little knowing that I had embarked on the most responsible assignment of my whole nursing career. . . .

Next morning as we drove through the muddy streets Doctor Hammond explained that while the patient appeared to be making steady progress, his condition was such as to cause continued concern, and that every precaution must therefore be taken to assure him uninterrupted rest and quiet. When we arrived before the gates, there were soldiers on guard there, as there had been ever since the night of the attack, but the officer in charge passed Doctor Hammond's carriage through without challenge. A moment later the coachman drew up before the entrance and we stepped down and entered the hallway, proceeding at once to the family living quarters on the second floor and on down the corridor to the extreme western end, where the sick-room was located. Adjoining the latter was a much smaller room that had been assigned to the nurses. For the next several weeks I shared this small chamber with my associate, an amiable, middle-aged woman named Margaret White, each of us serving on alternate shifts so that one or the other was constantly on call. . . .

During the first week a vigilant watch was maintained night and day. Except for the nurse on duty, and the doctors themselves, everyone was excluded from the sickroom, the one exception to this rule being the patient's wife, whose deep concern was evident to all, and who came and sat quietly at the bedside for an hour or more each afternoon. . . .

As the days passed and the wounded man's condition continued to improve, the strain and uncertainty that had gripped the household, and indeed the entire nation, gave place to a feeling of confidence which, cautious at first, daily grew more pronounced. Nowhere was this changing attitude more evident than in the sickroom itself. During the first few days after he was brought home the patient had seemed content to lie quietly in the darkened room, taking but little notice of what went on about him. As his strength returned, however, this enforced idleness daily grew more burdensome, and his protests against it, mild at first, presently became so insistent that the doctors were obliged to modify their order excluding all callers. The visitors were, however, limited to members of the immediate family: his wife of course and their two sons, the elder of whom was in his early twenties and the other a high-spirited lad of about twelve. The latter, who had long been allowed the run of the house, had found it hard to curb his normal habits during the days when the rule of silence was rigidly enforced. Now, however, no such restrictions were placed on his behavior during his daily visits to the bedside, and the result was that his boyish exuberance dispelled the gloom from the chamber and brought indulgent smiles to the wan face on the pillow. . . .

As he continued to mend, the responsibilities of his high office came to occupy an ever larger place in his thoughts, and the doctors, facing appeals that daily grew more urgent, had no choice but to agree to a gradual resumption of his official duties, although they were at pains to point out the danger of overtaxing his still feeble strength. Thus by mid-May he was permitted to sit up in bed for a limited period each morning while he discussed with his secretaries—both of whom customarily addressed him as "the Shogun"—such matters as could not prudently be longer postponed. Presently, too, the rule against visitors was further relaxed, so that soon the injured man was following an increasingly active schedule, with half his mornings given over to official business and the afternoons to a succession of visitors: cabinet officers, members of the Congress, officers of the Army and Navy, and a variety of friends, advisers and well-wishers.

Despite this busy program, or perhaps because of it, his recovery continued apace. Soon he was strong enough to leave his bed afternoons and receive callers while seated in an armchair before the windows, from which he could look out toward the Potomac and, closer at hand, admire the trees in the President's Park, the branches of which were now garlanded with the bright colors of spring. Then one day, toward the middle of the month, he asked that his clothing be brought in and proceeded to dress himself, rejecting all offers of assistance, whereupon, supported only by a cane, he made his way slowly down the hallway to his long-vacant study.

As it proved, this first visit to his study marked the virtual end of his illness, for he returned briefly to his study the next afternoon and again, for a much longer period, on the day following. That evening, it having grown clear that my services were no longer needed, Doctor Hammond stated that I was free to report back to my regular duties at the hospital. This I did the next day, much pleased that my special assignment had had so happy an outcome. . . .

SUMMER AT AUBURN, 1869: BEING EXCERPTS FROM THE DIARY OF MATTHEW BOSLEY, WITH ADDITIONS FROM VARIOUS SOURCES. COMPILED AND EDITED BY SYLVANUS SLADE

A NOTE ON THE EDITOR: *Sylvanus Slade was born at Auburn, California, on December 4, 1879, and died at Sacramento, August 19, 1949. For more than forty years he taught in the various California schools, attaining the rank of vice-principal of a Sacramento junior high school shortly before he retired in 1943. Throughout his long career he had an abiding interest in the history of his native state, an interest that was manifested not only by his membership in various California historical societies and his faithful attendance at their meetings (often in the role of speaker) but by his frequent contributions of historical studies to their publications.*

Summer at Auburn, 1869 *is the last of this series of papers he lived to complete, and, as he stated in a brief foreword to his manuscript, his interest in that now forgotten episode in California history was first engaged by a reading of the Diary of Matthew Bosley, which was owned by a granddaughter of its writer. Using that faded, pen-written document as a basis for his study, Slade, with characteristic industry and patience, searched through numerous books, newspapers, and periodicals of the period, located and interviewed the few then living who had personal knowledge of so remote a time, and, after two years of close application to his task, completed the carefully annotated, scholarly, and reasonably complete narrative that appears on the following pages.*

A BRIEF ACCOUNT OF THE CIRCUMSTANCES LEADING TO THE SHOGUN'S VISIT TO CALIFORNIA, TOGETHER WITH CERTAIN HAPPENINGS EN ROUTE

SOON *after the close of his second term, the Shogun received from an old California acquaintance, Brooke David, a new and urgent invitation to make his long-contemplated visit to the west coast. This time David had a forceful new argument to add to those he had employed earlier. The transcontinental railroad, begun during the early years of the Shogun's administration, and the progress of which he had followed with close interest, had recently been completed, and the overland passage to California, once long and arduous, could now be made in comparative comfort. Perhaps that was the deciding factor, for the Shogun's return to private life had failed to bring about the hoped-for improvement in his health, and it may be that his doctor had advised against his facing the heat and dust and jolt of so long a ride in the Concord stages.*

In any event, only a day or two after Brooke David's letter reached Springfield, he dispatched a reply accepting the Californian's invitation to spend a few weeks at the latter's summer home in the Sierra foothills, and stating that he planned to leave in about a fortnight. "One of the advantages of being on the shelf," he added, "is that I have no commitments urgent enough to demand my presence anywhere. . . . I can be idle in California quite as well as here, and perhaps more pleasantly. . . ."

He left home on June 2, traveling via the Illinois Central to Council Bluffs, where on the evening of the 3rd he boarded the cars of the Overland for the four-day trip. He was accompanied by Matthew Bosley. These excerpts from Bosley's diary tell something of the journey.

June 4 [1869]: The Shogun slept late and I, knowing that he rarely rests well in the sleeping cars, did not awaken him until, a few minutes before 8 o'clock, the conductor passed through and announced that we were due at North Platte in half an hour, where a 20-minute stop would be made for breakfast. When I carried the news to him, urging the need for haste, the Shogun, who had removed only his outer garments, sat up and began laboriously drawing on his pantaloons, complaining all the while that his bed was much too short and that he had been obliged to sleep doubled up like a jack-knife. . . .

He finished dressing while the train was drawing to a stop and he was pulling on his rumpled coat as he joined the group in the aisle. His manner was bleak and morose as we followed in the wake of the headlong rush to the station eating-house. He brightened measurably, however, when, we having found places at one of the long tables, pitchers of coffee were placed before us and these were followed by platters of eggs and bacon and fragrant mounds of cornbread fresh from the oven.

To this he did full justice, having eaten but sparingly the evening before, then joined in the lively talk at our end of the table, entertaining the group with anecdotes of the boarding-house at Vandalia where he had lived while a member of the Illinois legislature. This continued pleasantly enough until blasts of the locomotive summoned us back to the cars. He was in good spirits when we returned to our seats, his melancholy forgotten. . . .

June 5: News of the Shogun's presence having traveled through the train, our car has become a congregating place where at most hours of the day seldom less than half a dozen men—and an occasional woman—stand about, blocking the passageway so trainmen have difficulty pushing through. Most of these are curious idlers; they stand and stare for a few moments, then return contented to their cars, and their places are taken by others. This continued all morning and well into the afternoon, the crowd melting away only when some object on the prairie outside draws the curious to the windows.

The Shogun bears this inspection with tolerant good humor. He spent much of the morning dozing or looking out at the passing scenery, getting up from time to time and, in his halting gait, walking the length of the car to stretch his legs, which grow cramped in the confined space between the seats. This afternoon he took from his satchel a book by Artemus Ward and read it for an hour, chuckling now and again at the late humorist's drolleries and seemingly unaware of the group in the aisle. The latter were, therefore, taken aback when he suddenly closed the book and, looking musingly at his uninvited visitors, addressed them as follows:

"I've just been reading here," he said gravely, "something that reminded me of a preacher they used to tell about back in Indiana. This fellow rode into our village one day on a broken-down horse and started preaching in the schoolhouse. But only a few came to hear his sermons and after a few Sundays he got downright discouraged. But before giving up entirely he decided to make one last try, so he wrote out a little notice on a sheet of paper and tacked it up in front of the village store. The notice announced that after his sermon on the following Sunday he was going to have on exhibit in the schoolyard a very remarkable animal known as a *Bos domesticus*. That of course caused a good deal of curiosity, and when Sunday came the schoolhouse was crowded. The preacher delivered a long and very dull sermon, then led the congregation outside and pointed out a very ordinary-looking cow he had borrowed from a neighbor, explaining that *Bos domesticus* was the critter's Latin name. 'But that cow's no different from any other cow,' said one of the onlookers. The preacher admitted that that was so. 'Then why did you have us come out here and look at it?' they wanted to know. 'Well,' said the preacher, 'if you hadn't come and seen it with your own eyes you might have thought you were missing something worth looking at.' "

The Shogun put on his glasses and resumed his reading, and soon the crowd, catching the point of his yarn and looking a bit shamefaced, drifted away. But they were soon replaced by others. . . .

June 6: This morning we stopped at the village of Promontory, where the passengers were obliged to transfer, with their belongings, from the cars of the Union Pacific to those of the Central Pacific, which are to carry us on westward. There was a long delay while the west-bound train was being made ready to receive us. Meantime we stood about in shivering groups, exposed to a chill wind blowing off the Great Salt Lake, which lay before us, looking gray and cheerless in the dim sunlight.

The coaches of the western link of the road, when at length we were admitted to them, were distressingly cold, for the fires had not yet been kindled in the stoves. During the first hour or more after we left Promontory all sat bundled in coats and blankets, and a gloomy silence settled over the car, which was broken only when the half-frozen passengers voiced bitter complaints against the company's indifference to the comfort of its patrons.

The Shogun sat wrapped in silence, taking no part in this demonstration. But when an official of the road, who chanced to be aboard, presently put in an appearance and affably introduced himself, the Shogun greeted him with marked reserve. Undeterred by the formality of his reception, the official spoke volubly of the other's services to the railroad during the construction period, and expressed his regret that his superiors had not learned in advance that he was planning this trip. Had it been known, he declared, proper steps would have been taken to assure him a comfortable passage. One of the company's private cars, he went on, was always available for the use of distinguished travelers, and it would have been a pleasure to place it at his disposal.

The Shogun listened patiently to this voluble visitor, and when the latter had finished he remarked dryly that since he no longer held any official position in the government, he neither wished nor expected any services that were not available to all the traveling public. Then he added mildly that he would be obliged if the other would grant him one small favor: on his way back to his car would he mind tossing a few sticks of firewood into the stove?

Somewhat deflated, the official departed on this errand, and presently the car grew tolerably warm.

June 7: One of our fellow passengers is a man named Llewellyn, an inspector for the Post Office Department, on his way to California and Oregon on official business. He sat with us for an hour this afternoon and spoke entertainingly of his experiences in the South after the war, when the postal service was being re-established. Llewellyn expressed his astonishment at the Shogun's familiarity with this subject, saying that he seemed to have a complete knowledge of the inner workings of the department. The Shogun sighed. "During all the years I was in Washington," he replied, "half the visitors to my office came to urge me to appoint some friend or relative to the postmastership at some town or village in their home districts. Yes, first and last, I learned a great deal about the postal service. Sometimes I used to wonder what the country considered most important: getting the mails delivered or putting down the Rebellion."

During his conversation with Llewellyn, the Shogun revealed something I had not known before: that when he was a young man he had served for a time as postmaster at the frontier village where he lived. "It was my first government job," he recalled, "and in many ways it was more satisfactory than any I've held since. I ran the office to suit myself, with nobody to tell me what I must or must not do, or to point out how badly I was performing the job and how much better it could have been done by almost anybody else. Out at New Salem I carried the mail about in my hat, and if I felt like taking a day off and going off visiting, the people who had business to transact didn't mind waiting until I got back. I sometimes wonder if I shouldn't have followed that plan after I went to Washington instead of placing myself at the beck and call of every Tom, Dick, and Harry who had an ax to grind and looked to me to furnish the grindstone."

After Llewellyn had gone back to his car, the Shogun's thoughts continued to dwell on his frontier youth. He spoke of the wooded hills and valleys of Indiana and Illinois, so different from the barren plains through which we were passing. At one station where the train stopped for wood and water he looked out at a cattle-loading corral beside the track. Its high sides were made of boards.

"We seldom saw fences like that back home," he remarked. "Ours were all made out of rails that had to be cut and split by hand. It took us days of the hardest sort of work to do what the rudest of sawmills could have done in half an hour. For years I haven't been able to look at a rail fence without reflecting on all the toil and sweat that went into making it. And all because none of us had the enterprise, or the skill, to throw a dam across one of the brooks and rig up a water-operated mill."

"It seems odd, sir," I observed, "to hear you speak slightingly of fence-rails."

He smiled a bit sadly. "I know, Matt, I know," he replied. "I don't expect I'll ever live that story down. Perhaps it was wise politics that day in Chicago to carry those rails into the convention hall, although I'd hate to have to take an oath that they were the identical rails I once split. But I've never been altogether proud of that symbol. It's no great satisfaction to reflect that you're going to be remembered—as long as you're remembered at all—because you wasted your youth doing by hand a job that could have been done faster and better and far, far easier with the help of a simple piece of machinery."

A RETROSPECTIVE CHAPTER, DRAWN LARGELY FROM THE BOSLEY DIARY, BEARING ON EVENTS PRIOR TO THE SHOGUN'S COMING TO AUBURN

MATTHEW BOSLEY *was born, on September 23, 1844, near the village of Newark Valley, in southern New York State, close to the Pennsylvania border. At the outbreak of the Civil War he enlisted in an infantry company being recruited in that area, and took part in the Peninsula Campaign and in the Second Battle of Bull Run. By the summer of 1862 he was a mounted orderly attached to the staff of General Burnside, and in December of that year, as he was returning from carrying a dispatch to an advanced position during the Battle of Fredericksburg, his horse was struck by a Rebel shell.*

Bosley's left leg was caught beneath the animal as it fell, and broken in two places. He managed, however, to crawl to a dressing station, where he was placed in a mule-drawn ambulance and taken to a field hospital. Because of the congested roads, this short trip consumed many hours, and after his arrival he lay for a full day in the rain before the overburdened staff could give him attention. When at length he was lifted on the operating table, he was delirious with fever, and his leg was so badly infected that the surgeon had no choice but to amputate it.

His chances of recovery seemed remote, but after a few days, during which the issue remained in doubt, he began to mend. Early in 1863 he was transferred to the old Union Hotel in Georgetown, which had been converted into a military hospital. There he was presently fitted with a wooden leg, and it was there, in the early summer of the same year, that there took place a chance meeting that profoundly influenced his future.

The President, who as often as he could spare the time visited the military hospitals in and about Washington, rode up one morning while a group of convalescent soldiers was playing bsaeball in an adjacent field. He reined his horse beside the fence and looked on for a few minutes, then continued on to the hospital and made a tour of the wards, stopping from time to time to exchange a few words with the patients. But he had not forgotten the baseball game in the near-by field, and when he returned to the Chief Surgeon's office he asked to have brought in the patient who had been playing with so much agility despite the handicap of a peg leg.

Young Bosley was summoned, and after being questioned about how he had received his injury, he was asked his plans for the future. The youth replied that he was soon to be discharged from the hospital and returned to civilian life, but that he was hopeful of finding something that a one-legged man could do to help put down the Rebellion. At the end of the interview the President shook hands and complimented him on his pluck. But—as Bosley later recorded in his diary—no promises were made, and he was therefore surprised and mystified when, on receiving his discharge a few days later, he was handed a letter from one of the Presidential secretaries asking that he report next morning at the Executive Mansion.

The result was that Bosley became a White House messenger, a post he continued to occupy for three years. He was clearly a young man of ambition, for in the intervals when he was not carrying messages to and from the various governmental bureaus he mapped out a course of study designed to fill in the gaps in his education. He applied himself to such good purpose that when, in the spring of 1867, another clerk was added to the White House staff, he was chosen to fill the post.

Young Bosley did not begin keeping his diary until almost two years later —its first entry is dated January 1, 1869—and it is only by occasional reminiscent passages that he makes reference to events during the period that followed the close of the Rebellion. Once started, however, he kept his journal faithfully, rarely missing a day. During the first few weeks his entries are brief and perfunctory, being mainly concerned with the work of winding up the affairs of the outgoing administration and with preparations for turning over the White House to its new occupant in early March. As time went on, however, his daily stints grow longer, sometimes taking on a philosophical tone, and thus it grows clear that he came to look on his diary as a place not only to record each day's happenings but to reflect on their possible significance.

The document does not state precisely when and under what circumstances young Bosley agreed to enter the employ of his admired chief after the latter returned to private life. The arrangement must have been concluded before the beginning of February 1869, however, for on the 6th of that month the diary contains this extended passage:

This afternoon the Shogun called me into his study and, indicating an open drawer in the cabinet that stands behind his desk, asked me to run through the papers it contained, putting aside what might be worth preserving and sending what remained down to the basement to be burned.

When, an hour or two later, he got back from his drive, he returned, as is his custom, to his study for another period of work. In passing through the anteroom he seemed surprised to find me still at my task. He stood beside the table for a few moments, silently looking on. I was far from finished, for the drawer had been filled to the top with papers: drafts of speeches and messages, letters bearing on personal matters, odds and ends of notes, memoranda, and the like, all tossed together in a confused mass. The material that seemed to me of no particular value—mostly hastily scribbled notations on matters long since disposed of—I had thrown on the floor, placing the rest, according to its subject-matter, on one or another of several piles on the table.

He looked at these bulky stacks, then at the comparatively small number of discarded papers on the floor, and his face showed a half-humorous concern as he asked if I had any idea how much the railroads were going to charge to carry all his belongings out to Springfield. I replied that I supposed the expense would be considerable, but that many of the papers seemed to me worth preserving and that I would hate to be responsible for destroying them. At some future time, I added, it might be that someone would undertake to write a history of his administration and, if so, documents of that sort would come in very handy. This must have seemed to him a highly unlikely possibility, for his only answer was a sort of mirthless chuckle. But I could see that he was not displeased. "If that's the way you feel about it, Matt," he said, "go ahead and pack up whatever you like. No doubt we can find some corner out in Springfield where it can be stowed away. I don't suppose there's any harm in letting it gather dust for a few years before someone carries it outside and builds a bonfire."

I replied that I was sure the time would come when many of these writings would be looked on as valuable historical documents.

He put a hand on my shoulder and from the quizzical expression on his face I guessed that he was about to tell another of his stories. I was not disappointed.

"Matt," he said, "many years ago out in Illinois they used to tell about an old fellow named Jeff Presley. Presley had a hog farm and for years he worked hard trying to make a go of it. But no matter how much he tried, something always happened to spoil his plans. His hogs would get sick and die, or they would break through the fences and stray away into the woods, and whenever he took a load of them in to market, the prices were so low he could hardly give them away. Well, that went on for a long time and at last he lost his farm and had to move into a cabin on the edge of town, where he supported himself by doing whatever odd jobs he could find. One day a friend went out to visit him, and as he came up to the cabin, he was surprised to see a pen in the yard with a pig inside. 'Jeff, you've had nothing but bad luck with them critters,' his friend said. 'I should think you'd never want to lay eyes on one again.' 'Well,' said Jeff, 'I'll tell you how it is. I keep this animal around to remind myself that I'm no great shakes as a hog-farmer and that I'll be well advised to steer clear of that business in the future.'"

The Shogun chuckled at the memory and continued on to his study. But when he reached the door he paused and added gravely: "Matt, maybe it will be a good idea after all to send a few boxes of those papers out to Springfield."

Subsequent diary entries make it clear that during the final weeks in Washington, Bosley devoted several hours each day to this task, sorting out the official letters and documents, to be deposited in the national archives, destroying those personal papers that seemed of no importance, and putting what remained aside to be shipped out to Illinois.

The material that fell into this last category must have been a considerable bulk, for on February 12 Bosley writes that he had already filled three large wooden cases and that the job was far from finished. The diary entry of that date contains this passage:

Today is the Shogun's sixtieth birthday, but the event was little noticed by the public at large, although in late afternoon the members of the White House staff presented him with a stout walking-stick with a suitable inscription engraved on its silver head. He was much touched by this small gift and had a few words for each of us, saying that he would remember always the loyalty of our little group during the trying times we had all been through. . . .

Then the diarist adds this philosophical comment:

Those of us who see him daily cannot but observe how deeply he feels his present unpopularity, an unpopularity brought about by the jealousies and misrepresentations of his political enemies, many of them members of his own party. It is tragic but true that the Shogun prepares to leave office believing that his final term has been four years of failure, for he has about him constantly an air of melancholy and defeat. It is not that he regrets the policies he has advocated from the beginning and to which he has adhered despite the abuses of those who regard his leniency toward the vanquished as a sign of weakness and indecision. Rather, he feels that where he has erred was in his failure to convince the opposition that the harsh measures they advocated, and have so largely put into effect, have served only to prolong the strife that would otherwise have ended when the war itself drew to a close. . . .

The frequency with which the Shogun's simplest acts were distorted by his opponents was a constant annoyance to his hot-tempered young aide. The following excerpt from his diary of February 20 [1869] *is typical of numerous similar outbursts:*

The New York newspapers of yesterday carry accounts of a speech delivered at the Cooper Union Hall in that city on Thursday last, in which the speaker, a figure high in the counsels of the Radical Republicans, won the applause of his listeners by repeating the old charge that the Shogun's act in granting clemency to certain associates of the actor Booth was a deliberate and unjustified affront to the courts that had duly tried and convicted them. In particular this demagogue professed to deplore his intercession on behalf of Mrs. Surratt, ignoring the fact that but for his executive order the nation would have been under the painful necessity of sending that misguided woman to the gallows.

The last weeks in Washington, already gloomy enough, were further darkened by an episode that was widely heralded in the press, thus adding to the already heavy cares of the outgoing executive.

In mid-February the President's wife returned to Springfield to prepare the family home for occupancy, for it was felt that the excitement and confusion of the final leave-taking would aggravate her already highly nervous state. Bosley records that much difficulty was encountered in persuading her to leave, and that although the date of her departure was several times fixed, she each time changed her mind and insisted on remaining until March 4 in order to ride in the inaugural parade.

On February 25, however, the President drove with her to the depot and put her on the train. She was accompanied by their younger son, then fifteen, and by her personal maid, Harriet Slide, and arrangements were made to have her met at Chicago by her sister, Mrs. Edwards, who would continue on with her to Springfield.

On the morning she reached Chicago, however, Mrs. Edwards was delayed and did not reach the depot until some fifteen minutes after the train had arrived. This slight miscarriage of the carefully laid plans had an unfortunate result. The President's wife, finding no one to meet her, went to the station master's office and, in a state of high excitement, charged that she had been made the victim of a plot on the part of her enemies to spirit her out of Washington, and demanded that he provide means for her immediate return.

Mrs. Edwards, who had meantime arrived, managed to calm the overwrought woman and, with some difficulty, persuaded her to give up her plan of hurrying back to the capital. But the commotion had caused a crowd to gather outside the station master's office, and the result was that highly colored accounts of the episode were published in several Chicago journals and widely copied by antiadministration papers throughout the nation.

In his entry for February 28, Bosley gives a full account of that unhappy affair and ends with this comment:

The Shogun, who usually accepts with equanimity the slanders of the opposition press, was stirred to a mighty anger by this needless and ungallant action in heralding to the world the outbreak of a woman too harassed to be held responsible for her behavior. The dispatches filled him with rage, and he relieved his feelings by expressing in the strongest terms, liberally studded with frontier epithets, his abhorrence of those editors who stooped to make political capital by such means. He quickly regained his composure, however, although when I encountered him later in the day his air of dejection, which has been evident enough in recent months, had deepened measurably. I think, though, that he was aware of the unspoken sympathy of all of us, for he had a worn smile and a kindly word for each.

Young Bosley's desire for what he termed the vindication of his employer's policies did not grow less with the passage of time, and after the move to Springfield his diary often touches on that theme. The following passage was written on March 24:

In the mail this morning was a letter from the editor of *Harper's Monthly Magazine* suggesting a paper, or, should the length of the manuscript justify it, several papers, telling the story of the war years, "not from the viewpoint of the soldier in the field, but from the pen of one who, as Commander-in-Chief, had formulated those broad policies that led to victory for the Union forces."

It was a long letter, presenting what seemed to me unanswerable arguments in favor of writing such a narrative and pointing out both its present interest and its future value. I confess that I was elated at the proposal, and when I had finished reading it,[1] some of my eagerness must have shown in my face, for the Shogun regarded me quizzically for a moment before he motioned me to go on to the next letter.

I realized then that this offer, like many others, was to be rejected, and that another opportunity to see justice done would be lost. I knew it was futile to protest, but I could not forbear bursting out:

"Isn't it high time, sir, that you said a few words in your own defense?"

He shook his head. "No, Matt," he replied gravely. "Far too much has already been said. Let the others occupy themselves with trying to explain and justify their acts." Then he added with a wry smile: "Some of them have a good deal that needs explaining."

The Shogun's failure to take advantage of such opportunities as that offered by the Harper's *editor to set before the public the true story of his services during the years of crisis was a constant source of disappointment to his young secretary, as it was to the generality of his friends. In his frequent references to the subject Bosley does not always conceal his impatience at his chief's docile acceptance of his lot and at his seeming content with the neglect and obscurity to which he had been consigned by the forgetful public.*

One seldom picks up a magazine or newspaper [wrote Bosley on March 30] without being confronted with one or more articles dealing with the war and its blundering aftermath. Sometimes it seems that every general, and every politician, who had a part in the conflict, however brief or inconsequential, has hurried into print to tell the nation how, by his own unaided efforts, he saved the Union, or to air his wrong-headed opinions and belittle the accomplishments of his betters. Yet in the face of this barrage of egoism and rancor, the Shogun remains silent week after week, deep sunk in lethargy

[1] The Shogun's head-wound, as many know, affected the vision of his left eye, and to spare him needless strain on the other, Bosley was in the habit of reading his correspondence aloud to him. Once he remarked humorously to his one-legged secretary: "Matt, when your good eyes and my good legs are totaled up, the result is one sound man, with half a man left over!"

and indifference, lacking the spirit to speak out and deny the most blatant falsehoods. . . .

In conversation here last evening in the office he shares with his former law partner, someone spoke of the flood of war reminiscences now being thrust on the public, most of them from the pens of the Union military leaders. At length the Shogun, who had been listening in moody silence, remarked dryly: "If only the generals could have been made to fight then half as hard as they are writing now, the war might have been over in a matter of weeks."

A few days later [*April* 2] *Bosley returns to the same subject, although this time his tone is less vehement.*

The mail this morning had the usual quota of letters from strangers, the writers of which all have favors to ask. Most of them couch their pleas, not as requests, but in the form of commands, they seeming to be under the impression that because he once occupied the White House he has a moral obligation to accede to their demands, no matter how absurd they are.

Each letter receives an answer, although the task makes heavy demands on his time and strength—and on his finances, too, for he rarely disregards the pleas of former soldiers, or their dependents, who write of poverty and illness and state that they know of no one else to whom to turn.

It is useless to remind him that he is often imposed on, that some of the supplicants are professional beggars. Once when I made bold to point that out he shrugged good-naturedly and replied: "If their letters are not genuine, then the rascals deserve some reward for inventing such heart-rending yarns. As you grow older, Matt, you'll come to realize that the man who does his job well is mighty rare, so much so that he deserves to be encouraged regardless of how he chooses to use his talents. In a world so full of blunderers, it's almost a pleasure to be imposed on by experts."

Some of the letters are full of spleen, and these too the Shogun listens to with equanimity and answers with forbearance. In one of those received a few days ago, from a mill town in Massachusetts, the writer complained bitterly that the influx of liberated Negroes had so overrun the labor market that scores of whites were tramping the streets with empty pockets. For this situation he held the Shogun responsible, citing once more the old canard that his reason for freeing the slaves—and thus betraying the laboring classes—was the Negro blood in his veins.

When I protested that a letter so full of venom did not deserve an answer, he shook his head patiently. "No," he replied mildly, "you can't expect a man whose belly is empty to make distinctions between what's true and what's false. Perhaps nothing I can say will convince him of his error, but he'll like to have someone try to reason with him."

His reply consumed the greater part of an hour and occupied three pages. I remarked that I hoped the Massachusetts man would have the good sense to keep the letter, because someday it might have a value. This thought seemed to amuse him. "Have you got any idea, Matt," he asked, "how many letters I've written during the past forty years? When I think of their number it's hard to understand why the whole country's not suffering from a shortage of paper and ink and quill pens. No, Matt, anybody who tries to peddle my letters will have to bind them into bales and sell them by the hundredweight."

That young Bosley never expected his diary to be seen by others is evident from even a casual reading of its pages. Because his daily jottings were intended exclusively for his own eyes, it is not surprising that he sometimes recorded certain incidents and conversations he would otherwise have hesitated to commit to paper. Needless to say, it is not the intention to bring to light here any material that its writer would have wished to remain secret and confidential. Certain passages are so informative, however, and afford such candid glimpses of his chief's personal life that there seems no reason at this late date for withholding them from the restricted circulation they will receive from readers of this memoir. I have therefore elected to include, and thus make available to present and future scholars, a few excerpts from the diary that its author might have preferred to pass over in silence. The first was written in Springfield on May 26, less than a week before Bosley and his chief set off for Auburn.

The Shogun accompanied his wife to the depot this afternoon and saw her off on the 3 o'clock train, she having decided to visit relatives in Kentucky while he is absent in California. From the station he walked back to the office, and the sound of his footsteps as he came up the stairs caused his old-time partner, who was writing at his desk, to put down his pen and listen closely. When the Shogun appeared in the doorway, the other looked at him in unbelief. "Godalmighty, sir!" he exclaimed, "I couldn't believe my ears when I heard you skipping upstairs. It was almost like listening to a ghost. It must be ten years since you've taken those steps two at a time. It does my heart good, sir, to see you so spry again!"

The Shogun looked a bit abashed at the exuberance of this greeting. "Well, Billy," he said mildly, "I've just seen Mary off, and I confess I'm a bit relieved in my mind to know she'll be among friends in Lexington while I go gadding off to California. I didn't feel altogether happy about leaving her behind for so long, but she refused to consider venturing out into that heathen country and running the risk of being scalped by wild Indians."

The Shogun was carefree and buoyant all the rest of the afternoon, pausing from time to time as we worked on his mail to joke with Billy Herndon or to exchange pleasantries with visitors. We were all much heartened at his new-found lightness of spirit, the reason for which was clear enough, although of course we refrained from commenting on it. Once when someone mentioned his high good humor he grew silent and a look of guilt passed over his face. "Poor Mary," he mused pensively, "I do hope she enjoys her little outing."

The following entry is dated three days later:

There was another gathering last night in the office facing the Court House Square, as there has been each evening since the Shogun's lady set off for Kentucky. In these familiar surroundings, in the company of boon companions of other days, he seems to have recaptured the carefree gaiety of youth, shunting off the melancholy that has recently rested so heavily on his shoulders. The little room nightly grows thick with tobacco smoke as one by one these old-time cronies recall happenings out of the past, each story bringing forth shouts of laughter, in which the chief joins no less heartily than the others.

At one point last evening the conversation turned, as it often does at such gatherings, to youthful love affairs, and Billy Herndon, who had been taking frequent nips at the bottle that stood within reach on his desk, returned to his oft-mentioned plan of someday putting on paper his recollections of the Shogun's career. He now stated in a tone of exaggerated solemnity that in it he intended to bring to light a long-forgotten episode of the Shogun's youth: his romantic attachment for a New Salem maiden, the beauteous and charming Miss Rutledge. The name appeared to mean nothing to the others, and all turned to the chief, curious to see what his response might be. The latter's face was blank. "Rutledge?" he repeated, clearly puzzled. "Rutledge? I don't seem to recall anyone of that name. I'm afraid, Billy," he added mildly, "that someone has been taking advantage of your innocence by supplying you with false information." Then he added with a reminiscent chuckle: "Now, if you had been referring to Vandalia you would have been much closer to the truth. There was a young woman there who waited on table at the boarding-house where a group of us stayed, and we all took a tremendous shine to her. But she was a very cultured miss and she put such great store in refined behavior that she would have nothing to do with us rough backwoodsmen, whose talk and manners at table must have jarred her sensibilities. Anyhow, one day she ran off to Chicago with a handsome law clerk who wore store clothes and a gold stickpin. You should have seen our table the day we heard the news. Our cries of anguish were heartbreaking to hear." The chief joined in the laugh that greeted this tale, and presently the talk drifted into other channels. . . .

After the gathering broke up, I walked home with the Shogun, for the cottage where I had taken lodgings was a few squares beyond his house at Eighth and Jackson streets. Bill Herndon's latest reference to his contemplated memoir had remained in my mind and I ventured to inquire if the Shogun thought his remark had been seriously intended. He walked for a few paces in silence; then he laughed indulgently. "Yes, I suppose he meant it at the time," he replied dryly. "After a few drinks Billy can be counted on to think up a dozen such schemes, each one more outlandish than the one before. Fortunately for him, he forgets all about them the next morning."

"Then," said I, unable to conceal my disappointment, "the life he talks about so often will never be written?"

We had reached the Shogun's corner and he paused before the gate, regarding me musingly for a few moments before he answered. "Matt," he said gravely, "you can bank on this: no such work is ever going to be written, not by Billy Herndon or by anyone else." I started to protest, but he motioned me silent. "The odd part of it is," he added musingly, "that one might have been written—or perhaps even more than one—if one small happening had had a different ending." "And what, sir, was that?" I asked, mystified. "If only that fool actor had been a bit more accurate," he replied. "D'you know, Matt," he added, his tone half-comic, half-grim, "I've never really forgiven him for being such a bad shot."

In his entry for the next day, that of May 30, Bosley thus comments on his employer's singular remark of the evening before:

This is not the first time the Shogun has made reference to what he terms the lamentably poor marksmanship of his assailant, and although he speaks in a tone of grim humor, it is evident that he truly believes that the nation's welfare, to say nothing of his own place in the regard of the people, would have been more secure had the attack had the tragic outcome that was so narrowly averted.

In his thorough and orderly way the diarist then goes on to state the reasons why he believes this theory to be false. While he grants that his chief's last four years in office saw a marked decline in the support and personal esteem the great majority had accorded him throughout the war years, he contends that this was but a passing phase, one that was to be expected during the period of difficult readjustment to a peacetime footing. Bosley argues that once these bitter controversies were forgotten and partisan passions had cooled, the Shogun's policy of patience and moderation would be seen in its true light and that his countrymen would elevate him again to his rightful place in the public regard. He continues:

Had the Shogun died in 1865, leaving so much of his great task unfinished, who can doubt that his memory would have faded rapidly from the minds of the unheeding public, or that future generations, when they recalled him at all, would have assigned him but a minor place in the nation's annals? For although it would have been admitted that he served ably throughout the war years, there would ever have remained a reasonable doubt as to whether he would have adhered steadfastly to his principles during the violent quarrels of the reconstruction period, or if, yielding to the pressures brought to bear from so many quarters, he might have taken the easy road to popularity by following the dictates of political expediency. Because the assault of the would-be assassin failed of its purpose, that question has happily been answered, and the Shogun's place in history is consequently far more secure than it otherwise could have been.

Young Bosley concludes this well-reasoned—and clearly sound—argument with these prophetic words:

With the passage of the years the animosities that were abroad during so much of the Shogun's second term will fade from memory, and future historians will examine his record dispassionately and render this impartial verdict: that he served courageously and unselfishly what he conceived to be the best interests of all the people, knowing full well that his policies would visit on him the malice and scorn of the short-sighted majority. But the very qualities he then revealed are the ones that will win for him in the end a secure place as one who, while never quite reaching the front among our national leaders, yet during one of the most troubled periods in our nation's history conducted himself in a way that brought discredit neither to himself nor to the high office he was called on to occupy.

SOME SELECTIONS FROM THE REMINISCENCES OF HUBERT MCKNIGHT GANS, PLACER COUNTY PIONEER

ONE *of the few persons now living in Auburn who recall the summer of* 1869 *is Hubert M. Gans, who is now eighty-nine years old and for the past five years has been a patient at the Placer County Hospital. Gans's father had a dairy on the outskirts of the town, and it was one of the boy's jobs to deliver milk each morning to the David summer home, about a mile distant on the Truckee road. Young Gans made the trip on horseback, carrying two one-gallon cans, one on each side of his saddle. A few excerpts from his "Recollections," dictated to the editor of this narration, are given below.*

. . . I had to start on my regular route at six o'clock, and that meant that when old man David came up for the summer I had to get up an hour earlier to make the delivery to his place. But I enjoyed riding out into the country that early in the morning. The air was cool and fresh and I had the road to myself except for the squirrels and bluejays and cottontail rabbits. The David house was a bit off the road, on a knoll looking out over the valley. It was a two-story affair, painted white, with a slate roof, with some big oak trees in the yard and with the barn and stable in the back, down the hill a piece. I used to ride up and leave the milk outside the kitchen door and pick up the empties and hurry back to town.

Usually nobody was up yet when I got there, but one morning when I came into the yard I saw an old man sitting on one of the benches and looking at some gray squirrels playing in the big oak. They were racing round and round the trunk and jumping from limb to limb the way squirrels do, moving so fast you could hardly keep track of them. When I came closer my horse scared them and they ran away down the hill.

The stranger said good morning and I said good morning, and then he asked me what I was doing up so early and what I had in the cans. I told him I was from the Star Dairy and that I was delivering milk. He said it was very good milk and that he drank a glass at each meal. He wanted to know how many cows we kept and I told him sixteen, but that we were only milking eleven. Then I said I had to go because I still had my regular route and I didn't want to be late for school. He asked me what grade I was in and I told him I would be in the fifth next term. He said that was fine, that he never got beyond the third grade himself and that he was always glad to meet someone who was better educated than he was.

After that I used to see him almost every morning. Once I asked him why he got up ahead of everybody else, and he said he liked to come out and watch the squirrels. He said I ought to watch them too because if I could learn to jump from one thing to another the way they did and always land on my feet it would be useful to me later on, especially if I went into politics and got to be President. I told him that when I grew up I intended to be a railroad engineer, but that if that didn't work out I wouldn't mind being President. He shook his head and said no, that I had better stick to my original plan.

We got to be pretty friendly and I was always polite, although I didn't think very highly of him, especially his quitting school so early. I thought he was one of old man David's hired hands, and one morning I asked him what time he went to work. He said he wasn't working just then, that he had lost his job a few months before and hadn't found anything else. I told him my dad was looking for someone to help with the milking, but that if he was a drinking man there wouldn't be any use of his applying because Dad wouldn't allow any whisky on the place. He said he had never been a heavy drinker, so that wouldn't be any hardship, and he would think the matter over and let me know.

A day or two later I was walking down High Street on my way home from school and I saw old man David drive up and stop in front of the post office, and who was sitting in the buggy with him but my friend. I was surprised to see him riding into town with Mr. David because David was a rich man and I couldn't understand why he would have anything to do with a fellow who didn't have a job and had only got as far as the third grade. While old David went into the post office, my friend stayed in the buggy, sort of slumped down with his gray beard resting on his chest, and his hands on his knees. Pretty soon a man stopped and stood looking at him for a few minutes and then went over and introduced himself and the two shook hands. I moved closer and heard the man on the sidewalk say that he had fought at Shiloh and Chancellorsville, and that it was an honor to shake hands. My friend said no, that the honor was his, and then he asked what the other was doing out in California, and the man said he had a little farm out near Pilot Hill. Old man David came out then and my friend introduced him to the farmer and pretty soon they drove away. . . .

I had a birthday about that time, and when my mother asked what I wanted for a present I told her I wanted an autograph album. One of the boys at school had got an album for his birthday and he had been getting his friends to write their names in it, and the rest of us wanted to follow suit, the way kids do. One morning I took my book out to the David place, and when I rode up, my friend was sitting on the porch with his feet on the rail looking out over the valley. After I had left the milk and picked up the empties I went up on the porch and took the album out of my pocket and took off the paper I had wrapped around it to keep it clean and told him I would like him to write his name in it.

He took the book and admired its red plush cover and said he would be glad to sign it, but that his pen and ink were upstairs and he didn't like to go inside because it might disturb the others, who were all late sleepers. He asked if it would be all right for him to keep the book and sign it later, and I could pick it up the next morning. I told him that would be O.K. if he would promise not to get it dirty or smear the ink, and he said he would be careful about the ink and that he would be sure to wash his hands before he began. So I wrapped it up again and gave it to him, and I was halfway down the steps when I thought of something else and came back. I told him I'd rather he didn't sign it too near the front because I was saving the first few pages for some names I hadn't got yet. Some of the kids had been taking their albums down to the courthouse and getting the names of prominent people like the sheriff and the county clerk and the assessor, and I was planning to do the same and of course I wanted them up front where I could show them off. He said he understood how I felt and that he would remember to put his name well toward the back. He did, too, on the very last page, and he wrote it small and neat, just his initial and his last name, and underneath he wrote: "One candid friend is worth a bushel of flatterers."

I've often wished I had kept that little book. But I soon lost interest in autographs and I remember trading it with another boy for an agate marble I wanted to use for a taw. Of course it wasn't long until I lost the marble, but that's the sort of thing that's been happening to me all my life. . . .

"GLEANINGS FROM AN EDITOR'S NOTEBOOK," BEING AN INSTALLMENT OF THE RECOLLECTIONS OF C. E. HARGRAVES, REPRINTED FROM THE CALIFORNIA PLOWMAN OF OCTOBER 17, 1903

DURING *the summer of* 1869 *the editor of the Auburn* Weekly Sentinel *was* C. E. *Hargraves, then a young man in his middle twenties. Hargraves was later a well-known figure in California journalism, for many years the Sacramento political correspondent for several state papers, and subsequently the owner and editor of a farm journal called* The California Plowman, *published at San Francisco.*

In the early 1900's Hargraves wrote a series of reminiscent sketches that were first printed on the editorial page of his paper and later issued in pamphlet form under the title: Gleanings from an Editor's Notebook. *Some of his papers have to do with happenings during the period, more than thirty years earlier, when he had edited the little Auburn weekly. The following is quoted from* The California Plowman *of October 17, 1903, in which he outlines Brooke David's career and recalls his first meeting with David's summer guest.*

The town in those days was well known as a health resort, and there were a number of sanatoriums in the vicinity where sufferers from asthma and TB came to take the "cure." One regular visitor was the San Francisco journalist Ambrose Bierce, who now [1903] represents the *Examiner* and other Hearst papers at Washington, D.C. Another asthma victim who benefited by Auburn's salubrious climate was Brooke David. David, as old-timers will recall, was long a prominent figure in California politics, having espoused the newly formed Republican Party in 1856 and campaigned for Frémont on the national ticket and for Stanford for governor. Frémont was defeated by Buchanan in a close election, but Stanford was swept into office and David was rewarded by being appointed to the board that had supervision over the state's prisons.

Four years later David was a delegate to the Republican Convention at Chicago, and before he returned home he traveled down to Springfield to offer his congratulations and support to the successful candidate. That was the beginning of a friendship that sprang up between the two men and lasted many years. Early in 1862 David was appointed collector of customs at San Francisco, and during the time he held that office he had a great deal to say about federal patronage within the state. For years it was said that no Californian who wanted to be appointed postmaster, or marshal, or even federal judge would hope for a hearing at Washington unless he first got Brooke David's endorsement.

Of course David's political influence ended when the administration changed in 1869. He promptly resigned and, the following year, established, with Lloyd Hammill, the still-existing importing firm of David & Hammill. About 1865 he built a house near Auburn, where each year he spent most of June, July, and August to escape the summer fogs about the bay, which were bad for his asthma.

As related in last week's installment, I took over the Auburn *Sentinel* in the spring of '69, and I had been on the job only a short time when David came up as usual to spend the summer. Of course, the people of Auburn were interested to have so important a man living among them, and I made up my mind to go out to his place at the first opportunity and get an interview with him. But the job of getting out the paper on the antiquated press kept me busy, and several weeks passed before I found time to carry out that plan. Then, late one afternoon, I set out. It was hot walking up the dusty road, and when I turned in at the David place I saw a group sitting in the shade of a big oak tree, the ladies wearing white dresses and the men in their shirt-sleeves, all drinking glasses of lemonade.

David came forward to see what I wanted, and when I told him I was editor of the Auburn weekly he shook hands and took me over and introduced me to his wife and guests. Then he poured me a cool drink from the pitcher on the table and told me to sit down and make myself at home.

It was easy to see why Brooke David had been a success in politics, for he was a big, affable man with an easy flow of talk that inspired the confidence of strangers and put them at their ease. I was so much taken with him that I paid very little attention to the other members of the group. He asked me a few questions about the paper and inquired after certain friends in town, and when I had answered as best I could, the conversation became general.

It was then that I first noticed that most of the others' remarks were addressed to the man on my right, who was sitting straddle-fashion on a wooden bench, with one leg on each side of it. The bench was low and his legs were so long that his knees came up to his chin, which gave him an awkward appearance that was almost laughable. Although, as I have said, it was a warm afternoon and the other men were in their shirt-sleeves, he was wearing a knitted shawl over his shoulders, and this added to his oddity.

Somehow I had failed to catch this stranger's name when David introduced us, and although there seemed something very familiar about his long, homely face, as though I had met him somewhere, it was some time before I realized who he was. Then, when his identity became clear, my surprise was complete, and I was at a loss to know how a man so well known, who had been only a few months out of the White House, could have slipped into Auburn without anybody knowing about it. It was not until later that I learned that he had come two days earlier, arriving on the overland train that passed through Auburn in the early hours of the morning. That accounted for the fact that, except for David himself and the night telegraph operator, there had been no one at the depot who might have recognized him.

After that I paid far closer attention to David's guest, and I must say that my first impression was disappointing. Although I had cast my first ballot for him in '64, and although one of the earliest editorials I had written for the *Sentinel* had been a defense of his policies and an indictment of the Congress that had defeated his every effort to deal fairly with the South, I must confess that now I felt my former enthusiasm slipping away.

It was the first time I had seen in the flesh a political figure of national importance, and I was young enough to feel a sort of shocked surprise that he bore so little likeness to the knight in shining armor my imagination had pictured. That experience was so often repeated in later years that it ceased to trouble me, but its effect then was one of disillusion, as though someone had taken advantage of my confidence. Regarding the gangling figure on the bench, I told myself that he looked far less the statesman than the handsome and dignified Brooke David. Indeed, he seemed the least prepossessing member of the group, one who but for his odd clothes and grotesque posture would have passed unnoticed.

It was not long, however, before I found myself revising that first impression. The others addressed him as the Shogun, which, I subsequently learned, was a name conferred on him by one of his former secretaries, which had been brought out to Auburn by young Matt Bosley, who then occupied that post. The Shogun took little part in the conversation, contenting himself with following the talk of the others, and when he answered such questions as were put to him it was with a sort of indulgent and good-humored brevity.

But soon there came a change. This was brought about by the fact that Mrs. David, with a hostess's concern for the comfort of her guests, suggested that he move from his bench to a near-by camp chair. He replied that he was well content where he was, and went on to explain that in the backwoods where he had grown up chairs had been scarce articles and that most of his youth had been spent sitting astride a log, much as he was doing then.

This remark seemingly put him in a reminiscent mood, for he went on to recall stories bearing on the austerities of frontier life as he had known it long ago in Kentucky and Indiana, one incident suggesting another until presently he was holding our undivided attention. As he talked, the lassitude seemed to lift from his shoulders, and his face, which in repose had been stolid and dull, became alert, his deep-set eyes beneath their bushy brows full of animation, and his features, recently grim and stern, transformed as they broke into frequent, droll smiles.

He continued thus for some time, talking in an easy, informal, self-effacing manner that I found most engaging. As I listened to his rambling monologue, to the homely force of his diction and his frequent flashes of humor (the latter the more amusing issuing as they did from so dolorous a countenance), the disappointment I had felt at my first sight of him slipped away. Gradually I came under the spell of his oddly appealing personality, and it was no longer a mystery to me why during his last contentious years in office he had retained the grudging respect of his enemies.

It was not until the supper bell rang that he broke off his seemingly inexhaustible store of frontier anecdotes, and even then the group stood up with a reluctance that I fully shared. Brooke David hospitably asked me to stay and take potluck, and when I declined, explaining that the paper had to go to press that night, he walked down the driveway with me and, as we parted, confided that he had a favor to ask. The Shogun, he explained, had been in poor health—which his bent figure and deeply lined face made obvious enough—and he had come out on this visit because David had promised him unlimited rest and quiet. David went on to say that he was anxious to carry out his part of the pact, and that meant he wished to protect his guest from the demands that would be made on him once his presence in California became known. Would I, therefore, keep word of his visit out of my paper?

Of course I promised to respect his wishes, but I pointed out that news of this sort had a way of leaking out and that he couldn't hope to keep the secret for long. David replied that he was well aware of it; he merely wished to extend as much as possible the interval before his guest was again caught up in the activities that had been his lot for so many years. Then he added with a chuckle: "I haven't much hope that he'll allow us to keep him on the shelf indefinitely. The chances are he'll be craving action before he's here a fortnight. If nothing happens of its own accord, it won't surprise me if he goes out and stirs it up himself!"

Events were to prove that, in this instance at least, Brooke David was a trustworthy prophet. Next week's installment will deal with how Auburn's famous guest got involved in the town's Fourth of July celebration, and will tell something of the repercussions that followed.

Hargraves's reminiscent articles in The California Plowman *must have been closely read by the paper's subscribers, for each installment brought forth a number of letters, which were printed on another page of the weekly in a department called "The People's Forum." The editor's recollections of Auburn during the summer of* 1869 *had the usual response, and two weeks later, in the issue of October* 31, 1903, *a number of the letters in "The People's Forum" bore on this subject. Several of these seem to have enough general interest to warrant preserving, and they are accordingly reprinted below.*

Editor: Your article in this week's *Plowman* about your visit to Brooke David's house outside Auburn reminds me of the one and only time I laid eyes on David's distinguished guest.

I was then attending high school in Oakland and was spending the summer working for my uncle, Lester Wilcox, who had a 30-acre orchard, mostly Bartlett pears, some miles south of Auburn on the Placerville road.

One day I rode into town with my uncle, and after he had delivered his load of pears at the freight shed, we went into Lyman & Briggs's store to do some shopping.

There were a number of men back toward the rear of the store, sitting about on boxes or on the counter. While my uncle was waiting for the grocer to fill his order, I wandered back and stood at the edge of the group.

Almost at once my attention was drawn to a curious-looking individual who was leaning against the counter near the coffee-mill. There was a big sack of walnuts beside him and from time to time he helped himself to one. While he talked or listened, he would crack the nut with his strong, bony fingers and, having clapped the meat into his mouth, would deposit the shells in a neat pile on the counter.

He seemed to be the center of interest and everybody paid attention when he talked. The conversation was about the Civil War, and one of the group, a youngish-looking man wearing steel-rimmed eyeglasses, was telling about having once read a speech the stranger had made. It had, he said, been printed in a newspaper that had found its way into the army camp where he was stationed, and he had been so taken with it that he had cut it out and stowed it away in his knapsack.

The man by the coffee-mill seemed interested and asked the other if he recalled what the speech had been about and where it had been delivered. The first speaker said he didn't recollect just what the occasion had been, but he seemed to recall that it had had something to do with one of the battlefields. He was inclined to think that it might have been delivered at Antietam.

The old man picked up another walnut, and while he was cracking it he looked thoughtfully at the ceiling. Antietam? Yes, he said, he might have made some remarks at Antietam. He was expected to say a few words whenever he visited the soldiers in the field, but for the life of him he couldn't recall what he had talked about. Then he chuckled and said that it was probably just as well that he had forgotten the occasion, because it was the nature of politicians to make speeches, and nobody was much interested in what they had to say on the battlefields where the actual fighting had taken place.

I wanted to hear more, but my uncle had finished his shopping and I had to help carry the groceries back to the wagon. It wasn't until later that I learned who that peculiar-looking old man was.

After that whenever I went to town I made a point of going around to Lyman & Briggs's, but I never saw him there again. Then one day I read in the Auburn paper that he had gone back to his home in the East. . . .

Red Bluff, Cal. —Wm. S. Hicks
October 22, 1903

Editor: . . . Californians who are familiar with the high-handed methods of boss Brooke David were not surprised at his action in inviting to California and receiving as an honored guest the politician who, more than any other, was responsible for the abuse and humiliation meted out to the helpless people of the South. . . .

The record is clear, and only those whose vision is distorted by prejudice and blind partisanship can fail to read it. If, during those hapless years, the occupant of the White House had been possessed of even moderate firmness the nation would have been reunited and the wounds of war quickly healed. . . . It was a time when the country desperately needed a leader strong enough to curb the malice and greed of the party that, to the lasting shame of the nation, twice elected him to office. Instead, we had for eight long years a policy of weakness and vacillation that reached its climax when the so-called radical wing of the party gained control in 1866. . . .

The public at large has forgotten much of the misery that resulted from that catastrophe . . . but those who, like this writer, have personal knowledge of conditions in the South under the cynical rule of the Republicans will not soon forget, nor will we fail to register our resentment at the polls on November next. . . .

Petaluma, Cal. —A. L. Everett
October 19, 1903

Editor: It was a privilege to read, in the current issue, your memoir of Auburn during the summer of 1869, when that town played host to one of the least appreciated of the nation's public servants, a man who during his lifetime was so bitterly maligned that few today recognize the soundness of many of the measures he advocated toward the vanquished people of the South.

But it is one of the weaknesses of a democracy that, having first made national heroes of our leaders, we take delight in going to the other extreme and, having consigned them to obscurity and neglect, we attribute to them follies that they deserve even less than the uncritical adulation we once bestowed on them. . . .

It is a tribute to the stature of the man that, when you met him that summer at Auburn, he bore himself with fortitude, accepting his unpopularity with unconcern and showing no evidence of the bitterness and disillusion that might have been expected in a nature less generous.

His services to his country—and they were considerable—have been too long obscured by the prejudices of the postwar era. But few can doubt that in the end he will be assigned a modest but honorable place in the nation's history as a man of courage and integrity, as a reasonably able administrator, and as a leader whose humane policies time will doubtless vindicate.

Morgan Hill, Cal. —Richard R. Dixon
October 24, 1903

Editor: . . . It was my good fortune to be in Washington, D.C., when Edwin Booth opened his engagement at Grover's Theater on E Street in the spring of 1867. Probably there are few now living who recall the furor his coming aroused not only in the city itself but throughout the country.

That the actor would dare make a public appearance in the capital at such a time (for less than two years had passed since the irrational act that had brought disgrace on the entire Booth family) was denounced by some as brazen effrontery, while others professed to see in it a courageous gesture on the tragedian's part to make amends for his brother's folly.

At any rate, feeling was high for weeks in advance, and all over town posters announcing his coming were torn from walls and fences or scrawled over with abusive comments. I remember standing in line for several hours to gain admittance on the opening night, and from my seat in the gallery I listened to the whistles and catcalls from the predominantly hostile audience.

The curtain was late going up, and although the orchestra played patriotic airs during the interval, the crowd, further angered by the delay, grew steadily more restive. Then, when the situation seemed about to get completely out of hand, the musicians struck up "Hail to the Chief" and the curtain at the rear of the box on the left parted and the President and his guests entered and took their seats.

In an instant the temper of the audience changed. The shouts of derision died and were succeeded by a spontaneous burst of applause, for even the dullest-witted among them realized the significance and magnanimity of that moment.

The famous star excelled himself that night, and I observed that the President's applause was as prolonged and hearty as that of the others. The play was *Othello* (which in view of all the circumstances was not the happiest choice that might have been made), but all agreed that Booth's Iago was magnificent.

Stockton, Cal. —R. Harrington
October 20, 1903

JULY 4, 1869:
BEING THE RECORD OF A LONG-FORGOTTEN INCIDENT THAT BRIEFLY DREW NATIONAL ATTENTION TO THE TOWN OF AUBURN

When he urged his friend to visit him in California, Brooke David held forth a promise that he would find his stay in the little foothill town serene and restful, where he could take his ease in peaceful surroundings and forget the cares that had long been his lot.

During the greater part of his stay that promise was fulfilled. Ever the considerate host, David was at pains to see that his guest enjoyed uninterrupted repose. Although, like most men who have long been in public life, David liked nothing better than to surround himself with companions, during the Shogun's stay he limited visitors to a few friends of long standing, men whom he knew could be relied on to respect the privacy of the honored guest.

The result of his careful planning must have been all Brooke David had envisioned. The Shogun had of course been in feeble health before he set off for California, and the long journey had made further inroads on his slender reserves of strength. But a few days of rest and quiet brought about a heartening change. Nights of tranquil sleep in the big corner room, its windows open to the cool breezes that swept down from the mountains, had a beneficent effect, as did also the simple meals and the hours he spent each afternoon sitting beneath the oaks overlooking the canyon while the faithful Bosley read aloud from a favorite book, closing it quietly whenever his listener's head inclined forward in sleep, his gray beard touching his chest.

After less than a week of that placid routine it became clear to all that the Shogun was on the mend. In his diary Bosley makes daily note of his progress, although his gratitude at his chief's reviving strength and spirits is tempered by his concern that the old man's impatience with the role of invalid might lead him to resume too quickly his normal activities and thus cancel his physical gains. The Shogun's resiliency, often before demonstrated, was such, however, that he was presently following again his accustomed active schedule, with few signs of undue fatigue.

He resumed his lifelong habit of rising early, getting up before the rest of the household was astir and making his way downstairs into the cool freshness of the morning. There one can imagine him wandering slowly about the grounds, a tall, gaunt figure with bent shoulders and lined face, standing for long periods while he gazed out over the successive ridges of the hills into the haze-filled valley, or regarding with contemplative interest the colony of squirrels that, rarely visible at other hours of the day, then ventured down out of the oaks and playfully scurried along the paths, displaying no fear of the attentive watcher.

Bosley reports that the Shogun spoke often of these quiet interludes, saying that the solitude of early morning had a healing quality superior to any tonic known to the doctors, and saying too that these strolls beneath the trees awakened memories of his long-distant youth.

Since coming to this quiet retreat [wrote Bosley in late June] the Shogun's thoughts often turn toward times long past. It is as though the burdens of later years have been eased from his shoulders, leaving his mind free to range backward to the time when, a carefree backwoods youth, he had known the forests and villages of the frontier.

When he speaks of that period, as he often does, the signs of weariness disappear from his face, and his spirit grows buoyant and almost gay. This morning when he came in from his stroll he opened the door of my room and, finding me awake, came and sat at the foot of my bed. He remained silent for some moments while I waited quietly, knowing from the cast of his countenance that he had something he wished to say. At last he began, speaking in a half-humorous tone that presently grew quite serious.

"Matt," he said, "when I was a boy they used to tell about an old schoolmaster who lived down in Kentucky. He was a simple backwoodsman without much book learning, but he got along well enough as long as he confined himself to teaching his scholars how to read and write and cipher. But one day the members of the school board got the idea that he ought to branch out, so they ordered him to add another subject—geography—to the curriculum.

"The old teacher had no textbooks to consult, but he did the best he could under the circumstances. He had once made a trip down the Ohio, so every day for the next four months when it came time for the geography lesson he told them what he could recollect about the town of Louisville. By the time the term was over, his students had heard all they ever wanted to hear about that place. So on the last day the schoolmaster made an announcement. 'Next term,' he said, 'we're going to broaden out and take up the study of foreign geography, beginning with St. Louis.' "

He paused, chuckling at the memory, then after a moment he continued: "I've been thinking this morning that sometimes we're all inclined to take the view of that Kentucky schoolmaster, particularly those of us who go into national politics and get elected to office. After we've spent a few years in Washington, we begin to think that's all there is to the country, and that when things go wrong there, the nation itself is going to the dogs. There have been times when I have felt that there was nothing much to hope for, when the people seemed blind to everything except self-interest and ready to follow any leader who offered them a chance to profit at the expense of their countrymen. You've sometimes heard me in my blindness rail against the blindness of others, little realizing that this land is far too big and too strong to be much affected by the quarrels of the politicians. What the office-holders need is a smattering of foreign geography. I've been taking that course myself these past few weeks and I've come to realize what I should have known all along: that the people's welfare is not, and never can be, in the hands of any one man or group of men."

He had become quite earnest as he talked, and now he stood up and began pacing between the bed and the window, his hands clasped behind his back.

"There's one thing this outing has done, Matt," he continued, "and that is to make me realize that the wrongs we saw done these past few years, and that we were powerless to prevent, are not nearly so serious as they appeared at the time. One can't ride for days across the plains and mountains, as we have done, without having one's eyes opened and one's faith renewed. This morning I've been sitting under that great oak and meditating while I looked out over the hills and canyons toward the far ridges of the mountains. And as I looked, it came to me how foolish it is to imagine that any set of men, no matter how wrong-headed or selfish, or how much power they hold, can do the nation any lasting hurt. Their day will pass, and with it all the injustices of their making; the bitterness too will pass and be forgotten; but the nation will endure, never fear, and be so little marred by all this turmoil that in a few years, or in a few decades at the most, what seem to us now matters of such import will be seen in their true light, and all this striving and grief and disappointment will end in—what? At the most, in a few passing lines in the history books."

The Shogun paused before the door leading into the hall; his manner changed and a droll smile came over his face. "Matt," he added, "I hope you haven't minded having to listen to this harangue so early in the morning. But that's what you've got to expect from us politicians; once an idea gets into our heads we can never rest until we've had a chance to try it out on an audience."

The Shogun's habit of rising early not only inspired such philosophical observations as that reported above; it was also a contributing factor in the sequence of events that were to make his stay at Auburn memorable by bringing him again briefly to the notice of the entire nation.

The memoir of eighty-nine-year-old Hubert Gans, excerpts from which were quoted earlier in this narrative, recounts his meetings with the Shogun when the Auburn schoolboy rode out from his father's dairy each morning and delivered milk to the David summer home. This, however, was not the only friendship David's guest formed during those early-morning hours while the rest of the household slept. Several times each week the David housekeeper, Mrs. Odgers, made up a bundle of soiled linen and, before she went to bed, deposited it outside the kitchen door. Early the next morning it was picked up by the fourteen-year-old daughter of the Auburn washerwoman, who left in its place the freshly laundered pieces she had carried away on her last trip.

One morning not long after he arrived, the Shogun came upon the girl as she was lifting the heavy wicker basket down from her buckboard. He came forward and helped her carry it up on the back porch. This was the beginning of their friendship, the details of which have been preserved because the incident to which it led caused comment far beyond the confines of the town, stirring up a controversy so heated that it assumed an importance neither of them could have foreseen.

Among various accounts of the episode that found their way into print, that of the one-time Auburn editor C. E. Hargraves (whose article in the October 17, 1903 *issue of* The California Plowman *has already been quoted), states the facts more briefly than most. The version that follows is based on a later installment of Hargraves's reminiscences, that of October* 24, *which is mainly devoted to this matter.*

The editor begins by describing the first meeting between Maud Luning and the Shogun and then goes on to relate that in the course of their subsequent visits he won the confidence of the reticent child and learned something of her history. The latter was simple enough. She lived with her mother and younger sisters in a cottage on lower High Street, near the edge of Chinatown. Since her husband's death, some two years earlier, Mrs. Luning had supported her small family by taking in washing, and Maud, a slight, freckle-faced girl who looked less than her fourteen years, did her part by delivering the bundles before and after school. The vehicle in which she made her rounds was, states Hargraves, a dilapidated buckboard drawn by an ancient sorrel mare; both were familiar sights on Auburn's streets long before the events of July 4 *projected them into wider prominence. The family had come to California in the summer of* 1866 *and settled at Auburn in the hope that the town's climate would prove beneficial to the husband and father, Henry Luning, whose health had been shattered by four years in the Confederate Army, where he had served under Jubal Early and, after* 1864, *with Mosby's guerrillas.*

Hargraves goes on to state that one morning a week or two after their acquaintance began, the Shogun observed that his young friend, who was normally a quiet, uncommunicative child, seemed more than usually preoccupied. At first she offered no explanation of her silence, but under his kindly questioning she at length explained that a group of girls in her class at school were preparing to ride on a float in the town's coming Fourth of July parade. Thirteen girls had been selected for that honor, and each was to wear a costume representing one of the original thirteen colonies, a project that had aroused added interest among the girls because their class was then studying the history of the American Revolution.

Maud had not been one of those chosen to ride on the float, but that had disturbed her less than what she believed to be the reason why she had not been included. The other girls, she related, had gathered about her at recess the previous day and jeeringly addressed her as a Johnny Reb, adding that no one whose father had fought for old Jeff Davis would be permitted to take part in the celebration.

Having bit by bit drawn this story from the child, the Shogun reassured her as best he could, and at length she climbed into her buckboard and headed back to town, measurably cheered. Later that day he mentioned the incident to his host. Both men thought it likely that the whole matter was the result of a childish misunderstanding, but when Brooke David made inquiries in town that afternoon, he discovered that her version was substantially correct. The float, he learned, was being sponsored by the Auburn branch of the then dominant wing of the Shogun's party, and the county chairman, a staunch supporter of that faction's stern policy toward the South, had issued orders that no children of Southern sympathizers be allowed to participate.

When David related these facts at supper that night, the Shogun listened without comment, but the lines about his mouth took on an added grimness, and those familiar with that expression grew convinced that the matter would not be dropped. And so it proved, although if at first he had any definite plans in mind he took no one into his confidence. The result was that the means he employed to rebuke the narrow intolerance of the town's Radical Republicans was as much a surprise to David and his friends as it was to the generality of the citizens.

Only later did those close to him recall certain happenings that, had they given thought to them at the time, might have indicated that something was afoot. Soon after the Shogun's presence in Auburn had become known, the group in charge of the Independence Day celebration had invited him to view the parade from the reviewing stand and later to deliver the traditional Fourth of July oration. Bosley, in his reference to this, states that the Shogun's reply expressed his appreciation of the honor but he asked to be excused, pleading his uncertain health and adding with characteristic humor that in his opinion discarded politicians could best serve their country by maintaining a discreet silence on all public questions.

A day or two after his talk with the Luning girl, however, he mildly surprised his host by remarking that he had been thinking over the committee's invitation and had concluded that perhaps he had reached too hasty a decision. Would David get in touch with the committee chairman and tell him that, if their arrangements would permit a last-minute change, he would be happy to attend the parade. This offer was promptly accepted. Seldom had the town had the privilege of entertaining so well known a public figure, and news that he was to appear was duly heralded in the next issue of the Sentinel.

The committee had assumed that the Shogun's role in the exercises would be exclusively that of spectator, and a place had been reserved for him on the flag-draped stand at the head of High Street. But on the morning of the 4th, to the growing concern of the officials, his chair remained unoccupied when the sound of distant music announced that the parade was getting under way. Brooke David, who was among the guests on the stand, could throw no light on the Shogun's whereabouts. They had, he explained, driven in to town together, but he and his guest had parted immediately on their arrival, the latter setting off through the crowd after remarking casually that he had agreed to meet a friend on a little matter of business.

It was some time before those on the stand learned the nature of this business or the identity of the Shogun's friend. The first of the floats, led by the twelve-piece Auburn band, had reached and passed the reviewing stand, and still the chair of the honored guest remained vacant. Then from far down the street came a roar of applause from the sidewalk crowds. The cheers grew in volume moment by moment, interspersed with shouts of laughter, and all up High Street necks craned to learn what was causing so much hilarity.

Soon the dignitaries on the reviewing stand saw a curious sight. Well toward the end of the column and sandwiched between gaily decorated floats and uniformed marching teams was a vehicle that, despite the bunting draped from its sides and festooned from the bridle and reins of the horse, was instantly recognized as the familiar laundry wagon in which Maud Luning daily made her rounds. That young lady herself was driving, sitting erect and prim in her starched white frock, her corn-colored hair in two tight pigtails down her back, and her eyes straight ahead, seemingly oblivious of the tumult about her. But it was the odd figure on the seat beside her that captured the attention of the crowd. He, too, preserved a manner as decorous as that of his companion as he periodically doffed his stovepipe hat in acknowledgment of the cheers, his bearing as grave and formal as though this ancient vehicle had been the most elegant of open carriages.

Although the Shogun's presence at the David house was then generally known in Auburn, this was the first glimpse many of the townspeople had had of him. But portraits and caricatures of his homely, rough-hewn features had appeared so often in the public prints as to make them familiar to all. It was the unassuming informality of his first appearance among them that so captivated the onlookers, stirring them to continuous laughing applause as the little wagon and its oddly incongruous occupants filed past.

No was the reason for the Shogun's presence in this humble vehicle lost on the crowd, for news that Maud Luning had been refused permission to ride with her schoolmates had for days past been widely discussed. Having thoroughly debated the question pro and con, the great majority of the townspeople, whatever their political beliefs, had concluded that the float's sponsors had been clearly in the wrong to hold the child responsible for her father's having fought on the side of the Rebels. Thus the Shogun's unexpected presence in the parade, squiring the small figure about which this controversy had raged, made so strong an appeal to the spectators' sense of justice that the wagon's progress up Auburn's main street took on the aspect of a triumphal procession.

His gesture won, too, as events were to prove, the lively approbation of many thousands elsewhere, for news of the incident was not long restricted to that obscure California town. So deep-seated were the political animosities of the period that this small event, which in less contentious times would have passed unnoticed, was eagerly seized upon and its importance magnified until it was presently claiming national attention. The wires of the overland telegraph carried the story across the mountains, and during the next few days it was printed, often with editorial comment, in hundreds of newspapers.

What significance the various journals attached to the incident depended of course on their political affiliations. Those that during the years following the war had supported the administration in its policy of conciliation saw in it a gesture of friendship to all helpless victims of popular prejudice and a rebuke to those who sought to keep alive wartime enmities. On the other hand, the opposition papers—and these included many of the most influential in the land—professed to see in the episode a plot on the part of the so-called moderate wing of the party to curry the favor of the unrepentant Rebels in the hope of thus regaining its lost political influence.

No useful end would be served by relating here the full story of that long-forgotten controversy. Yet this small happening had consequences far out of proportion to its intrinsic importance. Whether or no the Shogun, when he took that means of delivering a well-deserved rebuke to the bigotry of a local political faction, foresaw its possible result can only be guessed at, but it seems probable that so astute a politician could not have been unaware that it might cause far more than local repercussions.

It is a truism that consequences of importance sometimes spring from small beginnings, and so it proved now. For the Shogun's ride with small Maud Luning in Auburn's Fourth of July parade had the effect, whether planned or not, of bringing dramatically to the country's notice the treatment too often dealt out to innocent victims of mass prejudice. That his protest struck a responsive chord in the hearts of so many was due in part to the fact that the enmities growing out of the war, and intensified during the years that followed, had grown increasingly burdensome. Thus the Shogun, whether by design or accident, had chosen well the time to make his forthright plea for the burial of old resentments. The war had been over for more than four years, and the bitter quarrels that had followed, reaching their climax during the national election of 1868, had run their course. The rank and file were everywhere in a mood to welcome a return of peace and tranquillity and eager for a leader to guide them back along the paths of harmony and good will.

That it was the Shogun who found himself abruptly elevated to this role is not surprising in view of the treatment we too often accord our leaders. For as a nation it has long been our habit alternately to place our public servants on a pedestal as paragons of wisdom and probity and then, having tired of hero-worship, to brand them as rogues and cast them into the outer darkness, only in the end to have another change of heart and restore them miraculously to public esteem.

Like others before him and since, it was the Shogun's lot to pass suc-

cessively through periods of phenomenal popularity and of equally complete disfavor. It is pleasant to reflect that, having completed the cycle, he enjoyed during the few brief months still allotted him the renewed regard of his fellows, who by common consent conferred on him the accolade he valued above all others: that of spokesman for the weak and oppressed everywhere, who with courage and humility and infinite patience supported to the end the doctrine of justice and equality for all.

It is perhaps fitting that this memoir be brought to a close by a final brief quotation from the diary of Matthew Bosley, written in mid-October 1869, *hardly three months after the Shogun's visit to Auburn ended.*

Among the scores of messages that have daily arrived during the past fortnight [he wrote] the most touching by far have been those that come, not from men who occupy high places in the affairs of the nation, but from humble citizens who, prompted by one can only surmise what feelings of sorrow and compassion, were moved to take their pens in hand and record their deep sense of personal loss. For these messages, coming as they have from every corner of the land, many of them crudely written and phrased, yet have one quality in common, and shining through even the least legible of their scrawls and investing them with a quiet dignity is their boundless admiration for a great and humble fellow American and their candid grief at his passing.

These simple, heartfelt tributes form an imperishable garland to his memory, for one and all they voice the confidence and trust that so often sustained and comforted him during the troubled years when he walked among us.

DEAD CENTER
by Judith Merril

CHAPTER ONE

THEY GAVE HIM SWEET ICES, and kissed him all round, and the Important People who had come to dinner all smiled in a special way as his mother took him from the living room and led him down the hall to his own bedroom.

"Great kid you got there," they said to Jock, his father, and "Serious little bugger, isn't he?" Jock didn't say anything, but Toby knew he would be grinning, looking pleased and embarrassed. Then their voices changed, and that meant they had begun to talk about the important events for which the important people had come.

In his own room, Toby wriggled his toes between crisp sheets, and breathed in the powder-and-perfume smell of his mother as she bent over him for a last hurried goodnight kiss. There was no use asking for a story tonight. Toby lay still and waited while she closed the door behind her and went off to the party, click-tap, tip-clack, hurrying on her high silver heels. She had heard the voices change back there too, and she didn't want to miss anything. Toby got up and opened his door just a crack, and set himself down in back of it, and listened.

In the big square living room, against the abstract patterns of gray and vermilion and chartreuse, the men and women moved in easy patterns of familiar acts. Coffee, brandy, cigarette, cigar. Find your partner, choose your seat. Jock sprawled with perfect relaxed contentment on the low couch with the deep red corduroy cover. Tim O'Heyer balanced nervously on the edge of the same couch, wreathed in cigar smoke, small and dark and alert. Gordon Kimberly dwarfed the big easy chair with the bulking importance of him. Ben Stein, shaggy and rumpled as ever, was running a hand through his hair till it too stood on end. He was leaning against a window frame, one hand on the back of the straight chair in which his wife Sue sat, erect and neat and proper and chic, dressed in smart black that set off perfectly her precise blonde beauty. Mrs. Kimberly, just enough overstuffed so that her pearls gave the appearance of *actually* choking her, was the only stranger to the house. She was standing near the doorway, politely admiring Toby's personal art gallery, as Allie Madero valiantly strove to explain each minor masterpiece.

Ruth Kruger stood still a moment, surveying her room and her guests. Eight of them, herself included, and all Very Important People. In the familiar comfort of her own living room, the idea made her giggle. Allie and Mrs. Kimberly both turned to her, questioning. She laughed and shrugged, helpless to explain, and they all went across the room to join the others.

"Guts," O'Heyer said through the cloud of smoke. "How do you do it, Jock? Walk out of a setup like this into . . . God knows what?"

"Luck," Jock corrected him. "A setup like this helps. I'm the world's pampered darling and I know it."

"Faith is what he means," Ben put in. "He just gets by believing that last year's luck is going to hold up. So it does."

"Depends on what you mean by *luck*. If you think of it as a vector sum composed of predictive powers and personal ability and accurate information and . . ."

"Charm and nerve and . . ."

"Guts," Tim said again, interrupting the interrupter.

"All right, all of them," Ben agreed. "*Luck* is as good a word as any to cover the combination."

"We're all lucky people." That was Allie, drifting into range, with Ruth behind him. "We just happened to get born at the right time with the right dream. Any one of us, fifty years ago, would have been called a wild-eyed visiona—"

"Any one of us," Kimberly said heavily, "fifty years ago, would have had a different dream—in time with the times."

Jock smiled, and let them talk, not joining in much. He listened to philosophy and compliments and speculations and comments, and lay sprawled across the comfortable couch in his own living room, with his wife's hand under his own, consciously letting his mind play back and forth between the two lives he lived: this, here . . . and the perfect mathematic bleakness of the metal beast that would be his home in three days' time.

He squeezed his wife's hand, and she turned and looked at him, and there was no doubt a man could have about what the world held in store.

When they had all gone, Jock walked down the hall and picked up the little boy asleep on the floor, and put him back into his bed. Toby woke up long enough to grab his father's hand and ask earnestly, out of the point in the conversation where sleep had overcome him:

"Daddy, if the universe hasn't got any ends to it, how can you tell where you are?"

"Me?" Jock asked. "I'm right next to the middle of it."

"How do you *know?*"

His father tapped him lightly on the chest.

"Because that's where the middle is." Jock smiled and stood up. "Go to sleep, champ. Good night."

And Toby slept, while the universe revolved in all its mystery about the small center Jock Kruger had assigned to it.

"Scared?" she asked, much later, in the spaceless silence of their bedroom.

He had to think about it before he could answer. "I guess not. I guess I think I ought to be, but I'm not. I don't think I'd do it at all if I wasn't *sure*." He was almost asleep, when the thought hit him, and he jerked awake and saw she was sure enough lying wide-eyed and sleepless beside him. "*Baby!*" he said, and it was almost an accusation. "Baby, *you're* not scared, are you?"

"Not if you're not," she said. But they never could lie to each other.

CHAPTER TWO

TOBY SAT ON THE PLATFORM, next to his grandmother. They were in the second row, right in back of his mother and father, so it was all right for him to wriggle a little bit, or whisper. They couldn't hear much of the speeches back there, and what they did hear mostly didn't make sense to Toby. But every now and then Grandma would grab his hand tight all of a sudden, and he understood what the whole thing was about: it was because Daddy was going away again.

His Grandma's hand was very white, with little red and tan dots in it, and big blue veins that stood out higher than the wrinkles in her skin, whenever she grabbed at his hand. Later, walking over to the towering sky-scraping rocket, he held his mother's hand; it was smooth and cool and tan, all one color, and she didn't grasp at him the way Grandma did. Later still, his father's two hands, picking him up to kiss, were bigger and darker tan than his mother's, not so smooth, and the fingers were stronger, but so strong it hurt sometimes.

They took him up in an elevator, and showed him all around the inside of the rocket, where Daddy would sit, and where all the food was stored, for emergency, they said, and the radio and everything. Then it was time to say goodbye.

Daddy was laughing at first, and Toby tried to laugh, too, but he didn't really want Daddy to go away. Daddy kissed him, and he felt like crying because it was scratchy against Daddy's cheek, and the strong fingers were hurting him now. Then Daddy stopped laughing and looked at him very seriously. "You take care of your mother, now," Daddy told him. "You're a big boy this time."

"Okay," Toby said. Last time Daddy went away in a rocket, he was not-quite-four, and they teased him with the poem in the book that said, *James James Morrison Morrison Weatherby George Dupree, Took great care of his mother, though he was only three. . . .* So Toby didn't much like Daddy saying that now, because he knew they didn't really mean it.

"Okay," he said, and then because he was angry, he said, "Only she's supposed to take care of me, isn't she?"

Daddy and Mommy both laughed, and so did the two men who were standing there waiting for Daddy to get done saying goodbye to him. He wriggled, and Daddy put him down.

"I'll bring you a piece of the moon, son," Daddy said, and Toby said, "All right, fine." He reached for his mother's hand, but he found himself hanging onto Grandma instead, because Mommy and Daddy were kissing each other, and both of them had forgotten all about him.

He thought they were never going to get done kissing.

Ruth Kruger stood in the glass control booth with her son on one side of her, and Gordon Kimberly breathing heavily on the other side. *Something's wrong,* she thought, *this time something's wrong.* And then swiftly, *I mustn't think that way!*

Jealous? she taunted herself. Do you *want* something to be wrong, just because this one isn't all yours, because Argent did some of it?

But if anything is wrong, she prayed, let it be now, right away, so he can't go. If anything's wrong let it be in the firing gear or the . . . what? Even now, it was too late. The beast was too big and too delicate and too precise. If something went wrong, even now, it was too late. It was . . .

You didn't finish that thought. Not if you were Ruth Kruger, and your husband was Jock Kruger, and nobody knew but the two of you how much of the courage that had gone twice round the moon, and was about to land on it, was yours. When a man knows his wife's faith is *unshakeable,* he can't help coming back. (But: "*Baby! You're* not scared, are you?")

Twice around the moon, and they called him Jumping Jock. There was never a doubt in anyone's mind who'd pilot the KIM-5, the bulky beautiful beast out there today. Kruger and Kimberly, O'Heyer and Stein. It was a combo. It won every time. *Every* time. Nothing to doubt. No room for doubt.

"Minus five . . ." someone said into a mike, and there was perfect quiet all around. "Four . . . three . . ."

(But he held me too tight, and he laughed too loud. . . .)

". . . two . . . one . . ."

(Only because he thought *I* was scared, she answered herself.)

". . . Mar—"

You didn't even hear the whole word, because the thunder-drumming roar of the beast itself split your ears.

Ringing quiet came down and she caught up Toby, held him tight, tight. . . .

"Perfect!" Gordon Kimberly sighed. "*Per*fect!"

So if anything *was* wrong, it hadn't showed up yet.

She put Toby down, then took his hand. "Come on," she said. "I'll buy you an ice-cream soda." He grinned at her. He'd been looking very strange all day, but now he looked real again. His hair had got messed up when she grabbed him.

"We're having cocktails for the press in the conference room," Kimberly said. "I think we could find something Toby would like."

"Wel-l-l-l . . ." She didn't want a cocktail, and she didn't want to talk to the press. "I think maybe we'll beg off this time. . . ."

"I think there might be some disappointment—" the man started; then Tim O'Heyer came dashing up.

"Come on, babe," he said. "Your old man told me to take personal charge while he was gone." He leered. On him it looked cute. She laughed. Then she looked down at Toby. "What would you rather, Tobe? Want to go out by ourselves, or go to the party?"

"I don't care," he said.

Tim took the boy's hand. "What we were thinking of was having a kind of party here, and then I think they're going to bring some dinner in, and anybody who wants to can stay up till your Daddy gets to the moon. That'll be pretty late. I guess you wouldn't want to stay up late like that, would you?"

Somebody else talking to Toby like that would be all wrong, but Tim was a friend, Toby's friend too. Ruth still didn't want to go to the party, but she remembered now that there had been plans for something like that all along, and since Toby was beginning to look eager, and it *was* important to keep the press on their side . . .

"You win, O'Heyer," she said. "Will somebody please send out for an ice-cream soda? Cherry syrup, I think it is this week . . ." She looked inquiringly at her son. ". . . and . . . *strawberry* ice cream?"

Tim shuddered. Toby nodded. Ruth smiled, and they all went in to the party.

"Well, young man!" Toby thought the redheaded man in the brown suit was probably what they called a reporter, but he wasn't sure. "How about it? You going along next time?"

"I don't know," Toby said politely. "I guess not."

"Don't you want to be a famous flier like your Daddy?" a strange woman in an evening gown asked him.

"I don't know," he muttered, and looked around for his mother, but he couldn't see her.

They kept asking him questions like that, about whether he wanted to go to the moon. Daddy said he was too little. You'd think all these people would know that much.

Jock Kruger came up swiftly out of dizzying darkness into isolation and clarity. As soon as he could move his head, before he fully remembered why, he began checking the dials and meters and flashing lights on the banked panel in front of him. He was fully aware of the ship, of its needs and strains and motion, before he came to complete consciousness of himself, his weightless body, his purpose, or his memories.

But he was aware of himself as a part of the ship before he remembered his name, so that by the time he knew he had a face and hands and innards, these parts were already occupied with feeding the beast's human brain a carefully prepared stimulant out of a nippled flask fastened in front of his head.

He pressed a button under his index finger in the arm rest of the couch that held him strapped to safety.

"Hi," he said. "Is anybody up besides me?"

He pressed the button under his middle finger and waited.

Not for long.

"Thank God!" a voice crackled out of the loudspeaker. "You really conked out this time, Jock. Nothing wrong?"

"Not so I'd know it. You want . . . How long was I out?"

"Twenty-three minutes, eighteen seconds, takeoff to reception. Yeah. Give us a log reading."

Methodically, in order, he read off the pointers and numbers on the control panel, the colors and codes and swinging needles and quiet ones that told him how each muscle and nerve and vital organ of the great beast was taking the trip. He did it slowly and with total concentration. Then, when he was all done, there was nothing else to do except sit back and start wondering about that big blackout.

It shouldn't have happened. It never happened before. There was nothing in the compendium of information he'd just sent back to Earth to account for it.

A different ship, different . . . different men. Two and a half years different. Years of easy living and . . . growing old? Too old for this game?

Twenty-three minutes!

Last time it was under ten. The first time maybe 90 seconds more. It didn't matter, of course, not at takeoff. There was nothing for him to do then. Nothing now. Nothing for four more hours. He was there to put the beast back down on . . .

He grinned, and felt like Jock Kruger again. Identity returned complete. *This* time he was there to put the beast down where no man or beast had ever been before. This time they were going to the moon.

CHAPTER THREE

RUTH KRUGER SIPPED AT A COCKTAIL and murmured responses to the admiring, the curious, the envious, the hopeful, and the hate-full ones who spoke to her. She was waiting for something, and after an unmeasurable stretch of time Allie Madero brought it to her.

First a big smile seeking her out across the room, so she knew it had come. Then a low-voiced confirmation.

"Wasn't it . . . an awfully long time?" she asked. She hadn't been watching the clock, on purpose, but she was sure it was longer than it should have been.

Allie stopped smiling. "Twenty-three," she said.

Ruth gasped. "What . . . ?"

"*You* figure it. I can't."

"There's nothing in the ship. I mean nothing was changed that would account for it." She shook her head slowly. This time she didn't know the ship well enough to talk like that. There *could* be something. Oh, *Jock!* "I don't know," she said. "Too many people worked on that thing. I . . ."

"Mrs. Kruger!" It was the redheaded reporter, the obnoxious one. "We just got the report on the blackout. I'd like a statement from you, if you don't mind, as designer of the ship—"

"I am not the designer of this ship," she said coldly.

"You worked on the design, didn't you?"

"Yes."

"Well, then, to the best of your knowledge . . . ?"

"To the best of my knowledge, there is no change in design to account for Mr. Kruger's prolonged unconsciousness. Had there been any such prognosis, the press would have been informed."

"Mrs. Kruger, I'd like to ask you whether you feel that the innovations made by Mr. Argent could—"

"Aw, lay off, will you?" Allie broke in, trying to be casual and kidding about it; but behind her own flaming cheeks, Ruth was aware of her friend's matching anger. "How much do you want to milk this for, anyhow? So the guy conked out an extra ten minutes. If you want somebody to crucify for it, why don't you pick on one of us who doesn't happen to be married to him?" She turned to Ruth before the man could answer. "Where's Toby? He's probably about ready to bust from cookies and carbonation."

"He's in the lounge," the reporter put in. "Or he was a few minutes—"

Ruth and Allie started off without waiting for the rest. The redhead had been talking to the kid. No telling how many of them were on top of him now.

"I thought Tim was with him," Ruth said hastily, then she thought of something, and turned back long enough to say: "For the record, Mr. . . . uh . . . I know of no criticism that can be made of any of the work done by Mr. Argent." Then she went to find her son.

There was nothing to do and nothing to see except the instrument meters and dials to check and log and check and log again. Radio stations all around Earth were beamed on him. He could have kibitzed his way to the moon, but he didn't want to. He was thinking.

Thinking back, and forward, and right in this moment. Thinking of the instant's stiffness of Ruth's body when she said she wasn't scared, and the rambling big house on the hill, and Toby politely agreeing when he offered to bring him back a piece of the moon.

Thinking of Toby growing up some day, and how little he really knew about his son, and what would they do, Toby and Ruth, if anything . . .

He'd never thought that way before. He'd never thought anything except to know he'd come back, because he couldn't stay away. It was always that simple. He couldn't stay away now, either. That hadn't changed. But as he sat there, silent and useless for the time, it occurred to him that he'd left something out of his calculations. *Luck*, they'd been talking about. Yes, he'd had luck. But—what was it Sue had said about a vector sum?—there was more to figure in than your own reflexes and the beast's strength. There was the *outside*. Space . . . environment . . . God . . . destiny. What difference does it make what name you give it?

He couldn't *stay* away . . . but maybe he could be *kept* away.

He'd never thought that way before.

"You tired, honey?"

"No," he said. "I'm just sick of this party. I want to go home."

"It'll be over pretty soon, Tobe. I think as long as we stayed this long, we better wait for . . . for the end of the party."

"It's a silly party. You said you'd buy me an ice-cream soda."

"I did, darling," she said patiently. "At least, if I didn't *buy* it, I got it for you. You had it, didn't you?"

"Yes, but you *said* we'd go *out* and have one."

"Look. Why don't you just put your head down on my lap and . . ."

"I'm no *baby!* Anyhow I'm not tired."

"All right. We'll go pretty soon. You just sit here on the couch, and you don't have to talk to anybody if you don't feel like it. I'll tell you what. I'll go find you a magazine or a book or something to look at, and—"

"I don't *want* a magazine. I want my own book with the pirates in it."

"You just stay put a minute, so I can find you. I'll bring you something."

She got up and went out to the other part of the building where the officers were, and collected an assortments of leaflets and folders with shiny bright pictures of mail rockets and freight transports and jets and visionary moon rocket designs, and took them back to the little lounge where she'd left him.

She looked at the clock on the way. Twenty-seven more minutes. There was *no* reason to believe that anything was wrong.

They were falling now. A man's body is not equipped to sense direction *toward* or *from*, *up* or *down*, without the help of landmarks or gravity. But the body of the beast was designed to know such things; and Kruger, at the nerve center, knew everything the beast knew.

Ship is extension of self, and self is—extension or limitation?—of ship. If Jock Kruger is the center of the universe—remember the late night after the party, and picking Toby off the floor?—then ship is extension of self, and the man is the brain of the beast. But if ship *is* universe—certainly continuum; that's universe, isn't it?—then the weakling man-thing in the couch is a limiting condition of the universe. A human brake. He was there to make it stop when it didn't "want" to.

Suppose it wouldn't stop? Suppose it had decided to be a self-determined, free-willed universe?

Jock grinned, and started setting controls. His time was coming. It was measurable in minutes, and then in seconds . . . *now!*

His hand reached for the firing lever (but *what* was she scared of?), groped, and touched, hesitated, clasped, and pulled.

Grown-up parties at home were fun. But other places, like this one, they were silly. Toby half-woke-up on the way home, enough to realize his Uncle Tim was driving them, and they weren't in their own car. He was sitting on the front seat next to his mother, with his head against her side, and her arm around him. He tried to come all the way awake, to listen to what they were saying, but they weren't talking, so he started to go back to sleep.

Then Uncle Tim said, "For God's sake, Ruth, he's safe, and whatever happened certainly wasn't *your* fault. He's got enough supplies to hold out till . . ."

"Shh!" his mother said sharply, and then, whispering, "I know."

Now he remembered.

"Mommy . . ."

"Yes, hon?"

"Did Daddy go to the moon all right?"

"Y . . . yes, dear."

Her voice was funny.

"Where is it?"

"Where's what?"

"The moon."

"Oh. We can't see it now, darling. It's around the other side of the earth."

"Well, when is he going to come *back?*"

Silence.

"*Mommy . . . when?*"

"As soon as . . . just as soon as he can, darling. Now go to sleep."

And now the moon was up, high in the sky, a gilded football dangling from Somebody's black serge lapel. When she was a little girl, she used to say she loved the man in the moon, and now the man in the moon loved her too, but if she was a little girl still, somebody would tuck her into bed, and pat her head and tell her to go to sleep, and she would sleep as easy, breathe as soft, as Toby did. . . .

But she wasn't a little girl, she was all grown up, and she married the man, the man in the moon, and sleep could come and sleep could go, but sleep could never stay with her while the moonwash swept the window panes.

She stood at the open window and wrote a letter in her mind and sent it up the path of light to the man in the moon. It said:

"Dear Jock: Tim says it wasn't my fault, and I can't explain it even to him. I'm sorry, darling. Please to stay alive till we can get to you. Faithfully yours, Cassandra."

CHAPTER FOUR

THE GLASSES AND ASHES and litter and spilled drinks had all been cleared away. The table top gleamed in polished stripes of light and dark, where the light came through the louvered plastic of the wall. The big chairs were empty, waiting, and at each place, arranged with the precision of a formal dinner-setting, was the inevitable pad of yellow paper, two freshly-sharpened pencils, a small neat pile of typed white sheets of paper, a small glass ashtray and a shining empty water glass. Down the center of the table, spaced for comfort, three crystal pitchers of ice and water stood in perfect alignment.

Ruth was the first one there. She stood in front of a chair, fingering the little stack of paper on which someone (Allie? She'd have had to be up early to get it done so quickly) had tabulated the details of yesterday's events. "To refresh your memory," was how they always put it.

She poured a glass of water, and guiltily replaced the pitcher on the exact spot where it had been; lit a cigarette, and stared with dismay at the burnt match marring the cleanliness of the little ashtray; pulled her chair in beneath her and winced at the screech of the wooden leg across the floor.

Get it over with! She picked up the typed pages, and glanced at them. Two at the bottom were headed "Recommendations of U. S. Rocket Corps to Facilitate Construction of KIM-VIII." That could wait. The three top sheets she'd better get through while she was still alone.

She read slowly and carefully, trying to memorize each sentence, so that when the time came to talk, she could think of what had happened this way, from outside, instead of remembering how it had been for *her*.

There was nothing in the report that she didn't already know.

Jock Kruger had set out in the KIM-5 at 5:39 P.M., C.S.T., just at sunset. First report after recovery from blackout came at 6:02-plus. First log readings gave no reason to anticipate any difficulty. Subsequent reports and radioed log readings were, for Kruger, unusually terse and formal, and surprisingly infrequent; but earth-to-ship contact at twenty-minute intervals had been acknowledged. No reason to believe Kruger was having trouble at any time during the trip.

At 11:54, an attempt to call the ship went unanswered for 56 seconds. The radioman here described Kruger's voice as "irritable" when the reply finally came, but all he said was, "Sorry. I was firing the first brake." Then a string of figures, and a quick log reading—everything just what you'd expect.

Earth acknowledged, and waited.

Eighteen seconds later:

"Second brake." More figures. Again, everything as it should be. But twenty seconds after that call was completed:

"This is Kruger. Anything wrong with the dope I gave you?"

"Earth to Kruger. Everything okay in our book. Trouble?"

"Track me, boy. I'm off."

"You want a course correction?"

"I can figure it quicker here. I'll keep talking as I go. Stop me if I'm wrong by your book." More figures, and Kruger's calculations coincided perfectly with the swift work done at the base. Both sides came to the same conclusion, and both sides knew what it meant. The man in the beast fired once more, and once again, and made a landing.

There was no reason to believe that either ship or pilot had been hurt. There was no way of finding out. By the best calculations, they were five degrees of arc around onto the dark side. And there was no possibility at all, after that second corrective firing that Kruger had enough fuel left to take off again. The last thing Earth had heard, before the edge of the moon cut off Kruger's radio, was:

"Sorry, boys. I guess I fouled up this time. Looks like you'll have to come and . . ."

One by one, they filled the seats: Gordon Kimberly at one end, and the Colonel at the other; Tim O'Heyer to one side of Kimberly, and Ruth at the other; Allie, with her pad and pencil poised, alongside Tim; the Colonel's aide next down the line, with his little silent stenotype in front of him; the Steins across from him, next to Ruth. With a minimum of formality, Kimberly opened the meeting and introduced Col. Swenson.

The Colonel cleared his throat. "I'd like to make something clear," he said. "Right from the start, I want to make this clear. I'm here to help. Not to get in the way. My presence does not indicate any—*criticism* on the part of the Armed Services. We are entirely satisfied with the work you people have been doing." He cleared his throat again, and Kimberly put in:

"You saw our plans, I believe, Colonel. Everything was checked and approved by your outfit ahead of time."

"Exactly. We had no criticism then, and we have none now. The rocket program is what's important. Getting Kruger back is important, not just for ordinary humanitarian reasons—pardon me, Mrs. Kruger, if I'm too blunt—but for the sake of the whole program. Public opinion, for one thing. That's your line, isn't it, Mr. O'Heyer? And then, *we have to find out what happened!*

"I came down here today to offer any help we can give you on the relief ship, and to make a suggestion to facilitate matters."

He paused deliberately this time.

"Go ahead, Colonel," Tim said. "We're listening."

"Briefly, the proposal is that you all accept temporary commissions while the project is going on. Part of that report in front of you embodies the details of the plan. I hope you'll find it acceptable. You all know there is a great deal of—necessary, I'm afraid—*red tape*, you'd call it, and 'going through channels,' and such in the Services. It makes cooperation between civilian and military groups difficult. If we can all get together as one outfit 'for the duration,' so to speak . . ."

This time nobody jumped into the silence. The Colonel cleared his throat once more.

"Perhaps you'd best read the full report before we discuss it any further. I brought the matter up now just to—to let you know the *attitude* with which we are submitting the proposal to you . . ."

"Thank you, Colonel." O'Heyer saved him. "I've already had a chance to look at the report. Don't know that anyone else has, except of course Miss Madero. But I personally, at least, appreciate your attitude. And I think I can speak for Mr. Kimberly too. . . ."

He looked sideways at his boss; Gordon nodded.

"What I'd like to suggest now," O'Heyer went on, "since I've seen the report already, and I believe everyone else would like to have a chance to bone up some—perhaps you'd like to have a first-hand look at some of our plant, Colonel? I could take you around a bit . . . ?"

"Thank you. I would like to." The officer stood up, his gold Rocket Corps uniform blazing in the louvered light. "If I may so so, Mr. O'Heyer, you seem remarkably sensible, for a—well, a *publicity* man."

"That's all right, Colonel." Tim laughed easily. "I don't even think it's a dirty word. You seem like an all-right guy yourself—for an *officer*, that is."

They all laughed then, and Tim led the blaze of glory out of the room while the rest of them settled down to studying the R.C. proposals. When they had all finished, Kimberly spoke slowly, voicing the general reaction:

"I hate to admit it, but it makes sense."

"They're being pretty decent about it, aren't they?" Ben said. "Putting it to us as a proposal instead of pulling a lot of weight."

He nodded. "I've had a little contact with this man Swenson before. He's a good man to work with. It . . . makes sense, that's all."

"On paper, anyhow," Sue put in.

"Well, Ruth . . ." the big man turned to her, waiting. "You haven't said anything."

"I . . . it seems all right to me," she said, and added: "Frankly, Gordon, I don't know that I ought to speak at all. I'm not quite sure why I'm here."

Allie looked up sharply, questioning, from her notes; Sue pushed back her chair and half-stood. "My God, you're not going to back out on us now?"

"I . . . look, you all know I didn't do any of the real work on the last one. It was Andy Argent's job, and a good one. I've got Toby to think about, and . . ."

"Kid, we *need* you," Sue protested. "Argent can't do this one; this is going to be another Three, only more so. Unmanned, remote-control stuff, and no returning atmosphere-landing problems. This is up your alley. It's . . ." She sank back; there was nothing else to say.

"That's true, Ruth." Tim had come back in during the last outburst. Now he sat down. "Speed is what counts, gal. That's why we're letting the gold braid in on the job—we are, aren't we?" Kimberly nodded; Tim went on: "With you on the job, we've got a working team. With somebody new —well, you know what a ruckus we had until Sue got used to Argent's blueprints, and how Ben's pencil notes used to drive Andy wild. And we can't even use him this time. It's not his field. He did do a good job, but we'd have to start in with somebody new all over again . . ." He broke off, and looked at Kimberly.

"I hope you'll decide to work with us, Ruth," he said simply.

"If . . . obviously, if it's the best way to get it done *quick*, I will," she said. "Twenty-eight hours a day if you like."

Tim grinned. "I guess we can let the braid back in now . . . ?" He got up and went to the door.

Another Three, only more so . . . Sue's words danced in her mind while the Colonel and the Colonel's aide marched in, and took their places, while voices murmured politely, exchanging good will.

Another Three—the first ship she had designed for Kimberly. The ship that made her rich and famous, but that was nothing, because it was the ship that brought Jock to her, that made him write the letter, that made her meet him, that led to the Five and Six and now . . .

"I've got some ideas for a manned ship," he'd written. "If we could get together to discuss it some time . . ."

". . . pleasure to know you'll be working with us, Mrs. Kruger." She shook her head sharply, and located in time and place.

"Thank you, Colonel. I want to do what I can, of course. . . ."

CHAPTER FIVE

James James Morrison's mother put on a golden gown . . .

Toby knew the whole thing, almost, by heart. The little boy in the poem *told* his mother not to *go down to the end of the town*, wherever that was, unless she took him along. And she said she wouldn't, but she put on that golden gown and went, and thought she'd be back in time for tea. Only she wasn't. She never came back at all. *Last seen wandering vaguely* . . . *King John said he was sorry* . . .

Who's King John? And what time is tea?

Toby sat quietly beside his mother on the front seat of the car, and looked obliquely at the golden uniform she wore, and could not find a way to ask the questions in his mind.

Where was James James's *father*? Why did James James have to be the one to keep his mother from going down to the end of the town?

"Are you in the Army now, Mommy?" he asked.

"Well . . . sort of. But not for long, darling. Just till Daddy comes home."

"When is Daddy coming home?"

"Soon. Soon, I hope. Not too long."

She didn't sound right. Her voice had a cracking sound like Grandma's, and other old ladies. She didn't look right, either, in that golden-gown uniform. When she kissed him goodbye in front of the school, she didn't *feel* right. She didn't even *smell* the same as she used to.

"'Bye, boy. See you tonight," she said—the same words she always said, but they sounded different.

"'Bye." He walked up the driveway and up the front steps and down the corridor and into the pretty-painted room where his teacher was waiting. Miss Callahan was nice. Today she was *too* nice. The other kids teased him, and called him teacher's pet. At lunch time he went back in the room before anybody else did, and made pictures all over the floor with the colored chalk. It was the worst thing he could think of to do. Miss Callahan made him wash it all up, and she wasn't nice any more for the rest of the afternoon.

When he went out front after school, he couldn't see the car anywhere. It was true then. His mother had put on that golden gown, and now she was gone. Then he saw Grandma waving to him out of *her* car, and he remembered Mommy had said Grandma would come and get him. He got in the car, and she grabbed at him like she always did. He pulled away.

"Is Daddy home yet?" he asked.

Grandma started the car. "Not yet," she said, and she was crying. He didn't dare ask about Mommy after that, but she wasn't home when they got there. It was a long time after that till dinner was ready.

She came home for dinner, though.

"You have to allow for the human factor. . . ."

Nobody had said it to her, of course. Nobody would. She wondered how much tougher it made the job for everybody, having her around. She wondered how she'd stay sane, if she didn't have the job to do.

Thank God Toby was in school now! She couldn't do it, if it meant leaving him with someone else all day—even his grandmother. As it was, having the old lady in the house so much was nerve-racking.

I ought to ask her if she'd like to sleep here for a while, Ruth thought, and shivered. Dinner time was enough.

Anyway, Toby liked having her there, and that's what counted.

I'll have to go in and see his teacher. Tomorrow, she thought. I've got to make time for it tomorrow. Let her know . . . but of course she knew. Jock Kruger's family's affairs were hardly private. Just the same, I better talk to her. . . .

Ruth got out of bed and stood at the window, waiting for the moon. Another ten minutes, fifteen, twenty maybe, and it would edge over the hills on the other side of town. The white hands on the clock said 2:40. She had to get some sleep. She couldn't stand here waiting for the moon. Get to sleep now, before it comes up. That's better. . . .

Oh, *Jock!*

". . . the human factor . . ." They didn't know. She wanted to go tell them all, find somebody right away, and shout it. "*It's not his fault. I did it!*"

"You're *not scared, are you, baby?*"

Oh, no! No, no! Don't be silly. Who, me? Just stiff and trembling. The cold, you know . . . ?

Stop that!

She stood at the window, waiting for the moon, the man, the man in the moon.

Human factor . . . well, there wouldn't be a human factor in this one. If she went out to the field on takeoff day and told KIM-VIII she was scared, it wouldn't matter at all.

Thank God I can do something, at least!

Abruptly, she closed the blind, so she wouldn't know when it came, and pulled out the envelope she'd brought home; switched on the bed light, and unfolded the first blueprints.

It was all familiar. Just small changes here and there. Otherwise, it was the Three all over again—the first unmanned ship to be landed successfully on the moon surface. The only important difference was that this one had to have some fancy gadgetry on the landing mech. Stein had given her the orbit calcs today. The rest of the job was hers and Sue's: design and production. Between them, they could do it. What they needed was a goldberg that would take the thing once around low enough to contact Jock, if . . . to contact him, that's all. Then back again, prepared for him to take over the landing by remote, according to instructions, if he wanted to. If he could. If his radio was working. If . . .

Twice around, and then down where they figured he was, if he hadn't tried to bring it down himself.

It was complicated, but only quantitatively. Nothing basically new, or untried. And no *human* factors to be allowed for, once it was off the ground.

She fell asleep, finally, with the light still on, and the blind drawn, and the blueprints spread out on the floor next to the bed.

Every day, she drove him to school, dressed in her golden gown. And every afternoon, he waited, telling himself she was sure to come home. That was a very silly little poem, and he wasn't three, he was six now. But it was a long time since Daddy went away.

"I'd rather not," she said stiffly.

"I'm sorry, Ruth. I know—well, I *don't* know, but I can imagine how you feel. I hate to ask it, but if you can do it at all . . . just be there and look confident, and . . . *you* know."

Look confident! I couldn't do it for Jock, she thought; why should I do it for *them?* But of course that was silly. They didn't know her the way Jock did. They couldn't read her smiles, or sense a barely present stiffness, or know anything except what she chose to show on the front of her face.

"Look confident? What difference does it make, Tim? If the thing works, they'll all know soon enough. If . . ."

She stopped.

"All right, I'll be blunt. If it *doesn't* work, it's going to make a hell of a difference what the public feeling was at the time it went off. If we have to try again. If—damn it, you want it straight, all right! If we can't save Jock, we're not going to give up the whole thing! We're not going to let space travel wait another half century while the psychological effects wear off.

And Jock wouldn't want us to! Don't forget that. It was his dream, too. It was yours, once upon a time. If . . ."

"All *right!*" She was startled by her voice. She was screaming, or almost.

"All right," she said bitterly, more quietly. "If you think I'll be holding up progress for fifty years by not dragging Toby along to a launching, I'll come."

"Oh, Ruth, I'm sorry. No, it's not that important. And I had no business talking that way. But listen, babe, you used to understand this—the way I feel, the way Jock fel—feels. Even a guy like Kimberly. You used to feel it too. Look: the single item of you showing your face at the takeoff doesn't amount to much. Neither does one ounce of fuel. But either one could be the little bit that makes the difference. Kid, we got to put *everything* we've got behind it this time."

"All right," she said again. "I told you I'd come."

"You do understand, don't you?" he pleaded.

"I don't know, Tim. I'm not sure I do. But you're right. I would have, once. Maybe—I don't know. It's different for a woman, I guess. But I'll come. Don't worry about it."

She turned and started out.

"Thanks, Ruth. And I *am* sorry. Uh—want me to come and pick you up?"

She nodded. "Thanks." She was glad she wouldn't have to drive.

CHAPTER SIX

HE KEPT WAITING for a chance to ask her. He couldn't do it in the house before they left, because right after she told him where they were going, she went to get dressed in her golden uniform, and he had to stay with Grandma all the time.

Then Mr. O'Heyer came with the car, and he couldn't ask because, even though he sat up front with Mommy, Mr. O'Heyer was there too.

When they got to the launching field, there were people around all the time. Once he tried to get her off by himself, but all she did was think he had to go to the bathroom. Then, bit by bit, he didn't *have* to ask, because he could tell from the way they were all talking, and the way the cameras were all pointed at her all the time, like they had been at Daddy the other time.

Then there was the speeches part again, and this time *she* got up and talked, so that settled it.

He was glad he hadn't asked. They probably all thought he knew. Maybe they'd even told him, and he'd forgotten, like he sometimes did. "Mommy," he listened to himself in his mind, "Mommy, are you going to the moon too?" Wouldn't that sound silly!

She'd come back for him, he told himself. The other times, when Daddy went some place—like when they first came here to live, and Daddy went first, then Mommy, and then they came back to get him, and some other time, he didn't remember just what—but when Daddy went away, Mommy always went to stay with him, and then they *always* came to get him too.

It wasn't any different from Mommy going back to be with Daddy at a party or something, instead of staying in his room to talk to him when she put him to bed. It didn't feel any worse than that, he told himself.

Only he didn't believe himself.

She never did tell me! I wouldn't of forgotten that! She should *of told me!*

She did not want to make a speech. Nobody had warned her that she would be called upon to make a speech. It was bad enough trying to answer reporters coherently. She stood up and went forward to the microphone dutifully, and shook hands with the President of the United States, and tried to look confident. She opened her mouth and nothing came out.

"Thank you," she said finally, though she didn't know just what for. "You've all been very kind." She turned to the mike, and spoke directly into it. "I feel that a good deal of honor is being accorded me today which is not rightfully mine. We gave ourselves a two-month limit to complete a job, and the fact that it was finished inside of six weeks instead . . ."

She had to stop because everybody was cheering, and they wouldn't have heard her.

". . . that fact is not something for which the designer of a ship can be thanked. The credit is due to all the people at Kimberly who worked so hard, and to the Rocket Corps personnel who helped so much. I think . . ."

This time she paused to find the right words. It had suddenly become very important to level with the crowd, to tell them what she honestly felt.

"I think it is I who should be doing the thanking. I happen to be a designer of rockets, but much more importantly, to me, I am Jock Kruger's wife. So I want to thank everyone who helped . . ."

Grandma's hand tightened around his, and then pulled away to get a handkerchief, because she was crying. Right up here on the platform! Then he realized what Mommy had just said. She said that being Jock Kruger's wife was more important to her than anything else.

It was funny that Grandma should feel bad about that. Everybody else seemed to think it was a right thing to say, the way they were yelling and clapping and shouting. It occurred to Toby with a small shock of surprise that maybe Grandma sometimes felt bad about things the same way he did.

He was sort of sorry he wouldn't have much chance to find out more about that.

She broke away from the reporters and V.I.P.'s, and went and got Toby, and asked him did he want to look inside the rocket before it left.

He nodded. He was certainly being quiet today. Poor kid—he must be pretty mixed up about the whole thing by now.

She tried to figure out what was going on inside the small brown head, but all she could think of was how *much* like Jock he looked today.

She took him up the elevator inside the rocket. There wasn't much room to move around, of course, but they'd rigged it so that all the big shots who were there could have a look. She was a little startled to see the President and her mother-in-law come up together in the next elevator, but between trying to answer Toby's questions, and trying to brush off reporters, she didn't have much time to be concerned about such oddities.

She had never seen Toby so intent on anything. He wanted to know *everything*. Where's this, and what's that for? And where are you going to sit, Mommy?

"I'm not, hon. You know that. There isn't room in this rocket for . . ."

"Mrs. Kruger, pardon me, but . . ."

"Just a minute, *please*."

"Oh, I'm sorry."

"What was it you wanted to know now, Toby?" There were too many people; there was too much talk. She felt slightly dizzy. "Look, hon, I want to go on down." It was hard to talk. She saw Mrs. Kruger on the ramp, and called her, and left Toby with her. Down at the bottom, she saw Sue Stein, and asked her if she'd go take over with Toby and try to answer his questions.

"Sure. Feeling rocky, kid?"

"Kind of." She tried to smile.

"You better go lie down. Maybe Allie can get something for you. I saw her over there. . . ." She waved a vague hand. "You look like hell, kid. Better lie down." Then she rushed off.

He got away from Grandma when Sue Stein came and said Mother wanted her to show him everything. Then he said he was tired and got away from *her*. He could find his Grandma all right, he said

He'd found the spot he wanted. He could just about wriggle into it, he thought.

The loudspeaker crackled over her head. Five minutes now.

The other women who'd been fixing their hair and brightening their lipstick snapped their bags shut and took a last look and ran out, to find places where they could see everything. Ruth stretched out on the couch and closed her eyes. Five minutes now, by herself, to get used to the idea that the job was done.

She had done everything she could do, including coming here today. There was nothing further she could do. From now on, or in five minutes' time, it was out of anyone's hands, but— Whose? And Jock's, of course. Once the relief rocket got there, it was up to him.

If it got there.

If he was there for it to get to

The way they had worked it, there was a chance at least they'd know the answer in an hour's time. If the rocket made its orbit once, and only once, it would mean he was alive and well and in control of his own ship, with the radio working, and . . .

And if it made a second orbit, there was still hope. It *might* mean nothing worse than that his radio was out. But that way they would have to wait . . .

God! It could take months, if the calculations as to where he'd come down were not quite right. If . . . *if* a million little things that would make it harder to get the fuel from one rocket to the other.

But if they only saw one orbit . . .

For the first time, she let herself, forced herself to, consider the possibility that Jock was dead. That he would not come back.

He's not dead, she thought. I'd know it if he was. Like I knew something was wrong last time. Like I'd know it now if . . .

"Sixty seconds before zero," said the speaker.

But there is! She sat bolt upright, not tired or dizzy any more. Now she had faced it, she didn't feel confused. There was something . . . something dreadfully *wrong*. . . .

She ran out, and as she came on to the open field, the speaker was saying, "Fifty-one."

She ran to the edge of the crowd, and couldn't get through, and had to run, keep running, around the edges, to find the aisle between the cords.

Stop it! she screamed, but not out loud, because she had to use all her breath for running.

And while she ran, she tried to think.

"Minus forty-seven."

She couldn't make them stop without a reason. They'd think she was hysterical . . .

". . . forty-five . . ."

Maybe she was, at that. Coolly, her mind considered the idea and rejected it. No; there was a problem that hadn't been solved, a question she hadn't answered.

But *what* problem? What . . .

"Minus forty."

She dashed down between the ropes, toward the control booth. The guard stepped forward, then recognized her, and stepped back. The corridor between the packed crowds went on forever.

"Minus thirty-nine . . . eight . . . thirty-seven."

She stopped outside the door of Control, and tried to think, think, *think!* What *was* it? What could she tell them? How could she convince them? *She knew*, but they'd want to know what, why . . .

You just didn't change plans at a moment like this.

But if they fired the rocket before she figured it out, before she remembered the problem, and then found an answer, it was as good as murdering Jock. They could never get another one up quickly enough if anything went wrong this time.

She pushed open the door.

"Stop!" she said. "Listen, you've got to stop. Wait! There's something . . ."

Tim O'Heyer came and took her arm, and smiled and said something. Something soothing.

"Minus nineteen," somebody said into a microphone, quietly.

She kept trying to explain, and Tim kept talking at her, and when she tried to pull away she realized the hand on her arm wasn't just there to comfort her. He was keeping her from making trouble. He . . .

Oh, God! If there was just some way to make them understand! If she could only remember *what* was wrong . . .

"Minus three . . . two . . ."

It was no use.

She stopped fighting, caught her breath, stood still, and saw Tim's approving smile, as the word and the flare went off together:

"*Mark!*"

Then, in a dead calm, she looked around and saw Sue.

"Where's Toby?" she asked.

She was looking in the reserved grandstand seats for Mrs. Kruger, when she heard the crowd sigh, and looked up and saw it happening.

CHAPTER SEVEN

THE CRASH FIRE did not damage the inside of the rocket at all. The cause of the crash was self-evident, as soon as they found Toby Kruger's body wedged into the empty space between the outer hull of the third stage, and the inner hull of the second.

The headlines were not as bad as might have been expected. Whether it was the tired and unholy calm on Ruth Kruger's face that restrained them, or Tim O'Heyer's emergency-reserve supply of Irish whisky that convinced them, the newsmen took it easy on the story. All America couldn't attend the funeral, but a representative hundred thousand citizens mobbed the streets when the boy was buried; the other hundred and eighty million saw the ceremonies more intimately on their TV sets.

Nobody who heard the quiet words spoken over the fresh grave—a historic piece of poetry to which the author, O'Heyer, could never sign his name—nobody who heard that simple speech remained entirely unmoved. Just where or when or with whom the movement started is still not known; probably it began spontaneously in a thousand different homes during the brief ceremony; maybe O'Heyer had something to do with that part of it, too. Whichever way, the money started coming in, by wire, twenty minutes afterwards; and by the end of the week "Bring Jock Back" was denting more paychecks than the numbers racket and the nylon industry combined.

The KIM-IX was finished in a month. They didn't have Ruth Kruger to design this time, but they didn't need her: the KIM-VIII plans were still good. O'Heyer managed to keep the sleeping-pill story down to a tiny back-page notice in most of the papers, and the funeral was not televised.

Later, they brought back the perfectly preserved, emaciated body of Jock Kruger, and laid him to rest next to his wife and son. He had been a good pilot and an ingenious man. The moon couldn't kill him; it took starvation to do that.

They made an international shrine of the house, and the garden where the three graves lay.

Now they are talking of making an interplanetary shrine of the lonely rocket on the wrong side of the moon.

LOST ART
by George O. Smith

Sargon of Akkad was holding court in all of his splendor in the Mesopotamia area, which he thought to be the center of the Universe. The stars to him were but holes in a black bowl which he called the sky. They were beautiful then, as they are now, but he thought that they were put there for his edification only; for was he not the ruler of Akkadia?

After Sargon of Akkad, there would come sixty centuries of climbing before men reached the stars and found not only that there had been men upon them, but that a civilization on Mars had reached its peak four thousand years before Christ and was now but a memory and a wealth of pictographs that adorned the semipreserved Temples of Canalopsis.

And sixty centuries after, the men of Terra wondered about the ideographs and solved them sufficiently to piece together the wonders of the long-dead Martian Civilization.

Sargon of Akkad did not know that the stars that he beheld carried on them wonders his mind would not, could not, accept.

Altas, the Martian, smiled tolerantly at his son. The young man boasted on until Altas said: "So you have memorized the contents of my manual? Good, Than, for I am growing old and I would be pleased to have my son fill my shoes. Come into the workshop that I may pass upon your proficiency."

Altas led Than to the laboratory that stood at the foot of the great tower of steel; Altas removed from a cabinet a replacement element from the great beam above their heads, and said: "Than, show me how to hook this up!"

Than's eyes glowed. From other cabinets he took small auxiliary parts. From hooks upon the wall, Than took lengths of wire. Working with a brilliant deftness that was his heritage as a Martian, Than spent an hour attaching the complicated circuits. After he was finished, Than stepped

Reprinted from *Astounding Science Fiction*.
Reprinted by permission of the author.

back and said: "There—and believe it or not, this is the first time you have permitted me to work with one of the beam elements."

"You have done well," said Altas with that same cryptic smile. "But now we shall see. The main question is: Does it work?"

"Naturally," said Than in youthful pride. "Is it not hooked up exactly as your manual says? It will work."

"We shall see," repeated Altas. "We shall see."

Barney Carroll and James Baler cut through the thin air of Mars in a driver-wing flier at a terrific rate of speed. It was the only kind of flier that would work on Mars with any degree of safety since it depended upon the support of its drivers rather than the wing surface. They were hitting it up at almost a thousand miles per hour on their way from Canalopsis to Lincoln Head; their trip would take an hour and a half.

As they passed over the red sand of Mars, endlessly it seemed, a glint of metal caught Barney's eye, and he shouted.

"What's the matter, Barney?" asked Jim.

"Roll her over and run back a mile or so," said Barney. "I saw something down there that didn't belong in this desert."

Jim snapped the plane around in a sharp loop that nearly took their heads off, and they ran back along their course.

"Yop," called Barney, "there she is!"

"What?"

"See that glint of shiny metal? That doesn't belong in this mess of erosion. Might be a crash."

"Hold tight," laughed Jim. "We're going down."

They did. Jim's piloting had all of the aspects of a daredevil racing pilot's, and Barney was used to it. Jim snapped the nose of the little flier down and they power-dived to within a few yards of the sand before he set the plane on its tail and skidded flatwise to kill speed. He leveled off, and the flier came screaming in for a perfect landing not many feet from the glinting object.

"This is no crash," said Baler. "This looks like the remains of an air-lane beacon of some sort."

"Does it? Not like any I've ever seen. It reminds me more of some of the gadgets they find here and there—the remnants of the Ancients. They used to build junk like this."

"Hook up the sand-blower," suggested Jim Baler. "We'll clear some of this rubble away and see what she really looks like. Can't see much more than what looks like a high-powered searchlight."

Barney hauled equipment out of the flier and hitched it to a small motor in the plane. The blower created a small storm for an hour or so, its blast directed by suit-clad Barney Carroll. Working with experience gained in uncovering the remains of a dozen dead and buried cities, Barney cleared the shifting sand from the remains of the tower.

The head was there, preserved by the dry sand. Thirty feet below the platform, the slender tower was broken off. No delving could find the lower portion.

"This is quite a find," said Jim. "Looks like some of the carvings on the Temple of Science at Canalopsis—that little house on the top of the spire with the three-foot runway around it; then this dingbat perched on top of the roof. Never did figure out what it was for."

"We don't know whether the Martians' eyes responded as ours do," suggested Barney. "This might be a searchlight that puts out with Martian visible spectrum. If they saw with infrared, they wouldn't be using Terran fluorescent lighting. If they saw with long heat frequencies, they wouldn't waste power with even a tungsten filament light, but would have invented something that cooked its most energy in the visible spectrum, just as we have in the last couple of hundred years."

"That's just a guess, of course."

"Naturally," said Barney. "Here, I've got the door cracked. Let's be the first people in this place for six thousand years Terran. Take it easy, this floor is at an angle of thirty degrees."

"I won't slide. G'wan in. I'm your shadow."

They entered the thirty-foot circular room and snapped on their torches. There was a bench that ran almost around the entire room. It was empty save for a few scraps of metal and a Martian book of several hundred metal pages.

"Nuts," said Barney, "we would have to find a thing like this but empty. That's our luck. What's the book, Jim?"

"Some sort of text, I'd say. Full of diagrams and what seems to be mathematics. Hard to tell, of course, but we've established the fact that mathematics is universal, though the characters can not possibly be."

"Any chance of deciphering it?" asked Barney.

"Let's get back in the flier and try. I'm in no particular hurry."

"Nor am I. I don't care whether we get to Lincoln Head tonight or the middle of next week."

"Now let's see that volume of diagrams," he said as soon as they were established in the flier.

Jim passed the book over, and Barney opened the book to the first page. "If we never find anything else," he said, "this will make us famous. I am now holding the first complete volume of Martian literature that anyone has ever seen. The darned thing is absolutely complete, from cover to cover!"

"That's a find," agreed Jim. "Now go ahead and transliterate it—you're the expert on Martian pictographs."

For an hour, Barney scanned the pages of the volume. He made copious notes on sheets of paper which he inserted between the metal leaves of the book. At the end of that time, during which Jim Baler had been inspecting the searchlight-thing on the top of the little house, he called to his friend, and Jim entered the flier lugging the thing on his shoulders.

"What'cha got?" he grinned. "I brought this along. Nothing else in that shack, so we're complete except for the remnants of some very badly corroded cable that ran from this thing to a flapping end down where the tower was broken."

Barney smiled and blinked. It was strange to see this big man working studiously over a book; Barney Carroll should have been leading a horde of Venusian engineers through the Palanortis country instead of delving into the artifacts of a dead civilization.

"I think that this thing is a sort of engineer's handbook," he said. "In the front there is a section devoted to mathematical tables. You know, a table of logs to the base twelve which is because the Martians had six fingers on each hand. There is what seems to be a table of definite integrals—at least if I were writing a handbook I'd place the table of integrals at the last part of the math section. The geometry and trig is absolutely recognizable because of the designs. So is the solid geom and the analyt for the same reason. The next section seems to be devoted to chemistry; the Martians used a hexagonal figure for a benzene ring, too, and so that's established. From that we find the key to the Periodic Chart of the Atoms which is run vertically instead of horizontally, but still unique. These guys were sharp, though; they seem to have hit upon the fact that isotopes are separate elements though so close in grouping to one another that they exhibit the same properties. Finding this will uncover a lot of mystery."

"Yeah," agreed Baler, "from a book of this kind we can decipher most anything. The keying on a volume of physical constants is perfect and almost infinite in number. What do they use for Pi?"

"Circle with a double dot inside."

"And Plank's Constant?"

"Haven't hit that one yet. But we will. But to get back to the meat of this thing, the third section deals with something strange. It seems to have a bearing on this gadget from the top of the tower. I'd say that the volume was a technical volume on the construction, maintenance, and repair of the tower and its functions—whatever they are."

Barney spread the volume out for Jim to see. "That dingbat is some sort of electronic device. Or, perhaps subelectronic. Peel away that rusted side and we'll look inside."

Jim peeled a six-inch section from the side of the big metal tube, and they inspected the insides. Barney looked thoughtful for a minute and then flipped the pages of the book until he came to a diagram.

"Sure," he said exultantly, "this is she. Look, Jim, they draw a cathode like this, and the grids are made with a series of fine parallel lines. Different, but more like the real grid than our symbol of a zigzag line. The plate is a round circle instead of a square, but that's so clearly defined that it comes out automatically. Here's your annular electrodes, and the . . . call 'em deflection plates. I think we can hook this do-boodle up as soon as we get to our place in Lincoln Head."

"Let's go then. Not only would I like to see this thing work, but I'd give anything to know what it's for!"

"You run the crate," said Barney, "and I'll try to decipher this mess into voltages for the electrode-supply and so on. Then we'll be in shape to go ahead and hook her up."

The trip to Lincoln Head took almost an hour. Barney and Jim landed in their landing yards and took the book and the searchlight-thing inside. They went to their laboratory, and called for sandwiches and tea. Jim's sister brought in the food a little later and found them tinkering with the big beam tube.

"What have you got this time?" she groaned.

"Name it and it's yours," laughed Barney.

"A sort of gadget that we found on the Red Desert."

"What does it do?" asked Christine Baler.

"Well," said Jim, "it's a sort of a kind of a dingbat that does things."

"Uh-huh," said Christine. "A dololly that plings the inghams."

"Right!"

"You're well met, you two. Have your fun. But for Pete's sake don't forget to eat. Not that you will, I know you, but a girl has got to make some sort of attempt at admonishment. I'm going to the moompicher. I'll see you when I return."

"I'd say stick around," said Barney. "But I don't think we'll have anything to show you for hours and hours. We'll have something by the time you return."

Christine left, and the men applied themselves to their problem. Barney had done wonders in unraveling the unknown. Inductances, he found, were spirals; resistance were dotted lines; capacitances were parallel squares.

"What kind of stuff do we use for voltages?" asked Jim.

"That's a long, hard trail," laughed Barney. "Basing my calculations on the fact that their standard voltage cell was the same as ours, we apply the voltages as listed on my schematic here."

"Can you assume that their standard is the same as ours?"

"Better," said Barney. "The Terran Standard Cell—the well-known Weston Cell—dishes out what we call 1.0183 volts at twenty degrees C. Since the Martian description of their Standard Cell is essentially the same as the Terran, they are using the same thing. Only they use sense and say that a volt is the unit of a standard cell, period. Calculating their figures on the numerical base of twelve is tricky, but I've done it."

"You're doing fine. How do you assume their standard is the same?"

"Simple," said Barney in a cheerful tone. "Thank God for their habit of drawing pictures. Here we have the well-known H tube. The electrodes are signified by the symbols for the elements used. The Periodic Chart in the first section came in handy here. But look, master mind, this dinky should be evacuated, don't you think?"

"If it's electronic or subelectronic, it should be. We can solder up this breach here and apply the hyvac pump. Rig us up a power supply whilst I repair the blowout."

"Where's the BFO?"

"What do you want with that?" asked Jim.

"The second anode takes about two hundred volts worth of eighty-four cycles," explained Barney. "Has a sign that seems to signify 'In Phase,' but I'll be darned if I know with what. Y'know, Jim, this dingbat looks an awful lot like one of the drivers we use in our spaceships and driver-wing fliers."

"Yeah," drawled Jim. "About the same recognition as the difference between Edison's first electric light and a twelve-element, electron multiplier, a power output tube. Similarity: They both have cathodes."

"Edison didn't have a cathode—"

"Sure he did. Just because he didn't hang a plate inside of the bottle doesn't stop the filament from being a cathode."

Barney snorted. "A monode, hey?"

"Precisely. After which come diodes, triodes, tetrodes, pentodes, hexodes, heptodes—"

"—and the men in the white coats. How's your patching job?"

"Fine. How's your power-supply job?"

"Good enough," said Barney. "This eighty-four cycles is not going to be a sine wave at two hundred volts; the power stage of the BFO overloads just enough to bring in a bit of second harmonic."

"A beat-frequency-oscillator was never made to run at that level," complained Jim Baler. "At least, not this one. She'll tick on a bit of second, I think."

"Are we ready for the great experiment?"

"Yup, and I still wish I knew what the thing was for. Go ahead, Barney. Crack the big switch!"

Altas held up a restraining hand as Than grasped the main power switch. "Wait," he said. "Does one stand in his sky flier and leave the ground at full velocity? Or does one start an internal combustion engine at full speed?"

"No," said the youngster. "We usually take it slowly."

"And like the others, we must tune our tube. And that we cannot do under full power. Advance your power lever one-tenth step and we'll adjust the deflection anodes."

"I'll get the equipment," said Than. "I forgot that part."

"Never mind the equipment," smiled Altas. "Observe."

Altas picked up a long screwdriverlike tool and inserted it into the maze of wiring that surrounded the tube. Squinting in one end of the big tube, he turned the tool until the cathode surface brightened slightly. He adjusted the instrument until the cathode was at its brightest, and then withdrew the tool.

"That will do for your experimental set-up," smiled Altas. "The operation in service is far more critical and requires equipment. As an experiment, conducted singly, the accumulative effect cannot be dangerous, though if the deflection plates are not properly served with their supply voltages, the experiment is a failure. The operation of the tube depends upon the perfection of the deflection-plate voltages."

"No equipment is required, then?"

"It should have been employed," said Altas modestly. "But in my years as a beam-tower attendant, I have learned the art of aligning the plates by eye. Now, son, we may proceed from there."

Barney Carroll took a deep breath and let the power switch fall home. Current meters swung across their scales for an instant, and then the lights went out in the house!

"Fuse blew," said Barney shortly. He fumbled his way through the dark house and replaced the fuse. He returned smiling. "Fixed that one," he told Jim. "Put a washer behind it."

"O.K. Hit the switch again."

Barney cranked the power over, and once more the meters climbed up across the scales. There was a groaning sound from the tube, and the smell of burning insulation filled the room. One meter blew with an audible sound as the needle hit the end stop, and immediately afterward the lights in the entire block went out.

"Fix that one by hanging a penny behind it," said Jim with a grin.

"That's a job for Martian Electric to do," laughed Barney.

Several blocks from there, an attendant in the substation found the open circuit-breaker and shoved it in with a grim smile. He looked up at the power-demand meter and grunted. High for this district, but not dangerous. Duration, approximately fifteen seconds. Intensity, higher than usual but not high enough to diagnose any failure of the wiring in the district. "Ah, well," he thought, "we can crank up the blow-point on this breaker if it happens again."

He turned to leave and the crashing of the breaker scared him out of a week's growth. He snarled and said a few choice words not fit for publication. He closed the breaker and screwed the blow-point control up by two-to-one. "That'll hold 'em," he thought, and then the ringing of the telephone called him to his office, and he knew that he was in for an explanatory session with some people who wanted to know why their lights were going on and off. He composed a plausible tale on his way to the phone. Meanwhile, he wondered about the unreasonable demand and concluded that one of the folks had just purchased a new power saw or something for their home workshop.

"Crack the juice about a half," suggested Barney. "That'll keep us on the air until we find out what kind of stuff this thing takes. The book claims about one tenth of the current-drain for this unit. Something we've missed, no doubt."

"Let's see that circuit," said Jim. After a minute, he said: "Look, guy, what are these screws for?"

"They change the side plate voltages from about three hundred to about three hundred and fifty. I've got 'em set in the middle of the range."

"Turn us on half voltage and diddle one of 'em."

"That much of a change shouldn't make the difference," objected Barney.

"Brother, we don't know what this thing is even for," reminded Jim. "Much less do we know the effect of anything on it. Diddle, I say."

"O.K., we diddle." Barney turned on half power and reached into the maze of wiring and began to tinker with one of the screws. "Hm-m-m," he said after a minute. "Does things, all right. She goes through some kind of resonance point or something. There is a spot of minimum current here. There! I've hit it. Now for the other one."

For an hour, Barney tinkered with first one screw and then the other one. He found a point where the minimum current was really low; the two screws were interdependent and only by adjusting them alternately was he able to reach the proper point on each. Then he smiled and thrust the power on full. The current remained at a sane value.

"Now what?" asked Barney.

"I don't know. Anything coming out of the business end?"

"Heat."

"Yeah, and it's about as lethal as a sun lamp. D'ye suppose the Martians used to artificially assist their crop by synthetic sunshine?"

Barney applied his eye to a spectroscope. It was one of the newer designs that encompassed everything from short ultraviolet to long infrared by means of fluorescent screens at the invisible wave lengths. He turned the instrument across the spectrum and shook his head. "Might be good for a chest cold," he said, "but you wouldn't get a sunburn off of it. It's all in the infra. Drops off like a cliff just below the deep red. Nothing at all in the visible or above. Gee," he said with a queer smile, "you don't suppose that they died off because of a pernicious epidemic of colds and they tried chest-cooking *en masse?*"

"I'd believe anything if this darned gadget were found in a populated district," said Jim. "But we know that the desert was here when the Martians were here, and that it was just as arid as it is now. They wouldn't try farming in a place where iron oxide abounds."

"Spinach?"

"You don't know a lot about farming, do you?" asked Jim.

"I saw a cow once."

"That does not qualify you as an expert on farming."

"I know one about the farmer's daughter, and—"

"Not even an expert on dirt farming," continued Jim. "Nope, Barney, we aren't even close."

Barney checked the book once more and scratched his nose.

"How about that eighty-four cycle supply," asked Jim.

"It's eighty-four, all right. From the Martian habit of using twelve as a base, I've calculated the number to be eighty-four."

"Diddle that, too," suggested Jim.

"O.K.," said Barney. "It doesn't take a lot to crank that one around from zero to about fifteen thousand c.p.s. Here she goes!"

Barney took the main dial of the beat-frequency oscillator and began to crank it around the scale. He went up from eighty-four to the top of the dial and then returned. No effect. Then he passed through eighty-four and started down toward zero.

He hit sixty cycles and the jackpot at the same time!

At exactly sixty cycles, a light near the wall dimmed visibly. The wallpaper scorched and burst into a smoldering flame on a wall opposite the dimmed light.

Barney removed the BFO from the vicinity of sixty cycles and Jim extinguished the burning wallpaper.

"Now we're getting somewhere," said Barney.

"This is definitely some sort of weapon," said Jim. "She's not very efficient right now, but we can find out why and then we'll have something hot."

"What for?" asked Barney. "Nobody hates anybody any more."

"Unless the birds who made this thing necessary return," said Jim soberly. His voice was ominous. "We know that only one race of Martians existed, and they were all amicable. I suspect an inimical race from outer space—"

"Could be. Some of the boys are talking about an expedition to Centauri right now. We could have had a visitor from somewhere during the past."

"If you define eternity as the time required for everything to happen once, I agree. In the past or in the future, we have or will be visited by a super race. It may have happened six thousand years ago."

"Did you notice that the electric light is not quite in line with the axis of the tube?" asked Barney.

"Don't turn it any closer," said Jim. "In fact, I'd turn it away before we hook it up again."

"There she is. Completely out of line with the light. Now shall we try it again?"

"Go ahead."

Barney turned the BFO gingerly, and at sixty cycles the thing seemed quite sane. Nothing happened. "Shall I swing it around?"

"I don't care for fires as a general rule," said Jim. "Especially in my own home. Turn it gently, and take care that you don't focus the tube full on that electric light."

Barney moved the tube slightly, and then with a cessation of noise, the clock on the wall stopped abruptly. The accustomed ticking had not been noticed by either man, but the unaccustomed lack-of-ticking became evident at once. Barney shut off the BFO immediately and the two men sat down to a head-scratching session.

"She's good for burning wallpaper, dimming electric lights, and stopping clocks," said Barney. "Any of which you could do without a warehouse full of cockeyed electrical equipment. Wonder if she'd stop anything more powerful than a clock."

"I've got a quarter-horse motor here. Let's wind that up and try it."

The motor was installed on a bench nearby, and the experiment was tried again. At sixty cycles the motor groaned to a stop, and the windings began to smolder. But at the same time the big tube began to exhibit the signs of strain. Meters raced up their scales once more, reached the stops and bent. Barney shut off the motor, but the strains did not stop in the tube. The apparent overload increased linearly and finally the lights went out all over the neighborhood once more.

"Wonderful," said Barney through the darkness. "As a weapon, this thing is surpassed by everything above a fly swatter."

"We might be able to cook a steak with it—if it would take the terrific overload," said Jim. "Or we could use it as an insect exterminator."

"We'd do better by putting the insect on an anvil and hitting it firmly with a five-pound hammer," said Barney. "Then we'd only have the anvil and hammer to haul around. This thing is like hauling a fifty-thousand-watt radio transmitter around. Power supplies, BFO, tube, meters, tools, and a huge truck full of spare fuses for the times when we miss the insect. Might be good for a central heating system."

"Except that a standard electric unit is more reliable and considerably less complicated. You'd have to hire a corps of engineers to run the thing."

The lights went on again, and the attendant in the substation screwed the blow-point control tighter. He didn't know it, but his level was now above the rating for his station. But had he known it he might not have cared. At least, his station was once more in operation.

"Well," said Barney, getting up from the table, "what have we missed?"

Altas said: "Now your unit is operating at its correct level. But, son, you've missed one thing. It is far from efficient. Those two leads must be isolated from one another. Coupling from one to the other will lead to losses."

"Gosh," said Than, "I didn't know that."

"No, for some reason the books assume that the tower engineer has had considerable experience in the art. Take it from me, son, there are a lot of things that are not in the books. Now isolate those leads from one another and we'll go on."

"While you're thinking," said Jim, "I'm going to lockstitch these cables together. It'll make this thing less messy." Jim got a roll of twelve-cord from the cabinet and began to bind the many supply leads into a neat cable.

Barney watched until the job was finished, and then said: "Look, chum, let's try that electric-light trick again."

They swung the tube around until it was in the original position, and turned the juice on. Nothing happened.

Barney looked at Jim, and then reached out and pointed the big tube right at the electric light.

Nothing happened.

"Check your anode voltages again."

"All O.K."

"How about that aligning job?"

Barney fiddled with the alignment screws for minutes, but his original setting seemed to be valid.

"Back to normal," said Barney. "Rip out your cabling."

"Huh?"

"Sure. You did something. I don't know what. But rip it out and fan out the leads. There is something screwy in the supply lines. I've been tied up on that one before; this thing looks like electronics, as we agree, and I've had occasion to remember coupling troubles."

"All right," said Jim, and he reluctantly ripped out his lock-stitching. He fanned the leads and they tried it again.

Obediently the light dimmed and the wallpaper burned.

"Here we go again," said Jim, killing the circuits and reaching for a small rug to smother the fire. "No wonder the Martians had this thing out in the middle of the desert. D'ye suppose that they were trying to find out how it works, too?"

"Take it easier this time and we'll fan the various leads," said Barney. "There's something tricky about the lead placement."

"Half power," announced Barney. "Now, let's get that sixty cycles."

The light dimmed slightly and a sheet of metal placed in front of the tube became slightly warm to the touch. The plate stopped the output of the tube, for the wallpaper did not scorch. Jim began to take supply line after supply line from the bundle of wiring. About halfway through the mess he hit the critical lead, and immediately the light went out completely, and the plate grew quite hot.

"Stop her!" yelled Barney.

"Why?"

"How do we know what we're overloading this time?"

"Do we care?"

"Sure. Let's point this thing away from that light. Then we can hop it up again and try it at full power."

"What do you want to try?"

"This energy-absorption thing."

"Wanna burn out my motor?"

"Not completely. This dingbat will stop a completely mechanical gadget like a clock. It seems to draw power from electric lights. It stops electromechanical power. I wonder just how far it will go toward absorbing power. And also I want to know where the power goes."

The tube was made to stop the clock again. The motor groaned under the load put upon it by the tube. Apparently the action of the tube was similar to a heavy load being placed on whatever its end happened to point to. Barney picked up a small metal block and dropped it over the table.

"Want to see if it absorbs the energy of a falling object— Look at that!"

The block fell until it came inside of the influence of the tube. Then it slowed in its fall and approached the table slowly. It did not hit the table, it touched and came to rest.

"What happens if we wind up a spring and tie it?" asked Jim.

They tried it. Nothing happened.

"Works on kinetic energy, not potential energy," said Barney.

He picked up a heavy hammer and tried to hit the table. "Like swinging a club through a tub of water," he said.

"Be a useful gadget for saving the lives of people who are falling," said Jim thoughtfully.

"Oh, sure. Put it on a truck and rush it out to the scene of the suicide."

"No. How about people jumping out of windows on account of fires? How about having one of the things around during a flier-training course? Think of letting a safe down on one of these beams, or taking a piano from the fifth floor of an apartment building."

"The whole apartment full of furniture could be pitched out of a window," said Barney.

"Mine looks that way now," said Jim, "and we've only moved a couple of times. No, Barney, don't give 'em any ideas."

Jim picked up the hammer and tried to hit the table. Then, idly, he swung the hammer in the direction of the tube's end.

Barney gasped. In this direction there was no resistance. Jim's swing continued, and the look on Jim's face indicated that he was trying to brake the swing in time to keep from hitting the end of the tube. But it seemed as though he were trying to stop an avalanche. The swing continued on and on and finally ended when the hammer head contacted the end of the tube.

There was a burst of fire. Jim swung right on through, whirling around off balance and coming to a stop only when he fell to the floor. He landed in darkness again. The burst of fire emanated from the insulation as it flamed under the heat of extreme overload.

This time the lights were out all over Lincoln Head. The whole city was in complete blackout!

Candles were found, and they inspected the tube anxiously. It seemed whole. But the hammer head was missing. The handle was cut cleanly, on an optically perfect surface.

Where the hammer head went, they couldn't say. But on the opposite wall there was a fracture in the plaster that Jim swore hadn't been there before. It extended over quite an area, and after some thought, Barney calculated that if the force of Jim's hammer blow had been evenly distributed over that area on the wall, the fracturing would have been just about that bad.

"A weapon, all right," said Barney.

"Sure. All you have to do is to shoot your gun right in this end and the force is dissipated over quite an area out of that end. In the meantime you blow out all of the powerhouses on the planet. If a hammer blow can raise such merry hell, what do you think the output of a sixteen-inch rifle would do? Probably stop the planet in its tracks. D'ye know what I think?"

"No, do you?"

"Barney, I think that we aren't even close as to the operation and use of this device."

"For that decision, Jim, you should be awarded the Interplanetary Award for Discovery and Invention—posthumously!"

"So what do we do now?"

"Dunno. How soon does this lighting situation get itself fixed?"

"You ask me . . . I don't know either."

"Well, let's see what we've found so far."

"That's easy," said Jim. "It might be a weapon, but it don't weap. We might use it for letting elevators down easy, except that it would be a shame to tie up a room full of equipment when the three-phase electric motor is so simple. We could toast a bit of bread, but the electric toaster has been refined to a beautiful piece of breakfast furniture that doesn't spray off and scorch the wallpaper. We could use it to transmit hammer blows, or to turn out electric lights, but both of those things have been done very simply; one by means of sending the hammerer to the spot, and the other by means of turning the switch. And then in the last couple of cases, there is little sense in turning out a light by short circuiting the socket and blowing all the fuses."

"That is the hard way," smiled Barney. "Like hitting a telephone pole to stop the car, or cutting the wings off a plane to return it to the ground."

"So we have a fairly lucid book that describes the entire hook-up of the thing except what it's for. It gives not only the use of this device, but also variations and replacements. Could we figure it out by sheer deduction?"

"I don't see how. The tower is in the midst of the Red Desert. There is nothing but sand that assays high in iron oxide between Canalopsis, at the junction of the Grand Canal and Lincoln Head. Might be hid, of course, just as this one was, and we'll send out a crew of expert sub-sand explorers with under-surface detectors to cover the ground for a few hundred miles in any direction from the place where we found this. Somehow, I doubt that we'll find much."

"And how do you . . . ah, there's the lights again . . . deduce that?" asked Jim.

"This gadget is or was of importance to the Martians. Yet in the Temple of Science and Industry at Canalopsis, there is scant mention of the towers."

"Not very much, hey?"

"Very little, in fact. Of course the pictographs on the Temple at Canalopsis show one tower between what appeared to be two cities. Wavy lines run from one city to the tower and to the other city. Say! I'll bet a cooky that this is some sort of signaling device!"

"A beam transmitter?" asked Jim skeptically. "Seems like a lot of junk for just signaling. Especially where such a swell job can be done with standard radio equipment. A good civilization—such as the Martians must have had—wouldn't piddle around with relay stations between two cities less than a couple of thousand miles apart. With all the juice this thing can suck, they'd be more than able to hang a straight broadcast station and cover halfway around the planet as ground-wave area. What price relay station?"

"Nevertheless, I'm going to tinker up another one of these and see if it is some sort of signaling equipment."

The door opened and Christine Baler entered. She waved a newspaper before her brother's eyes and said: "Boy, have you been missing it!"

"What?" asked Barney.

"Pixies or gremlins loose in Lincoln Head."

"Huh-huh. Read it," said Jim.

"Just a bunch of flash headlines. Fire on Manley Avenue. Three planes had to make dead-tube landings in the center of the city; power went dead for no good reason for about ten minutes. Façade of the City Hall caved in.

Power plants running wild all over the place. Ten thousand dollars' worth of electrical equipment blown out. Automobiles stalled in rows for blocks."

Jim looked at Barney. "Got a bear by the tail," he said.

"Could be," admitted Barney.

"Are you two blithering geniuses going to work all night?" asked Christine.

"Nope. We're about out of ideas. Except the one that Barney had about the gadget being some sort of signaling system."

"Why don't you fellows call Don Channing? He's the signaling wizard of the Solar System."

"Sure, call Channing. Every time someone gets an idea, everyone says, 'Call Channing!' He gets called for everything from Boy Scout wigwag ideas to super-cyclotronic-electron-stream beams to contact the outer planets. Based upon the supposition that people will eventually get there, of course."

"Well?"

"Well, I . . . we, I mean . . . found this thing and we're jolly well going to tinker it out. In spite of the fact that it seems to bollix up everything from electric lights to moving gears. I think we're guilty of sabotage. Façade of the City Hall, et cetera. Barney, how long do you think it will take to tinker up another one of these?"

"Few hours. They're doggoned simple things in spite of the fact that we can't understand them. In fact, I'm of the opinion that the real idea would be to make two; one with only the front end for reception, one for the rear end for transmission, and the one we found for relaying. That's the natural bent, I believe."

"Could be. Where are you going to cut them?"

"The transmitter will start just before the cathode and the receiver will end just after the . . . uh, cathode."

"Huh?"

"Obviously the cathode is the baby that makes with the end product. She seems to be a total intake from the intake end and a complete output from the opposite end. Right?"

"Right, but it certainly sounds like heresy."

"I know," said Barney thoughtfully, "but the thing is obviously different from anything that we know today. Who knows how she works?"

"I give up."

Christine, who had been listening in an interested manner, said: "You fellers are the guys responsible for the ruckus that's been going on all over Lincoln Head?"

"I'm afraid so."

"Well, brother warlocks, unless you keep your activities under cover until they're worth mentioning, you'll both be due for burning at the stake."

"O.K., Chris," said Jim. "We'll not let it out."

"But how are you going to tinker up that transmitter-relay-receiver system?"

"We'll take it from here to Barney's place across the avenue and into his garage. That should do it."

"O.K., but now I'm going to bed."

"Shall we knock off, too?" asked Jim.

"Yup. Maybe we'll dream a good thought."

"So long then. We'll leave the mess as it is. No use cleaning up now, we'll only have to mess it up again tomorrow with the same junk."

"And I'll have that—or those—other systems tinkered together by tomorrow noon. That's a promise," said Barney. "And you," he said to Christine, "will operate the relay station."

Altas said to Than: "Now that your system is balanced properly, and we have proved the worth of this tube as a replacement, we shall take it to the roof and install it. The present tube is about due for retirement."

"I've done well, then?" asked Than.

"Considering all, you've done admirably. But balancing the device in the tower, and hooked into the circuit as an integral part is another thing. Come, Than. We shall close the line for an hour whilst replacing the tube."

"Is that permissible?"

"At this time of the night the requirements are small. No damage will be done; they can get along without us for an hour. In fact, at this time of night, only the people who are running the city will know that we are out of service. And it is necessary that the tube be maintained at full capability. We can not chance a weakened tube; it might fail when it is needed the most."

Than carried the tube to the top of the tower, and Altas remained to contact the necessary parties concerning the shut-off for replacement purposes. He followed Than to the top after a time and said: "Now disconnect the old tube and put it on the floor. We shall replace the tube immediately, but it will be an hour before it is properly balanced again."

It was not long before Than had the tube connected properly. "Now," said Altas, "turn it on one-tenth power and we shall align it."

"Shall I use the meters?"

"I think it best. This requires perfect alignment now. We've much power and considerable distance, and any losses will create great amounts of heat."

"All right," said Than. He left the tower top to get the meters.

Barney Carroll spoke into a conveniently placed microphone. "Are you ready?" he asked.

"Go ahead," said Christine.

"We're waiting," said Jim.

"You're the bird on the transmitter," said Barney to Jim. "*You* make with the juice."

Power rheostats were turned up gingerly, until Jim shouted to stop. His shout was blotted out by cries from the other two. They met in Barney's place to confer.

"What's cooking?" asked Jim.

"The meters are all going crazy in my end," said Barney. "I seem to be sucking power out of everything in line with my tube."

"The so-called relay station is firing away at full power and doing nothing but draining plenty of power from the line," complained Christine.

"And on my end, I was beginning to scorch the wallpaper again. I don't understand it. With no receiver-end, how can I scorch wallpaper?"

"Ask the Martians. They know."

"You ask 'em. What shall we do, invent a time machine and go back sixty centuries?"

"Wish we could," said Barney. "I'd like to ask the bird that left this textbook why they didn't clarify it more."

"Speaking of Don Channing again," said Jim, "I'll bet a hat that one of his tube-replacement manuals for the big transmitters out on Venus Equilateral do not even mention that the transmitter requires a receiver before it is any good. We think we're modern. We are, and we never think that some day some poor bird will try to decipher our technical works. Why, if Volta himself came back and saw the most perfect machine ever invented—the transformer—he'd shudder. No connection between input and output, several kinds of shorted loops of wire; and instead of making a nice simple electromagnet, we short the lines of force and on top of that we use a lot of laminations piled on top of one another instead of a nice, soft iron core. We completely short the input, et cetera, but how do we make with a gadget like that?"

"I know. We go on expecting to advance. We forget the simple past. Remember the lines of that story: 'How does one chip the flint to make the best arrowhead?' I don't know who wrote it any more than I know how to skin a boar, but we do get on without making arrowheads or skinning boars or trimming birch-bark canoes."

"All right, but there's still this problem."

"Remember how we managed to align this thing? I wonder it it might not take another alignment to make it work as a relay."

"Could be," said Jim. "I'll try it. Christine, you work these screws at the same time we do, and make the current come out as low as we can."

They returned to their stations and began to work on the alignment screws. Jim came out first on the receiver. Christine was second on the transmitter, while Barney fumbled for a long time with the relay tube.

Then Christine called: "Fellows, my meter readings are climbing up again. Shall I diddle?"

"Wait a minute," said Barney. "That means I'm probably taking power out of that gadget you have in there. Leave 'em alone."

He fiddled a bit more, and then Jim called: "Whoa, Nellie. Someone just lost me a millimeter. She wound up on the far end."

"Hm-m-m," said Barney, "so we're relaying."

"Go ahead," said Jim. "I've got a ten-ampere meter on here now."

Barney adjusted his screws some more.

"Wait a minute," said Jim. "I'm going to shunt this meter up to a hundred amps."

"What?" yelled Barney.

"Must you yell?" asked Christine ruefully. "These phones are plenty uncomfortable without some loud-mouthed bird screaming."

"Sorry, but a hundred amps . . . *whoosh!* What have we got here, anyway?"

"Yeah," said Christine. "I was about to say that my input meter is running wild again."

"Gone?"

"Completely. You shouldn't have hidden it behind that big box. I didn't notice it until just now, but she's completely gone."

"I'll be over. I think we've got something here."

An hour passed, during which nothing of any great importance happened. By keying the transmitter tube, meters in the receiver tube were made to read in accordance. Then they had another conclave.

"Nothing brilliant," said Jim. "We could use super-output voice amplifiers and yell halfway across the planet if we didn't have radio. We can radio far better than this cockeyed system of signaling."

"We might cut the power."

"Or spread out quite a bit. I still say, however, that this is no signaling system."

"It works like one."

"So can a clothesline be made to serve as a transmitter of intelligence. But it's prime function is completely different."

"S'pose we have a super-clothesline here?" asked Christine.

"The way that hammer felt last night, I'm not too sure that this might not be some sort of tractor beam," said Jim.

"Tractor beams are mathematically impossible."

"Yeah, and they proved conclusively that a bird cannot fly," said Jim. "That was before they found the right kind of math. Up until Clerk Maxwell's time, radio was mathematically impossible. Then he discovered the electromagnetic equations, and we're squirting signals across the Inner System every day. And when math and fact do not agree, which changes?"

"The math. Galileo proved that. Aristotle said that a heavy stone will fall faster. Then Galileo changed the math of that by heaving a couple of boulders off the Leaning Tower. But what have we here?"

"Has anyone toyed with the transmission of power?"

"Sure. A lot of science-fiction writers have their imaginary planets crisscrossed with transmitted power. Some broadcast it, some have it beamed to the consumer. When they use planes, they have the beam coupled to an object-finder so as to control the direction of the beam. I prefer the broadcasting, myself. It uncomplicates the structure of the tale."

"I mean actually?"

"Oh, yes. But the losses are terrific. Useful power transmission is a minute percentage of the total output of the gadget. Absolutely impractical, especially when copper and silver are so plentiful to string along the scenery on steel towers. No good."

"But look at this cockeyed thing. Christine puts in a couple of hundred amps; I take them off my end. Believe it or not, the output meter at my end was getting a lot more soup than I was pouring in."

"And my gadget was not taking anything to speak of," said Barney. "Supposing it was a means of transmitting power. How on Mars did they use a single tower there in the middle of the Red Desert? We know there was a Martian city at Canalopsis, and another one not many miles from Lincoln Head. Scribbled on the outer cover of this book is the legend: 'Tower Station, Red Desert,' and though the Martians didn't call this the 'Red Desert,' the terminology will suffice for nomenclature."

"Well?" asked Jim.

"You notice they did not say: 'Station No. 1,' or '3' or '7.' That means to me that there was but one."

"Holy Smoke! Fifteen hundred miles with only one station? On Mars the curvature of ground would put such a station below the electrical horizon—" Jim thought that one over for a minute and then said: "Don't tell me they bent the beam?"

"Either they did that or they heated up the sand between," said Barney cryptically. "It doesn't mind going through nonconducting walls, but a nice, fat ground . . . blooey, or I miss my guess. That'd be like grounding a high line."

"You're saying that they did bend— *Whoosh*, again!"

"What was that alignment problem? Didn't we align the deflecting anodes somehow?"

"Yeah, but you can't bend the output of a cathode ray tube externally of the deflection plates."

"But this is not electron-beam stuff," objected Barney. "This is as far ahead of cathode-ray tubes as they are ahead of the Indian signal drum or the guy who used to run for twenty-four miles from Ghent to Aix."

"That one was from Athens to Sparta," explained Christine, "the Ghent to Aix journey was a-horseback, and some thousand-odd years after."

"Simile's still good," said Barney. "There's still a lot about this I do not understand."

"A masterpiece of understatement, if I ever heard one," laughed Jim. "Well, let's work on it from that angle. Come on, gang, to horse!"

"Now," said Altas, "you will find that the best possible efficiency is obtained when the currents in these two resistances are equal and opposite in direction. That floats the whole tube on the system, and makes it possible to run the tube without any external power source. It requires a starter-source for aligning and for standby service, and for the initial surge; then it is self-sustaining. Also the in-phase voltage can not better be obtained than by exciting the phasing anode with some of the main-line power. That must always be correctly phased. We now need the frequency generator no longer, and by increasing the power rheostat to full, the tube will take up the load. Watch the meters, and when they read full power, you may throw the cut-over switch and make the tube self-sustaining. Our tower will then be in perfect service, and you and I may return to our home below."

Than performed the operations, and then they left, taking the old tube with them.

And on Terra, Sargon of Akkad watched ten thousand slaves carry stone for one of his public buildings. He did not know that on one of the stars placed in the black bowl of the evening sky for his personal benefit, men were flinging more power through the air than the total output of all of his slaves combined. Had he been told, he would have had the teller beheaded for lying because Sargon of Akkad couldn't possibly have understood it—

"You know, we're missing a bet," said Jim. "This in-phase business here. Why shouldn't we hang a bit of the old wall-socket juice in here?"

"That might be the trick," said Barney.

Jim made the connections, and they watched the meters read up and up and up—and from the street below them a rumbling was heard. Smoke issued from a crevasse in the pavement, and then with a roar, the street erupted and a furrow three feet wide and all the way across the street from Jim Baler's residence to Barney Carroll's garage lifted out of the ground. It blew straight up and fell back, and from the bottom of the furrow the smoldering of burned and tortured wiring cast a foul smell.

"*Wham!*" said Barney, looking at the smoking trench. "What was that?"

"I think we'll find that it was the closest connection between our places made by the Electric Co.," said Jim.

"But what have we done?"

"I enumerate," said Christine, counting off on her fingers. "We've blasted in the façade of the City Hall. We've caused a couple of emergency flier-landings within the city limits. We've blown fuses and circuit breakers all the way from here to the main powerhouse downtown. We've stalled a few dozen automobiles. We've torn or burned or cut the end off of one hammer and have fractured the wall with it . . . where did that go, anyway, the hammerhead? We've burned wallpaper. We've run our electric bill up to about three hundred dollars, I'll bet. We've bunged up a dozen meters. And now we've ripped up a trench in the middle of the street."

"Somewhere in this set-up, there is a return circuit," said Jim thoughtfully. "We've been taking power out of the line, and I've been oblivious of the fact that a couple of hundred amperes is too high to get out of our power line without trouble. What we've been doing is taking enough soup out of the public utility lines to supply the losses only. The power we've been seeing on our meters is the build-up, recirculated!"

"Huh?"

"Sure. Say we bring an amp in from the outside and shoot it across the street. It goes to the wires and comes back because of some electrical urge in our gadgets here, and then goes across the street inphase with the original. That makes two amps total crossing our beam. The two come back and we have two plus two. Four come back, and we double again and again until the capability of our device is at saturation. All we have to do is to find the ground-return and hang a load in there. We find the transmitter-load input, and supply that with a generator. Brother, we can beam power all the way from here to Canalopsis on one relay tower!"

Barney looked at his friend. "Could be."

"Darned right. What other item can you think of that fits this tower any better? We've run down a dozen ideas, but this works. We may be arrested for wrecking Lincoln Head, but we'll get out as soon as this dingbat hits the market. Brother, what a find!"

"Fellows, I think you can make your announcement now," smiled Christine. "They won't burn you at the stake if you can bring electric power on a beam of pure nothing. This time you've hit the jackpot!"

It is six thousand Terran Years since Sargon of Akkad held court that was lighted by torch. It is six thousand years, Terran, since Than and Altas replaced the link in a power system that tied their cities together.

It is six thousand years since the beam tower fell into the Red Desert and the mighty system of beamed power became lost as an art. But once again the towers dot the plains, not only of Mars, but of Venus and Terra, too.

And though they are of a language understood by the peoples of three worlds, the manuals of instruction would be as cryptic to Than as his manual was to Barney Carroll and Jim Baler.

People will never learn.

THE OTHER SIDE OF THE SKY

by Arthur C. Clarke

SPECIAL DELIVERY

I CAN STILL REMEMBER the excitement, back in 1957, when Russia launched the first artificial satellites and managed to hang a few pounds of instruments up here above the atmosphere. Of course, I was only a kid at the time, but I went out in the evening like everyone else, trying to spot those little magnesium spheres as they zipped through the twilight sky hundreds of miles above my head. It's strange to think that some of them are still there—but that now they're *below* me, and I'd have to look down toward Earth if I wanted to see them. . . .

Yes, a lot has happened in the last forty years, and sometimes I'm afraid that you people down on Earth take the space stations for granted, forgetting the skill and science and courage that went to make them. How often do you stop to think that all your long-distance phone calls, and most of your TV programs, are routed through one or the other of the satellites? And how often do you give any credit to the meteorologists up here for the fact that weather forecasts are no longer the joke they were to our grandfathers, but are dead accurate ninety-nine per cent of the time?

It was a rugged life, back in the seventies, when I went up to work on the outer stations. They were being rushed into operation to open up the millions of new TV and radio circuits which would be available as soon as we had transmitters out in space that could beam programs to anywhere on the globe.

The first artificial satellites had been very close to Earth, but the three stations forming the great triangle of the Relay Chain had to be twenty-two thousand miles up, spaced equally around the equator. At this altitude—and at no other—they would take exactly a day to go around their orbit, and so would stay poised forever over the same spot on the turning Earth.

In my time I've worked on all three of the stations, but my first tour of duty was aboard Relay Two. That's almost exactly over Entebbe, Uganda, and provides service for Europe, Africa, and most of Asia. Today it's a huge structure hundreds of yards across, beaming thousands of simultaneous programs down to the hemisphere beneath it as it carries the radio traffic of half the world. But when I saw it for the first time from the port of the ferry rocket that carried me up to orbit, it looked like a junk pile adrift in space. Prefabricated parts were floating around in hopeless confusion, and it seemed impossible that any order could ever emerge from this chaos.

Accommodation for the technical staff and assembling crews was primitive, consisting of a few unserviceable ferry rockets that had been stripped of everything except air purifiers. "The Hulks," we christened them; each man had just enough room for himself and a couple of cubic feet of personal belongings. There was a fine irony in the fact that we were living in the midst of infinite space—and hadn't room to swing a cat.

It was a great day when we heard that the first pressurized living quarters were on their way up to us—complete with needle-jet shower baths that would operate even here, where water—like everything else—had no weight. Unless you've lived aboard an overcrowded spaceship, you won't appreciate what that meant. We could throw away our damp sponges and feel really clean at last. . . .

Nor were the showers the only luxury promised us. On the way up from Earth was an inflatable lounge spacious enough to hold no fewer than eight people, a microfilm library, a magnetic billiard table, lightweight chess sets, and similar novelties for bored spacemen. The very thought of all these comforts made our cramped life in the Hulks seem quite unendurable, even though we were being paid about a thousand dollars a week to endure it.

Starting from the Second Refueling Zone, two thousand miles above Earth, the eagerly awaited ferry rocket would take about six hours to climb up to us with its precious cargo. I was off duty at the time, and stationed myself at the telescope where I'd spent most of my scanty leisure. It was impossible to grow tired of exploring the great world hanging there in space beside us; with the highest power of the telescope, one seemed to be only a few miles above the surface. When there were no clouds and the seeing was good, objects the size of a small house were easily visible. I had never been to Africa, but I grew to know it well while I was off duty in Station Two. You may not believe this, but I've often spotted elephants moving across the plains, and the immense herds of zebras and antelopes were easy to see as they flowed back and forth like living tides on the great reservations.

But my favorite spectacle was the dawn coming up over the mountains in the heart of the continent. The line of sunlight would come sweeping across the Indian Ocean, and the new day would extinguish the tiny, twinkling galaxies of the cities shining in the darkness below me. Long before the sun had reached the lowlands around them, the peaks of Kilimanjaro and Mount Kenya would be blazing in the dawn, brilliant stars still surrounded by the night. As the sun rose higher, the day would march swiftly down their slopes and the valleys would fill with light. Earth would then be at its first quarter, waxing toward full.

Twelve hours later, I would see the reverse process as the same mountains caught the last rays of the setting sun. They would blaze for a little while in the narrow belt of twilight; then Earth would spin into darkness, and night would fall upon Africa.

It was not the beauty of the terrestrial globe I was concerned with now. Indeed, I was not even looking at Earth, but at the fierce blue-white star high above the western edge of the planet's disk. The automatic freighter was eclipsed in Earth's shadow; what I was seeing was the incandescent flare of its rockets as they drove it up on its twenty-thousand-mile climb.

I had watched ships ascending to us so often that I knew every stage of their maneuver by heart. So when the rockets didn't wink out, but continued to burn steadily, I knew within seconds that something was wrong. In sick, helpless fury I watched all our longed-for comforts—and, worse still, our mail!—moving faster and faster along the unintended orbit. The freighter's autopilot had jammed; had there been a human pilot aboard, he could have overridden the controls and cut the motor, but now all the fuel that should have driven the ferry on its two-way trip was being burned in one continuous blast of power.

By the time the fuel tanks had emptied, and that distant star had flickered and died in the field of my telescope, the tracking stations had confirmed what I already knew. The freighter was moving far too fast for Earth's gravity to recapture it—indeed, it was heading into the cosmic wilderness beyond Pluto. . . .

It took a long time for morale to recover, and it only made matters worse when someone in the computing section worked out the future history of our errant freighter. You see, nothing is ever really lost in space. Once you've calculated its orbit, you know where it is until the end of eternity. As we watched our lounge, our library, our games, our mail receding to the far horizons of the solar system, we knew that it would all come back one day, in perfect condition. If we have a ship standing by it will be easy to intercept it the second time it comes around the sun—quite early in the spring of the year A.D. 15,862.

FEATHERED FRIEND

To THE BEST OF MY KNOWLEDGE, there's never been a regulation that forbids one to keep pets in a space station. No one ever thought it was necessary—and even had such a rule existed, I am quite certain that Sven Olsen would have ignored it.

With a name like that, you will picture Sven at once as a six-foot-six Nordic giant, built like a bull and with a voice to match. Had this been so, his chances of getting a job in space would have been very slim; actually he was a wiry little fellow, like most of the early spacers, and managed to qualify easily for the 150-pound bonus that kept so many of us on a reducing diet.

Sven was one of our best construction men, and excelled at the tricky and specialized work of collecting assorted girders as they floated around in free fall, making them do the slow-motion, three-dimensional ballet that would get them into their right positions, and fusing the pieces together when they were precisely dovetailed into the intended pattern. I never tired of watching him and his gang as the station grew under their hands like a giant jigsaw puzzle; it was a skilled and difficult job, for a space suit is not the most convenient of garbs in which to work. However, Sven's team had one great advantage over the construction gangs you see putting up skyscrapers down on Earth. They could step back and admire their handiwork without being abruptly parted from it by gravity. . . .

Don't ask me why Sven wanted a pet, or why he chose the one he did. I'm not a psychologist, but I must admit that his selection was very sensible. Claribel weighed practically nothing, her food requirements were infinitesimal—and she was not worried, as most animals would have been, by the absence of gravity.

I first became aware that Claribel was aboard when I was sitting in the little cubbyhole laughingly called my office, checking through my lists of technical stores to decide what items we'd be running out of next. When I heard the musical whistle beside my ear, I assumed that it had come over the station intercom, and waited for an announcement to follow. It didn't; instead, there was a long and involved pattern of melody that made me look up with such a start that I forgot all about the angle beam just behind my head. When the stars had ceased to explode before my eyes, I had my first view of Claribel.

She was a small yellow canary, hanging in the air as motionless as a hummingbird—and with much less effort, for her wings were quietly folded along her sides. We stared at each other for a minute; then, before I had quite recovered my wits, she did a curious kind of backward loop I'm sure no earthbound canary had ever managed, and departed with a few leisurely flicks. It was quite obvious that she'd already learned how to operate in the absence of gravity, and did not believe in doing unnecessary work.

Sven didn't confess to her ownership for several days, and by that time it no longer mattered, because Claribel was a general pet. He had smuggled her up on the last ferry from Earth, when he came back from leave—partly, he claimed, out of sheer scientific curiosity. He wanted to see just how a bird would operate when it had no weight but could still use its wings.

Claribel thrived and grew fat. On the whole, we had little trouble concealing our unauthorized guest when VIP's from Earth came visiting. A space station has more hiding places than you can count; the only problem was that Claribel got rather noisy when she was upset, and we sometimes had to think fast to explain the curious peeps and whistles that came from ventilating shafts and storage bulkheads. There were a couple of narrow escapes—but then who would dream of looking for a canary in a space station?

We were now on twelve-hour watches, which was not as bad as it sounds, since you need little sleep in space. Though of course there is no "day" and "night" when you are floating in permanent sunlight, it was still convenient to stick to the terms. Certainly when I woke up that "morning" it felt like 6:00 A.M. on Earth. I had a nagging headache, and vague memories of fitful, disturbed dreams. It took me ages to undo my bunk straps, and I was still only half awake when I joined the remainder of the duty crew in the mess. Breakfast was unusually quiet, and there was one seat vacant.

"Where's Sven?" I asked, not very much caring.

"He's looking for Claribel," someone answered. "Says he can't find her anywhere. She usually wakes him up."

Before I could retort that she usually woke me up, too, Sven came in through the doorway, and we could see at once that something was wrong. He slowly opened his hand, and there lay a tiny bundle of yellow feathers, with two clenched claws sticking pathetically up into the air.

"What happened?" we asked, all equally distressed.

"I don't know," said Sven mournfully. "I just found her like this."

"Let's have a look at her," said Jock Duncan, our cook-doctor-dietitian. We all waited in hushed silence while he held Claribel against his ear in an attempt to detect any heartbeat.

Presently he shook his head. "I can't hear anything, but that doesn't prove she's dead. I've never listened to a canary's heart," he added rather apologetically.

"Give her a shot of oxygen," suggested somebody, pointing to the green-banded emergency cylinder in its recess beside the door. Everyone agreed that this was an excellent idea, and Claribel was tucked snugly into a face mask that was large enough to serve as a complete oxygen tent for her.

To our delighted surprise, she revived at once. Beaming broadly, Sven removed the mask, and she hopped onto his finger. She gave her series of "Come to the cookhouse, boys" trills—then promptly keeled over again.

"I don't get it," lamented Sven. "What's wrong with her? She's never done this before."

For the last few minutes, something had been tugging at my memory. My mind seemed to be very sluggish that morning, as if I was still unable to cast off the burden of sleep. I felt that I could do with some of that oxygen—but before I could reach the mask, understanding exploded in my brain. I whirled on the duty engineer and said urgently:

"Jim! There's something wrong with the air! That's why Claribel's passed out. I've just remembered that miners used to carry canaries down to warn them of gas."

"Nonsense!" said Jim. "The alarms would have gone off. We've got duplicate circuits, operating independently."

"Er—the second alarm circuit isn't connected up yet," his assistant reminded him. That shook Jim; he left without a word, while we stood arguing and passing the oxygen bottle around like a pipe of peace.

He came back ten minutes later with a sheepish expression. It was one of those accidents that couldn't possibly happen; we'd had one of our rare eclipses by Earth's shadow that night; part of the air purifier had frozen up, and the single alarm in the circuit had failed to go off. Half a million dollars' worth of chemical and electronic engineering had let us down completely. Without Claribel, we should soon have been slightly dead.

So now, if you visit any space station, don't be surprised if you hear an inexplicable snatch of bird song. There's no need to be alarmed: on the contrary, in fact, it will mean that you're being doubly safeguarded, at practically no extra expense.

TAKE A DEEP BREATH

A LONG TIME AGO I discovered that people who've never left Earth have certain fixed ideas about conditions in space. Everyone "knows," for example, that a man dies instantly and horribly when exposed to the vacuum that exists beyond the atmosphere. You'll find numerous gory descriptions of exploded space travelers in the popular literature, and I won't spoil your appetite by repeating them here. Many of those tales, indeed, are basically true. I've pulled men back through the air lock who were very poor advertisements for space flight.

Yet, at the same time, there are exceptions to every rule—even this one. I should know, for I learned the hard way.

We were on the last stages of building Communications Satellite Two; all the main units had been joined together, the living quarters had been pressurized, and the station had been given the slow spin around its axis that had restored the unfamiliar sensation of weight. I say "slow," but at its rim our two-hundred-foot-diameter wheel was turning at thirty miles an hour. We had, of course, no sense of motion, but the centrifugal force caused by this spin gave us about half the weight we would have possessed on Earth. That was enough to stop things from drifting around, yet not enough to make us feel uncomfortably sluggish after our weeks with no weight at all.

Four of us were sleeping in the small cylindrical cabin known as Bunkhouse Number 6 on the night that it happened. The bunkhouse was at the very rim of the station; if you imagine a bicycle wheel, with a string of sausages replacing the tire, you have a good idea of the layout. Bunkhouse Number 6 was one of these sausages, and we were slumbering peacefully inside it.

I was awakened by a sudden jolt that was not violent enough to cause me alarm, but which did make me sit up and wonder what had happened. Anything unusual in a space station demands instant attention, so I reached for the intercom switch by my bed. "Hello, Central," I called. "What was that?"

There was no reply; the line was dead.

Now thoroughly alarmed, I jumped out of bed—and had an even bigger shock. *There was no gravity*. I shot up to the ceiling before I was able to grab a stanchion and bring myself to a halt, at the cost of a sprained wrist.

It was impossible for the entire station to have suddenly stopped rotating. There was only one answer; the failure of the intercom and, as I quickly discovered, of the lighting circuit as well forced us to face the appalling truth. We were no longer part of the station; our little cabin had somehow come adrift, and had been slung off into space like a raindrop falling on a spinning flywheel.

There were no windows through which we could look out, but we were not in complete darkness, for the battery-powered emergency lights had come on. All the main air vents had closed automatically when the pressure dropped. For the time being, we could live in our own private atmosphere, even though it was not being renewed. Unfortunately, a steady whistling told us that the air we did have was escaping through a leak somewhere in the cabin.

There was no way of telling what had happened to the rest of the station. For all we knew, the whole structure might have come to pieces, and all our colleagues might be dead or in the same predicament as we—drifting through space in leaking cans of air. Our one slim hope was the possibility that we were the only cast-aways, that the rest of the station was intact and had been able to send a rescue team to find us. After all, we were receding at no more than thirty miles an hour, and one of the rocket scooters could catch up to us in minutes.

It actually took an hour, though without the evidence of my watch I should never have believed that it was so short a time. We were now gasping for breath, and the gauge on our single emergency oxygen tank had dropped to one division above zero.

The banging on the wall seemed like a signal from another world. We banged back vigorously, and a moment later a muffled voice called to us through the wall. Someone outside was lying with his space-suit helmet pressed against the metal, and his shouted words were reaching us by direct conduction. Not as clear as radio—but it worked.

The oxygen gauge crept slowly down to zero while we had our council of war. We would be dead before we could be towed back to the station; yet the rescue ship was only a few feet away from us, with its air lock already open. Our little problem was to cross that few feet—*without* space suits.

We made our plans carefully, rehearsing our actions in the full knowledge that there could be no repeat performance. Then we each took a deep, final swig of oxygen, flushing out our lungs. When we were all ready, I banged on the wall to give the signal to our friends waiting outside.

There was a series of short, staccato raps as the power tools got to work on the thin hull. We clung tightly to the stanchions, as far away as possible from the point of entry, knowing just what would happen. When it came, it was so sudden that the mind couldn't record the sequence of events. The cabin seemed to explode, and a great wind tugged at me. The last trace of air gushed from my lungs, through my already-opened mouth. And then—utter silence, and the stars shining through the gaping hole that led to life.

Believe me, I didn't stop to analyze my sensations. I think—though I can never be sure that it wasn't imagination—that my eyes were smarting and there was a tingling feeling all over my body. And I felt very cold, perhaps because evaporation was already starting from my skin.

The only thing I can be certain of is that uncanny silence. It is never completely quiet in a space station, for there is always the sound of machinery or air pumps. But this was the absolute silence of the empty void, where there is no trace of air to carry sound.

Almost at once we launched ourselves out through the shattered wall, into the full blast of the sun. I was instantly blinded—but that didn't matter, because the men waiting in space suits grabbed me as soon as I emerged and hustled me into the air lock. And there, sound slowly returned as the air rushed in, and we remembered we could breathe again. The entire rescue, they told us later, had lasted just twenty seconds. . . .

Well, we were the founding members of the Vacuum-Breathers' Club. Since then, at least a dozen other men have done the same thing, in similar emergencies. The record time in space is now two minutes; after that, the blood begins to form bubbles as it boils at body temperature, and those bubbles soon get to the heart.

In my case, there was only one aftereffect. For maybe a quarter of a minute I had been exposed to *real* sunlight, not the feeble stuff that filters down through the atmosphere of Earth. Breathing space didn't hurt me at all—but I got the worst dose of sunburn I've ever had in my life.

FREEDOM OF SPACE

NOT MANY OF YOU, I suppose, can imagine the time before the satellite relays gave us our present world communications system. When I was a boy, it was impossible to send TV programs across the oceans, or even to establish reliable radio contact around the curve of the Earth without picking up a fine assortment of crackles and bangs on the way. Yet now we take interference-free circuits for granted, and think nothing of seeing our friends on the other side of the globe as clearly as if we were standing face to face. Indeed, it's a simple fact that without the satellite relays, the whole structure of world commerce and industry would collapse. Unless we were up here on the space stations to bounce their messages around the globe, how do you think any of the world's big business organizations could keep their widely scattered electronic brains in touch with each other?

But all this was still in the future, back in the late seventies, when we were finishing work on the Relay Chain. I've already told you about some of our problems and near disasters; they were serious enough at the time, but in the end we overcame them all. The three stations spaced around Earth were no longer piles of girders, air cylinders, and plastic pressure chambers. Their assembly had been completed, we had moved aboard, and could now work in comfort, unhampered by space suits. And we had gravity again, now that the stations had been set slowly spinning. Not real gravity, of course; but centrifugal force feels exactly the same when you're out in space. It was pleasant being able to pour drinks and to sit down without drifting away on the first air current.

Once the three stations had been built, there was still a year's solid work to be done installing all the radio and TV equipment that would lift the world's communications networks into space. It was a great day when we established the first TV link between England and Australia. The signal was beamed up to us in Relay Two, as we sat above the center of Africa, we flashed it across to Three—poised over New Guinea—and they shot it down to Earth again, clear and clean after its ninety-thousand-mile journey.

These, however, were the engineers' private tests. The official opening of the system would be the biggest event in the history of world communication—an elaborate global telecast, in which every nation would take part. It would be a three-hour show, as for the first time the live TV camera roamed around the world, proclaiming to mankind that the last barrier of distance was down.

The program planning, it was cynically believed, had taken as much effort as the building of the space stations in the first place, and of all the problems the planners had to solve, the most difficult was that of choosing a compère or master of ceremonies to introduce the items in the elaborate global show that would be watched by half the human race.

Heaven knows how much conniving, blackmail, and downright character assassination went on behind the scenes. All we knew was that a week before the great day, a nonscheduled rocket came up to orbit with Gregory Wendell aboard. This was quite a surprise, since Gregory wasn't as big a TV personality as, say, Jeffers Jackson in the U.S. or Vince Clifford in Britain. However, it seemed that the big boys had canceled each other out, and Gregg had got the coveted job through one of those compromises so well known to politicians.

Gregg had started his career as a disc jockey on a university radio station in the American Midwest, and had worked his way up through the Hollywood and Manhattan night-club circuits until he had a daily, nation-wide program of his own. Apart from his cynical yet relaxed personality, his biggest asset was his deep velvet voice, for which he could probably thank his Negro blood. Even when you flatly disagreed with what he was saying—even, indeed, when he was tearing you to pieces in an interview—it was still a pleasure to listen to him.

We gave him the grand tour of the space station, and even (strictly against regulations) took him out through the air lock in a space suit. He loved it all, but there were two things he liked in particular. "This air you make," he said, "it beats the stuff we have to breathe down in New York. This is the first time my sinus trouble has gone since I went into TV." He also relished the low gravity; at the station's rim, a man had half his normal, Earth weight—and at the axis he had no weight at all.

However, the novelty of his surroundings didn't distract Gregg from his job. He spent hours at Communications Central, polishing his script and getting his cues right, and studying the dozens of monitor screens that would be his windows on the world. I came across him once while he was running through his introduction of Queen Elizabeth, who would be speaking from Buckingham Palace at the very end of the program. He was so intent on his rehearsal that he never even noticed I was standing beside him.

Well, that telecast is now part of history. For the first time a billion human beings watched a single program that came "live" from every corner of the Earth, and was a roll call of the world's greatest citizens. Hundreds of cameras on land and sea and air looked inquiringly at the turning globe; and at the end there was that wonderful shot of the Earth through a zoom lens on the space station, making the whole planet recede until it was lost among the stars. . . .

There were a few hitches, of course. One camera on the bed of the Atlantic wasn't ready on cue, and we had to spend some extra time looking at the Taj Mahal. And owing to a switching error Russian subtitles were superimposed on the South American transmission, while half the U.S.S.R. found itself trying to read Spanish. But this was nothing to what *might* have happened.

Through the entire three hours, introducing the famous and the unknown with equal ease, came the mellow yet never orotund flow of Gregg's voice. He did a magnificent job; the congratulations came pouring up the beam the moment the broadcast finished. But he didn't hear them; he made one short, private call to his agent, and then went to bed.

Next morning, the Earth-bound ferry was waiting to take him back to any job he cared to accept. But it left without Gregg Wendell, now junior station announcer of Relay Two.

"They'll think I'm crazy," he said, beaming happily, "but why should I go back to that rat race down there? I've all the universe to look at, I can breathe smog-free air, the low gravity makes me feel a Hercules, and my three darling ex-wives can't get at me." He kissed his hand to the departing rocket. "So long, Earth," he called. "I'll be back when I start pining for Broadway traffic jams and bleary penthouse dawns. And if I get homesick, I can look at anywhere on the planet just by turning a switch. Why, I'm more in the middle of things here than I could ever be on Earth, yet I can cut myself off from the human race whenever I want to."

He was still smiling as he watched the ferry begin the long fall back to Earth, toward the fame and fortune that could have been his. And then, whistling cheerfully, he left the observation lounge in eight-foot strides to read the weather forecast for Lower Patagonia.

PASSER-BY

IT'S ONLY FAIR TO WARN YOU, right at the start, that this is a story with no ending. But it has a definite beginning, for it was while we were both students at Astrotech that I met Julie. She was in her final year of solar physics when I was graduating, and during our last year at college we saw a good deal of each other. I've still got the woolen tam-o'shanter she knitted so that I wouldn't bump my head against my space helmet. (No, I never had the nerve to wear it.)

Unfortunately, when I was assigned to Satellite Two, Julie went to the Solar Observatory—at the same distance from Earth, but a couple of degrees eastward along the orbit. So there we were, sitting twenty-two thousand miles above the middle of Africa—but with nine hundred miles of empty, hostile space between us.

At first we were both so busy that the pang of separation was somewhat lessened. But when the novelty of life in space had worn off, our thoughts began to bridge the gulf that divided us. And not only our thoughts, for I'd made friends with the communications people, and we used to have little chats over the interstation TV circuit. In some ways it made matters worse seeing each other face to face and never knowing just how many other people were looking in at the same time. There's not much privacy in a space station. . . .

Sometimes I'd focus one of our telescopes onto the distant, brilliant star of the observatory. In the crystal clarity of space, I could use enormous magnifications, and could see every detail of our neighbors' equipment—the solar telescopes, the pressurized spheres of the living quarters that housed the staff, the slim pencils of visiting ferry rockets that had climbed up from Earth. Very often there would be space-suited figures moving among the maze of apparatus, and I would strain my eyes in a hopeless attempt at identification. It's hard enough to recognize anyone in a space suit when you're only a few feet apart—but that didn't stop me from trying.

We'd resigned ourselves to waiting, with what patience we could muster, until our Earth leave was due in six months' time, when we had an unexpected stroke of luck. Less than half our tour of duty had passed when the head of the transport section suddenly announced that he was going outside with a butterfly net to catch meteors. He didn't become violent, but had to be shipped hastily back to Earth. I took over his job on a temporary basis and now had—in theory at least—the freedom of space.

There were ten of the little low-powered rocket scooters under my proud command, as well as four of the larger interstation shuttles used to ferry stores and personnel from orbit to orbit. I couldn't hope to borrow one of *those*, but after several weeks of careful organizing I was able to carry out the plan I'd conceived some two micro-seconds after being told I was now head of transport.

There's no need to tell how I juggled duty lists, cooked logs and fuel registers, and persuaded my colleagues to cover up for me. All that matters is that, about once a week, I would climb into my personal space suit, strap myself to the spidery framework of a Mark III Scooter, and drift away from the station at minimum power. When I was well clear, I'd go over to full throttle, and the tiny rocket motor would hustle me across the nine-hundred-mile gap to the observatory.

The trip took about thirty minutes, and the navigational requirements were elementary. I could see where I was going and where I'd come from, yet I don't mind admitting that I often felt—well, a trifle lonely—around the mid-point of the journey. There was no other solid matter within almost five hundred miles—and it looked an awfully long way down to Earth. It was a great help, at such moments, to tune the suit radio to the general service band, and to listen to all the back-chat between ships and stations.

At mid-flight I'd have to spin the scooter around and start braking, and ten minutes later the observatory would be close enough for its details to be visible to the unaided eye. Very shortly after that I'd drift up to a small, plastic pressure bubble that was in the process of being fitted out as a spectroscopic laboratory—and there would be Julie, waiting on the other side of the air lock. . . .

I won't pretend that we confined our discussions to the latest results in astrophysics, or the progress of the satellite construction schedule. Few things, indeed, were further from our thoughts; and the journey home always seemed to flash by at a quite astonishing speed.

It was around mid-orbit on one of those homeward trips that the radar started to flash on my little control panel. There was something large at extreme range, and it was coming in fast. A meteor, I told myself—maybe even a small asteroid. Anything giving such a signal should be visible to the eye: I read off the bearings and searched the star fields in the indicated direction. The thought of a collision never even crossed my mind; space is so inconceivably vast that I was thousands of times safer than a man crossing a busy street on Earth.

There it was—a bright and steadily growing star near the foot of Orion. It already outshone Rigel, and seconds later it was not merely a star, but had begun to show a visible disk. Now it was moving as fast as I could turn my head; it grew to a tiny, misshaped moon, then dwindled and shrank with that same silent, inexorable speed.

I suppose I had a clear view of it for perhaps half a second, and that half-second has haunted me all my life. The—object—had already vanished by the time I thought of checking the radar again, so I had no way of gauging how close it came, and hence how large it really was. It could have been a small object a hundred feet away—or a very large one, ten miles off. There is no sense of perspective in space, and unless you know what you are looking at, you cannot judge its distance.

Of course, it *could* have been a very large and oddly shaped meteor; I can never be sure that my eyes, straining to grasp the details of so swiftly moving an object, were not hopelessly deceived. I may have imagined that I saw that broken, crumpled prow, and the cluster of dark ports like the sightless sockets of a skull. Of one thing only was I certain, even in that brief and fragmentary vision. If it *was* a ship, it was not one of ours. Its shape was utterly alien, and it was very, very old.

It may be that the greatest discovery of all time slipped from my grasp as I struggled with my thoughts midway between the two space stations. But I had no measurements of speed or direction; whatever it was that I had glimpsed was now lost beyond recapture in the wastes of the solar system.

What should I have done? No one would ever have believed me, for I would have had no proof. Had I made a report, there would have been endless trouble. I should have become the laughingstock of the Space Service, would have been reprimanded for misuse of equipment—and would certainly not have been able to see Julie again. And to me, at that age, nothing else was as important. If you've been in love yourself, you'll understand; if not, then no explanation is any use.

So I said nothing. To some other man (how many centuries hence?) will go the fame for proving that we were not the first-born of the children of the sun. Whatever it may be that is circling out there on its eternal orbit can wait, as it has waited ages already.

Yet I sometimes wonder. Would I have made a report, after all—had I known that Julie was going to marry someone else?

THE CALL OF THE STARS

Down there on earth the twentieth century is dying. As I look across at the shadowed globe blocking the stars, I can see the lights of a hundred sleepless cities, and there are moments when I wish that I could be among the crowds now surging and singing in the streets of London, Capetown, Rome, Paris, Berlin, Madrid. . . . Yes, I can see them all at a single glance, burning like fireflies against the darkened planet. The line of midnight is now bisecting Europe: in the eastern Mediterranean a tiny, brilliant star is pulsing as some exuberant pleasure ship waves her searchlights to the sky. I think she is deliberately aiming at us; for the past few minutes the flashes have been quite regular and startlingly bright. Presently I'll call the communications center and find out who she is, so that I can radio back our own greetings.

Passing into history now, receding forever down the stream of time, is the most incredible hundred years the world has ever seen. It opened with the conquest of the air, saw at its mid-point the unlocking of the atom—and now ends with the bridging of space.

(For the past five minutes I've been wondering what's happening to Nairobi; now I realize that they are putting on a mammoth fireworks display. Chemically fueled rockets may be obsolete out here—but they're still using lots of them down on Earth tonight.)

The end of a century—and the end of a millennium. What will the hundred years that begin with two and zero bring? The planets, of course; floating there in space, only a mile away, are the ships of the first Martian expedition. For two years I have watched them grow, assembled piece by piece, as the space station itself was built by the men I worked with a generation ago.

Those ten ships are ready now, with all their crews aboard, waiting for the final instrument check and the signal for departure. Before the first day of the new century has passed its noon, they will be tearing free from the reins of Earth, to head out toward the strange world that may one day be man's second home.

As I look at the brave little fleet that is now preparing to challenge infinity, my mind goes back forty years, to the days when the first satellites were launched and the moon still seemed very far away. And I remember—indeed, I have never forgotten—my father's fight to keep me down on Earth.

There were not many weapons he had failed to use. Ridicule had been the first: "Of course they can do it," he had sneered, "but what's the point? Who wants to go out into space while there's so much to be done here on Earth? There's not a single planet in the solar system where men can live. The moon's a burnt-out slag heap, and everywhere else is even worse. *This* is where we were meant to live."

Even then (I must have been eighteen or so at the time) I could tangle him up in points of logic. I can remember answering, "How do you know where we were meant to live, Dad? After all, we were in the sea for about a billion years before we decided to tackle the land. Now we're making the next big jump: I don't know where it will lead—nor did that first fish when it crawled up on the beach, and started to sniff the air."

So when he couldn't outargue me, he had tried subtler pressures. He was always talking about the dangers of space travel, and the short working life of anyone foolish enough to get involved in rocketry. At that time, people were still scared of meteors and cosmic rays; like the "Here Be Dragons" of the old map makers, they were the mythical monsters on the still-blank celestial charts. But they didn't worry me; if anything, they added the spice of danger to my dreams.

While I was going through college, Father was comparatively quiet. My training would be valuable whatever profession I took up in later life, so he could not complain—though he occasionally grumbled about the money I wasted buying all the books and magazines on astronautics that I could find. My college record was good, which naturally pleased him; perhaps he did not realize that it would also help me to get my way.

All through my final year I had avoided talking of my plans. I had even given the impression (though I am sorry for that now) that I had abandoned my dream of going into space. Without saying anything to him, I put in my application to Astrotech, and was accepted as soon as I had graduated.

The storm broke when that long blue envelope with the embossed heading "Institute of Astronautical Technology" dropped into the mailbox. I was accused of deceit and ingratitude, and I do not think I ever forgave my father for destroying the pleasure I should have felt at being chosen for the most exclusive—and most glamorous—apprenticeship the world has ever known.

The vacations were an ordeal; had it not been for Mother's sake, I do not think I would have gone home more than once a year, and I always left again as quickly as I could. I had hoped that Father would mellow as my training progressed and as he accepted the inevitable, but he never did.

Then had come that stiff and awkward parting at the spaceport, with the rain streaming down from leaden skies and beating against the smooth walls of the ship that seemed so eagerly waiting to climb into the eternal sunlight beyond the reach of storms. I know now what it cost my father to watch the machine he hated swallow up his only son: for I understand many things today that were hidden from me then.

He knew, even as we parted at the ship, that he would never see me again. Yet his old, stubborn pride kept him from saying the only words that might have held me back. I knew that he was ill, but how ill, he had told no one. That was the only weapon he had not used against me, and I respect him for it.

Would I have stayed had I known? It is even more futile to speculate about the unchangeable past than the unforeseeable future; all I can say now is that I am glad I never had to make the choice. At the end he let me go; he gave up his fight against my ambition, and a little while later his fight with Death.

So I said good-by to Earth, and to the father who loved me but knew no way to say it. He lies down there on the planet I can cover with my hand; how strange it is to think that of the countless billion human beings whose blood runs in my veins, I was the very first to leave his native world. . . .

The new day is breaking over Asia; a hairline of fire is rimming the eastern edge of Earth. Soon it will grow into a burning crescent as the sun comes up out of the Pacific—yet Europe is preparing for sleep, except for those revelers who will stay up to greet the dawn.

And now, over there by the flagship, the ferry rocket is coming back for the last visitors from the station. Here comes the message I have been waiting for: CAPTAIN STEVENS PRESENTS HIS COMPLIMENTS TO THE STATION COMMANDER. BLAST-OFF WILL BE IN NINETY MINUTES; HE WILL BE GLAD TO SEE YOU ABOARD NOW.

Well, Father, now I know how you felt: time has gone full circle. Yet I hope that I have learned from the mistakes we both made, long ago. I shall remember you when I go over there to the flagship *Starfire* and say good-by to the grandson you never knew.

THE MAN WHO SOLD THE MOON

by Robert A. Heinlein

CHAPTER ONE

"You've got to be a believer!"

George Strong snorted at his partner's declaration. "Delos, why don't you give up? You've been singing this tune for years. Maybe someday men will get to the Moon, though I doubt it. In any case, you and I will never live to see it. The loss of the power satellite washes the matter up for our generation."

D. D. Harriman grunted. "We won't see it if we sit on our fat behinds and don't do anything to make it happen. But we can make it happen."

"Question number one: how? Question number two: why?"

" 'Why?' The man asks 'why.' George, isn't there anything in your soul but discounts, and dividends? Didn't you ever sit with a girl on a soft summer night and stare up at the Moon and wonder what was there?"

"Yeah, I did once. I caught a cold."

Harriman asked the Almighty why he had been delivered into the hands of the Philistines. He then turned back to his partner. "I could tell you why, the real 'why,' but you wouldn't understand me. You want to know why in terms of cash, don't you? You want to know how Harriman & Strong and Harriman Enterprises can show a profit, don't you?"

"Yes," admitted Strong, "and don't give me any guff about tourist trade and fabulous lunar jewels. I've had it."

"You ask me to show figures on a brand-new type of enterprise, knowing I can't. It's like asking the Wright brothers at Kitty Hawk to estimate how much money Curtiss-Wright Corporation would someday make out of building airplanes. I'll put it another way. You didn't want us to go into plastic houses, did you? If you had had your way we would still be back in Kansas City, subdividing cow pastures and showing rentals."

Strong shrugged.

"How much has New World Homes made to date?"

Strong looked absent-minded while exercising the talent he brought to the partnership. "Uh . . . $172,946,004.62, after taxes, to the end of the last fiscal year. The running estimate to date is—"

"Never mind. What was our share in the take?"

"Well, uh, the partnership, exclusive of the piece you took personally and then sold to me later, has benefited from New World Homes during the same period by $13,010,437.20, ahead of personal taxes. Delos, this double taxation has got to stop. Penalizing thrift is a sure way to run this country straight into—"

"Forget it, forget it! How much have we made out of Skyblast Freight and Antipodes Transways?"

Strong told him.

"And yet I had to threaten you with bodily harm to get you to put up a dime to buy control of the injector patent. You said rockets were a passing fad."

"We were lucky," objected Strong. "You had no way of knowing that there would be a big uranium strike in Australia. Without it, the Skyways group would have left us in the red. For that matter New World Homes would have failed, too, if the roadtowns hadn't come along and given us a market out from under local building codes."

"Nuts on both points. Fast transportation will pay; it always has. As for New World, when ten million families need new houses and we can sell 'em cheap, they'll buy. They won't let building codes stop them, not permanently. We gambled on a certainty. Think back, George: what ventures have we lost money on and what ones have paid off? Everyone of my crack-brain ideas has made money, hasn't it? And the only times we've lost our ante was on conservative, blue-chip investments."

"But we've made money on some conservative deals, too," protested Strong.

"Not enough to pay for your yacht. Be fair about it, George; the Andes Development Company, the integrating pantograph patent, every one of my wildcat schemes I've had to drag you into—and every one of them paid."

"I've had to sweat blood to make them pay," Strong grumbled.

"That's why we are partners. I get a wildcat by the tail; you harness him and put him to work. Now we go to the Moon—and you'll make it pay."

"Speak for yourself. I'm not going to the Moon."

"I am."

"Hummph! Delos, granting that we have gotten rich by speculating on your hunches, it's a steel-clad fact that if you keep on gambling you lose your shirt. There's an old saw about the pitcher that went once too often to the well."

"Damn it, George—I'm going to the Moon! If you won't back me up, let's liquidate and I'll do it alone."

Strong drummed on his desk top. "Now, Delos, nobody said anything about not backing you up."

"Fish or cut bait. Now is the opportunity and my mind's made up. I'm going to be the Man in the Moon."

"Well . . . let's get going. We'll be late to the meeting."

As they left their joint office, Strong, always penny conscious, was careful to switch off the light. Harriman had seen him do so a thousand times; this time he commented. "George, how about a light switch that turns off automatically when you leave a room?"

"Hmm—but suppose someone were left in the room?"

"Well . . . hitch it to stay on only when someone was *in* the room—key the switch to the human body's heat radiation, maybe."

"Too expensive and too complicated."

"Needn't be. I'll turn the idea over to Ferguson to fiddle with. It should be no larger than the present light switch and cheap enough so that the power saved in a year will pay for it."

"How would it work?" asked Strong.

"How should I know? I'm no engineer; that's for Ferguson and the other educated laddies."

Strong objected, "It's no good commercially. Switching off a light when you leave a room is a matter of temperament. I've got it; you haven't. If a man hasn't got it, you can't interest him in such a switch."

"You can if power continues to be rationed. There is a power shortage now; and there will be a bigger one."

"Just temporary. This meeting will straighten it out."

"George, there is nothing in this world so permanent as a temporary emergency. The switch will sell."

Strong took out a notebook and stylus. "I'll call Ferguson in about it tomorrow."

Harriman forgot the matter, never to think of it again. They had reached the roof; he waved to a taxi, then turned to Strong. "How much could we realize if we unloaded our holdings in Roadways and in Belt Transport Corporation—yes, and in New World Homes?"

"Huh? Have you gone crazy?"

"Probably. But I'm going to need all the cash you can shake loose for me. Roadways and Belt Transport are no good anyhow; we should have unloaded earlier."

"You *are* crazy! It's the one really conservative venture you've sponsored."

"But it wasn't conservative when I sponsored it. Believe me, George, roadtowns are on their way out. They are growing moribund, just as the railroads did. In a hundred years there won't be a one left on the continent. What's the formula for making money, George?"

"Buy low and sell high."

"That's only half of it . . . *your* half. We've got to guess which way things are moving, give them a boost, and see that we are cut in on the ground floor. Liquidate that stuff, George; I'll need money to operate." The taxi landed; they got in and took off.

The taxi delivered them to the roof of the Hemisphere Power Building; they went to the power syndicate's board room, as far below ground as the landing platform was above—in those days, despite years of peace, tycoons habitually came to rest at spots relatively immune to atom bombs. The room did not seem like a bomb shelter; it appeared to be a chamber in a luxurious penthouse, for a "view window" back of the chairman's end of the table looked out high above the city, in convincing, live stereo, relayed from the roof.

The other directors were there before them. Dixon nodded as they came in, glanced at his watch finger and said, "Well, gentlemen, our bad boy is here, we may as well begin." He took the chairman's seat and rapped for order.

"The minutes of the last meeting are on your pads as usual. Signal when ready." Harriman glanced at the summary before him and at once flipped a switch on the table top; a small green light flashed on at his place. Most of the directors did the same.

"Who's holding up the procession?" inquired Harriman, looking around. "Oh—you, George. Get a move on."

"I like to check the figures," his partner answered testily, then flipped his own switch. A larger green light showed in front of Chairman Dixon, who then pressed a button; a transparency, sticking an inch or two above the table top in front of him lit up with the word RECORDING.

"Operations report," said Dixon and touched another switch. A female voice came out from nowhere. Harriman followed the report from the next sheet of paper at his place. Thirteen Curie-type power piles were now in operation, up five from the last meeting. The Susquehanna and Charleston piles had taken over the load previously borrowed from Atlantic Roadcity and the roadways of that city were now up to normal speed. It was expected that the Chicago-Angeles road could be restored to speed during the next fortnight. Power would continue to be rationed but the crisis was over.

All very interesting but of no direct interest to Harriman. The power crisis that had been caused by the explosion of the power satellite was being satisfactorily met—very good, but Harriman's interest in it lay in the fact that the cause of interplanetary travel had thereby received a setback from which it might not recover.

When the Harper-Erickson isotopic artificial fuels had been developed three years before it had seemed that, in addition to solving the dilemma of an impossibly dangerous power source which was also utterly necessary to the economic life of the continent, an easy means had been found to achieve interplanetary travel.

The Arizona power pile had been installed in one of the largest of the Antipodes rockets, the rocket powered with isotopic fuel created in the power pile itself, and the whole thing was placed in an orbit around the Earth. A much smaller rocket had shuttled between satellite and Earth, carrying supplies to the staff of the power pile, bringing back synthetic radioactive fuel for the power-hungry technology of Earth.

As a director of the power syndicate Harriman had backed the power satellite—with a private ax to grind: he expected to power a Moon ship with fuel manufactured in the power satellite and thus to achieve the first trip to the Moon almost at once. He had not even attempted to stir the Department of Defense out of its sleep; he wanted no government subsidy—

the job was a cinch; anybody could do it—and Harriman *would* do it. He had the ship; shortly he would have the fuel.

The ship had been a freighter of his own Antipodes line, her chem-fuel motors replaced, her wings removed. She still waited, ready for fuel—the recommissioned *Santa Maria,* nee *City of Brisbane.*

But the fuel was slow in coming. Fuel had to be earmarked for the shuttle rocket; the power needs of a rationed continent came next—and those needs grew faster than the power satellite could turn out fuel. Far from being ready to supply him for a "useless" Moon trip, the syndicate had seized on the safe but less efficient low temperature uranium-salts and heavy water, Curie-type power piles as a means of using uranium directly to meet the ever growing need for power, rather than build and launch more satellites.

Unfortunately the Curie piles did not provide the fierce star-interior conditions necessary to breeding the isotopic fuels needed for an atomic-powered rocket. Harriman had reluctantly come around to the notion that he would have to use political pressure to squeeze the necessary priority for the fuels he wanted for the *Santa Maria.*

Then the power satellite had blown up.

Harriman was stirred out of his brown study by Dixon's voice. "The operations report seems satisfactory, gentlemen. If there is no objection, it will be recorded as accepted. You will note that in the next ninety days we will be back up to the power level which existed before we were forced to close down the Arizona pile."

"But with no provision for future needs," pointed out Harriman. "There have been a lot of babies born while we have been sitting here."

"Is that an objection to accepting the report, D.D.?"

"No."

"Very well. Now the public relations report—let me call attention to the first item, gentlemen. The vice-president in charge recommends a schedule of annuities, benefits, scholarships and so forth for dependents of the staff of the power satellite and of the pilot of the *Charon:* see appendix 'C'."

A director across from Harriman—Phineas Morgan, chairman of the food trust, Cuisine, Incorporated—protested, "What is this, Ed? Too bad they were killed of course, but we paid them skyhigh wages and carried their insurance to boot. Why the charity?"

Harriman grunted. "Pay it—I so move. It's peanuts. 'Do not bind the mouths of the kine who tread the grain.' "

"I wouldn't call better than nine hundred thousand 'peanuts,' " protested Morgan.

"Just a minute, gentlemen—" It was the vice-president in charge of public relations, himself a director. "If you'll look at the breakdown, Mr. Morgan, you will see that eighty-five percent of the appropriation will be used to publicize the gifts."

Morgan squinted at the figures. "Oh—why didn't you say so? Well, I suppose the gifts can be considered unavoidable overhead, but it's a bad precedent."

"Without them we have nothing to publicize."

"Yes, but—"

Dixon rapped smartly. "Mr. Harriman has moved acceptance. Please signal your desires." The tally board glowed green; even Morgan, after hesitation, okayed the allotment. "We have a related item next," said Dixon. "A Mrs. —uh, Garfield, through her attorneys, alleges that we are responsible for the congenital crippled condition of her fourth child. The putative facts are that her child was being born just as the satellite exploded and that Mrs. Garfield was then on the meridian underneath the satellite. She wants the court to award her half a million."

Morgan looked at Harriman. "Delos, I suppose that *you* will say to settle out of court."

"Don't be silly. We fight it."

Dixon looked around, surprised. "Why, D.D.? It's my guess we could settle for ten or fifteen thousand—and that was what I was about to recommend. I'm surprised that the legal department referred it to publicity."

"It's obvious why; it's loaded with high explosive. But we should fight, regardless of bad publicity. It's not like the last case; Mrs. Garfield and her brat are not our people. And any dumb fool knows you can't mark a baby by radioactivity at birth; you have to get at the germ plasm of the previous generation at least. In the third place, if we let this get by, we'll be sued for every double-yolked egg that's laid from now on. This calls for an open allotment for defense and not one damned cent for compromise."

"It might be very expensive," observed Dixon.

"It'll be more expensive not to fight. If we have to, we should buy the judge."

The public relations chief whispered to Dixon, then announced, "I support Mr. Harriman's view. That's my department's recommendation."

It was approved. "The next item," Dixon went on, "is a whole sheaf of suits arising out of slowing down the roadcities to divert power during the crisis. They alleged loss of business, loss of time, loss of this and that, but they are all based on the same issue. The most touchy, perhaps, is a stockholder's suit which claims that Roadways and this company are so interlocked that the decision to divert the power was not done in the interests of the stockholders of Roadways. Delos, this is your pidgin; want to speak on it?"

"Forget it."

"Why?"

"Those are shotgun suits. This corporation is not responsible; I saw to it that Roadways volunteered to sell the power because I anticipated this. And the directorates don't interlock; not on paper, they don't. That's why dummies were born. Forget it—for every suit you've got there, Roadways has a dozen. We'll beat them."

"What makes you so sure?"

"Well—" Harriman lounged back and hung a knee over the arm of his chair. "—a good many years ago I was a Western Union messenger boy. While waiting around the office I read everything I could lay hands on, including the contract on the back of the telegram forms. Remember those? They used to come in big pads of yellow paper; by writing a message on the face of the form you accepted the contract in the fine print on the back—only most people didn't realize that. Do you know what that contract obligated the company to do?"

"Send a telegram, I suppose."

"It didn't promise a durn thing. The company offered to *attempt* to deliver the message, by camel caravan or snail back, or some equally streamlined method, if convenient, but in event of failure, the company was not responsible. I read that fine print until I knew it by heart. It was the loveliest piece of prose I had ever seen. Since then all my contracts have been worded on the same principle. Anybody who sues Roadways will find that Roadways can't be sued on the element of time, because time is not of the essence. In the event of complete non-performance—which hasn't happened yet—Roadways is financially responsible only for freight charges or the price of the personal transportation tickets. So forget it."

Morgan sat up. "D.D., suppose I decided to run up to my country place tonight, by the roadway, and there was a failure of some sort so that I didn't get there until tomorrow? You mean to say Roadways is not liable?"

Harriman grinned. "Roadways is not liable even if you starve to death on the trip. Better use your copter." He turned back to Dixon. "I move that we stall these suits and let Roadways carry the ball for us."

"The regular agenda being completed," Dixon announced later, "time is allotted for our colleague, Mr. Harriman, to speak on a subject of his own choosing. He has not listed a subject in advance, but we will listen until it is your pleasure to adjourn."

Morgan looked sourly at Harriman. "I move we adjourn."

Harriman grinned. "For two cents I'd second that and let you die of curiosity." The motion failed for want of a second. Harriman stood up.

"Mr. Chairman, friends—" He then looked at Morgan. "—and associates. As you know, I am interested in space travel."

Dixon looked at him sharply. "Not that again, Delos! If I weren't in the chair, I'd move to adjourn myself."

"'That again'," agreed Harriman. "Now and forever. Hear me out. Three years ago, when we were crowded into moving the Arizona power pile out into space, it looked as if we had a bonus in the shape of interplanetary travel. Some of you here joined with me in forming Spaceways, Incorporated, for experimentation, exploration—and exploitation.

"Space was conquered; rockets that could establish orbits around the globe could be modified to get to the Moon—and from there, anywhere! It was just a matter of doing it. The problems remaining were financial—and political.

"In fact, the real engineering problems of space travel have been solved since World World II. Conquering space has long been a matter of money and politics. But it did seem that the Harper-Erickson process, with its concomitant of a round-the-globe rocket and a practical economical rocket fuel, had at last made it a very present thing, so close indeed that I did not object when the early allotments of fuel from the satellite were earmarked for industrial power."

He looked around. "I shouldn't have kept quiet. I should have squawked and brought pressure and made a hairy nuisance of myself until you allotted fuel to get rid of me. For now we have missed our best chance. The satellite is gone; the source of fuel is gone. Even the shuttle rocket is gone. We are back where we were in 1950. Therefore—"

He paused again. "Therefore—I propose that we build a space ship and send it to the Moon!"

Dixon broke the silence. "Delos, have you come unzipped? You just said that it was no longer possible. Now you say to build one."

"I didn't say it was impossible; I said we had missed our best chance. The time is overripe for space travel. This globe grows more crowded every day. In spite of technical advances the daily food intake on this planet is lower than it was thirty years ago—and we get 46 new babies every minute, 65,000 every day, 25,000,000 every year. Our race is about to burst forth to the planets; if we've got the initiative God promised an oyster we will help it along!

"Yes, we missed our best chance—but the engineering details can be solved. The real question is who's going to foot the bill? That is why I address you gentlemen, for right here in this room is the financial capital of this planet."

Morgan stood up. "Mr. Chairman, if all *company* business is finished, I ask to be excused."

Dixon nodded. Harriman said, "So long, Phineas. Don't let me keep you. Now, as I was saying, it's a money problem and here is where the money is. I move we finance a trip to the Moon."

The proposal produced no special excitement; these men knew Harriman. Presently Dixon said, "Is there a second to D.D.'s proposal?"

"Just a minute, Mr. Chairman—" It was Jack Entenza, president of Two-Continents Amusement Corporation. "I want to ask Delos some questions." He turned to Harriman. "D.D., you know I strung along when you set up Spaceways. It seemed like a cheap venture and possibly profitable in educational and scientific values—I never did fall for space liners plying between planets; that's fantastic. I don't mind playing along with your dreams to a moderate extent, but how do you propose to get to the Moon? As you say, you are fresh out of fuel."

Harriman was still grinning. "Don't kid me, Jack, I know why you came along. You weren't interested in science; you've never contributed a dime to science. You expected a monopoly on pix and television for your chain. Well, you'll get 'em, if you stick with me—otherwise I'll sign up 'Recreations, Unlimited'; they'll pay just to have you in the eye."

Entenza looked at him suspiciously. "What will it cost me?"

"Your other shirt, your eye teeth, and your wife's wedding ring—unless 'Recreations' will pay more."

"Damn you, Delos, you're crookeder than a dog's hind leg."

"From you, Jack, that's a compliment. We'll do business. Now as to how I'm going to get to the Moon, that's a silly question. There's not a man in here who can cope with anything more complicated in the way of machinery than a knife and fork. You can't tell a left-handed monkey wrench from a reaction engine, yet you ask me for blue prints of a space ship.

"Well, I'll tell you how I'll get to the Moon. I'll hire the proper brain boys, give them everything they want, see to it that they have all the money they can use, sweet talk them into long hours—then stand back and watch them produce. I'll run it like the Manhattan Project—most of you remember the A-bomb job; shucks, some of you can remember the Mississippi Bubble. The chap that headed up the Manhattan Project didn't know a neutron from Uncle George—but he got results. They solved that trick *four ways*. That's why I'm not worried about fuel; we'll get a fuel. We'll get several fuels."

Dixon said, "Suppose it works? Seems to me you're asking us to bankrupt the company for an exploit with no real value, aside from pure science, and a one-shot entertainment exploitation. I'm not against you—I wouldn't mind putting in ten, fifteen thousand to support a worthy venture—but I can't see the thing as a business proposition."

Harriman leaned on his fingertips and stared down the long table. "Ten or fifteen thousand gum drops! Dan, I mean to get into you for a couple of megabucks *at least*—and before we're through you'll be hollering for more stock. This is the greatest real estate venture since the Pope carved up the New World. Don't ask me what we'll make a profit on; I can't itemize the assets—but I can lump them. The assets are a planet—a *whole planet*, Dan, that's never been touched. And more planets beyond it. If we can't figure out ways to swindle a few fast bucks out of a sweet set-up like that then you and I had better both go on relief. It's like having Manhattan Island offered to you for twenty-four dollars and a case of whiskey."

Dixon grunted. "You make it sound like the chance of a lifetime."

"Chance of a lifetime, nuts! This is the greatest chance in all history. It's raining soup; grab yourself a bucket."

Next to Entenza sat Gaston P. Jones, director of Trans-America and half a dozen other banks, one of the richest men in the room. He carefully removed two inches of cigar ash, then said dryly, "Mr. Harriman, I will sell you all of my interest in the Moon, present and future, for fifty cents."

Harriman looked delighted. "Sold!"

Entenza had been pulling at his lower lip and listening with a brooding expression on his face. Now he spoke up. "Just a minute, Mr. Jones—I'll give you a dollar for it."

"Dollar fifty," answered Harriman.

"Two dollars," Entenza answered slowly.

"Five!"

They edged each other up. At ten dollars Entenza let Harriman have it and sat back, still looking thoughtful. Harriman looked happily around. "Which one of you thieves is a lawyer?" he demanded. The remark was rhetorical; out of seventeen directors the normal percentage—eleven, to be exact—were lawyers. "Hey, Tony," he continued, "draw me up an instrument right *now* that will tie down this transaction so that it couldn't be broken before the Throne of God. All of Mr. Jones' interests, rights, title, natural interest, future interests, interests held directly or through ownership of stock, presently held or to be acquired, and so forth and so forth. Put lots of Latin in it. The idea is that every interest in the Moon that Mr. Jones now has or may acquire is mine—for a ten spot, cash in hand paid." Harriman slapped a bill down on the table. "That right, Mr. Jones?"

Jones smiled briefly. "That's right, young fellow." He pocketed the bill. "I'll frame this for my grandchildren—to show them how easy it is to make money." Entenza's eyes darted from Jones to Harriman.

"Good!" said Harriman. "Gentlemen, Mr. Jones has set a market price for one human being's interest in our satellite. With around three billion persons on this globe that sets a price on the Moon of thirty billion dollars." He hauled out a wad of money. "Any more suckers? I'm buying every share that's offered, ten bucks a copy."

"I'll pay twenty!" Entenza rapped out.

Harriman looked at him sorrowfully. "Jack—don't do that! We're on the same team. Let's take the shares together, at ten."

Dixon pounded for order. "Gentlemen, please conduct such transactions after the meeting is adjourned. Is there a second to Mr. Harriman's motion?"

Gaston Jones said, "I owe it to Mr. Harriman to second his motion, without prejudice. Let's get on with a vote."

No one objected; the vote was taken. It went eleven to three against Harriman—Harriman, Strong, and Entenza for; all others against. Harriman popped up before anyone could move to adjourn and said, "I expected that. My real purpose is this: since the company is no longer interested in space travel, will it do me the courtesy of selling me what I may need of patents, processes, facilities, and so forth now held by the company but relating to space travel and not relating to the production of power on this planet? Our brief honeymoon with the power satellite built up a backlog; I want to use it. Nothing formal—just a vote that it is the policy of the company to assist me in any way not inconsistent with the primary interest of the company. How about it, gentlemen? It'll get me out of your hair."

Jones studied his cigar again. "I see no reason why we should not accommodate him, gentlemen . . . and I speak as the perfect disinterested party."

"I think we can do it, Delos," agreed Dixon, "only we won't sell you anything, we'll *lend* it to you. Then, if you happen to hit the jackpot, the company still retains an interest. Has anyone any objection?" he said to the room at large.

There was none; the matter was recorded as company policy and the meeting was adjourned. Harriman stopped to whisper with Entenza and, finally, to make an appointment. Gaston Jones stood near the door, speaking privately with Chairman Dixon. He beckoned to Strong, Harriman's partner. "George, may I ask a personal question?"

"I don't guarantee to answer. Go ahead."

"You've always struck me as a level-headed man. Tell me—why do you string along with Harriman? Why, the man's mad as a hatter."

Strong looked sheepish. "I ought to deny that, he's my friend . . . but I can't. But dawggone it! Every time Delos has a wild hunch, it turns out to be the real thing. I hate to string along—it makes me nervous—but I've learned to trust his hunches rather than another man's sworn financial report."

Jones cocked one brow. "The Midas touch, eh?"

"You could call it that."

"Well, remember what happened to King Midas—in the long run. Good day, gentlemen."

Harriman had left Entenza; Strong joined him. Dixon stood staring at them, his face very thoughtful.

CHAPTER TWO

HARRIMAN'S HOME had been built at the time when everyone who could was decentralizing and going underground. Above ground there was a perfect little Cape Cod cottage—the clapboards of which concealed armor plate—and most delightful, skillfully landscaped grounds; below ground there was four or five times as much floorspace, immune to anything but a direct hit and possessing an independent air supply with reserves for one thousand hours. During the Crazy Years the conventional wall surrounding the grounds had been replaced by a wall which looked the same but which would stop anything short of a broaching tank—nor were the gates weak points; their gadgets were as personally loyal as a well-trained dog.

Despite its fortress-like character the house was comfortable. It was also very expensive to keep up.

Harriman did not mind the expense; Charlotte liked the house and it gave her something to do. When they were first married she had lived uncomplainingly in a cramped flat over a grocery store; if Charlotte now liked to play house in a castle, Harriman did not mind.

But he was again starting a shoe-string venture; the few thousand per month of ready cash represented by the household expenses might, at some point in the game, mean the difference between success and the sheriff's bailiffs. That night at dinner, after the servants fetched the coffee, and port, he took up the matter.

"My dear, I've been wondering how you would like a few months in Florida."

His wife stared at him. "Florida? Delos, is your mind wandering? Florida is unbearable at this time of the year."

"Switzerland, then. Pick your own spot. Take a real vacation, as long as you like."

"Delos, you are up to something."

Harriman sighed. Being "up to something" was the unnameable and unforgivable crime for which any American male could be indicted, tried, convicted, and sentenced in one breath. He wondered how things had gotten rigged so that the male half of the race must always behave to suit feminine rules and feminine logic, like a snotty-nosed school boy in front of a stern teacher.

"In a way, perhaps. We've both agreed that this house is a bit of a white elephant. I was thinking of closing it, possibly even of disposing of the land—it's worth more now than when we bought it. Then, when we get around to it, we could build something more modern and a little less like a bombproof."

Mrs. Harriman was temporarily diverted. "Well, I *have* thought it might be nice to build another place, Delos—say a little chalet tucked away in the mountains, nothing ostentatious, not more than two servants, or three. But we won't close this place until it's built, Delos—after all, one must live somewhere."

"I was not thinking of building right away," he answered cautiously.

"Why not? We're not getting any younger, Delos; if we are to enjoy the good things of life we had better not make delays. You needn't worry about it; I'll manage everything."

Harriman turned over in his mind the possibility of letting her build to keep her busy. If he earmarked the cash for her "little chalet," she would live in a hotel nearby wherever she decided to build it—and he could sell this monstrosity they were sitting in. With the nearest roadcity now less than ten miles away, the land should bring more than Charlotte's new house would cost and he would be rid of the monthly drain on his pocketbook.

"Perhaps you are right," he agreed. "But suppose you do build at once; you won't be living here; you'll be supervising every detail of the new place. I say we should unload this place; it's eating its head off in taxes, upkeep, and running expenses."

She shook her head. "Utterly out of the question, Delos. This is my home."

He ground out an almost unsmoked cigar. "I'm sorry, Charlotte, but you can't have it both ways. If you build, you can't stay here. If you stay here, we'll close these below-ground catacombs, fire about a dozen of the parasites I keep stumbling over, and live in the cottage on the surface. I'm cutting expenses."

"Discharge the servants? Delos, if you think that I will undertake to make a home for you without a proper staff, you can just—"

"Stop it." He stood up and threw his napkin down. "It doesn't take a squad of servants to make a home. When we were first married you had *no* servants—and you washed and ironed my shirts in the bargain. But we had a home then. This place is owned by that staff you speak of. Well, we're getting rid of them, all but the cook and a handy man."

She did not seem to hear. "Delos! sit down and behave yourself. Now what's all this about cutting expenses? Are you in some sort of trouble? Are you? Answer me!"

He sat down wearily and answered, "Does a man have to be in trouble to want to cut out unnecessary expenses?"

"In your case, yes. Now what is it? Don't try to evade me."

"Now see here, Charlotte, we agreed a long time ago that I would keep business matters in the office. As for the house, we simply don't need a house this size. It isn't as if we had a passel of kids to fill up—"

"*Oh!* Blaming me for *that* again!"

"Now see here, Charlotte," he wearily began again, "I never did blame you and I'm not blaming you now. All I ever did was suggest that we both see a doctor and find out what the trouble was we didn't have any kids. And for twenty years you've been making me pay for that one remark. But that's all over and done with now; I was simply making the point that two people don't fill up twenty-two rooms. I'll pay a reasonable price for a new house, if you want it, and give you an ample household allowance." He started to say how much, then decided not to. "Or you can close this place and live in the cottage above. It's just that we are going to quit squandering money—for a while."

She grabbed the last phrase. "'For a while.' What's going on, Delos? What are *you* going to squander money on?" When he did not answer she went on. "Very well, if you won't tell me, I'll call George. He will tell me."

"Don't do that, Charlotte. I'm warning you. I'll—"

"You'll what!" She studied his face. "I don't need to talk to George; I can tell by looking at you. You've got the same look on your face you had when you came home and told me that you had sunk all our money in those crazy rockets."

"Charlotte, that's not fair. Skyways paid off. It's made us a mint of money."

"That's beside the point. I know why you're acting so strangely; you've got that old trip-to-the-Moon madness again. Well, I won't stand for it, do you hear? I'll stop you; I don't have to put up with it. I'm going right down in the morning and see Mr. Kamens and find out what has to be done to make you behave yourself." The cords of her neck jerked as she spoke.

He waited, gathering his temper before going on. "Charlotte, you have no real cause for complaint. No matter what happens to me, your future is taken care of."

"Do you think I want to be a widow?"

He looked thoughtfully at her. "I wonder."

"Why— Why, you heartless *beast*." She stood up. "We'll say no more about it; do you mind?" She left without waiting for an answer.

His "man" was waiting for him when he got to his room. Jenkins got up hastily and started drawing Harriman's bath. "Beat it," Harriman grunted. "I can undress myself."

"You require nothing more tonight, sir?"

"Nothing. But don't go unless you feel like it. Sit down and pour yourself a drink. Ed, how long you been married?"

"Don't mind if I do." The servant helped himself. "Twenty-three years, come May, sir."

"How's it been, if you don't mind me asking?"

"Not bad. Of course there have been times—"

"I know what you mean. Ed, if you weren't working for me, what would you be doing?"

"Well, the wife and I have talked many times of opening a little restaurant, nothing pretentious, but good. A place where a gentleman could enjoy a quiet meal of good food."

"Stag, eh?"

"No, not entirely, sir—but there would be a parlor for gentlemen only. Not even waitresses, I'd tend that room myself."

"Better look around for locations, Ed. You're practically in business."

CHAPTER THREE

STRONG ENTERED THEIR JOINT OFFICES the next morning at a precise nine o'clock, as usual. He was startled to find Harriman there before him. For Harriman to fail to show up at all meant nothing; for him to beat the clerks in was significant.

Harriman was busy with a terrestrial globe and a book—the current Nautical Almanac, Strong observed. Harriman barely glanced up. "Morning, George. Say, who've we got a line to in Brazil?"

"Why?"

"I need some trained seals who speak Portuguese, that's why. And some who speak Spanish, too. Not to mention three or four dozen scattered around in this country. I've come across something very, very interesting. Look here . . . according to these tables the Moon only swings about twenty-eight, just short of twenty-nine degrees north and south of the equator." He held a pencil against the globe and spun it. "Like that. That suggest anything?"

"No. Except that you're getting pencil marks on a sixty dollar globe."

"And you an old real estate operator! What does a man own when he buys a parcel of land?"

"That depends on the deed. Usually mineral rights and other subsurface rights are—"

"Never mind that. Suppose he buys the works, without splitting the rights: how far down does he own? How far up does he own?"

"Well, he owns a wedge down to the center of the Earth. That was settled in the slant-drilling and off-set oil lease cases. Theoretically he used to own the space above the land, too, out indefinitely, but that was modified by a series of cases after the commercial airlines came in—and a good thing, for us, too, or we would have to pay tolls every time one of our rockets took off for Australia."

"No, no, no, George! you didn't read those cases right. Right of passage was established—but *ownership* of the space above the land remained unchanged. And even right of passage was not absolute; you can build a thousand-foot tower on your own land right where airplanes, or rockets, or whatever, have been in the habit of passing and the ships will thereafter have to go above it, with no kick back on you. Remember how we had to lease the air south of Hughes Field to insure that our approach wasn't built up?"

Strong looked thoughtful. "Yes. I see your point. The ancient principle of land ownership remains undisturbed—down to the center of the Earth, up to infinity. But what of it? It's a purely theoretical matter. You're not planning to pay tolls to operate those spaceships you're always talking about, are you?" He grudged a smile at his own wit.

"Not on your tintype. Another matter entirely. George—*who owns the Moon?*"

Strong's jaw dropped, literally. "Delos, you're joking."

"I am not. I'll ask you again: if basic law says that a man owns the wedge of sky above his farm out to infinity, *who owns the Moon?* Take a look at this globe and tell me."

Strong looked. "But it can't mean anything, Delos. Earth laws wouldn't apply to the Moon."

"They apply here and that's where I am worrying about it. The Moon stays constantly over a slice of Earth bounded by latitude twenty-nine north and the same distance south; if one man owned all that belt of Earth—it's roughly the tropical zone—then he'd own the Moon, too, wouldn't he? By all the theories of real property ownership that our courts pay any attention to. And, by direct derivation, according to the sort of logic that lawyers like, the various owners of that belt of land have title—good vendable title—to the Moon somehow lodged collectively in them. The fact that the distribution of the title is a little vague wouldn't bother a lawyer; they grow fat on just such distributed titles every time a will is probated."

"It's fantastic!"

"George, when are you going to learn that 'fantastic' is a notion that doesn't bother a lawyer?"

"You're not planning to try to buy the entire tropical zone—that's what you would have to do."

"No," Harriman said slowly, "but it might not be a bad idea to buy right, title and interest in the Moon, as it may appear, from each of the sovereign countries in that belt. If I thought I could keep it quiet and not run the market up, I might try it. You can buy a thing awful cheap from a man if he thinks it's worthless and wants to sell before you regain your senses.

"But that's not the plan," he went on. "George, I want corporations—local corporations—in every one of those countries. I want the legislatures of each of those countries to grant franchises to its local corporation for lunar exploration, exploitation, et cetera, and the right to claim lunar soil on behalf of the country—with fee simple, naturally, being handed on a silver platter to the patriotic corporation that thought up the idea. And I want all this done quietly, so that the bribes won't go too high. We'll own the corporations, of course, which is why I need a flock of trained seals. There is going to be one hell of a fight one of these days over who owns the Moon; I want the deck stacked so that we win no matter how the cards are dealt."

"It will be ridiculously expensive, Delos. And you don't even know that you will ever get to the Moon, much less that it will be worth anything after you get there."

"We'll get there! It'll be more expensive not to establish these claims. Anyhow it need not be very expensive; the proper use of bribe money is a homoeopathic art—you use it as a catalyst. Back in the middle of the last century four men went from California to Washington with $40,000; it was all they had. A few weeks later they were broke—but Congress had awarded them a billion dollars' worth of railroad right of way. The trick is not to run up the market."

Strong shook his head. "Your title wouldn't be any good anyhow. The Moon doesn't stay in one place; it passes *over* owned land certainly—but so does a migrating goose."

"And nobody has title to a migrating bird. I get your point—but the Moon *always* stays over that one belt. If you move a boulder in your garden, do you lose title to it? Is it still real estate? Do the title laws still stand? This is like that group of real estate cases involving wandering islands in the Mississippi, George—the land moved as the river cut new channels, *but somebody always owned it.* In this case I plan to see to it that we are the 'somebody.'"

Strong puckered his brow. "I seem to recall that some of those island-and-riparian cases were decided one way and some another."

"We'll pick the decisions that suit us. That's why lawyers' wives have mink coats. Come on, George; let's get busy."

"On what?"

"Raising the money."

"Oh." Strong looked relieved. "I thought you were planning to use *our* money."

"I am. But it won't be nearly enough. We'll use our money for the senior financing to get things moving; in the meantime we've got to work out ways to keep the money rolling in." He pressed a switch at his desk; the face of Saul Kamens, their legal chief of staff, sprang out at him. "Hey, Saul, can you slide in for a pow-wow?"

"Whatever it is, just tell them 'no,'" answered the attorney. "I'll fix it."

"Good. Now come on in—they're moving Hell and I've got an option on the first ten loads."

Kamens showed up in his own good time. Some minutes later Harriman had explained his notion for claiming the Moon ahead of setting foot on it. "Besides those dummy corporations," he went on, "we need an agency that can receive contributions without having to admit any financial interest on the part of the contributor—like the National Geographic Society."

Kamens shook his head. "You can't buy the National Geographic Society."

"Damn it, who said we were going to? We'll set up our own."

"That's what I started to say."

"Good. As I see it, we need at least one tax-free, non-profit corporation headed up by the right people—we'll hang on to voting control, of course. We'll probably need more than one; we'll set them up as we need them.

And we've got to have at least one new ordinary corporation, *not* tax-free—but it won't show a profit until we are ready. The idea is to let the non-profit corporations have all of the prestige and all of the publicity—and the other gets all of the profits, if and when. We swap assets around between corporations, always for perfectly valid reasons, so that the non-profit corporations pay the expenses as we go along. Come to think about it, we had better have at least two ordinary corporations, so that we can let one of them go through bankruptcy if we find it necessary to shake out the water. That's the general sketch. Get busy and fix it up so that it's legal, will you?"

Kamens said, "You know, Delos, it would be a lot more honest if you did it at the point of a gun."

"A lawyer talks to me of honesty! Never mind, Saul; I'm not actually going to cheat anyone—"

"Humph!"

"—and I'm just going to make a trip to the Moon. That's what everybody will be paying for; that's what they'll get. Now fix it up so that it's legal, that's a good boy."

"I'm reminded of something the elder Vanderbilt's lawyer said to the old man under similar circumstances: 'It's beautiful the way it is; why spoil it by making it legal?' Okeh, brother gonoph, I'll rig your trap. Anything else?"

"Sure. Stick around, you might have some ideas. George, ask Montgomery to come in, will you?" Montgomery, Harriman's publicity chief, had two virtues in his employer's eyes: he was personally loyal to Harriman, and, secondly, he was quite capable of planning a campaign to convince the public that Lady Godiva wore a *Caresse*-brand girdle during her famous ride . . . or that Hercules attributed his strength to Crunchies for breakfast.

He arrived with a large portfolio under his arm. "Glad you sent for me, Chief. Get a load of this—" He spread the folder open on Harriman's desk and began displaying sketches and layouts. "Kinsky's work—is that boy hot!"

Harriman closed the portfolio. "What outfit is it for?"

"Huh? New World Homes."

"I don't want to see it; we're dumping New World Homes. Wait a minute—don't start to bawl. Have the boys go through with it; I want the price kept up while we unload. But open your ears to another matter." He explained rapidly the new enterprise.

Presently Montgomery was nodding. "When do we start and how much do we spend?"

"Right away and spend what you need to. Don't get chicken about expenses; this is the biggest thing we've ever tackled." Strong flinched; Harriman went on, "Have insomnia over it tonight; see me tomorrow and we'll kick it around."

"Wait a sec, Chief. How are you going to sew up all those franchises from the, uh—the Moon states, those countries the Moon passes over, while a big publicity campaign is going on about a trip to the Moon and how big a thing it is for everybody? Aren't you about to paint yourself into a corner?"

"Do I look stupid? We'll get the franchise *before* you hand out so much as a filler—*you*'ll get 'em, you and Kamens. That's your first job."

"Hmmm. . . ." Montgomery chewed a thumb nail. "Well, all right—I can see some angles. How soon do we have to sew it up?"

"I give you six weeks. Otherwise just mail your resignation in, written on the skin off your back."

"I'll write it right now, if you'll help me by holding a mirror."

"Damn it, Monty, I know you can't do it in six weeks. But make it fast; we can't take a cent in to keep the thing going until you sew up those franchises. If you dilly-dally, we'll all starve—and we won't get to the Moon, either."

Strong said, "D.D., why fiddle with those trick claims from a bunch of moth-eaten tropical countries? If you are dead set on going to the Moon, let's call Ferguson in and get on with the matter."

"I like your direct approach, George," Harriman said, frowning. "Mmmm . . . back about 1845 or '46 an eager-beaver American army officer captured California. You know what the State Department did?"

"No."

"They made him hand it back. Seems he hadn't touched second base, or something. So they had to go to the trouble of capturing it all over again a few months later. Now I don't want that to happen to us. It's not enough just to set foot on the Moon and claim it; we've got to validate that claim in terrestrial courts—or we're in for a peck of trouble. Eh, Saul?"

Kamens nodded. "Remember what happened to Columbus."

"Exactly. We aren't going to let ourselves be rooked the way Columbus was."

Montgomery spat out some thumb nail. "But, Chief—you know damn well those banana-state claims won't be worth two cents after I do tie them up. Why not get a franchise right from the U.N. and settle the matter? I'd as lief tackle that as tackle two dozen cockeyed legislatures. In fact I've got an angle already—we work it through the Security Council and—"

"Keep working on that angle; we'll use it later. You don't appreciate the full mechanics of the scheme, Monty. Of course those claims are worth nothing—except nuisance value. But their nuisance value is all important. Listen: we get to the Moon, or appear about to. Every one of those countries puts up a squawk; we goose them into it through the dummy corporations they have enfranchised. Where do they squawk? To the U.N., of course. Now the big countries on this globe, the rich and important ones, are all in the northern temperate zone. They see what the claims are based on and they take a frenzied look at the globe. Sure enough, the Moon does not pass over a one of them. The biggest country of all—Russia—doesn't own a spadeful of dirt south of twenty-nine north. So they reject all the claims.

"Or do they?" Harriman went on. "The U.S. balks. *The Moon passes over Florida and the southern part of Texas.* Washington is in a tizzy. Should they back up the tropical countries and support the traditional theory of land title or should they throw their weight to the idea that the Moon belongs to everyone? Or should the United States try to claim the whole thing, seeing as how it was Americans who actually got there first?

"At this point we creep out from under cover. It seems that the Moon ship was owned and the expenses paid by a non-profit corporation chartered by the U.N. itself—"

"Hold it," interrupted Strong. "I didn't know that the U.N. could create corporations?"

"You'll find it can," his partner answered. "How about it, Saul?" Kamens nodded. "Anyway," Harriman continued, "I've already got the corporation. I had it set up several years ago. It can do most anything of an educational or scientific nature—and brother, that covers a lot of ground! Back to the point—this corporation, the creature of the U.N., asks its parent to declare the lunar colony autonomous territory, under the protection of the U.N. We won't ask for outright membership at first because we want to keep it simple—"

"Simple, he calls it!" said Montgomery.

"Simple. This new colony will be a *de facto* sovereign state, holding title to the entire Moon, and—listen closely!—capable of buying, selling, passing laws, issuing title to land, setting up monopolies, collecting tariffs, et cetera without end. *And we own it.*"

"The reason we get all this is because the major states in the U.N. can't think up a claim that sounds as legal as the claim made by the tropical states, they can't agree among themselves as to how to split up the swag if they were to attempt brute force and the other major states aren't willing to see the United States claim the whole thing. They'll take the easy way out of their dilemma by appearing to retain title in the U.N. itself. The real title, the title controlling all economic and legal matters, will revert to us. Now do you see my point, Monty?"

Montgomery grinned. "Damned if I know if it's necessary, Chief, but I love it. It's beautiful."

"Well, I don't think so," Strong grumbled. "Delos, I've seen you rig some complicated deals—some of them so devious that they turned even my stomach—but this one is the worst yet. I think you've been carried away by the pleasure you get out of cooking up involved deals in which somebody gets double-crossed."

Harriman puffed hard on his cigar before answering, "I don't give a damn, George. Call it chicanery, call it anything you want to. *I'm going to the Moon!* If I have to manipulate a million people to accomplish it, I'll do it."

"But it's not necessary to do it this way."

"Well, how would you do it?"

"Me? I'd set up a straightforward corporation. I'd get a resolution in Congress making my corporation the chosen instrument of the United States—"

"Bribery?"

"Not necessarily. Influence and pressure ought to be enough. Then I would set about raising the money and make the trip."

"And the United States would then own the Moon?"

"Naturally," Strong answered a little stiffly.

Harriman got up and began pacing. "You don't see it, George, you don't see it. The Moon was not meant to be owned by a single country, even the United States."

"It was meant to be owned by *you,* I suppose."

"Well, if I own it—for a short while—I won't misuse it and I'll take care that others don't. Damnation, nationalism should stop at the stratosphere. Can you see what would happen if the United States lays claim to the Moon? The other nations won't recognize the claim. It will become a permanent bone of contention in the Security Council—just when we were beginning to get straightened out to the point where a man could do business planning without having his elbow jogged by a war every few years. The other nations —quite rightfully—will be scared to death of the United States. They will be able to look up in the sky any night and see the main atom-bomb rocket base of the United States staring down the backs of their necks. Are they going to hold still for it? No, sirree—they are going to try to clip off a piece of the Moon for their own national use. The Moon is too big to hold, all at once. There will be other bases established there and presently there will be the worst war this planet has ever seen—and we'll be to blame.

"No, it's got to be an arrangement that everybody will hold still for—and that's why we've got to plan it, think of all the angles, and be devious about it until we are in a position to make it work.

"Anyhow, George, if we claim it in the name of the United States, do you know where we will be, as business men?"

"In the driver's seat," answered Strong.

"In a pig's eye! We'll be dealt right out of the game. The Department of National Defense will say, 'Thank you, Mr. Harriman. Thank you, Mr. Strong. We are taking over in the interests of national security; you can go home now.' And that's just what we would have to do—go home and wait for the next atom war.

"I'm not going to do it, George. I'm not going to let the brass hats muscle in. I'm going to set up a lunar colony and then nurse it along until it is big enough to stand on its own feet. I'm telling you—all of you!—this is the biggest thing for the human race since the discovery of fire. Handled right, it can mean a new and braver world. Handle it wrong and it's a one-way ticket to Armageddon. It's coming, it's coming soon, whether we touch it or not. But I plan to be the Man in the Moon myself—and give it my personal attention to see that it's handled right."

He paused. Strong said, "Through with your sermon, Delos?"

"No, I'm not," Harriman denied testily. "You don't see this thing the right way. Do you know what we may find up there?" He swung his arm in an arc toward the ceiling. "*People!*"

"On the *Moon?*" said Kamens.

"Why not on the Moon?" whispered Montgomery to Strong.

"No, not on the Moon—at least I'd be amazed if we dug down and found anybody under that airless shell. The Moon has had its day; I was speaking of the other planets—Mars and Venus and the satellites of Jupiter. Even maybe out at the stars themselves. Suppose we do find people? Think what it will mean to us. We've been alone, all alone, the only intelligent race in the only world we know. We haven't even been able to talk with dogs or apes. Any answers we got we had to think up by ourselves, like deserted orphans. But suppose we find *people,* intelligent people, who have done some thinking in their own way. *We wouldn't be alone any more!* We could look up at the stars and never be afraid again."

He finished, seeming a little tired and even a little ashamed of his outburst, like a man surprised in a private act. He stood facing them, searching their faces.

"Gee whiz, Chief," said Montgomery, "I can use that. How about it?"

"Think you can remember it?"

"Don't need to—I flipped on your 'silent steno.'"

"Well, damn your eyes!"

"We'll put it on video—in a play I think."

Harriman smiled almost boyishly. "I've never acted, but if you think it'll do any good, I'm game."

"Oh, no, not you, Chief," Montgomery answered in horrified tones. "You're not the type. I'll use Basil Wilkes-Booth, I think. With his organ-like voice and that beautiful archangel face, he'll really send 'em."

Harriman glanced down at his paunch and said gruffly, "O.K.—back to business. Now about money. In the first place we can go after straight donations to one of the non-profit corporations, just like endowments for colleges. Hit the upper brackets, where tax deductions really matter. How much do you think we can raise that way?"

"Very little," Strong opined. "That cow is about milked dry."

"It's never milked dry, as long as there are rich men around who would rather make gifts than pay taxes. How much will a man pay to have a crater on the Moon named after him?"

"I thought they all had names?" remarked the lawyer.

"Lots of them don't—and we have the whole back face that's not touched yet. We won't try to put down an estimate today; we'll just list it. Monty, I want an angle to squeeze dimes out of the school kids, too. Forty million school kids at a dime a head is $4,000,000.00—we can use that."

"Why stop at a dime?" asked Monty. "If you get a kid really interested he'll scrape together a dollar."

"Yes, but what do we offer him for it? Aside from the honor of taking part in a noble venture and so forth?"

"Mmmm. . . ." Montgomery used up more thumb nail. "Suppose we go after both the dimes and the dollars. For a dime he gets a card saying that he's a member of the Moonbeam club—"

"No, the 'Junior Spacemen'."

"O.K., the Moonbeams will be girls—and don't forget to rope the Boy Scouts and Girl Scouts into it, too. We give each kid a card; when he kicks in another dime, we punch it. When he's punched out a dollar, we give him a certificate, suitable for framing, with his name and some process engraving, and on the back a picture of the Moon."

"On the *front,*" answered Harriman. "Do it in one print job; it's cheaper and it'll look better. We give him something else, too, a steelclad guarantee that his name will be on the rolls of the Junior Pioneers of the Moon, which same will be placed in a monument to be erected on the Moon at the landing site of the first Moon ship—in microfilm, of course; we have to watch weight."

"Fine!" agreed Montgomery. "Want to swap jobs, Chief? When he gets up to ten dollars we give him a genuine, solid gold-plated shooting star pin and he's a senior Pioneer, with the right to vote or something or other. And his name goes *outside* of the monument—microengraved on a platinum strip."

Strong looked as if he had bitten a lemon. "What happens when he reaches a hundred dollars?" he asked.

"Why, then," Montgomery answered happily, "we give him another card and he can start over. Don't worry about it, Mr. Strong—if any kid goes that high, he'll have his reward. Probably we will take him on an inspection tour of the ship before it takes off and give him, absolutely free, a picture of himself standing in front of it, with the pilot's own signature signed across the bottom by some female clerk."

"Chiseling from kids. Bah!"

"Not at all," answered Montgomery in hurt tones. "Intangibles are the most honest merchandise anyone can sell. They are always worth whatever you are willing to pay for them and they never wear out. You can take them to your grave untarnished."

"Hmmmph!"

Harriman listened to this, smiling and saying nothing. Kamens cleared his throat. "If you two ghouls are through cannibalizing the youth of the land, I've another idea."

"Spill it."

"George, you collect stamps, don't you?"

"Yes."

"How much would a cover be worth which had been to the Moon and been cancelled there?"

"Huh? But you couldn't, you know."

"I think we could get our Moon ship declared a legal post office sub-station without too much trouble. What would it be worth?"

"Uh, that depends on how rare they are."

"There must be some optimum number which will fetch a maximum return. Can you estimate it?"

Strong got a faraway look in his eye, then took out an old-fashioned pencil and commenced to figure. Harriman went on, "Saul, my minor success in buying a share in the Moon from Jones went to my head. How about selling building lots on the Moon?"

"Let's keep this serious, Delos. You can't do that until you've landed there."

"I am serious. I know you are thinking of that ruling back in the 'forties that such land would have to be staked out and accurately described. I want to sell land on the Moon. You figure out a way to make it legal. I'll sell the whole Moon, if I can—surface rights, mineral rights, anything."

"Suppose they want to occupy it?"

"Fine. The more the merrier. I'd like to point out, too, that we'll be in a position to assess taxes on what we have sold. If they don't use it and won't pay taxes, it reverts to us. Now you figure out how to offer it, without going to jail. You may have to advertise it abroad, then plan to peddle it personally in this country, like Irish Sweepstakes tickets."

Kamens looked thoughtful. "We could incorporate the land company in Panama and advertise by video and radio from Mexico. Do you really think you can sell the stuff?"

"You can sell snowballs in Greenland," put in Montgomery. "It's a matter of promotion."

Harriman added, "Did you ever read about the Florida land boom, Saul? People bought lots they had never seen and sold them at tripled prices without ever having laid eyes on them. Sometimes a parcel would change hands a dozen times before anyone got around to finding out that the stuff was ten-foot deep in water. We can offer bargains better than that—an acre, a guaranteed dry acre with plenty of sunshine, for maybe ten dollars—or a thousand acres at a dollar an acre. Who's going to turn down a bargain like that? Particularly after the rumor gets around that the Moon is believed to be loaded with uranium?"

"Is it?"

"How should I know? When the boom sags a little we will announce the selected location of Luna City—and it will just happen to work out that the land around the site is still available for sale. Don't worry, Saul, if it's real estate, George and I can sell it. Why, down in the Ozarks, where the land stands on edge, we used to sell both sides of the same acre." Harriman looked thoughtful. "I think we'll reserve mineral rights—there just might actually be uranium there!"

Kamens chuckled. "Delos, you are a kid at heart. Just a great big, overgrown, lovable—juvenile delinquent."

Strong straightened up. "I make it half a million," he said.

"Half a million what?" asked Harriman.

"For the cancelled philatelic covers, of course. That's what we were talking about. Five thousand is my best estimate of the number that could be placed with serious collectors and with dealers. Even then we will have to discount them to a syndicate and hold back until the ship is built and the trip looks like a probability."

"Okay," agreed Harriman. "You handle it. I'll just note that we can tap you for an extra half million toward the end."

"Don't I get a commission?" asked Kamens. "I thought of it."

"You get a rising vote of thanks—and ten acres on the Moon. Now what other sources of revenue can we hit?"

"Don't you plan to sell stock?" asked Kamens.

"I was coming to that. Of course—but no preferred stock; we don't want to be forced through a reorganization. Participating common, non-voting—"

"Sounds like another banana-state corporation to me."

"Naturally—but I want some of it on the New York Exchange, and you'll have to work that out with the Securities Exchange Commission somehow. Not too much of it—that's our show case and we'll have to keep it active and moving up."

"Wouldn't you rather I swam the Hellespont?"

"Don't be like that, Saul. It beats chasing ambulances, doesn't it?"

"I'm not sure."

"Well, that's what I want you—wups!" The screen on Harriman's desk had come to life. A girl said, "Mr. Harriman, Mr. Dixon is here. He has no appointment but he says that you want to see him."

"I thought I had that thing shut off," muttered Harriman, then pressed his key and said, "O.K., show him in."

"Very well, sir—oh, Mr. Harriman, Mr. Entenza came in just this second."

"Look who's talking," said Kamens.

Dixon came in with Entenza behind him. He sat down, looked around, started to speak, then checked himself. He looked around again, especially at Entenza.

"Go ahead, Dan," Harriman encouraged him. " 'Tain't nobody here at all but just us chickens."

Dixon made up his mind. "I've decided to come in with you, D.D.," he announced. "As an act of faith I went to the trouble of getting this." He took a formal-looking instrument from his pocket and displayed it. It was a sale of lunar rights, from Phineas Morgan to Dixon, phrased in exactly the same fashion as that which Jones had granted to Harriman.

Entenza looked startled, then dipped into his own inner coat pocket. Out came three more sales contracts of the same sort, each from a director of the power syndicate. Harriman cocked an eyebrow at them. "Jack sees you and raises you two, Dan. You want to call?"

Dixon smiled ruefully. "I can just see him." He added two more to the pile, grinned and offered his hand to Entenza.

"Looks like a stand off." Harriman decided to say nothing just yet about seven telestated contracts now locked in his desk—after going to bed the night before he had been quite busy on the phone almost till midnight. "Jack, how much did you pay for those things?"

"Standish held out for a thousand; the others were cheap."

"Damn it, I warned you not to run the price up. Standish will gossip. How about you, Dan?"

"I got them at satisfactory prices."

"So you won't talk, eh? Never mind—gentlemen, how serious are you about this? How much money did you bring with you?"

Entenza looked to Dixon, who answered, "How much does it take?"

"How much can you raise?" demanded Harriman.

Dixon shrugged. "We're getting no place. Let's use figures. A hundred thousand."

Harriman sniffed. "I take it what you really want is to reserve a seat on the first regularly scheduled Moon ship. I'll sell it to you at that price."

"Let's quit sparring, Delos. How much?"

Harriman's face remained calm but he thought furiously. He was caught short, with too little information—he had not even talked figures with his chief engineer as yet. Confound it! Why had he left that phone hooked in? "Dan, as I warned you, it will cost you at least a million just to sit down in this game."

"So I thought. How much will it take to *stay* in the game?"

"All you've got."

"Don't be silly, Delos. I've got more than you have."

Harriman lit a cigar, his only sign of agitation. "Suppose you match us, dollar for dollar."

"For which I get two shares?"

"Okay, okay, you chuck in a buck whenever each of us does—share and share alike. But I run things."

"You run the operations," agreed Dixon. "Very well, I'll put up a million now and match you as necessary. You have no objection to me having my own auditor, of course."

"When have I ever cheated you, Dan?"

"Never and there is no need to start."

"Have it your own way—but be damned sure you send a man who can keep his mouth shut."

"He'll keep quiet. I keep his heart in a jar in my safe."

Harriman was thinking about the extent of Dixon's assets. "We just might let you buy in with a second share later, Dan. This operation will be expensive."

Dixon fitted his finger tips carefully together. "We'll meet that question when we come to it. I don't believe in letting an enterprise fold up for lack of capital."

"Good." Harriman turned to Entenza. "You heard what Dan had to say, Jack. Do you like the terms?"

Entenza's forehead was covered with sweat. "I can't raise a million that fast."

"That's all right, Jack. We don't need it this morning. Your note is good; you can take your time liquidating."

"But you said a million is just the beginning. I can't match you indefinitely; you've got to place a limit on it. I've got my family to consider."

"No annuities, Jack? No monies transferred in an irrevocable trust?"

"That's not the point. You'll be able to squeeze me—freeze me out."

Harriman waited for Dixon to say something. Dixon finally said, "We wouldn't squeeze you, Jack—as long as you could prove you had converted every asset you hold. We would let you stay in on a pro rata basis."

Harriman nodded. "That's right, Jack." He was thinking that any shrinkage in Entenza's share would give himself and Strong a clear voting majority.

Strong had been thinking of something of the same nature, for he spoke up suddenly, "I don't like this. Four equal partners—we can be deadlocked too easily."

Dixon shrugged. "I refuse to worry about it. I am in this because I am betting that Delos can manage to make it profitable."

"We'll get to the Moon, Dan!"

"I didn't say that. I am betting that you will show a profit whether we get to the Moon or not. Yesterday evening I spent looking over the public records of several of your companies; they were very interesting. I suggest we resolve any possible deadlock by giving the Director—that's you, Delos—the power to settle ties. Satisfactory, Entenza?"

"Oh, sure!"

Harriman was worried but tried not to show it. He did not trust Dixon, even bearing gifts. He stood up suddenly. "I've got to run, gentlemen. I leave you to Mr. Strong and Mr. Kamens. Come along, Monty." Kamens, he was sure, would not spill anything prematurely, even to nominal full partners. As for Strong—George, he knew, had not even let his left hand know how many fingers there were on his right.

He dismissed Montgomery outside the door of the partners' personal office and went across the hall. Andrew Ferguson, chief engineer of Harriman Enterprises, looked up as he came in. "Howdy, Boss. Say, Mr. Strong gave me an interesting idea for a light switch this morning. It did not seem practical at first but—"

"Skip it. Let one of the boys have it and forget it. You know the line we are on now."

"There have been rumors," Ferguson answered cautiously.

"Fire the man that brought you the rumor. No—send him on a special mission to Tibet and keep him there until we are through. Well, let's get on with it. I want you to build a Moon ship as quickly as possible."

Ferguson threw one leg over the arm of his chair, took out a pen knife and began grooming his nails. "You say that like it was an order to build a privy."

"Why not? There have been theoretically adequate fuels since way back in '49. You get together the team to design it and the gang to build it; you build it—I pay the bills. What could be simpler?"

Ferguson stared at the ceiling. " 'Adequate fuels—' " he repeated dreamily.

"So I said. The figures show that hydrogen and oxygen are enough to get a step rocket to the Moon and back—it's just a matter of proper design."

" 'Proper design,' he says," Ferguson went on in the same gentle voice, then suddenly swung around, jabbed the knife into the scarred desk top and bellowed, "What do you know about proper design? Where do I get the steels? What do I use for a throat liner? How in the hell do I burn enough tons of your crazy mix per second to keep from wasting all my power breaking loose? How can I get a decent mass-ratio with a step rocket? Why in the hell didn't you let me build a proper ship when we had the fuel?"

Harriman waited for him to quiet down, then said, "What do we do about it, Andy?"

"Hmmm. . . . I was thinking about it as I lay abed last night—and my old lady is sore as hell at you; I had to finish the night on the couch. In the first place, Mr. Harriman, the proper way to tackle this is to get a research appropriation from the Department of National Defense. Then you—"

"Damn it, Andy, you stick to engineering and let me handle the political and financial end of it. I don't want your advice."

"Damn it, Delos, don't go off half-cocked. This *is* engineering I'm talking about. The government owns a whole mass of former art about rocketry—all classified. Without a government contract you can't even get a peek at it."

"It can't amount to very much. What can a government rocket do that a Skyways rocket can't do? You told me yourself that Federal rocketry no longer amounted to anything."

Ferguson looked supercilious. "I am afraid I can't explain it in lay terms. You will have to take it for granted that we need those government research reports. There's no sense in spending thousands of dollars in doing work that has already been done."

"Spend the thousands."

"Maybe millions."

"Spend the millions. Don't be afraid to spend money. Andy, I don't want this to be a military job." He considered elaborating to the engineer the involved politics back of his decision, thought better of it. "How bad do you actually need that government stuff? Can't you get the same results by hiring engineers who used to work for the government? Or even hire them away from the government right now?"

Ferguson pursed his lips. "If you insist on hampering me, how can you expect me to get results?"

"I am not hampering you. I am telling you that this is not a government project. If you won't attempt to cope with it on those terms, let me know now, so that I can find somebody who will."

Ferguson started playing mumblety-peg on his desk top. When he got to "noses"—and missed—he said quietly, "I mind a boy who used to work for the government at White Sands. He was a very smart lad indeed—design chief of section."

"You mean he might head up your team?"

"That was the notion."

"What's his name? Where is he? Who's he working for?"

"Well, as it happened, when the government closed down White Sands, it seemed a shame to me that a good boy should be out of a job, so I placed him with Skyways. He's maintenance chief engineer out on the Coast."

"Maintenance? What a hell of a job for a creative man! But you mean he's working for us now? Get him on the screen. No—call the coast and have them send him here in a special rocket; we'll all have lunch together."

"As it happens," Ferguson said quietly, "I got up last night and called him—that's what annoyed the Missus. He's waiting outside. Coster—Bob Coster."

A slow grin spread over Harriman's face. "Andy! You black-hearted old scoundrel, why did you pretend to balk?"

"I wasn't pretending. I like it here, Mr. Harriman. Just as long as you don't interfere, I'll do my job. Now my notion is this: we'll make young

Coster chief engineer of the project and give him his head. I won't joggle his elbow; I'll just read the reports. Then you leave him alone, d'you hear me? Nothing makes a good technical man angrier than to have some incompetent nitwit with a check book telling him how to do his job."

"Suits. And I don't want a penny-pinching old fool slowing him down, either. Mind you don't interfere with him, either, or I'll jerk the rug out from under you. Do we understand each other?"

"I think we do."

"Then get him in here."

Apparently Ferguson's concept of a "lad" was about age thirty-five, for such Harriman judged Coster to be. He was tall, lean, and quietly eager. Harriman braced him immediately after shaking hands with, "Bob, can you build a rocket that will go to the Moon?"

Coster took it without blinking. "Do you have a source of X-fuel?" he countered, giving the rocket man's usual shorthand for the isotope fuel formerly produced by the power satellite.

"No."

Coster remained perfectly quiet for several seconds, then answered, "I can put an unmanned messenger rocket on the face of the Moon."

"Not good enough. I want it to go there, land, and come back. Whether it lands here under power or by atmosphere braking is unimportant."

It appeared that Coster never answered promptly; Harriman had the fancy that he could hear wheels turning over in the man's head. "That would be a very expensive job."

"Who asked you how much it would cost? Can you do it?"

"I could try."

"Try, hell. Do you think you can *do* it? Would you bet your shirt on it? Would you be willing to risk your neck in the attempt? If you don't believe in yourself, man, you'll always lose."

"How much will *you* risk, sir? I told you this would be expensive—and I doubt if you have any idea how expensive."

"And I told you not to worry about money. Spend what you need; it's my job to pay the bills. Can you do it?"

"I can do it. I'll let you know later how much it will cost and how long it will take."

"Good. Start getting your team together. Where are we going to do this, Andy?" he added, turning to Ferguson. "Australia?"

"No." It was Coster who answered. "It can't be Australia; I want a mountain catapult. That will save us one step-combination."

"How big a mountain?" asked Harriman. "Will Pikes Peak do?"

"It ought to be in the Andes," objected Ferguson. "The mountains are taller and closer to the equator. After all, we own facilities there—or the Andes Development Company does."

"Do as you like, Bob," Harriman told Coster. "I would prefer Pikes Peak, but it's up to you." He was thinking that there were tremendous business advantages to locating Earth's space port #1 inside the United States—and he could visualize the advertising advantage of having Moon ships blast off from the top of Pikes Peak, in plain view of everyone for hundreds of miles to the East.

"I'll let you know."

"Now about salary. Forget whatever it was we were paying you; how much do you want?"

Coster actually gestured, waving the subject away. "I'll work for coffee and cakes."

"Don't be silly."

"Let me finish. Coffee and cakes and one other thing: I get to make the trip."

Harriman blinked. "Well, I can understand that," he said slowly. "In the meantime I'll put you on a drawing account." He added, "Better calculate for a three-man ship, unless you are a pilot."

"I'm not."

"Three men, then. You see, I'm going along, too."

CHAPTER FOUR

"A GOOD THING YOU DECIDED to come in, Dan," Harriman was saying, "or you would find yourself out of a job. I'm going to put an awful crimp in the power company before I'm through with this."

Dixon buttered a roll. "Really? How?"

"We'll set up high-temperature piles, like the Arizona job, just like the one that blew up, around the corner on the far face of the Moon. We'll remote-control them; if one explodes it won't matter. And I'll breed more X-fuel in a week than the company turned out in three months. Nothing personal about it; it's just that I want a source of fuel for interplanetary liners. If we can't get good stuff here, we'll have to make it on the Moon."

"Interesting. But where do you propose to get the uranium for six piles? The last I heard the Atomic Energy Commission had the prospective supply earmarked twenty years ahead."

"Uranium? Don't be silly; we'll get it on the Moon."

"On the Moon? Is there uranium on the Moon?"

"Didn't you know? I thought that was why you decided to join up with me?"

"No, I didn't know," Dixon said deliberately. "What proof have you?"

"Me? I'm no scientist, but it's a well-understood fact. Spectroscopy, or something. Catch one of the professors. But don't go showing too much interest; we aren't ready to show our hand." Harriman stood up. "I've got to run, or I'll miss the shuttle for Rotterdam. Thanks for the lunch." He grabbed his hat and left.

Harriman stood up. "Suit yourself, Mynheer van der Velde. I'm giving you and your colleagues a chance to hedge your bets. Your geologists all agree that diamonds result from volcanic action. What do you think we will find *there?*" He dropped a large photograph of the Moon on the Hollander's desk.

The diamond merchant looked impassively at the pictured planet, pock-marked by a thousand giant craters. "If you get there, Mr. Harriman."

Harriman swept up the picture. "We'll get there. And we'll find diamonds—though I would be the first to admit that it may be twenty years or even forty before there is a big enough strike to matter. I've come to you because I believe that the worst villain in our social body is a man who introduces a major new economic factor without planning his innovation in such a way as to permit peaceful adjustment. I don't like panics. But all I can do is warn you. Good day."

"Sit down, Mr. Harriman. I'm always confused when a man explains how he is going to do *me* good. Suppose you tell me instead how this is going to do *you* good? Then we can discuss how to protect the world market against a sudden influx of diamonds from the Moon."

Harriman sat down.

Harriman liked the Low Countries. He was delighted to locate a dog-drawn milk cart whose young master wore real wooden shoes; he happily took pictures and tipped the child heavily, unaware that the set-up was arranged for tourists. He visited several other diamond merchants but without speaking of the Moon. Among other purchases he found a brooch for Charlotte—a peace offering.

Then he took a taxi to London, planted a story with the representatives of the diamond syndicate there, arranged with his London solicitors to be insured by Lloyd's of London through a dummy, *against* a successful Moon flight, and called his home office. He listened to numerous reports, especially those concerning Montgomery, and found that Montgomery was in New Delhi. He called him there, spoke with him at length, then hurried to the port just in time to catch his ship. He was in Colorado the next morning.

At Peterson Field, east of Colorado Springs, he had trouble getting through the gate, even though it was now his domain, under lease. Of course he could have called Coster and gotten it straightened out at once, but he wanted to look around before seeing Coster. Fortunately the head guard knew him by sight; he got in and wandered around for an hour or more, a tri-colored badge pinned to his coat to give him freedom.

The machine shop was moderately busy, so was the foundry . . . but most of the shops were almost deserted. Harriman left the shops, went into the main engineering building. The drafting room and the loft were fairly active, as was the computation section. But there were unoccupied desks in the structures group and a churchlike quiet in the metals group and in the adjoining metallurgical laboratory. He was about to cross over into the chemicals and materials annex when Coster suddenly showed up.

"Mr. Harriman! I just heard you were here."

"Spies everywhere," remarked Harriman. "I didn't want to disturb you."

"Not at all. Let's go up to my office."

Settled there a few moments later Harriman asked, "Well—how's it going?"

Coster frowned. "All right, I guess."

Harriman noted that the engineer's desk baskets were piled high with papers which spilled over onto the desk. Before Harriman could answer, Coster's desk phone lit up and a feminine voice said sweetly, "Mr. Coster—Mr. Morgenstern is calling."

"Tell him I'm busy."

After a short wait the girl answered in a troubled voice, "He says he's just got to speak to you, sir."

Coster looked annoyed. "Excuse me a moment, Mr. Harriman—O.K., put him on."

The girl was replaced by a man who said, "Oh there you are—what was the hold up? Look, Chief, we're in a jam about these trucks. Every one of them that we leased needs an overhaul and now it turns out that the White Fleet company won't do anything about it—they're sticking to the fine print in the contract. Now the way I see it, we'd do better to cancel the contract and do business with Peak City Transport. They have a scheme that looks good to me. They guarantee to—"

"Take care of it," snapped Coster. "You made the contract and you have authority to cancel. You know that."

"Yes, but Chief, I figured this would be something you would want to pass on personally. It involves policy and—"

"Take care of it! I don't give a damn what you do as long as we have transportation when we need it." He switched off.

"Who is that man?" inquired Harriman.

"Who? Oh, that's Morgenstern, Claude Morgenstern."

"Not his name—what does he do?"

"He's one of my assistants—buildings, grounds, and transportation."

"Fire him!"

Coster looked stubborn. Before he could answer a secretary came in and stood insistently at his elbow with a sheaf of papers. He frowned, initialed them, and sent her out.

"Oh, I don't mean that as an order," Harriman added, "but I do mean it as serious advice. I won't give orders in your backyard,—but will you listen to a few minutes of advice?"

"Naturally," Coster agreed stiffly.

"Mmm . . . this your first job as top boss?"

Coster hesitated, then admitted it.

"I hired you on Ferguson's belief that you were the engineer most likely to build a successful Moon ship. I've had no reason to change my mind. But top administration ain't engineering, and maybe I can show you a few tricks there, if you'll let me." He waited. "I'm not criticizing," he added. "Top bossing is like sex; until you've had it, you don't know about it." Harriman had the mental reservation that if the boy would not take advice, he would suddenly be out of a job, whether Ferguson liked it or not.

Coster drummed on his desk. "I don't know what's wrong and that's a fact. It seems as if I can't turn anything over to anybody and have it done properly. I feel as if I were swimming in quicksand."

"Done much engineering lately?"

"I try to." Coster waved at another desk in the corner. "I work there, late at night."

"That's no good. I hired you as an engineer. Bob, this setup is all wrong. The joint ought to be jumping—and it's not. Your office ought to be quiet as a grave. Instead your office is jumping and the plant looks like a graveyard."

Coster buried his face in his hands, then looked up. "I know it. I know what needs to be done—but every time I try to tackle a technical problem some bloody fool wants me to make a decision about trucks—or telephones—or some damn thing. I'm sorry, Mr. Harriman. I thought I could do it."

Harriman said very gently, "Don't let it throw you, Bob. You haven't had much sleep lately, have you? Tell you what—we'll put over a fast one on Ferguson. I'll take that desk you're at for a few days and build you a set-up to protect you against such things. I want that brain of yours thinking about reaction vectors and fuel efficiencies and design stresses, not about contracts for trucks." Harriman stepped to the door, looked around the outer office and spotted a man who might or might not be the office's chief clerk. "Hey, you! C'mere."

The man looked startled, got up, came to the door and said, "Yes?"

"I want that desk in the corner and all the stuff that's on it moved to an empty office on this floor, right away."

The clerk raised his eyebrows. "And who are you, if I may ask?"

"Damn it—"

"Do as he tells you, Weber," Coster put in.

"I want it done inside of twenty minutes," added Harriman. "Jump!"

He turned back to Coster's other desk, punched the phone, and presently was speaking to the main offices of Skyways. "Jim, is your boy Jock Berkeley around? Put him on leave and send him to me, at Peterson Field, right away, special trip. I want the ship he comes in to raise ground ten minutes after we sign off. Send his gear after him." Harriman listened for a moment, then answered, "No, your organization won't fall apart if you lose Jock—or, if it does, maybe we've been paying the wrong man the top salary . . . okay, okay, you're entitled to one swift kick at my tail the next time you catch up with me but send Jock. So long."

He supervised getting Coster and his other desk moved into another office, saw to it that the phone in the new office was disconnected, and, as an afterthought, had a couch moved in there, too. "We'll install a projector, and a drafting machine and bookcases and other junk like that tonight," he told Coster. "Just make a list of anything you need—to work on *engineering*. And call me if you want anything." He went back to the nominal chief-engineer's office and got happily to work trying to figure where the organization stood and what was wrong with it.

Some four hours later he took Berkeley in to meet Coster. The chief engineer was asleep at his desk, head cradled on his arms. Harriman started to back out, but Coster roused. "Oh! Sorry," he said, blushing, "I must have dozed off."

"That's why I brought you the couch," said Harriman. "It's more restful. Bob, meet Jock Berkeley. He's your new slave. You remain chief engineer and top, undisputed boss. Jock is Lord High Everything Else. From now on you've got absolutely nothing to worry about—except for the little detail of building a Moon ship."

They shook hands. "Just one thing I ask, Mr. Coster," Berkeley said seriously, "bypass me all you want to—you'll have to run the technical show—but for God's sake record it so I'll know what's going on. I'm going to have a switch placed on your desk that will operate a sealed recorder at my desk."

"Fine!" Coster was looking, Harriman thought, younger already.

"And if you want something that is not technical, don't do it yourself. Just flip a switch and whistle; it'll get done!" Berkeley glanced at Harriman. "The Boss says he wants to talk with you about the real job. I'll leave you and get busy." He left.

Harriman sat down; Coster followed suit and said, "Whew!"

"Feel better?"

"I like the looks of that fellow Berkeley."

"That's good; he's your twin brother from now on. Stop worrying; I've used him before. You'll think you're living in a well-run hospital. By the way, where do you live?"

"At a boarding house in the Springs."

"That's ridiculous. And you don't even have a place here to sleep?" Harriman reached over to Coster's desk, got through to Berkeley. "Jock—get a suite for Mr. Coster at the Broadmoor, under a phony name."

"Right."

"And have this stretch along here adjacent to his office fitted out as an apartment."

"Right. Tonight."

"Now, Bob, about the Moon ship. Where do we stand?"

They spent the next two hours contentedly running over the details of the problem, as Coster had laid them out. Admittedly very little work had been done since the field was leased but Coster had accomplished considerable theoretical work and computation before he had gotten swamped in administrative details. Harriman, though no engineer and certainly not a mathematician outside the primitive arithmetic of money, had for so long devoured everything he could find about space travel that he was able to follow most of what Coster showed him.

"I don't see anything here about your mountain catapult," he said presently.

Coster looked vexed. "Oh, that! Mr. Harriman, I spoke too quickly."

"Huh? How come? I've had Montgomery's boys drawing up beautiful pictures of what things will look like when we are running regular trips. I intend to make Colorado Springs the spaceport capital of the world. We hold the franchise of the old cog railroad now; what's the hitch?"

"Well, it's both time and money."

"Forget money. That's my pidgin."

"Time then. I still think an electric gun is the best way to get the initial acceleration for a chem-powered ship. Like this—" He began to sketch rapidly. "It enables you to omit the first step-rocket stage, which is bigger than all the others put together and is terribly inefficient, as it has such a poor mass-ratio. But what do you have to do to get it? You can't build a tower, not a tower a couple of miles high, strong enough to take the thrusts—not this year, anyway. So you have to use a mountain. Pikes Peak is as good as any; it's accessible, at least.

"But what do you have to do to use it? First, a tunnel in through the side, from Manitou to just under the peak, and big enough to take the loaded ship—"

"Lower it down from the top," suggested Harriman.

Coster answered, "I thought of that. Elevators two miles high for loaded space ships aren't exactly built out of string, in fact they aren't built out of any available materials. It's possible to gimmick the catapult itself so that the accelerating coils can be reversed and timed differently to do the job, but believe me, Mr. Harriman, it will throw you into other engineering problems quite as great . . . such as a giant railroad up to the top of the ship. And it still leaves you with the shaft of the catapult itself to be dug. It can't be as small as the ship, not like a gun barrel for a bullet. It's got to be considerably larger; you don't compress a column of air two miles high with impunity. Oh, a mountain catapult could be built, but it might take ten years—or longer."

"Then forget it. We'll build it for the future but not for this flight. No, wait—how about a *surface* catapult. We scoot up the side of the mountain and curve it up at the end?"

"Quite frankly, I think something like that is what will eventually be used. But, as of today, it just creates new problems. Even if we could devise an electric gun in which you could make that last curve—we can't, at present—the ship would have to be designed for terrific side stresses and all the additional weight would be parasitic so far as our main purpose is concerned, the design of a rocket ship."

"Well, Bob, what *is* your solution?"

Coster frowned. "Go back to what we know how to do—build a step rocket."

CHAPTER FIVE

"MONTY—"

"Yeah, Chief?"

"Have you ever heard this song?" Harriman hummed, "*The Moon belongs to everyone; the best things in life are free*—," then sang it, badly off key.

"Can't say as I ever have."

"It was before your time. I want it dug out again. I want it revived, plugged until Hell wouldn't have it, and on everybody's lips."

"O.K." Montgomery took out his memorandum pad. "When do you want it to reach its top?"

Harriman considered. "In, say, about three months. Then I want the first phrase picked up and used in advertising slogans."

"A cinch."

"How are things in Florida, Monty?"

"I thought we were going to have to buy the whole damned legislature until we got the rumor spread around that Los Angeles had contracted to have a City-Limits-of-Los-Angeles sign planted on the Moon for publicity pix. Then they came around."

"Good." Harriman pondered. "You know, that's not a bad idea. How much do you think the Chamber of Commerce of Los Angeles would pay for such a picture?"

Montgomery made another note. "I'll look into it."

"I suppose you are about ready to crank up Texas, now that Florida is loaded?"

"Most any time now. We're spreading a few snide rumors first."

Headline from Dallas-Fort Worth *Banner*:

"THE MOON BELONGS TO TEXAS!!!"

"—and that's all for tonight, kiddies. Don't forget to send in those box tops, or reasonable facsimiles. Remember—first prize is a thousand-acre ranch on the Moon itself, free and clear; the second prize is a six-foot scale model of the actual Moon ship, and there are fifty, count them, fifty third prizes, each a saddle-trained Shetland pony. Your hundred word composition 'Why I want to go to the Moon' will be judged for sincerity and originality, not on literary merit. Send those boxtops to Uncle Taffy, Box 214, Juarez, Old Mexico."

Harriman was shown into the office of the president of the Moka-Coka Company ("Only a Moke is truly a coke"— "Drink the Cola drink with the Lift"). He paused at the door, some twenty feet from the president's desk and quickly pinned a two-inch wide button to his lapel.

Patterson Griggs looked up. "Well, this is really an honor, D.D. Do come in and—" The soft-drink executive stopped suddenly, his expression changed. "What are you doing wearing *that?*" he snapped. "Trying to annoy me?"

"That" was the two-inch disc; Harriman unpinned it and put it in his pocket. It was a celluloid advertising pin, in plain yellow; printed on it in black, almost covering it, was a simple

the trademark of Moka-Coka's only serious rival.

"No," answered Harriman, "though I don't blame you for being irritated. I see half the school kids in the country wearing these silly buttons. But I came to give you a friendly tip, not to annoy you."

"What do you mean?"

"When I paused at your door that pin on my lapel was just the size—to you, standing at your desk—as the full Moon looks when you are standing in your garden, looking up at it. You didn't have any trouble reading what was on the pin, did you? I know you didn't; you yelled at me before either one of us stirred."

"What about it?"

"How would you feel—and what would the effect be on your sales—if there was 'six-plus' written across the face of the Moon instead of just on a school kid's sweater?"

Griggs thought about it, then said, "D.D., don't make poor jokes. I've had a bad day."

"I'm not joking. As you have probably heard around the Street, I'm behind this Moon trip venture. Between ourselves, Pat, it's quite an expensive undertaking, even for me. A few days ago a man came to me—you'll pardon me if I don't mention names? You can figure it out. Anyhow, this man represented a client who wanted to buy the advertising concession for the Moon. He knew we weren't sure of success; but he said his client would take the risk.

"At first I couldn't figure out what he was talking about; he set me straight. Then I thought he was kidding. Then I was shocked. Look at this—" Harriman took out a large sheet of paper and spread it on Griggs' desk. "You see the equipment is set up anywhere near the center of the Moon, as we see it. Eighteen pyrotechnics rockets shoot out in eighteen directions, like the spokes of a wheel, but to carefully calculated distances. They hit and the bombs they carry go off, spreading finely divided carbon black for calculated distances. There's no air on the Moon, you know, Pat—a fine powder will throw just as easily as a javelin. Here's your result." He turned the paper over; on the back there was a picture of the Moon, printed lightly. Overlaying it, in black, heavy print was:

"So it *is* that outfit—those poisoners!"

"No, no, I didn't say so! But it illustrates the point; six-plus is only two symbols; it can be spread large enough to be read on the face of the Moon."

Griggs stared at the horrid advertisement. "I don't believe it will work!"

"A reliable pyrotechnics firm has guaranteed that it will—provided I can deliver their equipment to the spot. After all, Pat, it doesn't take much of a pyrotechnics rocket to go a long distance on the Moon. Why, you could throw a baseball a couple of miles yourself—low gravity, you know."

"People would never stand for it. It's sacrilege!"

Harriman looked sad. "I wish you were right. But they stand for sky-writing—and video commercials."

Griggs chewed his lip. "Well, I don't see why you come to me with it," he exploded. "You know damn well the name of my product won't go on the face of the Moon. The letters would be too small to read."

Harriman nodded. "That's exactly why I came to you. Pat, this isn't just a business venture to me; it's my heart and soul. It just made me sick to think of somebody actually wanting to use the face of the Moon for advertising. As you say, it's sacrilege. But somehow, these jackals found out I was pressed for cash. They came to me when they knew I would have to listen.

"I put them off. I promised them an answer on Thursday. Then I went home and lay awake about it. After a while I thought of you."

"Me?"

"You. You and your company. After all, you've got a good product and you need legitimate advertising for it. It occurred to me that there are more ways to use the Moon in advertising than by defacing it. Now just suppose that your company bought the same concession, but with the public-spirited promise of never letting it be used. Suppose you featured that fact in your ads? Suppose you ran pictures of a boy and girl, sitting out under the Moon, sharing a bottle of Moke? Suppose Moke was the only soft drink carried on the first trip to the Moon? But I don't have to tell you how to do it." He glanced at his watch finger. "I've got to run and I don't want to rush you. If you want to do business just leave word at my office by noon tomorrow and I'll have our man Montgomery get in touch with your advertising chief."

The head of the big newspaper chain kept him waiting the minimum time reserved for tycoons and cabinet members. Again Harriman stopped at the threshold of a large office and fixed a disc to his lapel.

"Howdy, Delos," the publisher said, "how's the traffic in green cheese today?" He then caught sight of the button and frowned. "If that is a joke, it is in poor taste."

Harriman pocketed the disc; it displayed not

but the hammer-and-sickle.

"No," he said, "it's not a joke; it's a nightmare. Colonel, you and I are among the few people in this country who realize that communism is still a menace."

Sometime later they were talking as chummily as if the Colonel's chain had not obstructed the Moon venture since its inception. The publisher waved a cigar at his desk. "How did you come by those plans? Steal them?"

"They were copied," Harriman answered with narrow truth. "But they aren't important. The important thing is to get there first; we can't risk having an enemy rocket base on the Moon. For years I've had a recurrent nightmare of waking up and seeing headlines that the Russians had landed on the Moon and declared the Lunar Soviet—say thirteen men and two female scientists—and had petitioned for entrance into the U.S.S.R.—and the petition had, of course, been graciously granted by the Supreme Soviet. I used to wake up and tremble. I don't know that they would actually go through with painting a hammer and sickle on the face of the Moon, but it's consistent with their psychology. Look at those enormous posters they are always hanging up."

The publisher bit down hard on his cigar. "We'll see what we can work out. Is there any way you can speed up your take-off?"

CHAPTER SIX

"MR. HARRIMAN?"

"Yes?"

"That Mr. LeCroix is here again."

"Tell him I can't see him."

"Yes, sir—uh, Mr. Harriman, he did not mention it the other day but he says he is a rocket pilot."

"Send him around to Skyways. I don't hire pilots."

A man's face crowded into the screen, displacing Harriman's reception secretary. "Mr. Harriman—I'm Leslie LeCroix, relief pilot of the *Charon*."

"I don't care if you are the Angel Gab— Did you say *Charon*?"

"I said *Charon*. And I've got to talk to you."

"Come in."

Harriman greeted his visitor, offered him tobacco, then looked him over with interest. The *Charon*, shuttle rocket to the lost power satellite, had been the nearest thing to a space ship the world had yet seen. Its pilot, lost in the same explosion that had destroyed the satellite and the *Charon* had been the first, in a way, of the coming breed of spacemen.

Harriman wondered how it had escaped his attention that the *Charon* had alternating pilots. He had known it, of course—but somehow he had forgotten to take the fact into account. He had written off the power satellite, its shuttle rocket and everything about it, ceased to think about them. He now looked at LeCroix with curiosity.

He saw a small, neat man with a thin, intelligent face, and the big, competent hands of a jockey. LeCroix returned his inspection without embarrassment. He seemed calm and utterly sure of himself.

"Well, Captain LeCroix?"

"You are building a Moon ship."

"Who says so?"

"A Moon ship is being built. The boys all say you are behind it."

"Yes?"

"I want to pilot it."

"Why should you?"

"I'm the best man for it."

Harriman paused to let out a cloud of tobacco smoke. "If you can prove that, the billet is yours."

"It's a deal." LeCroix stood up. "I'll leave my name and address outside."

"Wait a minute. I said 'if.' Let's talk. I'm going along on this trip myself; I want to know more about you before I trust my neck to you."

They discussed Moon flight, interplanetary travel, rocketry, what they might find on the Moon. Gradually Harriman warmed up, as he found another spirit so like his own, so obsessed with the Wonderful Dream. Subconsciously he had already accepted LeCroix; the conversation began to assume that it would be a joint venture.

After a long time Harriman said, "This is fun, Les, but I've got to do a few chores yet today, or none of us will get to the Moon. You go on out to Peterson Field and get acquainted with Bob Coster—I'll call him. If the pair of you can manage to get along, we'll talk contract." He scribbled a chit and handed it to LeCroix. "Give this to Miss Perkins as you go out and she'll put you on the payroll."

"That can wait."

"Man's got to eat."

LeCroix accepted it but did not leave. "There's one thing I don't understand, Mr. Harriman."

"Huh?"

"Why are you planning on a chemically powered ship? Not that I object; I'll herd her. But why do it the hard way? I know you had the *City of Brisbane* refitted for X-fuel—"

Harriman stared at him. "Are you off your nut, Les? You're asking why pigs don't have wings—there isn't any X-fuel and there won't be any more until we make some ourselves—on the Moon."

"Who told you that?"

"What do you mean?"

"The way I heard it, the Atomic Energy Commission allocated X-fuel, under treaty, to several other countries—and some of them weren't prepared to make use of it. But they got it just the same. What happened to it?"

"Oh, *that!* Sure, Les, several of the little outfits in Central America and South America were cut in for a slice of pie for political reasons, even though they had no way to eat it. A good thing, too—we bought it back and used it to ease the immediate power shortage." Harriman frowned. "You're right, though. I should have grabbed some of the stuff then."

"Are you *sure* it's all gone?"

"Why, of course, I'm— No, I'm not. I'll look into it. G'bye, Les."

His contacts were able to account for every pound of X-fuel in short order—save for Costa Rica's allotment. That nation had declined to sell back its supply because its power plant, suitable for X-fuel, had been almost finished at the time of the disaster. Another inquiry disclosed that the power plant had never been finished.

Montgomery was even then in Managua; Nicaragua had had a change in administration and Montgomery was making certain that the special position of the local Moon corporation was protected. Harriman sent him a coded message to proceed to San José, locate X-fuel, buy it and ship it back—at any cost. He then went to see the chairman of the Atomic Energy Commission.

That official was apparently glad to see him and anxious to be affable. Harriman got around to explaining that he wanted a license to do experimental work in isotopes—X-fuel, to be precise.

"This should be brought up through the usual channels, Mr. Harriman."

"It will be. This is a preliminary inquiry. I want to know your reactions."

"After all, I am not the only commissioner . . . and we almost always follow the recommendations of our technical branch."

"Don't fence with me, Carl. You know dern well you control a working majority. Off the record, what do you say?"

"Well, D.D.—off the record—you can't get any X-fuel, so why get a license?"

"Let me worry about that."

"Mmmm . . . we weren't required by law to follow every millicurie of X-fuel, since it isn't classed as potentially suitable for mass weapons. Just the same, we knew what happened to it. There's none available."

Harriman kept quiet.

"In the second place, you can have an X-fuel license, if you wish—for any purpose but rocket fuel."

"Why the restriction?"

"You are building a Moon ship, aren't you?"

"Me?"

"Don't *you* fence with me, D.D. It's my business to know things. You can't use X-fuel for rockets, even if you can find it—which you can't." The chairman went to a vault back of his desk and returned with a quarto volume, which he laid in front of Harriman. It was titled: *Theoretical Investigation into the Stability of Several Radioisotopic Fuels—With Notes on the* Charon-*Power-Satellite Disaster*. The cover had a serial number and was stamped: *SECRET*.

Harriman pushed it away. "I've got no business looking at that—and I wouldn't understand it if I did."

The chairman grinned. "Very well, I'll tell you what's in it. I'm deliberately tying your hands, D.D., by trusting you with a defense secret—"

"I won't have it, I tell you!"

"Don't try to power a space ship with X-fuel, D.D. It's a lovely fuel—but it may go off like a firecracker anywhere out in space. That report tells why."

"Confound it, we ran the *Charon* for nearly three years!"

"You were lucky. It is the official—but utterly confidential—opinion of the government that the *Charon* set off the power satellite, rather than the satellite setting off the *Charon*. We had thought it was the other way around at first, and of course it could have been, but there was the disturbing matter of the radar records. It seemed as if the ship had gone up a split second before the satellite. So we made an intensive theoretical investigation. X-fuel is too dangerous for rockets."

"That's ridiculous! For every pound burned in the *Charon* there were at least a hundred pounds used in power plants on the surface. How come *they* didn't explode?"

"It's a matter of shielding. A rocket necessarily uses less shielding than a stationary plant, but the worst feature is that it operates out in space. The disaster is presumed to have been triggered by primary cosmic radiation. If you like, I'll call in one of the mathematical physicists to elucidate."

Harriman shook his head. "You know I don't speak the language." He considered. "I suppose that's all there is to it?"

"I'm afraid so. I'm really sorry." Harriman got up to leave. "Uh, one more thing, D.D.—you weren't thinking of approaching any of my subordinate colleagues, were you?"

"Of course not. Why should I?"

"I'm glad to hear it. You know, Mr. Harriman, some of our staff may not be the most brilliant scientists in the world—it's very hard to keep a first-class scientist happy in the conditions of government service. But there is one thing I am sure of; all of them are utterly incorruptible. Knowing that, I would take it as a personal affront if anyone tried to influence one of my people—a very personal affront."

"So?"

"Yes. By the way, I used to box light-heavyweight in college. I've kept it up."

"Hmmm . . . well, I never went to college. But I play a fair game of poker." Harriman suddenly grinned. "I won't tamper with your boys, Carl. It would be too much like offering a bribe to a starving man. Well, so long."

When Harriman got back to his office he called in one of his confidential clerks. "Take another coded message to Mr. Montgomery. Tell him to ship the stuff to Panama City, rather than to the States." He started to dictate another message to Coster, intending to tell him to stop work on the *Pioneer*, whose skeleton was already reaching skyward on the Colorado prairie, and shift to the *Santa Maria*, formerly the *City of Brisbane*.

He thought better of it. Take-off would have to be outside the United States; with the Atomic Energy Commission acting stuffy, it would not do to try to move the *Santa Maria:* it would give the show away.

Nor could she be moved without refitting her for chem-powered flight. No, he would have another ship of the *Brisbane* class taken out of service and sent to Panama, and the power plant of the *Santa Maria* could be disassembled and shipped there, too. Coster could have the new ship ready in six weeks, maybe sooner . . . and he, Coster, and LeCroix would start for the Moon!

The devil with worries over primary cosmic rays! The *Charon* operated for three years, didn't she? They would make the trip, they would prove it could be done, then, if safer fuels were needed, there would be the incentive to dig them out. The important thing was to do it, make the trip. If Columbus had waited for decent ships, we'd all still be in Europe. A man had to take some chances or he never got anywhere.

Contentedly he started drafting the messages that would get the new scheme underway.

He was interrupted by a secretary. "Mr. Harriman, Mr. Montgomery wants to speak to you."

"Eh? Has he gotten my code already?"

"I don't know, sir."

"Well, put him on."

Montgomery had not received the second message. But he had news for Harriman: Costa Rica had sold all its X-fuel to the English Ministry of Power, soon after the disaster. There was not an ounce of it left, neither in Costa Rica, nor in England.

Harriman sat and moped for several minutes after Montgomery had cleared the screen. Then he called Coster. "Bob? Is LeCroix there?"

"Right here—we were about to go out to dinner together. Here he is, now."

"Howdy, Les. Les, that was a good brain storm of yours, but it didn't work. Somebody stole the baby."

"Eh? Oh, I get you. I'm sorry."

"Don't ever waste time being sorry. We'll go ahead as originally planned. We'll get there!"

"Sure we will."

CHAPTER SEVEN

FROM THE JUNE ISSUE of *Popular Technics* magazine: "URANIUM PROSPECTING ON THE MOON—A Fact Article about a soon-to-come Major Industry."

From HOLIDAY: "*Honeymoon on the Moon*—A Discussion of the Miracle Resort that your children will enjoy, as told to our travel editor."

From the *American Sunday Magazine:* "DIAMONDS ON THE MOON? —A World Famous Scientist Shows Why Diamonds Must Be Common As Pebbles in the Lunar Craters."

"Of course, Clem, I don't know anything about electronics, but here is the way it was explained to me. You can hold the beam of a television broadcast down to a degree or so these days, can't you?"

"Yes—if you use a big enough reflector."

"You'll have plenty of elbow room. Now Earth covers a space two degrees wide, as seen from the Moon. Sure, it's quite a distance away, but you'd have no power losses and absolutely perfect and unchanging conditions for transmission. Once you made your set-up, it wouldn't be any more expensive than broadcasting from the top of a mountain here, and a derned sight less expensive than keeping copters in the air from coast to coast, the way you're having to do now."

"It's a fantastic scheme, Delos."

"What's fantastic about it? Getting to the Moon is my worry, not yours. Once we are there, there's going to be television back to Earth, you can bet your shirt on that. It's a natural set-up for line-of-sight transmission. If you aren't interested, I'll have to find someone who is."

"I didn't say I wasn't interested."

"Well, make up your mind. Here's another thing, Clem—I don't want to go sticking my nose into your business, but haven't you had a certain amount of trouble since you lost the use of the power satellite as a relay station?"

"You know the answer; don't needle me. Expenses have gone out of sight without any improvement in revenue."

"That wasn't quite what I meant. How about censorship?"

The television executive threw up his hands. "Don't say that word! How anybody expects a man to stay in business with every two-bit wowser in the country claiming a veto over what we can say and can't say and what we can show and what we can't show—it's enough to make you throw up. The whole principle is wrong; it's like demanding that grown men live on skim milk because the baby can't eat steak. If I were able to lay my hands on those confounded, prurient-minded, slimy—"

"Easy! Easy!" Harriman interrupted. "Did it ever occur to you that there is absolutely no way to interfere with a telecast from the Moon—and that boards of censorship on Earth won't have jurisdiction in any case?"

"What? Say that again."

" 'LIFE goes to the Moon.' LIFE-TIME Inc. is proud to announce that arrangements have been completed to bring LIFE'S readers a personally conducted tour of the first trip to our satellite. In place of the usual weekly feature 'LIFE Goes to a Party' there will commence, immediately after the return of the first successful—"

"ASSURANCE FOR THE NEW AGE"

(An excerpt from an advertisement of the North Atlantic Mutual Insurance and Liability Company)

"—the same looking-to-the-future that protected our policy-holders after the Chicago Fire, after the San Francisco Fire, after every disaster since the War of 1812, now reaches out to insure you from unexpected loss *even on the Moon—*"

"THE UNBOUNDED FRONTIERS OF TECHNOLOGY"

"When the Moon ship *Pioneer* climbs skyward on a ladder of flame, twenty-seven essential devices in her 'innards' will be powered by especially-engineered *DELTA* batteries—"

"Mr. Harriman, could you come out to the field?"

"What's up, Bob?"

"Trouble," Coster answered briefly.

"What sort of trouble?"

Coster hesitated. "I'd rather not talk about it by screen. If you can't come, maybe Les and I had better come there."

"I'll be there this evening."

When Harriman got there he saw that LeCroix's impassive face concealed bitterness, Coster looked stubborn and defensive. He waited until the three were alone in Coster's workroom before he spoke. "Let's have it, boys."

LeCroix looked at Coster. The engineer chewed his lip and said, "Mr. Harriman, you know the stages this design has been through."

"More or less."

"We had to give up the catapult idea. Then we had this—" Coster rummaged on his desk, pulled out a perspective treatment of a four-step rocket, large but rather graceful. "Theoretically it was a possibility; practically it cut things too fine. By the time the stress group boys and the auxiliary group and the control group got through adding things we were forced to come to this—" He hauled out another sketch; it was basically like the first, but squattier, almost pyramidal. "We added a fifth stage as a ring around the fourth stage. We even managed to save some weight by using most of the auxiliary and control equipment for the fourth stage to control the fifth stage. And it still had enough sectional density to punch through the atmosphere with no important drag, even if it was clumsy."

Harriman nodded. "You know, Bob, we're going to have to get away from the step rocket idea before we set up a schedule run to the Moon."

"I don't see how you can avoid it with chem-powered rockets."

"If you had a decent catapult you could put a single-stage chem-powered rocket into an orbit around the Earth, couldn't you?"

"Sure."

"That's what we'll do. Then it will refuel in that orbit."

"The old space-station set-up. I suppose that makes sense—in fact I know it does. Only the ship wouldn't refuel and continue on to the Moon. The economical thing would be to have special ships that never landed anywhere make the jump from there to another fueling station around the Moon. Then—"

LeCroix displayed a most unusual impatience. "All that doesn't mean anything now. Get on with the story, Bob."

"Right," agreed Harriman.

"Well, this model should have done it. And, damn it, it still should do it."

Harriman looked puzzled. "But, Bob, that's the approved design, isn't it? That's what you've got two-thirds built right out there on the field."

"Yes." Coster looked stricken. "But it won't do it. It won't work."

"Why not?"

"Because I've had to add in too much dead weight, that's why. Mr. Harriman, you aren't an engineer; you've no idea how fast the performance falls off when you have to clutter up a ship with anything but fuel and power plant. Take the landing arrangements for the fifth-stage power ring. You use that stage for a minute and a half, then you throw it away. But you don't dare take a chance of it falling on Wichita or Kansas City. We have to include a parachute sequence. Even then we have to plan on tracking it by radar and cutting the shrouds by radio control when it's over empty countryside and not too high. That means more weight, besides the parachute. By the time we are through, we don't get a net addition of a mile a second out of that stage. It's not enough."

Harriman stirred in his chair. "Looks like we made a mistake in trying to launch it from the States. Suppose we took off from someplace unpopulated, say the Brazil coast, and let the booster stages fall in the Atlantic; how much would that save you?"

Coster looked off in the distance, then took out a slide rule. "Might work."

"How much of a chore will it be to move the ship, at this stage?"

"Well . . . it would have to be disassembled completely; nothing less would do. I can't give you a cost estimate off hand, but it would be expensive."

"How long would it take?"

"Hmm . . . shucks, Mr. Harriman, I can't answer off hand. Two years—eighteen months, with luck. We'd have to prepare a site. We'd have to build shops."

Harriman thought about it, although he knew the answer in his heart. His shoe string, big as it was, was stretched to the danger point. He couldn't keep up the promotion, on talk alone, for another two years; he *had* to have a successful flight and soon—or the whole jerry-built financial structure would burst. "No good, Bob."

"I was afraid of that. Well, I tried to add still a sixth stage." He held up another sketch. "You see that monstrosity? I reached the point of diminishing returns. The final effective velocity is actually less with this abortion than with the five-step job."

"Does that mean you are whipped, Bob? You can't build a Moon ship?"

"No, I—"

LeCroix said suddenly, "Clear out Kansas."

"Eh?" asked Harriman.

"Clear everybody out of Kansas and Eastern Colorado. Let the fifth and fourth sections fall anywhere in that area. The third section falls in the Atlantic; the second section goes into a permanent orbit—and the ship itself goes on to the Moon. You could do it if you didn't have to waste weight on the parachuting of the fifth and fourth sections. Ask Bob."

"So? How about it, Bob?"

"That's what I said before. It was the parasitic penalties that whipped us. The basic design is all right."

"Hmmm . . . somebody hand me an Atlas." Harriman looked up Kansas and Colorado, did some rough figuring. He stared off into space, looking surprisingly, for the moment, as Coster did when the engineer was thinking about his own work. Finally he said, "It won't work."

"Why not?"

"Money. I told you not to worry about money—for the ship. But it would cost upward of six or seven million dollars to evacuate that area even for a day. We'd have to settle nuisance suits out of hand; we couldn't wait. And there would be a few diehards who just couldn't move anyhow."

LeCroix said savagely, "If the crazy fools won't move, let them take their chances."

"I know how you feel, Les. But this project is too big to hide and too big to move. Unless we protect the bystanders we'll be shut down by court order and force. I can't buy all the judges in two states. Some of them wouldn't be for sale."

"It was a nice try, Les," consoled Coster.

"I thought it might be an answer for all of us," the pilot answered.

Harriman said, "You were starting to mention another solution, Bob?"

Coster looked embarrassed. "You know the plans for the ship itself—a three-man job, space and supplies for three."

"Yes. What are you driving at?"

"It doesn't have to be three men. Split the first step into two parts, cut the ship down to the bare minimum for one man and jettison the remainder. That's the only way I see to make this basic design work." He got out another sketch. "See? One man and supplies for less than a week. No airlock—the pilot stays in his pressure suit. No galley. No bunks. The bare minimum to keep one man alive for a maximum of two hundred hours. It will work."

"It will work," repeated LeCroix, looking at Coster.

Harriman looked at the sketch with an odd, sick feeling at his stomach. Yes, no doubt it would work—and for the purposes of the promotion it did not matter whether one man or three went to the Moon and returned. Just to do it was enough; he was dead certain that one successful flight would cause money to roll in so that there would be capital to develop to the point of practical, passenger-carrying ships.

The Wright brothers had started with less.

"If that is what I have to put up with, I suppose I have to," he said slowly.

Coster looked relieved. "Fine! But there is one more hitch. You know the conditions under which I agreed to tackle this job—I was to go along. Now Les here waves a contract under my nose and says *he* has to be the pilot."

"It's not just that," LeCroix countered. "You're no pilot, Bob. You'll kill yourself and ruin the whole enterprise, just through bull-headed stubbornness."

"I'll learn to fly it. After all, I designed it. Look here, Mr. Harriman, I hate to let you in for a suit—Les says he will sue—but my contract antedates his. I intend to enforce it."

"Don't listen to him, Mr. Harriman. Let him do the suing. I'll fly that ship and bring her back. He'll wreck it."

"Either I go or I don't build the ship," Coster said flatly.

Harriman motioned both of them to keep quiet. "Easy, easy, both of you. You can both sue me if it gives you any pleasure. Bob, don't talk nonsense; at this stage I can hire other engineers to finish the job. You tell me it has to be just one man."

"That's right."

"You're looking at him."

They both stared.

"Shut your jaws," Harriman snapped. "What's funny about that? You both knew I meant to go. You don't think I went to all this trouble just to give you two a ride to the Moon, do you? *I intend to go.* What's wrong with me as a pilot? I'm in good health, my eyesight is all right, I'm still smart enough to learn what I have to learn. If I have to drive my own buggy, I'll do it. I won't step aside for anybody, not anybody, d'you hear me?"

Coster got his breath first. "Boss, you don't know what you are saying."

Two hours later they were still wrangling. Most of the time Harriman had stubbornly sat still, refusing to answer their arguments. At last he went out of the room for a few minutes, on the usual pretext. When he came back in he said, "Bob, what do you weigh?"

"Me? A little over two hundred."

"Close to two twenty, I'd judge. Les, what do you weigh?"

"One twenty-six."

"Bob, design the ship for a net load of one hundred and twenty-six pounds."

"Huh? Now wait a minute, Mr. Harriman—"

"*Shut up!* If I can't learn to be a pilot in six weeks, neither can you."

"But I've got the mathematics and the basic knowledge to—"

"Shut up I said! Les has spent as long learning his profession as you have learning yours. Can he become an engineer in six weeks? Then what gave you the conceit to think that you can learn his job in that time? I'm not going to have you wrecking my ship to satisfy your swollen ego. Anyhow, you gave out the real key to it when you were discussing the design. The real limiting factor is the actual weight of the passenger or passengers, isn't it? Everything—*everything* works in proportion to that one mass. Right?"

"Yes, but—"

"Right or wrong?"

"Well . . . yes, that's right. I just wanted—"

"The smaller man can live on less water, he breathes less air, he occupies less space. Les goes." Harriman walked over and put a hand on Coster's shoulder. "Don't take it hard, son. It can't be any worse on you than it is on me. This trip has got to succeed—and that means you and I have got to give up the honor of being the first man on the Moon. But I promise you this: we'll go on the second trip, we'll go with Les as our private chauffeur. It will be the first of a lot of passenger trips. Look, Bob—you can be a big man in this game, if you'll play along now. How would you like to be chief engineer of the first lunar colony?"

Coster managed to grin. "It might not be so bad."

"You'd like it. Living on the Moon will be an engineering problem; you and I have talked about it. How'd you like to put your theories to work? Build the first city? Build the big observatory we'll found there? Look around and know that you were the man who had done it?"

Coster was definitely adjusting himself to it. "You make it sound good. Say, what will *you* be doing?"

"Me? Well, maybe I'll be the first mayor of Luna City." It was a new thought to him; he savored it. "The Honorable Delos David Harriman, Mayor of Luna City. Say, I like that! You know, I've never held any sort of public office; I've just owned things." He looked around. "Everything settled?"

"I guess so," Coster said slowly. Suddenly he stuck his hand out at LeCroix. "You fly her, Les; I'll build her."

LeCroix grabbed his hand. "It's a deal. And you and the Boss get busy and start making plans for the next job—big enough for all of us."

"Right!"

Harriman put his hand on top of theirs. "That's the way I like to hear you talk. We'll stick together and we'll found Luna City together."

"I think we ought to call it "Harriman," LeCroix said seriously.

"Nope, I've thought of it as Luna City ever since I was a kid; Luna City it's going to be. Maybe we'll put Harriman Square in the middle of it," he added.

"I'll mark it that way in the plans," agreed Coster.

Harriman left at once. Despite the solution he was terribly depressed and did not want his two colleagues to see it. It had been a Pyrrhic victory; he had saved the enterprise but he felt like an animal who has gnawed off his own leg to escape a trap.

CHAPTER EIGHT

STRONG WAS ALONE in the offices of the partnership when he got a call from Dixon. "George, I was looking for D.D. Is he there?"

"No, he's back in Washington—something about clearances. I expect him back soon."

"Hmmm. . . . Entenza and I want to see him. We're coming over."

They arrived shortly. Entenza was quite evidently very much worked up over something; Dixon looked sleekly impassive as usual. After greetings Dixon waited a moment, then said, "Jack, you had some business to transact, didn't you?"

Entenza jumped, then snatched a draft from his pocket.

"Oh, yes! George, I'm not going to have to pro-rate after all. Here's my payment to bring my share up to full payment to date."

Strong accepted it. "I know that Delos will be pleased." He tucked it in a drawer.

"Well," said Dixon sharply, "aren't you going to receipt for it?"

"If Jack wants a receipt. The cancelled draft will serve." However, Strong wrote out a receipt without further comment; Entenza accepted it.

They waited a while. Presently Dixon said, "George, you're in this pretty deep, aren't you?"

"Possibly."

"Want to hedge your bets?"

"How?"

"Well, candidly, I want to protect myself. Want to sell one half of one percent of your share?"

Strong thought about it. In fact he was worried—worried sick. The presence of Dixon's auditor had forced them to keep on a cash basis—and only Strong knew how close to the line that had forced the partners. "Why do you want it?"

"Oh, I wouldn't use it to interfere with Delos's operations. He's our man; we're backing him. But I would feel a lot safer if I had the right to call a halt if he tried to commit us to something we couldn't pay for. You know Delos; he's an incurable optimist. We ought to have some sort of a brake on him."

Strong thought about it. The thing that hurt him was that he agreed with everything Dixon said; he had stood by and watched while Delos dissipated two fortunes, painfully built up through the years. D.D. no longer seemed to care. Why, only this morning he had refused even to look at a report on the H & S automatic household switch—after dumping it on Strong.

Dixon leaned forward. "Name a price, George. I'll be generous."

Strong squared his stooped shoulders. "I'll sell—"

"Good!"

"—if Delos okays it. Not otherwise."

Dixon muttered something. Entenza snorted. The conversation might have gone acrimoniously further, had not Harriman walked in.

No one said anything about the proposal to Strong. Strong inquired about the trip; Harriman pressed a thumb and finger together. "All in the groove! But it gets more expensive to do business in Washington every day." He turned to the others. "How's tricks? Any special meaning to the assemblage? Are we in executive session?"

Dixon turned to Entenza. "Tell him, Jack."

Entenza faced Harriman. "What do you mean by selling television rights?"

Harriman cocked a brow. "And why not?"

"Because you promised them to me, that's why. That's the original agreement; I've got it in writing."

"Better take another look at the agreement, Jack. And don't go off half-cocked. You have the exploitation rights for radio, television, and other amusement and special feature ventures in connection with the first trip to the Moon. You've still got 'em. Including broadcasts from the ship, provided we are able to make any." He decided that this was not a good time to mention that weight considerations had already made the latter impossible; the *Pioneer* would carry no electronic equipment of any sort not needed in astrogation. "What I sold was the franchise to erect a television station on the Moon, later. By the way, it wasn't even an exclusive franchise, although Clem Haggerty thinks it is. If you want to buy one yourself, we can accommodate you."

"*Buy* it! Why you—"

"Wups! Or you can have it free, if you can get Dixon and George to agree that you are entitled to it. I won't be a tightwad. Anything else?"

Dixon cut in. "Just where do we stand now, Delos?"

"Gentlemen, you can take it for granted that the *Pioneer* will leave on schedule—next Wednesday. And now, if you will excuse me, I'm on my way to Peterson Field."

After he had left his three associates sat in silence for some time, Entenza muttering to himself, Dixon apparently thinking, and Strong just waiting. Presently Dixon said, "How about that fractional share, George?"

"You didn't see fit to mention it to Delos."

"I see." Dixon carefully deposited an ash. "He's a strange man, isn't he?"

Strong shifted around. "Yes."

"How long have you known him?"

"Let me see—he came to work for me in—"

"*He* worked for *you?*"

"For several months. Then we set up our first company." Strong thought back about it. "I suppose he had a power complex, even then."

"No," Dixon said carefully. "No, I wouldn't call it a power complex. It's more of a Messiah complex."

Entenza looked up. "He's a crooked son of a bitch, that's what he is!"

Strong looked at him mildly. "I'd rather you wouldn't talk about him that way. I'd really rather you wouldn't."

"Stow it, Jack," ordered Dixon. "You might force George to take a poke at you. One of the odd things about him," went on Dixon, "is that he seems to be able to inspire an almost feudal loyalty. Take yourself. I know you are cleaned out, George—yet you won't let me rescue you. That goes beyond logic; it's personal."

Strong nodded. "He's an odd man. Sometimes I think he's the last of the Robber Barons."

Dixon shook his head. "Not the last. The last of them opened up the American West. He's the first of the *new* Robber Barons—and you and I won't see the end of it. Do you ever read Carlyle?"

Strong nodded again. "I see what you mean, the 'Hero' theory, but I don't necessarily agree with it."

"There's something to it, though," Dixon answered. "Truthfully, I don't think Delos knows what he is doing. He's setting up a new imperialism.

There'll be the devil to pay before it's cleaned up." He stood up. "Maybe we should have waited. Maybe we should have balked him—*if* we could have. Well, it's done. We're on the merry-go-round and we can't get off. I hope we enjoy the ride. Come on, Jack."

CHAPTER NINE

THE COLORADO PRAIRIE was growing dusky. The Sun was behind the peak and the broad white face of Luna, full and round, was rising in the east. In the middle of Peterson Field the *Pioneer* thrust toward the sky. A barbed-wire fence, a thousand yards from its base in all directions, held back the crowds. Just inside the barrier guards patrolled restlessly. More guards circulated through the crowd. Inside the fence, close to it, trunks and trailers for camera, sound, and television equipment were parked and, at the far ends of cables, remote-control pick-ups were located both near and far from the ship on all sides. There were other trucks near the ship and a stir of organized activity.

Harriman waited in Coster's office; Coster himself was out on the field, and Dixon and Entenza had a room to themselves. LeCroix, still in a drugged sleep, was in the bedroom of Coster's on-the-job living quarters.

There was a stir and a challenge outside the door. Harriman opened it a crack. "If that's another reporter, tell him 'no.' Send him to Mr. Montgomery across the way. Captain LeCroix will grant no unauthorized interviews."

"Delos! Let me in."

"Oh—you, George. Come in. We've been hounded to death."

Strong came in and handed Harriman a large and heavy handbag. "Here it is."

"Here is what?"

"The cancelled covers for the philatelic syndicate. You forgot them. That's half a million dollars, Delos," he complained. "If I hadn't noticed them in your coat locker we'd have been in the soup."

Harriman composed his features. "George, you're a brick, that's what you are."

"Shall I put them in the ship myself?" Strong said anxiously.

"Huh? No, no. Les will handle them." He glanced at his watch. "We're about to waken him. I'll take charge of the covers." He took the bag and added, "Don't come in now. You'll have a chance to say goodbye on the field."

Harriman went next door, shut the door behind him, waited for the nurse to give the sleeping pilot a counteracting stimulant by injection, then chased her out. When he turned around the pilot was sitting up, rubbing his eyes. "How do you feel, Les?"

"Fine. So this is it."

"Yup. And we're all rooting for you, boy. Look, you've got to go out and face them in a couple of minutes. Everything is ready—but I've got a couple of things I've got to say to you."

"Yes?"

"See this bag?" Harriman rapidly explained what it was and what it signified.

LeCroix looked dismayed. "But I *can't* take it, Delos. It's all figured to the last ounce."

"Who said you were going to take it? Of course you can't; it must weigh sixty, seventy pounds. I just plain forgot it. Now here's what we do: for the time being I'll just hide it in here—" Harriman stuffed the bag far back into a clothes closet. "When you land, I'll be right on your tail. Then we pull a sleight-of-hand trick and you fetch it out of the ship."

LeCroix shook his head ruefully. "Delos, you beat me. Well, I'm in no mood to argue."

"I'm glad you're not; otherwise I'd go to jail for a measly half million dollars. We've already spent that money. Anyhow, it doesn't matter," he went on. "Nobody but you and me will know it—and the stamp collectors will get their money's worth." He looked at the younger man as if anxious for his approval.

"Okay, okay," LeCroix answered. "Why should I care what happens to a stamp collector—tonight? Let's get going."

"One more thing," said Harriman and took out a small cloth bag. "This you take with you—and the weight *has* been figured in. I saw to it. Now here is what you do with it." He gave detailed and very earnest instructions.

LeCroix was puzzled. "Do I hear you straight? I let it be found—then I tell the exact truth about what happened?"

"That's right."

"Okay." LeCroix zipped the little bag into a pocket of his coveralls. "Let's get out to the field. H-hour minus twenty-one minutes already."

Strong joined Harriman in the control blockhouse after LeCroix had gone up inside the ship. "Did they get aboard?" he demanded anxiously. "LeCroix wasn't carrying anything."

"Oh, sure," said Harriman. "I sent them ahead. Better take your place. The ready flare has already gone up."

Dixon, Entenza, the Governor of Colorado, the Vice-President of the United States, and a round dozen of V.I.P.'s were already seated at periscopes, mounted in slits, on a balcony above the control level. Strong and Harriman climbed a ladder and took the two remaining chairs.

Harriman began to sweat and realized he was trembling. Through his periscope out in front he could see the ship; from below he could hear Coster's voice, nervously checking departure station reports. Muted through a speaker by him was a running commentary of one of the newscasters reporting the show. Harriman himself was the—well, the admiral, he decided—of the operation, but there was nothing more he could do, but wait, watch, and try to pray.

A second flare arched up in the sky, burst into red and green. Five minutes.

The seconds oozed away. At minus two minutes Harriman realized that he could not stand to watch through a tiny slit; he had to be outside, take part in it himself—he had to. He climbed down, hurried to the exit of the blockhouse. Coster glanced around, looked startled, but did not try to stop him; Coster could not leave his post no matter what happened. Harriman elbowed the guard aside and went outdoors.

To the east the ship towered skyward, her slender pyramid sharp black against the full Moon. He waited.

And waited.

What had gone wrong? There had remained less than two minutes when he had come out; he was sure of that—yet there she stood, silent, dark, unmoving. There was not a sound, save the distant ululation of sirens warning the spectators behind the distant fence. Harriman felt his own heart stop, his breath dry up in his throat. Something had failed. Failure.

A single flare rocket burst from the top of the blockhouse; a flame licked at the base of the ship.

It spread, there was a pad of white fire around the base. Slowly, almost lumberingly, the *Pioneer* lifted, seemed to hover for a moment, balanced on a pillar of fire—then reached for the sky with acceleration so great that she was above him almost at once, overhead at the zenith, a dazzling circle of flame. So quickly was she above, rather than out in front, that it seemed as if she were arching back over him and must surely fall on him. Instinctively and futilely he threw a hand in front of his face.

The sound reached him.

Not as sound—it was a white noise, a roar in all frequencies, sonic, subsonic, supersonic, so incredibly loaded with energy that it struck him in the chest. He heard it with his teeth and with his bones as well as with his ears. He crouched his knees, bracing against it.

Following the sound at the snail's pace of a hurricane came the backwash of the splash. It ripped at his clothing, tore his breath from his lips. He stumbled blindly back, trying to reach the lee of the concrete building, was knocked down.

He picked himself up coughing and strangling and remembered to look at the sky. Straight overhead was a dwindling star. Then it was gone.

He went into the blockhouse.

The room was a babble of high-tension, purposeful confusion. Harriman's ears, still ringing, heard a speaker blare, "Spot One! Spot One to blockhouse! Step five loose on schedule—ship and step five showing separate blips—" and Coster's voice, high and angry, cutting in with, "Get Track One! Have they picked up step five yet? Are they tracking it?"

In the background the news commentator was still blowing his top. "A great day, folks, a great day! The mighty *Pioneer*, climbing like an angel of the Lord, flaming sword at hand, is even now on her glorious way to our sister planet. Most of you have seen her departure on your screens; I wish you could have seen it as I did, arching up into the evening sky, bearing her precious load of—"

"Shut that thing off!" ordered Coster, then to the visitors on the observation platform, "And pipe down up there! Quiet!"

The Vice-President of the United States jerked his head around, closed his mouth. He remembered to smile. The other V.I.P.'s shut up, then resumed again in muted whispers. A girl's voice cut through the silence, "Track One to Blockhouse—step five tracking high, plus two." There was a stir in the corner. There a large canvas hood shielded a heavy sheet of Plexiglass from direct light. The sheet was mounted vertically and was edge-lighted; it displayed a coordinate map of Colorado and Kansas in fine white lines; the cities and towns glowed red. Unevacuated farms were tiny warning dots of red light.

A man behind the transparent map touched it with a grease pencil; the reported location of step five shone out. In front of the map screen a youngish man sat quietly in a chair, a pear-shaped switch in his hand, his thumb lightly resting on the button. He was a bombardier, borrowed from the Air Forces; when he pressed the switch, a radio-controlled circuit in step five should cause the shrouds of step five's landing 'chute to be cut and let it plummet to Earth. He was working from radar reports alone with no fancy computing bombsight to think for him. He was working almost by instinct—or, rather, by the accumulated subconscious knowledge of his trade, integrating in his brain the meager data spread before him, deciding where the tons of step five would land if he were to press his switch at any particular instant. He seemed unworried.

"Spot One to Blockhouse!" came a man's voice again. "Step four free on schedule," and almost immediately following, a deeper voice echoed, "Track Two, tracking step four, instantaneous altitude nine-five-one miles, predicted vector."

No one paid any attention to Harriman.

Under the hood the observed trajectory of step five grew in shining dots of grease, near to, but not on, the dotted line of its predicted path. Reaching out from each location dot was drawn a line at right angles, the reported altitude for that location.

The quiet man watching the display suddenly pressed down hard on his switch. He then stood up, stretched, and said, "Anybody got a cigaret?"

"Track Two!" he was answered. "Step four—first impact prediction—forty miles west of Charleston, South Carolina."

"Repeat!" yelled Coster.

The speaker blared out again without pause, "Correction, correction—forty miles east, repeat *east*."

Coster sighed. The sigh was cut short by a report. "Spot One to Blockhouse—step three free, minus five seconds," and a talker at Coster's control desk called out, "Mr. Coster, *Mister Coster*—Palomar Observatory wants to talk to you."

"Tell 'em to go—no, tell 'em to wait." Immediately another voice cut in with, "Track One, auxiliary range Fox—Step one about to strike near Dodge City, Kansas."

"*How near?*"

There was no answer. Presently the voice of Track One proper said, "Impact reported approximately fifteen miles southwest of Dodge City."

"Casualties?"

Spot One broke in before Track One could answer, "Step two free, step two free—the ship is now on its own."

"Mr. Coster—*please*, Mr. Coster—"

And a totally new voice: "Spot Two to Blockhouse—we are now tracking the ship. Stand by for reported distances and bearings. Stand by—"

"Track Two to Blockhouse—step four will definitely land in Atlantic, estimated point of impact oh-five-seven miles east of Charleston bearing oh-nine-three. I will repeat—"

Coster looked around irritably. "Isn't there any drinking water anywhere in this dump?"

"Mr. Coster, please—Palomar says they've just *got* to talk to you."

Harriman eased over to the door and stepped out. He suddenly felt very much let down, utterly weary, and depressed.

The field looked strange without the ship. He had watched it grow; now suddenly it was gone. The Moon, still rising, seemed oblivious—and space travel was as remote a dream as it had been in his boyhood.

There were several tiny figures prowling around the flash apron where the ship had stood—souvenir hunters, he thought contemptuously. Someone came up to him in the gloom. "Mr. Harriman?"

"Eh?"

"Hopkins—with the A.P. How about a statement?"

"Uh? No, no comment. I'm bushed."

"Oh, now, just a word. How does it feel to have backed the first successful Moon flight—if it is successful."

"It will be successful." He thought a moment, then squared his tired shoulders and said, "Tell them that this is the beginning of the human race's greatest era. Tell them that every one of them will have a chance to follow in Captain LeCroix's footsteps, seek out new planets, wrest a home for themselves in new lands. Tell them that this means new frontiers, a shot in the arm for prosperity. It means—" He ran down. "That's all tonight. I'm whipped, son. Leave me alone, will you?"

Presently Coster came out, followed by the V.I.P.'s. Harriman went up to Coster. "Everything all right?"

"Sure. Why shouldn't it be? Track three followed him out to the limit of range—all in the groove." Coster added, "Step five killed a cow when it grounded."

"Forget it—we'll have steak for breakfast." Harriman then had to make conversation with the Governor and the Vice-President, had to escort them out to their ship. Dixon and Entenza left together, less formally; at last Coster and Harriman were alone save for subordinates too junior to constitute a strain and for guards to protect them from the crowds. "Where you headed, Bob?"

"Up to the Broadmoor and about a week's sleep. How about you?"

"If you don't mind, I'll doss down in your apartment."

"Help yourself. Sleepy pills in the bathroom."

"I won't need them." They had a drink together in Coster's quarters, talked aimlessly, then Coster ordered a copter cab and went to the hotel. Harriman went to bed, got up, read a day-old copy of the Denver *Post* filled with pictures of the *Pioneer*, finally gave up and took two of Coster's sleeping capsules.

CHAPTER TEN

SOMEONE WAS SHAKING HIM. "Mr. Harriman! Wake up—Mr. Coster is on the screen."

"Huh? Wazza? Oh, all right." He got up and padded to the phone. Coster was looking tousle-headed and excited. "Hey, Boss—*he made it!*"

"Huh? What do you mean?"

"Palomar just called me. They saw the mark and now they've spotted the ship itself. He—"

"Wait a minute, Bob. Slow up. He *can't* be there yet. He just left last night."

Coster looked disconcerted. "What's the matter, Mr. Harriman? Don't you feel well? He left Wednesday."

Vaguely, Harriman began to be oriented. No, the take-off had not been the night before—fuzzily he recalled a drive up into the mountains, a day spent dozing in the sun, some sort of a party at which he had drunk too much. What day was today? He didn't know. If LeCroix had landed on the Moon, then—never mind. "It's all right, Bob—I was half asleep. I guess I dreamed the take-off all over again. Now tell me the news, slowly."

Coster started over. "LeCroix has landed, just west of Archimedes crater. They can see his ship, from Palomar. Say that was a great stunt you thought up, marking the spot with carbon black. Les must have covered two acres with it. They say it shines out like a billboard, through the Big Eye."

"Maybe we ought to run down and have a look. No—later," he amended. "We'll be busy."

"I don't see what more we can do, Mr. Harriman. We've got twelve of our best ballistic computers calculating possible routes for you now."

Harriman started to tell the man to put on another twelve, switched off the screen instead. He was still at Peterson Field, with one of Skyways' best stratoships waiting for him outside, waiting to take him to whatever point on the globe LeCroix might ground. LeCroix was in the upper stratosphere, had been there for more than twenty-four hours. The pilot was slowly, cautiously wearing out his terminal velocity, dissipating the incredible kinetic energy as shock wave and radiant heat.

They had tracked him by radar around the globe and around again—and again . . . yet there was no way of knowing just where and what sort of landing the pilot would choose to risk. Harriman listened to the running radar reports and cursed the fact that they had elected to save the weight of radio equipment.

The radar figures started coming closer together. The voice broke off and started again: "He's in his landing glide!"

"Tell the field to get ready!" shouted Harriman. He held his breath and waited. After endless seconds another voice cut in with, "The Moon ship is now landing. It will ground somewhere west of Chihuahua in Old Mexico."

Harriman started for the door at a run.

Coached by radio en route, Harriman's pilot spotted the *Pioneer* incredibly small against the desert sand. He put his own ship quite close to it, in a beautiful landing. Harriman was fumbling at the cabin door before the ship was fairly stopped.

LeCroix was sitting on the ground, resting his back against a skid of his ship and enjoying the shade of its stubby triangular wings. A paisano sheepherder stood facing him, open-mouthed. As Harriman trotted out and lumbered toward him LeCroix stood up, flipped a cigaret butt away and said, "Hi, Boss!"

"Les!" The older man threw his arms around the younger. "It's good to see you, boy."

"It's good to see *you*. Pedro here doesn't speak my language." LeCroix glanced around; there was no one else nearby but the pilot of Harriman's ship. "Where's the gang? Where's Bob?"

"I didn't wait. They'll surely be along in a few minutes—hey, there they come now!" It was another stratoship, plunging in to a landing. Harriman turned to his pilot. "Bill—go over and meet them."

"Huh? They'll come, never fear."

"Do as I say."

"You're the doctor." The pilot trudged through the sand, his back expressing disapproval. LeCroix looked puzzled. "Quick, Les—help me with this."

"This" was the five thousand cancelled envelopes which were supposed to have been to the Moon. They got them out of Harriman's stratoship and into the Moon ship, there to be stowed in an empty food locker, while their actions were still shielded from the later arrivals by the bulk of the stratoship. "Whew!" said Harriman. "That was close. Half a million dollars. We need it, Les."

"Sure, but look, Mr. Harriman, the di—"

"Sssh! The others are coming. How about the other business? Ready with your act?"

"Yes. But I was trying to tell you—"

"Quiet!"

It was not their colleagues; it was a shipload of reporters, camera men, mike men, commentators, technicians. They swarmed over them.

Harriman waved to them jauntily. "Help yourselves, boys. Get a lot of pictures. Climb through the ship. Make yourselves at home. Look at anything you want to. But go easy on Captain LeCroix—he's tired."

Another ship had landed, this time with Coster, Dixon and Strong. Entenza showed up in his own chartered ship and began bossing the TV, pix, and radio men, in the course of which he almost had a fight with an unauthorized camera crew. A large copter transport grounded and spilled out nearly a platoon of khaki-clad Mexican troops. Fom somewhere—out of the sand apparently—several dozen native peasants showed up. Harriman broke away from reporters, held a quick and expensive discussion with the captain of the local troops and a degree of order was restored in time to save the *Pioneer* from being picked to pieces.

"Just let that be!" It was LeCroix's voice, from inside the *Pioneer*. Harriman waited and listened. "None of your business!" the pilot's voice went on, rising higher, "and put them back!"

Harriman pushed his way to the door of the ship. "What's the trouble, Les?"

Inside the cramped cabin, hardly large enough for a TV booth, three men stood, LeCroix and two reporters. All three men looked angry. "What's the trouble, Les?" Harriman repeated.

LeCroix was holding a small cloth bag which appeared to be empty. Scattered on the pilot's acceleration rest between him and the reporters were several small, dully brilliant stones. A reporter held one such stone up to the light.

"These guys were poking their noses into things that didn't concern them," LeCroix said angrily.

The reporter looked at the stone said, "You told us to look at what we liked, didn't you, Mr. Harriman?"

"Yes."

"Your pilot here—" He jerked a thumb at LeCroix. "—apparently didn't expect us to find these. He had them hidden in the pads of his chair."

"What of it?"

"They're diamonds."

"What makes you think so?"

"They're diamonds all right."

Harriman stopped and unwrapped a cigar. Presently he said, "Those diamonds were where you found them because I put them there."

A flashlight went off behind Harriman; a voice said, "Hold the rock up higher, Jeff."

The reporter called Jeff obliged, then said, "That seems an odd thing to do, Mr. Harriman."

"I was interested in the effect of outer space radiations on raw diamonds. On my orders Captain LeCroix placed that sack of diamonds in the ship."

Jeff whistled thoughtfully. "You know, Mr. Harriman, if you did not have that explanation, I'd think LeCroix had found the rocks on the Moon and was trying to hold out on you."

"Print that and you will be sued for libel. I have every confidence in Captain LeCroix. Now give me the diamonds."

Jeff's eyebrows went up. "But not confidence enough in him to let him keep them, maybe?"

"Give me the stones. Then get out."

Harriman got LeCroix away from the reporters as quickly as possible and into Harriman's own ship. "That's all for now," he told the news and pictures people. "See us at Peterson Field."

Once the ship raised ground he turned to LeCroix. "You did a beautiful job, Les."

"That reporter named Jeff must be sort of confused."

"Eh? Oh, *that*. No, I mean the flight. You did it. You're head man on this planet."

LeCroix shrugged it off. "Bob built a good ship. It was a cinch. Now about those diamonds—"

"Forget the diamonds. You've done your part. We placed those rocks in the ship; now we tell everybody we did—truthful as can be. It's not our fault if they don't believe us."

"But Mr. Harriman—"

"What?"

LeCroix unzipped a pocket in his coveralls, hauled out a soiled handkerchief, knotted into a bag. He untied it—and spilled into Harriman's hands many more diamonds than had been displayed in the ship—larger, finer diamonds.

Harriman stared at them. He began to chuckle.

Presently he shoved them back at LeCroix. "Keep them."

"I figure they belong to all of us."

"Well, keep them for us, then. And keep your mouth shut about them. No, wait." He picked out two large stones. "I'll have rings made from these two, one for you, one for me. But keep your mouth shut, or they won't be worth anything, except as curiosities."

It was quite true, he thought. Long ago the diamond syndicate had realized that diamonds in plentiful supply were worth little more than glass, except for industrial uses. Earth had more than enough for that, more than enough for jewels. If Moon diamonds were literally "common as pebbles" then they were just that—pebbles.

Not worth the expense of bringing them to earth.

But now take uranium. If that were plentiful—

Harriman sat back and indulged in daydreaming.

Presently LeCroix said softly, "You know, Boss, it's wonderful there."

"Eh? Where?"

"Why, on the Moon of course. I'm going back. I'm going back just as soon as I can. We've got to get busy on the new ship."

"Sure, sure! And this time we'll build one big enough for all of us. This time I go, too!"

"You bet."
"Les—" The older man spoke almost diffidently. "What does it look like when you look back and see the Earth?"
"Huh? It looks like— It looks—" LeCroix stopped. "Hell's bells, Boss, there isn't any way to tell you. It's wonderful, that's all. The sky is black and—well, wait until you see the pictures I took. Better yet, wait and see it yourself."
Harriman nodded. "But it's hard to wait."

CHAPTER ELEVEN

"FIELDS OF DIAMONDS ON THE MOON!!!"
"BILLIONAIRE BACKER DENIES DIAMOND STORY
Says Jewels Taken Into Space for Science Reasons"
"MOON DIAMONDS: HOAX OR FACT?"
"—but consider this, friends of the invisible audience: why would anyone take diamonds *to* the moon? Every ounce of that ship and its cargo was calculated; diamonds would not be taken along without reason. Many scientific authorities have pronounced Mr. Harriman's professed reason an absurdity. It is easy to guess that diamonds might be taken along for the purpose of 'salting' the Moon, so to speak, with earthly jewels, with the intention of convincing us that diamonds exist on the Moon—but Mr. Harriman, his pilot Captain LeCroix, and everyone connected with the enterprise have sworn from the beginning that the diamonds *did not* come from the Moon. But it is an absolute certainty that the diamonds were in the space ship when it landed. Cut it how you will; this reporter is going to try to buy some lunar diamond mining stock—"

Strong was, as usual, already in the office when Harriman came in. Before the partners could speak, the screen called out, "Mr. Harriman, Rotterdam calling."
"Tell them to go plant a tulip."
"Mr. van der Velde is waiting, Mr. Harriman."
"Okay."
Harriman let the Hollander talk, then said, "Mr. van der Velde, the statements attributed to me are absolutely correct. I put those diamonds the reporters saw into the ship before it took off. They were mined right here on Earth. In fact I bought them when I came over to see you; I can prove it."
"But Mr. Harriman—"
"Suit yourself. There may be more diamonds on the Moon than you can run and jump over. I don't guarantee it. But I do guarantee that those diamonds the newspapers are talking about came from Earth."
"Mr. Harriman, why would you send diamonds to the Moon? Perhaps you intended to fool us, no?"

"Have it your own way. But I've said all along that those diamonds came from Earth. Now see here: you took an option—an option on an option, so to speak. If you want to make the second payment on that option and keep it in force, the deadline is nine o'clock Thursday, New York time, as specified in the contract. Make up your mind."

He switched off and found his partner looking at him sourly. "What's eating you?"

"I wondered about those diamonds, too, Delos. So I've been looking through the weight schedule of the *Pioneer*."

"Didn't know you were interested in engineering."

"I can read figures."

"Well, you found it, didn't you? Schedule F-17-c, two ounces, allocated to me personally."

"I found it. It sticks out like a sore thumb. But I didn't find something else."

Harriman felt a cold chill in his stomach. "What?"

"I didn't find a schedule for the cancelled covers." Strong stared at him.

"It must be there. Let me see that weight schedule."

"It's not there, Delos. You know, I thought it was funny when you insisted on going to meet Captain LeCroix by yourself. What happened, Delos? Did you sneak them aboard?" He continued to stare while Harriman fidgeted. "We've put over some sharp business deals—but this will be the first time that anyone can say that the firm of Harriman and Strong has cheated."

"George—I would cheat, lie, steal, beg, bribe—do *anything* to accomplish what we have accomplished."

Harriman got up and paced the room. "We *had* to have that money, or the ship would never have taken off. We're cleaned out. You know that, don't you?"

Strong nodded. "But those covers should have gone to the Moon. That's what we contracted to do."

"I just forgot it. Then it was too late to figure the weight in. But it doesn't matter. I figured that if the trip was a failure, if LeCroix cracked up, nobody would know or care that the covers hadn't gone. And I knew if he made it, it wouldn't matter; we'd have plenty of money. And we will, George, we will!"

"We've got to pay the money back."

"Now? Give me time, George. Everybody concerned is happy the way it is. Wait until we recover our stake; then I'll buy every one of those covers back—out of my own pocket. That's a promise."

Strong continued to sit. Harriman stopped in front of him. "I ask you, George, is it worth while to wreck an enterprise of this size for a purely theoretical point?"

Strong sighed and said, "When the time comes, use the firm's money."

"That's the spirit! But I'll use my own, I promise you."

"No, the firm's money. If we're in it together, we're in it together."

"O.K., if that's the way you want it."

Harriman turned back to his desk. Neither of the two partners had anything to say for a long while. Presently Dixon and Entenza were announced.

"Well, Jack," said Harriman. "Feel better now?"

"No thanks to you. I had to fight for what I did put on the air—and some of it was pirated as it was. Delos, there should have been a television pick-up in the ship."

"Don't fret about it. As I told you, we couldn't spare the weight this time. But there will be the next trip, and the next. Your concession is going to be worth a pile of money."

Dixon cleared his throat. "That's what we came to see you about, Delos. What are your plans?"

"Plans? We go right ahead. Les and Coster and I make the next trip. We set up a permanent base. Maybe Coster stays behind. The third trip we send a real colony—nuclear engineers, miners, hydroponics experts, communications engineers. We'll found Luna City, first city on another planet."

Dixon looked thoughtful. "And when does this begin to pay off?"

"What do you mean by 'pay off'? Do you want your capital back, or do you want to begin to see some return on your investment? I can cut it either way."

Entenza was about to say that he wanted his investment back; Dixon cut in first, "Profits, naturally. The investment is already made."

"Fine!"

"But I don't see how you expect profits. Certainly, LeCroix made the trip and got back safely. There is honor for all of us. But where are the royalties?"

"Give the crop time to ripen, Dan. Do I look worried? What are our assets?" Harriman ticked them off on his fingers. "Royalties on pictures, television, radio—"

"Those things go to Jack."

"Take a look at the agreement. He has the concession, but he pays the firm—that's all of us—for them."

Dixon said, "Shut up, Jack!" before Entenza could speak, then added, "What else? That won't pull us out of the red."

"Endorsements galore. Monty's boys are working on that. Royalties from the greatest best seller yet—I've got a ghost writer and a stenographer following LeCroix around this very minute. A franchise for the first and only space line—"

"From whom?"

"We'll get it. Kamens and Montgomery are in Paris now, working on it. I'm joining them this afternoon. And we'll tie down that franchise with a franchise from *the other end*, just as soon as we can get a permanent colony there, no matter how small. It will be the autonomous state of Luna, under the protection of the United Nations—and no ship will land or take off in its territory without its permission. Besides that we'll have the right to franchise a dozen other companies for various purposes—and tax them, too—just as soon as we set up the Municipal Corporation of the City of Luna under the laws of the State of Luna. We'll sell everything but vacuum—we'll even sell vacuum, for experimental purposes. And don't forget—we'll still have a big chunk of real estate, sovereign title in us—as a state—and not yet sold. The Moon is *big*."

"Your ideas are rather big, too, Delos," Dixon said dryly. "But what actually happens next?"

"First we get title confirmed by the U.N. The Security Council is now in secret session; the Assembly meets tonight. Things will be popping; that's why I've got to be there. When the United Nations decides—as it will!—that its own non-profit corporation has the only real claim to the Moon, then I get busy. The poor little weak non-profit corporation is going to grant a number of things to some real honest-to-god corporations with hair on their chests—in return for help in setting up a physics research lab, an astronomical observatory, a lunography institute and some other perfectly proper non-profit enterprises. That's our interim pitch until we get a permanent colony with its own laws. Then we—"

Dixon gestured impatiently. "Never mind the legal shenanigans, Delos. I've known you long enough to know that you can figure out such angles. What do we actually have to *do* next?"

"Huh? We've got to build another ship, a bigger one. Not actually bigger, but effectively bigger. Coster has started the design of a surface catapult—it will reach from Manitou Springs to the top of Pikes Peak. With it we can put a ship in free orbit around the Earth. Then we'll use such a ship to fuel more ships—it amounts to a space station, like the power station. It adds up to a way to get there on chemical power without having to throw away nine-tenths of your ship to do it."

"Sounds expensive."

"It will be. But don't worry; we've got a couple of dozen piddling little things to keep the money coming in while we get set up on a commercial basis, then we sell stock. We sold stock before; now we'll sell a thousand dollars' worth where we sold ten before."

"And you think that will carry you through until the enterprise as a whole is on a paying basis? Face it, Delos, the thing as a whole doesn't pay off until you have ships plying between here and the Moon on a paying basis, figured in freight and passenger charges. That means customers, with cash. What is there on the Moon to ship—and who pays for it?"

"Dan, don't you believe there will be? If not, why are you here?"

"I believe in it, Delos—or I believe in you. But what's your time schedule? What's your budget? What's your prospective commodity? And please don't mention diamonds; I think I understand that caper."

Harriman chewed his cigar for a few moments. "There's one valuable commodity we'll start shipping at once."

"What?"

"Knowledge."

Entenza snorted. Strong looked puzzled. Dixon nodded. "I'll buy that. Knowledge is always worth something—to the man who knows how to exploit it. And I'll agree that the Moon is a place to find new knowledge. I'll assume that you can make the next trip pay off. What's your budget and your time table for that?"

Harriman did not answer. Strong searched his face closely. To him Harriman's poker face was as revealing as large print—he decided that his partner had been crowded into a corner. He waited, nervous but ready to back Harriman's play. Dixon went on, "From the way you describe it, Delos, I judge that you don't have money enough for your next step—and you don't know where you will get it. I believe in you, Delos—and I told you at the start that I did not believe in letting a new business die of anemia. I'm ready to buy in with a fifth share."

Harriman stared. "Look," he said bluntly, "you own Jack's share now, don't you?"

"I wouldn't say that."

"You vote it. It sticks out all over."

Entenza said, "That's not true. I'm independent. I—"

"Jack, you're a damn liar," Harriman said dispassionately. "Dan, you've got fifty percent now. Under the present rules I decide deadlocks, which gives me control as long as George sticks by me. If we sell you another share, you vote three-fifths—and are boss. Is that the deal you are looking for?"

"Delos, as I told you, I have confidence in you."

"But you'd feel happier with the whip hand. Well, I won't do it. I'll let space travel—*real* space travel, with established runs—wait another twenty years before I'll turn loose. I'll let us all go broke and let us live on glory before I'll turn loose. You'll have to think up another scheme."

Dixon said nothing. Harriman got up and began to pace. He stopped in front of Dixon. "Dan, if you really understood what this is all about, I'd let you have control. But you don't. You see this is just another way to money and to power. I'm perfectly willing to let you vultures get rich—but I keep control. I'm going to see this thing developed, not milked. The human race is heading out to the stars—and this adventure is going to present new problems compared with which atomic power was a kid's toy. Unless the whole matter is handled carefully, it will be fouled up. *You'll* foul it up, Dan, if I let you have the deciding vote in it—because you don't understand it."

He caught his breath and went on, "Take safety for instance. Do you know *why* I let LeCroix take that ship out instead of taking it myself? Do you think I was afraid? No! I wanted it to come back—*safely*. I didn't want space travel getting another set-back. Do you know why we have to have a monopoly, for a few years at least? Because every so-and-so and his brother is going to want to build a Moon ship, now that they know it can be done. Remember the first days of ocean flying? After Lindbergh did it, every so-called pilot who could lay hands on a crate took off for some over-water point. Some of them even took their kids along. And most of them landed in the drink. Airplanes get a reputation for being dangerous. A few years after that the airlines got so hungry for quick money in a highly competitive field that you couldn't pick up a paper without seeing headlines about another airliner crash.

"That's not going to happen to space travel! I'm not going to let it happen.

Space ships are too big and too expensive; if they get a reputation for being unsafe as well, we might as well have stayed in bed. I run things."

He stopped. Dixon waited and then said, "I said I believed in you, Delos. How much money do you need?"

"Eh? On what terms?"

"Your note."

"My note? Did you say *my note?*"

"I'd want security, of course."

Harriman swore. "I knew there was a hitch in it. Dan, you know everything I've got is tied up in this venture."

"You have insurance. You have quite a lot of insurance, I know."

"Yes, but that's all made out to my wife."

"I seem to have heard you say something about that sort of thing to Jack Entenza," Dixon said. "Come, now—if I know your tax-happy sort, you have at least one irrevocable trust, or paid-up annuities, or something, to keep Mrs. Harriman out of the poor house."

Harriman thought fiercely about it. "When's the call date on this note?"

"In the sweet bye and bye. I want a no-bankruptcy clause, of course."

"Why? Such a clause has no legal validity."

"It would be valid with *you*, wouldn't it?"

"Mmm . . . yes. Yes, it would."

"Then get out your policies and see how big a note you can write."

Harriman looked at him, turned abruptly and went to his safe. He came back with quite a stack of long, stiff folders. They added them up together; it was an amazingly large sum—for those days. Dixon then consulted a memorandum taken from his pocket and said, "One seems to be missing—a rather large one. A North Atlantic Mutual policy, I think."

Harriman glared at him. "Am I going to have to fire every confidential clerk in my force?"

"No," Dixon said mildly, "I don't get my information from your staff.

Harriman went back to the safe, got the policy and added it to the pile. Strong spoke up, "Do you want mine, Mr. Dixon?"

"No," answered Dixon, "that won't be necessary." He started stuffing the policies in his pocket. "I'll keep these, Delos, and attend to keeping up the premiums. I'll bill you of course. You can send the note and the change-of-beneficiary forms to my office. Here's your draft." He took out another slip of paper; it was the draft—already made out in the amount of the policies.

Harriman looked at it. "Sometimes," he said slowly, "I wonder who's kidding who?" He tossed the draft over to Strong. "O.K., George, take care of it. I'm off to Paris, boys. Wish me luck." He strode out as jauntily as a fox terrier.

Strong looked from the closed door to Dixon, then at the note. "I ought to tear this thing up!"

"Don't do it," advised Dixon. "You see, I really do believe in him." He added, "Ever read Carl Sandburg, George?"

"I'm not much of a reader."

"Try him some time. He tells a story about a man who started a rumor that they had struck oil in hell. Pretty soon everybody has left for hell, to get in on the boom. The man who started the rumor watches them all go, then scratches his head and says to himself that there just *might* be something in it, after all. So he left for hell, too."

Strong waited, finally said, "I don't get the point."

"The point is that I just want to be ready to protect myself if necessary, George—and so should you. Delos might begin believing his own rumors. Diamonds! Come, Jack."

CHAPTER TWELVE

THE ENSUING MONTHS were as busy as the period before the flight of the *Pioneer* (now honorably retired to the Smithsonian Institution). One engineering staff and great gangs of men were working on the catapult; two more staffs were busy with two new ships; the *Mayflower*, and the *Colonial*; a third ship was on the drafting tables. Ferguson was chief engineer for all of this; Coster, still buffered by Jock Berkeley, was engineering consultant, working where and as he chose. Colorado Springs was a boom town; the Denver-Trinidad roadcity settlements spread out at the Springs until they surrounded Peterson Field.

Harriman was as busy as a cat with two tails. The constantly expanding exploitation and promotion took eight full days a week of his time, but, by working Kamens and Montgomery almost to ulcers and by doing without sleep himself, he created frequent opportunities to run out to Colorado and talk things over with Coster.

Luna City, it was decided, would be founded on the very next trip. The *Mayflower* was planned for a pay-load not only of seven passengers, but with air, water and food to carry four of them over to the next trip; they would live in an aluminum Quonset-type hut, sealed, pressurized, and buried under the loose soil of Luna until—and assuming—they were succored.

The choice of the four extra passengers gave rise to another contest, another publicity exploitation—and more sale of stock. Harriman insisted that they be two married couples, over the united objections of scientific organizations everywhere. He gave in only to the extent of agreeing that there was no objection to all four being scientists, providing they constituted two married couples. This gave rise to several hasty marriages—and some divorces, after the choices were announced.

The *Mayflower* was the maximum size that calculations showed would be capable of getting into a free orbit around the Earth from the boost of the catapult, plus the blast of her own engines. Before she took off, four other ships, quite as large, would precede her. But they were not space ships; they were mere tankers—nameless. The most finicky of ballistic calculations, the most precise of launchings, would place them in the same orbit at the same spot. There the *Mayflower* would rendezvous and accept their remaining fuel.

This was the trickiest part of the entire project. If the four tankers could be placed close enough together, LeCroix, using a tiny maneuvering reserve, could bring his new ship to them. If not—well, it gets very lonely out in space.

Serious thought was given to placing pilots in the tankers and accepting as a penalty the use of enough fuel from one tanker to permit a get-away boat, a life boat with wings, to decelerate, reach the atmosphere and brake to a landing. Coster found a cheaper way.

A radar pilot, whose ancestor was the proximity fuse and whose immediate parents could be found in the homing devices of guided missiles, was given the task of bringing the tankers together. The first tanker would not be so equipped, but the second tanker through its robot would smell out the first and home on it with a pint-sized rocket engine, using the smallest of vectors to bring them together. The third would home on the first two and the fourth on the group.

LeCroix should have no trouble—if the scheme worked.

CHAPTER THIRTEEN

STRONG WANTED TO SHOW HARRIMAN the sales reports on the H & S automatic household switch; Harriman brushed them aside.

Strong shoved them back under his nose. "You'd better start taking an interest in such things, Delos. *Somebody* around this office had better start seeing to it that some money comes in—some money that belongs to us, personally—or you'll be selling apples on a street corner."

Harriman leaned back and clasped his hands back of his head. "George, how can you talk that way on a day like this? Is there no poetry in your soul? Didn't you hear what I said when I came in? *The rendezvous worked.* Tankers one and two are as close together as Siamese twins. We'll be leaving within the week."

"That's as may be. Business has to go on."

"You keep it going; I've got a date. When did Dixon say he would be over?"

"He's due now."

"Good!" Harriman bit the end off a cigar and went on, "You know, George, I'm not sorry I didn't get to make the first trip. Now I've still got it to do. I'm as expectant as a bridegroom—and as happy." He started to hum.

Dixon came in without Entenza, a situation that had obtained since the day Dixon had dropped the pretence that he controlled only one share. He shook hands. "You heard the news, Dan?"

"George told me."

"This is it—or almost. A week from now, more or less, I'll be on the Moon. I can hardly believe it."

Dixon sat down silently. Harriman went on, "Aren't you even going to congratulate me? Man, this is a great day!"

Dixon said, "D.D., why are you going?"

"Huh? Don't ask foolish questions. This is what I have been working toward."

"It's not a foolish question. I asked why *you* were going. The four colonists have an obvious reason, and each is a selected specialist observer as well. LeCroix is the pilot. Coster is the man who is designing the permanent colony. But why are *you* going? What's your function?"

"My function? Why, I'm the guy who runs things. Shucks, I'm going to run for mayor when I get there. Have a cigar, friend—the name's Harriman. Don't forget to vote." He grinned.

Dixon did not smile. "I did not know you planned on staying."

Harriman looked sheepish. "Well, that's still up in the air. If we get the shelter built in a hurry, we may save enough in the way of supplies to let me sort of lay over until the next trip. You wouldn't begrudge me that, would you?"

Dixon looked him in the eye. "Delos, I can't let you go at all."

Harriman was too startled to talk at first. At last he managed to say, "Don't joke, Dan. I'm going. You can't stop me. Nothing on Earth can stop me."

Dixon shook his head. "I can't permit it, Delos. I've got too much sunk in this. If you go and anything happens to you, I lose it all."

"That's silly. You and George would just carry on, that's all."

"Ask George."

Strong had nothing to say. He did not seem anxious to meet Harriman's eyes. Dixon went on, "Don't try to kid your way out of it, Delos. This venture is you and you are this venture. If you get killed, the whole thing folds up. I don't say space travel folds up; I think you've already given that a boost that will carry it along even with lesser men in your shoes. But as for this venture—our company—it will fold up. George and I will have to liquidate at about half a cent on the dollar. It would take sale of patent rights to get that much. The tangible assets aren't worth anything."

"Damn it, it's the intangibles we sell. You knew that all along."

"You are the intangible asset, Delos. You are the goose that lays the golden eggs. I want you to stick around until you've laid them. You must not risk your neck in space flight until you have this thing on a profit-making basis, so that any competent manager, such as George or myself, thereafter can keep it solvent. I mean it, Delos. I've got too much in it to see you risk it in a joy ride."

Harriman stood up and pressed his fingers down on the edge of his desk. He was breathing hard. "You can't stop me!" he said slowly and forcefully. "Not all the forces of heaven or hell can stop me."

Dixon answered quietly, "I'm sorry, Delos. But I can stop you and I will. I can tie up that ship out there."

"Try it! I own as many lawyers as you do—and better ones!"

"I think you will find that you are not as popular in American courts as you once were—not since the United States found out it didn't own the Moon after all."

"Try it, I tell you. I'll break you and I'll take your shares away from you, too."

"Easy, Delos! I've no doubt you have some scheme whereby you could milk the basic company right away from George and me if you decided to. But it won't be necessary. Nor will it be necessary to tie up the ship. I want the flight to take place as much as you do. But you won't be on it, because you will decide not to go."

"I will, eh? Do I look crazy from where you sit?"

"No, on the contrary."

"Then why won't I go?"

"Because of your note that I hold. I want to collect it."

"What? There's no due date."

"No. But I want to be sure to collect it."

"Why, you dumb fool, if I get killed you collect it sooner than ever."

"Do I? You are mistaken, Delos. If you are killed—on a flight to the Moon—I collect nothing. I know; I've checked with every one of the companies underwriting you. Most of them have escape clauses covering experimental vehicles that date back to early aviation. In any case all of them will cancel and fight it out in court if you set foot inside that ship."

"You put them up to this!"

"Calm down, Delos. You'll be bursting a blood vessel. Certainly I queried them, but I was legitimately looking after my own interests. I don't want to collect on that note—not now, not by your death. I want you to pay it back out of your own earnings, by staying here and nursing this company through till it's stable."

Harriman chucked his cigar, almost unsmoked and badly chewed, at a waste basket. He missed. "I don't give a hoot if you lose on it. If you hadn't stirred them up, they'd have paid without a quiver."

"But it did dig up a weak point in your plans, Delos. If space travel is to be a success, insurance will have to reach out and cover the insured anywhere."

"Confound it, one of them does now—N. A. Mutual."

"I've seen their ad and I've looked over what they claim to offer. It's just window dressing, with the usual escape clause. No, insurance will have to be revamped, all sorts of insurance."

Harriman looked thoughtful. "I'll look into it. George, call Kamens. Maybe we'll have to float our own company."

"Never mind Kamens," objected Dixon. "The point is you can't go on this trip. You have too many details of that sort to watch and plan for and nurse along."

Harriman looked back at him. "You haven't gotten it through your head, Dan, that *I'm going!* Tie up the ship if you can. If you put sheriffs around it, I'll have goons there to toss them aside."

Dixon looked pained. "I hate to mention this point, Delos, but I am afraid you will be stopped even if I drop dead."

"How?"

"Your wife."

"What's she got to do with it?"

"She's ready to sue for separate maintenance right now—she's found out about this insurance thing. When she hears about this present plan, she'll force you into court and force an accounting of your assets."

"*You put her up to it!*"

Dixon hesitated. He knew that Entenza had spilled the beans to Mrs. Harriman—maliciously. Yet there seemed no point in adding to a personal feud. "She's bright enough to have done some investigating on her own account. I won't deny I've talked to her—but she sent for me."

"I'll fight both of you!" Harriman stomped to a window, stood looking out—it was a real window; he liked to look at the sky.

Dixon came over and put a hand on his shoulder, saying softly, "Don't take it this way, Delos. Nobody's trying to keep you from your dream. But you can't go just yet; you can't let us down. We've stuck with you this far; you owe it to us to stick with us until it's done."

Harriman did not answer; Dixon went on, "If you don't feel any loyalty toward me, how about George? He's stuck with you *against* me, when it hurt him, when he thought you were ruining him—and you surely were, unless you finish this job. How about George, Delos? Are you going to let him down, too?"

Harriman swung around, ignoring Dixon and facing Strong. "What about it, George? Do you think I should stay behind?"

Strong rubbed his hands and chewed his lip. Finally he looked up. "It's all right with me, Delos. You do what you think is best."

Harriman stood looking at him for a long moment, his face working as if he were going to cry. Then he said huskily, "Okay, you rats. Okay. I'll stay behind."

CHAPTER FOURTEEN

IT WAS ONE OF THOSE GLORIOUS EVENINGS so common in the Pikes Peak region, after a day in which the sky has been well scrubbed by thunderstorms. The track of the catapult crawled in a straight line up the face of the mountain, whole shoulders having been carved away to permit it. At the temporary space port, still raw from construction, Harriman, in company with visiting notables, was saying good-bye to the passengers and crew of the *Mayflower*.

The crowds came right up to the rail of the catapult. There was no need to keep them back from the ship; the jets would not blast until she was high over the peak. Only the ship itself was guarded, the ship and the gleaming rails.

Dixon and Strong, together for company and mutual support, hung back at the edge of the area roped off for passengers and officials. They watched Harriman jollying those about to leave: "Good-bye, Doctor. Keep an eye on him, Janet. Don't let him go looking for Moon Maidens." They saw him engage Coster in private conversation, then clap the younger man on the back.

"Keeps his chin up, doesn't he?" whispered Dixon.

"Maybe we should have let him go," answered Strong.

"Eh? Nonsense! We've got to have him. Anyway, his place in history is secure."

"He doesn't care about history," Strong answered seriously, "he just wants to go to the Moon."

"Well, confound it—he can go to the Moon . . . as soon as he gets his job done. After all, it's his job. He made it."

"I know."

Harriman turned around, saw them, started toward them. They shut up. "Don't duck," he said jovially. "It's all right. I'll go on the next trip. By then I plan to have it running itself. You'll see." He turned back toward the *Mayflower*. "Quite a sight, isn't she?"

The outer door was closed; ready lights winked along the track and from the control tower. A siren sounded.

Harriman moved a step or two closer.

"*There she goes!*"

It was a shout from the whole crowd. The great ship started slowly, softly up the track, gathered speed, and shot toward the distant peak. She was already tiny by the time she curved up the face and burst into the sky.

She hung there a split second, then a plume of light exploded from her tail. Her jets had fired.

Then she was a shining light in the sky, a ball of flame, then—nothing. She was gone, upward and outward, to her rendezvous with her tankers.

The crowd had pushed to the west end of the platform as the ship swarmed up the mountain. Harriman had stayed where he was, nor had Dixon and Strong followed the crowd. The three were alone, Harriman most alone for he did not seem aware that the others were near him. He was watching the sky.

Strong was watching him. Presently Strong barely whispered to Dixon, "Do you read the Bible?"

"Some."

"He looks as Moses must have looked, when he gazed out over the promised land."

Harriman dropped his eyes from the sky and saw them. "You guys still here?" he said. "Come on—there's work to be done."

MAGIC CITY
by Nelson S. Bond

CHAPTER ONE

Out of the sweet, dark emptiness of sleep there was a pressure on her arm and a voice whispering an urgent plea.

"Rise, O Mother! O Mother, rise and come quickly!"

Meg woke with a start. The little sleep-imp in her brain stirred fretfully, resentful of being thus rudely banished. He made one last effort to hold Meg captive, tossing a mist of slumber-dust into her eyes, but Meg shook her head resolutely. The sleep-imp, sulky, forced her lips open in a great gape, climbed from her mouth, and sped away.

Sullen shadows lingered in the corners of the *hoam*, but the windows were gray-limned with approaching dawn. Meg glanced at the cot beside her own, where Daiv, her mate, lay in undisturbed rest. His tawny mane was tousled, and on his lips hovered the memory of a smile. His face was curiously, endearingly boyish, but the bronzed arms and shoulders that lay exposed were the arms and shoulders of a fighting man.

"Quickly, O Mother—"

Meg said, "Peace, Jain; I come." She spoke calmly, gravely, as befitted the matriarch of the Jinnia Clan, but a thin, cold fear-thought touched her heart. So many were the duties of a Mother; so many and so painful. Meg the Priestess had not guessed the troubles that lay beyond the days of her novitiate. Now the aged, kindly tribal Mother was dead; into Meg's firm, white hands had been placed the guidance of her clan's destiny. It was so great a task, and this—*this* was the hardest task of all.

She drew a deep breath. "Elnor?" she asked.

"Yes, Mother. Even now the Evil Ones circle about, seeking to steal the breath from her nostrils. He bides His time, but He is impatient. There is no time to waste."

"I come," said Meg. From a shelf she took a rattle made of a dry gourd wound with the tresses of a virgin; from another a fire-rock, a flaked piece of god-metal and a strip of parchment upon which a sacred stick, dipped into midnight water, had left its spoor of letters.

These things she touched with reverence, and Jain's eyes were great with awe. The worker captain shuddered, hid her face in her hands lest the sight of these holy mysteries blind her.

Dry fern rustled. Daiv, eyes heavy-lidded, propped himself up on one elbow.

"What is it, Golden One?"

"Elnor," replied Meg quietly. "He has come to take her. I must do what I can."

Impatience etched tiny lines on Daiv's forehead.

"With those things, Golden One? I've told you time and again, they won't bother Him—"

"Hush!" Meg made a swift, appeasing gesture lest He, hearing Daiv's impious words, take offense. Daiv's boldness often frightened Meg. He held the gods in so little awe it was a marvel they let him live. Of course he came from a sacred place himself, from the Land of the Escape. That might have something to do with it.

She said again, "I must do what I can, Daiv. Come, Jain."

They left the Mother's hoam, walked swiftly down the deserted walk-avenue. The morning symphony of the birds was in its tune-up stage. The sky was dim, gray, overcast. One hoam was lighted, that of the stricken worker, Elnor.

Meg opened the door, motioned Jain quickly inside, closed the door again behind her that no breath of foul outside air taint the hot, healthy closeness of the sickroom. She noted with approval that the windows had been closed and tightly sealed, that strong-scented ox-grease candles filled the room with their potent, demon-chasing odor.

Yet despite these precautions, the Evil Ones did—as Jain had told—vie for possession of Elnor's breath. On a narrow cot in the middle of the room lay the dying worker. Her breath choked, ragged and uneven as the song of the jay. Her cheeks, beneath their coat of tan, were bleached; her eyes were hot coals in murky pockets. Her flesh was dry and harsh; she tossed restlessly, eyes roving as if watching some unseen presence.

Jain said fearfully, "See, O Mother? She sees Him. He is here."

Meg nodded. Her jaw tightened. Two women and Bil, Elnor's mate, huddled about the sickbed. She motioned them away. "I will do battle with Him," she said grimly.

She poised a moment, tense for the conflict. Elnor moaned. Then Meg, with a great, reverberant cry, struck the sacred stones together, the bit of fire-rock and the rasp of god-metal. A shower of golden sparks leaped from her hands. Her watchers cried aloud their awe, fell back trembling.

Meg raised the gourd. Holding it high, shaking it, the scrap of parchment clenched in her right hand, she began chanting the magic syllables written thereon. She cried out reverently, for these were mighty words of healing power, no one knew how old, but they had been handed down through long ages. They were a rite of the Ancient Ones.

"'I swear,'" she intoned, "'by Apollo the physician and Aesculapius, and Health, and All-heal, and all the gods and goddesses, that, according to my ability and judgment, I will keep this Oath and stipulation—'"

The gourd challenged the demons who haunted Elnor. Meg crossed her eyes and crept widdershins three times about Elnor's cot.

"'—I will give no deadly med-sun to anyone—'"

The sonorous periods rolled and throbbed; sweat ran down Meg's cheeks and throat. Beneath her blankets, Elnor tossed. In the corner, Bil muttered fearfully.

"'—will not cut persons laboring under the Stone, but will leave this to be done by men who are practitioners of this work—'"

The candle guttered, and a drop of wax spilled on the floor as the door behind her opened, closed gently. Meg dared not glance at the newcomer, dared not risk halting the incantation. Some of the hectic color appeared to have left Elnor's cheeks. Perhaps, then, He was leaving? Without His prey?

"'—while I continue to keep this Oath unviolated, may it be granted to me—'"

Meg's voice swelled with hope. Oh, mighty was the magic of the Ancient Ones! The spell was succeeding! In a vast, triumphant clamor of the gourd, tone shrill and joyful, she broke into the peroration.

"'—to enjoy life and the practice of the Art, respected by all—'"

A sudden, blood-chilling sound interrupted her. It was Elnor. A gasp of pain, a stifled cry, one lunging twist of a pain-racked body. And then—

"It is too late, Golden One," said Daiv. "Elnor is dead."

The women in the corner began keening a dirge. The man, Bil, ceased his muttering. He moved to the side of his dead mate, knelt there wordlessly, staring at Meg with mute, reproachful eyes.

Choking, Meg stammered the words required of her. "'Aamé, the gods, have mercy on her soul.'" Then she fled from the hoam of sorrow. It was not permitted that anyone should see the Mother in tears.

Daiv followed her. Even in his arms, there was but little comfort—

Later, in their own hoam, Daiv sat watching in respectful silence as Meg performed the daily magic that was an obligation of the Mother.

Having offered a brief prayer to the gods, Meg took into her right hand a stick. This she let drink from a pool of midnight in a dish before her, then scratched it across a scroll of smooth, bleached calfskin. Where it moved it left its spoor, a spidery trail of black.

She finished, and Daiv gazed at her admiringly. He was proud of this mate of his who held the knowledge of many lost mysteries. He said, "It is done, Golden One? Read it. Let me hear the speech-without-words."

Meg read, somberly.

"Report of the fourteenth day of the month of June, 3485 A.D.

"Our work is going forward very well. Today Evalin returned from her visit to the Zurrie territory. There, she says, her message was received with astonishment and wonder, but for the most part with approval. There is some dissent, especially amongst the older women, but the Mother has heard the Revelation with understanding, and has given her promise that the Slooie Clan will immediately attempt to communicate peace and a knowledge of the new order to the Wild Ones.

"Our crops ripen, and soon Lima will have completed the new dam across the Ronoak River. We have now fourscore cattle, fifty horses, and our clan numbers three hundred and twenty-nine. All of our women are supplied with mates.

"We lost a most valuable worker today, when He came for Elnor, Lootent of the Field Coar. We could ill afford to lose her, but He would not be denied—"

Meg's voice broke. She stopped reading, tossed the scroll on a jumbled heap with countless others, some shining new, some yellow with age, written in the painstaking script of Mothers long dead and long forgotten.

Daiv said consolingly, "Do not grieve, Golden One. You tried to save her. But eventually He comes for each of us. The aged, the weak, the hurt—"

Meg cried, "Why, Daiv, why? Why should He come for Elnor? We know He takes the aged because in their weakness is His strength; He takes the wounded because He scents flowing blood from afar.

"But Elnor was young and strong and healthy. There were no wounds or sores upon her body. She did not taste of His berries in the fields, nor had she touched, at any time, a person already claimed by Him.

"Yet—she died! Why? Why, Daiv?"

"I do not know, Golden One. But I am curious. For I am Daiv, known as He-who-would-learn. There is a mystery here far greater than all your magic spells. Perhaps it is even greater than the wisdom of the Ancient Ones."

"I am afraid, Daiv. He is so ever-near; we are so weak. You know I have tried to be a good Mother. It was I who made a pilgrimage to the Place of the Gods, learned the secret that the gods were men, and established a new order, that men and women should live together again, as it was in the old days.

"I have worked to spread this knowledge throughout the world, through all of Tizathy. One day we will reclaim all the Wild Ones of the forests, bring them into our camps and together we and they will rebuild the world.

"Only one stands in our way. Him! He who strikes down our warriors with an invisible sword, reaps an endless harvest amongst our workers. He is our arch-foe. A grim, mocking, unseen enemy, against whom we are powerless."

Daiv grunted. There were small, hard lines on his forehead, between his eyes. His lips were not up-curved in their usual happy look.

He said, "You are right, Meg. He, alone, destroys more of us each year than the forest beasts or our occasional invaders. Could we but find and kill Him our people would increase in knowledge and power swiftly."

He shook his head. "But we do not know where to seek Him, Golden One."

Meg drew a swift, deep breath. Her eyes glinted, suddenly excited.
"*I know*, Daiv!"
"You know where He lives, Golden One?"
"Yes. The old Mother told me, many years ago when I was a student priestess. She spoke and warned me against a forbidden city to the north and eastward—the city known as the City of Death! That is, must be, His lair!"
There was a moment of strident silence.
Then Daiv said, tightly, "Can you tell me how to reach this spot, Meg? Can you draw me a marker-of-places that will enable me to find it?"
"I can! It lies where the great creet highways of the Ancient Ones meet with a river and an island at a vast, salt sea. But . . . but why, Daiv?"
Daiv said, "Draw me the marker-of-places, Meg. He must be destroyed. I will go to His city to find Him."
"No!" It was not Meg the priestess who cried out; it was Meg the woman. "No, Daiv! It is an accursed city. I cannot let you go!"
"You cannot stop me, Golden One."
"But you know no spells, no incantations. He will destroy you—"
"I will destroy Him, first." The happy look clung to the corners of Daiv's lips. He drew Meg into his bronze arms, woke fire in her veins with the touching-of-mouths he had taught her. "My arm is strong, Meg; my sword keen. He must feel its bite if we are to live and prosper. You cannot change my mind."
Then Meg decided.
"Very well, Daiv. You shall go. But I will make you no marker-of-places."
"Come now, Golden One! Without it I shall not be able to find—"
Meg's voice was firm, unequivocal. "Because I shall go with you! Together we shall seek and destroy—Him!"

CHAPTER TWO

So STARTED MEG AND DAIV for the City of Death. It was not a happy parting, theirs with the men and women of the Jinnia Clan. There were tears and lamentations and sad mutterings, for all knew the law that the eastern cities of the Ancient Ones were forbidden.
There was bravery, too, and loyalty. Stern-jawed Lora, Captain of the Warriors, confronted Meg at the gate. She was clad for battle; her leathern plates and buckler were newly refurbished, her sword hung at her side. Behind her stood a squad of picked warriors, packed for trek.
"We are ready, O Mother!" said Lora succinctly.
Meg smiled, a sweet, proud smile. She knew only too well the mental terror, the physical qualms of fear these women had overcome to thus offer themselves. Her heart lifted within her, but she leaned forward and with her own fingers unbuckled Lora's scabbard.

"You are needed here, my daughter," she said. "You must guard the clan till I return. And"—she faltered an instant, continued swiftly—"and if it is the will of the gods I return not, then you must continue to see that the law is obeyed until the young priestess, Haizl, is finished her novitiate and can assume leadership.

"Peace be with you all!" She pressed her lips to Lora's forehead lightly. It seemed strange to none of them that she should call the harsh-visaged chieftain, many years her senior, "My daughter." For she was the Mother, and the Mother was ageless and of all time.

Others came forward then, each in their turn to ask a farewell blessing, to offer silent prayers to the gods for Meg's safe return. Young Haizl, the clear-eyed, inquisitive twelve-year-old maiden whom Meg had selected to succeed her as matriarch of the Jinnia Clan whispered: "Be strong, O Mother, but not too daring. Return safely, for never can I take your place."

"But you can, my daughter. Study diligently, learn the speech-without-words and the magic of the numbers. Keep the law and learn the rituals."

"I try, O Mother. But the little pain-demons dwell in my head, behind my eyes. They dance and make the letters move strangely."

"Pursue your course and they will go away."

Came 'Ana, who had been a breeding-mother before the Revelation, and who was now a happily wedded mate. Her eyes were red with weeping and she could not speak. Came Izbel, strongest of the workers, who with her bare hands had crushed the life from a mountain cat. But there was no strength in her hands now; they trembled as they touched Meg's doeskin boots. Also came Bil, eyes smoldering with hot demand.

"I would go with you to destroy Him, O Mother! It is my right. You cannot refuse me!"

"But I can and do, Bil."

Bil said rebelliously, "I am a man, strong, brave. I fought beside Daiv when the Japcans attacked. Ask him if I am not a great fighter."

"That I know without asking. But now we fight an invisible foe. Of all the clan, only Daiv and I can stand before Him. I am a Mother, inviolate; Daiv is sprung of an ancient, sacred tribe. The Kirki tribe, dwelling in the Land of the Escape.

"And now—farewell—"

But after they had left the town, Daiv repeated his objections, voiced many times in the hours preceding this.

"Go back, Golden One! This is a man's task. He is a potent enemy. Go back to the clan, wait for my return—"

Meg said, as if not hearing him, "See, the road lies before us. The broken creet road of the Ancient Ones."

It was not a long journey. Only eight days' march, according to Meg's calculations. Scarce one fifth of the distance she had covered in her pilgrimage to the Place of the Gods in 'Kota territory a year before. And Daiv was an experienced traveler; alone, he had wandered through most of Tizathy from sun-parched 'Vadah to bleak Wyomin, from the lush jungles of Flarduh to the snow-crested mountains of Orgen. Only this one path he had never trod, for all tribes in wide Tizathy knew the law, that the east was forbidden.

So their journey was one filled with many wonders. It was difficult walking on the crumbled creet highways of the Ancient Ones, so Meg and Daiv walked in the fields but kept the white rock roadbed in sight. They passed through an abandoned village named Lextun or Veémi—the old name for it was confused in the records—and another known as Stantn. Only by the intersections of the roads could they tell these towns had once been. No hoams stood; grass ran riot where once had been fertile fields and pasture land.

On the morning of the fourth day they took a wrong turning, departed from the high plateau and climbed eastward into a blue and smoky ridge of mountain. Here they found a great marvel. High in the hills they came upon the broken walls of an ancient shrine, stone heaped upon stone, creet holding the blocks together. Spiked with god-metal on one wall was a green-molded square. Daiv, scraping this out of curiosity, uncovered oddly shaped letters in the language. The letters read:

URAY CAVER
—dmiss———One dol—

Beyond the shrine was a huge hole, leading deep into the bowels of the earth. Daiv would have gone into it, seeking a fuller explanation of this wonder, but cold dampness seeped from the vent, and the stir of his footsteps at the entrance roused a myriad of loathsome bats from below.

Meg understood, then, and dragged Daiv from the accursed spot hastily. "This is the abode of one of their Evil Gods," she explained. "The bats are souls of his worshipers. We must not tarry here."

And they fled, retracing their steps to the point at which they had made the wrong turning. But as they ran, Meg, to be on the safe side, made a brief, apologetic prayer to the dark god, Uray Caver.

Oh, many were the wonders of that journey. Perhaps most wondrous of all—at least most unexpected of all—was their discovery of a clan living far to the north and east, near the end of their sixth day's travel.

It was Daiv who first noted signs of human habitation. They had crossed a narrow strip of land which, from a rusted place of god-metal Meg identified as part of the Maerlun territory, when Daiv suddenly halted his priestess with a silencing gesture.

"Golden One—a fire! A campfire!"

Meg looked, and a slow, shuddering apprehension ran through her veins. He was right in all save one thing. It could not be a *campfire*. Flame there was, and smoke. But in this forbidden territory smoke and flame could mean only—a charnel fire! For they were nearing His abode. Meg's nostrils sought the air delicately, half-afraid of the scent that might reach them.

Then, surprisingly, a happy sound was breaking from Daiv's throat, he was propelling her forward.

"They are men, Golden One! Men and women living in peace and harmony! The message of the Revelation must somehow have penetrated even these forbidden regions. Come!"

But a great disappointment awaited them. For when they met the strange clanspeople, they found themselves completely unable to converse with them. Only one thing could Meg and Daiv learn. That they called their village Lankstr. Their tribal name they never revealed, though Daiv believed they called themselves Nikvars.

Meg was bitterly chagrined.

"If they could only speak the language, Daiv, they could tell us something about His city. They live so near. But perhaps—" She looked doubtful. "Do you think maybe they worship—Him?"

Daiv shook his head.

"No, Golden One. These Nikvars speak a coarse, animal tongue, but I think they are a kindly folk. They have never received the Revelation, yet they live together in the fashion of the Ancient Ones. They plow the fields and raise livestock. They have sheltered and fed us, offered us fresh clothing. They cannot be His disciples. This is another of the many, many mysteries of Tizathy. One that we must some day solve."

And the next morning they left the camp of their odd hosts. They bore with them friendly gifts of salt and bacca, and a damp-pouch filled with a strange food, krowt. And with the quaint Nikvar farewell ringing in their ears, "Veedzain! O Veedzain!", they continued their way east into a territory avoided and feared for thrice five centuries.

Through Lebnun and Alntun, skirting a huge pile of masonry that Meg's marker-of-places indicated as "Lizbeth," up the salt-swept marshes of the Joysy flatlands. The salt air stung their inland nostrils strangely, and the flatland air oppressed Meg's mountain-bred lungs, but she forgot her physical discomforts in the marvels to be seen.

And then, on the morning of the tenth day, the red lance of the dawning sun shattered itself on a weird, light-reflecting dreadfulness a scant ten miles away. Something so strange, so unnatural, so absolutely incredible that it took Meg's breath away, and she could only clutch her mate's arm, gasping and pointing.

Hoams! But such hoams! Great, towering buildings that groped sharded fingers into the very bosom of the sky; hoams of god-metal and creet—red with water-hurt, true—but still intact. Some of them—Meg closed her eyes, then opened them again and found it was still so—must have been every bit of two hundred, three hundred feet in height!

And as from afar, she heard Daiv's voice repeating the ancient description.

"'It lies where the great creet highways of the Ancient Ones meet with a river and an island at a vast, salt sea.' This is it, Meg! We have found it, my Golden One!"

The sun lifted higher, spilling its blood upon the forbidden village. There was ominous portent in that color, and for the first time fear crept from its secret lurking place in Meg's heart, ran on panicky feet to her brain. She faltered, "It . . . it is His city, Daiv. See, even the hoams are bleached skeletons from which He has stripped the flesh. Think you, we should go on?"

Daiv made a happy sound deep in his throat. Still it was not altogether a happy sound; there was anger in it, and courage, and defiance.

He said, "We go on, Golden One! My sword thirsts for His defeat!"

And swiftly, eagerly, he pressed onward. Thus came Meg and Daiv to the City of Death.

CHAPTER THREE

It was not so easy to effect entry into the city as Meg had expected. According to the old marker-of-places she had brought, the city was connected with the road by a tunl. Meg did not know what a tunl was, but clearly it had to be some sort of bridge or roadway.

There was nothing such here. The road ended abruptly at a great hole in the ground, similar to that which they had seen at the shrine of Uray Caver, except that this one was begemmed with glistening creet platters, and everywhere about it were queer oblongs of god-metal scored with cryptic runes. Prayers. "O Left Tur," said one; "O Parki," another.

Daiv glanced at Meg querulously, but she shook her head. These were —or appeared to be—in the language, but their meanings were lost in the mists of time. Lost, too, was the significance of that gigantic magic spell carven in solid stone at the mouth of the hole—

N.Y.—MCMXXVII—N.J.

Discouraged but undaunted, Meg and Daiv turned away from the hole. Fortunately this was uncivilized territory; the forest ran right down to the water's edge. It eased the task of hewing small trees, building a raft with which they might cross the river.

This they did in the daytime, working with muffled axes lest He hear, investigate, and thwart their plans to invade His domain.

At night they crept back into the forest to build a camp. While Daiv went out and caught game, a fat young wild pig, Meg baked fresh biscuit, boiled maters she found growing wild in a nearby glade, and brewed cawfee from their rapidly dwindling store of that fragrant bean.

The next day they worked again on their craft, and the day after that. And at last the job was completed, Daiv looked upon it and pronounced it good. So at dusk they pushed it into the water. And when the icy moon invaded the sky, forcing the tender sun to flee before its barrage of silver hoarshakings, they set out for the opposite shore.

Without incident, they attained their goal. Behind a thicket, Daiv moored their rough craft; each committed the location to memory. Then they climbed the stone-rubbled bank, and stood at last in the City of Death, on the very portals of His lair.

Nor was there any doubt that this *was* Death's city. So far as the eye could see or the ear hear, there was no token of life. Harsh, jumbled blocks of creet scraped tender their soles, and there was no blade of grass to soften that moon-frozen severity. About and around and before them were countless aged hoams; their doors were gasping mouths, their shutterless windows like vast, blank eyes. They moved blindly forward, but no hare sprang, startled, from an unseen warren before them; no night bird broke the tomblike silence with a melancholy cry.

Only the faint breath of the wind, stirring through the great avenues of emptiness, whispered them caution in a strange, sad sigh.

A great unease weighted Meg's mind, and in the gloom her hand caught that of Daiv as they pressed ever forward into the heart of Death's citadel. High corridors abutted them on either side; by instinct, rather than sense, they pursued a northward path.

A thousand questions filled Meg's heart, but in this hallowed place she could not stir her lips to motion. But as she walked, she wondered, marveled, at the Ancient Ones who, it was told, had built and lived in this great stone village.

Perhaps the creet roadbed on which they walked had once been smooth, as the legends told, though Meg doubted it. Surely not even the ages could have so torn creet into jagged boulders, deep-pitted and sore. And why should the Ancient Ones have deliberately pockmarked their roads with holes, and at the bottom of these holes placed broken tubes of red god-metal?

Why, too, should the Ancient Ones have built hoams that, probing the sky, still were roofless, and had in many places had their façades stripped away so that beneath the exterior showed little square cubicles, like rooms? Or why should the Ancient Ones have placed long laths of metal in the middle of their walk-avenues? Was it, Meg wondered, because they feared the demons? And had placed these bars to fend them off? All demons, Meg knew, feared god-metal, and would not cross it—

How long they trod those deserted thoroughfares Meg could not tell. Their path was generally northward, but it was a devious one because Daiv, great-eyed with wonder, was ever moved to explore some mysterious alley. Once, even, he braved destruction by creeping furtively into the entrance of a hoam consecrated to a god with a harsh-sounding foreign name, Mcmxl, but from there Meg begged him to withdraw, lest He somehow divine their presence.

Yet it was Daiv's insatiable curiosity that found a good omen for them. Well within the depths of the city, he stumbled across the first patch of life they had found. It was a tiny square of green, surmounted on all sides by bleak desolation. Yet from its breast of high, rank jungle grass soared a dozen mighty trees, defiantly quick in the city of the dead. Meg dropped to her knees at this spot, kissed the earth and made a prayer to the familiar gods of her clan.

And she told Daiv, "Remember well this spot. It is a refuge, a sanctuary. Perhaps, then, even He is not invulnerable, if life persists in His fortress. Should we ever be parted, let us meet here."

She marked the spot on her marker-of-places. From a plaque of the Ancient Ones, she learned its name. It was called Madinsqua.

Through the long night they trod the city streets, but when the first faint edge of gray lifted night's shadow in the east, Daiv strangled in his throat and made a tired mouth. Then Meg, suddenly aware of her own fatigue, remembered they must not meet their powerful foe in this state.

"We must rest, Daiv. We must be strong and alert when we come face to face with Him."

Daiv demanded, "But where, Golden One? You will not enter one of the hoams—"

"The hoams are taboo," said Meg piously, "but there are many temples. Behold, there lies a great one before us now. I am a Priestess and a Mother; all temples are refuge to me. We shall go there."

So they went into the mighty, colonnaded building. And it was, indeed, a temple. Through a long corridor they passed, down many steps, and at last into the towering vault of the sacristan.

Here, once, on the high niches about the walls, there had stood statues of the gods. Now most of these had been dislodged, their shards lay upon the cracked tiles beneath. Yet a few stood, and beneath centuries of dust and dirt the adventurers could still see the faded hues of ancient paint.

The floor of the sacristan was one, vast crater; a wall had crashed to earth and covered the confessionals of the priests. But above their heads was suspended an awesome object—a huge, round face around the rim of which appeared symbols familiar to Meg.

Daiv's eyes asked Meg for an answer.

"It is a holy sign," Meg told him. "Those are the numbers that make and take away. I had to learn them when I was a priestess. There is great magic in them." And while Daiv stood silent and respectful, she chanted them as it was ordained, "One—two—three—"

The size of this temple wakened greater awe in Meg than anything she had heretofore seen. She knew, now, that it must have been a great and holy race that lived here before the Great Disaster, for thousands could stand in the sacristan alone without crowding; in addition, there were a dozen smaller halls and prayer rooms, many of which had once been provided with seats. The western wall of the cathedral was lined with barred gates; on these depended metal placards designating the various sects who were permitted to worship here. One such, more legible than the rest, bore the names of communities vaguely familiar to Meg.

THE SPORTSMAN—12:01
Newark
Philadelphia
Washington
Cincinnati

This was, of course, the ancient language, but Meg thought she could detect some similarity to names of present-day clans. She and Daiv had, themselves, come through a town called Noork on their way here, and the elder legends told of a Fideffia, the City of Endless Sleep, and a Sinnaty, where once had ruled a great people known as the Reds.

But it would have been sacrilege to sleep in these hallowed halls. At Meg's advice they sought refuge in one of the smaller rooms flanking the corridor through which they had entered the temple. There were many of these, and one was admirably adapted to their purpose; it was the tiny prayer room of a forgotten god, Ited-Ciga. There was, in this room, a miraculously undamaged dais on which they could sleep.

They had eaten, but had not slaked their thirst in many hours. Daiv was overjoyed to find a black drink-fountain set into one of the walls, complete with a mouthpiece and a curiously shaped cup, but try as he might, he could not force the spring to flow.

It, too, was magic; at its base was a dial of god-metal marked with the numbers and letters of the language. Meg made an incantation over it, and when the water refused to come, Daiv, impatient, beat upon the mouth part. Rotten wood split from the wall, the entire fountain broke from its foundation and tumbled to the floor, disclosing a nest of inexplicable wires and metal fragments.

As it fell, from somewhere within it tumbled many circles of stained metal, large and small. Meg, seeing one of these, prayed the gods to forgive Daiv's impatience.

"The fountain would not flow," she explained, "because you did not make the fitting sacrifice. See? These are the tributes of the Ancient Ones. White pieces, carven with the faces of the gods: the Red god, the buffalo god"—her voice deepened with awe—"even great Taamuz, himself! I remember his face from the Place of the Gods.

"Aie, Daiv, but they were a humble and god-fearing race, the Ancient Ones!"

And there, in the massive pantheon of Ylvania Stat, they slept—

Meg started from slumber suddenly, some inner awareness rousing her to a sense of indefinable malease. The sun was high in the heavens, the night-damp had passed. But as she sat up, her keen ears caught again the sound that had awakened her, and fear clutched her kidneys.

Daiv, too, had been awakened by the sound. Beside her he sat upright, motioning her to silence. His lips made voiceless whisper.

"Footsteps!"

Meg answered, fearfully, "His footsteps?"

Daiv slipped to the doorway, disappeared. Minutes passed, and continued to pass until Meg, no longer able to await his return, followed him. He was crouched behind the doorway of the temple, staring down the avenue up which they had marched the preceding night. He felt her breath on his shoulder, pointed silently.

It was not Him. But it was someone almost as dangerous. A little band of His worshipers—all men. It was obvious that they were His followers, for in addition to the usual breechclout and sandals worn by all clansmen, these wore a gruesome decoration—necklaces of human bone! Each of them —and there must have been six or seven—carried as a weapon His traditional arm, a razor-edged sword, curved in the shape of a scythe!

They had halted beside the entrance to a hooded cavern, similar to dozens such which Meg and Daiv had passed the night before, but had not dared investigate. Now two of them ducked suddenly into the cavernous depths. After a brief period of time, two sounds split the air simultaneously. The triumphant cry of masculine voices, and the high, shrill scream of a woman!

And from the cave mouth, their lips drawn back from their teeth in evil happy looks, emerged the raiders. Behind them they dragged the fighting, clawing figure of a woman.

Meg gasped, her thoughts churned into confusion by a dozen conflicting emotions. Amazement that in this City of Death should be found living humans. The ghouls, His followers, she could understand. But not the fact that this woman seemed as normal as her own Jinnians.

Second, a frightful anger that anyone, *anything*, should thus dare lay forceful hands upon a woman. Meg was of the emancipated younger generation; she had accepted the new principle that men were women's equals. But, still—

Her desire to do something labored with her fright. But before either could gain control of her muscles, action quickened the tableau. There came loud cries from below the ground, the sound of clanking harness, the surge of racing feet. And from the cavern's gorge charged the warriors of this stranger clan, full-panoplied, enraged, to the rescue of their comrade.

The invaders were ready for them. One had taken a position at each side of the entrance, another had leaped to its metallic roof. As the first warrior burst from the cave mouth, three scythe swords swung as one. Blood spurted. A headless torso lurched forward a shambling pace, pitched to earth, lay still. Again the scythes lifted.

Daiv could stand no more. A rage-choked roar broke from his lips, his swift motion upset Meg. And on feet that flew, sword drawn, clenched in his right fist, bellowing his wrath, he charged forward into the unequal fray!

CHAPTER FOUR

NOR WAS MEG far behind him. She was a Priestess and a Mother, but in her veins, as in the veins of all Jinnians, flowed ever the quicksilver battle lust. Her cry was as loud as his, her charge as swift. Like twin lances of vengeance they bore down upon the invaders from the rear.

The minions of Death spun, startled. For an instant stark incredulity stunned them to quiescence; that immobility cost their leader his life. For even as his scattered wits reassembled, his lips framed commands to his followers, Daiv was upon him.

It was no hooked and awkward scythe Daiv wielded; it was a long sword, keen and true. Its gleaming blade flashed in the sunlight, struck at the leader's breast like the fang of a water viper—and when it met sunlight again, its gleam was crimson.

Now Daiv's sword parried an enemy hook; his foeman, weaponless and mad with fright, screamed aloud and tried to stave off the dripping edge of doom. His bare hands gripped Daiv's blade in blind, inchoate defense. The edge bit deep, grotesque-angled fingers fell to the ground like bloodworms crawling, bright ribbons of blood spurted from severed palms.

All this in the single beat of a pulse. Then Meg, too, was upon the invaders; her sword thirsted and drank beside that of her mate. And the battle was over almost before it began. Even as the vanguard of clanswomen, taking heart at this unexpected relief, came surging from the cave mouth, a half dozen bodies lay motionless on the creet, their blood enscarleting its drab. But one remained, and he, eyes wide, mouth slack in awestruck fear, turned and fled down the long avenue on feet lent wings by terror.

Then rose the woman whom the invaders had attempted to linber; in her eyes was a vast respect. She stared first at Daiv, uncertain, unbelieving. Then she turned to Meg and made low obeisance.

"Greetings and thanks, O Woman from Nowhere! Emma, Gard of the Be-Empty, pledges now her life and hand, which are truly yours."

She knelt to kiss Meg's hand. Then deepened her surprise, for she gasped: "But . . . but you are a Mother! You wear the Mother's ring!"

Meg said quietly, "Yes, my daughter. I am Meg, the Mother of the Jinnia Clan, newly come to the City of Death."

"Jinnia Clan!" It was the foremost of the rescuers who spoke now; by her trappings Meg knew her to be a lootent of her tribe. "What is this Jinnia Clan, O Mother? Whence come you, and how—"

Meg said, "Peace, woman! It is not fitting that a clanswoman should make queries of a Mother. But lead me to your Mother. With her I would speak."

The lootent flushed. Apologetically, "Forgive me, Mother. Swiftly shall I lead you to our Mother, Alis. But what—" She glanced curiously at Daiv who, the battle over, was now methodically wiping his stained blade on the hem of his clout. "But what shall I do with this man-thing? It is surely not a breeding-male; it fights and acts like a Wild One."

Meg smiled.

"He is not a man-thing, my child. He is a man—a true man. Take me to your Mother, and to her I will explain this mystery."

Thus it was that, shortly after, Meg and Daiv spoke with Alis in her private chamber deep in the bowels of the earth beneath the City of Death. There was great wonder in the Mother's eyes and voice, but there was respect, too, and understanding in the ear she lent Meg's words.

Meg told her the tale of the Revelation. Of how she, when yet Meg the Priestess, had made pilgrimage, as was the custom of her clan, to the far-off Place of the Gods.

"Through blue-swarded Tucky and Zurrie I traveled, O Alis; many days

I walked through the flat fields of Braska territory. In this journey was I accompanied by Daiv, then a stranger, now my mate, who had rescued me from a Wild One. And at last I reached the desolate grottoes of distant 'Kota, and there, with my own eyes, looked upon the carven stone faces of the gods of the Ancient Ones. Grim Jarg, the sad-eyed Ibrim, ringleted Taamuz, and far-seeing Tedhi, He who laughs—"

Alis made a holy sign.

"You speak a mighty wonder, O Meg. These are gods of our clan, too, though none made your pilgrimage. But we worship still another god, whose temple lies not far away. The mighty god, Granstoom. But—this secret you learned?"

"Hearken well, Alis, and believe," said Meg, "for I tell you truth. The gods of the Ancient Ones—were *men!*"

"Men!" Alis half rose from her seat. Her hands trembled. "But surely, Meg, you are mistaken—"

"No. The mistake occurred centuries ago, Mother of another clan. Daiv, who comes from the sacred Land of the Escape, has taught me the story.

"Long, long ago, all Tizathy was ruled by the great Ancient Ones. Mighty were they, and skilled in forgotten magics. They could run on the ground with the speed of the woodland doe; great, wheeled horses they built for this purpose. They could fly in the air on birds made of god-metal. Their hoams probed the clouds, they never labored except on the play-field; their life was one of gay amusement, spent in chanting into boxes that carried their voices everywhere and looking at pictures-that-ran.

"But in another world across the salt water from Tizathy were still other men and women. Amongst them were evil ones, restless, impatient, fretful, greedy. These, in an attempt to rule the world, created a great war. We cannot conceive the war of the Ancient Ones. They brought all their magics into play.

"The men met on gigantic battlefields, killed each other with smoke and flame and acid and smell-winds. And at hoam, the women—in secret magic-chambers called labteries—made for them sticks-that-spit-fire and great eggs that hatched death."

"It is hard to believe, O Meg," breathed Alis, "but I do believe. I have read certain cryptic records of the Ancient Ones—but go on."

"Came at last the day," continued Meg, "when Tizathy itself entered this war. But when their mates and children had gone to Him by the scores of scores of scores, the women rebelled. They banded together, exiled all men forevermore, set up the matriarchal form of government, keeping only a few weak and infant males as breeders.

"When they could no longer get the fire-eggs or the spit-sticks, the men came back to Tizathy. Then ensued years of another great war between the sexes—but in the end, the women were triumphant.

"The rest you know. The men, disorganized, became Wild Ones, roving the jungles in search of food, managing to recreate themselves with what few clanswomen they linberred from time to time. Our civilization persisted, but many of the old legends and most of the old learning was gone. We finally came to believe that *never* had the men ruled; that it was right and proper for women to rule; that the very gods were women.

"But this," said Meg stanchly, "is not so. For I have brought back from the Place of the Gods the Revelation. Now I spread the word. It is the duty of all clans to bring the Wild Ones out of the forests, make them their mates, so our people may one day reclaim our deserved heritage."

There was a long silence.

Then asked Alis, "I must think deeply on this, O Meg. But you spoke of the Land of the Escape. What is that?"

"It is the hot lands to the south. Daiv comes from there. It is a sacred place, for from there—from the heart of Zoni—long ago a Wise One named Renn foresaw the end of the civilization of the Ancient Ones.

"In the bowels of a monstrous bird, he and a chosen few escaped Earth itself, flying to the evening star. They have never been heard of since. But some day they will come back. We must prepare for their coming; such is the law."

Alis nodded somberly.

"I hear and understand, O Mother to whom the truth has been revealed. But . . . but I fear that never can we make peace with the Wild Ones of Loalnyawk. You have seen them, fought them. You know they are vicious and untamed."

Meg had been so engrossed in spreading the news of the Revelation, she had almost forgotten her true mission. Now it flooded back upon her like an ominous pall. And she nodded.

"Loalnyawk? Is that what you call the City of Him? Perhaps you are right, Mother Alis. It would be impossible to mate with the children who worship Death as a master."

"Death?" Alis' head lifted sharply. "Death, Meg? I do not understand. They do not worship Death, but Death's mistress. They worship the grim and savage warrior goddess, the fearful goddess, Salibbidy."

"Her," said Meg dubiously, "I never heard of. But you speak words unhappy to my ear, O Alis. A long way have Daiv and I come to do battle with Him who nips the fairest buds of our clan. Now you tell me this is not His city—

"Aie, but you must be mistaken! Of a certainty it is His city. His tumbled desolation reigns everywhere."

Alis made a thought-mouth.

"You force me to wonder, Meg. Perhaps He is here. Of a truth, He takes many of us to whom He has no right. A moon ago He claimed the Priestess Kait who was young, happy, in wondrous good health.

"A sweet and holy girl, inspired by the gods. Only the day before had she been in commune with them; her tender young body atremble with ecstasy, her eyes rapt, her lips wet with the froth of their knowledge. Oft did she experience these sacred spells, and I had planned a great future for her. But—" Alis sighed and shook her head. "He came and took her even as she communed with the gods. It was a foul deed and brutal."

Daiv said grimly, "And by that we know that this *is* His city, indeed. For where else would He be so powerful and so daring?"

"Yes," said Alis, "the more I think on it, the more I believe you are right. Above ground must be His domains. We have not guessed the truth, because for countless ages we have dwelt in the tiled corridors of Be-Empty."

"Tell us more," demanded Daiv, He-who-would-learn, "about the halls of Be-Empty. Why are they called that?"

"I know not, Daiv. It is the ancient name, yet the corridors are *not* empty. They are a vast network of underground passages, built by the Ancient Ones for mystic rites we no longer know. Great wonders are here, as I will later show you.

"These corridors are tiled with shining creet, and upon their roadbeds lie parallels of god-metal, red and worn. Aie, and there is a greater wonder still! From place to place I can show you ancient hoams, with doors and many windows and seats. These hoams were tied together with rods of god-metal, and whensoever the Ancient Ones would move, they had but to push their hoams along the parallels to a new location!

"Once we were not all one clan, but many. There were the Women of the In-Deeps, and there were the Aiyartees. But we were the strongest, and we welded all the livers-underground into one strong clan.

"We have many villages, wide creet plateaus built on the sunken roadways of the Ancient Ones. Each village has its entrance to the city above, forbidden Loalnyawk, but we use these only when urgency presses. For there are openings aplenty to the sun, there are streams of fresh water. Safe from the Wild Ones above, we raise our vegetables and a few meat-animals.

"Yet," continued Alis proudly, "there is no spot in all Loalnyawk to which we have not ready access should it be necessary to get there. Above ground there are many shrines like that of great Granstoom and the fallen tower of Arciay. There is also the Citadel of Clumby to the north, and not far from where we now sit could I show you the Temple of Shoobut, where each year the Ancient Ones sacrificed a thousand virgins to their gods. There is the forbidden altar of Slukes—"

The Mother's mouth stayed in midsentence. Her eyes widened.

"Slukes!" she repeated awfully.

"Well?" Meg and Daiv leaned forward, intent.

"That must be it! In the ancient legends it tells that there was where He visited most often. That must be His present lair and hiding place!"

"Then there," proclaimed Daiv, "we must go!"

CHAPTER FIVE

MEG STUMBLED on a sharp stone, lurched against Daiv and steadied herself on his reassuring presence. Her eyes had become somewhat accustomed to the endless gloom, now, though they ached and burned with the concentration of peering into murky blackness, then having the blackness lighted from time to time, unexpectedly, by a shaft of golden sunlight flooding into the corridors of Be-Empty from the city above.

Her feet, though, thought Meg disconsolately, would never accustom themselves to this jagged, uneven roadbed. She had been told to walk between the parallels of god-metal, for that was the best, driest, safest walking. Maybe it was. But it was treacherous. For there were creet crossties on which her doeskin-clad feet bruised themselves, and ever and again there were rocks and boulders lying unsuspectedly in the road.

How far they had come, Meg had no way of guessing. It must have been many miles. They had passed, easily, twoscore tiny, raised villages of the Be-Empty Clan. At each of these they had tarried a moment while the warrior lootent, under whose guidance Alis had dispatched a small foray party at Meg's disposal, made known herself and her mission.

Meg panted, hating the heavy, stuffy air her lungs labored to suck in, fuming at the slowness of their march, eager only to reach their destination. It did not improve her temper to slip on a round rock, submerge one foot to the ankle in a stream of sluggish water. Of the lootent she demanded, "How much farther, my daughter?"

"We are nearly there, O Mother."

Daiv grunted. It was a think-grunt. Meg tried to see him, but in the darkness his face was a white blur.

"Yes, Daiv?"

"There's more to this than meets the eye, Golden One. These passageways are not the purposeless corridors Alis thought. I was wondering—"

"Yes?"

"Well—it sounds ridiculous. But do you remember those hoams on wheels? The ones with the windows? Suppose the Ancient Ones had the magic power to make them run like horses along these parallels?"

Meg shrugged.

"But why should they, Daiv? When it would have been so much simpler to make them run on top of the earth? These grottoes were built for some sacred purpose, my mate."

"I suppose you're right," acknowledged Daiv. But he didn't sound convinced. Sometimes Meg grew a little impatient with Daiv. He was, like all men, such a hard creature to convince. He couldn't reason things out in the cold, clear logical fashion of a woman; he kept insisting that his "masculine intuition" told him otherwise.

Much time had passed. They had broken fast at the hoam of the Mother, and had eaten a midday meal here in the depths of Be-Empty. The last opening under which they had passed revealed that the sun was being swallowed by the westward clouds; for twelve hours it would pass through the belly of the sky, then miraculously, tomorrow, a new sun would be reborn in the east.

So it was almost night when the lootent halted at a tiny, deserted creet platform, turned and touched her forehead to Meg.

"This is it, O Mother."

"This?" Meg glanced about. There was nothing unusual about this location.

"Above this spot lies the forbidden altar of Slukes. I . . . I fear—" The lootent's eyes were troubled. "I fear I dare take you no farther, O Mother. You and your man are inviolate; I and my warriors are but humble women. That which lies above would be destruction for us to gaze upon."

Meg nodded complacently.

"So be it, my daughter. We shall leave you now, go to dare Him in His den."

The lootent said, "We shall wait, Mother—"

"Wait not, my child. Return to your village."

"Very well, Mother. Your blessing ere we leave?"

Meg gave it, touching her fingers to the lips and the forehead of the kneeling lootent, chanting the hallowed phrases of the Ancient Ones' blessing. " 'My country, Tizathy; sweet land of liberty—' " Then there were stifled footsteps in the gloom and Meg and Daiv were alone.

Only briefly did Meg consider the possibility of entering His temple at this time—and then she abandoned the project. It would be suicidal. Everyone knew He was strongest at night. His powers waned with the waxing sun. So she and Daiv built a tiny fire in the quarters of a long-vanished warrior named Private Keepout, and there huddled together through the long, dank, fearsome night.

They awakened with the sun, broke their fast with unleavened biscuit given them by Alis. Daiv, who was expert at such matters, then examined with painstaking care their swords and hurling-leathers. He approved these. And as if feeling within his own breast an echo of the dread that fluttered in Meg's, he pressed his lips hard against hers in a touching-of-mouths. Then, hand in hand, they climbed a long flight of steps, into the sunlight, forward to the threshold of His stronghold.

It was a majestic building.

How many footsteps long and wide it was, Meg could not even conceive. It reached half as far as the eye would reach in one direction; in the other, it branched into many smaller buildings. And it was pine-high. An awe-inspiring sight.

Daiv, standing beside her, stared dubiously at the main portal. He said, "This may not be the place, Meg. Alis said the name of the temple was Slukes, didn't she? This is called—" He glanced again at the weather-worn carving atop the doorway. "This is called Stlukes."

Again, as oft before, Meg felt swift pride at her mate's intelligence. Daiv was a living proof that men were the equals—or almost, anyway—of women. It had taken her many, many summers to learn the art of reading the speech-without-words; he had assimilated the knowledge from her in a tenth the time.

"It is the right place, Daiv," she whispered. "The Ancient Ones were often careless in putting down the language. But can you not *feel* that this is His abode?"

For she could. Those grim, gray walls breathed an atmosphere of death and decay. The bleached walls were like the picked bones of a skeleton lying in some forgotten field. And the great, gaping vents of windows, the sagging lintels, the way one portion of roof had fallen in—there were marks of His dominance. Meg did not even need the omen of the red-throated carrion buzzard wheeling lazily ever and ever about the horrid altar of Slukes.

"Come," she said, "let us enter."

Daiv held back. There were anxious lines about his eyes. "He does not speak, Meg?"

"No one has ever heard His voice, Daiv. Why?"

"I thought I heard voices. But I must have made a mistake. Well"—he shrugged—"it does not matter."

Thus they entered the secret hiding place of Death.

All the great courts lay silent.

What Meg had expected to see, she did not rightly know. Perhaps a charnel house of human bodies, dismembered and gory, raw with frightful cicatrices, oozing filth from sick and rotting sores. Or perhaps that even more dreadful thing, chambers in which were imprisoned the mournful souls of the dead. Against flesh and blood, no matter how frightful, Meg knew her courage would hold. But she did not know whether her nerves would stand before the dim restlessness of the gray unalive.

She found neither of these in the temple of Slukes. She found only floors and walls and ceilings which had once been shining white, but were now gray with ages of floating dust. She found her footsteps muffled beneath her upon a mat of substance, now crumbling, but still resilient to the soles. She found silence, silence, silence that beat upon her eardrums until it was a tangible, terrifying sound.

And finding that, she took comfort in Daiv's keen, questing, ever-forward search for Him.

Down a long hallway they strode on catlike feet; a chamber they passed in which heaped dust outlined the seats and stools of Ancient Ones. Past a god-metal counter they walked, and saw within its confines not one but a half-dozen water fountains like that Daiv had wrenched from the wall of Ited-Ciga's shrine.

Above their heads, from time to time, they glimpsed strange, magic pendants of green and red god-metal; beneath one of these was a greater marvel still—a pear-shaped ball with wire seeds coiled within. Transparent was the skin of this fruit, and slippery to the touch. Daiv tried to split it, hungering for a taste of its newness, but it exploded in his hands with a fearful *pop!* —and there was nothing but its stem and seeds!

The fruit itself had vanished, but the skin, as if angered, had bit Daiv's palm until the blood flowed.

Meg blessed the wound, and begged forgiveness in a swift prayer to the gods of the harvest at having destroyed the magic pear.

And they went on.

Either side of the corridor through which they moved was lined with doorways. Into one of these they looked, believing He might have hid there, but the rooms were vacant except for strange, four-legged god-metal objects humped in the middle, on which reposed parasitic coils and twists of metal twined inextricably together. Dust lay over all, and in one room more carefully shuttered, barred and sealed than the others, they saw tatters of something like homespun covering the coils. But when Meg attempted to touch this, the wind from her motion swept the gossamer cloth into nothingness.

Aie, but it was a mighty and mysterious place, this altar of Slukes, where dwelt Him who steals away the breath! There were rooms in which reposed great urns and pans of god-metal; these rooms held, also, huge metal boxes with handles on the front, and their platters were crusted with flaked and ancient grease. Meg shuddered. "Here," she whispered to Daiv, "He burnt the flesh of them He took." In the same room was a massive white box with a door. Daiv opened this, and they saw within neat metal racks. "And here," whispered Meg, "must He have stored the dwindled souls until again He hungered. But now He does not use this closet. I wonder why?"

And they went on.

Until at last, having climbed many flights of steps, Meg and Daiv came at last to the chamber they had been seeking. It lay on the story nearest the roof. Oh, but He was a methodical destroyer. The compartments in which he imprisoned His victims were all carefully labeled in the language. Contagious Ward, Infants' Ward, Maternity Ward—all these Meg saw and read, and shuddered to recognize. And this, His holy of holies, was symbolized as His workroom by the sign, Operating Room.

Once it had been a high, lofted chamber; now it wore the roof of infinity, for some antique cataclysm had opened it to the skies. Crumbled plaster and shards of brick heaped the floor.

But in its center, beneath a gigantic weapon defying description or understanding, was His bed. It could be nothing else, for even now, upon it, lay the lately-slain body of a woman. Her face was a mask of frozen agony; His touch had drawn taut her throat muscles and arched her back in the final paroxysm. Her lifeless fingers gripped the sides of the bed in unrelaxing fervor.

And the room bore, amidst its clutter and confusion, unmistakable signs of recent habitation! The trappings of the newly slaughtered woman had been tossed carelessly into a corner, along with countless others. Feet, many feet, had beaten firm the rubble on the floor; in one corner, not too long since, had been a fire. And the blood that had gushed from the dead woman when her heart had been roughly hewn from her bosom still clotted the floor!

Meg cried, a little cry of terror and dismay.

"He is here, Daiv!"

Then all things happened at once. Her cry wakened ominous echoes in chambers adjacent to this. Daiv's arm was about her, pulling her away. There came the patter of footsteps, voices lifted, and the door at the farther end of the room jerked open.

And Daiv cried, "Not only He, but His ghouls! Behind me, Golden One!"

Then the deluge. A horde of Wild Ones of the same tribe as those whom they had fought two days before, charged into the room.

CHAPTER SIX

THERE WAS NO TAINT of cowardice in the heart of Meg the Mother. Had she any fault, it was that of excess bravery. Oft before had she proven this, to her own peril. This time, Daiv's speed left her no opportunity to become a courageous sacrifice to His minions.

His quick eye measured the number of their adversaries, his battle-trained judgment worked instinctively. For an instant he hesitated, just long enough to strike down with flailing long sword the foremost of their attackers. Then he swept Meg backward with his mighty right arm, thrust her irresistibly toward a doorway at the other end of the room.

"Flee, Golden One!"

Meg had no choice. For Daiv was on her heels; his body a bulwark of defense against hers and a battering-ram of force. They reached the door, crashed it shut in the face of the charging ghouls. Daiv braced himself against it stanchly, his eyes sweeping the small chamber in which they found themselves.

"That!" he commanded. "And that other, Golden One. And that!"

His nods designated objects of furniture within the room; heavy, solid braces of god-metal. Meg bent to the task, and before Daiv's strength could fail under the now clamorous pounding on the doorway, the portal was braced and secured with the massive frames that once had been chairs, a desk, a cabinet.

Now there was time for breathing and inspection of their refuge. And Meg's soul sickened, seeing the trap into which they had let themselves.

"But, Daiv—there is no way out! There is but one door to the room. The one through which we entered!"

Daiv said, "There is a window—" and strode to it. She saw the swift, dazed shock that creased his brows, moved to his side and peered from the window.

It was an eagle's aerie in which they stood! Down, down, down, far feet below, was the sun-lit courtyard of this building. But the wall was sheer and smooth as the jowls of lean youth; no crawling insect could have dared that descent.

Daiv looked at her somberly, and his arm crept about her.

"Since we cannot flee, we must outwait them, Golden One. If we cannot get out, they, at least, cannot get in."

He did not mention the thought uppermost in his mind and in hers.

That their food pouches lay far below them, in the murky grotto of Be-Empty; that they had no water. And that the shortest of sieges would render them impotent before their adversaries.

For he was Daiv, known as He-who-would-learn. And even in this moment when things looked darkest, he was roused to curiosity by the chamber in which they were immured.

It was a small and cluttered room. More dusty than most, and that was odd, because it was not open to the dust-laden air.

But Daiv, questing, discovered the reason for this. The floor was gray not with rock dust, but with the fragments of things which—which—

"This is a great mystery, Meg. What are, or were, these things?"

Meg, too, had been staring about her. A faint suspicion was growing in her mind. She remembered a word she had heard but once in her life, and that when she was but a young girl, neophyte priestess under the former Mother.

"Shelves," she whispered. "Many long shelves, all of water-hurt god-metal. Desks. And crumbled fragments of parchment.

"Daiv, long ago the Ancient Ones had houses, rooms, in which they kept, pressed flat between cloth and boards, parchment marked with the speech-without-words. These they called—" She cudgeled her brain for the elusive word. "These they called 'lyberries.' The flat scrolls were known as 'books.' This room must have been the lyberry of Slukes."

"And in these books," said Daiv in hallowed tones, "they kept their records?"

"Aie, more than that. In them they kept all their secret knowledge. The story of their spells and magic, and of their foretelling-of-dreams."

Daiv groaned in pain as an unhappy-imp prodded his heart.

"We stand at the heart of their mysteries, but He who withers all has ripped their parchment into motes! Meg, it is a sad and bitter thing."

He saw, now, that she spoke truth. For he pawed through the piles of rotted debris; in one spot he found a frayed leather oblong from which, as he lifted it, granules of charred black sifted. Once, again, he found a single bit of parchment marked with the language, but it fell into ten million bits at the touch of his fingers.

"There have been fire and flame in this room," Meg said. "Water-hurt, and the winds of the ages. That is why no books remain. It must have happened in the wars, when the fire-eggs fell upon the building. Daiv! What are you doing?"

For Daiv, still pawing the ruins, had uncovered a large, metal cabinet deep-set in the wall. This alone seemed to have escaped, unhurt, whatever holocaust had destroyed all else. With a swift grunt of satisfaction, he was tearing at the handle of this cabinet.

"Don't open it, Daiv! It is a forbidden thing! It may be a trick of the Ancient Ones. Of Him—"

But Meg's warning was futile. For Daiv's fumbling fingers had solved the secret of the antique lock; creaking in protest, the door swung open to reveal, in an unlighted chamber from which a faint, musty breath of wind stirred—*books!*

Books! Books as Meg had described them. Books as Meg had learned of them from the lips of the elder Mother. Books, still encased in jackets of cloth and leather, unhurt through thrice five centuries of time, preserved, by a whim of the gods, in a locked and airless cabinet!

And again it became Meg's lot to save Daiv's life and soul, for he, man-like, impatient, paused not to placate the gods, but groped instantly for the nearest of the forbidden volumes.

Fervent were the prayers Meg made then, and swiftly, that the gods destroy him not for his eagerness. And she was rewarded graciously, for Daiv did not fall, mortally stricken, as he knelt there muttering over his find.

"Behold, Meg—the secrets of the Ancient Ones! Ah, Golden One, hurry—read to me! This speech-without-words is too mighty for my powers; only the knowledge of a Mother can tell its meaning. But, lo! here are drawings! Look, Golden One! Here is a man like me! But, behold, this is a mystery! The flesh has been stripped from his body, disclosing hordes of tiny red worms covering his carcass—but he still stands erect!

"And, see, Meg—here is a woman with white sheets of bandage about her head. What means this? And behold this man's head! It lays open from front to back, but Meg, there is no village of tiny pain-imps, and like-imps and hate-imps dwelling within! Only red worms and blue, and inside his nostrils a sponge—"

Meg took the book with trembling hands. It was as Daiv said. Here were drawings without number of men and women who, their bodies dismembered horribly, still smiled and stood erect. Little arrows pierced them, and at the end of the arrows were feathers of the language, saying magic words. *Serratus magnus—Poupart's ligament—transplyoric plane.*

And the name of the book was "Fundamental Anatomy."

In their moment of wild excitement, both Meg and Daiv had quite forgotten the danger of their situation. Now they were rudely reawakened to a memory of that danger. For the sounds outside the door of the lyberry, which had never quite ceased, now sharpened in tone. There came the sound of a voice raised in command, cries of labor redoubled, and with an echoing crash, something struck the door of their refuge!

The door trembled; the braces gave a fraction of an inch. And again the crash, the creak, the strain.

"A ram! Daiv, they are forcing the door!"

Daiv the dreamer became, swiftly, Daiv the man of action. With a single bound he was on his feet, his sword in hand. His brows were anxious.

"Take you the right side of the door, Golden One; I will guard the other. When these ghouls burst in upon us, we shall split them like pea pods—"

But a great idea had been born to Meg.

Her face glowing with a sudden happy look, she spun to face her mate.

"No, Daiv. Open the door!"

"What? Golden One, has fear softened your brain?"

"Not my brain nor my heart, beloved! But do as I say! Look you! I am a Mother and a Priestess, is it not so?"

"Yes, but—"

"And I have just discovered a mighty secret. The secret of the knowledge of the Ancient Ones."

"Still—" said Daiv.

"Would not even the underlings of Him," cried Meg, "pay greatly for this knowledge? Open the door for them, my mate! We will parley with them or with Death, Himself, for an exchange. Our lives in payment for the sharing of this secret!" Daiv might have withstood her logic, but he could not refuse the eager demand of her eyes. Like a man bedazed, he moved to the door, started, scraping the bulwark away even as the horde outside continued their assault.

When he had almost completed, the door shook before imminent collapse—

"Stand you out of sight, Daiv. I would meet them face to face."

And she took her post squarely before the door. In the hollow of her left arm she cradled the Book of Secrets. On her face was the smile of triumph, and a look of exalted glory. The door trembled; this time it split away from its hinges. Once more, now! Came the final crash, and—

"*Hold!*" cried Meg, the Priestess.

Through the oblong of the door, faces frightful with fury and blood lust, tumbled the ghouls of Death. Their hook-shaped scythes swung ready in their hands; a scream of triumph hovered on their lips. Hovered there—then trembled—then died!

And of a sudden, a miracle occurred. For the flame died from their eyes, their sword-arms fell, and as one man the attackers tumbled to their knees, groveling before Meg. A low muttering arose, was carried from man to man as the breath of the night wind is passed through the forest by the sad and whispering pines.

It was a murmur, then a cry, of fear and adoration.

"Mercy, O Goddess! Slay not your children, O Everlasting. O Goddess—great Goddess Salibbidy!"

CHAPTER SEVEN

Not in her most hopeful moment had Meg expected so sudden and complete a victory as this.

For her plan she had entertained great hopes, true, but she had wagered her life and Daiv's on the balance of an exchange. But here, suddenly, inexplicably, was utter capitulation. Surrender so complete that the leader of His warriors dared not even lift his eyes to meet hers as he slobbered his worship at her feet.

She glanced swiftly at Daiv, but for once Daiv had no knowledge in his eyes; they were as blank and questioning as her own.

Still, Meg was a Priestess and a Mother. She was a woman, too, and an opportunist. And instinct governed her actions.

She stepped to the leader's side, touched his brow with cool fingers.

"Rise, O Man! Your Goddess gives you grace."

The ghoul rose, shaken and fearful. His voice was the winnowed chaff of hope.

"Be merciful unto us, O Goddess. We did not know—we did not dream—we dared not hope for a Visitation."

Meg chose her words carefully, delivered them as a Mother intones a sacred chant, in a tone calculated to inspire dreadful awe in the hearts of her listeners.

"You have sinned mightily, O Man! You have laid siege to the holy refuge of the Goddess. You have linberred and slain women of the Be-Empty Clan, a grievous deed. You have forgotten the Faith, and have bowed down in worship before Him, the arch-enemy, Death—"

"No, O Goddess!" The contradiction was humble but sincere. "These other sins we confess, but not this last! Never have we worshiped Him! Never!"

"You dwell in His citadel."

"His citadel!" There was horror in the Wild One's voice. "We did not know it was His, O sweet Salibbidy! We live many places as we journey through Loalnyawk. Today we rested here because we had a sacrifice to make unto thee; a woman unfit for mating whom we linberred last night." His eyes pleaded with Meg's. "Was the sacrifice unpleasing to thee, gracious Salibbidy?"

"It was foul in my nostrils," said Meg sternly. "Her blood is a wound upon my heart. This is the law from this time henceforward! There shall be no more linberring or slaying of women. Instead, there shall be a new order. You shall go to the women and make peace. They will receive you with singing and soft hands, for unto them I have given the law.

"Together, you shall form a new city. They shall come out of the caverns of Be-Empty. You and they shall reclaim the hoams of the Ancient Ones. When again I visit the village of Loalnyawk, I shall expect to see men and women living together in peace and harmony as it was in the days of old.

"Do you understand the law?"

"Yes, mighty Goddess!" The cry rose from each man.

"You will obey it?"

"We will obey it, sweet Salibbidy."

"Then go in peace, and sin no more."

The vanquished worshipers, intoning prayers of thanksgiving, crawled backward from the chamber. When the last had disappeared, and they were again alone, Meg turned to her mate. His strong arms soothed the belated trembling of her body.

"Fear not, Golden One," he whispered. "Today have you performed a miracle. In bloodless victory you have borne the Revelation to the last outpost. To the accursed and forbidden city of the Ancient Ones. To the stronghold of Him."

"But they said they did not worship Him, Daiv! And they dared not lie, believing me their Goddess. If He does not rule them, if He reigns not here, then where is He, Daiv? And why did they accept me as their Goddess? Why?"

Daiv shook his head. This was unimportant now, he thought. It was sufficient that the enemy had been overcome. There were great things to do. He returned to his cabinet, and drew from it its precious store of books—

Afterward, in the hoam of Alis, Meg learned part of the answer to her questions. When she had told Alis what had happened, and received the Mother's pledge to accept the Wild Ones' envoys in peace and good will, she told again of their sudden surrender.

"I sought but to parley with them, Mother Alis. At the door I stood, and thus I stood, waiting calmly—"

She struck the pose. Book cradled in her arm, the other arm lifted high above her head, chin lifted proudly.

And then Alis nodded. But in her eyes, too, came unexpectedly a worship-look, and she whispered brokenly, "Now I understand, O Goddess who chooses to call herself Meg, the Mother. From the beginning I felt your sanctity. I should have known then—"

She rose, led Meg to the surface above Be-Empty, now no longer forbidden territory to the women. Once there had been many and great buildings here, but ancient strife had stricken them as the whirlwind hews a path through solid woodland.

Far to the southward, where the green ocean waters met the creet shores of Loalnyawk there was a figure, dimly visible. But not so dimly visible that Meg and Daiv could not recognize it.

"There is thy image, sweet Salibbidy," whispered the Mother, Alis. "Still it stands, as it did in the days of the Ancient Ones. Forever will it stand, and you remain the Goddess of broad Tizathy."

Meg cried petulantly, "Alis, do not call me by this name, Salibbidy! I am Meg, Mother of the Jinnia Clan. Like yourself, a woman—"

A smile of mysterious understanding touched Alis' lips.

"As you will—Mother Meg," she said.

But it was strange that her head should still be bowed—

Thus it was, that with the breaking of the new dawn over the creet walls of Loalnyawk, Meg and Daiv said farewell to these friends and converts, and turned their faces south and west to the remembered green hills of Jinnia.

Nor was this a sad parting. An envoy of the men had come this morning; long had he and the Mother parleyed, and an understanding had been reached. As ever, there were women who demurred, and women who disapproved—but Meg had seen a young maiden looking with gentle, speculative eyes upon the envoy. And a grim warrior had spoken with unusually gentle warmth to one of the envoy's guards—a bristle-jowled man of fighting mold.

These things would take care of themselves, thought Meg. The new order would come about, inevitably, because the men and women, both, would wish it so—

Then the last farewell had been spoken, the final blessing given. And once more Meg and Daiv were striding the long highway to Jinnia.

Daiv was strangely silent. And strangely inattentive, too, for he was attempting a difficult task. Trying to march without watching the road before him. His eyes were in one of the many books he had brought with him; the others he wore like a huge hump on his back. He stumbled for the hundredth time, and while Meg helped him reset the pack on his shoulders she said, ruefully:

"There is but one thing I regret, Daiv! Much we accomplished, but not that one thing we came to do. We found not Him, nor destroyed Him, as we willed. And our problem is still great, for ever and again will He pluck the ripest from our harvest of living."

But Daiv shook his head.

"Not so, Golden One."

"No?"

"No, my Priestess. It has come to me that we have more than fulfilled our mission. For you see—"

Daiv looked at the sky and the trees and the clouds that floated above. He took a deep breath, and the air was sweet. Life flowed strongly and true in his veins, and the knowledge he was eking, laboriously, from the magical books was potent liquid in his brain.

"You see, Golden One, we were wrong. He does not, nor ever did, live in Loalnyawk. He has no hoam, for He is everywhere, waiting to claim those who violate His barriers."

Meg cried bitterly, "Then, Daiv, we are forever at His mercy! If He cannot be found and destroyed—"

"He cannot be slain, Meg—and that is well. Else the crippled, the sick, the mad, would live forever, in endless torment. But He can be fought—and in these books it tells the ways in which to do battle with Him.

"They are not the ways of magic, Golden One. Or of any magic you know. These are new ways we must study. These magics are called by strange names—serum, and vaccination, and physic. But the way of each is told in these books. One day we shall understand all the mysteries, and Death's hand will be stayed.

"Boiled water He fears, and fresh air, and cleanliness. We shall not fight Him with swords and stones, but with sunshine and fresh water and the soap of boiled fats. For so it was in the old days—"

And a great vision was in Daiv's eyes; a vision Meg saw there, and, seeing, read with wonder. Of a day to come when men and women, hand in hand, should some day climb again to assail the very heights lost by the madness of the Ancient Ones.

His shoulder touched hers, and the day was warm and the road long. Meg was afire with impatience to get back to Jinnia, to bring this new knowledge to her clan. But there was other fire within her, too, and the message could wait a little while if she and Daiv tarried in the cool of a leafy tree.

Her hands met his and clung, and she turned her lips to his in the touching-of-mouths. She was Meg, and he was Daiv, and they were man and woman. And the grass was soft and cool.

So, too, it was in the old days—

THE MORNING OF THE DAY THEY DID IT

by E. B. White

MY PURPOSE is to tell how it happened and to set down a few impressions of that morning while it is fresh in memory. I was in a plane that was in radio communication with the men on the platform. To put the matter briefly, what was intended as a military expedient turned suddenly into a holocaust. The explanation was plain enough to me, for, like millions of others, I was listening to the conversation between the two men and was instantly aware of the quick shift it took. That part is clear. What is not so clear is how I myself survived, but I am beginning to understand that, too. I shall not burden the reader with an explanation, however, as the facts are tedious and implausible. I am now in good health and fair spirits, among friendly people on an inferior planet, at a very great distance from the sun. Even the move from one planet to another has not relieved me of the nagging curse that besets writing men—the feeling that they must produce some sort of record of their times.

The thing happened shortly before twelve noon. I came out of my house on East Harding Boulevard at quarter of eight that morning swinging my newspaper and feeling pretty good. The March day was mild and springlike, the warmth and the smells doubly welcome after the rotten weather we'd been having. A gentle wind met me on the Boulevard, frisked me, and went on. A man in a leather cap was loading bedsprings into a van in front of No. 220. I remember that as I walked along I worked my tongue around the roof of my mouth, trying to dislodge a prune skin. (These details have no significance; why write them down?)

A few blocks from home there was a Contakt plane station and I hurried in, caught the 8:10 plane, and was soon aloft. I always hated a jet-assist takeoff right after breakfast, but it was one of the discomforts that went with my job. At ten thousand feet our small plane made contact with the big one, we passengers were transferred, and the big ship went on up to fifty thousand, which was the height television planes flew at. I was a script writer for one of the programs. My tour of duty was supposed to be eight hours.

I should probably explain here that at the period of which I am writing, the last days of the planet earth, telecasting was done from planes circling the stratosphere.This eliminated the coaxial cable, a form of relay that had given endless trouble. Coaxials worked well enough for a while, but eventually they were abandoned, largely because of the extraordinary depredations of earwigs. These insects had developed an alarming resistance to bugspray and were out of control most of the time. Earwigs increased in size and in numbers, and the forceps at the end of their abdomen developed so that they could cut through a steel shell. They seemed to go unerringly for coaxials. Whether the signals carried by the cables had anything to do with it I don't know, but the bugs fed on these things and were enormously stimulated. Not only did they feast on the cables, causing the cables to disintegrate, but they laid eggs in them in unimaginable quantities, and as the eggs hatched the television images suffered greatly, there was more and more flickering on the screen, more and more eyestrain and nervous tension among audiences, and of course a further debasement of taste and intellectual life in general. Finally the coaxials were given up, and after much experimenting by Westinghouse and the Glenn Martin people a satisfactory substitute was found in the high-flying planes. A few of these planes, spotted around the country, handled the whole television load nicely. Known as Stratovideo planes, they were equipped with studios; many programs originated in the air and were transmitted directly, others were beamed to the aircraft from ground stations and then relayed. The planes flew continuously, twenty-four hours a day, were refuelled in air, and dropped down to ten thousand feet every eight hours to meet the Contakt planes and take on new shifts of workers.

I remember that as I walked to my desk in the Stratoship that morning, the nine-o'clock news had just ended and a program called "Author, Please!" was going on, featuring Melonie Babson, a woman who had written a best-seller on the theme of euthanasia, called "Peace of Body." The program was sponsored by a dress-shield company.

I remember, too, that a young doctor had come aboard the plane with the rest of us. He was a newcomer, a fellow named Cathcart, slated to be the physician attached to the ship. He had introduced himself to me in the Contakt plane, had asked the date of my Tri-D shot, and had noted it down in his book. (I shall explain about these shots presently.) This doctor certainly had a brief life in our midst. He had hardly been introduced around and shown his office when our control room got a radio call asking if there was a doctor in the stratosphere above Earthpoint F-plus-6, and requesting medical assistance at the scene of an accident.

F-plus-6 was almost directly below us, so Dr. Cathcart felt he ought to respond, and our control man gave the word and asked for particulars and instructions. It seems there had been a low-altitude collision above F-plus-6 involving two small planes and killing three people. One plane was a Diaheliper, belonging to an aerial diaper service that flew diapers to rural homes by helicopter. The other was one of the familiar government-owned sprayplanes that worked at low altitudes over croplands, truck gardens, and commercial orchards, delivering a heavy mist of the deadly Tri-D solution, the pesticide that had revolutionized agriculture, eliminated the bee from nature, and given us fruits and vegetables of undreamed-of perfection but very high toxicity.

The two planes had tangled and fallen onto the observation tower of a whooping-crane sanctuary, scattering diapers over an area of half a mile and releasing a stream of Tri-D. Cathcart got his medical kit, put on his parachute, and paused a moment to adjust his pressurizer, preparatory to bailing out. Knowing that he wouldn't be back for a while, he asked if anybody around the shop was due for a Tri-D shot that morning, and it turned out that Bill Foley was. So the Doctor told Foley to come along, and explained that he would give him his injection on the way down. Bill threw me a quick look of mock anguish, and started climbing into his gear. This must have been six or seven minutes past nine.

It seems strange that I should feel obliged to explain Tri-D shots. They were a commonplace at this time—as much a part of a person's life as his toothbrush. The correct name for them was Anti-Tri-D, but people soon shortened the name. They were simply injections that everyone had to receive at regular twenty-one-day intervals, to counteract the lethal effect of food, and the notable thing about them was the great importance of the twenty-one-day period. To miss one's Tri-D shot by as much as a couple of hours might mean serious consequences, even death. Almost every day there were deaths reported in the papers from failure to get the injection at the proper time. The whole business was something like insulin control in diabetes. You can easily imagine the work it entailed for doctors in the United States, keeping the entire population protected against death by poisoning.

As Dr. Cathcart and Bill eased themselves out of the plane through the chute exit, I paused briefly and listened to Miss Babson, our author of the day.

"It is a grand privilege," she was saying, "to appear before the television audience this morning and face this distinguished battery of critics, including my old sparring partner, Ralph Armstrong, of the *Herald Tribune*. I suppose after Mr. Armstrong finishes with me I will be a pretty good candidate for euthanasia myself. Ha. But seriously, ladies and gentlemen, I feel that a good book is its own defense."

The authoress had achieved a state of exaltation already. I knew that her book, which she truly believed to be great, had been suggested to her by an agent over a luncheon table and had been written largely by somebody else, whom the publisher had had to bring in to salvage the thing. The final result was a run-of-the-can piece of rubbish easily outselling its nearest competitor.

Miss Babson continued, her exaltation stained with cuteness:

"I have heard my novel criticized on the ground that the theme of euthanasia is too daring, and even that it is anti-Catholic. Well, I can remember, way back in the dark ages, when a lot of things that are accepted as commonplace today were considered daring or absurd. My own father can recall the days when dairy cows were actually bred by natural methods. The farmers of those times felt that the artificial-breeding program developed by our marvellous experiment stations was highfalutin nonsense. Well, we all know what has happened to the dairy industry, with many of our best milch cows giving milk continuously right around the clock, in a steady stream. True, the cows do have to be propped up and held in position in special stanchions and fed intravenously, but I always say it isn't the hubbub that counts, it's the butterfat. And I doubt if even Mr. Armstrong here would want to return to the days when a cow just gave a bucket of milk and then stopped to rest."

Tiring of the literary life, I walked away and looked out a window. Below, near the layer of cumulus, the two chutes were visible. With the help of binoculars I could see Bill manfully trying to slip his chute over next to the Doc, and could see Cathcart fumbling for his needle. Our telecandid man was at another window, filming the thing for the next newscast, as it was a new wrinkle in the Tri-D world to have somebody getting his shot while parachuting.

I had a few chores to do before our program came on, at eleven-five. "Town Meeting of the Upper Air" was the name of it. "Town Meeting" was an unrehearsed show, but I was supposed to brief the guests, distribute copies of whatever prepared scripts there were, explain the cuing, and make everybody happy generally. The program we were readying that morning had had heavy advance billing, and there was tremendous interest in it everywhere, not so much because of the topic ("Will the fear of retaliation stop aggression?") or even the cast of characters, which included Major General Artemus T. Recoil, but because of an incidental stunt we were planning to pull off. We had arranged a radio hookup with the space platform, a gadget the Army had succeeded in establishing six hundred miles up, in the regions of the sky beyond the pull of gravity. The Army, after many years of experimenting with rockets, had not only got the platform established but had sent two fellows there in a Spaceship, and also a liberal supply of the New Weapon.

The whole civilized world had read about this achievement, which swung the balance of power so heavily in our favor, and everyone was aware that the damned platform was wandering around in its own orbit at a dizzy distance from the earth and not subject to gravitational pull. Every kid in America had become an astrophysicist overnight and talked knowingly of exhaust velocities, synergy curves, and Keplerian ellipses. Every subway rider knew that the two men on the platform were breathing oxygen thrown off from big squash vines that they had taken along. The *Reader's Digest* had added to the fun by translating and condensing several German treatises on rockets and space travel, including the great *Wege zur Raumschiffahrt*. But to date, because of security regulations and technical difficulties, there had been no radio-television hookup. Finally we got clearance from Washington, and

General Recoil agreed to interview the officers on the platform as part of the "Town Meeting" program. This was big stuff—to hear directly from the Space Platform for Checking Aggression, known pretty generally as the SPCA.

I was keyed up about it myself, but I remember that all that morning in the plane I felt disaffected, and wished I were not a stratovideo man. There were often days like that in the air. The plane, with its queer cargo and its cheap goings on, would suddenly seem unaccountably remote from the world of things I admired. In a physical sense we were never very remote: the plane circled steadily in a fixed circle of about ten miles diameter, and I was never far from my own home on East Harding Boulevard. I could talk to Ann and the children, if I wished, by radiophone.

In many respects mine was a good job. It paid two hundred and twenty-five dollars a week, of which two hundred and ten was withheld. I should have felt well satisfied. Almost everything in the way of social benefits was provided by the government—medical care, hospitalization, education for the children, accident insurance, fire and theft, old-age retirement, Tri-D shots, vacation expense, amusement and recreation, welfare and well-being, Christmas and good will, rainy-day resource, staples and supplies, beverages and special occasions, babysitzfund—it had all been worked out. Any man who kept careful account of his pin money could get along all right, and I guess I should have been happy. Ann never complained much, except about one thing. She found that no matter how we saved and planned, we never could afford to buy flowers. One day, when she was a bit lathered up over household problems, she screamed, "God damn it, I'd rather live dangerously and have one dozen yellow freesias!" It seemed to prey on her mind.

Anyway, this was one of those oppressive days in the air for me. Something about the plane's undeviating course irritated me; the circle we flew seemed a monstrous excursion to nowhere. The engine noise (we flew at subsonic speed) was an unrelieved whine. Usually I didn't notice the engines, but today the ship sounded in my ears every minute, reminding me of a radiotherapy chamber, and there was always the palpable impact of vulgar miracles—the very nature of television—that made me itchy and fretful.

Appearing with General Recoil on "Town Meeting of the Upper Air" were to be Mrs. Florence Gill, president of the Women's Auxiliary of the Sons of Original Matrons; Amory Buxton, head of the Economics and Withholding Council of the United Nations; and a young man named Tollip, representing one of the small, ineffectual groups that advocated world federation. I rounded up this stable of intellects in the reception room, went over the procedure with them, gave the General a drink (which seemed to be what was on his mind), and then ducked out to catch the ten-o'clock news and to have a smoke.

I found Pete Everhardt in the control room. He looked bushed. "Quite a morning, Nuncle," he said. Pete not only had to keep his signal clean on the nine-o'clock show (Melonie Babson was a speaker who liked to range all over the place when she talked) but he had to keep kicking the ball around with the two Army officers on the space platform, for fear he would lose them just as they were due to go on. And on top of that he felt obliged to stay in touch with Dr. Cathcart down below, as a matter of courtesy, and also to pick up incidental stuff for subsequent newscasts.

I sat down and lit a cigarette. In a few moments the day's authoress wound up her remarks and the news started, with the big, tense face of Ed Peterson on the screen dishing it out. Ed was well equipped by nature for newscasting; he had the accents of destiny. When he spread the news, it penetrated in depth. Each event not only seemed fraught with meaning, it seemed fraught with Ed. When he said "I predict . . ." you felt the full flow of his pipeline to God.

To the best of my recollection the ten-o'clock newscast on this awful morning went as follows:

(Announcer) "Good morning. Tepky's Hormone-Enriched Dental Floss brings you Ed Peterson and the news."

(Ed) "Flash! Three persons were killed and two others seriously injured a few minutes ago at Earthpoint F-plus-6 when a government sprayplane collided with a helicopter of the Diaheliper Company. Both pilots were thrown clear. They are at this moment being treated by a doctor released by parachute from Stratovideo Ship 3, from which I am now speaking. The sprayplane crashed into the observation tower of a whooping-crane sanctuary, releasing a deadly mist of Tri-D and instantly killing three wardens who were lounging there watching the love dance of the cranes. Diapers were scattered widely over the area, and these sterile garments proved invaluable to Dr. Herbert L. Cathcart in bandaging the wounds of the injured pilots, Roy T. Bliss and Homer Schenck. [Here followed a newsreel shot showing Cathcart winding a diaper around the head of one of the victims.] You are now at the scene of the disaster," droned Ed. "This is the first time in the history of television that an infant's napkin has appeared in the role of emergency bandage. Another first for American Tel. & Vid.!

"Washington! A Senate committee, with new facts at its disposal, will reopen the investigation to establish the blame for Pearl Harbor.

"Chicago! Two members of the Department of Sanitation were removed from the payroll today for refusal to take the loyalty oath. Both are members of New Brooms, one of the four hundred thousand organizations on the Attorney General's subversive list.

"Hollywood! It's a boy at the Roscoe Pews. Stay tuned to this channel for a closeup of the Caesarean section during the eleven-o'clock roundup!

"New York! Flash! The Pulitzer Prize in editorial writing has been awarded to Frederick A. Mildly, of the New York *Times*, for his nostalgic editorial 'The Old Pumphandle.'

"Flash! Donations to the Atlantic Community Chest now stand at a little over seven hundred billion dollars. Thanks for a wonderful job of giving—I mean that from my heart.

"New York! The vexing question of whether Greek athletes will be allowed to take part in next year's Olympic Games still deadlocks the Security Council. In a stormy session yesterday the Russian delegate argued that the presence of Greek athletes at the games would be a threat to world peace. Most of the session was devoted to a discussion of whether the question was a procedural matter or a matter of substance.

"Flash! Radio contact with the two United States Army officers on the Space Platform for Checking Aggression, known to millions of listeners as the SPCA, has definitely been established, despite rumors to the contrary. The television audience will hear their voices in a little more than one hour from this very moment. You will *not* see their faces. Stay tuned! This is history, ladies and gentlemen—the first time a human voice freed from the pull of gravity has been heard on earth. The spacemen will be interviewed by Major General Artemus T. Recoil on the well-loved program 'Town Meeting of the Upper Air.'

"I predict: that because of SPCA and the Army's Operation Space, the whole course of human destiny will be abruptly changed, and that the age-old vision of peace is now on the way to becoming a reality."

Ed finished and went into his commercial, which consisted of digging a piece of beef gristle out of his teeth with dental floss.

I rubbed out my cigarette and walked back toward my cell. In the studio next ours, "The Bee" was on the air, and I paused for a while to watch. "The Bee" was a program sponsored by the Larry Cross Pollination Company, aimed principally at big orchardists and growers—or rather at their wives. It was an interminable mystery-thriller sort of thing, with a character called the Bee, who always wore a green hood with two long black feelers. Standing there in the aisle of the plane, looking into the glass-enclosed studio, I could see the Bee about to strangle a red-haired girl in slinky pajamas. This was America's pollination hour, an old standby, answer to the housewife's dream. The Larry Cross outfit was immensely rich. I think they probably handled better than eighty per cent of all fertilization in the country. Bees, as I have said, had become extinct, thanks to the massive doses of chemicals, and of course this had at first posed a serious agricultural problem, as vast areas were without natural pollination. The answer came when the Larry Cross firm was organized, with the slogan "We Carry the Torch for Nature." The business mushroomed, and branch offices sprang up all over the nation. During blossom time, field crews of highly trained men fanned out and pollinized everything by hand—a huge job and an arduous one. The only honey in the United States was synthetic—a blend of mineral oil and papaya juice. Ann hated it with a morbid passion.

When I reached my studio I found everybody getting ready for the warm-up. The Town Crier, in his fusty costume, stood holding his bell by the clapper, while the makeup man touched up his face for him. Mrs. Gill, the S.O.M. representative, sat gazing contemptuously at young Tollip. I had riffled through her script earlier, curious to find out what kind of punch she was going to throw. It was about what I expected. Her last paragraph contained the suggestion that all persons who advocated a revision of the Charter of the United Nations be automatically deprived of their citizenship. "If these well-meaning but misguided persons," ran the script, "with their utopian plans for selling this nation down the river are so anxious to acquire world citizenship, I say let's make it easy for them—let's take away the citizenship they've already got and see how they like it. As a lineal descendant of one of the Sons of Original Matrons, I am sick and tired of these cuckoo notions of one world, which come dangerously close to simple treachery. We've enough to do right here at home without . . ."

And so on. In my mind's ear I could already hear the moderator's salutary and impartial voice saying, "Thank you, Mrs. Florence Gill."

At five past eleven, the Crier rang his bell. "Hear ye! See ye! Town Meetin' today! Listen to both sides and make up your own minds!" Then George Cahill, the moderator, started the ball rolling.

I glanced at Tollip. He looked as though his stomach were filling up with gas. As the program got under way, my own stomach began to inflate, too, the way it often did a few hours after breakfast. I remember very little of the early minutes of that morning's Town Meeting. I recall that the U.N. man spoke first, then Mrs. Gill, then Tollip (who looked perfectly awful). Finally the moderator introduced General Recoil, whose stomach enjoyed the steadying effects of whiskey and who spoke in a loud, slow, confident voice, turning frequently to smile down on the three other guests.

"We in the Army," began the General, "don't pretend that we know all the answers to these brave and wonderful questions. It is not the Army's business to know whether aggression is going to occur or not. Our business is to put on a good show if it *does* occur. The Army is content to leave to the United Nations and to idealists like Mr. Tollip the troublesome details of political progress. I certainly don't know, ladies and gentlemen, whether the fear of retaliation is going to prevent aggression, but I *do* know that there is no moss growing on we of Operation Space. As for myself, I guess I am what you might call a retaliatin' fool. [Laughter in the upper air.] Our enemy is well aware that we are now in a most unusual position to retaliate. That knowledge on the part of our enemy is, in my humble opinion, a deterrent to aggression. If I didn't believe that, I'd shed this uniform and get into a really well-paid line of work, like professional baseball."

Will this plane never quit circling? (*I thought*). *Will the words never quit going round and round? Is there no end to this noisy carrousel of indigestible ideas? Will no one ever catch the brass ring?*

"But essentially," continued the General, "our job is not to deal with the theoretical world of Mr. Tollip, who suggests that we merge in some vast superstate with every Tom, Dick, and Harry, no matter what their color or race or how underprivileged they are, thus pulling down our standard of living to the level of the lowest common denominator. Our job is not to deal with the diplomatic world of Mr. Buxton, who hopes to find a peaceful solution around a conference table. No, the Army must face the world as it is. We know the enemy is strong. In our dumb way, we think it is just horse sense for us to be stronger. And I'm proud, believe me, ladies and gentlemen, proud to be at one end of the interplanetary conversation that is about to take place on this very, *very* historic morning. The achievement of the United States Army in establishing the space platform—which is literally a man-made planet—is unparalleled in military history. We have led the way into space. We have given Old Lady Gravity the slip. We have got there, and we have got there fustest with the mostest. [Applause.]

"I can state without qualification that the New Weapon, in the capable hands of the men stationed on our platform, brings the *en*tire globe under our dominion. We can pinpoint any spot, anywhere, and sprinkle it with our particular brand of thunder. Mr. Moderator, I'm ready for this interview if the boys out there in space are ready."

Everyone suspected that there might be a slipup in the proceedings at this point, that the mechanical difficulties might prove insuperable. I glanced at the studio clock. The red sweep hand was within a few jumps of eleven-thirty—the General had managed his timing all right. Cahill's face was tenser than I had ever seen it before. Because of the advance buildup, a collapse at this moment would put him in a nasty hole, even for an old experienced m.c. But at exactly eleven-thirty the interview started, smooth as silk. Cahill picked it up from the General.

"And now, watchers of television everywhere, you will hear a conversation between Major General Artemus T. Recoil, who pioneered Operation Space, and two United States Army officers on the platform—Major James Obblington, formerly of Brooklyn, New York, now of Space, and Lieutenant Noble Trett, formerly of Sioux City, Iowa, now of Space. Go ahead, General Recoil!"

"Come in, Space!" said the General, his tonsils struggling in whiskey's undertow, his eyes bearing down hard on the script. "Can you hear me, Major Obblington and Lieutenant Trett?"

"I hear you," said a voice. "This is Trett." The voice, as I remember it, astonished me because of a certain laconic quality that I had not expected. I believe it astonished everyone. Trett's voice was cool, and he sounded as though he were right in the studio.

"Lieutenant Trett," continued the General, "tell the listeners here on earth, tell us, in your position far out there in free space, do you feel the pull of gravity?"

"No, sir, I don't," answered Trett. In spite of the "sir," Trett sounded curiously listless, almost insubordinate.

"Yet you are perfectly comfortable, sitting there on the platform, with the whole of earth spread out before you like a vast target?"

"Sure I'm comfortable."

The General waited a second, as though expecting amplification, but it failed to come. "Well, ah, how's the weather up there?" he asked heartily.

"There isn't any," said Trett.

"No weather? No weather in space? That's very interesting."

"The hell it is," said Trett. "It's God-damn dull. This place is a dump. Worse than some of the islands in the Pacific."

"Well, I suppose it must get on your nerves a bit. That's all part of the game. Tell us, Lieutenant, what's it like to be actually a part of the solar system, with your own private orbit?"

"It's all right, except I'd a damn sight rather get drunk," said Trett.

I looked at Cahill. He was swallowing his spit. General Recoil took a new hold on his script.

"And you say you don't feel the pull of gravity, not even a little?"

"I just told you I didn't feel any pull," said Trett. His voice now had a surly quality.

"Well, ah," continued the General, who was beginning to tremble, "can you describe, briefly, for the television audience—" But it was at this point that Trett, on the platform, seemed to lose interest in talking with General Recoil and started chinning with Major Obblington, his sidekick in space. At first the three voices clashed and blurred, but the General, on a signal from the moderator, quit talking, and the conversation that ensued between Trett and Obblington was audible and clear. Millions of listeners must have heard the dialogue.

"Hey, Obie," said Trett, "you want to know something else I don't feel the pull of, besides gravity?"

"What?" asked his companion.

"Conscience," said Trett cheerfully. "I don't feel my conscience pulling me around."

"Neither do I," said Obblington. "I ought to feel some pulls but I don't."

"I also don't feel the pull of duty."

"Check," said Obblington.

"And what is even more fantastic, I don't feel the pull of dames."

Cahill made a sign to the General. Stunned and confused by the turn things had taken, Recoil tried to pick up the interview and get it back on the track. "Lieutenant Trett," he commanded, "you will limit your remarks to the—"

Cahill waved him quiet. The next voice was the Major's.

"Jesus, now that you mention it, I don't feel the pull of dames, either! Hey, Lieutenant—you suppose gravity has anything to do with sex?"

"God damn if *I* know," replied Trett. "I know I don't *weigh* anything, and when you don't weigh anything, you don't seem to *want* anything."

The studio by this time was paralyzed with attention. The General's face was swollen, his mouth was half open, and he struggled for speech that wouldn't come.

Then Trett's cool, even voice again: "See that continent down there, Obie? That's where old Fatso Recoil lives. You feel drawn toward that continent in any special way?"

"Naa," said Obblington.

"You feel like doing a little shooting, Obie?"

"You're rootin' tootin' I feel like shootin'."

"Then what are we waiting for?"

I am, of course, reconstructing this conversation from memory. I am trying to report it faithfully. When Trett said the words "Then what are we waiting for?" I quit listening and dashed for the phones in the corridor. As I was leaving the studio, I turned for a split second and looked back. The General had partially recovered his power of speech. He was mumbling something to Cahill. I caught the words "phone" and "Defense Department."

The corridor was already jammed. I had only one idea in my head—to speak to Ann. Pete Everhardt pushed past me. He said crisply, "This is it." I nodded. Then I glanced out of a window. High in the east a crazy ribbon of light was spreading upward. Lower down, in a terrible parabola, another streak began burning through. The first blast was felt only slightly in the plane. It must have been at a great distance. It was followed immediately by two more. I saw a piece of wing break up, saw one of the starboard engines shake itself loose from its fastenings and fall. Near the phone booths, the Bee, still in costume, fumbled awkwardly for a parachute. In the crush one of his feelers brushed my face. I never managed to reach a phone. All sorts of things flashed through my mind. I saw Ann and the children, their heads in diapers. I saw again the man in the leather cap, loading bedsprings. I heard again Pete's words, "This is it," only I seemed to hear them in translation: "Until the whole wide world to nothingness do sink." (How durable the poets are!) As I say, I never managed the phone call. My last memory of the morning is of myriads of bright points of destruction where the Weapon was arriving, each pyre in the characteristic shape of an artichoke. Then a great gash, and the plane tumbling. Then I lost consciousness.

I cannot say how many minutes or hours after that the earth finally broke up. I do not know. There is, of course, a mild irony in the fact that it was the United States that was responsible. Insofar as it can be said of any country that it had human attributes, the United States was well-meaning. Of that I am convinced. Even I, at this date and at this distance, cannot forget my country's great heart and matchless ingenuity. I can't in honesty say that I believe we were wrong to send the men to the platform—it's just that in any matter involving love, or high explosives, one can never foresee all the factors. Certainly I can't say with any assurance that Tollip's theory was right; it seems hardly likely that anyone who suffered so from stomach gas could have been on the right track. I did feel sympathetic toward some of his ideas, perhaps because I suffered from flatulence myself. Anyway, it was inevitable that it should have been the United States that developed the space platform and the new weapon that made the H-bomb obsolete. It was inevitable that what happened, at last, was conceived in good will.

Those times—those last days of earth! I think about them a lot. A sort of creeping ineptitude had set in. Almost everything in life seemed wrong to me, somehow, as though we were all hustling down a blind alley. Many of my friends seemed mentally confused, emotionally unstable, and I have an idea I seemed the same to them. In the big cities, horns blew before the light changed, and it was clear that motorists no longer had the capacity to endure the restrictions they had placed on their own behavior. When the birds became extinct (all but the whooping crane), I was reasonably sure that human beings were on the way out, too. The cranes survived only because of their dance—which showmen were quick to exploit. (Every sanctuary had its television transmitter, and the love dance became a more popular spectacle then heavy weight prizefighting.) Birds had always been the symbol of freedom. As soon as I realized that they were gone, I felt that the significance had gone from my own affairs. (I was a cranky man, though—I must remember that, too—and am not trying here to suggest anything beyond a rather strong personal sadness at all this.)

Those last days! There were so many religions in conflict, each ready to save the world with its own dogma, each perfectly intolerant of the other. Every day seemed a mere skirmish in the long holy war. It was a time of debauch and conversion. Every week the national picture magazines, as though atoning for past excesses, hid their cheesecake carefully away among four-color reproductions of the saints. Television was the universal peepshow—in homes, schools, churches, bars, stores, everywhere. Children early formed the habit of gaining all their images at second hand, by looking at a screen; they grew up believing that anything perceived directly was vaguely fraudulent. Only what had been touched with electronics was valid and real. I think the decline in the importance of direct images dated from the year television managed to catch an eclipse of the moon. After that, nobody ever looked at the sky, and it was as though the moon had joined the shabby company of buskers. There was really never a moment when a child, or even a man, felt free to look away from the television screen—for fear he might miss the one clue that would explain everything.

In many respects I like the planet I'm on. The people here have no urgencies, no capacity for sustained endeavor, but merely tackle things by fits and starts, leaving undone whatever fails to hold their interest, and so, by witlessness and improvidence, escape many of the errors of accomplishment. I like the apples here better than those on earth. They are often wormy, but with a most wonderful flavor. There is a saying here: "Even a very lazy man can eat around a worm."

But I would be lying if I said I didn't miss that other life, I loved it so.

PIGGY BANK
by Henry Kuttner

BALLARD'S DIAMONDS were being stolen as fast as he could make new ones. Insurance companies had long since given him up as a bad risk. Detective agencies were glad to offer their services, at a high fee, but, since the diamonds were invariably stolen, anyhow, this was simply more money down the drain. It couldn't keep up. Ballard's fortune was founded on diamonds, and the value of gems increases in inverse proportion to their quantity and availability. In ten years or so, at the present rate of theft, unflawed blue-whites would be almost worthless.

"So what I need is a perfect safe," Ballard said, sipping a liqueur. He stared across the table at Joe Gunther, who only smiled.

"Sure," Gunther said. "Well?"

"You're a technician. Figure it out. What do I pay you for?"

"You pay me for making diamonds and not telling anybody I can make 'em."

"I hate lazy people," Ballard remarked. "You graduated top man at the Institute in 1990. What have you done since then?"

"Practiced hedonism," Gunther said. "Why should I work my head off when I can get everything I want just by making diamonds for you? What does any man want? Security, freedom, a chance to indulge his whims. I got that. Just by finding a formula for the Philosopher's Stone. Too bad Cain never guessed the potentialities of his patent. Too bad for him; lucky for me."

"Shut up," Ballard said with soft intensity.

Gunther grinned and glanced around the gigantic dining hall. "Nobody can hear us." He was a little drunk. A lock of lank dark hair fell over his forehead; his thin face looked sharp and mocking. "Besides, I like to talk. It makes me realize I'm as much of a big shot as you are. Swell stuff for my soul."

"Then talk. When you're quite finished, I'll get on with what I've got to say."

Gunther drank brandy. "I'm a hedonist, and I've got a high I.Q. When I graduated, I looked around for the best way of supporting Joe Gunther without working. Building something new from scratch wastes time. The best system is to find a structure already built, and add something more. Ergo, the Patent Office. I spent two years going through the files, looking for pay dirt. I found it in Cain's formula. He didn't know what it was. A theory about thermodynamics—*he* thought. Never realized he could make diamonds simply by developing the idea a bit. So," Gunther finished, "for twenty years that formula has been buried in the Patent Office, and I found it. And sold it to you, on condition that I keep my mouth shut and let the world believe your diamonds were real."

"Finished?" Ballard asked.

"Sure."

"Why do you recapitulate the obvious on an average of once a month?"

"To keep you reminded," Gunther said. "You'd kill me if you dared. Then your secret would be quite safe. The way I figure it, ever so often you work out a method of getting rid of me, and it biases your judgment. You're apt to go off half-cocked, get me killed, and then realize your mistake. When I'm dead, the formula will be made public, and everybody can make diamonds. Where'll you be, then?"

Ballard shifted his bulky body, half closing his eyes and clasping large, well-shaped hands behind his neck. He regarded Gunther coolly.

"Symbiosis," he said. "You'll keep your mouth shut, because diamonds are your security, too. Credits, currency, bonds—they're all apt to become worthless under current economic conditions. But diamonds are rare. I want to keep 'em that way. I've got to stop these thefts."

"If one man builds a safe, another man can crack it. You know the history of that. In the old days, somebody invented a combination lock. Right away, somebody else figured out the answer—listening to the fall of the tumblers. Tumblers were made noiseless; then a crook used a stethoscope. The answer to that was a time lock. Nitroglycerin canceled that. Stronger metals were used, and precision jointures. O.K.—thermite. One guy used to take off the dial, slip a piece of carbon paper under it, replace it—and come back a day later, after the combination had been scratched on the carbon. Today it's X rays, and so forth."

"A perfect safe can be made," Ballard said.

"How?"

"There are two methods. One, lock the diamonds in an absolutely uncrackable safe."

"No such thing."

"Two, leave the diamonds in plain sight, guarded by men who never take their eyes from them."

"You tried that, too. It didn't work. The men were gassed once. The second time, a ringer got in, disguised as one of the detectives."

Ballard ate an olive. "When I was a kid, I had a piggy bank made of glass. I could see the coins, but I couldn't get 'em out without breaking the pig. That's what I want. Only—I want a pig who can run."

Gunther looked up, his eyes suddenly sharp. "Eh?"

"A pig who's conditioned to flight—self-preservation. One who specializes in the art of running away. Animals do it—herbivores chiefly. There's an African deer that reacts to movement before it's made. Better than split-second reaction. A fox is another example. Can a man catch a fox?"

"He'd use dogs and horses."

"Uh-huh. So foxes run through herds of sheep, and cross water, to spoil the scent. My pig must do that, too."

"You're talking about a robot," Gunther said.

"The Metalman people will make us one to order, with the radioatomic type of brain. A seven-foot robot, studded with diamonds, conditioned to running away. An intelligent robot."

Gunther rubbed his jaw. "Lovely. Except for one thing. The intelligence must be limited. Metalman *have* made robots of human mind-power, but each one covers a city block. Mobility's lost as intelligence increases. They haven't yet found a substitute for the colloid brain. However—" He stared at his fingernails. "Yeah. It could be done. The robot must be conditioned in one line only, self-preservation. It must be able to build logically from that motivation, and that's all it needs."

"Would that be enough?"

"Yes, because a robot's logical. You can drive a seal or a deer into a trap. Or a tiger. The tiger hears the beaters behind him, and runs from them. To him, that's the only danger he knows, till he falls in the pit that's been dug for him. A fox might be smarter. He might think of both the menace behind him and the one in front. A robot—he wouldn't stampede blindly. If he was driven toward a cul-de-sac, he'd use logic and wonder what was up that blind alley."

"And escape?"

"He'd have split-second—in fact, instantaneous reaction. Radioatomic brains think fast. You've set me a beautiful problem, Bruce, but I think it can be done. A diamond-studded robot, parading around here—psychologically, it's right up your alley."

Ballard shrugged. "I like ostentation. As a kid I had a hell of an inferiority complex. I'm compensating for that now. Why do you suppose I built the castle? It's a showplace. I need an army of servants to keep it going. The worst thing I can imagine is being a nonentity."

"Which in your mind is synonymous with poverty," Gunther murmured. "You're essentially imitative, Bruce. You built your economic empire through imitation. I don't think you've ever had an original thought in your life."

"What about this robot?"

"Induction—simple addition. You figured out your requirements and added them up. The result is a diamond-studded robot conditioned to flight." Gunther hesitated. "Flight isn't enough. It's got to be escape—self-preservation. Sometimes offense is the best defense. The robot should run as long as that's feasible and logical—and then try escape in other ways."

"You mean giving him armament?"

"Uh-huh. If we started that, we couldn't stop. We want a mobile unit, not a tank. The robot's intelligence, based on flight logic, should enable him to make use of whatever he needs, the tools that are at hand. Squirt his brain full of the basic patterns, and he'll do the rest. I'll get at it immediately."

Ballard wiped his lips with a napkin. "Good."

Gunther got up. "I'm not really signing my death warrant, you know," he said conversationally. "If you have a theft-proof safe like the robot, you won't need me to make more diamonds. There'll be enough on the robot to satisfy all your needs till you die. If you kill me, then, your diamond monopoly's safe—nobody can make them but me. However, I wouldn't make that robot without taking precautions. The Patent Office formula isn't listed under the name of Cain, and it isn't really a thermodynamic principle."

"Naturally," Ballard said. "I checked on that, without telling my investigators exactly what I was after. The patent number is your secret."

"And I'm safe as long as it remains my secret. It will, until I die. Then it'll be broadcast, and a lot of people will have their suspicions confirmed. There's a pretty widespread rumor that your diamonds are artificial, but nobody can prove it. I know one guy who'd like to."

"Ffoulkes?"

"Barney Ffoulkes, of Mercantile Alloys. He hates your insides as much as you hate his. But you're a bigger man than he is, just now. Yeah, Ffoulkes would love to smash you, Bruce."

"Get busy on the robot," Ballard said, rising. "See if you can finish it before there's another robbery."

Gunther's grin was sardonic. Ballard didn't smile, but the skin crinkled around his eyes. The two men understood each other thoroughly—which was probably the reason they were both still alive.

"Metalman, eh?" Barney Ffoulkes said to his chief of staff, Dangerfield. "Making a diamond-studded robot for Ballard, eh? Bloody show-off!"

Dangerfield didn't say anything.

"How big?"

"Seven feet, perhaps."

"And *studded*—wonder how thickly? Ballard's going to tie up a lot of rocks in that sandwich man. Wonder if he'll have the diamonds spell out, 'Hurrah for Bruce Ballard'?" Ffoulkes got up from his desk and buzzed around the room like a mosquito, a ginger-haired, partially bald little man with a wrinkled rat-trap face, soured in brine. "Get an offensive ready. Revise it daily. Chart a complete economic front, so we can jump on Ballard from all directions when we get the tip-off."

Dangerfield still said nothing, but his eyebrows lifted inquiringly in the sallow, blank face.

Ffoulkes scuttled toward him, twitching. "Do I have to make a blueprint? Whenever we've had Ballard in a spot before, he's wriggled out—insurance companies, loan flotations, more diamonds. No insurance company will handle him now. His diamonds can't be inexhaustible, unless they're artificial. If they are, he'll find it harder and harder to float a loan. See?"

Dangerfield nodded dubiously.

"Hm-m-m. He'll have a lot of gems tied up in this robot. It'll be stolen, naturally. And that time we'll strike."

Dangerfield pursed his lips.

"O.K.," Ffoulkes said. "So it may not work. It hasn't worked before. But in this game the whole trick is to keep hammering till the wall's breached. This time may be the charm. If we can once catch Ballard insolvent, he'll go under. Anyhow, we've got to try. Prepare an offensive. Stocks, bonds, utilities, agricultures, ores—everything. What we want to do is force Ballard to buy on margin when he can't cover. Meantime, be sure our protection's paid. Hand the boys a bonus."

Dangerfield made a circle with thumb and forefinger. Ffoulkes chuckled nastily as his chief of staff went out.

It was a time of booms and panics, of unstable economics and utterly crazy variables. Man hours, as usual, remained the base. But what in theory seemed effective in practice was somewhat different. Man hours, fed into the hopper of the social culture, emerged in fantastic forms. Science had done that—science enslaved.

The strangle hold of the robber barons was still strong. Each one wanted a monopoly, but, because they were all at war, a species of toppling chaos was the result. They tried desperately to keep their own ships afloat while sinking the enemy fleet. Science and government were handicapped by the Powers, which were really industrial empires, completely self-contained if not self-supporting units. Their semanticists and propagandists worked on the people, ladling out soothing sirup. All would be well later—when Ballard, or Ffoulkes, or All-Steel, or Unlimited Power, took over. Meantime—

Meantime the technicians of the robber barons, well subsidized, kept throwing monkey wrenches into the machinery. It was the time preceding the Scientific Revolution, and akin to the Industrial Revolution in its rapid shifting of economic values. All-Steel's credit was based chiefly on the Hallwell Process. Unlimited Power's scientists discovered a better, more effective method that scrapped the Hallwell Process. Result, the bottom fell out of All-Steel, and there was a brief period of frantic readjustment, during which All-Steel yanked certain secret patents out into the open and utilized them, playing hell with Ffoulkes, whose Gatun Bond Issue was based on a law of supply and demand which was automatically revised by the new All-Steel patents. Meantime each company was trying to catch the others with their pants down. Each one wanted to be master. When that enviable day arrived, the economic mess would settle, it was hoped, under the central control, and there would be Utopia.

The structure grew like the Tower of Babel. It couldn't stop—naturally. Crime kept pace with it.

Because crime was a handy weapon. The old protection racket had been revived. All-Steel would pay the Donner gang plenty to keep their hands off All-Steel interests. If the Donner boys happened to concentrate on robberies that would weaken Ffoulkes or Ballard or Unlimited Power—fine! Enough spectacular thefts would lead to a panic during which enemy stocks would drop to the bottom, one asked, nothing bid.

And if a man went down, he was lost. His holdings would go to the wolves, and he himself would be too potentially dangerous ever to be allowed power again. *Vae victis!*

But diamonds were increasingly rare—and so, till now, Bruce Ballard's empire had been safe.

The robot was sexless, but gave the impression of masculinity. Neither Ballard nor Gunther ever used the neuter pronoun in reference to the creature. Metalman Products had done their usual satisfactory job, and Gunther improved on it.

So Argus came to the castle, for final conditioning. Rather surprisingly, the robot was not vulgarly ostentatious. He was functional, a towering, symmetrical figure of gold, studded with diamonds. He was patterned on an armored knight, seven feet tall, with a cuirass of bright gold, golden greaves, golden gauntlets that looked clumsy but which contained remarkably sensitive nerve-endings. His eyes had diamond lenses, specially chosen for their refractive powers, and, logically, Ballard called him Argus.

He was blazingly beautiful, a figure out of myth. In a bright light he resembled Apollo more than Argus. He was a god come to Earth, the shower of gold that Danae saw.

Gunther sweated over the conditioning process. He worked in a maze of psychological charts, based on the mentalities of the creatures that lived by flight. Automatic reactions had to have voluntary cut-offs, controlled by logic, when reasoning power took over—reasoning power based on the flight-instinct. Self-preservation was the prime factor. The robot had it in a sufficient amount.

"So he can't be caught," Ballard said, regarding Argus.

Gunther grunted. "How? He automatically adjusts to the most logical solution, and readjusts instantly to any variable. Logic and superswift reactions make him a perfect flight machine."

"You've implanted the routine?"

"Sure. Twice a day he makes his round of the castle. He won't leave the castle for any reason—which is a safeguard. If crooks could lure Argus outside, they *might* set an ingenious trap. But even if they captured the castle, they couldn't hold it long enough to immobilize Argus. What have you got burglar alarms for?"

"You're sure the tour's a good idea?"

"You wanted it. Once in the afternoon, once at night—so Argus could show off to the guests. If he meets danger during his round, he'll adjust to it."

Ballard fingered the diamonds on the robot's cuirass. "I'm still not sure about—sabotage."

"Diamonds are pretty tough. They'll resist a lot of heat. And under the gold plate is a casing that'll resist fire and acid—not forever, but long enough to give Argus his chance. The point is that Argus can't be immobilized long enough to let himself be destroyed. Sure, you could play a flame thrower on him—but for how long? One second, and then he'd scram."

"If he could. What about cornering him?"

"He won't go into corners if he can help it. And his radioatomic brain is *good!* He's a thinking machine devoted to one purpose: self-preservation."

"Hm-m-m."

"And he's strong," Gunther said. "Don't forget that. It's important. He can rip metal, if he can get leverage. He's not a superdooper, of course—if he were, he couldn't be mobile. He's subject to normal physical laws. But he is beautifully adaptive; he's very strong; he has super-swift reactive powers; he's not too vulnerable. And we're the only guys who can immobilize Argus."

"That helps," Ballard said.

Gunther shrugged. "Might as well start. The robot's ready." He jerked a wire free from the golden helm. "It takes a minute or so for the automatic controls to take over. Now—"

The immense figure stirred. On light, rubberoid soles, it moved away, so quickly that its legs almost blurred. Then it stood motionless once more.

"We were too close," Gunther said, licking his lips. "He reacts to the vibrations sent out by our brains. There's your piggy bank, Bruce!"

A little smile twisted Ballard's lips. "Yeah. Let's see—" He walked toward the robot. Argus slid away quietly.

"Try the combination," Gunther suggested.

Ballard said softly, almost whispering, "All is not gold that glitters." He approached the robot again, but it reacted by racing noiselessly into a distant corner. Before Ballard could say anything, Gunther murmured, "Say it louder."

"Suppose someone overhears? That's—"

"So what? You'll change the key phrase, and when you do, you can get close enough to Argus to whisper it."

"All is not gold that glitters." Ballard's voice rose. This time, when he went to the robot, the giant figure did not stir.

Ballard pressed a concealed stud in the golden helm and murmured, "These are pearls that were his eyes." He touched the button again, and the robot fled into another corner. "Uh-huh. It works, all right."

"Don't give him such obvious combinations," Gunther suggested. "Suppose one of your guests starts quoting Shakespeare? Mix up your quotations."

Ballard tried again. "What light through yonder window breaks I come here to bury Caesar now is the time for all good men."

"Nobody's going to say that by accident," Gunther remarked. "Fair enough. Now I'm going out and enjoy myself. I need relaxation. Write me a check."

"How much?"

"Couple of thousand. I'll tele-call you if I need more."

"What about testing the robot?"

"Go ahead and test him. You won't find anything wrong."

"Well, take your guards."

Gunther grinned sardonically and headed for the door.

An hour later the air taxi grounded atop a New York skyscraper. Gunther emerged, flanked by two husky protectors. Ballard was running no risks of having his colleague abducted by a rival. As Gunther paid the air cabman, the detectives glanced at their wrist spotters and punched the red button set into each case. They reported thus, every five minutes, that all was well. One of Ballard's control centers in New York received the signals and learned that all was well—that there was no need to send out a rush rescue squad. It was complicated, but effective. No one else could use the spotters, for a new code was used each day. This time the key ran: first hour, report every five minutes; second hour, every eight minutes; third hour, every six minutes. And, at the first hint of danger, the detectives could instantly send in an alarm.

But this time it didn't work out successfully. When the three men got into the elevator, Gunther said, "The Fountain Room," and licked his lips in anticipation. The door swung shut, and as the elevator started its breakneck race down, anaesthetic gas flooded the little cubicle. One of the detectives managed to press the alarm warning on his spotter, but he was unconscious before the car slowed at the basement. Gunther didn't even realize he was being gassed before he lost consciousness.

He woke up fettered securely to a metal chair. The room was windowless, and a spotlight was focused on Gunther's face. He manipulated sticky eyelids, wondering how long he had been out. Scowling, he twisted his arm so that his wrist watch was visible.

Two men loomed, shadowy beyond the lamp. One wore a physician's white garment. The other was a little man, ginger-haired, with a hard rat trap of a face.

"Hi, Ffoulkes," Gunther said. "You saved me a hangover."

The little man chuckled. "Well, we've done it at last. Lord knows I've been trying long enough to get you away from Ballard's watchdogs."

"What day is this?"

"Wednesday. You've been unconscious for about twenty hours."

Gunther frowned. "Well, start talking."

"I'll do that, first, if you like. Are Ballard's diamonds artificial?"

"Don't you wish you knew?"

"I'll offer you about anything you want if you'll cross up Ballard."

"I wouldn't dare," Gunther said candidly. "You wouldn't have to keep your word. It'd be more logical for you to kill me, after I'd talked."

"Then we'll have to use scopolamin."

"It won't work. I've been immunized."

"Try it, anyway. Lester!"

The white-gowned man came forward and put a hypodermic deftly into Gunther's arm. After a while he shrugged.

"Complete immunization. Scop is no good, Mr. Ffoulkes."

Gunther smiled. "Well?"

"Suppose I try torture?"

"I don't think you'd dare. Torture and murder are capital crimes."

The little man moved nervously around the room. "Does Ballard himself know how to make the diamonds? Or are you the only one?"

"The Blue Fairy makes 'em," Gunther said. "She's got a magic wand."

"I see. Well, I won't try torture yet. I'll use duress. You'll have plenty to eat and drink. But you'll stay here till you talk. It'll get rather dull after a month or so."

Gunther didn't answer, and the two men went out. An hour passed, and another.

The white-gowned physician brought in a tray and deftly fed the prisoner. After he had vanished, Gunther looked at his watch again. A worried frown showed on his forehead.

He grew steadily more nervous.

The watch read 9:15 when another meal was served. This time Gunther waited till the physician had left, and then recovered the fork he had managed to secrete in his sleeve. He hoped its absence wouldn't be noticed immediately. A few minutes was all he wanted, for Gunther knew the construction of these electromagnetic prison chairs. If he could short circuit the current—

It wasn't too difficult, even though Gunther's arms were prisoned by metal clamps. He knew where the wires were. After a bit, there was a crackling flash, and Gunther swore at the pain in his seared fingertips. But the clamps slid free from his arms and legs.

He stood up, looking again at his wrist watch. Scowling, he prowled around the room till he found what he wanted—the window buttons. As he pressed these, panels in the blank walls slid aside, revealing the lighted towers of New York.

Gunther glanced at the door warily. He opened a window and peered down. The height was dizzying, but a ledge provided easy egress. Gunther eased himself over the sill and slid along to his right till he reached another window.

It was locked. He looked down, hesitating. There was another ledge below, but he wasn't sure he could make it. Instead, he went on to the next window.

Locked.

But the one after that was open. Gunther peered into the dimness. He could make out a bulky desk, and the glimmer of a telepanel. Sighing with relief, he crawled into the office, with another glance at his watch.

He went directly to the televisor and fingered a number. When a man's face appeared on the panel, Gunther merely said, "Reporting. O.K.," and broke the connection. His consciousness recorded a tiny click.

He called Ballard then, but the castle's secretary answered.

"Where's Ballard?"

"Not here, sir. Can I—"

Gunther went white, remembering the click he had heard. He broke the connection experimentally, and heard it again. Ballard—

"Hell!" Gunther said under his breath. He returned to the window, crawled out, hung by his hands, and let himself drop. He almost missed the ledge one story below. Skin ripped from his fingertips as he fought for a grip.

But he got it at last. He kicked his way through the window before him and dived in, glass showering. No televisor here. But there was a door dimly defined in the wall.

Gunther opened it, finding what he wanted on the other side. He switched on a lamp, riffling through the drawers till he was certain that this office wasn't another plant. After that, he used the televisor, fingering the same number he had called before.

There was no answer.

"Uh-huh," Gunther said, and made another call.

He had just broken the connection when a man in a surgeon's gown came in and shot him through the head.

The man who looked like Ffoulkes scrubbed make-up from his face. He glanced up when the physician entered.

"O.K.?"

"Yeah. Let's go."

"Did they trace Gunther's call?"

"That's not our pie. Come on."

A gray-haired man, tied securely in his chair, swore as the hypodermic pierced his skin. Ballard waited a minute and then jerked his head at the two guards behind him.

"Get out."

They obeyed. Ballard turned to the prisoner.

"Gunther was supposed to report to you every day. If he failed, you were told to release a certain message he gave you. Where's the message?"

"Where's Gunther?" the gray-haired man said. His voice was thick, the words slurring as the scopolamin began its work.

"Gunther's dead. I arranged matters so that he'd telecall you on a tapped beam. I traced the call. Now where's the message?"

It took a little while, but at last Ballard unscrewed a hollow table leg and took out a thin roll of recording wire tape, carefully sealed.

"Know what's in this?"

"No. No. No—"

Ballard went to the door. "Kill him," he said to the guards, and waited till he heard the muffled shot. Then he sighed with heartfelt relief.

He was, at last, impregnable.

Barney Ffoulkes called his chief of staff. "I hear Ballard's robot is finished. Clamp down. Put the squeeze on him. Force him to liquidate. Tell the Donner boys about the robot."

Dangerfield's face showed no expression as he made thumb and forefinger into a circle.

What Gunther had called Cain's thermodynamic patent was in reality something different, as the wire tape showed. Actually it was "McNamara, Torsion Process, Patent No. R-735-V-22." Ballard recorded that in his capacious memory and looked up the patent himself. This time he wished to share the secret with no one. He was enough of a scientist, he thought, to be able to work out the details himself. Besides, Gunther's machines for diamond-making were already set up in the castle laboratory.

Ballard immediately ran into an annoying, though not serious, hitch. The original McNamara process was not designed to create artificial diamonds. It was a method of developing certain electronic alterations in matter, and through torsion changing the physical structure involved. Gunther had taken McNamara's system, applied it to carbon, and made diamonds.

Ballard felt certain he could do the same, but it would take time. As a matter of fact, it took exactly two weeks. Once the new application was discovered, the rest was incredibly easy. Ballard started to make diamonds.

There was one other difficulty. The annealing process took nearly a month. If the carbon was removed from the chamber before that time, it would be merely carbon. In the past, Gunther had kept a supply of diamonds on hand for emergencies; that supply was depleted now, most of the gems having gone to cover the golden robot. Ballard sat back and shrugged. In a month—

Long before that Ffoulkes struck. He clamped down with both hands. Propaganda, whispering campaigns, releasing of new patents that rendered Ballard's worthless—all the weapons of economic warfare were unleashed against the diamond king. Holdings depreciated. There were strikes in Ballard's mines and factories. An unexpected civil war knocked the bottom out of certain African stocks he held. Word began to go around that the Ballard empire was collapsing.

Margin was the answer—that, and security. Diamonds were excellent collateral. Ballard used up his small hoard lavishly, trying to plug the leaks in the dike, buying on margin, using the tactics that had always succeeded for him in the past. His obvious confidence stemmed the tide for a while. Not for long. Ffoulkes kept hitting, hard and fast.

By the end of the month, Ballard knew, he would have all the diamonds he needed, and could re-establish his credit. In the meantime—

The Donner gang tried to steal Argus. They didn't know the robot's capabilities. Argus fled from room to room, clanging an alarm, ignoring bullets, until the Donners decided to give it up as a bad job and escape. But by that time the police had arrived, and they failed.

Ballard had been too busy pulling strings to enjoy his golden plaything. The advent of the Donners gave him a new idea. It would be a shame to mar the robot, but the diamonds could be replaced later. And what good was a bank except for emergencies?

Ballard found a canvas bag and went into the robot's room, locking the doors behind him. Argus stood motionless in a corner, his diamond eyes inscrutable. Ballard took out a tiny chisel, shook his head rather sadly, and said in a firm voice, "What light through yonder window breaks—"

He finished the scrambled quotation and walked toward the robot. Argus silently went away.

Ballard moved his shoulders impatiently. He repeated the key sentence louder. How many decibels were necessary? A good many—

Argus still ran away. This time Ballard yelled the key at the top of his voice.

And the robot's flight mechanism continued to operate. The automatic alarm began to work. The siren screech hooted deafeningly through the room.

Ballard noticed that a little envelope was protruding from a slot in Argus' cuirass. Automatically he reached for it—and the robot fled.

Ballard lost his temper and began to follow Argus around the room. The robot kept at a safe distance. Eventually Argus, since he was untiring, won the race. Panting, Ballard unlocked the door and rang for help. The alarm siren died.

When servants came, Ballard ordered them to surround the robot. The circle of humanity closed in gradually, until Argus, unable to retreat within himself, chose the most logical solution and walked through the living wall, brushing the servants aside casually. He continued toward the door and through it, in a crackling of splintered mahogany panels. Ballard looked after the retreating figure without saying anything.

The envelope had been brushed free by the encounter with the door, and Ballard picked it up. The brief note inside read:

Dear Bruce:

I'm taking no chances. Unless I make a certain adjustment on Argus daily, he reverts to a different code phrase from the one you give him. Since I'm the only guy who knows that code, you'll have a sweet time catching Argus in case you cut my throat. Honesty is the best policy.

Love,

Joe Gunther.

Ballard tore the note into tiny fragments. He dismissed the servants and followed the robot, who had become immobile in the next room.

He went out, after a while, and televised his divorced wife in Chicago.

"Jessie?"

"Hello," Jessie said. "What's up?"

"You heard about my golden robot?"

"Sure. Build as many as you want, as long as you keep on paying my alimony. What's this I hear about your hitting the skids?"

"Ffoulkes is behind that," Ballard said grimly. "If you want your alimony to continue, do me a favor. I want to register my robot in your name. Sign it over to you for a dollar. That way, I won't lose the robot even if there's a foreclosure."

"Is it that bad?"

"It's plenty bad. But as long as I've got the robot, I'm safe. It's worth several fortunes. I want you to sell the robot back to me for a dollar, of course, but we'll keep that document quiet."

"You mean you don't trust me, Bruce?"

"Not with a diamond-studded robot," Ballard said.

"Then I want two dollars. I've got to make a profit on the transaction. O.K. I'll attend to it. Send me the papers and I'll sign 'em."

Ballard broke the beam. That was done, anyhow. The robot was unequivocally his, and not even Ffoulkes could take it away from him.

Even if he went broke before the month was up and the new diamonds ready, the robot would put him on his feet again in no time. However, it was first necessary to catch Argus—

There were many telecalls that day. People wanted collateral. Brokers wanted margin covered. Ballard frantically juggled his holdings, liquidating, attempting flotations, trying to get loans. He received a visit from two bulky men who made a business of supplying credit, at exorbitant rates.

They had heard of the robot. But they demanded to see it.

Ballard was gratified by their expressions. "What do you need credit for, Bruce? You've got plenty tied up in that thing."

"Sure. But I don't want to dismantle it. So you'll help me out till after the first—"

"Why the first?"

"I'm getting a new shipment of diamonds then."

"Uh-huh," said the taller of the two men. "That robot runs away, doesn't he?"

"That's why he's burglar-proof."

The two brokers exchanged glances. "Mind if we make a closer examination?" They went forward, and Argus fled.

Ballard said hastily, "Stopping him is rather a complicated process. And it takes time to start him again. Those stones are perfect."

"How do we know? Turn off the juice, or whatever makes the thing tick. You don't object to our making a closer examination, do you?"

"Of course not," Ballard said. "But it takes time—"

"I smell a rat," one of the brokers remarked. "You can have all the credit you want, but I insist on testing those diamonds. Call me when you're ready."

They both went out. Ballard cursed silently. The telescreen in the corner flickered. Ballard didn't bother to answer; he knew very well what the purport of the message would be. Collateral—

Ffoulkes was closing in for the kill.

Ballard's lips tightened. He glared at the robot, spun on his heel, and summoned his secretary. He issued swift orders.

The secretary, a dapper, youngish man with yellow hair and a perpetually worried expression, went into action. He, in turn, issued orders. People began to come to the castle—workmen and technicians.

Ballard consulted with the technicians. None of them could suggest a certain method for immobilizing the robot. Yet they were far too optimistic. It didn't seem difficult to them to catch a machine.

"Flame throwers?"

Ballard considered. "There's an alloy casing under the gold plate."

"Suppose we can corner it long enough to burn through to the brain? That should do the trick."

"Well, try it. I can afford to lose a few diamonds if I can get my hands on the rest of 'em."

Ballard watched as six men, armed with flame throwers, maneuvered Argus into a corner. He warned them finally, "You're close enough. Don't go any nearer, or he'll break through you."

"Yes, sir. Ready? One . . . two—"

The nozzles blasted fire in unison. It took an appreciable time for the flame to reach the robot's head—some fractional part of a second, perhaps. By that time, Argus had ducked, and, safely under the flames, was running out of his corner. Crouching, he burst through the line of men, his alarm siren screeching. He fled into the next room and relapsed into contented immobility.

"Try it again," Ballard said glumly, but he knew it wouldn't work. It didn't. The robot's reactions were instantaneous. The men could not correct their aim with sufficient speed to hit Argus. A good deal of valuable furniture was destroyed, however.

The secretary touched Ballard's sleeve. "It's nearly two."

"Eh? Oh—that's right. Call the men off, Johnson. Is the trapdoor ready?"

"Yes, sir."

The robot suddenly turned and headed for a door. It was time for his first tour of the castle that day. Since his route was prearranged and never swerved an iota from its course, it had been easy to set a trap. Ballard hadn't really expected the flame throwers to work, anyhow.

He followed, with Johnson, as Argus moved slowly through the ornate rooms of the castle. "His weight will spring the trapdoor, and he'll drop into the room below. Can he get out of that room?"

"No, sir. The walls are reinforced metal. He'll stay put."

"Fair enough."

"But . . . uh . . . won't he keep dodging around that room?"

"He may," Ballard said grimly, "till I pour quick-setting concrete in on him. That'll immobilize the so-and-so. It'll be easy after that to drill through the concrete and get the diamonds."

Johnson smiled weakly. He was a little afraid of the huge, glittering robot.

"How wide is the trap?" Ballard asked abruptly.

"Ten feet."

"So. Well, call the men with the flame throwers. Tell 'em to close in behind us. If Argus doesn't fall into the trap, we want to be able to drive him in."

Johnson hesitated. "Wouldn't he simply smash his way through the men?"

"We'll see. Put the men on both sides of the trap, so we'll have Argus cornered. Hop to it!"

The secretary raced away. Ballard followed the robot through room after room. Eventually Johnson and three of the flame-throwing crew appeared. The others had circled around to flank the robot.

They turned into the passage. It was narrow, but long. Halfway along it was the trapdoor, concealed by a rich Bokhara rug. In the distance Ballard could see three men waiting, flame throwers ready, watching as the robot approached them. Within minutes now the trap would be sprung.

"Turn it on, boys," Ballard said, on a sudden impulse. The crew of three walking in front of him obeyed. Fire jutted out from the nozzles they held.

The robot increased its pace. It had eyes in the back of its head, Ballard remembered. Well, eyes wouldn't help Argus now. The rug—

A golden foot came down. The robot began to shift its weight forward, and suddenly froze as instantaneous reactions warned it of the difference in pressure between the solid floor and the trap. There was no time for the door to drop down, before Argus had instantly readjusted, withdrew his foot, and stood motionless on the verge of the rug. The flame throwers gushed out toward the robot's back. Ballard yelled a command.

The three men beyond the trapdoor began to run forward, fire spouting from their hoses. The robot bent its legs, shifted balance, and jumped. It wasn't at all bad for a standing broad jump. Since Argus could control his movements with the nicest accuracy, and since his metal body had strength in excess of his weight, the golden figure sprang across the ten-foot gap with inches to spare. Flame lashed out at him.

Argus moved fast—very fast. His legs were a blinding blur of speed. Ignoring the fire that played on his body, he ran toward the three men and through them. Then he slowed down to a normal walk and continued mildly on his way. The alarm siren was screaming Ballard realized, just as it died.

For Argus, the danger was over. Here and there on his metal body the gold had melted into irregular blobs. That was all.

Johnson gulped. "He must have seen the trap."

"He felt it," Ballard said, his voice low with fury. "Hell! If we could just immobilize Argus long enough to pour concrete on him—"

That was tried an hour later. A metal-sheathed ceiling collapsed on the robot, a ceiling of mesh metal through which concrete could be poured. Ballard simply had liquid concrete run into the room above till the platform collapsed under the weight. The robot was below—

Was below. The difference in air pressure warned Argus, and he knew what to do about it. He lunged through the door and escaped, leaving a frightful mess behind him.

Ballard cursed. "We can't shoot concrete at the devil. If he's sensitized to differences in air pressure—hell! I don't know. There must be some way. Johnson! Get me Plastic Products, quick!"

A short while later Ballard was closeted with a representative of Plastic Products.

"I don't quite understand. A quick-drying cement—"

"To be squirted out of hoses, and to harden as soon as it hits the robot. That's what I said."

"If it dries that quickly, it'll dry as soon as air hits it. I think we've got almost what you want. A very strong liquid cementoid; it'll harden half a minute after being exposed to air."

"That should work. Yeah. How soon—"

"Tomorrow morning."

The next morning, Argus was herded into one of the huge halls downstairs. A ring of thirty men surrounded the robot, each armed with a tank, filled with the quick-drying cementoid. Ballard and Johnson watched from the side lines.

"The robot's pretty strong, sir," Johnson hazarded.

"So's the cementoid. Quantity will do it. The men will keep spraying the stuff on till Argus is in a cocoon. Without leverage he can't break out. Like a mammoth in a tar pit."

Johnson made a clicking noise with his lips. "That's an idea. If this shouldn't work, perhaps I—"

"Save it," Ballard said. He looked around at the doors. Before each one was stationed a group of men, also armed with cementoid tanks.

In the center of the room stood Argus, blankly impassive, waiting. Ballard said, "O.K.," and from thirty positions around the robot streams of cementoid converged on his golden body.

The warning siren screamed deafeningly. Argus began to turn around.

That was all. He kept turning around. But—fast!

He was a machine, and could develop tremendous power. He spun on his longitudinal axis, a blazing, shining, glittering blur of light, far too fast for the eye to follow. He was like a tiny world spinning through space—but a world has gravitation. Argus' gravitational pull was negligible. There was, however, centrifugal force.

It was like throwing an egg into an electric fan. The streams of cementoid hit Argus, and bounced, repelled by the centrifuge. Ballard got a gob of the stuff in his middle. It had hardened enough to be painful.

Argus kept on spinning. He didn't try to run, this time. His alarm kept screeching deafeningly. The men, plastered with cementoid, continued to squirt the stuff at Argus for a while.

But the cementoid stuck to them when it was flung back. It hardened on them. Within seconds the scene resembled a Mack Sennett pie-throwing comedy.

Ballard roared commands. His voice went unheard in the uproar. But the men did not continue their hopeless task for long. They, not Argus, were becoming immobilized.

Presently the warning siren stopped. Argus slowed down in his mad spinning. He was no longer the target of cementoid streams.

He went quietly out of the room, and nobody tried to stop him.

One man almost strangled before the hardened cementoid could be dislodged from his mouth and nostrils. Aside from that, there were no casualties, save to Ballard's temper.

It was Johnson who suggested the next experiment. Quicksand would immobilize anything. It was difficult to introduce quicksand into the castle, but a substitute was provided—a gooey, tarry mess poured into an improvised tank twenty-five feet wide. All that remained was to lure Argus into the quicksand.

"Traps won't work," Ballard said glumly. "Maybe stringing a wire to trip him—"

"I think he'd react instantly to that, too, sir," Johnson vetoed. "If I may make a suggestion, it should not be difficult to drive Argus into the pit, once he's maneuvered into a passage leading to it."

"How? Flame throwers again? He automatically reacts away from the most serious danger. When he came to the pit, he'd turn around and go the other way. Break right through the men."

"His strength is limited, isn't it?" Johnson asked. "He couldn't pass a tank."

Ballard didn't see the point immediately. "A midget tractor? Not too small, though—some of the castle's passages are plenty wide. If we got a tank just broad enough to fill the hall—a pistol that would drive Argus into the quicksand—"

Measurements were made, and a powerful tractor brought into the castle. It fitted the passage, leaving no room to spare—at least, not enough to accommodate the robot. Once Argus was driven into that particular passage, he could go only one way.

The tractor, at Johnson's suggestion, was camouflaged, so the robot's flight-conditioned brain would not recognize and consider it as a serious factor. But the machine was ready to roll into the passage instantly.

The trick would probably have succeeded, had it not been for one difficulty. The consistency of the artificial quicksand had been calculated carefully. It had to be soft enough to drag the robot down, and stiff enough so that Argus would be helpless. The robot could walk safely under water; that had been proved days ago, in an abortive early experiment.

So the mix had surface tension, though not enough to bear Argus' great weight.

The robot was maneuvered into the passage without trouble, and the tractor swung after it, blocking Argus' escape. It rumbled slowly on, driving the robot before it. Argus seemed untroubled. When he reached the edge of the artificial quicksand, he bent and tested the consistency with one golden hand.

After that, he lay flat on his face, legs bent like a frog's, feet braced against one wall of the passage, head pointed out over the quicksand. He thrust strongly.

Had Argus walked into the goo feet first, he would have sunk. But his weight was spread over a far larger surface area now. Not enough to sustain him indefinitely, but long enough for his purposes. He simply didn't have time to sink. Argus skimmed over the quicksand like a skiff or a sandboat. His powerful initial thrust gave him sufficient impetus. No human could have done it, and, while Argus weighed more than a human, he had also had more strength.

So he shot out, angling across the tank, buoyed by surface tension and carried on by his impetus. The quicksand got hold at last and bogged him down, but by that time Argus' powerful hands reached their destination, the edge of the tank. Another door was in the wall at that point, and Ballard and Johnson were standing on the threshold, watching.

They dodged before Argus trampled them in his automatic fight-reaction away from the quicksand tank.

The robot dripped goo over a dozen valuable rugs before he dried. But after that he was no longer so dazzling a spectacle. However, his abilities were unimpaired.

Ballard tried the quicksand trick again, with a larger tank and smooth walls, on which the robot could get no grip. Yet Argus seemed to learn through experience. Before entering a passage now, he would make certain that there were no tractors within reach. Ballard concealed a tractor in an adjoining room where Argus could not see it, and the robot was induced to go into the fatal passage; but he ran out again the moment the tractor clanked into movement. Argus had an excellent sense of hearing.

"Well—" Johnson said doubtfully.

Ballard moved his lips silently. "Eh? Get that stuff from the quicksand washed off Argus. He's supposed to be a showpiece!"

Johnson looked after Ballard's retreating figure. His eyebrows lifted quizzically.

Ballard had a tough session with the televisor. His enemies were closing in from all sides. If only the end of the month would come, when he could get the new diamonds! His holdings were falling in ruin around him. And that damned robot held the key to—everything!

He gave such orders as he could and wandered upstairs, to Argus' room. The robot, newly cleaned, stood by the window in a blaze of sunlight, a figure of fantastic beauty. Ballard noticed his own reflection in a nearby mirror. Instinctively he drew himself up.

It was a singularly futile gesture. The silent presence of Argus was like a rebuke. Ballard looked at the robot.

"Oh, damn you!" he said. "Damn you!"

Through the visor the impassive face of Argus ignored him. A whim had made Ballard shape the robot to resemble a knight. Somehow the idea seemed less satisfactory now.

Ballard's long-suppressed inferiority complex was suffering badly.

The golden knight stood there, towering, beautiful, mighty. There was dignity in its silence. It was a machine, Ballard told himself, merely a machine that man had made. He was certainly better than a machine.

But he wasn't.

Within its specialized limits, the robot had greater intelligence than his own. It had security, for it was invulnerable. It had wealth—it *was* wealth, a Midas without the Midas curse. And it had beauty. Calm, huge, utterly self-confident, Argus stood ignoring Ballard.

If Ballard could have destroyed the robot then, he might have done so. If only the damned thing wouldn't *ignore* him! It was wrecking his life, his power, his empire—and doing so unconsciously. Malice and hatred Ballard could have faced; as long as a man is important enough to be hated, he is not a cipher. But, to Argus, Ballard simply did not exist.

The sunlight blazed yellow from the golden cuirass. The diamonds sent out rainbow rays into the still air of the room. Ballard did not realize that his lips had drawn back into a snarling rictus—

After that events moved swiftly. The most notable was the impounding of the castle, a result of Ballard's avalanching economic collapse. He had to move out. Before he did so, he risked opening the annealing chamber on the new diamonds, a week before the process was finished. The result was worthless carbon. But Ballard could not have waited a week, for by that time the castle and all it contained would have been out of his possession.

Except the robot. That was still his own—or, rather, it belonged technically to his divorced wife. The documents he and Jessica had signed were thoroughly waterproof and legal. Ballard secured a court judgment; he was permitted to enter the castle and take away the robot at any convenient time. If he could find a way of immobilizing Argus long enough to dismantle the creature.

In time he might hit on a way. Maybe. Maybe—

Ffoulkes summoned Ballard to a conference, superficially a luncheon engagement. For a time Ffoulkes talked of casual matters, but there was a sardonic gleam in his eyes.

At last he said, "How are you getting on with that robot of yours, Bruce?"

"All right." Ballard was wary. "Why?"

"The castle's impounded, isn't it?"

"That's right. But I can get the robot whenever I like. The court ruled in my favor—special circumstances."

"Think you can catch the thing. *I* don't. Gunther was a smart man. If he made that robot invulnerable. I'll bet you won't be able to get your hands on it. Unless you know the key phrase, of course."

"I—" Ballard stopped. His eyes changed. "How'd you know—"

"That there was a code? Gunther phoned me just before he . . . ah . . . met his unfortunate accident. He suspected you were going to kill him.

I do not know the ins and outs of the thing, but I got a telecall from him that night. All he said was to tell you what the key code was—but not to tell you till the right time. Gunther was pretty farsighted."

"You know the code?" Ballard said, his voice expressionless.

Ffoulkes shook his head. "No."

"Just what do you mean?"

"Gunther said this: 'Tell Ballard that the key code is what he finds on the wire tape—the name and number of the patent for making artificial diamonds.' "

Ballard looked at his fingernails. The wire tape. The secret he had found only by tricking and killing Gunther. Only in his mind now did that information exist—"McNamara, Torsion Process, Patent No. R-735-V-22."

And Gunther must have keyed the robot to that chain of phrases before he died.

"Finished?" Ffoulkes asked.

"Yeah." Ballard got up, crumpling his napkin.

"This is on me. . . . One more point, Bruce. It would be distinctly to my advantage if diamonds became valueless. I've sold out all my diamond holdings, but plenty of my competitors have interests in the African mines. If the bottom falls out of the market, I can do some good for myself."

"Well?"

"Would you tell me that patent number?"

"No."

"I thought not," Ffoulkes said, sighing. "Well, good-by."

Ballard commandeered a truck, well armored, and hired a dozen guards. He drove out to the castle. The officer at the gate nodded agreeably.

"Want to go in, sir?"

"Yes. I have permission—"

"I know that, sir. Go right ahead. You're after your robot?"

Ballard didn't answer. The castle, after he had entered, seemed strange to him. Already there had been alterations, rugs removed, pictures stored, furniture carried away. It was no longer his.

He glanced at his watch. Five after two. Argus would be making his rounds. The great hall—

Ballard headed for it. He caught sight of the golden robot emerging into the hall and beginning its slow circuit. Two men followed it, just beyond the circle of reaction. They were police guards.

Ballard walked toward them. "I'm Bruce Ballard."

"Yes, sir."

"What . . . what the devil! Aren't you Dangerfield? Ffoulkes' chief of staff? Wh—"

Dangerfield's blank face didn't change expression. "I've been sworn in as special deputy. The authorities consider your robot too valuable to be left unguarded. We're detailed to keep an eye on it."

Ballard didn't move for a moment. Then he said, "Well, your job's finished. I'm taking the robot away."

"Very well, sir."

"You can leave."

"Sorry, sir. My orders were not to leave the robot unguarded for a moment."

"Ffoulkes gave you those orders," Ballard said, his voice not quite under control.

"Sir?"

Ballard looked at the other guard. "Are you Ffoulkes' man, too?"

"Sir?"

Dangerfield said, "You're quite free to remove your robot whenever you wish, but until it's out of the castle, we mustn't take our eyes off those diamonds."

They had, as they talked, been following Argus. Now the robot moved on into the next hall and commenced its slow circuit. Ballard ran around in front of the creature. Covering his lips with one hand, he whispered, "McNamara, Torsion Process, Patent No. R-735-V-22."

The robot kept on walking. Dangerfield said, "You'll have to say it louder, won't you?"

He was holding a little notebook and stylo.

Ballard stared at the other for a moment. Then he ran in toward Argus, beginning to whisper the code phrase again. But the robot instantly fled till it was beyond Ballard's triggering nearness.

He couldn't get close enough to whisper the code. And if he said it loudly enough for Argus to hear, Dangerfield was ready to carry the formula to Ffoulkes. What Ffoulkes would do was obvious—publicize the process, so that the bottom would fall out of the diamond market.

The trio moved on, leaving Ballard where he was. Could there be a way out? Was there any way of trapping the robot?

The man knew that there was none—none he could employ in a house no longer his own. With power and wealth, he might eventually figure out a way. But time was important.

Even yet, he could re-establish himself. A month from now he could not. By that time the strings of empire would have passed forever from his hands. Frantically his mind doubled back on its tracks, seeking escape.

Suppose he used the process to make more diamonds?

He might try. But he was no longer Bruce Ballard, the robber baron. He did not have the invulnerability of the very wealthy. Ffoulkes could have him shadowed, could trace his every movement. There was no possibility of secrecy. Whatever he did from now on would be an open book to Ffoulkes. So, if he made more diamonds, Ffoulkes' men would discover the method. There was no escape that way.

Escape. So easy for the robot. He had lost invulnerability, but the robot was invulnerable. He had lost wealth; Argus was Midas. His intelligence could not help him now in this greatest crisis of his life. For an insane moment he wondered what Argus would do in his place—Argus whose infallible metal brain was so far superior to the brain that had brought it into being.

But Argus would never be in this position—Argus cared for nothing on

Earth but Argus' own magnificent golden hide, studded with flashing glory. Even now he was stalking on his way through the castle, uncaring and unheeding.

Ballard drew an unsteady breath and went down to the cellar, where he found a heavy sledge hammer. After that he went up to look for Argus.

He found him in the dining hall, moving with a slow, majestic tread as light from the windows slid softly over his golden mail, splintered into rainbows from his jewels.

Ballard was sweating, though not with exertion. He got in front of Argus and said, "Stop right there, you—" He called the robot an unprintable name.

Argus moved to circle him. Ballard in a clear, carrying voice said, "McNamara, Torsion Process, Patent No. R-735-V-22."

Dangerfield's stylo moved swiftly. The robot stopped. It was like stopping some inexorable force of nature, as if an avalanche had halted halfway down a mountain. In the unnatural silence Ballard heard the other guard ask:

"Got it?"

"Yeah," said Dangerfield. "Let's go."

They went out. Ballard hefted the sledge. He walked toward Argus on the balls of his feet. Argus towered over him, serene and blind.

The first blow sent diamonds showering and flashing, gouged gold from the robot's massive chest. With tremendous dignity Argus rocked backward from the blow. The thunder of his fall echoed through the silent hall.

Ballard lifted the sledge and brought it down again. He couldn't break through the almost impermeable casing beneath the gold plate, of course, nor crush the gems, but his furious blows ripped diamonds free and tore great furrows and gouges in the golden armor.

"You . . . damned . . . machine!" Ballard shouted, wielding the sledge in a blind, clamorous fury of meaningless destruction. "You . . . damned . . . *machine!*"

LETTERS FROM LAURA
by Mildred Clingerman

Monday

Dear Mom:

Stop *worrying*. There isn't a bit of danger. Nobody ever dies or gets hurt or anything like that while time traveling. The young man at the Agency explained it all to me in detail, but I've forgotten most of it. His eyebrows move in the most fascinating way. So I'm going this weekend. I've already bought my ticket. I haven't the faintest idea where I'm going, but that's part of the fun. Grab Bag Tours, they call them. It costs $60 for one day and night, and the Agency supplies you with food concentrates and water capsules—a whole bag full of stuff they send right along with you. I certainly do *not* want Daddy to go with me. I'll tell him all about it when I get back, and then he can go himself, if he still wants to. The thing Daddy forgets is that all the history he reads is mostly just a pack of lies. Everybody says so nowadays, since time travel. He'd spoil everything arguing with the natives, telling them how they were supposed to act. I have to stop now, because the young man from the Agency is going to take me out to dinner and explain about insurance for the trip.

Love,
Laura

Tuesday

Dear Mom:

I can't *afford* to go first class. The Grab Bag Tours are not the leavings. They're perfectly all right. It's just that you sorta have to rough it. They've been thoroughly explored. I mean somebody has been there at least once before. I never heard of a native attacking a girl traveler. Just because I won't have a guide you start worrying about that. Believe me, some of those guides from what I hear wouldn't be very safe, either. Delbert explained it all to me. He's the boy from the Agency. Did you know that insurance is a very interesting subject?

Love,

Laura

Friday

Dear Mom:

Everything is set for tomorrow. I'm so excited. I spent three hours on the couch at the Agency's office—taking the hypno-course, you know, so I'll be able to speak the language. Later Delbert broke a rule and told me my destination, so I rushed over to the public library and read bits here and there. It's ancient Crete! Dad will be so pleased. I'm going to visit the Minotaur in the Labyrinth. Delbert says he is really off the beaten track of the tourists. I like unspoiled things, don't you? The Agency has a regular little room all fixed up right inside the cave, but hidden, so as not to disturb the regular business of the place. The Agency is very particular that way. Time travelers, Delbert says, have to agree to make themselves as inconspicuous as possible. Delbert says that will be very difficult for me to do. Don't you think *subtle* compliments are the nicest? I've made myself a darling costume —I sat up late to finish it. I don't know that it's exactly right, historically, but it doesn't really matter, since I'm not supposed to leave the cave. I have to stay close to my point of arrival, you understand. Delbert says I'm well covered now with insurance, so don't worry. I'll write the minute I get back.

Love,

Laura

Friday

Dear Prue:

Tomorrow I take my first time travel tour. I wish you could see my costume. Very fetching! It's cut so that my breasts are displayed in the style of ancient Crete. A friend of mine doubts the authenticity of the dress but says the charms it shows off are *really* authentic! Next time I see you I'll lend you the pattern for the dress. But I honestly think, darling, you ought to get one of those Liff-Up operations first. I've been meaning to tell you. Of course, I don't need it myself. I'll tell you all about it (the trip I mean) when I get back.

Love,

Laura

Monday

Dear Prue:

I had the *stinkiest* time! I'll never know why I let that character at the travel agency talk me into it. The accommodations were lousy. If you want to know what I think, it's all a gyp. These Grab Bag Tours, third-class, are just the *leavings*, that they can't sell any other way. I hate salesmen. Whoever heard of ancient Crete anyway? And the Minotaur. You would certainly expect him to be a red-blooded he-man, wouldn't you? He looked like one. Not cute, you know, but built like a bull, practically. Prue, you just can't *tell* anymore. But I'm getting ahead of myself.

You've heard about that funny dizziness you feel for the first few minutes on arrival? That part is true. Everything is supposed to look black at first, but things kept on looking black even after the dizziness wore off. Then I remembered it was a cave I was in, but I did expect it to be lighted. I was lying on one of those beastly little cots that wiggle everytime your heart beats, and mine was beating plenty fast. Then I remembered the bag the Agency packs for you, and I sat up and felt around till I found it. I got out a perma-light and attached it to the solid rock wall and looked around. The floor was just plain old dirty dirt. That Agency had me stuck off in a little alcove, furnished with that sagging cot and a few coat hangers. The air in the place was rather stale. Let's be honest—it smelled. To console myself I expanded my wrist mirror and put on some more makeup. I was wearing my costume, but I had forgotten to bring a coat. I was freezing. I draped the blanket from the cot around me and went exploring. What a place! One huge room just outside my cubbyhole and corridors taking off in all directions, winding away into the dark. I had a perma-light with me, and naturally I couldn't get lost with my earrings tuned to point of arrival, but it was *weird* wandering around all by myself. I discovered that the corridor I was in curved downward. Later I found there were dozens of levels in the Labyrinth. Very confusing.

I was just turning to go back when something reached out and grabbed for me, from one of those alcoves. I was *thrilled*. I flicked off the light, dropped my blanket, and ran.

From behind I heard a man's voice. "All right, sis, we'll play games."

Well, Prue, I hadn't played hide-and-seek in years, (except once or twice at office parties) but I was still pretty good at it. That part was fun. After a time my eyes adjusted to the dark so that I could see well enough to keep from banging into the walls. Sometimes I'd deliberately make a lot of noise to keep things interesting. But do you know what? That character would blunder right by me, and way down at the end of the corridor he'd make noises like "Oho" or "Aha." Frankly, I got discouraged. Finally I heard him grumbling his way back in my direction. I knew the dope would never catch me, so I just stepped out in front of him and said "Wellll?" You know, in that drawly, sarcastic way I have.

He reached out and grabbed me, and then he staggered back—like you've seen actors do in those old, old movies. He kept pounding his forehead with his fist, and then he yelled, "Cheated! Cheated again!" I almost slapped him. Instead I snapped on my perma-light and let him look me over good.

"Well, Buster," I said very coldly, "what do you mean, cheated?"

He grinned at me and shaded his eyes from the light. "Darling," he said, "you look luscious, indeed, but what the hell are you doing here?"

"I'm sight-seeing," I said. "Are you one of the sights?"

"Listen, baby, I *am* the sight. Meet the Minotaur." He stuck out his huge paw, and I shook it.

"Who did you think I was?" I asked him.

"Not *who*, but *what*," he said. "Baby, you ain't no virgin."

Well, Prue, really. How can you argue a thing like that? He was completely *wrong*, of course, but I simply refused to discuss it.

"I only gobble virgins," he said.

Then he led me down into his rooms, which were really quite comfortable. I couldn't forgive the Agency for that cot, so when I spied his lovely, soft couch draped in pale blue satin, I said, "I'll borrow that if you don't mind."

"It's all yours, kid," the Minotaur said. He meant it, too. You remember how pale blue is one of my best colors? There I was lolling on the couch, looking like the Queen of the Nile, flapping my eyelashes, and what does this churl want to do?

"I'm simply starved for talk," he says. And about what? Prue, when a working girl spends her hard-earned savings on time travel, she has a right to expect something besides *politics*. I have heard there are men, a few shy ones, who will talk very fast to you about science and all that highbrow stuff, hoping maybe you won't notice some of the things they're doing in the *meantime*. But not the Minotaur. Who cares about the government a room's length apart? Lying there, twiddling my fingers and yawning, I tried to remember if Daddy had ever mentioned anything about the Minotaur's being so persnickety. That's the trouble with books. They leave out all the important details.

For instance, did you know that at midnight every night the Minotaur makes a grand tour of the Labyrinth? He wouldn't let me go along. That's another thing. He just says "no" and grins and means it. Now isn't that a typical male trait? I thought so, and when he locked me in his rooms the evening looked like turning into fun. I waited for him to come back with bated breath. But you can't bate your breath forever, and he was gone hours. When he did come back I'd fallen asleep and he woke me up *belching*.

"Please," I said, "do you have to do that?"

"Sorry, kid," he said. "It's these gaunt old maids. Awful souring to the stomach." It seems this windy diet was one of the things wrong with the government. He was very bitter about it all. Tender virgins, he said, had always been in short supply and now he was out of favor with the new regime. I rummaged around in my wrist bag and found an anti-acid pill. He was delighted. Can you imagine going into a transport over pills?

"Any cute males ever find their way into this place?" I asked him. I got up and walked around. You can loll on a couch just so long, you know.

"No boys!" The Minotaur jumped up and shook his fist at me. I cowered behind some hangings, but I needn't have bothered. He didn't even jerk me out from behind them. Instead he paced up and down and raved about the lies told on him. He swore he'd never eaten boys—hadn't cared for them at all. That creep, Theseus, was trying to ruin him politically. "I've worn myself thin," he yelled, "in all these years of service—" At that point I walked over and poked him in his big, fat stomach. Then I gathered my things together and walked out.

He puffed along behind me wanting to know what was the matter. "Gee, kid," he kept saying, "don't go home mad." I didn't say goodbye to him at all. A spider fell on him and it threw him into a hissy. The last I saw of him he was cursing the government because they hadn't sent him an exterminator.

Well, Prue, so much for the bogey man. Time travel in the raw!

Love,
Laura

Monday

Dear Mom:

Ancient Crete was nothing but politics, not a bit exciting. You didn't have a single cause to worry. Those people are just as particular about girls as you are.

Love,
Laura

Tuesday

Dear Mr. Delbert Barnes:

Stop calling me or I will complain to your boss. You cad. I see it all now. You and your fine talk about how your Agency "fully protects its clients." That's a very high-sounding name for it. Tell me, how many girls do you talk into going to ancient Crete? And do you provide all of them with the same kind of insurance? Mr. Barnes, I don't want any more insurance from you. But I'm going to send you a client for that trip—the haggiest old maid I know. She has buck teeth and whiskers. Insure *her*.

Laura

P.S. Just in case you're feeling smug about me, put this in your pipe and smoke it. The Minotaur *knew*, I can't imagine how, but *you*, Mr. Barnes, *are no Minotaur*.

THE STARS MY DESTINATION
by Alfred Bester

PART 1

Tiger! Tiger! burning bright
In the forests of the night,
What immortal hand or eye
Could frame thy fearful symmetry?
Blake

PROLOGUE

THIS WAS A GOLDEN AGE, a time of high adventure, rich living, and hard dying . . . but nobody thought so. This was a future of fortune and theft, pillage and rapine, culture and vice . . . but nobody admitted it. This was an age of extremes, a fascinating century of freaks . . . but nobody loved it.

All the habitable worlds of the solar system were occupied. Three planets and eight satellites and eleven million million people swarmed in one of the most exciting ages ever known, yet minds still yearned for other times, as always. The solar system seethed with activity . . . fighting, feeding, and breeding, learning the new technologies that spewed forth almost before the old had been mastered, girding itself for the first exploration of the far stars in deep space; but—

"Where are the new frontiers?" the Romantics cried, unaware that the frontier of the mind had opened in a laboratory on Callisto at the turn of the twenty-fourth century. A researcher named Jaunte set fire to his bench and himself (accidentally) and let out a yell for help with particular reference to a fire extinguisher. Who so surprised as Jaunte and his colleagues when he found himself standing alongside said extinguisher, seventy feet removed from his lab bench.

They put Jaunte out and went into the whys and wherefores of his instantaneous seventy-foot journey. Teleportation . . . the transportation of oneself through space by an effort of the mind alone . . . had long been a theoretic concept, and there were a few hundred badly documented proofs that it had happened in the past. This was the first time that it had ever taken place before professional observers.

They investigated the Jaunte Effect savagely. This was something too earth-shaking to handle with kid gloves, and Jaunte was anxious to make his name immortal. He made his will and said farewell to his friends. Jaunte knew he was going to die because his fellow researchers were determined to kill him, if necessary. There was no doubt about that.

Twelve psychologists, parapsychologists and neurometrists of varying specialization were called in as observers. The experimenters sealed Jaunte into an unbreakable crystal tank. They opened a water valve, feeding water into the tank, and let Jaunte watch them smash the valve handle. It was impossible to open the tank; it was impossible to stop the flow of water.

The theory was that if it had required the threat of death to goad Jaunte into teleporting himself in the first place, they'd damned well threaten him with death again. The tank filled quickly. The observers collected data with the tense precision of an eclipse camera crew. Jaunte began to drown. Then he was outside the tank, dripping and coughing explosively. He'd teleported again.

The experts examined and questioned him. They studied graphs and X-rays, neural patterns and body chemistry. They began to get an inkling of how Jaunte had teleported. On the technical grapevine (this had to be kept secret) they sent out a call for suicide volunteers. They were still in the primitive stage of teleportation; death was the only spur they knew.

They briefed the volunteers thoroughly. Jaunte lectured on what he had done and how he thought he had done it. Then they proceeded to murder the volunteers. They drowned them, hanged them, burned them; they invented new forms of slow and controlled death. There was never any doubt in any of the subjects that death was the object.

Eighty per cent of the volunteers died, and the agonies and remorse of their murderers would make a fascinating and horrible study, but that has no place in this history except to highlight the monstrosity of the times. Eighty per cent of the volunteers died, but 20 per cent jaunted. (The name became a word almost immediately.)

"Bring back the romantic age," the Romantics pleaded, "when men could risk their lives in high adventure."

The body of knowledge grew rapidly. By the first decade of the twenty-fourth century the principles of jaunting were established and the first school was opened by Charles Fort Jaunte himself, then fifty-seven, immortalized, and ashamed to admit that he had never dared jaunte again. But the primitive days were past; it was no longer necessary to threaten a man with death to make him teleport. They had learned how to teach man to recognize, discipline, and exploit yet another resource of his limitless mind.

How, exactly, did man teleport? One of the most unsatisfactory explanations was provided by Spencer Thompson, publicity representative of the Jaunte Schools, in a press interview.

THOMPSON: Jaunting is like seeing; it is a natural aptitude of almost every human organism, but it can only be developed by training and experience.

REPORTER: You mean we couldn't see without practice?

THOMPSON: Obviously you're either unmarried or have no children . . . preferably both.

(*Laughter*)

REPORTER: I don't understand.

THOMPSON: Anyone who's observed an infant learning to use its eyes, would.

REPORTER: But what *is* teleportation?

THOMPSON: The transportation of oneself from one locality to another by an effort of the mind alone.

REPORTER: You mean we can *think* ourselves from . . . say . . . New York to Chicago?

THOMPSON: Precisely; provided one thing is clearly understood. In jaunting from New York to Chicago it is necessary for the person teleporting himself to know exactly where he is when he starts and where he's going.

REPORTER: How's that?

THOMPSON: If you were in a dark room and unaware of where you were, it would be impossible to jaunte anywhere with safety. And if you knew where you were but intended to jaunte to a place you had never seen, you would never arrive alive. One cannot jaunte from an unknown departure point to an unknown destination. *Both* must be known, memorized and visualized.

REPORTER: But if we know where we are and where we're going . . . ?

THOMPSON: We can be pretty sure we'll jaunte and arrive.

REPORTER: Would we arrive naked?

THOMPSON: If you started naked.

(*Laughter*)

REPORTER: I mean, would our clothes teleport with us?

THOMPSON: When people teleport, they also teleport the clothes they wear and whatever they are strong enough to carry. I hate to disappoint you, but even ladies' clothes would arrive with them.

(*Laughter*)

REPORTER: But how do we do it?

THOMPSON: How do we think?

REPORTER: With our minds.

THOMPSON: And how does the mind think? What is the thinking process? Exactly how do we remember, imagine, deduce, create? Exactly how do the brain cells operate?

REPORTER: I don't know. Nobody knows.

THOMPSON: And nobody knows exactly how we teleport either, but we know we can do it—just as we know that we can think. Have you ever heard of Descartes? He said: *Cogito ergo sum*. I think, therefore I am. We say: *Cogito ergo jaunteo*. I think, therefore I jaunte.

If it is thought that Thompson's explanation is exasperating, inspect this report of Sir John Kelvin to the Royal Society on the mechanism of jaunting:

> We have established that the teleportative ability is associated with the Nissl bodies, or Tigroid Substance in nerve cells. The Tigroid Substance is easiest demonstrated by Nissl's method using 3.75 g. of methylen blue and 1.75 g. of Venetian soap dissolved in 1,000 cc. of water.
> Where the Tigroid Substance does not appear, jaunting is impossible. Teleportation is a Tigroid Function.
> (*Applause*)

Any man was capable of jaunting provided he developed two faculties, visualization and concentration. He had to visualize, completely and precisely, the spot to which he desired to teleport himself; and he had to concentrate the latent energy of his mind into a single thrust to get him there. Above all, he had to have faith . . . the faith that Charles Fort Jaunte never recovered. He had to believe he would jaunte. The slightest doubt would block the mind-thrust necessary for teleportation.

The limitations with which every man is born necessarily limited the ability to jaunte. Some could visualize magnificently and set the co-ordinates of their destination with precision, but lacked the power to get there. Others had the power but could not, so to speak, see where they were jaunting. And space set a final limitation, for no man had ever jaunted further than a thousand miles. He could work his way in jaunting jumps over land and water from Nome to Mexico, but no jump could exceed a thousand miles.

By the 2420's, this form of employment application blank had become a commonplace:

This space reserved for retina pattern identification ( )

NAME (Capital Letters):.........................
Last Middle First

RESIDENCE (Legal):...........................
Continent Country County

JAUNTE CLASS (Official Rating: Check one Only):

M (1,000 miles):.....	**L (50 miles):.....**
D (500 miles):	**X (10 miles):.....**
C (100 miles):	**V(5 miles): ......**

The old Bureau of Motor Vehicles took over the new job and regularly tested and classed jaunte applicants, and the old American Automobile Association changed its initials to AJA.

Despite all efforts, no man had ever jaunted across the voids of space, although many experts and fools had tried. Helmut Grant, for one, who spent a month memorizing the co-ordinates of a jaunte stage on the moon and visualized every mile of the two hundred and forty thousand-mile trajectory from Times Square to Kepler City. Grant jaunted and disappeared. They never found him. They never found Enzio Dandridge, a Los Angeles revivalist looking for Heaven; Jacob Maria Freundlich, a paraphysicist who should have known better than to jaunte into deep space searching for metadimensions; Shipwreck Cogan, a professional seeker after notoriety; and hundreds of others, lunatic-fringers, neurotics, escapists and suicides. Space was closed to teleportation. Jaunting was restricted to the surfaces of the planets of the solar system.

But within three generations the entire solar system was on the jaunte. The transition was more spectacular than the change-over from horse and buggy to gasoline age four centuries before. On three planets and eight satellites, social, legal, and economic structures crashed while the new customs and laws demanded by universal jaunting mushroomed in their place.

There were land riots as the jaunting poor deserted slums to squat in plains and forests, raiding the livestock and wildlife. There was a revolution in home and office building: labyrinths and masking devices had to be introduced to prevent unlawful entry by jaunting. There were crashes and panics and strikes and famines as pre-jaunte industries failed.

Plagues and pandemics raged as jaunting vagrants carried disease and vermin into defenseless countries. Malaria, elephantiasis, and the breakbone fever came north to Greenland; rabies returned to England after an absence of three hundred years. The Japanese beetle, the citrous scale, the chestnut blight, and the elm borer spread to every corner of the world, and from one forgotten pesthole in Borneo, leprosy, long imagined extinct, reappeared.

Crime waves swept the planets and satellites as their underworlds took to jaunting with the night around the clock, and there were brutalities as the police fought them without quarter. There came a hideous return to the worst prudery of Victorianism as society fought the sexual and moral dangers of jaunting with protocol and taboo. A cruel and vicious war broke out between the Inner Planets—Venus, Terra and Mars—and the Outer Satellites . . . a war brought on by the economic and political pressures of teleportation.

Until the Jaunte Age dawned, the three Inner Planets (and the Moon) had lived in delicate economic balance with the seven inhabited Outer Satellites: Io, Europa, Ganymede, and Callisto of Jupiter; Rhea and Titan of Saturn; and Lassell of Neptune. The United Outer Satellites supplied raw materials for the Inner Planets' manufactories, and a market for their finished goods. Within a decade this balance was destroyed by jaunting.

The Outer Satellites, raw young worlds in the making, had bought 70 per cent of the I.P. transportation production. Jaunting ended that. They had bought 90 per cent of the I.P. communications production. Jaunting ended that too. In consequence I.P. purchase of O.S. raw materials fell off.

With trade exchange destroyed it was inevitable that the economic war would degenerate into a shooting war. Inner Planets' cartels refused to ship manufacturing equipment to the Outer Satellites, attempting to protect themselves against competition. The O.S. confiscated the planets already in operation on their worlds, broke patent agreements, ignored royalty obligations . . . and the war was on.

It was an age of freaks, monsters, and grotesques. All the world was misshapen in marvelous and malevolent ways. The Classicists and Romantics who hated it were unaware of the potential greatness of the twenty-fifth century. They were blind to a cold fact of evolution . . . that progress stems from the clashing merger of antagonistic extremes, out of the marriage of pinnacle freaks. Classicists and Romantics alike were unaware that the Solar System was trembling on the verge of a human explosion that would transform man and make him the master of the universe.

It is against this seething background of the twenty-fifth century that the vengeful history of Gulliver Foyle begins.

CHAPTER ONE

He was one hundred and seventy days dying and not yet dead. He fought for survival with the passion of a beast in a trap. He was delirious and rotting, but occasionally his primitive mind emerged from the burning nightmare of survival into something resembling sanity. Then he lifted his mute face to Eternity and muttered: "What's a matter, me? Help, you goddamn gods! Help, is all."

Blasphemy came easily to him: it was half his speech, all his life. He had been raised in the gutter school of the twenty-fifth century and spoke nothing but the gutter tongue. Of all brutes in the world he was among the least valuable alive and most likely to survive. So he struggled and prayed in blasphemy; but occasionally his raveling mind leaped backward thirty years to his childhood and remembered a nursery jingle:

Gully Foyle is my name
And Terra is my nation.
Deep space is my dwelling place
And death's my destination.

He was Gulliver Foyle, Mechanic's Mate 3rd Class, thirty years old, big boned and rough . . . and one hundred and seventy days adrift in space. He was Gully Foyle, the oiler, wiper, bunkerman; too easy for trouble, too slow for fun, too empty for friendship, too lazy for love. The lethargic outlines of his character showed in the official Merchant Marine records:

FOYLE, GULLIVER ------- AS-128/127:006

EDUCATION: NONE
SKILLS: NONE
MERITS: NONE
RECOMMENDATIONS: NONE

(PERSONNEL COMMENTS)

A man of physical strength and intellectual potential stunted by lack of ambition. Energizes at minimum. The stereotype Common Man. Some unexpected shock might possibly awaken him, but Psych cannot find the key. Not recommended for promotion. Has reached a dead end.

He had reached a dead end. He had been content to drift from moment to moment of existence for thirty years like some heavily armored creature, sluggish and indifferent—Gully Foyle, the stereotype Common Man—but now he was adrift in space for one hundred and seventy days, and the key to his awakening was in the lock. Presently it would turn and open the door to holocaust.

The spaceship "Nomad" drifted halfway between Mars and Jupiter. Whatever war catastrophe had wrecked it had taken a sleek steel rocket, one hundred yards long and one hundred feet broad, and mangled it into a skeleton on which was mounted the remains of cabins, holds, decks and bulkheads. Great rents in the hull were blazes of light on the sunside and frosty blotches of stars on the darkside. The S.S. "Nomad" was a weightless emptiness of blinding sun and jet shadow, frozen and silent.

The wreck was filled with a floating conglomerate of frozen debris that hung within the destroyed vessel like an instantaneous photograph of an explosion. The minute gravitational attraction of the bits of rubble for each other was slowly drawing them into clusters which were periodically torn apart by the passage through them of the one survivor still alive on the wreck, Gulliver Foyle, AS-128/127:006.

He lived in the only airtight room left intact in the wreck, a tool locker off the main-deck corridor. The locker was four feet wide, four feet deep and nine feet high. It was the size of a giant's coffin. Six hundred years before, it had been judged the most exquisite Oriental torture to imprison a man in a cage that size for a few weeks. Yet Foyle had existed in this lightless coffin for five months, twenty days, and four hours.

"Who are you?"
"Gully Foyle is my name."
"Where are you from?"
"Terra is my nation."
"Where are you now?"
"Deep space is my dwelling place."
"Where are you bound?"

"Death's my destination."

On the one hundred and seventy-first day of his fight for survival, Foyle answered these questions and awoke. His heart hammered and his throat burned. He groped in the dark for the air tank which shared his coffin with him and checked it. The tank was empty. Another would have to be moved in at once. So this day would commence with an extra skirmish with death which Foyle accepted with mute endurance.

He felt through the locker shelves and located a torn spacesuit. It was the only one aboard "Nomad" and Foyle no longer remembered where or how he had found it. He had sealed the tear with emergency spray, but had no way of refilling or replacing the empty oxygen cartridges on the back. Foyle got into the suit. It would hold enough air from the locker to allow him five minutes in vacuum . . . no more.

Foyle opened the locker door and plunged out into the black frost of space. The air in the locker puffed out with him and its moisture congealed into a tiny snow cloud that drifted down the torn main-deck corridor. Foyle heaved at the exhausted air tank, floated it out of the locker and abandoned it. One minute was gone.

He turned and propelled himself through the floating debris toward the hatch to the ballast hold. He did not run: his gait was the unique locomotion of free-fall and weightlessness . . . thrusts with foot, elbow and hand against deck, wall and corner, a slow-motion darting through space like a bat flying under water. Foyle shot through the hatch into the darkside ballast hold. Two minutes were gone.

Like all spaceships, "Nomad" was ballasted and stiffened with the mass of her gas tanks laid down the length of her keel like a long lumber raft tapped at the sides by a labyrinth of pipe fittings. Foyle took a minute disconnecting an air tank. He had no way of knowing whether it was full or already exhausted; whether he would fight it back to his locker only to discover that it was empty and his life was ended. Once a week he endured this game of space roulette.

There was a roaring in his ears; the air in his spacesuit was rapidly going foul. He yanked the massy cylinder toward the ballast hatch, ducked to let it sail over his head, then thrust himself after it. He swung the tank through the hatch. Four minutes had elapsed and he was shaking and blacking out. He guided the tank down the main-deck corridor and bulled it into the tool locker.

He slammed the locker door, dogged it, found a hammer on a shelf and swung it thrice against the frozen tank to loosen the valve. Foyle twisted the handle grimly. With the last of his strength he unsealed the helmet of his spacesuit, lest he suffocate within the suit while the locker filled with air . . . if this tank contained air. He fainted, as he had fainted so often before, never knowing whether this was death.

"Who are you?"

"Gully Foyle."

"Where are you from?"

"Terra."
"Where are you now?"
"Space."
"Where are you bound?"
He awoke. He was alive. He wasted no time on prayer or thanks but continued the business of survival. In the darkness he explored the locker shelves where he kept his rations. There were only a few packets left. Since he was already wearing the patched spacesuit he might just as well run the gantlet of vacuum again and replenish his supplies.
He flooded his spacesuit with air from the tank, resealed his helmet and sailed out into the frost and light again. He squirmed down the main-deck corridor and ascended the remains of a stairway, to the control deck which was no more than a roofed corridor in space. Most of the walls were destroyed.
With the sun on his right and the stars on his left, Foyle shot aft toward the galley storeroom. Halfway down the corridor he passed a door frame still standing foursquare between deck and roof. The leaf still hung on its hinges, half-open, a door to nowhere. Behind it was all space and the steady stars.
As Foyle passed the door he had a quick view of himself reflected in the polished chrome of the leaf . . . Gully Foyle, a giant black creature, bearded, crusted with dried blood and filth, emaciated, with sick, patient eyes . . . and followed always by a stream of floating debris, the raffle disturbed by his motion and following him through space like the tail of a festering comet.
Foyle turned into the galley storeroom and began looting with the methodical speed of five months' habit. Most of the bottled goods were frozen solid and exploded. Much of the canned goods had lost their containers, for tin crumbles to dust in the absolute zero of space. Foyle gathered up ration packets, concentrates, and a chunk of ice from the burst water tank. He threw everything into a large copper cauldron, turned and darted out of the storeroom, carrying the cauldron.
At the door to nowhere Foyle glanced at himself again, reflected in the chrome leaf framed in the stars. Then he stopped his motion in bewilderment. He stared at the stars behind the door which had become familiar friends after five months. There was an intruder among them; a comet, it seemed, with an invisible head and a short, spurting tail. Then Foyle realized he was staring at a spaceship, stern rockets flaring as it accelerated on a sunward course that must pass him.
"No," he muttered. "No, man. No."
He was continually suffering from hallucinations. He turned to resume the journey back to his coffin. Then he looked again. It was still a spaceship, stern rockets flaring as it accelerated on a sunward course which must pass him. He discussed the illusion with Eternity.
"Six months already," he said in his gutter tongue. "Is it now? You listen a me, lousy gods. I talkin' a deal, is all. I look again, sweet prayer-men. If it's a ship, I'm your's. You own me. But if it's a gaff, man . . . if it's no ship . . . I unseal right now and blow my guts. We both ballast level, us. Now reach me the sign, yes or no, is all."
He looked for a third time. For the third time he saw a spaceship, stern

rockets flaring as it accelerated on a sunward course which must pass him.

It was the sign. He believed. He was saved.

Foyle shoved off and went hurtling down control-deck corridor toward the bridge. But at the companionway stairs he restrained himself. He could not remain conscious for more than a few more moments without refilling his spacesuit. He gave the approaching spaceship one pleading look, then shot down to the tool locker and pumped his suit full.

He mounted to the control bridge. Through the starboard observation port he saw the spaceship, stern rockets still flaring, evidently making a major alteration in course, for it was bearing down on him very slowly.

On a panel marked FLARES, Foyle pressed the DISTRESS button. There was a three-second pause during which he suffered. Then white radiance blinded him as the distress signal went off in three triple bursts, nine prayers for help. Foyle pressed the button twice again, and twice more the flares flashed in space while the radioactives incorporated in their combustion set up a static howl that must register on any waveband of any receiver.

The stranger's jets cut off. He had been seen. He would be saved. He was reborn. He exulted.

Foyle darted back to his locker and replenished his spacesuit again. He began to weep. He started to gather his possessions—a faceless clock which he kept wound just to listen to the ticking, a lug wrench with a hand-shaped handle which he would hold in lonely moments, an egg slicer upon whose wires he would pluck primitive tunes. . . . He dropped them in his excitement, hunted for them in the dark, then began to laugh at himself.

He filled his spacesuit with air once more and capered back to the bridge. He punched a flare button labelled: RESCUE. From the hull of the "Nomad" shot a sunlet that burst and hung, flooding miles of space with harsh white light.

"Come on, baby you," Foyle crooned. "Hurry up, man. Come on, baby baby you."

Like a ghost torpedo, the stranger slid into the outermost rim of light, approaching slowly, looking him over. For a moment Foyle's heart constricted; the ship was behaving so cautiously that he feared she was an enemy vessel from the Outer Satellites. Then he saw the famous red and blue emblem on her side, the trademark of the mighty industrial clan of Presteign; Presteign of Terra, powerful, munificent, beneficent. And he knew this was a sister ship, for the "Nomad" was also Presteign-owned. He knew this was an angel from space hovering over him.

"Sweet sister," Foyle crooned. "Baby angel, fly away home with me."

The ship came abreast of Foyle, illuminated ports along its side glowing with friendly light, its name and registry number clearly visible in illuminated figures on the hull: Vorga-T:1339. The ship was alongside him in a moment, passing him in a second, disappearing in a third.

The sister had spurned him; the angel had abandoned him.

Foyle stopped dancing and crooning. He stared in dismay. He leaped to the flare panel and slapped buttons. Distress signals, landing, take-off, and quarantine flares burst from the hull of the "Nomad" in a madness of white, red and green light, pulsing, pleading . . . and "Vorga-T:1339" passed silently and implacably, stern jets flaring again as it accelerated on a sunward course.

So, in five seconds, he was born, he lived, and he died. After thirty years of existence and six months of torture, Gully Foyle, the stereotype Common Man, was no more. The key turned in the lock of his soul and the door was opened. What emerged expunged the Common Man forever.

"You pass me by," he said with slow mounting fury. "You leave me rot like a dog. You leave me die, 'Vorga' . . . 'Vorga-T:1339.' No. I get out of here, me. I follow you, 'Vorga.' I find you, 'Vorga.' I pay you back, me. I rot you. I kill you, 'Vorga.' I kill you filthy."

The acid of fury ran through him, eating away the brute patience and sluggishness that had made a cipher of Gully Foyle, precipitating a chain of reactions that would make an infernal machine of Gully Foyle. He was dedicated.

" 'Vorga,' I kill you filthy."

He did what the cipher could not do; he rescued himself.

For two days he combed the wreckage in five-minute forays, and devised a harness for his shoulders. He attached an air tank to the harness and connected the tank to his spacesuit helmet with an improvised hose. He wriggled through space like an ant dragging a log, but he had the freedom of the "Nomad" for all time.

He thought.

In the control bridge he taught himself to use the few navigation instruments that were still unbroken, studying the standard manuals that littered the wrecked navigation room. In the ten years of his service in space he had never dreamed of attempting such a thing, despite the rewards of promotion and pay; but now he had "Vorga-T:1339" to reward him.

He took sights. The "Nomad" was drifting in space on the ecliptic, three hundred million miles from the sun. Before him were spread the constellations Perseus, Andromeda and Pisces. Hanging almost in the foreground was a dusty orange spot that was Jupiter, distinctly a planetary disc to the naked eye. With any luck he could make a course for Jupiter and rescue.

Jupiter was not, could never be habitable. Like all the outer planets beyond the asteroid orbits, it was a frozen mass of methane and ammonia; but its four largest satellites swarmed with cities and populations now at war with the Inner Planets. He would be a war prisoner, but he had to stay alive to settle accounts with "Vorga-T:1339."

Foyle inspected the engine room of the "Nomad." There was Hi-Thrust fuel remaining in the tanks and one of the four tail jets was still in operative condition. Foyle found the engine room manuals and studied them. He repaired the connection between fuel tanks and the one jet chamber. The tanks were on the sunside of the wreck and warmed above freezing point.

The Hi-Thrust was still liquid, but it would not flow. In free-fall there was no gravity to draw the fuel down the pipes.

Foyle studied a space manual and learned something about theoretical gravity. If he could put the "Nomad" into a spin, centrifugal force would impart enough gravitation to the ship to draw fuel down into the combustion chamber of the jet. If he could fire the combustion chamber, the unequal thrust of the one jet would impart a spin to the "Nomad."

But he couldn't fire the jet without first having the spin; and he couldn't get the spin without first firing the jet.

He thought his way out of the deadlock; he was inspired by "Vorga."

Foyle opened the drainage petcock in the combustion chamber of the jet and tortuously filled the chamber with fuel by hand. He had primed the pump. Now, if he ignited the fuel, it would fire long enough to impart the spin and start gravity. Then the flow from the tanks would commence and the rocketing would continue.

He tried matches.

Matches will not burn in the vacuum of space.

He tried flint and steel.

Sparks will not glow in the absolute zero of space.

He thought of red-hot filaments.

He had no electric power of any description aboard the "Nomad" to make a filament red hot.

He found texts and read. Although he was blacking out frequently and close to complete collapse, he thought and planned. He was inspired to greatness by "Vorga."

Foyle brought ice from the frozen galley tanks, melted it with his own body heat, and added water to the jet combustion chamber. The fuel and the water were nonmiscible, they did not mix. The water floated in a thin layer over the fuel.

From the chemical stores Foyle brought a silvery bit of wire, pure sodium metal. He poked the wire through the open petcock. The sodium ignited when it touched the water and flared with high heat. The heat touched off the Hi-Thrust which burst in a needle flame from the petcock. Foyle closed the petcock with a wrench. The ignition held in the chamber and the lone aft jet slammed out flame with a soundless vibration that shook the ship.

The off-center thrust of the jet twisted the "Nomad" into a slow spin. The torque imparted a slight gravity. Weight returned. The floating debris that cluttered the hull fell to decks, walls and ceilings; and the gravity kept the fuel feeding from tanks to combustion chamber.

Foyle wasted no time on cheers. He left the engine room and struggled forward in desperate haste for a final, fatal observation from the control bridge. This would tell him whether the "Nomad" was committed to a wild plunge out into the no-return of deep space, or a course for Jupiter and rescue.

The slight gravity made his air tank almost impossible to drag. The sudden forward surge of acceleration shook loose masses of debris which flew backward through the "Nomad." As Foyle struggled up the companionway stairs to the control deck, the rubble from the bridge came hurtling back down the corridor and smashed into him. He was caught up in this tumbleweed in space, rolled back the length of the empty corridor, and brought up against the galley bulkhead with an impact that shattered his last hold on consciousness. He lay pinned in the center of half a ton of wreckage, helpless, barely alive, but still raging for vengeance.

"Who are you?"

"Where are you from?"

"Where are you now?"

"Where are you bound?"

CHAPTER TWO

BETWEEN MARS AND JUPITER is spread the broad belt of the asteroids. Of the thousands, known and unknown, most unique to the Freak Century was the Sargasso Asteroid, a tiny planet manufactured of natural rock and wreckage salvaged by its inhabitants in the course of two hundred years.

They were savages, the only savages of the twenty-fourth century; descendants of a research team of scientists that had been lost and marooned in the asteroid belt two centuries before when their ship had failed. By the time their descendants were rediscovered they had built up a world and a culture of their own, and preferred to remain in space, salvaging and spoiling, and practicing a barbaric travesty of the scientific method they remembered from their forebears. They called themselves The Scientific People. The world promptly forgot them.

S.S. "Nomad" looped through space, neither on a course for Jupiter nor the far stars, but drifting across the asteroid belt in the slow spiral of a dying animalcule. It passed within a mile of the Sargasso Asteroid, and it was immediately captured by The Scientific People to be incorporated into their little planet. They found Foyle.

He awoke once while he was being carried in triumph on a litter through the natural and artificial passages within the scavenger asteroid. They were constructed of meteor metal, stone, and hull plates. Some of the plates still bore names long forgotten in the history of space travel: INDUS QUEEN, TERRA; SYRTUS RAMBLER, MARS; THREE RING CIRCUS, SATURN. The passages led to great halls, storerooms, apartments, and homes, all built of salvaged ships cemented into the asteroid.

In rapid succession Foyle was borne through an ancient Ganymede scow, a Lassell ice borer, a captain's barge, a Callisto heavy cruiser, a twenty-second-century fuel transport with glass tanks still filled with smoky rocket fuel. Two centuries of salvage were gathered in this hive: armories of weapons, libraries of books, museums of costumes, warehouses of machinery, tools, rations, drink, chemicals, synthetics, and surrogates.

A crowd around the litter was howling triumphantly. "Quant Suff!" they shouted. A woman's chorus began an excited bleating:

Ammonium bromide	gr. 1½
Potassium bromide	gr. 3
Sodium bromide	gr. 2
Citric acid	quant. suff.

"Quant Suff!" The Scientific People roared. "Quant Suff!"

Foyle fainted.

He awoke again. He had been taken out of his spacesuit. He was in the greenhouse of the asteroid where plants were grown for fresh oxygen. The hundred-yard hull of an old ore carrier formed the room, and one wall had been entirely fitted with salvaged windows . . . round ports, square ports, diamond, hexagonal . . . every shape and age of port had been introduced until the vast wall was a crazy quilt of glass and light.

The distant sun blazed through; the air was hot and moist. Foyle gazed around dimly. A devil face peered at him. Cheeks, chin, nose, and eyelids were hideously tattooed like an ancient Maori mask. Across the brow was tattooed JOSEPH. The "O" in JOSEPH had a tiny arrow thrust up from the right shoulder, turning it into the symbol of Mars, used by scientists to designate male sex.

"We are the Scientific Race," Joseph said. "I am Joseph; these are my people."

He gestured. Foyle gazed at the grinning crowd surrounding his litter. All faces were tattooed into devil masks; all brows had names blazoned across them.

"How long did you drift?" Joseph asked.

"Vorga," Foyle mumbled.

"You are the first to arrive alive in fifty years. You are a puissant man. Very. Arrival of the fittest is the doctrine of Holy Darwin. Most scientific."

"Quant Suff!" the crowd bellowed.

Joseph seized Foyle's elbow in the manner of a physician taking a pulse. His devil mouth counted solemnly up to ninety-eight.

"Your pulse. Ninety-eight-point-six," Joseph said, producing a thermometer and shaking it reverently. "Most scientific."

"Quant Suff!" came the chorus.

Joseph proffered an Erlenmeyer flask. It was labeled: *Lung, Cat, c.s., hematoxylin & eosin*. "Vitamin?" Joseph inquired.

When Foyle did not respond, Joseph removed a large pill from the flask, placed it in the bowl of a pipe, and lit it. He puffed once and then gestured. Three girls appeared before Foyle. Their faces were hideously tattooed. Across each brow was a name: JOAN and MOIRA and POLLY. The "O" of each name had a tiny cross at the base.

"Choose." Joseph said. "The Scientific People practice Natural Selection. Be scientific in your choice. Be genetic."

As Foyle fainted again, his arm slid off the litter and glanced against Moira.

"Quant Suff!"

He was in a circular hall with a domed roof. The hall was filled with rusting antique apparatus: a centrifuge, an operating table, a wrecked fluoroscope, autoclaves, cases of corroded surgical instruments.

They strapped Foyle down on the operating table while he raved and rambled. They fed him. They shaved and bathed him. Two men began turning the ancient centrifuge by hand. It emitted a rhythmic clanking like the pounding of a war drum. Those assembled began tramping and chanting.

They turned on the ancient autoclave. It boiled and geysered, filling the hall with howling steam. They turned on the old fluoroscope. It was short-circuited and spat sizzling bolts of lightning across the steaming hall.

A ten foot figure loomed up to the table. It was Joseph on stilts. He wore a surgical cap, a surgical mask, and a surgeon's gown that hung from his shoulders to the floor. The gown was heavily embroidered with red and black thread illustrating anatomical sections of the body. Joseph was a lurid tapestry out of a surgical text.

"I pronounce you Nomad!" Joseph intoned.

The uproar became deafening. Joseph tilted a rusty can over Foyle's body. There was the reek of ether.

Foyle lost his tatters of consciousness and darkness enveloped him. Out of the darkness "Vorga-T:1339" surged again and again, accelerating on a sunward course that burst through Foyle's blood and brains until he could not stop screaming silently for vengeance.

He was dimly aware of washings and feedings and trampings and chantings. At last he awoke to a lucid interval. There was silence. He was in a bed. The girl, Moira, was in bed with him.

"Who you?" Foyle croaked.

"Your wife, Nomad."

"What?"

"Your wife. You chose me, Nomad. We are gametes."

"What?"

"Scientifically mated," Moira said proudly. She pulled up the sleeve of her nightgown and showed him her arm. It was disfigured by four ugly slashes. "I have been inoculated with something old, something new, something borrowed and something blue."

Foyle struggled out of the bed.

"Where we now?"

"In our home."

"What home?"

"Yours. You are one of us, Nomad. You must marry every month and beget many children. That will be scientific. But I am the first."

Foyle ignored her and explored. He was in the main cabin of a small rocket launch of the early 2300's . . . once a private yacht. The main cabin had been converted into a bedroom.

He lurched to the ports and looked out. The launch was sealed into the mass of the asteroid, connected by passages to the main body. He went aft. Two smaller cabins were filled with growing plants for oxygen. The engine room had been converted into a kitchen. There was Hi-Thrust in the fuel tanks, but it fed the burners of a small stove atop the rocket chambers. Foyle went forward. The control cabin was now a parlor, but the controls were still operative.

He thought.

He went aft to the kitchen and dismantled the stove. He reconnected the fuel tanks to the original jet combustion chambers. Moira followed him curiously.

"What are you doing, Nomad?"

"Got to get out of here, girl." Foyle mumbled. "Got business with a ship called 'Vorga.' You dig me, girl? Going to ram out in this boat, is all."

Moira backed away in alarm. Foyle saw the look in her eyes and leaped for her. He was so crippled that she avoided him easily. She opened her mouth and let out a piercing scream. At that moment a mighty clangor filled the launch; it was Joseph and his devil-faced Scientific People outside, banging on the metal hull, going through the ritual of a scientific charivari for the newlyweds.

Moira screamed and dodged while Foyle pursued her patiently. He trapped her in a corner, ripped her nightgown off and bound and gagged her with it. Moira made enough noise to split the asteroid open, but the scientific charivari was louder.

Foyle finished his rough patching of the engine room; he was almost an expert by now. He picked up the writhing girl and took her to the main hatch.

"Leaving," he shouted in Moira's ear. "Takeoff. Blast right out of asteroid. Hell of a smash, girl. Maybe all die, you. Everything busted wide open. Guesses for grabs what happens. No more air. No more asteroid. Go tell'm. Warn'm. Go, girl."

He opened the hatch, shoved Moira out, slammed the hatch and dogged it. The charivari stopped abruptly.

At the controls Foyle pressed ignition. The automatic take-off siren began a howl that had not sounded in decades. The jet chambers ignited with dull concussions. Foyle waited for the temperature to reach firing heat. While he waited he suffered. The launch was cemented into the asteroid. It was surrounded by stone and iron. Its rear jets were flush on the hull of another ship packed into the mass. He didn't know what would happen when his jets began their thrust, but he was driven to gamble by "Vorga."

He fired the jets. There was a hollow explosion as Hi-Thrust flamed out of the stern of the ship. The launch shuddered, yawed, heated. A squeal of metal began. Then the launch grated forward. Metal, stone and glass split asunder and the ship burst out of the asteroid into space.

The Inner Planets navy picked him up ninety thousand miles outside Mars's orbit. After seven months of shooting war, the I.P. patrols were alert but reckless. When the launch failed to answer and give recognition countersigns, it should have been shattered with a blast and questions could have been asked of the wreckage later. But the launch was small and the cruiser crew was hot for prize money. They closed and grappled.

They found Foyle inside, crawling like a headless worm through a junk heap of spaceship and home furnishings. He was bleeding again, ripe with stinking gangrene, and one side of his head was pulpy. They brought him into the sick bay aboard the cruiser and carefully curtained his tank. Foyle was no sight even for the tough stomachs of lower deck navy men.

They patched his carcass in the amniotic tank while they completed their tour of duty. On the jet back to Terra, Foyle recovered consciousness and bubbled words beginning with V. He knew he was saved. He knew that only time stood between him and vengeance. The sick bay orderly heard him exulting in his tank and parted the curtains. Foyle's filmed eyes looked up. The orderly could not restrain his curiosity.

"You hear me, man?" he whispered.

Foyle grunted. The orderly bent lower.

"What happened? Who in hell done that to you?"

"What?" Foyle croaked.

"Don't you know?"

"What? What's a matter, you?"

"Wait a minute, is all."

The orderly disappeared as he jaunted to a supply cabin, and reappeared alongside the tank five seconds later. Foyle struggled up out of the fluid. His eyes blazed.

"It's coming back, man. Some of it. Jaunte. I couldn't jaunte on the 'Nomad,' me."

"What?"

"I was off my head."

"Man, you didn't have no head left, you."

"I couldn't jaunte. I forgot how, is all. I forgot everything, me. Still don't remember much. I—"

He recoiled in terror as the orderly thrust the picture of a hideous tattooed face before him. It was a Maori mask. Cheeks, chin, nose, and eyelids were decorated with stripes and swirls. Across the brow was blazoned NOMAD. Foyle stared, then cried out in agony. The picture was a mirror. The face was his own.

CHAPTER THREE

"Bravo, Mr. Harris! Well done! L-E-S, gentlemen. Never forget. Location. Elevation. Situation. That's the only way to remember your jaunte co-ordinates. *Etre entre le marteau et l'enclume*. *French*. Don't jaunte yet, Mr. Peters. Wait your turn. Be patient, you'll all be C class by and by. Has anyone seen Mr. Foyle? He's missing. *Oh, look at that heavenly brown thrasher. Listen to him.* Oh dear, I'm thinking all over the place . . . or have I been speaking, gentlemen?"

"Half and half, m'am."

"It does seem unfair. One-way telepathy is a nuisance. I do apologize for shrapneling you with my thoughts."

"We like it, m'am. You think pretty."

"*How sweet of you, Mr. Gorgas.* All right, class; all back to school and we start again. Has Mr. Foyle jaunted already? I never can keep track of him."

Robin Wednesbury was conducting her re-education class in jaunting on its tour through New York City, and it was as exciting a business for the cerebral cases as it was for the children in her primer class. She treated the adults like children and they rather enjoyed it. For the past month they had been memorizing jaunte stages at street intersections, chanting: "L-E-S, m'am. Location. Elevation. Situation."

She was a tall, lovely Negro girl, brilliant and cultivated, but handicapped by the fact that she was a telesend, a one-way telepath. She could broadcast her thoughts to the world, but could receive nothing. This was a disadvantage that barred her from more glamorous careers, yet suited her for teaching. Despite her volatile temperament, Robin Wednesbury was a thorough and methodical jaunte instructor.

The men were brought down from General War Hospital to the jaunte school, which occupied an entire building in the Hudson Bridge at 42nd Street. They started from the school and marched in a sedate crocodile to the vast Times Square jaunte stage, which they earnestly memorized. Then they all jaunted to the school and back to Times Square. The crocodile re-formed and they marched up to Columbus Circle and memorized its co-ordinates. Then all jaunted back to school via Times Square and returned by the same route to Columbus Circle. Once more the crocodile formed and off they went to Grand Army Plaza to repeat the memorizing and the jaunting.

Robin was re-educating the patients (all head injuries who had lost the power to jaunte) to the express stops, so to speak, of the public jaunte stages. Later they would memorize the local stops at street intersections. As their horizons expanded (and their powers returned) they would memorize jaunte stages in widening circles, limited as much by income as ability; for one thing was certain: you had to actually see a place to memorize it, which meant you first had to pay for the transportation to get you there. Even 3-D photographs would not do the trick. The Grand Tour had taken on a new significance for the rich.

"Location. Elevation. Situation," Robin Wednesbury lectured, and the class jaunted by express stages from Washington Heights to the Hudson Bridge and back again in primer jumps of a quarter mile each; following their lovely Negro teacher earnestly.

The little technical sergeant with the platinum skull suddenly spoke in the gutter tongue: "But there ain't no elevation, m'am. We're on the ground, us."

"*Isn't, Sgt. Logan. 'Isn't any' would be better.* I beg your pardon. Teaching becomes a habit and I'm having trouble controlling my thinking today. The war news is so bad. We'll get to Elevation when we start memorizing the stages on top of skyscrapers, Sgt. Logan."

The man with the rebuilt skull digested that, then asked: "We hear you when you think, is a matter you?"

"Exactly."

"But you don't hear us?"

"Never. I'm a one-way telepath."

"We all hear you, or just I, is all?"

"That depends, Sgt. Logan. When I'm concentrating, just the one I'm thinking at; when I'm at loose ends, anybody and everybody . . . poor souls. Excuse me." Robin turned and called: "Don't hesitate before jaunting, Chief Harris. That starts doubting, and doubting ends jaunting. Just step up and bang off."

"I worry sometimes, m'am," a chief petty officer with a tightly bandaged head answered. He was obviously stalling at the edge of the jaunte stage.

"Worry? About what?"

"Maybe there's gonna be somebody standing where I arrive. Then there'll be a hell of a real bang, m'am. Excuse me."

"Now I've explained that a hundred times. Experts have gauged every jaunte stage in the world to accommodate peak traffic. That's why private jaunte stages are small, and the Times Square stage is two hundred yards wide. It's all been worked out mathematically and there isn't one chance in ten million of a simultaneous arrival. That's less than your chance of being killed in a jet accident."

The bandaged C.P.O. nodded dubiously and stepped up on the raised stage. It was of white concrete, round, and decorated on its face with vivid black and white patterns as an aid to memory. In the center was an illuminated plaque which gave its name and jaunte co-ordinates of latitude, longitude, and elevation.

At the moment when the bandaged man was gathering courage for his primer jaunte, the stage began to flicker with a sudden flurry of arrivals and departures. Figures appeared momentarily as they jaunted in, hesitated while they checked their surroundings and set new co-ordinates, and then disappeared as they jaunted off. At each disappearance there was a faint "Pop" as displaced air rushed into the space formerly occupied by a body.

"Wait, class," Robin called. "There's a rush on. Everybody off the stage, please."

Laborers in heavy work clothes, still spattered with snow, were on their way south to their homes after a shift in the north woods. Fifty white clad dairy clerks were headed west toward St. Louis. They followed the morning from the Eastern Time Zone to the Pacific Zone. And from eastern Greenland, where it was already noon, a horde of white-collar office workers was pouring into New York for their lunch hour.

The rush was over in a few moments. "All right, class," Robin called. "We'll continue. Oh dear, where *is* Mr. Foyle? He always seems to be missing."

"With a face like he's got, him, you can't blame him for hiding it, m'am. Up in the cerebral ward we call him Boogey."

"He does look dreadful, doesn't he, Sgt. Logan. Can't they get those marks off?"

"They're trying, Miss Robin, but they don't know how yet. It's called 'tattooing' and it's sort of forgotten, is all."

"Then how did Mr. Foyle acquire his face?"

"Nobody knows, Miss Robin. He's up in cerebral because he's lost his mind, him. Can't remember nothing. Me personal, if I had a face like that I wouldn't want to remember nothing too."

"It's a pity. He looks frightful. Sgt. Logan, d'you suppose I've let a thought about Mr. Foyle slip and hurt his feelings?"

The little man with the platinum skull considered. "No, m'am. You wouldn't hurt nobody's feelings, you. And Foyle ain't got none to hurt, him. He's just a big, dumb ox, is all."

"I have to be so careful, Sgt. Logan. You see, no one likes to know what another person really thinks about him. We imagine that we do, but we don't. *This telesending of mine makes me loathed. And lonesome. I—Please don't listen to me. I'm having trouble controlling my thinking.* Ah! There you are, Mr. Foyle. Where in the world have you been wandering?"

Foyle had jaunted in on the stage and stepped off quietly, his hideous face averted. "Been practicing, me," he mumbled.

Robin repressed the shudder of revulsion in her and went to him sympathetically. She took his arm. "You really should be with us more. We're all friends and having a lovely time. Join in."

Foyle refused to meet her glance. As he pulled his arm away from her sullenly, Robin suddenly realized that his sleeve was soaking wet. His entire hospital uniform was drenched.

"Wet? He's been in the rain somewhere. But I've seen the morning weather reports. No rain east of St. Louis. Then he must have jaunted further than that. But he's not supposed to be able. He's supposed to have lost all memory and ability to jaunte. He's malingering."

Foyle leapt at her. "Shut up, you!" The savagery of his face was terrifying.

"Then you are malingering."

"How much do you know?"

"That you're a fool. Stop making a scene."

"Did they hear you?"

"I don't know. Let go of me." Robin turned away from Foyle. "All right, class. We're finished for the day. All back to school for the hospital bus. You jaunte first, Sgt. Logan. Remember: L-E-S. Location. Elevation. Situation . . ."

"What do you want?" Foyle growled, "A pay-off, you?"

"Be quiet. Stop making a scene. Now don't hesitate, Chief Harris. Step up and jaunte off."

"I want to talk to you."

"*Certainly not.* Wait your turn, Mr. Peters. Don't be in such a hurry."

"You going to report me in the hospital?"

"*Naturally.*"

"I want to talk to you."

"*No.*"

"They gone now, all. We got time. I'll meet you in your apartment."

"My apartment?" Robin was genuinely frightened.

"In Green Bay, Wisconsin."

"*This is absurd. I've got nothing to discuss with this—*"

"You got plenty, Miss Robin. You got a family to discuss."

Foyle grinned at the terror she radiated. "Meet you in your apartment," he repeated.

"You can't possibly know where it is," she faltered.

"Just told you, didn't I?"

"Y-You couldn't possibly jaunte that far. You—"

"No?" The mask grinned. "You just told me I was mal—that word. You told the truth, you. We got half an hour. Meet you there."

Robin Wednesbury's apartment was in a massive building set alone on the shore of Green Bay. The apartment house looked as though a magician had removed it from a city residential area and abandoned it amidst the Wisconsin pines. Buildings like this were a commonplace in the jaunting world. With self-contained heat and light plants, and jaunting to solve the transportation problem, single and multiple dwellings were built in desert, forest, and wilderness.

The apartment itself was a four-room flat, heavily insulated to protect neighbors from Robin's telesending. It was crammed with books, music, paintings, and prints . . . all evidence of the cultured and lonely life of this unfortunate wrong-way telepath.

Robin jaunted into the living room of the apartment a few seconds after Foyle who was waiting for her with ferocious impatience.

"So now you know for sure," he began without preamble. He seized her arm in a painful grip. "But you ain't gonna tell nobody in the hospital about me, Miss Robin. Nobody."

"Let go of me!" Robin lashed him across his face. "*Beast! Savage! Don't you dare touch me!*"

Foyle released her and stepped back. The impact of her revulsion made him turn away angrily to conceal his face.

"So you've been malingering. You knew how to jaunte. You've been jaunting all the while you've been pretending to learn in the primer class . . . taking big jumps around the country; around the world, for all I know."

"Yeah. I go from Times Square to Columbus Circle by way of . . . most anywhere, Miss Robin."

"And that's why you're always missing. But why? Why? What are you up to?"

An expression of possessed cunning appeared on the hideous face. "I'm holed up in General Hospital, me. It's my base of operations, see? I'm settling something, Miss Robin. I got a debt to pay off, me. I had to find out where a certain ship is. Now I got to pay her back. Not I rot you, 'Vorga.' I kill you, 'Vorga.' I kill you filthy!"

He stopped shouting and glared at her in wild triumph. Robin backed away in alarm.

"For God's sake, what are you talking about?"

"'Vorga.' 'Vorga-T:1339.' Ever hear of her, Miss Robin? I found out where she is from Bo'ness & Uig's ship registry. Bo'ness & Uig are out in SanFran. I went there, me, the time when you was learning us the crosstown jaunte stages. Went out to SanFran, me. Found 'Vorga,' me. She's in Vancouver shipyards. She's owned by Presteign of Presteign. Heard of him, Miss Robin? Presteign's the biggest man on Terra, is all. But he won't stop me. I'll kill 'Vorga' filthy. And you won't stop me neither, Miss Robin."

Foyle thrust his face close to hers. "Because I cover myself, Miss Robin. I cover every weak spot down the line. I got something on everybody who could stop me before I kill 'Vorga' . . . including you, Miss Robin."

"No."

"Yeah. I found out where you live. They know up at the hospital. I come here and looked around. I read your diary, Miss Robin. You got a family on Callisto, mother and two sisters."

"For God's sake!"

"So that makes you alien-belligerent. When the war started you and all the rest was given one month to get out of the Inner Planets and go home. Any which didn't became spies by law." Foyle opened his hand. "I got you right here, girl." He clenched his hand.

"My mother and sisters have been trying to leave Callisto for a year and a half. We belong here. We—"

"Got you right here," Foyle repeated. "You know what they do to spies? They cut information out of them. They cut you apart, Miss Robin. They take you apart, piece by piece—"

The Negro girl screamed. Foyle nodded happily and took her shaking shoulders in his hands. "I got you, is all, girl. You can't even run from me because all I got to do is tip Intelligence and where are you? There ain't nothing nobody can do to stop me; not the hospital or even Mr. Holy Mighty Presteign of Presteign."

"*Get out, you filthy, hideous . . . thing. Get out!*"

"You don't like my face, Miss Robin? There ain't nothing you can do about that either."

Suddenly he picked her up and carried her to a deep couch. He threw her down on the couch.

"Nothing," he repeated.

Devoted to the principle of conspicuous waste, on which all society is based, Presteign of Presteign had fitted his Victorian mansion in Central Park with elevators, house phones, dumb-waiters and all the other labor-saving devices which jaunting had made obsolete. The servants in that giant gingerbread castle walked dutifully from room to room, opening and closing doors, and climbing stairs.

Presteign of Presteign arose, dressed with the aid of his valet and barber, descended to the morning room with the aid of an elevator, and breakfasted, assisted by a butler, footman, and waitresses. He left the morning room and entered his study. In an age when communication systems were virtually extinct—when it was far easier to jaunte directly to a man's office for a discussion than to telephone or telegraph—Presteign still maintained an antique telephone switchboard with an operator in his study.

"Get me Dagenham," he said.

The operator struggled and at last put a call through to Dagenham Couriers, Inc. This was a hundred million credit organization of bonded jaunters guaranteed to perform any public or confidential service for any principal. Their fee was ¢r 1 per mile. Dagenham guaranteed to get a courier around the world in eighty minutes.

Eighty seconds after Presteign's call was put through, a Dagenham courier appeared on the private jaunte stage outside Presteign's home, was identified and admitted through the jaunte-proof labyrinth behind the entrance. Like every member of the Dagenham staff, he was an M class jaunter, capable of teleporting a thousand miles a jump indefinitely, and familiar with thousands of jaunte co-ordinates. He was a senior specialist in chicanery and cajolery, trained to the incisive efficiency and boldness that characterized Dagenham Couriers and reflected the ruthlessness of its founder.

"Presteign?" he said, wasting no time on protocol.

"I want to hire Dagenham."

"Ready, Presteign."

"Not you. I want Saul Dagenham himself."

"Mr. Dagenham no longer gives personal service for less than ¢r 100,000."

"The amount will be five times that."

"Fee or percentage?"

"Both. Quarter of a million fee, and a quarter of a million guaranteed against 10 per cent of the total amount at risk."

"Agreed. The matter?"

"PyrE."

"Spell it, please."

"The name means nothing to you?"

"No."

"Good. It will to Dagenham. PyrE. Capital P-y-r Capital E. Pronounced "pyre" as in funeral pyre. Tell Dagenham we've located the PyrE. He's engaged to get it . . . at all costs . . . through a man named Foyle. Gulliver Foyle."

The courier produced a tiny silver pearl, a memo-bead, repeated Presteign's instructions into it, and left without another word. Presteign turned to his telephone operator. "Get me Regis Sheffield," he directed.

Ten minutes after the call went through to Regis Sheffield's law office, a young law clerk appeared on Presteign's private jaunte stage, was vetted and admitted through the maze. He was a bright young man with a scrubbed face and the expression of a delighted rabbit.

"Excuse the delay, Presteign," he said. "We got your call in Chicago and I'm still only a D class five hundred miler. Took me a while getting here."

"Is your chief trying a case in Chicago?"

"Chicago, New York *and* Washington. He's been on the jaunte from court to court all morning. We fill in for him when he's in another court."

"I want to retain him."

"Honored, Presteign, but Mr. Sheffield's pretty busy."

"Not too busy for PyrE."

"Sorry, sir; I don't quite—"

"No, you don't, but Sheffield will. Just tell him: PyrE as in funeral pyre, and the amount of his fee."

"Which is?"

"Quarter of a million retainer and a quarter of a million guaranteed against 10 per cent of the total amount at risk."

"And what performance is required of Mr. Sheffield?"

"To prepare every known legal device for kidnaping a man and holding him against the army, the navy and the police."

"Quite. And the man?"

"Gulliver Foyle."

The law clerk muttered quick notes into a memo-bead, thrust the bead into his ear, listened, nodded and departed. Presteign left the study and ascended the plush stairs to his daughter's suite to pay his morning respects.

In the homes of the wealthy, the rooms of the female members were blind, without windows or doors, open only to the jaunting of intimate members of the family. Thus was morality maintained and chastity defended. But since Olivia Presteign was herself blind to normal sight, she could not jaunte. Consequently her suite was entered through doors closely guarded by ancient retainers in the Presteign clan livery.

Olivia Presteign was a glorious albino. Her hair was white silk, her skin was white satin, her nails, her lips, and her eyes were coral. She was beautiful and blind in a wonderful way, for she could see in the infrared only, from 7,500 angstroms to one millimeter wavelengths. She saw heat waves, magnetic fields, radio waves, radar, sonar, and electromagnetic fields.

She was holding her Grand Levee in the drawing room of the suite. She sat in a brocaded wing chair, sipping tea, guarded by her duenna, holding court, chatting with a dozen men and women standing about the room. She looked like an exquisite statue of marble and coral, her blind eyes flashing as she saw and yet did not see.

She saw the drawing room as a pulsating flow of heat emanations ranging from hot highlights to cool shadows. She saw the dazzling magnetic patterns of clocks, phones, lights, and locks. She saw and recognized people by the characteristic heat patterns radiated by their faces and bodies. She saw, around each head, an aura of the faint electromagnetic brain pattern, and sparkling through the heat radiation of each body, the everchanging tone of muscle and nerve.

Presteign did not care for the artists, musicians, and fops Olivia kept about her, but he was pleased to see a scattering of society notables this morning. There was a Sears-Roebuck, a Gillet, young Sidney Kodak who would one day be Kodak of Kodak, a Houbigant, Buick of Buick, and R. H. Macy XVI, head of the powerful Saks-Gimbel clan.

Presteign paid his respects to his daughter and left the house. He set off for his clan headquarters at 99 Wall Street in a coach and four driven by a coachman assisted by a groom, both wearing the Presteign trademark of red, black, and blue. That black "P" on a field of scarlet and cobalt was one of the most ancient and distinguished trademarks in the social register, rivaling the "57" of the Heinz clan and the "RR" of the Rolls-Royce dynasty in antiquity.

The head of the Presteign clan was a familiar sight to New York jaunters. Iron gray, handsome, powerful, impeccably dressed and mannered in the old-fashioned style, Presteign of Presteign was the epitome of the socially elect, for he was so exalted in station that he employed coachmen, grooms, hostlers, stableboys, and horses to perform a function for him which ordinary mortals performed by jaunting.

As men climbed the social ladder, they displayed their position by their refusal to jaunte. The newly adopted into a great commercial clan rode an expensive bicycle. A rising clansman drove a small sports car. The captain of a sept was transported in a chauffeur-driven antique from the old days, a vintage Bentley or Cadillac or a towering Lagonda. An heir presumptive in direct line of succession to the clan chieftainship staffed a yacht or a plane. Presteign of Presteign, head of the clan Presteign, owned carriages, cars, yachts, planes, and trains. His position in society was so lofty that he had not jaunted in forty years. Secretly he scorned the bustling new-rich like the Dagenhams and Sheffields who still jaunted and were unshamed.

Presteign entered the crenelated keep at 99 Wall Street that was Castle Presteign. It was staffed and guarded by his famous Jaunte-Watch, all in clan livery. Presteign walked with the stately gait of a chieftain as they piped him to his office. Indeed he was grander than a chieftain, as an importunate government official awaiting audience discovered to his dismay. That unfortunate man leaped forward from the waiting crowd of petitioners as Presteign passed.

"Mr. Presteign," he began. "I'm from the Internal Revenue Department, I must see you this morn—" Presteign cut him short with an icy stare.

"There are thousands of Presteigns," he pronounced. "All are addressed as Mister. But I am Presteign of Presteign, head of house and sept, first of the family, chieftain of the clan. I am addressed as Presteign. Not 'Mister' Presteign. Presteign."

He turned and entered his office where his staff greeted him with a muted chorus: "Good morning, Presteign."

Presteign nodded, smiled his basilisk smile and seated himself behind the enthroned desk while the Jaunte-Watch skirled their pipes and ruffled their drums. Presteign signaled for the audience to begin. The Household Equerry stepped forward with a scroll. Presteign disdained memo-beads and all mechanical business devices.

"Report on Clan Presteign enterprises," the Equerry began. "Common

Stock: High—201½, Low—201¼. Average quotations New York, Paris, Ceylon, Tokyo—"

Presteign waved his hand irritably. The Equerry retired to be replaced by Black Rod.

"Another Mr. Presto to be invested, Presteign."

Presteign restrained his impatience and went through the tedious ceremony of swearing in the 497th Mr. Presto in the hierarchy of Presteign Prestos who managed the shops in the Presteign retail division. Until recently the man had had a face and body of his own. Now, after years of cautious testing and careful indoctrination, he had been elected to join the prestos.

After six months of surgery and psycho-conditioning, he was identical with the other 496 Mr. Prestos and to the idealized portrait of Mr. Presto which hung behind Presteign's dais . . . a kindly, honest man resembling Abraham Lincoln, a man who instantly inspired affection and trust. Around the world purchasers entered an identical Presteign store and were greeted by an identical manager, Mr. Presto. He was rivaled, but not surpassed, by the Kodak clan's Mr. Kwik and Montgomery Ward's Uncle Monty.

When the ceremony was completed, Presteign arose abruptly to indicate that the public investiture was ended. The office was cleared of all but the high officials. Presteign paced, obviously repressing his seething impatience. He never swore, but his restraint was more terrifying than profanity.

"Foyle," he said in a suffocated voice. "A common sailor. Dirt. Dregs. Gutter scum. But that man stands between me and—"

"If you please, Presteign," Black Rod interrupted timidly. "It's eleven o'clock Eastern time; eight o'clock Pacific time."

"What?"

"If you please, Presteign, may I remind you that there is a launching ceremony at nine, Pacific time? You are to preside at the Vancouver shipyards."

"Launching?"

"Our new freighter, the Presteign 'Princess.' It will take some time to establish three dimensional broadcast contact with the shipyard so we had better—"

"I will attend in person."

"In person!" Black Rod faltered. "But we cannot possibly fly to Vancouver in an hour, Presteign. We—"

"I will jaunte," Presteign of Presteign snapped. Such was his agitation.

His appalled staff made hasty preparations. Messengers jaunted ahead to warn the Presteign offices across the country, and the private jaunte stages were cleared. Presteign was ushered to the stage within his New York office. It was a circular platform in a black-hung room without windows—a masking and concealment necessary to prevent unauthorized persons from discovering and memorizing co-ordinates. For the same reason, all homes and offices had one-way windows and confusion labyrinths behind their doors.

To jaunte it was necessary (among other things) for a man to know exactly where he was and where he was going, or there was little hope of arriving anywhere alive. It was as impossible to jaunte from an undetermined starting point as it was to arrive at an unknown destination. Like shooting a pistol, one had to know where to aim and which end of the gun to hold. But a glance through a window or door might be enough to enable a man to memorize the L-E-S co-ordinates of a place.

Presteign stepped on the stage, visualized the co-ordinates of his destination in the Philadelphia office, seeing the picture clearly and the position accurately. He relaxed and energized one concentrated thrust of will and belief toward the target. He jaunted. There was a dizzy moment in which his eyes blurred. The New York stage faded out of focus; the Philadelphia stage blurred into focus. There was a sensation of falling down, and then up. He arrived. Black Rod and others of his staff arrived a respectful moment later.

So, in jauntes of one and two hundred miles each, Presteign crossed the continent, and arrived outside the Vancouver shipping yards at exactly nine o'clock in the morning, Pacific time. He had left New York at 11 A.M. He had gained two hours of daylight. This, too, was a commonplace in a jaunting world.

The square mile of unfenced concrete (what fence could bar a jaunter?) comprising the shipyard, looked like a white table covered with black pennies neatly arranged in concentric circles. But on closer approach, the pennies enlarged into the hundred-foot mouths of black pits dug deep into the bowels of the earth. Each circular mouth was rimmed with concrete buildings, offices, check rooms, canteens, changing rooms.

These were the take-off and landing pits, the drydock and construction pits of the shipyards. Spaceships, like sailing vessels, were never designed to support their own weight unaided against the drag of gravity. Normal terran gravity would crack the spine of a spaceship like an eggshell. The ships were built in deep pits, standing vertically in a network of catwalks and construction grids, braced and supported by anti-gravity screens. They took off from similar pits, riding the anti-grav beams upward like motes mounting the vertical shaft of a searchlight until at last they reached the Roche Limit and could thrust with their own jets. Landing spacecraft cut drive jets and rode the same beams downward into the pits.

As the Presteign entourage entered the Vancouver yards they could see which of the pits were in use. From some the noses and hulls of spaceships extruded, raised a quarterway or halfway above ground by the anti-grav screen as workmen in the pits below brought their aft sections to particular operational levels. Three Presteign V-class transports, "Vega," "Vestal," and "Vorga," stood partially raised near the center of the yards, undergoing flaking and replating, as the heat-lightning flicker of torches around "Vorga" indicated.

At the concrete building marked: ENTRY, the Presteign entourage stopped before a sign that read:

YOU ARE ENDANGERING YOUR LIFE
IF YOU ENTER THESE PREMISES UN-
LAWFULLY. *YOU HAVE BEEN WARNED!*

Visitor badges were distributed to the party, and even Presteign of Presteign received a badge. He dutifully pinned it on for he well knew what the result of entry without such a protective badge would be. The entourage continued, winding its way through pits until it arrived at o-3, where the pit mouth was decorated with bunting in the Presteign colors and a small grandstand had been erected.

Presteign was welcomed and, in turn, greeted his various officials. The Presteign band struck up the clan song, bright and brassy, but one of the instruments appeared to have gone insane. It struck a brazen note that blared louder and louder until it engulfed the entire band and the surprised exclamations. Only then did Presteign realize that it was not an instrument sounding, but the shipyard alarm.

An intruder was in the yard, someone not wearing an identification or visitor's badge. The radar field of the protection system was tripped and the alarm sounded. Through the raucous bellow of the alarm, Presteign could hear a multitude of "pops" as the yard guards jaunted from the grandstand and took positions around the square mile of concrete field. His own Jaunte-Watch closed in around him, looking wary and alert.

A voice began blaring on the P.A., co-ordinating defense. "UNKNOWN IN YARD. UNKNOWN IN YARD AT E FOR EDWARD NINE. E FOR EDWARD NINE MOVING WEST ON FOOT."

"Someone must have broken in," Black Rod shouted.

"I'm aware of that," Presteign answered calmly.

"He must be a stranger if he's not jaunting in here."

"I'm aware of that also."

"UNKNOWN APPROACHING D FOR DAVID FIVE. D FOR DAVID FIVE. STILL ON FOOT. D FOR DAVID FIVE ALERT."

"What in God's name is he up to?" Black Rod exclaimed.

"You are aware of my rule, sir," Presteign said coldly. "No associate of the Presteign clan may take the name of the Divinity in vain. You forget yourself."

"UNKNOWN NOW APPROACHING C FOR CHARLEY FIVE. NOW APPROACHING C FOR CHARLEY FIVE."

Black Rod touched Presteign's arm. "He's coming this way, Presteign. Will you take cover, please?"

"I will not."

"Presteign, there have been assassination attempts before. Three of them. If—"

"How do I get to the top of this stand?"

"Presteign!"

"Help me up."

Aided by Black Rod, still protesting hysterically, Presteign climbed to the top of the grandstand to watch the power of the Presteign clan in action against danger. Below he could see workmen in white jumpers swarming out of the pits to watch the excitement. Guards were appearing as they jaunted from distant sectors toward the focal point of the action.

"UNKNOWN MOVING SOUTH TOWARD B FOR BAKER THREE. B FOR BAKER THREE."

Presteign watched the B-3 pit. A figure appeared, dashing swiftly toward the pit, veering, dodging, bulling forward. It was a giant man in hospital blues with a wild thatch of black hair and a distorted face that appeared, in the distance, to be painted in livid colors. His clothes were flickering like heat lightning as the protective induction field of the defense system seared him.

"B FOR BAKER THREE ALERT. B FOR BAKER THREE CLOSE IN."

There were shouts and a distant rattle of shots, the pneumatic whine of scope guns. Half a dozen workmen in white leaped for the intruder. He scattered them like ninepins and drove on and on toward B-3 where the nose of "Vorga" showed. He was a lightning bolt driving through workmen and guards, pivoting, bludgeoning, boring forward implacably.

Suddenly he stopped, reached inside his flaming jacket and withdrew a black cannister. With the convulsive gesture of an animal writhing in death throes, he bit the end of the cannister and hurled it, straight and true on a high arc toward "Vorga." The next instant he was struck down.

"EXPLOSIVE. TAKE COVER. EXPLOSIVE. TAKE COVER. COVER."

"Presteign!" Black Rod squawked.

Presteign shook him off and watched the cannister curve up and then down toward the nose of "Vorga," spinning and glinting in the cold sunlight. At the edge of the pit it was caught by the anti-grav beam and flicked upward as by a giant invisible thumbnail. Up and up and up it whirled, one hundred, five hundred, a thousand feet. Then there was a blinding flash, and an instant later a titanic clap of thunder that smote ears and jarred teeth and bone.

Presteign picked himself up and descended the grandstand to the launching podium. He placed his finger on the launching button of the Presteign "Princess."

"Bring me that man, if he's still alive," he said to Black Rod. He pressed the button. "I christen thee . . . the Presteign 'Power,'" he called in triumph.

CHAPTER FOUR

THE STAR CHAMBER in Castle Presteign was an oval room with ivory panels picked out with gold, high mirrors, and stained glass windows. It contained a gold organ with robot organist by Tiffany, a gold-tooled library with android librarian on library ladder, a Louis Quinze desk with android secretary before a manual memo-bead recorder, an American bar with robot bartender. Presteign would have preferred human servants, but androids and robots kept secrets.

"Be seated, Captain Yeovil," he said courteously. "This is Mr. Regis Sheffield, representing me in this matter. That young man is Mr. Sheffield's assistant."

"Bunny's my portable law library," Sheffield grunted.

Presteign touched a control. The still life in the star chamber came alive. The organist played, the librarian sorted books, the secretary typed, the bartender shook drinks. It was spectacular; and the impact, carefully calculated by industrial psychometrists, established control for Presteign and put visitors at a disadvantage.

"You spoke of a man named Foyle, Captain Yeovil?" Presteign prompted.

Captain Peter Y'ang-Yeovil of Central Intelligence was a lineal descendant of the learned Mencius and belonged to the Intelligence Tong of the Inner Planets Armed Forces. For two hundred years the IPAF had entrusted its intelligence work to the Chinese who, with a five thousand-year history of cultivated subtlety behind them, had achieved wonders. Captain Y'ang-Yeovil was a member of the dreaded Society of Paper Men, an adept of the Tientsin Image Makers, a Master of Superstition, and fluent in the Secret Speech. He did not look Chinese.

Y'ang-Yeovil hesitated, fully aware of the psychological pressures operating against him. He examined Presteign's ascetic, basilisk face; Sheffield's blunt, aggressive expression; and the eager young man named Bunny whose rabbit features had an unmistakable Oriental cast. It was necessary for Yeovil to re-establish control or effect a compromise.

He opened with a flanking movement. "Are we related anywhere within fifteen degrees of consanguinity?" he asked Bunny in the Mandarin dialect. "I am of the house of the learned Meng-Tse whom the barbarians call Mencius."

"Then we are hereditary enemies," Bunny answered in faltering Mandarin. "For the formidable ancestor of my line was deposed as governor of Shantung in 342 B.C. by the earth pig Meng-Tse."

"With all courtesy I shave your ill-formed eyebrows," Y'ang-Yeovil said.

"Most respectfully I singe your snaggle teeth." Bunny laughed.

"Come, sirs," Presteign protested.

"We are reaffirming a three thousand-year blood feud," Y'ang-Yeovil explained to Presteign, who looked sufficiently unsettled by the conversation and the laughter which he did not understand. He tried a direct thrust. "When will you be finished with Foyle?" he asked.

"What Foyle?" Sheffield cut in.

"What Foyle have you got?"

"There are thirteen of that name associated with the clan Presteign."

"An interesting number. Did you know I was a Master of Superstition? Some day I must show you the Mirror-And-Listen Mystery. I refer to the Foyle involved in a reported attempt on Mr. Presteign's life this morning."

"Presteign," Presteign corrected. "I am not 'Mister.' I am Presteign of Presteign."

"Three attempts have been made on Presteign's life," Sheffield said. "You'll have to be more specific."

"Three this morning? Presteign must have been busy." Y'ang-Yeovil sighed. Sheffield was proving himself a resolute opponent. The Intelligence man tried another diversion. "I do wish our Mr. Presto had been more specific."

"*Your* Mr. Presto!" Presteign exclaimed.

"Oh yes. Didn't you know one of your five hundred Prestos was an agent of ours? That's odd. We took it for granted you'd find out and went ahead with a confusion operation."

Presteign looked appalled. Y'ang-Yeovil crossed his legs and continued to chat breezily. "That's the basic weakness in routine intelligence procedure; you start finessing before finesse is required."

"He's bluffing," Presteign burst out. "None of our Prestos could possibly have any knowledge of Gulliver Foyle."

"Thank you." Y'ang-Yeovil smiled. "That's the Foyle I want. When can you let us have him?"

Sheffield scowled at Presteign and then turned on Y'ang-Yeovil. "Who's 'us'?" he demanded.

"Central Intelligence."

"Why do you want him?"

"Do you make love to a woman before or after you take your clothes off?"

"That's a damned impertinent question to ask."

"And so was yours. When can you let us have Foyle?"

"When you show cause."

"To whom?"

"To me." Sheffield hammered a heavy forefinger against his palm. "This is a civilian matter concerning civilians. Unless war material, war personnel, or the strategy and tactics of a war-in-being are involved, civilian jurisdiction shall always prevail."

"303 Terran Appeals 191," murmured Bunny.

"The 'Nomad' was carrying war material."

"The 'Nomad' was transporting platinum bullion to Mars Bank," Presteign snapped. "If money is a—"

"*I* am leading this discussion," Sheffield interrupted. He swung around on Y'ang-Yeovil. "Name the war material."

This blunt challenge knocked Y'ang-Yeovil off balance. He knew that the crux of the "Nomad" situation was the presence on board the ship of 20 pounds of PyrE, the total world supply, which was probably irreplaceable now that its discoverer had disappeared. He knew that Sheffield knew that they both knew this. He had assumed that Sheffield would prefer to keep PyrE unnamed. And yet, here was the challenge to name the unnamable.

He attempted to meet bluntness with bluntness. "All right, gentlemen, I'll name it now. The 'Nomad' was transporting twenty pounds of a substance called PyrE."

Presteign started; Sheffield silenced him. "What's PyrE?"

"According to our reports—"

"From Presteign's Mr. Presto?"

"Oh, that was bluff," Y'ang-Yeovil laughed, and momentarily regained control. "According to Intelligence, PyrE was developed for Presteign by a man who subsequently disappeared. PyrE is a Misch Metal, a pyrophore. That's all we know for a fact. But we've had vague reports about it . . . Unbelievable reports from reputable agents. If a fraction of our inferences are correct, PyrE could make the difference between a victory and a defeat."

"Nonsense. No war materiel has ever made that much difference."

"No? I cite the fission bomb of 1945. I cite the Null-G anti-gravity installations of 2022. Talley's All-Field Radar Trip Screen of 2194. Material can often make the difference, especially when there's the chance of the enemy getting it first."

"There's no such chance now."

"Thank you for admitting the importance of PyrE."

"I admit nothing; I deny everything."

"Central Intelligence is prepared to offer an exchange. A man for a man. The inventor of PyrE for Gully Foyle."

"You've got him?" Sheffield demanded. "Then why badger us for Foyle?"

"Because we've got a corpse!" Y'ang-Yeovil flared. "The Outer Satellites command had him on Lassell for six months trying to carve information out of him. We pulled him out with a raid at a cost of 79 per cent casualties. We rescued a corpse. We still don't know if the Outer Satellites were having a cynical laugh at our expense letting us recapture a body. We still don't know how much they ripped out of him."

Presteign sat bolt upright at this. His merciless fingers tapped slowly and sharply.

"Damn it," Y'ang-Yeovil stormed. "Can't you recognize a crisis, Sheffield? We're on a tightrope. What the devil are you doing backing Presteign in this shabby deal? You're the leader of the Liberal party . . . Terra's archpatriot. You're Presteign's political archenemy. Sell him out, you fool, before he sells us all out."

"Captain Yeovil," Presteign broke in with icy venom. "These expressions cannot be countenanced."

"We want and need PyrE," Y'ang-Yeovil continued. "We'll have to investigate that twenty pounds of PyrE, rediscover the synthesis, learn to apply it to the war effort . . . and all this before the O.S. beats us to the punch, if they haven't already. But Presteign refuses to co-operate. Why? Because he's opposed to the party in power. He wants no military victories for the Liberals. He'd rather we lost the war for the sake of politics because rich men like Presteign never lose. Come to your senses, Sheffield. You've been retained by a traitor. What in God's name are you trying to do?"

Before Sheffield could answer, there was a discreet tap on the door of the Star Chamber and Saul Dagenham was ushered in. Time was when Dagenham was one of the Inner Planets' research wizards, a physicist with inspired intuition, total recall, and a sixth-order computer for a brain. But there was an accident at Tycho Sands, and the fission blast that should have killed him did not. Instead it turned him dangerously radioactive; it turned him "hot"; it transformed him into a twenty-fourth century "Typhoid Mary."

He was paid ¢r 25,000 a year by the Inner planets government to take precautions which they trusted him to carry out. He avoided physical contact with any person for more than five minutes per day. He could not occupy any room other than his own for more than thirty minutes a day. Commanded and paid by the IP to isolate himself, Dagenham had abandoned research and built the colossus of Dagenham Couriers, Inc.

When Y'ang-Yeovil saw the short blond cadaver with leaden skin and death's-head smile enter the Star Chamber, he knew he was assured of defeat in this encounter. He was no match for the three men together. He arose at once.

"I'm getting an Admiralty order for Foyle," he said. "As far as Intelligence is concerned, all negotiations are ended. From now on it's war."

"Captain Yeovil is leaving," Presteign called to the Jaunte-Watch officer who had guided Dagenham in. "Please see him out through the maze."

Y'ang-Yeovil waited until the officer stepped alongside him and bowed. Then, as the man courteously motioned to the door, Y'ang-Yeovil looked directly at Presteign, smiled ironically, and disappeared with a faint Pop!

"Presteign!" Bunny exclaimed. "He jaunted. This room isn't blind to him. He—"

"Evidently," Presteign said icily. "Inform the Master of the Household," he instructed the amazed Watch officer. "The co-ordinates of the Star Chamber are no longer secret. They must be changed within twenty-four hours. And now, Mr. Dagenham . . ."

"One minute," Dagenham said. "There's that Admiralty order."

Without apology or explanation he disappeared too. Presteign raised his eyebrows. "Another party to the Star Chamber secret," he murmured. "But at least he had the tact to conceal his knowledge until the secret was out."

Dagenham reappeared. "No point wasting time going through the motions of the maze," he said. "I've given orders in Washington. They'll hold Yeovil up; two hours guaranteed, three hours probably, four hours possible."

"How will they hold him up?" Bunny asked.

Dagenham gave him his deadly smile. "Standard FFCC Operation of Dagenham Couriers. Fun, fantasy, confusion, catastrophe. . . . We'll need all four hours. Damn! I've disrupted your dolls, Presteign." The robots were suddenly capering in lunatic fashion as Dagenham's hard radiation penetrated their electronic systems. "No matter, I'll be on my way."

"Foyle?" Presteign asked.

"Nothing yet." Dagenham grinned his death's-head smile. "He's really unique. I've tried all the standard drugs and routines on him . . . Nothing. Outside, he's just an ordinary spaceman . . . if you forget the tattoo on his face . . . but inside he's got steel guts. Something's got hold of him and he won't give."

"What's got hold of him?" Sheffield asked.

"I hope to find out."

"How?"

"Don't ask; you'd be an accessory. Have you got a ship ready, Presteign?"

Presteign nodded.

"I'm not guaranteeing there'll be any 'Nomad' for us to find, but we'll have to get a jump on the navy if there is. Law ready, Sheffield?"

"Ready. I'm hoping we won't have to use it."

"I'm hoping too; but again, I'm not guaranteeing. All right. Stand by for instructions. I'm on my way to crack Foyle."

"Where have you got him?"

Dagenham shook his head. "This room isn't secure." He disappeared.

He jaunted Cincinnati-New Orleans-Monterey to Mexico City, where he appeared in the Psychiatry Wing of the giant hospital of the Combined Terran Universities. Wing was hardly an adequate name for this section which occupied an entire city in the metropolis which was the hospital. Dagenham jaunted up to the 43rd floor of the Therapy Division and looked into the isolated tank where Foyle floated, unconscious. He glanced at the distinguished bearded gentlemen in attendance.

"Hello, Fritz."

"Hello, Saul."

"Hell of a thing, the Head of Psychiatry minding a patient for me."

"I think we owe you favors, Saul."

"You still brooding about Tycho Sands, Fritz? I'm not. Am I lousing your wing with radiation?"

"I've had everything shielded."

"Ready for the dirty work?"

"I wish I knew what you were after."

"Information."

"And you have to turn my therapy department into an inquisition to get it?"

"That was the idea."

"Why not use ordinary drugs?"

"Tried them already. No good. He's not an ordinary man."

"You know this is illegal."

"I know. Changed your mind? Want to back out? I can duplicate your equipment for a quarter of a million."

"No, Saul. We'll always owe you favors."

"Then let's go. Nightmare Theater first."

They trundled the tank down a corridor and into a hundred feet square padded room. It was one of therapy's by-passed experiments. Nightmare Theater had been an early attempt to shock schizophrenics back into the objective world by rendering the phantasy world into which they were withdrawing uninhabitable. But the shattering and laceration of patients' emotions had proved to be too cruel and dubious a treatment.

For Dagenham's sake, the head of Psychiatry had dusted off the 3D visual projectors and reconnected all sensory projectors. They decanted Foyle from his tank, gave him a reviving shot and left him in the middle of the floor. They removed the tank, turned off the lights and entered the concealed control booth. There, they turned on the projectors.

Every child in the world imagines that its phantasy world is unique to itself. Psychiatry knows that the joys and terrors of private phantasies are a common heritage shared by all mankind. Fears, guilts, terrors, and shames could be interchanged, from one man to the next, and none would notice the difference. The therapy department at Combined Hospital had recorded thousands of emotional tapes and boiled them down to one all-inclusive all-terrifying performance in Nightmare Theater.

Foyle awoke, panting and sweating, and never knew that he had awakened. He was in the clutch of the serpent-haired bloody-eyed Eumenides. He was pursued, entrapped, precipitated from heights, burned, flayed, bowstringed, vermin-covered, devoured. He screamed. He ran. The radar Hobble-Field in the Theater clogged his steps and turned them into the ghastly slow motion of dream-running. And through the cacophony of grinding, shrieking, moaning, pursuing that assailed his ears, muttered the thread of a persistent voice.

"Where is 'Nomad' where is 'Nomad' where is 'Nomad' where is 'Nomad' where is 'Nomad'?"

" 'Vorga,' " Foyle croaked. " 'Vorga.' "

He had been inoculated by his own fixation. His own nightmare had rendered him immune.

"Where is 'Nomad'? where have you left 'Nomad'? what happened to 'Nomad'? where is 'Nomad'?"

" 'Vorga,' " Foyle shouted. " 'Vorga.' 'Vorga.' 'Vorga.' "

In the control booth, Dagenham swore. The head of psychiatry, monitoring the projectors, glanced at the clock. "One minute and forty-five seconds, Saul. He can't stand much more."

"He's got to break. Give him the final effect."

They buried Foyle alive, slowly, inexorably, hideously. He was carried down into black depths and enclosed in stinking slime that cut off light and air. He slowly suffocated while a distant voice boomed: "WHERE IS 'NOMAD'? WHERE HAVE YOU LEFT 'NOMAD'? YOU CAN ESCAPE IF YOU FIND 'NOMAD.' WHERE IS 'NOMAD'?"

But Foyle was back aboard "Nomad" in his lightless, airless coffin, floating comfortably between deck and roof. He curled into a tight foetal ball and prepared to sleep. He was content. He would escape. He would find "Vorga."

"Impervious bastard!" Dagenham swore. "Has anyone ever resisted Nightmare Theater before, Fritz?"

"Not many. You're right. That's an uncommon man, Saul."

"He's got to be ripped open. All right, to hell with any more of this. We'll try the Megal Mood next. Are the actors ready?"

"All ready."

"Then let's go."

There are six directions in which delusions of grandeur can run. The Megal (short for Megalomania) Mood was therapy's dramatic diagnosis technique for establishing and plotting the particular course of megalomania.

Foyle awoke in a luxurious four-poster bed. He was in a bedroom hung with brocade, papered in velvet. He glanced around curiously. Soft sunlight filtered through latticed windows. Across the room a valet was quietly laying out clothes.

"Hey . . ." Foyle grunted.

The valet turned. "Good morning, Mr. Fourmyle," he murmured.

"What?"

"It's a lovely morning, sir. I've laid out the brown twill and the cordovan pumps, sir."

"What's a matter, you?"

"I've—" The valet gazed at Foyle curiously. "Is anything wrong, Mr. Fourmyle?"

"What you call me, man?"

"By your name, sir."

"My name is . . . Fourmyle?" Foyle struggled up in the bed. "No, it's not. It's Foyle. Gully Foyle, that's my name, me."

The valet bit his lip. "One moment, sir . . ." He stepped outside and called. Then he murmured. A lovely girl in white came running into the bedroom and sat down on the edge of the bed. She took Foyle's hands and gazed into his eyes. Her face was distressed.

"Darling, darling, darling," she whispered. "You aren't going to start all that again, are you? The doctor swore you were over it."

"Start what again?"

"All that Gulliver Foyle nonsense about your being a common sailor and—"

"I am Gully Foyle. That's my name, Gully Foyle."

"Sweetheart, you're not. That's just a delusion you've had for weeks. You've been overworking and drinking too much."

"Been Gully Foyle all my life, me."

"Yes, I know darling. That's the way it's seemed to you. But you're not. You're Geoffrey Fourmyle. *The* Geoffrey Fourmyle. You're— Oh, what's the sense telling you? Get dressed, my love. You've got to come downstairs. Your office has been frantic."

Foyle permitted the valet to dress him and went downstairs in a daze. The lovely girl, who evidently adored him, conducted him through a giant studio littered with drawing tables, easels, and half-finished canvases. She took him into a vast hall filled with desks, filing cabinets, stock tickers, clerks, secretaries, office personnel. They entered a lofty laboratory cluttered with glass and chrome. Burners flickered and hissed; bright colored liquids bubbled and churned; there was a pleasant odor of interesting chemicals and odd experiments.

"What's all this?" Foyle asked.

The girl seated Foyle in a plush armchair alongside a giant desk littered with interesting papers scribbled with fascinating symbols. On some Foyle saw the name: Geoffrey Fourmyle, scrawled in an imposing, authoritative signature.

"There's some crazy kind of mistake, is all," Foyle began.

The girl silenced him. "Here's Doctor Regan. He'll explain."

An impressive gentleman with a crisp, comforting manner, came to Foyle, touched his pulse, inspected his eyes, and nodded in satisfaction.

"Good," he said. "Excellent. You are close to complete recovery, Mr. Fourmyle. Now you will listen to me for a moment, eh?"

Foyle nodded.

"You remember nothing of the past. You have only a false memory. You were overworked. You are an important man and there were too many demands on you. You started to drink heavily a month ago— No, no, denial is useless. You drank. You lost yourself."

"I—"

"You became convinced you were not the famous Jeff Fourmyle. An infantile attempt to escape responsibility. You imagined you were a common spaceman named Foyle. Gulliver Foyle, yes? With an odd number . . ."

"Gully Foyle. AS:128/127:006. But that's me. That's—"

"It is not you. *This* is you." Dr. Regan waved at the interesting offices they could see through the transparent glass wall.

"You can only recapture the true memory if you discharge the old. All this glorious reality is yours, if we can help you discard the dream of the spaceman." Dr. Regan leaned forward, his polished spectacles glittering hypnotically. "Reconstruct this false memory of yours in detail, and I will tear it down. Where do you imagine you left the spaceship 'Nomad'? How did you escape? Where do you imagine the 'Nomad' is now?"

Foyle wavered before the romantic glamour of the scene which seemed to be just within his grasp.

"It seems to me I left 'Nomad' out in—" He stopped short.

A devil-face peered at him from the highlights reflected in Dr. Regan's spectacles . . . a hideous tiger mask with NOMAD blazoned across the distorted brow. Foyle stood up.

"Liars!" he growled. "It's real, me. This here is phoney. What happened to me is real. I'm real, me."

Saul Dagenham walked into the laboratory. "All right," he called. "Strike. It's a washout."

The bustling scene in laboratory, office, and studio ended. The actors quietly disappeared without another glance at Foyle. Dagenham gave Foyle his deadly smile. "Tough, aren't you? You're really unique. My name is Saul Dagenham. We've got five minutes for a talk. Come into the garden."

The Sedative Garden atop the Therapy Building was a triumph of therapeutic planning. Every perspective, every color, every contour had been designed to placate hostility, soothe resistance, melt anger, evaporate hysteria, absorb melancholia and depression.

"Sit down," Dagenham said, pointing to a bench alongside a pool in which crystal waters tinkled. "Don't try to jaunte—you're drugged. I'll have to walk around a bit. Can't come too close to you. I'm 'hot.' D'you know what that means?"

Foyle shook his head sullenly. Dagenham cupped both hands around the flaming blossom of an orchid and held them there for a moment. "Watch that flower," he said. "You'll see."

He paced up a path and turned suddenly. "You're right, of course. Everything that happened to you is real. . . . Only what did happen?"

"Go to hell," Foyle growled.

"You know, Foyle, I admire you."

"Go to hell."

"In your own primitive way you've got ingenuity and guts. You're cro-Magnon, Foyle. I've been checking on you. That bomb you threw in the Presteign shipyards was lovely, and you nearly wrecked General Hospital getting the money and material together." Dagenham counted fingers. "You looted lockers, stole from the blind ward, stole drugs from the pharmacy, stole apparatus from the lab stockrooms."

"Go to hell, you."

"But what have you got against Presteign? Why'd you try to blow up his shipyard? They tell me you broke in and went tearing through the pits like a wild man. What were you trying to do, Foyle?"

"Go to hell."

Dagenham smiled. "If we're going to chat," he said. "You'll have to hold up your end. Your conversation's getting monotonous. What happened to 'Nomad'?"

"I don't know about 'Nomad,' nothing."

"The ship was last reported over seven months ago. Are you the sole survivor? And what have you been doing all this time? Having your face decorated?"

"I don't know about 'Nomad,' nothing."

"No, no, Foyle, that won't do. You show up with 'Nomad' tattooed across your face. Fresh tattooed. Intelligence checks and finds you were aboard 'Nomad' when she sailed. Foyle, Gulliver: AS:128/127:006, Mechanic's Mate, 3rd Class. As if all this isn't enough to throw Intelligence into a tizzy, you come back in a private launch that's been missing fifty years. Man, you're cooking in the reactor. Intelligence wants the answers to all these questions. And you ought to know how Central Intelligence butchers its answers out of people."

Foyle started. Dagenham nodded as he saw his point sink home. "Which is why I think you'll listen to reason. We want information, Foyle. I tried to trick it out of you; admitted. I failed because you're too tough; admitted. Now I'm offering an honest deal. We'll protect you if you'll co-operate. If you don't, you'll spend five years in an Intelligence lab having information chopped out of you."

It was not the prospect of the butchery that frightened Foyle, but the thought of the loss of freedom. A man had to be free to avenge himself, to raise money and find "Vorga" again, to rip and tear and gut "VORGA."

"What kind of deal?" he asked.

"Tell us what happened to 'Nomad' and where you left her."

"Why, man?"

"Why? Because of the salvage, man."

"There ain't nothing to salvage. She's a wreck, is all."

"Even a wreck's salvagable."

"You mean you'd jet out a million miles to pick up pieces? Don't joker me, man."

"All right," Dagenham said in exasperation. "There's the cargo."

"She was split wide open. No cargo left."

"It was a cargo you don't know about," Dagenham said confidentially. " 'Nomad' was transporting platinum bullion to Mars Bank. Every so often, banks have to adjust accounts. Normally, enough trade goes on between planets so that accounts can be balanced on paper. The war's disrupted normal trade, and Mars Bank found that Presteign owed them twenty odd million credits without any way of getting the money short of actual delivery. Presteign was delivering the money in bar platinum aboard the 'Nomad.' It was locked in the purser's safe."

"Twenty million," Foyle whispered.

"Give or take a few thousand. The ship was insured, but that just means that the underwriters, Bo'ness and Uig, get the salvage rights and they're even tougher than Presteign. However, there'll be a reward for you. Say . . . twenty thousand credits."

"Twenty million," Foyle whispered again.

"We're assuming that an O.S. raider caught up with 'Nomad' somewhere on course and let her have it. They couldn't have boarded and looted or you wouldn't have been left alive. This means that the purser's safe is still— Are you listening, Foyle?"

But Foyle was not listening. He was seeing twenty million . . . not twenty thousand . . . twenty million in platinum bullion as a broad highway to "Vorga." No more petty thefts from lockers and labs; twenty million for the taking and the razing of "Vorga."

"Foyle!"

Foyle awoke. He looked at Dagenham. "I don't know about 'Nomad,' nothing," he said.

"What the hell's got into you now? Why're you dummying up again?"

"I don't know about 'Nomad,' nothing."

"I'm offering a fair reward. A spaceman can go on a hell of a tear with twenty thousand credits . . . a one-year tear. What more do you want?"

"I don't know about 'Nomad,' nothing."

"It's us or Intelligence, Foyle."

"You ain't so anxious for them to get me, or you wouldn't be flipping through all this. But it ain't no use, anyway. I don't know about 'Nomad,' nothing."

"You son of a——" Dagenham tried to repress his anger. He had revealed just a little too much to this cunning, primitive creature. "You're right," he said. "We're not anxious for Intelligence to get you. But we've made our own preparations." His voice hardened. "You think you can dummy up and stand us off. You think you can leave us to whistle for 'Nomad.' You've even got an idea that you can beat us to the salvage."

"No," Foyle said.

"Now listen to this. We've got a lawyer waiting in New York. He's got a criminal prosecution for piracy pending against you; piracy in space, murder, and looting. We're going to throw the book at you. Presteign will get a conviction in twenty-four hours. If you've got a criminal record of any kind, that means a lobotomy. They'll open up the top of your skull and burn out half your brain to stop you from ever jaunting again."

Dagenham stopped and looked hard at Foyle. When Foyle shook his head, Dagenham continued.

"If you haven't got a record, they'll hand you ten years of what is laughingly known as medical treatment. We don't punish criminals in our enlightened age, we cure 'em; and the cure is worse than punishment. They'll stash you in a black hole in one of the cave hospitals. You'll be kept in permanent darkness and solitary confinement so you can't jaunte out. They'll go through the motions of giving you shots and therapy, but you'll be rotting in the dark. You'll stay there and rot until you decide to talk. We'll keep you there forever. So make up your mind."

"I don't know nothing about 'Nomad.' Nothing!" Foyle said.

"All right," Dagenham spat. Suddenly he pointed to the orchid blossom he had enclosed with his hands. It was blighted and rotting. "That's what's going to happen to you."

CHAPTER FIVE

SOUTH OF SAINT-GIRONS near the Spanish-French border is the deepest abyss in France, the Gouffre Martel. Its caverns twist for miles under the Pyrenees. It is the most formidable cavern hospital on Terra. No patient has ever jaunted out of its pitch darkness. No patient has ever succeeded in getting his bearings and learning the jaunte co-ordinates of the black hospital depths.

Short of prefrontal lobotomy, there are only three ways to stop a man from jaunting: a blow on the head producing concussion, sedation which prevents concentration, and concealment of jaunte co-ordinates. Of the three, the jaunting age considered concealment the most practical.

The cells that line the winding passages of Gouffre Martel are cut out of living rock. They are never illuminated. The passages are never illuminated. Infrared lamps flood the darkness. It is black light visible only to guards and attendants wearing snooper goggles with specially treated lenses. For the patients there is only the black silence of Gouffre Martel broken by the distant rush of underground waters.

For Foyle there was only the silence, the rushing, and the hospital routine. At eight o'clock (or it may have been any hour in this timeless abyss) he was awakened by a bell. He arose and received his morning meal, slotted into the cell by pneumatic tube. It had to be eaten at once, for the china surrogate of cups and plates was timed to dissolve in fifteen minutes. At eight-thirty the cell door opened and Foyle and hundreds of others shuffled blindly through the twisting corridors to Sanitation.

Here, still in darkness, they were processed like beef in a slaughter house: cleansed, shaved, irradiated, disinfected, dosed, and inoculated. Their paper uniforms were removed and sent back to the shops to be pulped. New uniforms were issued. Then they shuffled back to their cells which had been automatically scrubbed out while they were in Sanitation. In his cell, Foyle listened to interminable therapeutic talks, lectures, moral and ethical guidance for the rest of the morning. Then there was silence again, and nothing but the rush of distant water and the quiet steps of goggled guards in the corridors.

In the afternoon came occupational therapy. The TV screen in each cell illuminated and the patient thrust his hands into the shadow frame of the screen. He saw three-dimensionally and he felt the broadcast objects and tools. He cut hospital uniforms, sewed them, manufactured kitchen utensils, and prepared foods. Although actually he touched nothing, his motions were transmitted to the shops where the work was accomplished by remote control. After one short hour of this relief came the darkness and silence again.

But every so often . . . once or twice a week (or perhaps once or twice a year) came the muffled thud of a distant explosion. The concussions were startling enough to distract Foyle from the furnace of vengeance that he stoked all through the silences. He whispered questions to the invisible figures around him in Sanitation.

"What's them explosions?"

"Explosions?"

"Blow-ups. Hear 'em a long way off, me."

"Them's Blue Jauntes."

"What?"

"Blue Jauntes. Every sometime a guy gets fed up with old Jeffrey. Can't take it no more, him. Jauntes into the wild blue yonder."

"Jesus."

"Yep. Don't know where they are, them. Don't know where they're going. Blue Jaunte into the dark . . . and we hear 'em exploding in the mountains. Boom! Blue Jaunte."

He was appalled, but he could understand. The darkness, the silence, the monotony destroyed sense and brought on desperation. The loneliness was intolerable. The patients buried in Gouffre Martel prison hospital looked forward eagerly to the morning Sanitation period for a chance to whisper a word and hear a word. But these fragments were not enough, and desperation came. Then there would be another distant explosion.

Sometimes the suffering men would turn on each other and then a savage fight would break out in Sanitation. These were instantly broken up by the goggled guards, and the morning lecture would switch on the Moral Fiber record preaching the Virtue of Patience.

Foyle learned the records by heart, every word, every click and crack in the tapes. He learned to loathe the voices of the lecturers: the Understanding Baritone, the Cheerful Tenor, the Man-to-Man Bass. He learned to deafen himself to the therapeutic monotony and perform his occupational therapy mechanically, but he was without resources to withstand the endless solitary hours. Fury was not enough.

He lost count of the days, of meals, of sermons. He no longer whispered in

Sanitation. His mind came adrift and he began to wander. He imagined he was back aboard "Nomad," reliving his fight for survival. Then he lost even this feeble grasp on illusion and began to sink deeper and deeper into the pit of catatonia: of womb silence, womb darkness, and womb sleep.

There were fleeting dreams. An angel hummed to him once. Another time she sang quietly. Thrice he heard her speak: "Oh God . . ." and "God damn!" and "Oh . . ." in a heart-rending descending note.

He sank into his abyss, listening to her.

"There is a way out," his angel murmured in his ear, sweetly, comforting. Her voice was soft and warm, yet it burned with anger. It was the voice of a furious angel. "There is a way out."

It whispered in his ear from nowhere, and suddenly, with the logic of desperation, it came to him that there was a way out of Gouffre Martel. He had been a fool not to see it before.

"Yes," he croaked. "There's a way out."

There was a soft gasp, then a soft question: "Who's there?"

"Me, is all," Foyle said. "You know me."

"Where are you?"

"Here. Where I always been, me."

"But there's no one. I'm alone."

"Got to thank you for helping me."

"Hearing voices is bad," the furious angel murmured. "The first step off the deep end. I've got to stop."

"You showed me the way out. Blue Jaunte."

"Blue Jaunte! My God, this must be real. You're talking the gutter lingo. You must be real. Who are you?"

"Gully Foyle."

"But you're not in my cell. You're not even near. Men are in the north quadrant of Gouffre Martel. Women are in the south. I'm South-900. Where are you?"

"North-111."

"You're a quarter of a mile away. How can we— Of course! It's the Whisper Line. I always thought that was a legend, but it's true. It's working now."

"Here I go, me," Foyle whispered. "Blue Jaunte."

"Foyle, listen to me. Forget the Blue Jaunte. Don't throw this away. It's a miracle."

"What's a miracle?"

"There's an acoustical freak in Gouffre Martel . . . they happen in underground caves . . . a freak of echoes, passages and whispering galleries. Old-timers call it the Whisper Line. I never believed them. No one ever did, but it's true. We're talking to each other over the Whisper Line. No one can hear us but us. We can talk, Foyle. We can plan. Maybe we can escape."

Her name was Jisbella McQueen. She was hot-tempered, independent, intelligent, and she was serving five years of cure in Gouffre Martel for larceny. Jisbella gave Foyle a cheerfully furious account of her revolt against society.

"You don't know what jaunting's done to women, Gully. It's locked us up, sent us back to the seraglio."

"What's seraglio, girl?"

"A harem. A place where women are kept on ice. After a thousand years of civilization (it says here) we're still property. Jaunting's such a danger to our virtue, our value, our mint condition, that we're locked up like gold plate in a safe. There's nothing for us to do . . . nothing respectable. No jobs. No careers. There's no getting out, Gully, unless you bust out and smash all the rules."

"Did you have to, Jiz?"

"I had to be independent, Gully. I had to live my own life, and that's the only way society would let me. So I ran away from home and turned crook." And Jiz went on to describe the lurid details of her revolt: the Temper Racket, the Cataract Racket, the Honeymoon and Obituary Robs, the Badger Jaunte, and the Glim-Drop.

Foyle told her about "Nomad" and "Vorga," his hatred and his plans. He did not tell Jisbella about his face or the twenty millions in platinum bullion waiting out in the asteroids.

"What happened to 'Nomad'?" Jisbella asked. "Was it like that man, Dagenham, said? Was she blasted by an O.S. raider?"

"I don't know, me. Can't remember, girl."

"The blast probably wiped out your memory. Shock. And being marooned for six months didn't help. Did you notice anything worth salvaging from 'Nomad'?"

"No."

"Did Dagenham mention anything?"

"No," Foyle lied.

"Then he must have another reason for hounding you into Gouffre Martel. There must be something else he wants from 'Nomad.' "

"Yeah, Jiz."

"But you were a fool trying to blow up 'Vorga' like that. You're like a wild beast trying to punish the trap that injured it. Steel isn't alive. It doesn't think. You can't punish 'Vorga.' "

"Don't know what you mean, girl. 'Vorga' passed me by."

"You punish the brain, Gully. The brain that sets the trap. Find out who was aboard 'Vorga.' Find out who gave the order to pass you by. Punish him."

"Yeah. How?"

"Learn to think, Gully. The head that could figure out how to get 'Nomad' under way and how to put a bomb together ought to be able to figure that out. But no more bombs; brains instead. Locate a member of 'Vorga's' crew. He'll tell you who was aboard. Track them down. Find out who gave the order. Then punish him. But it'll take time, Gully . . . time and money; more than you've got."

"I got a whole life, me."

They murmured for hours across the Whisper Line, their voices sounding small yet close to the ear. There was only one particular spot in each cell where the other could be heard, which was why so much time had passed before they discovered the miracle. But now they made up for lost time. And Jisbella educated Foyle.

"If we ever break out of Gouffre Martel, Gully, it'll have to be together, and I'm not trusting myself to an illiterate partner."

"Who's illiterate?"

"You are," Jisbella answered firmly. "I have to talk gutter a you half the time, me."

"I can read and write."

"And that's about all . . . which means that outside of brute strength you'll be useless."

"Talk sense, you," he said angrily.

"I am talking sense, me. What's the use of the strongest chisel in the world if it doesn't have an edge? We've got to sharpen your wits, Gully. Got to educate you, man, is all."

He submitted. He realized she was right. He would need training not only for the bust-out but for the search for "Vorga" as well. Jisbella was the daughter of an architect and had received an education. This she drilled into Foyle, leavened with the cynical experience of five years in the underworld. Occasionally he rebelled against the hard work, and then there would be whispered quarrels, but in the end he would apologize and submit again. And sometimes Jisbella would tire of teaching, and then they would ramble on, sharing dreams in the dark.

"I think we're falling in love, Gully."

"I think so too, Jiz."

"I'm an old hag, Gully. A hundred and five years old. What are you like?"

"Awful."

"How awful?"

"My face."

"You make yourself sound romantic. Is it one of those exciting scars that make a man attractive?"

"No. You'll see when we meet, us. That's wrong, isn't it, Jiz? Just plain: 'When we meet.' Period."

"Good boy."

"We will meet some day, won't we, Jiz?"

"Soon, I hope, Gully." Jisbella's faraway voice became crisp and businesslike. "But we've got to stop hoping and get down to work. We've got to plan and prepare."

From the underworld, Jisbella had inherited a mass of information about Gouffre Martel. No one had ever jaunted out of the cavern hospitals, but for decades the underworld had been collecting and collating information about them. It was from this data that Jisbella had formed her quick recognition of the Whisper Line that joined them. It was on the basis of this information that she began to discuss escape.

"We can pull it off, Gully. Never doubt that for a minute. There must be dozens of loopholes in their security system."

"No one's ever found them before."

"No one's ever worked with a partner before. We'll pool our information and we'll make it."

He no longer shambled to Sanitation and back. He felt the corridor walls, noted doors, noted their texture, counted, listened, deduced, and reported. He made a note of every separate step in the Sanitation pens and reported them to Jiz. The questions he whispered to the men around him in the shower and scrub rooms had purpose. Together, Foyle and Jisbella built up a picture of the routine of Gouffre Martel and its security system.

One morning, on the return from Sanitation, he was stopped as he was about to step back into his cell.

"Stay in line, Foyle."

"This is North-111. I know where to get off by now."

"Keep moving."

"But—" He was terrified. "You're changing me?"

"Visitor to see you."

He was marched up to the end of the north corridor where it met the three other main corridors that formed the huge cross of the hospital. In the center of the cross were the administration offices, maintenance workshops, clinics, and plants. Foyle was thrust into a room, as dark as his cell. The door was shut behind him. He became aware of a faint shimmering outline in the blackness. It was no more than the ghost of an image with a blurred body and a death's head. Two black discs on the skull face were either eye sockets or infrared goggles.

"Good morning," said Saul Dagenham.

"You?" Foyle exclaimed.

"Me. I've got five minutes. Sit down. Chair behind you."

Foyle felt for the chair and sat down slowly.

"Enjoying yourself?" Dagenham inquired.

"What do you want, Dagenham?"

"There's been a change," Dagenham said dryly. "Last time we talked your dialogue consisted entirely of 'Go to hell.'"

"Go to hell, Dagenham, if it'll make you feel any better."

"Your repartee's improved; your speech, too. You've changed," Dagenham said. "Changed a damned sight too much and a damned sight too fast. I don't like it. What's happened to you?"

"I've been going to night school."

"You've had ten months in this night school."

"Ten months!" Foyle echoed in amazement. "That long?"

"Ten months without sight and without sound. Ten months in solitary. You ought to be broke."

"Oh, I'm broke, all right."

"You ought to be whining. I was right. You're unusual. At this rate it's going to take too long. We can't wait. I'd like to make a new offer."

"Make it."

"Ten per cent of 'Nomad's' bullion. Two million."

"Two million!" Foyle exclaimed. "Why didn't you offer that in the first place?"

"Because I didn't know your caliber. Is it a deal?"

"Almost. Not yet."

"What else?"

"I get out of Gouffre Martel."

"Naturally."

"And someone else, too."

"It can be arranged." Dagenham's voice sharpened. "Anything else?"

"I get access to Presteign's files."

"Out of the question. Are you insane? Be reasonable."

"His shipping files."

"What for?"

"A list of personnel aboard one of his ships."

"Oh." Dagenham's eagerness revived. "That, I can arrange. Anything else?"

"No."

"Then it's a deal." Dagenham was delighted. The ghostly blur of light arose from its chair. "We'll have you out in six hours. We'll start arrangements for your friend at once. It's a pity we wasted this time, but no one can figure you, Foyle."

"Why didn't you send in a telepath to work me over?"

"A telepath? Be reasonable, Foyle. There aren't ten full telepaths in all the Inner Planets. Their time is earmarked for the next ten years. We couldn't persuade one to interrupt his schedule for love or money."

"I apologize, Dagenham. I thought you didn't know your business."

"You very nearly hurt my feelings."

"Now I know you're just lying."

"You're flattering me."

"You could have hired a telepath. For a cut in twenty million you could have hired one easy."

"The government would never—"

"They don't all work for the government. No. You've got something too hot to let a telepath get near."

The blur of light leaped across the room and seized Foyle. "How much do you know, Foyle? What are you covering? Who are you working for?" Dagenham's hands shook. "Christ! What a fool I've been. Of course you're unusual. You're no common spaceman. I asked you: who are you working for?"

Foyle tore Dagenham's hands away from him. "No one," he said. "No one, except myself."

"No one, eh? Including your friend in Gouffre Martel you're so eager to rescue? By God, you almost swindled me, Foyle. Tell Captain Y'ang-Yeovil I congratulate him. He's got a better staff than I thought."

"I never heard of any Y'ang-Yeovil."

"You and your colleague are going to rot here. It's no deal. You'll fester here. I'll have you moved to the worst cell in the hospital. I'll sink you to the bottom of Gouffre Martel. I'll— Guard, here! G—"

Foyle grasped Dagenham's throat, dragged him down to the floor and hammered his head on the flagstones. Dagenham squirmed once and then was still. Foyle ripped the goggles off his face and put them on. Sight returned in soft red and rose lights and shadows.

He was in a small reception room with a table and two chairs. Foyle stripped Dagenham's jacket off and put it on with two quick jerks that split the shoulders. Dagenham's cocked highwayman's hat lay on the table. Foyle clapped it over his head and pulled the brim down before his face.

On opposite walls were two doors. Foyle opened one a crack. It led out to the north corridor. He closed it, leaped across the room and tried the other. It opened onto a jaunte-proof maze. Foyle slipped through the door and entered the maze. Without a guide to lead him through the labyrinth, he was immediately lost. He began to run around the twists and turns and found himself back at the reception room. Dagenham was struggling to his knees.

Foyle turned back into the maze again. He ran. He came to a closed door and thrust it open. It revealed a large workshop illuminated by normal light. Two technicians working at a machine bench looked up in surprise.

Foyle snatched up a sledge hammer, leaped on them like a caveman, and felled them. Behind him he heard Dagenham shouting in the distance. He looked around wildly, dreading the discovery that he was trapped in a cul-de-sac. The workshop was L-shaped. Foyle tore around the corner, burst through the entrance of another jaunte-proof maze and was lost again. The Gouffre Martel alarm system began clattering. Foyle battered at the walls of the labyrinth with the sledge, shattered the thin plastic masking, and found himself in the infrared-lit south corridor of the women's quadrant.

Two women guards came up the corridor, running hard. Foyle swung the sledge and dropped them. He was near the head of the corridor. Before him stretched a long perspective of cell doors, each bearing a glowing red number. Overhead the corridor was lit by glowing red globes. Foyle stood on tiptoe and clubbed the globe above him. He hammered through the socket and smashed the current cable. The entire corridor went dark . . . even to goggles.

"Evens us up; all in the dark now," Foyle gasped and tore down the corridor feeling the wall as he ran and counting cell doors. Jisbella had given him an accurate word picture of the South Quadrant. He was counting his way toward South-900. He blundered into a figure, another guard. Foyle hacked at her once with his sledge. She shrieked and fell. The women patients began shrieking. Foyle lost count, ran on, stopped.

"Jiz!" he bellowed.

He heard her voice. He encountered another guard, disposed of her, ran, located Jisbella's cell.

"Gully, for God's sake . . ." Her voice was muffled.

"Get back, girl. Back." He hammered thrice against the door with his sledge and it burst inward. He staggered in and fell against a figure.

"Jiz?" he gasped. "Excuse me . . . Was passing by. Though I'd drop in."

"Gully, in the name of—"

"Yeah. Hell of a way to meet, eh? Come on. Out, girl. Out!" He dragged her out of the cell. "We can't try a break through the offices. They don't like me back there. Which way to your Sanitation pens?"

"Gully, you're crazy."

"Whole quadrant's dark. I smashed the power cable. We've got half a chance. Go, girl. Go."

He gave her a powerful thrust and she led him down the passages to the automatic stalls of the women's Sanitation pens. While mechanical hands removed their uniforms, soaped, soaked, sprayed and disinfected them, Foyle felt for the glass pane of the medical observation window. He found it, swung the sledge and smashed it.

"Get in, Jiz."

He hurled her through the window and followed. They were both stripped, greasy with soap, slashed and bleeding. Foyle slipped and crashed through the blackness searching for the door through which the medical officers entered.

"Can't find the door, Jiz. Door from the clinic. I—"

"Shh!"

"But—"

"Be quiet, Gully."

A soapy hand found his mouth and clamped over it. She gripped his shoulder so hard that her fingernails pierced his skin. Through the bedlam in the caverns sounded the clatter of steps close at hand. Guards were running blindly through the Sanitation stalls. The infrared lights had not yet been repaired.

"They may not notice the window," Jisbella hissed. "Be quiet."

They crouched on the floor. Steps trampled through the pens in bewildering succession. Then they were gone.

"All clear, now," Jisbella whispered. "But they'll have searchlights any minute. Come on, Gully. Out."

"But the door to the clinic, Jiz. I thought—"

"There is no door. They use spiral stairs and they pull them up. They've thought of this escape too. We'll have to try the laundry lift. God knows what good it'll do us. Oh Gully, you fool! You utter fool!"

They climbed through the observation window back into the pens. They searched through the darkness for the lifts by which soiled uniforms were removed and fresh uniforms issued. And in the darkness the automatic hands again soaped, sprayed and disinfected them. They could find nothing.

The caterwauling of a siren suddenly echoed through the caverns, silencing all other sound. There came a hush as suffocating as the darkness.

"They're using the G-phone to track us, Gully."

"The what?"

"Geophone. It can trace a whisper through half a mile of solid rock. That's why they've sirened for silence."

"The laundry lift?"

"Can't find it."

"Then come on."

"Where?"

"We're running."

"Where?"

"I don't know, but I'm not getting caught flat-footed. Come on. The exercise'll do you good."

Again he thrust Jisbella before him and they ran, gasping and stumbling, through the blackness, down into the deepest reaches of South Quadrant. Jisbella fell twice, blundering against turns in the passages. Foyle took the lead and ran, holding the twenty-pound sledge in his hand, the handle extended before him as an antenna. Then they crashed into a blank wall and realized they had reached the dead end of the corridor. They were boxed, trapped.

"What now?"

"Don't know. Looks like the dead end of my ideas, too. We can't go back for sure. I clobbered Dagenham in the offices. Hate that man. Looks like a poison label. You got a flash, girl?"

"Oh Gully . . . Gully . . ." Jisbella sobbed.

"Was counting on you for ideas. 'No more bombs,' you said. Wish I had one now. Could— Wait a minute." He touched the oozing wall against which they were leaning. He felt the checkerboard indentations of mortar seams. "Bulletin from G. Foyle. This isn't a natural cave wall. It's made. Brick and stone. Feel."

Jisbella felt the wall. "So?"

"Means this passage don't end here. Goes on. They blocked it off. Out of the way."

He shoved Jisbella up the passage, ground his hands into the floor to grit his soapy palms, and began swinging the sledge against the wall. He swung in steady rhythm, grunting and gasping. The steel sledge struck the wall with the blunt concussion of stones struck under water.

"They're coming," Jiz said. "I hear them."

The blunt blows took on a crumbling, crushing overtone. There was a whisper, then a steady pebble-fall of loose mortar. Foyle redoubled his efforts. Suddenly there was a crash and a gush of icy air blew in their faces.

"Through," Foyle muttered.

He attacked the edges of the hole pierced through the wall with ferocity. Bricks, stones, and old mortar flew. Foyle stopped and called Jisbella.

"Try it."

He dropped the sledge, seized her, and held her up to the chest-high opening. She cried out in pain as she tried to wriggle past the sharp edges. Foyle pressed her relentlessly until she got her shoulders and then her hips through. He let go of her legs and heard her fall on the other side.

Foyle pulled himself up and tore himself through the jagged breach in the wall. He felt Jisbella's hands trying to break his fall as he crashed down in a mass of loose brick and mortar. They were both through into the icy blackness of the unoccupied caverns of Gouffre Martel . . . miles of unexplored grottos and caves.

"By God, we'll make it yet," Foyle mumbled.

"I don't know if there's a way out, Gully." Jisbella was shaking with cold. "Maybe this is all cul-de-sac, walled off from the hospital."

"There has to be a way out."

"I don't know if we can find it."

"We've got to find it. Let's go, girl."

They blundered forward in the darkness. Foyle tore the useless set of goggles from his eyes. They crashed against ledges, corners, low ceilings; they fell down slopes and steep steps. They climbed over a razor-back ridge to a level plain and their feet shot from under them. Both fell heavily to a glassy floor. Foyle felt it and touched it with his tongue.

"Ice," he muttered. "Good sign. We're in an ice cavern, Jiz. Underground glacier."

They arose shakily, straddling their legs and worked their way across the ice that had been forming in the Gouffre Martel abyss for millenia. They climbed into a forest of stone saplings that were stalagmites and stalactites thrusting up from the jagged floor and down from the ceilings. The vibrations of every step loosened the huge stalactites; ponderous stone spears thundered down from overhead. At the edge of the forest, Foyle stopped, reached out and tugged. There was a clear metallic ring. He took Jisbella's hand and placed the long tapering cone of a stalagmite in it.

"Cane," he grunted. "Use it like a blind man."

He broke off another and they went tapping, feeling, stumbling through the darkness. There was no sound but the gallop of panic . . . their gasping breath and racing hearts, the taps of their stone canes, the multitudinous drip of water, the distant rushing of the underground river beneath Gouffre Martel.

"Not that way, girl," Foyle nudged her shoulder. "More to the left."

"Have you the faintest notion where we're headed, Gully?"

"Down, Jiz. Follow any slope that leads down."

"You've got an idea?"

"Yeah. Surprise, surprise! Brains instead of bombs."

"Brains instead of—" Jisbella shrieked with hysterical laughter. "You exploded into South Quadrant w-with a sledge hammer and th-that's your idea of b-brains instead of b-b-b—" She brayed and hooted beyond all control until Foyle grasped her and shook her.

"Shut up, Jiz. If they're tracking us by G-phone they could hear you from Mars."

"S-sorry, Gully. Sorry. I . . ." She took a breath. "Why down?"

"The river, the one we hear all the time. It must be near. It probably melts off the glacier back there."

"The river?"

"The only sure way out. It must break out of the mountain somewhere. We'll swim."

"Gully, you're insane!"

"What's a matter, you? You can't swim?"

"I can swim, but—"

"Then we've got to try. Got to, Jiz. Come on."

The rush of the river grew louder as their strength began to fail. Jisbella pulled to a halt at last, gasping.

"Gully, I've got to rest."

"Too cold. Keep moving."

"I can't."

"Keep moving." He felt for her arm.

"Get your hands off me," she cried furiously. In an instant she was all spitfire. He released her in amazement.

"What's the matter with you? Keep your head, Jiz, I'm depending on you."

"For what? I told you we had to plan . . . work out an escape . . . and now you've trapped us into this."

"I was trapped myself. Dagenham was going to change my cell. No more Whisper Line for us. I had to, Jiz . . . and we're out, aren't we?"

"Out where? Lost in Gouffre Martel. Looking for a damned river to drown in. You're a fool, Gully, and I'm an idiot for letting you trap me into this. Damn you! Damn you! You pull everything down to your imbecile level and you've pulled me down too. Run. Fight. Punch. That's all you know. Beat. Break. Blast. Destroy— Gully!"

Jisbella screamed. There was a clatter of loose stone in the darkness, and her scream faded down and away to a heavy splash. Foyle heard the thrash of her body in water. He leaped forward, shouted: "Jiz!" and staggered over the edge of a precipice.

He fell and struck the water flat with a stunning impact. The icy river enclosed him, and he could not tell where the surface was. He struggled, suffocated, felt the swift current drag him against the chill slime of rocks, and then was borne bubbling to the surface. He coughed and shouted. He heard Jisbella answer, her voice faint and muffled by the roaring torrent. He swam with the current, trying to overtake her.

He shouted and heard her answering voice growing fainter and fainter. The roaring grew louder, and abruptly he was shot down the hissing sheet of a waterfall. He plunged to the bottom of a deep pool and struggled once more to the surface. The whirling current entangled him with a cold body bracing itself against a smooth rock wall.

"Jiz!"

"Gully! Thank God!"

They clung together for a moment while the water tore at them.

"Gully . . ." Jisbella coughed. "It goes through here."

"The river?"

"Yes."

He squirmed past her, bracing himself against the wall, and felt the mouth of an underwater tunnel. The current was sucking them into it.

"Hold on," Foyle gasped. He explored to the left and the right. The walls of the pool were smooth, without handhold.

"We can't climb out. Have to go through."

"There's no air, Gully. No surface."

"Couldn't be forever. We'll hold our breath."

"It could be longer than we can hold our breath."

"Have to gamble."

"I can't do it."

"You must. No other way. Pump your lungs. Hold on to me."

They supported each other in the water, gasping for breath, filling their lungs. Foyle nudged Jisbella toward the underwater tunnel. "You go first. I'll be right behind. . . . Help you if you get into trouble."

"Trouble!" Jisbella cried in a shaking voice. She submerged and permitted the current to suck her into the tunnel mouth. Foyle followed. The fierce waters drew them down, down, down, caroming from side to side of a tunnel that had been worn glass-smooth. Foyle swam close behind Jisbella, feeling her thrashing legs beat his head and shoulders.

They shot through the tunnel until their lungs burst and their blind eyes started. Then there was a roaring again and a surface, and they could breathe. The glassy tunnel sides were replaced by jagged rocks. Foyle caught Jisbella's leg and seized a stone projection at the side of the river.

"Got to climb out here," he shouted.

"What?"

"Got to climb out. You hear that roaring up ahead? Cataracts. Rapids. Be torn to pieces. Out, Jiz."

She was too weak to climb out of the water. He thrust her body up onto the rocks and followed. They lay on the dripping stones, too exhausted to speak. At last Foyle got wearily to his feet.

"Have to keep on," he said. "Follow the river. Ready?"

She could not answer; she could not protest. He pulled her up and they went stumbling through the darkness, trying to follow the bank of the torrent. The boulders they traversed were gigantic, standing like dolmens, heaped, jumbled, scattered into a labyrinth. They staggered and twisted through them and lost the river. They could hear it in the darkness; they could not get back to it. They could get nowhere.

"Lost . . ." Foyle grunted in disgust. "We're lost again. Really lost this time. What are we going to do?"

Jisbella began to cry. She made helpless yet furious sounds. Foyle lurched to a stop and sat down, drawing her down with him.

"Maybe you're right, girl," he said wearily. "Maybe I am a damned fool. I got us trapped into this no-jaunte jam, and we're licked."

She didn't answer.

"So much for brainwork. Hell of an education you gave me." He hesitated. "You think we ought to try backtracking to the hospital?"

"We'll never make it."

"Guess not. Was just practicing m'brain. Should we start a racket? Make a noise so they can track us by G-phone?"

"They'd never hear us . . . Never find us in time."

"We could make enough noise. You could knock me around a little. Be a pleasure for both of us."

"Shut up."

"What a mess!" He sagged back, cushioning his head on a tuft of soft grass. "At least I had a chance aboard 'Nomad.' There was food and I could see where I was trying to go. I could—" He broke off and sat bolt upright. "Jiz!"

"Don't talk so much."

He felt the ground under him and clawed up sods of earth and tufts of grass. He thrust them into her face.

"Smell this," he laughed. "Taste it. It's grass, Jiz. Earth and grass. We must be out of Gouffre Martel."

"What?"

"It's night outside. Pitch-black. Overcast. We came out of the caves and never knew it. We're out, Jiz! We made it."

They leaped to their feet, peering, listening, sniffing. The night was impenetrable, but they heard the soft sigh of night winds, and the sweet scent of green growing things came to their nostrils. Far in the distance a dog barked.

"My God, Gully," Jisbella whispered incredulously. "You're right. We're out of Gouffre Martel. All we have to do is wait for dawn."

She laughed. She flung her arms about him and kissed him, and he returned the embrace. They babbled excitedly. They sank down on the soft grass again, weary, but unable to rest, eager, impatient, all life before them.

"Hello, Gully, darling Gully. Hello Gully, after all this time."

"Hello, Jiz."

"I told you we'd meet some day . . . some day soon. I told you, darling. And this is the day."

"The night."

"The night, so it is. But no more murmuring in the night along the Whisper Line. No more night for us, Gully, dear."

Suddenly they became aware that they were nude, lying close, no longer separated. Jisbella fell silent but did not move. He clasped her, almost angrily, and enveloped her with a desire that was no less than hers.

When dawn came, he saw that she was lovely: long and lean with smoky red hair and a generous mouth.

But when dawn came, she saw his face.

CHAPTER SIX

Harley baker, m.d., had a small general practice in Montana-Oregon which was legitimate and barely paid for the diesel oil he consumed each weekend participating in the rallies for vintage tractors which were the vogue in Sahara. His real income was earned in his Freak Factory in Trenton to which

Baker jaunted every Monday, Wednesday, and Friday night. There, for enormous fees and no questions asked, Baker created monstrosities for the entertainment business and refashioned skin, muscle, and bone for the underworld.

Looking like a male midwife, Baker sat on the cool veranda of his Spokane mansion listening to Jiz McQueen finish the story of her escape.

"Once we hit the open country outside Gouffre Martel it was easy. We found a shooting lodge, broke in, and got some clothes. There were guns there too . . . lovely old steel things for killing with explosives. We took them and sold them to some locals. Then we bought rides to the nearest jaunte stage we had memorized."

"Which?"

"Biarritz."

"Traveled by night, eh?"

"Naturally."

"Do anything about Foyle's face?"

"We tried makeup but that didn't work. The damned tattooing showed through. Then I bought a dark skin-surrogate and sprayed it on."

"Did that do it?"

"No," Jiz said angrily. "You have to keep your face quiet or else the surrogate cracks and peels. Foyle couldn't control himself. He never can. It was hell."

"Where is he now?"

"Sam Quatt's got him in tow."

"I thought Sam retired from the rackets."

"He did," Jisbella said grimly, "But he owes me a favor. He's minding Foyle. They're circulating on the jaunte to stay ahead of the cops."

"Interesting," Baker murmured. "Haven't seen a tattoo case in all my life. Thought it was a dead art. I'd like to add him to my collection. You know I collect curios, Jiz?"

"Everybody knows that zoo of yours in Trenton, Baker. It's ghastly."

"I picked up a genuine fraternal cyst last month," Baker began enthusiastically.

"I don't want to hear about it," Jiz snapped. "And I don't want Foyle in your zoo. Can you get the muck off his face? Clean it up? He says they were stymied at General Hospital."

"They haven't had my experience, dear. Hmm. I seem to remember reading something once . . . somewhere . . . Now where did I—? Wait a minute." Baker stood up and disappeared with a faint pop. Jisbella paced the veranda furiously until he reappeared twenty minutes later with a tattered book in his hands and a triumphant expression on his face.

"Got it," Baker said. "Saw it in the Caltech stacks three years ago. You may admire my memory."

"To hell with your memory. What about his face?"

"It can be done." Baker flipped the fragile pages and meditated. "Yes, it can be done. Indigotin disulphonic acid. I may have to synthesize the acid but . . ." Baker closed the text and nodded emphatically. "I can do it. Only it seems a pity to tamper with that face if it's as unique as you describe."

"Will you get off your hobby," Jisbella exclaimed in exasperation. "We're hot, understand? The first that ever broke out of Gouffre Martel. The cops won't rest until they've got us back. This is extra-special for them."

"But—"

"How long d'you think we can stay out of Gouffre Martel with Foyle running around with that tattooed face?"

"What are you so angry about?"

"I'm not angry. I'm explaining."

"He'd be happy in the zoo," Baker said persuasively. "And he'd be under cover there. I'd put him in the room next to the cyclops girl—"

"The zoo is out. That's definite."

"All right, dear. But why are you worried about Foyle being recaptured? It won't have anything to do with you."

"Why should you worry about me worrying? I'm asking you to do a job. I'm paying for the job."

"It'll be expensive, dear, and I'm fond of you. I'm trying to save you money."

"No you're not."

"Then I'm curious."

"Then let's say I'm grateful. He helped me; now I'm helping him."

Baker smiled cynically. "Then let's help him by giving him a brand new face."

"No."

"I thought so. You want his face cleaned up because you're interested in his face."

"Damn you, Baker, will you do the job or not?"

"It'll cost five thousand."

"Break that down."

"A thousand to synthesize the acid. Three thousand for the surgery. And one thousand for—"

"Your curiosity?"

"No, dear." Baker smiled again. "A thousand for the anesthetist."

"Why anesthesia?"

Baker reopened the ancient text. "It looks like a painful operation. You know how they tattoo? They take a needle, dip it in dye, and hammer it into the skin. To bleach that dye out I'll have to go over his face with a needle, pore by pore, and hammer in the indigotin disulphonic. It'll hurt."

Jisbella's eyes flashed. "Can you do it without the dope?"

"I can, dear, but Foyle—"

"To hell with Foyle. I'm paying four thousand. No dope, Baker. Let Foyle suffer."

"Jiz! You don't know what you're letting him in for."

"I know. Let him suffer." She laughed so furiously that she startled Baker. "Let his face make him suffer too."

Baker's Freak Factory occupied a round brick threestory building that had once been the roundhouse in a suburban railway yard before jaunting ended the need for suburban railroads. The ancient ivy-covered roundhouse was alongside the Trenton rocket pits, and the rear windows looked out on the mouths of the pits thrusting their anti-grav beams upward, and Baker's patients could amuse themselves watching the spaceships riding silently up and down the beams, their portholes blazing, recognition signals blinking, their hulls rippling with St. Elmo's fire as the atmosphere carried off the electrostatic charges built up in outer space.

The basement floor of the factory contained Baker's zoo of anatomical curiosities, natural freaks and monsters bought, and/or abducted. Baker, like the rest of his world, was passionately devoted to these creatures and spent long hours with them, drinking in the spectacle of their distortions the way other men saturated themselves with the beauty of art. The middle floor of the roundhouse contained bedrooms for post-operative patients, laboratories, staff rooms, and kitchens. The top floor contained the operating theaters.

In one of the latter, a small room usually used for retinal experiments, Baker was at work on Foyle's face. Under a harsh battery of lamps, he bent over the operating table working meticulously with a small steel hammer and a platinum needle. Baker was following the pattern of the old tattooing on Foyle's face, searching out each minute scar in the skin, and driving the needle into it. Foyle's head was gripped in a clamp, but his body was unstrapped. His muscles writhed at each tap of the hammer, but he never moved his body. He gripped the sides of the operating table.

"Control," he said through his teeth. "You wanted me to learn control, Jiz. I'm practicing." He winced.

"Don't move," Baker ordered.

"I'm playing it for laughs."

"You're doing all right, son," Sam Quatt said, looking sick. He glanced sidelong at Jisbella's furious face. "What do you say, Jiz?"

"He's learning."

Baker continued dipping and hammering the needle.

"Listen, Sam," Foyle mumbled, barely audible. "Jiz told me you own a private ship. Crime pays, huh?"

"Yeah. Crime pays. I got a little four-man job. Twin-jet. Kind they call a Saturn Weekender."

"Why Saturn Weekender?"

"Because a weekend on Saturn would last ninety days. She can carry food and fuel for three months."

"Just right for me," Foyle muttered. He writhed and controlled himself. "Sam, I want to rent your ship."

"What for?"

"Something hot."

"Legitimate?"

"No."

"Then it's not for me, son. I've lost my nerve. Jaunting the circuit with you, one step ahead of the cops, showed me that. I've retired for keeps. All I want is peace."

"I'll pay fifty thousand. Don't you want fifty thousand? You could spend Sundays counting it."

The needle hammered remorselessly. Foyle's body was twitching at each impact.

"I already got fifty thousand. I got ten times that in cash in a bank in Vienna." Quatt reached into his pocket and took out a ring of glittering radioactive keys. "Here's the key for the bank. This is the key to my place in Joburg. Twenty rooms; twenty acres. This here's the key to my Weekender in Montauk. You ain't temptin' me, son. I quit while I was ahead. I'm jaunting back to Joburg and live happy for the rest of my life."

"Let me have the Weekender. You can sit safe in Joburg and collect."

"Collect when?"

"When I get back."

"You want my ship on trust and a promise to pay?"

"A guarantee."

Quatt snorted. "What guarantee?"

"It's a salvage job in the asteroids. Ship named 'Nomad.'"

"What's on the 'Nomad'? What makes the salvage pay off?"

"I don't know."

"You're lying."

"I don't know," Foyle mumbled stubbornly. "But there has to be something valuable. Ask Jiz."

"Listen," Quatt said, "I'm going to teach you something. We do business legitimate, see? We don't slash and scalp. We don't hold out. I know what's on your mind. You got something juicy but you don't want to cut anybody else in on it. That's why you're begging for favors . . ."

Foyle writhed under the needle, but, still gripped in the vice of his possession, was forced to repeat: "I don't know, Sam. Ask Jiz."

"If you've got an honest deal, make an honest proposition," Quatt said angrily. "Don't come prowling around like a damned tattooed tiger figuring how to pounce. We're the only friends you got. Don't try to slash and scalp—"

Quatt was interrupted by a cry torn from Foyle's lips.

"Don't move," Baker said in an abstracted voice. "When you twitch your face I can't control the needle." He looked hard and long at Jisbella. Her lips trembled. Suddenly she opened her purse and took out two ¢r 500 banknotes. She dropped them alongside the beaker of acid.

"We'll wait outside," she said.

She fainted in the hall. Quatt dragged her to a chair, and found a nurse who revived her with aromatic ammonia. She began to cry so violently that Quatt was frightened. He dismissed the nurse and hovered until the sobbing subsided.

"What the hell has been going on?" he demanded. "What was that money supposed to mean?"

"It was blood money."

"For what?"

"I don't want to talk about it."

"Are you all right?"
"No."
"Anything I can do?"
"No."
There was a long pause. Then Jisbella asked in a weary voice: "Are you going to make that deal with Gully?"
"Me? No. It sounds like a thousand-to-one shot."
"There has to be something valuable on the 'Nomad.' Otherwise Dagenham wouldn't have hounded Gully."
"I'm still not interested. What about you?"
"Me? Not interested either. I don't want any part of Gully Foyle again."
After another pause, Quatt asked: "Can I go home now?"
"You've had a rough time, haven't you, Sam?"
"I think I died about a thousand times nurse-maidin' that tiger around the circuit."
"I'm sorry, Sam."
"I had it coming to me after what I did to you when you were copped in Memphis."
"Running out on me was only natural, Sam."
"We always do what's natural, only sometimes we shouldn't do it."
"I know, Sam. I know."
"And you spend the rest of your life trying to make up for it. I figure I'm lucky, Jiz. I was able to square it tonight. Can I go home now?"
"Back to Joburg and the happy life?"
"Uh-huh."
"Don't leave me alone, yet, Sam. I'm ashamed of myself."
"What for?"
"Cruelty to dumb animals."
"What's that supposed to mean?"
"Never mind. Hang around a little. Tell me about the happy life. What's so happy about it?"
"Well," Quatt said reflectively. "It's having everything you wanted when you were a kid. If you can have everything at fifty that you wanted when you were fifteen, you're happy. Now when I was fifteen . . ." And Quatt went on and on describing the symbols, ambitions, and frustrations of his boyhood which he was now satisfying until Baker came out of the operating theater.
"Finished?" Jisbella asked eagerly.
"Finished. After I put him under I was able to work faster. They're bandaging his face now. He'll be out in a few minutes."
"Weak?"
"Naturally."
"How long before the bandages come off?"
"Six or seven days."
"His face'll be clean?"
"I thought you weren't interested in his face, dear. It ought to be clean.

I don't think I missed a spot of pigment. You may admire my skill, Jisbella . . . also my sagacity. I'm going to back Foyle's salvage trip."

"What?" Quatt laughed. "You taking a thousand-to-one gamble, Baker? I thought you were smart."

"I am. The pain was too much for him and he talked under the anesthesia. There's twenty million in platinum bullion aboard the 'Nomad.' "

"Twenty million!" Sam Quatt's face darkened and he turned on Jisbella. But she was furious too.

"Don't look at me, Sam. I didn't know. He held out on me too. Swore he never knew why Dagenham was hounding him."

"It was Dagenham who told him," Baker said. "He let that slip too."

"I'll kill him," Jisbella said. "I'll tear him apart with my own two hands and you won't find anything inside his carcass but black rot. He'll be a curio for your zoo, Baker; I wish to God I'd let you have him!"

The door of the operating theater opened and two orderlies wheeled out a trolley on which Foyle lay, twitching slightly. His entire head was one white globe of bandage.

"Is he conscious?" Quatt asked Baker.

"I'll handle this," Jisbella burst out. "I'll talk to the son of a—— Foyle!"

Foyle answered faintly through the mask of bandage. As Jisbella drew a furious breath for her onslaught, one wall of the hospital disappeared and there was a clap of thunder that knocked them to their feet. The entire building rocked from repeated explosions, and through the gaps in the walls uniformed men began jaunting in from the streets outside, like rooks swooping into the gut of a battlefield.

"Raid!" Baker shouted. "Raid!"

"Christ Jesus!" Quatt shook.

The uniformed men were swarming all over the building, shouting: "Foyle! Foyle! Foyle! Foyle!" Baker disappeared with a pop. The attendants jaunted too, deserting the trolley on which Foyle waved his arms and legs feebly, making faint sounds.

"It's a goddamn raid!" Quatt shook Jisbella. "Go, girl! Go!"

"We can't leave Foyle!" Jisbella cried.

"Wake up, girl! Go!"

"We can't run out on him."

Jisbella seized the trolley and ran it down the corridor. Quatt pounded alongside her. The roaring in the hospital grew louder: "Foyle! Foyle! Foyle!"

"Leave him, for God's sake!" Quatt urged. "Let them have him."

"No."

"It's a lobo for us, girl, if they get us."

"We can't run out on him."

They skidded around a corner into a shrieking mob of post-operative patients, bird men with fluttering wings, mermaids dragging themselves along the floor like seals, hermaphrodites, giants, pygmies, two-headed twins, centaurs, and a mewling sphinx. They clawed at Jisbella and Quatt in terror.

"Get him off the trolley," Jisbella yelled.

Quatt yanked Foyle off the trolley. Foyle came to his feet and sagged. Jisbella took his arm, and between them Sam and Jiz hauled him through a door into a ward filled with Baker's temporal freaks . . . subjects with accelerated time sense, darting about the ward with the lightning rapidity of humming birds and emitting piercing batlike squeals.

"Jaunte him out, Sam."

"After the way he tried to cross and scalp us?"

"We can't run out on him, Sam. You ought to know that by now. Jaunte him out. Caister's place!"

Jisbella helped Quatt haul Foyle to his shoulder. The temporal freaks seemed to fill the ward with shrieking streaks. The ward doors burst open. A dozen bolts from pneumatic guns whined through the ward, dropping the temporal patients in their gyrations. Quatt was slammed back against a wall, dropping Foyle. A black and blue bruise appeared on his temple.

"Get to hell out of here," Quatt roared. "I'm done."

"Sam!"

"I'm done. Can't jaunte. Go, girl!"

Trying to shake off the concussion that prevented him from jaunting, Quatt straightened and charged forward, meeting the uniformed men who poured into the ward. Jisbella took Foyle's arm and dragged him out the back of the ward, through a pantry, a clinic, a laundry supply, and down flights of ancient stairs that buckled and threw up clouds of termite dust.

They came into a victual cellar. Baker's zoo had broken out of their cells in the chaos and were raiding the cellar like bees glutting themselves with honey in an attacked hive. A Cyclops girl was cramming her mouth with handfuls of butter scooped from a tub. Her single eye above the bridge of her nose leered at them.

Jisbella dragged Foyle through the victual cellar, found a bolted wooden door and kicked it open. They stumbled down a flight of crumbling steps and found themselves in what once had been a coal cellar. The concussions and roarings overhead sounded deeper and hollow. A chute slot on one side of the cellar was barred with an iron door held by iron clamps. Jisbella placed Foyle's hands on the clamps. Together they opened them and climbed out of the cellar through the coal chute.

They were outside the Freak Factory, huddled against the rear wall. Before them were the Trenton rocket pits, and as they gasped for breath, Jiz saw a freighter come sliding down an anti-grav beam into a waiting pit. Its portholes blazed and its recognition signals blinked like a lurid neon sign, illuminating the back wall of the hospital.

A figure leaped from the roof of the hospital. It was Sam Quatt, attempting a desperate flight. He sailed out into space, arms and legs flailing, trying to reach the up-thrusting anti-grav beam of the nearest pit which might catch him in midflight and cushion his fall. His aim was perfect. Seventy feet above ground he dropped squarely into the shaft of the beam. It was not in operation. He fell and was smashed on the edge of the pit.

Jisbella sobbed. Still automatically retaining her grip on Foyle's arm, she ran across the seamed concrete to Sam Quatt's body. There she let go of

Foyle and touched Quatt's head tenderly. Her fingers were stained with blood. Foyle tore at the bandage before his eyes, working eye holes through the gauze. He muttered to himself, listening to Jisbella weep and hearing the shouts behind him from Baker's factory. His hands fumbled at Quatt's body, then he arose and tried to pull Jisbella up.

"Got to go," he croaked. "Got to get out. They've seen us."

Jisbella never moved. Foyle mustered all his strength and pulled her upright.

"Times Square," he muttered. "Jaunte, Jiz!"

Uniformed figures appeared around them. Foyle shook Jisbella's arm and jaunted to Times Square where masses of jaunters on the gigantic stage stared in amazement at the huge man with the white bandaged globe for a head. The stage was the size of two football fields. Foyle stared around dimly through the bandages. There was no sign of Jisbella but she might be anywhere. He lifted his voice to a shout.

"Montauk, Jiz! Montauk! The Folly Stage!"

Foyle jaunted with a last thrust of energy and a prayer. An icy nor'easter was blowing in from Block Island and sweeping brittle ice crystals across the stage on the site of a medieval ruin known as Fisher's folly. There was another figure on the stage. Foyle tottered to it through the wind and the snow. It was Jisbella, looking frozen and lost.

"Thank God," Foyle muttered. "Thank God. Where does Sam keep his Weekender?" He shook Jisbella's elbow. "Where does Sam keep his Weekender?"

"Sam's dead."

"Where does he keep that Saturn Weekender?"

"He's retired, Sam is. He's not scared any more."

"Where's the ship, Jiz?"

"In the yards down at the lighthouse."

"Come on."

"Where?"

"To Sam's ship." Foyle thrust his big hand before Jisbella's eyes; a bunch of radiant keys lay in his palm. "I took his keys. Come on."

"He gave them to you?"

"I took them off his body."

"Ghoul!" She began to laugh. "Liar . . . Lecher . . . Tiger . . . Ghoul. The walking cancer . . . Gully Foyle."

Nevertheless she followed him through the snowstorm to Montauk Light.

To three acrobats wearing powdered wigs, four flamboyant women carrying pythons, a child with golden curls and a cynical mouth, a professional duellist in medieval armor, and a man wearing a hollow glass leg in which goldfish swam, Saul Dagenham said: "All right, the operation's finished. Call the rest off and tell them to report back to Courier headquarters."

The side show jaunted and disappeared. Regis Sheffield rubbed his eyes and asked: "What was that lunacy supposed to be, Dagenham?"

"Disturbs your legal mind, eh? That was part of the cast of our FFCC operation. Fun, fantasy, confusion, and catastrophe." Dagenham turned to Presteign and smiled his death's-head smile. "I'll return your fee if you like, Presteign."

"You're not quitting?"

"No, I'm enjoying myself. I'll work for nothing. I've never tangled with a man of Foyle's caliber before. He's unique."

"How?" Sheffield demanded.

"I arranged for him to escape from Gouffre Martel. He escaped, all right, but not my way. I tried to keep him out of police hands with confusion and catastrophe. He ducked the police, but not my way . . . his own way. I tried to keep him out of Central Intelligence's hands with fun and fantasy. He stayed clear . . . again his own way. I tried to detour him into a ship so he could make his try for 'Nomad.' He wouldn't detour, but he got his ship. He's on his way out now."

"You're following?"

"Naturally." Dagenham hesitated. "But what was he doing in Baker's factory?"

"Plastic surgery?" Sheffield suggested. "A new face?"

"Not possible. Baker's good, but he can't do a plastic that quick. It was minor surgery. Foyle was on his feet with his head bandaged."

"The tattoo," Presteign said.

Dagenham nodded and the smile left his lips. "That's what's worrying me. You realize, Presteign, that if Baker removed the tattooing we'll never recognize Foyle?"

"My dear Dagenham, his face won't be changed."

"We've never seen his face . . . only the mask."

"I haven't met the man at all," Sheffield said. "What's the mask like?"

"Like a tiger. I was with Foyle for two long sessions. I ought to know his face by heart, but I don't. All I know is the tattooing."

"Ridiculous," Sheffield said bluntly.

"No. Foyle has to be seen to be believed. However, it doesn't matter. He'll lead us out to 'Nomad.' He'll lead us to your bullion and PyrE, Presteign. I'm almost sorry it's all over. Or nearly. As I said, I've been enjoying myself. He really is unique."

CHAPTER SEVEN

THE SATURN WEEKENDER was built like a pleasure yacht; it was ample for four, spacious for two, but not spacious enough for Foyle and Jiz McQueen. Foyle slept in the main cabin; Jiz kept to herself in the stateroom.

On the seventh day out, Jisbella spoke to Foyle for the second time: "Let's get those bandages off, Ghoul."

Foyle left the galley where he was sullenly heating coffee, and kicked back to the bathroom. He floated in after Jisbella and wedged himself into the alcove before the washbasin mirror. Jisbella braced herself on the basin, opened an ether capsule and began soaking and stripping the bandage off with hard, hating hands. The strips of gauze peeled slowly. Foyle was in agony of suspense.

"D'you think Baker did the job?" he asked.

No answer.

"Could he have missed anywhere?"

The stripping continued.

"It stopped hurting two days ago."

No answer.

"For God's sake, Jiz! Is it still war between us?"

Jisbella's hands stopped. She looked at Foyle's bandaged face with hatred. "What do you think?"

"I asked you."

"The answer is yes."

"Why?"

"You'll never understand."

"Make me understand."

"Shut up."

"If it's war, why'd you come with me?"

"To get what's coming to Sam and me."

"Money?"

"Shut up."

"You didn't have to. You could have trusted me."

"Trusted you? You?" Jisbella laughed without mirth and recommenced the peeling. Foyle struck her hands away.

"I'll do it myself."

She lashed him across his bandaged face. "You'll do what I tell you. Be still, Ghoul!"

She continued unwinding the bandage. A strip came away revealing Foyle's eyes. They stared at Jisbella, dark and brooding. The eyelids were clean; the bridge of the nose was clean. A strip came away from Foyle's chin. It was blue-black. Foyle, watching intently in the mirror, gasped.

"He missed the chin!" he exclaimed. "Baker goofed—"

"Shut up," Jiz answered shortly. "That's beard."

The innermost strips came away quickly, revealing cheeks, mouth, and brow. The brow was clean. The cheeks under the eyes were clean. The rest was covered with a blue-black seven day beard.

"Shave," Jiz commanded.

Foyle ran water, soaked his face, rubbed in shave ointment, and washed the beard off. Then he leaned close to the mirror and inspected himself, unaware that Jisbella's head was close to his as she too stared into the mirror. Not a mark of tattooing remained. Both sighed.

"It's clean," Foyle said. "Clean. He did the job." Suddenly he leaned further forward and inspected himself more closely. His face looked new to him, as new as it looked to Jisbella. "I'm changed. I don't remember looking like this. Did he do surgery on me too?"

"No," Jisbella said. "What's inside you changed it. That's the ghoul you're seeing, along with the liar and the cheat."

"For God's sake! Lay off. Let me alone!"

"Ghoul," Jisbella repeated, staring at Foyle's face with glowing eyes. "Liar. Cheat."

He took her shoulders and shoved her out into the companionway. She went sailing down into the main lounge, caught a guide bar and spun herself around. "Ghoul!" she cried. "Liar! Cheat! Ghoul! Lecher! Beast!"

Foyle pursued her, seized her again and shook her violently. Her red hair burst out of the clip that gathered it at the nape of her neck and floated out like a mermaid's tresses. The burning expression on her face transformed Foyle's anger into passion. He enveloped her and buried his new face in her breast.

"Lecher," Jiz murmured. "Animal . . ."

"Oh, Jiz . . ."

"The light," Jisbella whispered. Foyle reached out blindly toward the wall switches and pressed buttons, and the Saturn Weekender drove on toward the asteroids with darkened portholes.

They floated together in the cabin, drowsing, murmuring, touching tenderly for hours.

"Poor Gully," Jisbella whispered. "Poor darling Gully . . ."

"Not poor," he said. "Rich . . . soon."

"Yes, rich and empty. You've got nothing inside you, Gully dear . . . Nothing but hatred and revenge."

"It's enough."

"Enough for now. But later?"

"Later? That depends."

"It depends on your inside, Gully; what you get hold of."

"No. My future depends on what I get rid of."

"Gully . . . why did you hold out on me in Gouffre Martel? Why didn't you tell me you knew there was a fortune aboard 'Nomad'?"

"I couldn't."

"Didn't you trust me?"

"It wasn't that. I couldn't help myself. That's what's inside me . . . what I have to get rid of."

"Control again, eh Gully? You're driven."

"Yes, I'm driven. I can't learn control, Jiz. I want to, but I can't."

"Do you try?"

"I do. God knows, I do. But then something happens, and—"

"And then you pounce like a tiger."

"If I could carry you in my pocket, Jiz . . . to warn me . . . stick a pin in me . . ."

"Nobody can do it for you, Gully. You have to learn yourself."

He digested that for a long moment. Then he spoke hesitantly: "Jiz . . . about the money . . . ?"

"To hell with the money."

"Can I hold you to that?"

"Oh, Gully."

"Not that I . . . that I'm trying to hold out on you. If it wasn't for 'Vorga,' I'd give you all you wanted. All! I'll give you every cent left over when I'm finished. But I'm scared, Jiz. 'Vorga' is tough . . . what with Presteign and Dagenham and that lawyer, Sheffield. I've got to hold on to every cent, Jiz. I'm afraid if I let you take one credit, that could make the difference between 'Vorga' and I."

"Me."

"Me." He waited. "Well?"

"You're all possessed," she said wearily. "Not just a part of you, but all of you."

"No."

"Yes, Gully. All of you. It's just your skin making love to me. The rest is feeding on 'Vorga.'"

At that moment the radar alarm in the forward control cabin burst upon them, unwelcome and warning.

"Destination zero," Foyle muttered, no longer relaxed, once more possessed. He shot forward into the control cabin.

So he returned to the freak planetoid in the asteroid belt between Mars and Jupiter, the Sargasso planet manufactured of rock and wreckage and the spoils of space disaster salvaged by The Scientific People. He returned to the home of Joseph and his People who had tattooed NOMAD across his face and scientifically mated him to the girl named Moira.

Foyle overran the asteroid with the sudden fury of a Vandal raid. He came blasting out of space, braked with a spume of flame from the forward jets, and kicked the Weekender into a tight spin around the junkheap. They whirled around, passing the blackened ports, the big hatch from which Joseph and his Scientific People emerged to collect the drifting debris of space, the new crater Foyle had torn out of the side of the asteroid in his first plunge back to Terra. They whipped past the giant patchwork windows of the asteroid greenhouse and saw hundreds of faces peering out at them, tiny white dots mottled with tattooing.

"So I didn't murder them," Foyle grunted. "They've pulled back into the asteroid . . . Probably living deep inside while they get the rest repaired."

"Will you help them, Gully?"

"Why?"

"You did the damage."

"To hell with them. I've got my own problems. But it's a relief. They won't be bothering us."

He circled the asteroid once more and brought the Weekender down in the mouth of the new crater.

"We'll work from here," he said. "Get into a suit, Jiz. Let's go! Let's go!"

He drove her, mad with impatience; he drove himself. They corked up in their spacesuits, left the Weekender, and went sprawling through the debris in the crater into the bleak bowels of the asteroid. It was like squirming through the crawling tunnels of giant worm-holes. Foyle switched on his micro-wave suit set and spoke to Jiz.

"Be easy to get lost in here. Stay with me. Stay close."

"Where are we going, Gully?"

"After 'Nomad.' I remember they were cementing her into the asteroid when I left. Don't remember where. Have to find her."

The passages were airless, and their progress was soundless, but the vibrations carried through metal and rock. They paused once for breath alongside the pitted hull of an ancient warship. As they leaned against it they felt the vibrations of signals from within, a rhythmic knocking.

Foyle smiled grimly. "That's Joseph and The Scientific People inside," he said. "Requesting a few words. I'll give 'em an evasive answer." He pounded twice on the hull. "And now a personal message for my wife." His face darkened. He smote the hull angrily and turned away. "Come on. Let's go."

But as they continued the search, the signals followed them. It became apparent that the outer periphery of the asteroid had been abandoned; the tribe had withdrawn to the center. Then, far down a shaft wrought of beaten aluminum, a hatch opened, light blazed forth, and Joseph appeared in an ancient spacesuit fashioned of glass cloth. He stood in the clumsy sack, his devil face staring, his hands clutched in supplication, his devil mouth making motions.

Foyle stared at the old man, took a step toward him, and then stopped, fists clenched, throat working as fury arose within him. And Jisabella, looking at Foyle, cried out in horror. The old tattooing had returned to his face, blood red against the pallor of the skin, scarlet instead of black, truly a tiger mask in color as well as design.

"Gully!" she cried. "My God! Your face!"

Foyle ignored her and stood glaring at Joseph while the old man made beseeching gestures, motioned to them to enter the interior of the asteroid, and then disappeared. Only then did Foyle turn to Jisbella and ask: "What? What did you say?"

Through the clear globe of the helmet she could see his face distinctly. And as the rage within Foyle died away, Jisbella saw the blood-red tattooing fade and disappear.

"Did you see that joker?" Foyle demanded. "That was Joseph. Did you see him begging and pleading after what he did to me . . . ? What did you say?"

"Your face, Gully. I know what's happened to your face."

"What are you talking about?"

"You wanted something that would control you, Gully. Well, you've got it. Your face. It—" Jisbella began to laugh hysterically. "You'll have to learn control now, Gully. You'll never be able to give way to emotion . . . any emotion . . . because—"

But he was staring past her and suddenly he shot up the aluminum shaft with a yell. He jerked to a stop before an open door and began to whoop in triumph. The door opened into a tool locker, four by four by nine. There were shelves in the locker and a jumble of old provisions and discarded containers. It was Foyle's coffin aboard the "Nomad."

Joseph and his people had succeeded in sealing the wreck into their asteroid before the holocaust of Foyle's escape had rendered further work impossible. The interior of the ship was virtually untouched. Foyle took Jisbella's arm and dragged her on a quick tour of the ship and finally to the purser's locker where Foyle tore at the windrows of wreckage and debris until he disclosed a massive steel face, blank and impenetrable.

"We've got a choice," he panted. "Either we tear the safe out of the hull and carry it back to Terra where we can work on it, or we open it here. I vote for here. Maybe Dagenham was lying. All depends on what tools Sam has in the Weekender anyway. Come back to the ship, Jiz."

He never noticed her silence and preoccupation until they were back aboard the Weekender and he had finished his urgent search for tools.

"Nothing!" he exclaimed impatiently. "There isn't a hammer or a drill aboard. Nothing but gadgets for opening bottles and rations."

Jisbella didn't answer. She never took her eyes off his face.

"Why are you staring at me like that?" Foyle demanded.

"I'm fascinated," Jisbella answered slowly.

"By what?"

"I'm going to show you something, Gully."

"What?"

"How much I despise you."

Jisbella slapped him thrice. Stung by the blows, Foyle started up furiously. Jisbella picked up a hand mirror and held it before him.

"Look at yourself, Gully," she said quietly. "Look at your face."

He looked. He saw the old tattoo marks flaming blood-red under the skin, turning his face into a scarlet and white tiger mask. He was so chilled by the appalling spectacle that his rage died at once, and simultaneously the mask disappeared.

"My God . . ." he whispered. "Oh my God . . ."

"I had to make you lose your temper to show you," Jisbella said.

"What's it mean, Jiz? Did Baker goof the job?"

"I don't think so. I think you've got scars under the skin, Gully . . . from the original tattooing and then from the bleaching. Needle scars. They don't show normally, but they do show, blood red, when your emotions take over and your heart begins pumping blood . . . when you're furious or frightened or passionate or possessed . . . Do you understand?"

He shook his head, still staring at his face, touching it in bewilderment.

"You said you wished you could carry me in your pocket to stick pins in you when you lose control. You've got something better than that, Gully, or worse, poor darling. You've got your face."

"No!" he said. "No!"

"You can't ever lose control, Gully. You'll never be able to drink too much, eat too much, love too much, hate too much . . . You'll have to hold yourself with an iron grip."

"No!" he insisted desperately. "It can be fixed. Baker can do it, or somebody else. I can't walk around afraid to feel anything because it'll turn me into a freak!"

"I don't think this can be fixed, Gully."

"Skin-graft . . ."

"No. The scars are too deep for graft. You'll never get rid of this stigmata, Gully. You'll have to learn to live with it."

Foyle flung the mirror from him in sudden rage, and again the blood-red mask flared up under his skin. He lunged out of the main cabin to the main hatch where he pulled his spacesuit down and began to squirm into it.

"Gully! Where are you going? What are you going to do?"

"Get tools," he shouted. "Tools for the safe."

"Where?"

"In the asteroid. They've got dozens of warehouses stuffed with tools from wrecked ships. There have to be drills there, everything I need. Don't come with me. There may be trouble. How is my God damned face now? Showing it? By Christ, I hope there *is* trouble!"

He corked his suit and went into the asteroid. He found a hatch separating the habited core from the outer void. He banged on the door. He waited and banged again and continued the imperious summons until at last the hatch was opened. Arms reached out and yanked him in, and the hatch was closed behind him. It had no air lock.

He blinked in the light and scowled at Joseph and his innocent people gathering before him, their faces hideously decorated. And he knew that his own face must be flaming red and white for he saw Joseph start, and he saw the devil mouth shape the syllables: NOMAD.

Foyle strode through the crowd, scattering them brutally. He smashed Joseph with a backhand blow from his mailed fist. He searched through the inhabited corridors, recognizing them dimly, and he came at last to the chamber, half natural cave, half antique hull, where the tools were stored.

He rooted and ferreted, gathering up drills, diamond bits, acids, thermites, crystallants, dynamite jellies, fuses. In the gently revolving asteroid the gross weight of the equipment was reduced to less than a hundred pounds. He lumped it into a mass, roughly bound it together with cable, and started out of the store-cave.

Joseph and his Scientific People were waiting for him, like fleas waiting for a wolf. They darted at him and he battered through them, harried, delighted, savage. The armor of his spacesuit protected him from their attacks and he went down the passages searching for a hatch that would lead out into the void.

Jisbella's voice came to him, tinny on the earphones and agitated: "Gully, can you hear me? This is Jiz. Gully, listen to me."

"Go ahead."

"Another ship came up two minutes ago. It's drifting on the other side of the asteroid."

"What!"

"It's marked with yellow and black colors, like a hornet."

"Dagenham's colors!"

"Then we've been followed."

"What else? Dagenham's probably had a fix on me ever since we busted out of Gouffre Martel. I was a fool not to think of it. We've got to work fast, Jiz. Cork up in a suit and meet me aboard 'Nomad.' The purser's room. Go, girl."

"But Gully . . ."

"Sign off. They may be monitoring our waveband. Go!"

He drove through the asteroid, reached a barrel hatch, broke through the guard before it, smashed it open and went into the void of the outer passages. The Scientific People were too desperate getting the hatch closed to stop him. But he knew they would follow him; they were raging.

He hauled the bulk of his equipment through twists and turns to the wreck of the "Nomad." Jisbella was waiting for him in the purser's room. She made a move to turn on her micro-wave set and Foyle stopped her. He placed his helmet against hers and shouted: "No shortwave. They'll be monitoring and they'll locate us by D/F. You can hear me like this, can't you?"

She nodded.

"All right. We've got maybe an hour before Dagenham locates us. We've got maybe an hour before Joseph and his mob come after us. We're in a hell of a jam. We've got to work fast."

She nodded again.

"No time to open the safe and transport the bullion."

"If it's there."

"Dagenham's here, isn't he? That's proof it's there. We'll have to cut the whole safe out of the 'Nomad' and get it into the Weekender. Then we blast."

"But—"

"Just listen to me and do what I say. Go back to the Weekender. Empty it out. Jettison everything we don't need . . . all supplies except emergency rations."

"Why?"

"Because I don't know how many tons this safe weighs, and the ship may not be able to handle it when we come back to gravity. We've got to make allowances in advance. It'll mean a tough trip back but it's worth it. Strip the ship. Fast! Go, girl. Go!"

He pushed her away and without another glance in her direction, attacked the safe. It was built into the structural steel of the hull, a massive steel ball some four feet in diameter. It was welded to the strakes and ribs of the "Nomad" at twelve different spots. Foyle attacked each weld in turn with acids, drills, thermite, and refrigerants. He was operating on the theory of structural strain . . . to heat, freeze, and etch the steel until its crystalline structure was distorted and its physical strength destroyed. He was fatiguing the metal.

Jisbella returned and he realized that forty-five minutes had passed. He was dripping and shaking but the globe of the safe hung free of the hull with a dozen rough knobs protruding from its surface. Foyle motioned urgently to Jisbella and she strained her weight against the safe with him. They could not budge its mass together. As they sank back in exhaustion and despair, a quick shadow eclipsed the sunlight pouring through the rents in the "Nomad" hull. They stared up. A spaceship was circling the asteroid less than a quarter of a mile off.

Foyle placed his helmet against Jisbella's. "Dagenham," he gasped. "Looking for us. Probably got a crew down here combing for us too. Soon as they talk to Joseph they'll be here."

"Oh Gully . . . ."

"We've still got a chance. Maybe they won't spot Sam's Weekender until they've made a couple of revolutions. It's hidden in that crater. Maybe we can get the safe aboard in the meantime."

"How, Gully?"

"I don't know, damn it! I don't know." He pounded his fists together in frustration. "I'm finished."

"Couldn't we blast it out?"

"Blast . . . ? What, bombs instead of brains? Is this Mental McQueen speaking?"

"Listen. Blast it with something explosive. That would act like a rocket jet . . . give it a thrust."

"Yes, I've got that. But then what? How do we get it into the ship, girl? Can't keep blasting. Haven't got time."

"No, we bring the ship to the safe."

"What?"

"Blast the safe straight out into space. Then bring the ship around and let the safe sail right into the main hatch. Like catching a ball in your hat. See?"

He saw. "By God, Jiz, we can do it." Foyle leaped to the pile of equipment and began sorting out sticks of dynamite gelatine, fuses and caps.

"We'll have to use the short-wave. One of us stays with the safe; one of us pilots the ship. Man with the safe talks the man with the ship into position. Right?"

"Right. You'd better pilot, Gully. I'll do the talking."

He nodded, fixing explosive to the face of the safe, attaching caps and fuses. Then he placed his helmet against hers. "Vacuum fuses, Jiz. Timed for two minutes. When I give the word by short-wave, just pull off the fuse heads and get the hell out of the way. Right?"

"Right."

"Stay with the safe. Once you've talked it into the ship, come right after it. Don't wait for anything. It's going to be close."

He thumped her shoulder and returned to the Weekender. He left the outer hatch open, and the inner door of the airlock as well. The ship's air emptied out immediately. Airless and stripped by Jisbella, it looked dismal and forlorn.

Foyle went directly to the controls, sat down and switched on his microwave set. "Stand by," he muttered. "I'm coming out now."

He ignited the jets, blew the laterals for three seconds and then the forwards. The Weekender lifted easily, shaking debris from her back and sides like a whale surfacing. As she slid up and back, Foyle called: "Dynamite, Jiz! Now!"

There was no blast; there was no flash. A new crater opened in the asteroid below him and a flower of rubble sprang upward, rapidly outdistancing a dull steel ball that followed leisurely, turning in a weary spin.

"Ease off." Jisbella's voice came cold and competent over the earphones. "You're backing too fast. And incidentally, trouble's arrived."

He braked with the rear jets, looking down in alarm. The surface of the asteroid was covered with a swarm of hornets. They were Dagenham's crew in yellow and black banded spacesuits. They were buzzing around a single figure in white that dodged and spun and eluded them. It was Jisbella.

"Steady as you go," Jiz said quietly, although he could hear how hard she was breathing. "Ease off a little more . . . Roll a quarter turn."

He obeyed her almost automatically, still watching the struggle below. The flank of the Weekender cut off any view of the trajectory of the safe as it approached him, but he could still see Jisabella and Dagenham's men. She ignited her suit rocket . . . he could see the tiny spurt of flame shoot out from her back . . . and came sailing up from the surface of the asteroid. A score of flames burst out from the backs of Dagenham's men as they followed. Half a dozen dropped the pursuit of Jisbella and came up after the Weekender.

"It's going to be close, Gully," Jisbella was gasping now, but her voice was still steady. "Dagenham's ship came down on the other side, but they've probably signaled him by now and he'll be on his way. Hold your position, Gully. About ten seconds now . . ."

The hornets closed in and engulfed the tiny white suit.

"Foyle! Can you hear me? Foyle!" Dagenham's voice came in fuzzily and finally cleared. "This is Dagenham calling on your band. Come in, Foyle!"

"Jiz! Jiz! Can you get clear of them?"

"Hold your position, Gully . . . There she goes! It's a hole in one, son!"

A crushing shock racked the Weekender as the safe, moving slowly but massively, rammed into the main hatch. At the same moment the white suited figure broke out of the cluster of yellow wasps. It came rocketing up to the Weekender, hotly pursued.

"Come on, Jiz! Come on!" Foyle howled. "Come, girl! Come!"

As Jisbella disappeared from sight behind the flank of the Weekender, Foyle set controls and prepared for top acceleration.

"Foyle! Will you answer me? This is Dagenham speaking."

"To hell with you, Dagenham," Foyle shouted. "Give me the word when you're aboard, Jiz, and hold on."

"I can't make it, Gully."

"Come on, girl!"

"I can't get aboard. The safe's blocking the hatch. It's wedged in halfway . . ."

"Jiz!"

"There's no way in, I tell you," she cried in despair. "I'm blocked out."

He stared around wildly. Dagenham's men were boarding the hull of the Weekender with the menacing purpose of professional raiders. Dagenham's ship was lifting over the brief horizon of the asteroid on a dead course for him. His head began to spin.

"Foyle, you're finished. You and the girl. But I'll offer a deal . . ."

"Gully, help me. Do something, Gully. I'm lost!"

"Vorga," he said in a strangled voice. He closed his eyes and tripped the controls. The tail jets roared. The Weekender shook and shuddered forward. It broke free of Dagenham's boarders, of Jisbella, of warnings and pleas. It pressed Foyle back into the pilot's chair with the blackout of 10G acceleration, an acceleration that was less pressing, less painful, less treacherous than the passion that drove him.

And as he passed from sight there rose up on his face the blood-red stigmata of his possession.

PART 2

With a heart of furious fancies
Whereof I am commander,
With a burning spear and a horse of air,
To the wilderness I wander.
With a knight of ghosts and shadows
I summoned am to tourney,
Ten leagues beyond the wide world's end—
Me thinks it is no journey.

Tom-a-Bedlam

CHAPTER EIGHT

THE OLD YEAR SOURED as pestilence poisoned the planets. The war gained momentum and grew from a distant affair of romantic raids and skirmishes in space to a holocaust in the making. It became evident that the last of the World Wars was done and the first of the Solar Wars had begun.

The belligerents slowly massed men and materiel for the havoc. The Outer Satellites introduced universal conscription, and the Inner Planets perforce followed suit. Industries, trades, sciences, skills, and professions were drafted; regulations and oppressions followed. The armies and navies requisitioned and commanded.

Commerce obeyed, for this war (like all wars) was the shooting phase of a commercial struggle. But populations rebelled, and draft-jaunting and labor-jaunting became critical problems. Spy scares and invasion scares spread. The hysterical became informers and lynchers. An ominous foreboding paralyzed every home from Baffin Island to the Falklands. The dying year was enlivened only by the advent of the Four Mile Circus.

This was the popular nickname for the grotesque entourage of Geoffrey Fourmyle of Ceres, a wealthy young buffoon from the largest of the asteroids. Fourmyle of Ceres was enormously rich; he was also enormously amusing. He was the classic *nouveau riche* of all time. His entourage was a cross between a country circus and the comic court of a Bulgarian kinglet, as witness this typical arrival in Green Bay, Wisconsin.

Early in the morning a lawyer, wearing the stovepipe hat of a legal clan, appeared with a list of camp sites in his hand and a small fortune in his pocket. He settled on a four-acre meadow facing Lake Michigan and rented it for an exorbitant fee. He was followed by a gang of surveyors from the Mason & Dixon clan. In twenty minutes the surveyors had laid out a camp site and the word had spread that the Four Mile Circus was arriving. Locals from Wisconsin, Michigan, and Minnesota came to watch the fun.

Twenty roustabouts jaunted in, each carrying a tent pack on his back. There was a mighty overture of bawled orders, shouts, curses, and the tortured scream of compressed air. Twenty giant tents ballooned upward, their lac and latex surfaces gleaming as they dried in the winter sun. The spectators cheered.

A six-motor helicopter drifted down and hovered over a giant trampoline. Its belly opened and a cascade of furnishings came down. Servants, valets, chefs, and waiters jaunted in. They furnished and decorated the tents. The kitchens began smoking and the odor of frying, broiling, and baking pervaded the camp. Fourmyle's private police were already on duty, patrolling the four acres, keeping the huge crowd of spectators back.

Then, by plane, by car, by bus, by truck, by bike and by jaunte came Fourmyle's entourage. Librarians and books, scientists and laboratories, philosophers, poets, athletes. Racks of swords and sabres were set up, and judo mats and a boxing ring. A fifty-foot pool was sunk in the ground and filled by pump from the lake. An interesting altercation arose between two beefy athletes as to whether the pool should be warmed for swimming or frozen for skating.

Musicians, actors, jugglers, and acrobats arrived. The uproar became deafening. A crew of mechanics melted a greasepit and began revving up Fourmyle's collection of vintage diesel harvesters. Last of all came the camp followers: wives, daughters, mistresses, whores, beggars, chiselers, and grafters. By midmorning the roar of the circus could be heard for four miles, hence the nickname.

At noon, Fourmyle of Ceres arrived with a display of conspicuous transportation so outlandish that it had been known to make seven-year melancholics laugh. A giant amphibian thrummed up from the south and landed on the lake. An LST barge emerged from the plane and droned across the water to the shore. Its forward wall banged down into a drawbridge and out came a twentieth century staff car. Wonder piled on wonder for the delighted spectators, for the staff car drove a matter of twenty yards to the center of camp and then stopped.

"What can possibly come next? Bike?"

"No, roller skates."

"He'll come out on a pogo stick."

Fourmyle capped their wildest speculations. The muzzle of a circus cannon thrust up from the staff car. There was the bang of a black-powder explosion and Fourmyle of Ceres was shot out of the cannon in a graceful arc to the very door of his tent where he was caught in a net by four valets. The applause that greeted him could be heard for six miles. Fourmyle climbed onto his valets' shoulders and motioned for silence.

"Friends, Romans, Countrymen," Fourmyle began earnestly. "Lend me your ears, Shakespeare. 1564–1616. Damn!" Four white doves shook themselves out of Fourmyle's sleeves and fluttered away. He regarded them with astonishment, then continued. "Friends, greetings, salutations, *bonjour, bon ton, bon vivant, bon voyage, bon*— What the hell?" Fourmyle's pockets caught fire and rocketed forth Roman Candles. He tried to put himself out. Streamers and confetti burst from him. "Friends . . . Shut up! I'll get this speech straight. Quiet! Friends—!" Fourmyle looked down at himself in dismay. His clothes were melting away, revealing lurid scarlet underwear. "Kleinmann!" he bellowed furiously. "Kleinmann! What's happened to your goddamned hypno-training?"

A hairy head thrust out of a tent. "You stoodied for dis sbeech last night, Fourmyle?"

"Damn right. For two hours I stoodied. Never took my head out of the hypno-oven. Kleinmann on Prestidigitation."

"No, no, no!" the hairy man bawled. "How many times must I tell you? Prestidigitation is not sbeechmaking. Is magic. *Dumbkopf!* You haff the wrong hypnosis taken!"

The scarlet underwear began melting. Fourmyle toppled from the shoulders of his shaking valets and disappeared within his tent. There was a roar of laughter and cheering and the Four Mile Circus ripped into high gear. The kitchens sizzled and smoked. There was a perpetuity of eating and drinking. The music never stopped. The vaudeville never ceased.

Inside his tent, Fourmyle changed his clothes, changed his mind, changed again, undressed again, kicked his valets, and called for his tailor in a bastard tongue of French, Mayfair, and affectation. Halfway into a new suit, he recollected he had neglected to bathe. He slapped his tailor, ordered ten gallons of scent to be decanted into the pool, and was stricken with poetic inspiration. He summoned his resident poet.

"Take this down," Fourmyle commanded. "*Le roi est mort, les*— Wait. What rhymes to moon?"

"June," his poet suggested. "Croon, soon, dune, loon, noon, rune, tune, boon . . ."

"I forgot my experiment!" Fourmyle exclaimed. "Dr. Bohun! Dr. Bohun!"

Half-naked, he rushed pell-mell into the laboratory where he blew himself and Dr. Bohun, his resident chemist, halfway across the tent. As the chemist attempted to raise himself from the floor he found himself seized in a most painful and embarrassing strangle hold.

"Nogouchi!" Fourmyle shouted. "Hi! Nogouchi! I just invented a new judo hold."

Fourmyle stood up, lifted the suffocating chemist and jaunted to the judo mat where the little Japanese inspected the hold and shook his head.

"No, please." He hissed politely. "Hfffff. Pressure on windpipe are not perpetually lethal. Hfffff. I show you, please." He seized the dazed chemist, whirled him and deposited him on the mat in a position of perpetual self-strangulation. "You observe, please, Fourmyle?"

But Fourmyle was in the library bludgeoning his librarian over the head with Bloch's "*Das Sexual Leben*" (eight pounds, nine ounces) because that unhappy man could produce no text on the manufacture of perpetual motion machines. He rushed to his physics laboratory where he destroyed an expensive chronometer to experiment with cog wheels, jaunted to the bandstand where he seized a baton and led the orchestra into confusion, put on skates and fell into the scented swimming pool, was hauled out, swearing fulminously at the lack of ice, and was heard to express a desire for solitude.

"I wish to commute with myself," Fourmyle said, kicking his valets in all directions. He was snoring before the last of them limped to the door and closed it behind him.

The snoring stopped and Foyle arose. "That ought to hold them for today," he muttered, and went into his dressing room. He stood before a mirror, took a deep breath and held it, meanwhile watching his face. At the expiration of one minute it was still untainted. He continued to hold his breath, maintaining rigid control over pulse and muscle, mastering the strain with iron calm. At two minutes and twenty seconds the stigmata appeared, blood-red. Foyle let out his breath. The tiger mask faded.

"Better," he murmured. "Much better. The old fakir was right, Yoga is the answer. Control. Pulse, breath, bowels, brains."

He stripped and examined his body. He was in magnificent condition, but his skin still showed delicate silver seams in a network from neck to ankles. It looked as though someone had carved an outline of the nervous system into Foyle's flesh. The silver seams were the scars of an operation that had not yet faded.

That operation had cost Foyle a ¢r 200,000 bribe to the chief surgeon of the Mars Commando Brigade and had transformed him into an extraordinary fighting machine. Every nerve plexus had been rewired, miscroscopic transistors and transformers had been buried in muscle and bone, a minute platinum outlet showed at the base of his spine. To this Foyle affixed a power-pack the size of a pea and switched it on. His body began an internal electronic vibration that was almost mechanical.

"More machine than man," he thought. He dressed, rejected the extravagant apparel of Fourmyle of Ceres for the anonymous black coverall of action.

He jaunted to Robin Wednesbury's apartment in the lonely building amidst the Wisconsin pines. It was the real reason for the advent of the Four Mile Circus in Green Bay. He jaunted and arrived in darkness and empty space and immediately plummeted down. "Wrong co-ordinates!" he thought. "Misjaunted?" The broken end of a rafter dealt him a bruising blow and he landed heavily on a shattered floor upon the putrefying remains of a corpse.

Foyle leaped up in calm revulsion. He pressed hard with his tongue against his right upper first molar. The operation that had transformed half his body into an electronic machine, had located the control switchboard in his teeth. Foyle pressed a tooth with his tongue and the peripheral cells of his retina were excited into emitting a soft light. He looked down two pale beams at the corpse of a man.

The corpse lay in the apartment below Robin Wednesbury's flat. It was gutted. Foyle looked up. Above him was a ten-foot hole where the floor of Robin's living room had been. The entire building stank of fire, smoke, and rot.

"Jacked," Foyle said softly. "This place has been jacked. What happened?"

The jaunting age had crystallized the hoboes, tramps, and vagabonds of the world into a new class. They followed the night from east to west, always in darkness, always in search of loot, the leavings of disaster, carrion. If earthquake shattered a warehouse, they were jacking it the following night. If fire opened a house or explosion split the defenses of a shop, they jaunted in and scavenged. They called themselves Jack-jaunters. They were jackals.

Foyle climbed up through the wreckage to the corridor on the floor above. The Jack-jaunters had a camp there. A whole calf roasted before a fire which sparked up to the sky through a rent in the roof. There were a dozen men and three women around the fire, rough, dangerous, jabbering in the Cockney rhyming slang of the jackals. They were dressed in mismatched clothes and drinking potato beer from champagne glasses.

An ominous growl of anger and terror met Foyle's appearance as the big man in black came up through the rubble, his intent eyes emitting pale beams of light. Calmly, he strode through the rising mob to the entrance of Robin Wednesbury's flat. His iron control gave him an air of detachment.

"If she's dead," he thought, "I'm finished. I've got to use her. But if she's dead . . ."

Robin's apartment was gutted like the rest of the building. The living room was an oval of floor around the jagged hole in the center. Foyle searched for a body. Two men and a woman were in the bed in the bedroom. The men cursed. The woman shrieked at the apparition. The men hurled themselves at Foyle. He backed a step and pressed his tongue against his upper incisors. Neural circuits buzzed and every sense and response in his body was accelerated by a factor of five.

The effect was an instantaneous reduction of the external world to extreme slow motion. Sound became a deep garble. Color shifted down the spectrum to the red. The two assailants seemed to float toward him with dreamlike languor. To the rest of the world Foyle became a blur of action. He side-stepped the blow inching toward him, walked around the man, raised him and threw him toward the crater in the living room. He threw the second man after the first jackal. To Foyle's accelerated senses their bodies seemed to drift slowly, still in mid-stride, fists inching forward, open mouths emitting heavy clotted sounds.

Foyle whipped to the woman cowering in the bed.

"Wsthrabdy?" the blur asked.

The woman shrieked.

Foyle pressed his upper incisors again, cutting off the acceleration. The external world shook itself out of slow motion back to normal. Sound and color leaped up the spectrum and the two jackals disappeared through the crater and crashed into the apartment below.

"Was there a body?" Foyle repeated gently. "A Negro girl?" The woman was unintelligible. He took her by the hair and shook her, then hurled her through the crater in the living room floor.

His search for a clue to Robin's fate was interrupted by the mob from the hall. They carried torches and makeshift weapons. The Jack-jaunters were not professional killers. They only worried defenseless prey to death. "Don't bother me," Foyle warned quietly, ferreting intently through closets and under overturned furniture.

They edged closer, goaded by a ruffian in a mink suit and a tricornered hat, and inspired by the curses percolating up from the floor below. The man in the tricorne threw a torch at Foyle. It burned him. Foyle accelerated again and the Jack-jaunters were transformed into living statues. Foyle picked up half a chair and calmly clubbed the slow-motion figures. They remained upright. He thrust the man in the tricorne down on the floor and knelt on him. Then he decelerated.

Again the external world came to life. The jackals dropped in their tracks, pole-axed. The man in the tricorne hat and mink suit roared.

"Was there a body in here?" Foyle asked. "Negro girl. Very tall. Very beautiful."

The man writhed and attempted to gouge Foyle's eyes.

"You keep track of bodies," Foyle said gently. "Some of you Jacks like dead girls better than live ones. Did you find her body in here?"

Receiving no satisfactory answer, he picked up a torch and set fire to the mink suit. He followed the Jack-jaunter into the living room and watched him with detached interest. The man howled, toppled over the edge of the crater and flamed down into the darkness below.

"Was there a body?" Foyle called down quietly. He shook his head at the answer. "Not very deft," he murmured. "I've got to learn how to extract information. Dagenham could teach me a thing or two."

He switched off his electronic system and jaunted.

He appeared in Green Bay, smelling so abominably of singed hair and scorched skin that he entered the local Presteign shop (jewels, perfumes, cosmetics, ionics & surrogates) to buy a deodorant. But the local Mr. Presto had evidently witnessed the arrival of the Four Mile Circus and recognized him. Foyle at once awoke from his detached intensity and became the outlandish Fourmyle of Ceres. He clowned and cavorted, bought a twelve-ounce flagon of *Euge No. 5* at ¢r 100 the ounce, dabbed himself delicately and tossed the bottle into the street to the edification and delight of Mr. Presto.

The record clerk at the County Record Office was unaware of Foyle's identity and was obdurate and uncompromising.

"No, Sir. County Records Are Not Viewed Without Proper Court Order For Sufficient Cause. That Must Be Final."

Foyle examined him keenly and without rancor. "Asthenic type," he decided. "Slender, long-boned, no strength. Epileptoid character. Self-centered, pedantic, single-minded, shallow. Not bribable; too repressed and strait-laced. But repression's the chink in his armor."

An hour later six followers from the Four Mile Circus waylaid the record clerk. They were of the female persuasion and richly endowed with vice. Two hours later, the record clerk, dazed by flesh and the devil, delivered up his information. The apartment building had been opened to Jack-jaunting by a gas explosion two weeks earlier. All tenants had been forced to move. Robin Wednesbury was in protective confinement in Mercy Hospital near the Iron Mountain Proving Grounds.

"Protective confinement?" Foyle wondered. "What for? What's she done?"

It took thirty minutes to organize a Christmas party in the Four Mile Circus. It was made up of musicians, singers, actors, and rabble who knew the Iron Mountain co-ordinates. Led by their chief buffoon, they jaunted up with music, fireworks, firewater, and gifts. They paraded through the town spreading largess and laughter. They blundered into the radar field of the Proving Ground protection system and were driven out with laughter. Fourmyle of Ceres, dressed as Santa Claus, scattering bank notes from a huge sack over his shoulder and, leaping in agony as the induction field of the protection system burned his bottom, made an entrancing spectacle. They burst into Mercy Hospital, following Santa Claus who roared and cavorted with the detached calm of a solemn elephant. He kissed the nurses, made drunk the attendants, pestered the patients with gifts, littered the corridors with money, and abruptly disappeared when the happy rioting reached such heights that the police had to be called. Much later it was discovered that a patient had disappeared too, despite the fact that she had been under sedation and was incapable of jaunting. As a matter of fact she departed from the hospital inside Santa's sack.

Foyle jaunted with her over his shoulder to the hospital grounds. There, in a quiet grove of pines under a frosty sky, he helped her out of the sack. She wore severe white hospital pajamas and was beautiful. He removed his own costume, watching the girl intently, waiting to see if she would recognize him and remember him.

She was alarmed and confused; her telesending was like heat lightning: *"My God! Who is he? What's happened? The music. The uproar. Why kidnapped in a sack? Drunks slurring on trombones. 'Yes, Virginia, there is*

a Santa Claus.' Adeste Fidelis. What's he want from me? Who is he?"
"I'm Fourmyle of Ceres," Foyle said.
"What? Who? Fourmyle of—? Yes, of course. *The buffoon. The bourgeois gentilhomme. Vulgarity. Imbecility. Obscenity. The Four Mile Circus.* My God! Am I telesending? Can you hear me?"
"I hear you, Miss Wednesbury," Foyle said quietly.
"What have you done? Why? What do you want with me? I—"
"I want you to look at me."
"*Bonjour, Madame. Into my sack, Madame. Ecco! Look at me.* I'm looking," Robin said, trying to control the jangle of her thoughts. She gazed up into his face without recognition. "*It's a face. I've seen so many like it. The faces of men, oh God! The features of masculinity. Everyman in rut. Will God never save us from brute desire?*"
"My rutting season's over, Miss Wednesbury."
"I'm sorry you heard that. I'm terrified, naturally. I— You know me?"
"I know you."
"We've met before?" She scrutinized him closely, but still without recognition. Deep down inside Foyle there was a surge of triumph. If this woman of all women failed to remember him he was safe, provided he kept blood and brains and face under control.
"We've never met," he said. "I've heard of you. I want something from you. That's why we're here; to talk about it. If you don't like my offer you can go back to the hospital."
"You want something? *But I've got nothing . . . nothing. Nothing's left but shame and— Oh God! Why did the suicide fail? Why couldn't I—*"
"So that's it?" Foyle interrupted softly. "You tried to commit suicide, eh? That accounts for the gas explosion that opened the building . . . And your protective confinement. Attempted suicide. Why weren't you hurt in the explosion?"
"So many were hurt. So many died. But I didn't. I'm unlucky, I suppose. I've been unlucky all my life."
"Why suicide?"
"I'm tired. I'm finished. I've lost everything . . . I'm on the army gray list . . . suspected, watched, reported. No job. No family. No— Why suicide? Dear God, what else but suicide?"
"You can work for me."
"I can . . . What did you say?"
"I want you to work for me, Miss Wednesbury."
She burst into hysterical laughter. "For you? *Another camp follower in the Circus?* Work for you, Fourmyle?"
"You've got sex on the brain," he said gently. "I'm not looking for tarts. They look for me, as a rule."
"I'm sorry. *I'm obsessed by the brute who destroyed me. I*— I'll try to make sense." Robin calmed herself. "Let me understand you. You've taken me out of the hospital to offer me a job. You've heard of me. That means you want something special. My specialty is telesending."
"And charm."

"What?"

"I want to buy your charm, Miss Wednesbury."

"I don't understand."

"Why," Foyle said mildly. "It ought to be simple for you. I'm the buffoon. I'm vulgarity, imbecility, obscenity. That's got to stop. I want you to be my social secretary."

"You expect me to believe that? You could hire a hundred social secretaries . . . a thousand, with your money. You expect me to believe that I'm the only one for you? That you had to kidnap me from protective confinement to get me?"

Foyle nodded. "That's right, there are thousands, but only one that can telesend."

"What's that got to do with it?"

"You're going to be the ventriloquist; I'm going to be your dummy. I don't know the upper classes; you do. They have their own talk, their own jokes, their own manners. If a man wants to be accepted by them he's got to talk their language. I can't, but you can. You'll talk for me, through my mouth . . ."

"But you could learn."

"No. It would take too long. And charm can't be learned. I want to buy your charm, Miss Wednesbury. Now, about salary. I'll pay you a thousand a month."

Her eyes widened. "You're very generous, Fourmyle."

"I'll clean up this suicide charge for you."

"You're very kind."

"And I'll guarantee to get you off the army gray list. You'll be back on the white list by the time you finish working for me. You can start with a clean slate and a bonus. You can start living again."

Robin's lips trembled and then she began to cry. She sobbed and shook and Foyle had to steady her. "Well," he asked. "Will you do it?"

She nodded. "You're so kind . . . It's . . . I'm not used to kindness any more."

The dull concussion of a distant explosion made Foyle stiffen. "Christ!" he exclaimed in sudden panic. "Another Blue Jaunte. I—"

"No," Robin said. "I don't know what blue jaunte is, but that's the Proving Ground. They—" She looked up at Foyle's face and screamed. The unexpected shock of the explosion and the vivid chain of associations had wrenched loose his iron control. The blood-red scars of tattooing showed under his skin. She stared at him in horror, still screaming.

He touched his face once, then leaped forward and gagged her. Once again he had hold of himself.

"It shows, eh?" he murmured with a ghastly smile. "Lost my grip for a minute. Thought I was back in Gouffre Martel listening to a Blue Jaunte. Yes, I'm Foyle. The brute who destroyed you. You had to know, sooner or later, but I'd hoped it would be later, I'm Foyle, back again. Will you be quiet and listen to me?"

She shook her head frantically, trying to struggle out of his grasp. With detached calm he punched her jaw. Robin sagged. Foyle picked her up, wrapped her in his coat and held her in his arms, waiting for consciousness to return. When he saw her eyelids flutter he spoke again.

"Don't move or you'll be sick. Maybe I didn't pull that punch enough."

"*Brute . . . Beast . . .*"

"I could do this the wrong way," he said. "I could blackmail you. I know your mother and sisters are on Callisto, that you're classed as an alien belligerent by association. That puts you on the black list, *ipso facto*. Is that right? *Ipso facto*. 'By the very fact.' Latin. You can't trust hypno-learning. I could point out that all I have to do is send anonymous information to Central Intelligence and you wouldn't be just suspect any more. They'd be ripping information out of you inside twelve hours . . ."

He felt her shudder. "But I'm not going to do it that way. I'm going to tell you the truth because I want to turn you into a partner. Your mother's in the Inner Planets. She's in the Inner Planets," he repeated. "She may be on Terra."

"Safe?" she whispered.

"I don't know."

"Put me down."

"You're cold."

"Put me down."

He set her on her feet.

"You destroyed me once," she said in choked tones. "Are you trying to destroy me again?"

"No. Will you listen?"

She nodded.

"I was lost in space. I was dead and rotting for six months. A ship came up that could have saved me. It passed me by. It let me die. A ship named 'Vorga.' 'Vorga-T:1339.' Does that mean anything to you?"

"No."

"Jiz McQueen—a friend of mine who's dead now—once told me to find out why I was left to rot. That would be the answer to who gave the order. So I started buying information about 'Vorga.' Any information."

"What's that to do with my mother?"

"Just listen. Information was tough to buy. The 'Vorga' records were removed from the Bo'ness & Uig files. I managed to locate three names . . . three out of a standard crew of four officers and twelve men. Nobody knew anything or nobody would talk. And I found this." Foyle took a silver locket from his pocket and handed it to Robin. "It was pawned by some spaceman off the 'Vorga.' That's all I could find out."

Robin uttered a cry and opened the locket with trembling fingers. Inside was her picture and the pictures of two other girls. As the locket was opened, the 3D photos smiled and whispered: "Love from Robin, Mama . . . Love from Holly, Mama . . . Love from Wendy, Mama . . ."

"It is my mother's," Robin wept. "It . . . She . . . For pity's sake, where is she? What happened?"

"I don't know," Foyle said steadily. "But I can guess. I think your mother got out of that concentration camp . . . one way or another."

"And my sisters too. She'd never leave them."

"Maybe your sisters too. I think 'Vorga' was running refugees out of Callisto. Your family paid with money and jewelry to get aboard and be taken to the Inner Planets. That's how a spaceman off the 'Vorga' came to pawn this locket."

"Then where are they?"

"I don't know. Maybe they were dumped on Mars or Venus. Most probably they were sold to a labor camp on the Moon, which is why they haven't been able to get in touch with you. I don't know where they are, but 'Vorga' can tell us."

"Are you lying? Tricking me?"

"Is that locket a lie? I'm telling the truth . . . all the truth I know. I want to find out why they left me to die, and who gave the order. The man who gave the order will know where your mother and sisters are. He'll tell you . . . before I kill him. He'll have plenty of time. He'll be a long time dying."

Robin looked at him in horror. The passion that gripped him was making his face once again show the scarlet stigmata. He looked like a tiger closing in for the kill.

"I've got a fortune to spend . . . never mind how I got it. I've got three months to finish the job. I've learned enough maths to compute the probabilities. Three months is the outside before they figure that Fourmyle of Ceres is Gully Foyle. Ninety days. From New Year's to All Fools. Will you join me?"

"You?" Robin cried with loathing. "Join you?"

"All this Four Mile Circus is camouflage. Nobody ever suspects a clown. But I've been studying, learning, preparing for the finish. All I need now is you."

"Why?"

"I don't know where the hunt is going to lead me . . . society or slums. I've got to be prepared for both. The slums I can handle alone. I haven't forgotten the gutter, but I need you for society. Will you come in with me?"

"You're hurting me." Robin wrenched her arm out of Foyle's grasp.

"Sorry. I lose control when I think about 'Vorga.' Will you help me find 'Vorga' and your family?"

"I hate you," Robin burst out. "I despise you. You're rotten. You destroy everything you touch. Someday I'll pay you back."

"But we work together from New Year's to All Fools?"

"We work together."

CHAPTER NINE

ON NEW YEAR'S EVE, Geoffrey Fourmyle of Ceres made his onslaught on society. He appeared first in Canberra at the Government House ball, half an hour before midnight. This was a highly formal affair, bursting with color and pageantry, for it was the custom at formals for society to wear the evening dress that had been fashionable the year its clan was founded or its trademark patented.

Thus, the Morses (Telephone and Telegraph) wore nineteenth century frock coats and their women wore Victorian hoop skirts. The Skodas (Powder & Guns) harked back to the late eighteenth century, wearing Regency tights and crinolines. The daring Peenemundes (Rockets & Reactors), dating from the 1920's, wore tuxedos, and their women unashamedly revealed legs, arms, and necks in the décolleté of antique Worth and Mainbocher gowns.

Fourmyle of Ceres appeared in evening clothes, very modern and very black, relieved only by a white sunburst on his shoulder, the trademark of the Ceres clan. With him was Robin Wednesbury in a glittering white gown, her slender waist tight in whalebone, the bustle of the gown accentuating her long, straight back and graceful step.

The black and white contrast was so arresting that an orderly was sent to check the sunburst trademark in the Almanac of Peerages and Patents. He returned with the news that it was of the Ceres Mining Company, organized in 2250 for the exploitation of the mineral resources of Ceres, Pallos, and Vesta. The resources had never manifested themselves and the House of Ceres had gone into eclipse but had never become extinct. Apparently it was now being revived.

"Fourmyle? The clown?"

"Yes. The Four Mile Circus. Everybody's talking about him."

"Is that the same man?"

"Couldn't be. He looks human."

Society clustered around Fourmyle, curious but wary.

"Here they come," Foyle muttered to Robin.

"*Relax. They want the light touch. They'll accept anything if it's amusing. Stay tuned.*"

"Are you that dreadful man with the circus, Fourmyle?"

"Sure you are. Smile."

"I am, madam. You may touch me."

"Why, you actually seem proud. Are you proud of your bad taste?"

"*The problem today is to have any taste at all.*"

"The problem today is to have any taste at all. I think I'm lucky."

"Lucky but dreadfully indecent."

"Indecent but not dull."

"And dreadful but delightful. Why aren't you cavorting now?"

"I'm 'under the influence,' Madam."
"Oh dear. Are you drunk? I'm Lady Shrapnel. When will you be sober again?"
"I'm under your influence, Lady Shrapnel."
"You wicked young man. Charles! Charles, come here and save Fourmyle. I'm ruining him."
"That's Victor of RCA Victor."
"Fourmyle, is it? Delighted. What's that entourage of yours cost?"
"Tell him the truth."
"Forty thousand, Victor."
"Good *Lord!* A week?"
"A day."
"A day! What on earth d'you want to spend all that money for?"
"The truth!"
"For notoriety, Victor."
"Ha! Are you serious?"
"I told you he was wicked, Charles."
"Damned refreshing. Klaus! Here a moment. This impudent young man is spending forty thousand a day . . . for notoriety, if you please."
"Skoda of Skoda."
"Good evening, Fourmyle. I am much interested in this revival of the name. You are, perhaps, a cadet descendant of the original founding board of Ceres, Inc.?"
"Give him the truth."
"No, Skoda. It's a title by purchase. I bought the company. I'm an upstart."
"Good. Toujours de l'audace!"
"My word, Fourmyle! You're frank."
"Told you he was impudent. Very refreshing. There's a parcel of damned upstarts about, young man, but they don't admit it. Elizabeth, come and meet Fourmyle of Ceres."
"Fourmyle! I've been dying to meet you."
"Lady Elizabeth Citroen."
"Is it true you travel with a portable college?"
"The light touch here."
"A portable high school, Lady Elizabeth."
"But why on earth, Fourmyle?"
"Oh, madam, it's so difficult to spend money these days. We have to find the silliest excuses. If only someone would invent a new extravagance."
"You ought to travel with a portable inventor, Fourmyle."
"I've got one. Haven't I, Robin? But he wastes his time on perpetual motion. What I need is a resident spendthrift. Would any of your clans care to lend me a younger son?"
"Would any of us care to! There's many a clan would pay for the privilege of unloading."
"Isn't perpetual motion spendthrift enough for you, Fourmyle?"
"No. It's a shocking waste of money. The whole point of extravagance is to act like a fool and feel like a fool, but enjoy it. Where's the joy in per-

petual motion? Is there any extravagance in entropy? Millions for nonsense but not one cent for entropy. My slogan."

They laughed and the crowd clustering around Fourmyle grew. They were delighted and amused. He was a new toy. Then it was midnight, and as the great clock tolled in the New Year, the gathering prepared to jaunte with midnight around the world.

"Come with us to Java, Fourmyle. Regis Sheffield's giving a marvelous legal party. We're going to play 'Sober The Judge.'"

"Hong Kong, Fourmyle."

"Tokyo, Fourmyle. It's raining in Hong Kong. Come to Tokyo and bring your circus."

"Thank you, no. Shanghai for me. The Soviet Duomo. I promise an extravagant reward to the first one who discovers the deception of my costume. Meet you all in two hours. Ready, Robin?"

"*Don't jaunte. Bad manners. Walk out. Slowly. Languor is chic. Respects to the Governor . . . To the Commissioner . . . Their Ladies . . . Bien. Don't forget to tip the attendants. Not him, idiot! That's the Lieutenant Governor. All right. You made a hit. You're accepted. Now what?*"

"Now what we came to Canberra for."

"I thought we came for the ball."

"The ball *and* a man named Forrest."

"Who's that?"

"Ben Forrest, spaceman off the 'Vorga.' I've got three leads to the man who gave the order to let me die. Three names. A cook in Rome named Poggi; a quack in Shanghai named Orel; and this man, Forrest. This is a combined operation . . . society and search. Understand?"

"I understand."

"We've got two hours to rip Forrest open. D'you know the co-ordinates of the Aussie Cannery? The company town?"

"I don't want any part of your 'Vorga' revenge. I'm searching for my family."

"This is a combined operation . . . every way," he said with such detached savagery that she winced and at once jaunted. When Foyle arrived in his tent in the Four Mile Circus on Jervis Beach, she was already changing into travel clothes. Foyle looked at her. Although he forced her to live in his tent for security reasons, he had never touched her again. Robin caught his glance, stopped changing and waited.

He shook his head. "That's all finished."

"How interesting. You've given up rape?"

"Get dressed," he said, controlling himself. "Tell them they've got two hours to get the camp up to Shanghai."

It was twelve-thirty when Foyle and Robin arrived at the front office of the Aussie Cannery company town. They applied for identification tags and were greeted by the mayor himself.

"Happy New Year," he caroled. "Happy! Happy! Happy! Visiting? A pleasure to drive you around. Permit me." He bundled them into a lush helicopter and took off. "Lots of visitors tonight. Ours is a friendly town.

Friendliest company town in the world." The plane circled giant buildings. "That's our ice palace . . . Swimming baths on the left . . . Big dome is the ski jump. Snow all year 'round . . . Tropical gardens under that glass roof. Palms, parrots, orchids, fruit. There's our market . . . theater . . . got our own broadcasting company, too. 3D-5S. Take a look at the football stadium. Two of our boys made All-American this year. Turner at Right Rockne and Otis at Left Thorpe."

"Do tell," Foyle murmured.

"Yessir, we've got everything. Everything. You don't have to jaunte around the world looking for fun. Aussie Cannery brings the world to you. Our town's a little universe. Happiest little universe in the world."

"Having absentee problems, I see."

The mayor refused to falter in his sales pitch. "Look down at the streets. See those bikes? Motorcycles? Cars? We can afford more luxury transportation per capita than any other town on earth. Look at those homes. Mansions. Our people are rich and happy. We keep 'em rich and happy."

"But do you keep them?"

"What d'you mean? Of course we—"

"You can tell us the truth. We're not job prospects. Do you keep them?"

"We can't keep 'em more than six months," the mayor groaned. "It's a hell of a headache. We give 'em everything but we can't hold on to 'em. They get the wanderlust and jaunte. Absenteeism's cut our production by 12 per cent. We can't hold on to steady labor."

"Nobody can."

"There ought to be a law. Forrest, you said? Right here."

He landed them before a Swiss chalet set in an acre of gardens and took off, mumbling to himself. Foyle and Robin stepped before the door of the house, waiting for the monitor to pick them up and announce them. Instead, the door flashed red, and a white skull and crossbones appeared on it. A canned voice spoke: "WARNING. THIS RESIDENCE IS MAN-TRAPPED BY THE LETHAL DEFENSE CORPORATION OF SWEDEN. R:77-23. YOU HAVE BEEN LEGALLY NOTIFIED."

"What the hell?" Foyle muttered. "On New Year's Eve? Friendly fella. Let's try the back."

They walked around the chalet, pursued by the skull and crossbones flashing at intervals, and the canned warning. At one side, they saw the top of a cellar window brightly illuminated and heard the muffled chant of voices: "The Lord is my shepherd, I shall not want . . ."

"Cellar Christians!" Foyle exclaimed. He and Robin peered through the window. Thirty worshippers of assorted faiths were celebrating the New Year with a combined and highly illegal service. The twenty-fourth century had not yet abolished God, but it had abolished organized religion.

"No wonder the house is man-trapped," Foyle said. "Filthy practices like that. Look, they've got a priest and a rabbi, and that thing behind them is a crucifix."

"Did you ever stop to think what swearing is?" Robin asked quietly. "You say 'Jesus' and 'Jesus Christ.' Do you know what that is?"

"Just swearing, that's all. Like 'ouch' or 'damn.'"

"No, it's religion. You don't know it, but there are two thousand years of meaning behind words like that."

"This is no time for dirty talk," Foyle said impatiently. "Save it for later. Come on."

The rear of the chalet was a solid wall of glass, the picture window of a dimly lit, empty living room.

"Down on your face," Foyle ordered. "I'm going in."

Robin lay prone on the marble patio. Foyle triggered his body, accelerated into a lightning blur, and smashed a hole in the glass wall. Far down on the sound spectrum he heard dull concussions. They were shots. Quick projectiles laced toward him. Foyle dropped to the floor and tuned his ears, sweeping from low bass to supersonic until at last he picked up the hum of the Man-Trap control mechanism. He turned his head gently, pin-pointed the location by binaural D/F, wove in through the stream of shots and demolished the mechanism. He decelerated.

"Come in, quick!"

Robin joined him in the living room, trembling. The Cellar Christians were pouring up into the house somewhere, emitting the sounds of martyrs.

"Wait here," Foyle grunted. He accelerated, blurred through the house, located the Cellar Christians in poses of frozen flight, and sorted through them. He returned to Robin and decelerated.

"None of them is Forrest," he reported. "Maybe he's upstairs. The back way, while they're going out the front. Come on!"

They raced up the back stairs. On the landing they paused to take bearings.

"Have to work fast," Foyle muttered. "Between the shots and the religion riot, the world and his wife'll be jaunting around asking questions—" He broke off. A low mewling sound came from a door at the head of the stairs. Foyle sniffed.

"Analogue!" he exclaimed. "Must be Forrest. How about that? Religion in the cellar and dope upstairs."

"What are you talking about?"

"I'll explain later. In here. I only hope he isn't on a gorilla kick."

Foyle went through the door like a diesel tractor. They were in a large, bare room. A heavy rope was suspended from the ceiling. A naked man was entwined with the rope midway in the air. He squirmed and slithered down the rope, emitting a mewling sound and a musky odor.

"Python," Foyle said. "That's a break. Don't go near him. He'll mash your bones if he touches you."

Voices below began to call: "Forrest! What's all the shooting? Happy New Year, Forrest! Where in hell's the celebration?"

"Here they come," Foyle grunted "Have to jaunte him out of here. Meet you back at the beach. Go!"

He whipped a knife out of his pocket, cut the rope, swung the squirming man to his back and jaunted. Robin was on the empty Jervis beach a moment before him. Foyle arrived with the squirming man oozing over his neck and shoulders like a python, crushing him in a terrifying embrace. The red stigmata suddenly burst out on Foyle's face.

"Sinbad," he said in a strangled voice. "Old Man of the Sea. Quick girl! Right pockets. Three over. Two down. Sting ampule. Let him have it anywh—" His voice was choked off.

Robin opened the pocket, found a packet of glass beads and took them out. Each bead had a bee-sting end. She thrust the sting of an ampule into the writhing man's neck. He collapsed. Foyle shook him off and arose from the sand.

"Christ!" he muttered, massaging his throat. He took a deep breath. "Blood and bowels. Control," he said, resuming his air of detached calm. The scarlet tattooing faded from his face.

"What was all that horror?" Robin asked.

"Analogue. Psychiatric dope for psychotics. Illegal. A twitch has to release himself somehow, revert back to the primitive. He identifies with a particular kind of animal . . . gorilla, grizzly, brood bull, wolf . . . Takes the dope and turns into the animal he admires. Forrest was queer for snakes, seems as if."

"How do you know all this?"

"Told you I've been studying . . . preparing for 'Vorga.' This is one of the things I learned. Show you something else I've learned, if you're not chicken-livered. How to bring a twitch out of Analogue."

Foyle opened another pocket in his battle overalls and got to work on Forrest. Robin watched for a moment, then uttered a horrified cry, turned and walked to the edge of the water. She stood, staring blindly at the surf and the stars, until the mewling and the twisting ceased and Foyle called to her.

"You can come back now."

Robin returned to find a shattered creature seated upright on the beach gazing at Foyle with dull, sober eyes.

"You're Forrest?"

"Who the hell are you?"

"You're Ben Forrest, leading spaceman. Formerly aboard the Presteign 'Vorga.' "

Forrest cried out in terror.

"You were aboard the 'Vorga' on September 16, 2436."

The man sobbed and shook his head.

"On September sixteen you passed a wreck. Out near the asteroid belt. Wreck of the 'Nomad,' your sister ship. She signalled for help. 'Vorga' passed her by. Left her to drift and die. Why did 'Vorga' pass her by?"

Forrest began to scream hysterically.

"Who gave the order to pass her by?"

"Jesus, no! No! No!"

"The records are all gone from the Bo'ness & Uig files. Someone got to them before me. Who was that? Who was aboard 'Vorga'? Who shipped with you? I want officers and crew. Who was in command?"

"No," Forrest screamed. "No!"

Foyle held a sheaf of bank notes before the hysterical man's face. "I'll pay for the information. Fifty thousand. Analogue for the rest of your life. Who gave the order to let me die, Forrest? Who?"

The man smote the bank notes from Foyle's hand, leaped up and ran down the beach. Foyle tackled him at the edge of the surf. Forrest fell headlong, his face in the water. Foyle held him there.

"Who commanded 'Vorga,' Forrest? Who gave the order?"

"You're drowning him!" Robin cried.

"Let him suffer a little. Water's easier than vacuum. I suffered for six months. Who gave the order, Forrest?"

The man bubbled and choked. Foyle lifted his head out of the water. "What are you? Loyal? Crazy? Scared? Your kind would sell out for five thousand. I'm offering fifty. Fifty thousand for information, you son of a bitch, or you die slow and hard." The tattooing appeared on Foyle's face. He forced Forrest's head back into the water and held the struggling man. Robin tried to pull him off.

"You're murdering him!"

Foyle turned his terrifying face on Robin. "Get your hands off me, bitch! Who was aboard with you, Forrest? Who gave the order? Why?"

Forrest twisted his head out of the water. "Twelve of us on 'Vorga,'" he screamed. "Christ save me! There was me and Kemp—"

He jerked spasmodically and sagged. Foyle pulled his body out of the surf.

"Go on. You and who? Kemp? Who else? Talk."

There was no response. Foyle examined the body.

"Dead," he growled.

"Oh my God! My God!"

"One lead shot to hell. Just when he was opening up. What a damned break." He took a deep breath and drew calm about him like an iron cloak. The tattooing disappeared from his face. He adjusted his watch for 120 degrees east longitude. "Almost midnight in Shanghai. Let's go. Maybe we'll have better luck with Sergei Orel, pharmacist's mate off the 'Vorga.' Don't look so scared. This is only the beginning. Go, girl. Jaunte!"

Robin gasped. He saw that she was staring over his shoulder with an expression of incredulity. Foyle turned. A flaming figure loomed on the beach, a huge man with burning clothes and a hideously tattooed face. It was himself.

"Christ!" Foyle exclaimed. He took a step toward his burning image, and abruptly it was gone.

He turned to Robin, ashen and trembling. "Did you see that?"

"Yes."

"What was it?"

"You."

"For God's sake! Me? How's that possible? How—"

"It was you."

"But—" He faltered, the strength and furious possession drained out of him. "Was it illusion? Hallucination?"

"I don't know. I saw it too."

"Christ Almighty! To see yourself . . . face to face . . . The clothes were on fire. Did you see that? What in God's name was it?"

"It was Gully Foyle," Robin said, "burning in hell."

"All right," Foyle burst out angrily. "It was me in hell, but I'm still going through with it. If I burn in hell, Vorga'll burn with me." He pounded his palms together, stinging himself back to strength and purpose. "I'm still going through with it, by God! Shanghai next. Jaunte!"

CHAPTER TEN

AT THE COSTUME BALL in Shanghai, Fourmyle of Ceres electrified society by appearing as Death in Dürer's "Death and the Maiden" with a dazzling blonde creature clad in transparent veils. A Victorian society which stifled its women in purdah, and which regarded the 1920 gowns of the Peenemunde clan as excessively daring, was shocked, despite the fact that Robin Wednesbury was chaperoning the pair. But when Fourmyle revealed that the female was a magnificent android, there was an instant reversal of opinion in his favor. Society was delighted with the deception. The naked body, shameful in humans, was merely a sexless curiosity in androids.

At midnight, Fourmyle auctioned off the android to the gentlemen of the ball.

"The money to go to charity, Fourmyle?"

"Certainly not. You know my slogan: Not one cent for entropy. Do I hear a hundred credits for this expensive and lovely creature? One hundred, gentlemen? She's all beauty and highly adaptable. Two? Thank you. Three and a half? Thank you. I'm bid—Five? Eight? Thank you. Any more bids for this remarkable product of the resident genius of the Four Mile Circus? She walks. She talks. She adapts. She has been conditioned to respond to the highest bidder. Nine? Do I hear any more bids? Are you all done? Are you all through? Sold, to Lord Yale for nine hundred credits."

Tumultuous applause and appalled ciphering: "An android like that must have cost ninety thousand! How can he afford it?"

"Will you turn the money over to the android, Lord Yale? She will respond suitably. Until we meet again in Rome, ladies and gentlemen . . . The Borghese Palace at midnight. Happy New Year."

Fourmyle had already departed when Lord Yale discovered, to the delight of himself and the other bachelors, that a double deception had been perpetrated. The android was, in fact, a living, human creature, all beauty and highly adaptable. She responded magnificently to nine hundred credits. The trick was the smoking room story of the year. The stags waited eagerly to congratulate Fourmyle.

But Foyle and Robin Wednesbury were passing under a sign that read: "DOUBLE YOUR JAUNTING OR DOUBLE YOUR MONEY BACK" in seven languages, and entering the emporium of "DR. SERGEI OREL, CELESTIAL ENLARGER OF CRANIAL CAPABILITIES."

The waiting room was decorated with lurid brain charts demonstrating how Dr. Orel poulticed, cupped, balsamed, and electrolyzed the brain into double its capacity or double your money back. He also doubled your memory with antifebrile purgatives, magnified your morals with tonic roborants, and adjusted all anguished psyches with Orel's Epulotic Vulnerary.

The waiting room was empty. Foyle opened a door at a venture. He and Robin had a glimpse of a long hospital ward. Foyle grunted in disgust.

"A Snow Joint. Might have known he'd be running a dive for sick heads too."

This den catered to Disease Collectors, the most hopeless of neurotic-addicts. They lay in their hospital beds, suffering mildly from illegally induced para-measles, para-flu, para-malaria; devotedly attended by nurses in starched white uniforms, and avidly enjoying their illegal illness and the attention it brought.

"Look at them," Foyle said contemptuously. "Disgusting. If there's anything filthier than a religion-junkey, it's a disease-bird."

"Good evening," a voice spoke behind them.

Foyle shut the door and turned. Dr. Sergei Orel bowed. The good doctor was crisp and sterile in the classic white cap, gown, and surgical mask of the medical clans, to which he belonged by fraudulent assertion only. He was short, swarthy, and olive-eyed, recognizably Russian by his name alone. More than a century of jaunting had so mingled the many populations of the world that racial types were disappearing.

"Didn't expect to find you open for business on New Year's Eve," Foyle said.

"Our Russian New Year comes two weeks later," Dr. Orel answered. "Step this way, please." He pointed to a door and disappeared with a "pop." The door revealed a long flight of stairs. As Foyle and Robin started up the stairs, Dr. Orel appeared above them. "This way, please. Oh . . . one moment." He disappeared and appeared again behind them. "You forgot to close the door." He shut the door and jaunted again. This time he reappeared high at the head of the stairs. "In here, please."

"Showing off," Foyle muttered. "Double your jaunting or double your money back. All the same, he's pretty fast. I'll have to be faster."

They entered the consultation room. It was a glass-roofed penthouse. The walls were lined with gaudy but antiquated medical apparatus: a sedative-bath machine, an electric chair for administering shock treatment to schizophrenics, an EKG analyzer for tracing psychotic patterns, old optical and electronic microscopes.

The quack waited for them behind his desk. He jaunted to the door, closed it, jaunted back to his desk, bowed, indicated chairs, jaunted behind Robin's and held it for her, jaunted to the window and adjusted the shade, jaunted to the light switch and adjusted the lights, then reappeared behind his desk.

"One year ago," he smiled, "I could not jaunte at all. Then I discovered the secret, the Salutiferous Abstersive which . . ."

Foyle touched his tongue to the switchboard wired into the nerve endings of his teeth. He accelerated. He arose without haste, stepped to the slow-motion figure "Bloo-hwoo-fwaa-mawwing" behind the desk, took out a heavy sap, and scientifically smote Orel across the brow, concussing the frontal lobes and stunning the jaunte center. He picked the quack up and strapped him into the electric chair. All this took approximately five seconds. To Robin Wednesbury it was a blur of motion.

Foyle decelerated. The quack opened his eyes, stirred, discovered where he was, and started in anger and perplexity.

"You're Sergei Orel, pharmacist's mate off the 'Vorga'," Foyle said quietly. "You were aboard the 'Vorga' on September 16, 2436."

The anger and perplexity turned to terror.

"On September sixteen you passed a wreck. Out near the asteroid belt. It was the wreck of the 'Nomad.' She signalled for help and 'Vorga' passed her by. You left her to drift and die. Why?"

Orel rolled his eyes but did not answer.

"Who gave the order to pass me by? Who was willing to let me rot and die?"

Orel began to gibber.

"Who was aboard 'Vorga'? Who shipped with you? Who was in command? I'm going to get an answer. Don't think I'm not," Foyle said with calm ferocity. "I'll buy it or tear it out of you. Why was I left to die? Who told you to let me die?"

Orel screamed. "I can't talk abou— Wait I'll tell—"

He sagged.

Foyle examined the body.

"Dead," he muttered. "Just when he was ready to talk. Just like Forrest."

"Murdered."

"No. I never touched him. It was suicide." Foyle cackled without humor.

"You're insane."

"No, amused. I didn't kill them; I forced them to kill themselves."

"What nonsense is this?"

"They've been given Sympathetic Blocks. You know about SBs, girl? Intelligence uses them for espionage agents. Take a certain body of information you don't want told. Link it with the sympathetic nervous system that controls automatic respiration and heart beat. As soon as the subject tries to reveal that information, the block comes down, the heart and lungs stop, the man dies, your secret's kept. An agent doesn't have to worry about killing himself to avoid torture; it's been done for him."

"It was done to these men?"

"Obviously."

"But why?"

"How do I know? Refugee running isn't the answer. 'Vorga' must have been operating worse rackets than that to take this precaution. But we've got a problem. Our last lead is Poggi in Rome. Angelo Poggi, chef's assistant off the 'Vorga.' How are we going to get information out of him without—" He broke off.

His image stood before him, silent, ominous, face burning blood-red, clothes flaming.

Foyle was paralyzed. He took a breath and spoke in a shaking voice. "Who are you? What do you—"

The image disappeared.

Foyle turned to Robin, moistening his lips. "Did you see it?" Her expression answered him. "Was it real?"

She pointed to Sergei Orel's desk, alongside which the image had stood. Papers on the desk had caught fire and were burning briskly. Foyle backed away, still frightened and bewildered. He passed a hand across his face. It came away wet.

Robin rushed to the desk and tried to beat out the flames. She picked up wads of paper and letters and slammed helplessly. Foyle did not move.

"I can't stop it," she gasped at last. "We've got to get out of here."

Foyle nodded, then pulled himself together with power and resolution. "Rome," he croaked. "We jaunte to Rome. There's got to be some explanation for this. I'll find it, by God! And in the meantime I'm not quitting. Rome. Go, girl. Jaunte!"

Since the Middle Ages the Spanish Stairs have been the center of corruption in Rome. Rising from the Piazza di Spagna to the gardens of the Villa Borghese in a broad, long sweep, the Spanish Stairs are, have been, and always will be swarming with vice. Pimps lounge on the stairs, whores, perverts, lesbians, catamites. Insolent and arrogant, they display themselves and jeer at the respectables who sometimes pass.

The Spanish Stairs were destroyed in the fission wars of the late twentieth century. They were rebuilt and destroyed again in the war of the World Restoration in the twenty-first century. Once more they were rebuilt and this time covered over with blast-proof crystal, turning the stairs into a stepped Galleria. The dome of the Galleria cut off the view from the death chamber in Keats's house. No longer would visitors peep through the narrow window and see the last sight that met the dying poet's eyes. Now they saw the smoky dome of the Spanish Stairs, and through it the distorted figures of corruption below.

The Galleria of the Stairs was illuminated at night, and this New Year's Eve was chaotic. For a thousand years Rome has welcomed the New Year with a bombardment . . . firecrackers, rockets, torpedoes, gunshots, bottles, shoes, old pots and pans. For months Romans save junk to be hurled out of top-floor windows when midnight strikes. The roar of fireworks inside the Stairs, and the clatter of debris clashing on the Galleria roof, were deafening as Foyle and Robin Wednesbury climbed down from the carnival in the Borghese Palace.

They were still in costume: Foyle in the livid crimson-and-black tights and doublet of Cesare Borgia, Robin wearing the silver-encrusted gown of

Lucrezia Borgia. They wore grotesque velvet masks. The contrast between their Renaissance costumes and the modern clothes around them brought forth jeers and catcalls. Even the Lobos who frequented the Spanish Stairs, the unfortunate habitual criminals who had had a quarter of their brains burned out by prefrontal lobotomy, were aroused from their dreary apathy to stare. The mob seethed around the couple as they descended the Galleria.

"Poggi," Foyle called quietly. "Angelo Poggi?"

A bawd bellowed anatomical adjurations at him.

"Poggi? Angelo Poggi?" Foyle was impassive. "I'm told he can be found on the Stairs at night. Angelo Poggi?"

A whore maligned his mother.

"Angelo Poggi? Ten credits to anyone who brings me to him."

Foyle was ringed with extended hands, some filthy, some scented, all greedy. He shook his head. "Show me, first."

Roman rage crackled around him.

"Poggi? Angelo Poggi?"

After six weeks of loitering on the Spanish Stairs, Captain Peter Y'ang-Yeovil at last heard the words he had hoped to hear. Six weeks of tedious assumption of the identity of one Angelo Poggi, chef's assistant off the 'Vorga,' long dead, was finally paying off. It had been a gamble, first risked when Intelligence had brought the news to Captain Y'ang-Yeovil that someone was making cautious inquiries about the crew of the Presteign "Vorga," and paying heavily for information.

"It's a long shot," Y'ang-Yeovil had said, "But Gully Foyle, AS-128/127:006, *did* make that lunatic attempt to blow up 'Vorga.' And twenty pounds of PyrE is worth a long shot."

Now he waddled up the stairs toward the man in the Renaissance costume and mask. He had put on forty pounds weight with glandular shots. He had darkened his complexion with diet manipulation. His features, never of an Oriental cast but cut more along the hawklike lines of the ancient American Indian, easily fell into an unreliable pattern with a little muscular control.

The Intelligence man waddled up the Spanish Stairs, a gross cook with a larcenous countenance. He extended a package of soiled envelopes toward Foyle.

"Filthy pictures, signore? Cellar Christians, kneeling, praying, singing psalms, kissing cross? Very naughty. Very smutty, signore. Entertain your friends . . . Excite the ladies."

"No," Foyle brushed the pornography aside. "I'm looking for Angelo Poggi."

Y'ang-Yeovil signalled microscopically. His crew on the stairs began photographing and recording the interview without ceasing its pimping and whoring. The Secret Speech of the Intelligence Tong of the Inner Planets Armed Forces wig-wagged around Foyle and Robin in a hail of tiny tics, sniffs, gestures, attitudes, motions. It was the ancient Chinese sign language of eyelids, eyebrows, fingertips, and infinitesimal body motions.

"Signore?" Y'ang-Yeovil wheezed.

"Angelo Poggi?"
"Si, signore. I am Angelo Poggi."
"Chef's assistant off the 'Vorga'?" Expecting the same start of terror manifested by Forrest and Orel, which he at last understood, Foyle shot out a hand and grabbed Y'ang-Yeovil's elbow. "Yes?"
"Si, signore," Y'ang-Yeovil replied tranquilly. "How can I serve your worship?"
"Maybe this one can come through," Foyle murmured to Robin. "He's not scared. Maybe he knows a way around the Block. I want information from you, Poggi."
"Of what nature, signore, and at what price?"
"I want to buy all you've got. Anything you've got. Name your price."
"But signore! I am a man full of years and experience. I am not to be bought in wholesale lots. I must be paid item by item. Make your selection and I will name the price. What do you want?"
"You were aboard 'Vorga' on September 16, 2436?"
"The cost of that item is ¢r 10."
Foyle smiled mirthlessly and paid.
"I was, signore."
"I want to know about a ship you passed out near the asteroid belt. The wreck of the 'Nomad.' You passed her on September 16. 'Nomad' signalled for help and 'Vorga' passed her by. Who gave that order?"
"Ah, signore!"
"Who gave you that order, and why?"
"Why do you ask, signore?"
"Never mind why I ask. Name the price and talk."
"I must know why a question is asked before I answer, signore." Y'ang-Yeovil smiled greasily. "And I will pay for my caution by cutting the price. Why are you interested in 'Vorga' and 'Nomad' and this shocking abandonment in space? Were you, perhaps, the unfortunate who was so cruelly treated?"
"*He's not Italian! His accent's perfect, but the speech pattern's all wrong. No Italian would frame sentences like that.*"
Foyle stiffened in alarm. Y'ang-Yeovil's eyes, sharpened to detect and deduce from minutiae, caught the change in attitude. He realized at once that he had slipped somehow. He signalled to his crew urgently.
A white-hot brawl broke out on the Spanish Stairs. In an instant, Foyle and Robin were caught up in a screaming, struggling mob. The crews of the Intelligence Tong were past masters of this OP-I maneuver, designed to outwit a jaunting world. Their split-second timing could knock any man off balance and strip him for identification. Their success was based on the simple fact that between unexpected assault and defensive response there must always be a recognition lag. Within the space of that lag, the Intelligence Tong guaranteed to prevent any man from saving himself.
In three-fifths of a second Foyle was battered, kneed, hammered across the forehead, dropped to the steps and spread-eagled. The mask was plucked from his face, portions of his clothes torn away, and he was ripe and helpless

for the rape of the identification cameras. Then, for the first time in the history of the tong, their schedule was interrupted.

A man appeared, straddling Foyle's body . . . a huge man with a hideously tattooed face and clothes that smoked and flamed. The apparition was so appalling that the crew stopped dead and stared. A howl went up from the crowd on the Stairs at the dreadful spectacle.

"The Burning Man! Look! The Burning Man!"

"But *that's* Foyle," Y'ang-Yeovil whispered.

For perhaps a quarter of a minute the apparition stood, silent, burning, staring with blind eyes. Then it disappeared. The man spread-eagled on the ground disappeared too. He turned into a lightning blur of action that whipped through the crew, locating and destroying cameras, recorders, all identification apparatus. Then the blur seized the girl in the Renaissance gown and vanished.

The Spanish Stairs came to life again, painfully, as though struggling out of a nightmare. The bewildered Intelligence crew clustered around Y'ang-Yeovil.

"What in God's name was that, Yeo?"

"I think it was our man. Gully Foyle. You saw that tattooed face."

"And the burning clothes!"

"Looked like a witch at the stake."

"But if that burning man was Foyle, who in hell were we wasting our time on?"

"I don't know. Does the Commando Brigade have an Intelligence service they haven't bothered to mention to us?"

"Why the Commandos, Yeo?"

"You saw the way he accelerated, didn't you? He destroyed every record we made."

"I still can't believe my eyes."

"Oh, you can believe what you didn't see, all right. That was top secret Commando technique. They take their men apart and rewire and regear them. I'll have to check with Mars HQ and find out whether Commando Brigade's running a parallel investigation."

"Does the army tell the navy?"

"They'll tell Intelligence," Y'ang-Yeovil said angrily. "This case is critical enough without jurisdictional hassels. And another thing: there was no need to manhandle that girl in the maneuver. It was undisciplined and unnecessary." Y'ang-Yeovil paused, for once unaware of the significant glances passing around him. "I must find out who she is," he added dreamily.

"If she's been regeared too, it'll be real interesting, Yeo," a bland voice, markedly devoid of implication, said. "Boy Meets Commando."

Y'ang-Yeovil flushed. "All right," he blurted. "I'm transparent."

"Just repetitious, Yeo. All your romances start the same way. 'There's no need to manhandle that girl . . .' And then—Dolly Quaker, Jean Webster, Gwynn Roget, Marion—"

"No names, please!" a shocked voice interrupted. "Does Romeo tell Juliet?"

"You're all going on latrine assignment tomorrow," Y'ang-Yeovil said. "I'm damned if I'll stand for this salacious insubordination. No, not tomorrow; but as soon as this case is closed." His hawk face darkened. "My God, what a mess! Will you ever forget Foyle standing there like a burning brand? But where is he? What's he up to? What's it all mean?"

CHAPTER ELEVEN

PRESTEIGN OF PRESTEIGN'S MANSION in Central Park was ablaze for the New Year. Charming antique electric bulks with zigzag filaments and pointed tips shed yellow light. The jaunte-proof maze had been removed and the great door was open for the special occasion. The interior of the house was protected from the gaze of the crowd outside by a jeweled screen just inside the door.

The sightseers buzzed and exclaimed as the famous and near-famous of clan and sept arrived by car, by coach, by litter, by every form of luxurious transportation. Presteign of Presteign himself stood before the door, iron gray, handsome, smiling his basilisk smile, and welcomed society to his open house. Hardly had a celebrity stepped through the door and disappeared behind the screen when another, even more famous, came clattering up in a vehicle even more fabulous.

The Colas arrived in a band wagon. The Esso family (six sons, three daughters) was magnificent in a glass-topped Greyhound bus. But Greyhound arrived (in an Edison electric runabout) hard on their heels and there was much laughter and chaffing at the door. But when Edison of Westinghouse dismounted from his Esso-fueled gasoline buggy, completing the circle, the laughter on the steps turned into a roar.

Just as the crowd of guests turned to enter Presteign's home, a distant commotion attracted their attention. It was a rumble, a fierce chatter of pneumatic punches, and an outrageous metallic bellowing. It approached rapidly. The outer fringe of sightseers opened a broad lane. A heavy truck rumbled down the lane. Six men were tumbling baulks of timber out the back of the truck. Following them came a crew of twenty arranging the baulks neatly in rows.

Presteign and his guests watched with amazement. A giant machine, bellowing and pounding, approached, crawling over the ties. Behind it were deposited parallel rails of welded steel. Crews with sledges and pneumatic punches spiked the rails to the timber ties. The track was laid to Presteign's door in a sweeping arc and then curved away. The bellowing engine and crews disappeared into the darkness.

"Good God!" Presteign was distinctly heard to say. Guests poured out of the house to watch.

A shrill whistle sounded in the distance. Down the track came a man on a white horse, carrying a large red flag. Behind him panted a steam locomotive drawing a single observation car. The train stopped before Presteign's door. A conductor swung down from the car followed by a Pullman porter. The porter arranged steps. A lady and gentleman in evening clothes descended.

"Shan't be long," the gentleman told the conductor. "Come back for me in an hour."

"Good God!" Presteign exclaimed again.

The train puffed off. The couple mounted the steps.

"Good evening, Presteign," the gentleman said. "Terribly sorry about that horse messing up your grounds, but the old New York franchise still insists on the red flag in front of trains."

"Fourmyle!" the guests shouted.

"Fourmyle of Ceres!" the sightseers cheered.

Presteign's party was now an assured success.

Inside the vast velvet and plush reception hall, Presteign examined Fourmyle curiously. Foyle endured the keen iron-gray gaze with equanimity, meanwhile nodding and smiling to the enthusiastic admirers he had acquired from Canberra to New York, with whom Robin Wednesbury was chatting.

"*Control,*" he thought. "*Blood, bowels and brain. He grilled me in his office for one hour after that crazy attempt I made on 'Vorga.' Will he recognize me?* Your face is familiar, Presteign," Fourmyle said. "Have we met before?"

"I have not had the honor of meeting a Fourmyle until tonight," Presteign answered ambiguously. Foyle had trained himself to read men, but Presteign's hard, handsome face was inscrutable. Standing face to face, the one detached and compelled, the other reserved and indomitable, they looked like a pair of brazen statues at white heat on the verge of running molten.

"I'm told that you boast of being an upstart, Fourmyle."

"Yes. I've patterned myself after the first Presteign."

"Indeed?"

"You will remember that he boasted of starting the family fortune in the plasma blackmarket during the third World War."

"It was the second war, Fourmyle. But the hypocrites of our clan never acknowledge him. The name was Payne then."

"I hadn't known."

"And what was your unhappy name before you changed it to Fourmyle?"

"It was Presteign."

"Indeed?" The basilisk smile acknowledged the hit. "You claim a relationship with our clan?"

"I will claim it in time."

"Of what degree?"

"Let's say . . . a blood relationship."

"How interesting. I detect a certain fascination for blood in you, Fourmyle."

"No doubt a family weakness, Presteign."

"You're pleased to be cynical," Presteign said, not without cynicism, "but you speak the truth. We have always had a fatal weakness for blood and money. It is our vice. I admit it."

"And I share it."

"A passion for blood and money?"

"Indeed I do. Most passionately."

"Without mercy, without forgiveness, without hypocrisy?"

"Without mercy, without forgiveness, without hypocrisy."

"Fourmyle, you are a young man after my own heart. If you do not claim a relationship with our clan I shall be forced to adopt you."

"You're too late, Presteign. I've already adopted you."

Presteign took Foyle's arm. "You must be presented to my daughter, Lady Olivia. Will you allow me?"

They crossed the reception hall. Foyle hesitated, wondering whether he should call Robin to his side for impending emergencies, but he was too triumphant. *He doesn't know. He'll never know.* Then doubt came: *But I'll never know if he does know. He's crucible steel. He could teach me a thing or two about control.*

Acquaintances hailed Fourmyle.

"Wonderful deception you worked in Shanghai."

"Marvelous carnival in Rome, wasn't it? Did you hear about the burning man who appeared on the Spanish Stairs?"

"We looked for you in London."

"What a heavenly entrance that was," Harry Sherwin-Williams called. "Outdid us all, Fourmyle. Made us look like a pack of damned pikers."

"You forget yourself, Harry," Presteign said coldly. "You know I permit no profanity in my home."

"Sorry, Presteign. Where's the circus now, Fourmyle?"

"I don't know," Foyle said. "Just a moment."

A crowd gathered, grinning in anticipation of the latest Fourmyle folly. He took out a platinum watch and snapped open the case. The face of a valet appeared on the dial.

"Ahhh . . . whatever your name is . . . Where are we staying just now?"

The answer was tiny and tinny. "You gave orders to make New York your permanent residence, Fourmyle."

"Oh? Did I? And?"

"We bought St. Patrick's Cathedral, Fourmyle."

"And where is that?"

"Old St. Patrick's, Fourmyle. On Fifth Avenue and what was formerly 50th Street. We've pitched the camp inside."

"Thank you." Fourmyle closed the platinum Hunter. "My address is Old St. Patrick's, New York. There's one thing to be said for the outlawed religions . . . At least they built churches big enough to house a circus."

Olivia Presteign was seated on a dais, surrounded by admirers paying court to this beautiful albino daughter of Presteign. She was strangely and wonderfully blind, for she could see in the infrared only, from 7,500 angstroms to one millimeter wave lengths, far below the normal visible spectrum. She saw heat waves, magnetic fields, radio waves; she saw her admirers in a strange light of organic emanations against a background of red radiation.

She was a Snow Maiden, an Ice Princess with coral eyes and coral lips, imperious, mysterious, unattainable. Foyle looked at her once and lowered his eyes in confusion before the blind gaze that could only see him as electromagnetic waves and infrared light. His pulse began to beat faster; a hundred lightning fantasies about himself and Olivia Presteign flashed in his heart.

"*Don't be a fool!*" he thought desperately. "*Control yourself. Stop dreaming. This can be dangerous . . .*"

He was introduced; was addressed in a husky, silvery voice; was given a cool, slim hand; but the hand seemed to explode within his with an electric shock. It was almost a start of mutual recognition . . . almost a joining of emotional impact.

"This is insane. *She's a symbol. The Dream Princess . . . The Unattainable . . . Control!*"

He was fighting so hard that he scarcely realized he had been dismissed, graciously and indifferently. He could not believe it. He stood, gaping like a lout.

"What? Are you still here, Fourmyle?"

"I couldn't believe I'd been dismissed, Lady Olivia."

"Hardly that, but I'm afraid you *are* in the way of my friends."

"I'm not used to being dismissed. (*No. No. All wrong!*) At least by someone I'd like to count as a friend."

"Don't be tedious, Fourmyle. Do step down."

"How have I offended you?"

"Offended me? Now you're being ridiculous."

"Lady Olivia . . . (*Can't I say anything right? Where's Robin?*) Can we start again, please?"

"If you're trying to be gauche, Fourmyle, you're succeeding admirably."

"Your hand again, please. Thank you. I'm Fourmyle of Ceres."

"All right." She laughed. "I'll concede you're a clown. Now do step down. I'm sure you can find someone to amuse."

"What's happened this time?"

"Really, sir, are you trying to make me angry?"

"No. (*Yes, I am. Trying to touch you somehow . . . cut through the ice.*) The first time our handclasp was . . . violent. Now it's nothing. What happened?"

"Fourmyle," Olivia said wearily, "I'll concede that you're amusing, original, witty, fascinating . . . anything, if you will only go away."

He stumbled off the dais. "*Bitch. Bitch. Bitch. No. She's the dream just as I dreamed her. The icy pinnacle to be stormed and taken. To lay siege . . . invade . . . ravish . . . force to her knees . . .*"

He came face to face with Saul Dagenham.

He stood paralyzed, coercing blood and bowels.

"Ah, Fourmyle," Presteign said. "This is Saul Dagenham. He can only give us thirty minutes and he insists on spending one of them with you."

"Does he know? Did he send for Dagenham to make sure? Attack. Toujours de l'audace. What happened to your face, Dagenham?" Fourmyle asked with detached curiosity.

The death's head smiled. "And I thought I was famous. Radiation poisoning. I'm hot. Time was when they said 'Hotter than an pistol.' Now they say 'Hotter than Dagenham.'" The deadly eyes raked Foyle. "What's behind that circus of yours?"

"A passion for notoriety."

"I'm an old hand at camouflage myself. I recognize the signs. What's your larceny?"

"Did Dillinger tell Capone?" Foyle smiled back, beginning to relax, restraining his triumph. *"I've outfaced them both.* You look happier, Dagenham." Instantly he realized the slip.

Dagenham picked it up in a flash. "Happier than when? Where did we meet before?"

"Not happier than when; happier than me." Foyle turned to Presteign. "I've fallen desperately in love with Lady Olivia."

"Saul, your half hour's up."

Dagenham and Presteign, on either side of Foyle, turned. A tall woman approached, stately in an emerald evening gown, her red hair gleaming. It was Jisbella McQueen. Their glances met. Before the shock could seethe into his face, Foyle turned, ran six steps to the first door he saw, opened it and darted through.

The door slammed behind him. He was in a short blind corridor. There was a click, a pause, and then a canned voice spoke courteously: "You have invaded a private portion of this residence. Please retire."

Foyle gasped and struggled with himself.

"You have invaded a private portion of this residence. Please retire."

"I never knew . . . Thought she was killed out there . . . She recognized me . . ."

"You have invaded a private portion of this residence. Please retire."

"I'm finished . . . She'll never forgive me . . . Must be telling Dagenham and Presteign now."

The door from the reception hall opened, and for a moment Foyle thought he saw his flaming image. Then he realized he was looking at Jisbella's flaming hair. She made no move, just stood and smiled at him in furious triumph. He straightened.

"By God, I won't go down whining."

Without haste, Foyle sauntered out of the corridor, took Jisbella's arm and led her back to the reception hall. He never bothered to look around for Dagenham or Presteign. They would present themselves, with force and arms, in due time. He smiled at Jisbella; she smiled back, still in triumph.

"Thanks for running away, Gully. I never dreamed it could be so satisfying."

"Running away? My dear Jiz!"

"Well?"

"I can't tell you how lovely you're looking tonight. We've come a long way from Gouffre Martel, haven't we?" Foyle motioned to the ballroom. "Dance?"

Her eyes widened in surprise at his composure. She permitted him to escort her to the ballroom and take her in his arms.

"By the way, Jiz, how did you manage to keep out of Gouffre Martel?"

"Dagenham arranged it. So you dance now, Gully?"

"I dance, speak four languages miserably, study science and philosophy, write pitiful poetry, blow myself up with idiotic experiments, fence like a fool, box like a buffoon . . . In short, I'm the notorious Fourmyle of Ceres."

"No longer Gully Foyle."

"Only to you, dear, and whoever you've told."

"Just Dagenham. Are you sorry I blew your secret?"

"You couldn't help yourself any more than I could."

"No, I couldn't. Your name just popped out of me. What would you have paid me to keep my mouth shut?"

"Don't be a fool, Jiz. This accident's going to earn you about ¢r 17,980,000."

"What d'you mean?"

"I told you I'd give you whatever was left over after I finished 'Vorga'."

"You've finished 'Vorga'?" she said in surprise.

"No, dear, you've finished me. But I'll keep my promise."

She laughed. "Generous Gully Foyle. Be real generous, Gully. Make a run for it. Entertain me a little."

"Squealing like a rat? I don't know how, Jiz. I'm trained for hunting, nothing else."

"And I killed the tiger. Give me one satisfaction, Gully. Say you were close to 'Vorga.' I ruined you when you were half a step from the finish. Yes?"

"I wish I could, Jiz, but I can't. I'm nowhere. I was trying to pick up another lead here tonight."

"Poor Gully. Maybe I can help you out of this jam. I can say . . . oh . . . that I made a mistake . . . or a joke . . . that you really aren't Gully Foyle. I know how to confuse Saul. I can do it, Gully . . . if you still love me."

He looked down at her and shook his head. "It's never been love between us, Jiz. You know that. I'm too one-track to be anything but a hunter."

"Too one-track to be anything but a fool!"

"What did you mean, Jiz . . . Dagenham arranged to keep you out of Gouffre Martel . . . You know how to confuse Saul Dagenham? What have you got to do with him?"

"I work for him. I'm one of his couriers."

"You mean he's blackmailing you? Threatening to send you back if you don't . . ."

"No. We hit it off the minute we met. He started off capturing me; I ended up capturing him."

"How do you mean?"

"Can't you guess?"

He stared at her. Her eyes were veiled, but he understood. "Jiz! With *him?*"

"Yes."

"But how? He—"

"There are precautions. It's . . . I don't want to talk about it, Gully."

"Sorry. He's a long time returning."

"Returning?"

"Dagenham. With his army."

"Oh. Yes, of course." Jisabella laughed again, then spoke in a low, furious tone. "You don't know what a tightrope you've been walking, Gully. If you'd begged or bribed or tried to romance me . . . By God, I'd have ruined you. I'd have told the world who you were . . . Screamed it from the house-tops . . ."

"What are you talking about?"

"Saul isn't returning. He doesn't know. You can go to hell on your own."

"I don't believe you."

"D'you think it would take him *this* long to get you? Saul Dagenham?"

"But why didn't you tell him? After the way I ran out on you . . ."

"Because I don't want him going to hell with you. I'm not talking about 'Vorga.' I mean something else. PyrE. That's why they hunted you. That's what they're after. Twenty pounds of PyrE."

"What's that?"

"When you got the safe open was there a small box in it? Made of ILI . . . Inert Lead Isomer?"

"Yes."

"What was inside the ILI box?"

"Twenty slugs that looked like compressed iodine crystals."

"What did you do with the slugs?"

"Sent two out for analysis. No one could find out what they are. I'm trying to run an analysis on a third in my lab . . . when I'm not clowning for the public."

"Oh, you are, are you? Why?"

"I'm growing up, Jiz," Foyle said gently. "It didn't take much to figure out *that* was what Presteign and Dagenham were after."

"Where have you got the rest of the slugs?"

"In a safe place."

"They're not safe. They can't ever be safe. I don't know what PyrE is, but I know it's the road to hell, and I don't want Saul walking it."

"You love him that much?"

"I respect him that much. He's the first man that ever showed me an excuse for the double standard."

"Jiz, what *is* PyrE? You know."

"I've guessed. I've pieced together the hints I've heard. I've got an idea. And I could tell you, Gully, but I won't." The fury in her face was luminous. "I'm running out on *you*, this time. I'm leaving you to hang helpless in the dark. See what it feels like, boy! Enjoy!"

She broke away from him and swept across the ballroom floor. At that moment the first bombs fell.

They came in like meteor swarms; not so many, but far more deadly. They came in on the morning quadrant, that quarter of the globe in darkness from midnight to dawn. They collided head on with the forward side of the earth in its revolution around the sun. They had been traveling a distance of four hundred million miles.

Their excessive speed was matched by the rapidity of the Terran defense computors which traced and intercepted these New Year gifts from the Outer Satellites within the space of micro-seconds. A multitude of fierce new stars prickled in the sky and vanished; they were bombs detected and detonated five hundred miles above their target.

But so narrow was the margin between speed of defense and speed of attack that many got through. They shot through the aurora level, the meteor level, the twilight limit, the stratosphere, and down to earth. The invisible trajectories ended in titanic convulsions.

The first atomic explosion which destroyed Newark shook the Presteign mansion with an unbelievable quake. Floors and walls shuddered and the guests were thrown in heaps along with furniture and decorations. Quake followed quake as the random shower descended around New York. They were deafening, numbing, chilling. The sounds, the shocks, the flares of lurid light on the horizon were so enormous, that reason was stripped from humanity, leaving nothing but flayed animals to shriek, cower, and run. Within the space of five seconds Presteign's New Year party was transformed from elegance into anarchy.

Foyle arose from the floor. He looked at the struggling bodies on the ballroom parquet, saw Jisbella fighting to free herself, took a step toward her and then stopped. He revolved his head, dazedly, feeling it was no part of him. The thunder never ceased. He saw Robin Wednesbury in the reception hall, reeling and battered. He took a step toward her and then stopped again. He knew where he must go.

He accelerated. The thunder and lightning dropped down the spectrum to grinding and flickering. The shuddering quakes turned into greasy undulations. Foyle blurred through the giant house, searching, until at last he found her, standing in the garden, standing tiptoe on a marble bench looking like a marble statue to his accelerated senses . . . the statue of exaltation.

He decelerated. Sensation leaped up the spectrum again and once more he was buffeted by that bigger-than-death size bombardment.

"Lady Olivia," he called.

"Who is that?"

"The clown."

"Fourmyle?"

"Yes."

"And you came searching for me? I'm touched, really touched."

"You're insane to be standing out here like this. I beg you to let me—"

"No, no, no. It's beautiful . . . Magnificent!"

"Let me jaunte with you to some place that's safe."

"Ah, you see yourself as a knight in armor? Chivalry to the rescue. It doesn't suit you, my dear. You haven't the flair for it. You'd best go."

"I'll stay."

"As a beauty lover?"

"As a lover."

"You're still tedious, Fourmyle. Come, be inspired. This is Armageddon . . . Flowering Monstrosity. Tell me what you see."

"There's nothing much," he answered, looking around and wincing. "There's light all over the horizon. Quick clouds of it. Above, there's a . . . a sort of sparkling effect. Like Christmas lights twinkling."

"Oh, you see so little with your eyes. See what I see! There's a dome in the sky, a rainbow dome. The colors run from deep tang to brilliant burn. That's what I've named the colors I see. What would that dome be?"

"The radar screen," Foyle muttered.

"And then there are vasty shafts of fire thrusting up and swaying, weaving, dancing, sweeping. What are they?"

"Interceptor beams. You're seeing the whole electronic defense system."

"And I can see the bombs coming down too . . . quick streaks of what you call red. But not your red; mine. Why can I see them?"

"They're heated by air friction, but the inert lead casing doesn't show the color to us."

"See how much better you're doing as Galileo than Galahad. Oh! There's one coming down in the east. Watch for it! It's coming, coming, coming . . . Now!"

A flare of light on the eastern horizon proved it was not her imagination.

"There's another to the north. Very close. Very. Now!"

A shock tore down from the north.

"And the explosions, Fourmyle . . . They're not just clouds of light. They're fabrics, webs, tapestries of meshing colors. So beautiful. Like exquisite shrouds."

"Which they are, Lady Olivia."

"Are you afraid?"

"Yes."

"Then run away."

"No."

"Ah, you're defiant."

"I don't know what I am. I'm scared, but I won't run."

"Then you're brazening it out. Making a show of knightly courage." The husky voice sounded amused. "Just think, Fourmyle. How long does it take to jaunte? You could be safe in seconds . . . in Mexico, Canada, Alaska. So safe. There must be millions there now. We're probably the last left in the city."

"Not everybody can jaunte so far and so fast."

"Then we're the last left who count. Why don't you leave me? Be safe. I'll be killed soon. No one will ever know your pretense turned tail."

"Bitch!"

"Ah, you're angry. What shocking language. It's the first sign of weakness.

Why don't you exercise your better judgment and carry me off? That would be the second sign."

"Damn you!"

He stepped close to her, clenching his fists in rage. She touched his cheek with a cool, quiet hand, but once again there was that electric shock.

"No, it's too late, my dear," she said quietly. "Here comes a whole cluster of red streaks . . . down, down, down . . . directly at us. There'll be no escaping this. Quick, now! Run! Jaunte! Take me with you. Quick! Quick!"

He swept her off the bench. "Bitch! Never!"

He held her, found the soft coral mouth and kissed her; bruised her lips with his, waiting for the final blackout.

The concussion never came.

"Tricked!" he exclaimed. She laughed. He kissed her again and at last forced himself to release her. She gasped for breath, then laughed again, her coral eyes blazing.

"It's over," she said.

"It hasn't begun yet."

"What d'you mean?"

"The war between us."

"Make it a human war," she said fiercely. "You're the first not to be deceived by my looks. Oh God! The boredom of the chivalrous knights and their milk-warm passion for the fairy tale princess. But I'm not like that . . . inside. I'm not. I'm not. Never. Make it a savage war between us. Don't win me . . . destroy me!"

Suddenly she was Lady Olivia again, the gracious snow maiden. "I'm afraid the bombardment has finished, my dear Fourmyle. The show is over. But what an exciting prelude to the New Year. Good night."

"Good night?" he echoed incredulously.

"Good night," she repeated. "Really, my dear Fourmyle, are you so gauche that you never know when you're dismissed? You may go now. Good night."

He hesitated, searched for words, and at last turned and lurched out of the house. He was trembling with elation and confusion. He walked in a daze, scarcely aware of the confusion and disaster around him. The horizon now was lit with the light of red flames. The shock waves of the assault had stirred the atmosphere so violently that winds still whistled in strange gusts. The tremor of the explosions had shaken the city so hard that brick, cornice, glass, and metal were tumbling and crashing. And this despite the fact that no direct hit had been made on New York.

The streets were empty; the city was deserted. The entire population of New York, of every city, had jaunted in a desperate search for safety . . . to the limit of their ability . . . five miles, fifty miles, five hundred miles. Some had jaunted into the center of a direct hit. Thousands died in jaunte-explosions, for the public jaunte stages had never been designed to accommodate the crowding of mass exodus.

Foyle became aware of white-armored Disaster Crews appearing on the streets. An imperious signal directed at him warned him that he was about to be summarily drafted for disaster work. The problem of jaunting was not to get populations out of cities, but to force them to return and restore order. Foyle had no intention of spending a week fighting fire and looters. He accelerated and evaded the Disaster Crew.

At Fifth Avenue he decelerated; the drain of acceleration on his energy was so enormous that he was reluctant to maintain it for more than a few moments. Long periods of acceleration demanded days of recuperation.

The looters and Jack-jaunters were already at work on the avenue, singly, in swarms, furtive yet savage; jackals rending the body of a living but helpless animal. They descended on Foyle. Anything was their prey tonight.

"I'm not in the mood," he told them. "Play with somebody else."

He emptied the money out of his pockets and tossed it to them. They snapped it up but were not satisfied. They desired entertainment and he was obviously a helpless gentleman. Half a dozen surround Foyle and closed in to torment him.

"Kind gentleman," they smiled. "We're going to have a party."

Foyle had once seen the mutilated body of one of their party guests. He sighed and detached his mind from visions of Olivia Presteign.

"All right, jackals," he said. "Let's have a party."

They prepared to send him into a screaming dance. Foyle tripped the switchboard in his mouth and became for twelve devastating seconds the most murderous machine ever devised . . . the Commando killer. It was done without conscious thought or volition; his body merely followed the directive taped into muscle and reflex. He left six bodies stretched on the street.

Old St. Pat's still stood, unblemished, eternal, the distant fires flickering on the green copper of its roof. Inside, it was deserted. The tents of the Four Mile Circus filled the nave, illuminated and furnished, but the circus personnel was gone. Servants, chefs, valets, athletes, philosophers, camp followers and crooks had fled.

"But they'll be back to loot," Foyle murmured.

He entered his own tent. The first thing he saw was a figure in white, crouched on a rug, crooning sunnily to itself. It was Robin Wednesbury, her gown in tatters, her mind in tatters.

"Robin!"

She went on crooning wordlessly. He pulled her up, shook her, and slapped her. She beamed and crooned. He filled a syringe and gave her a tremendous shot of Niacin. The sobering wrench of the drug on her pathetic flight from reality was ghastly. Her satin skin turned ashen. The beautiful face twisted. She recognized Foyle, remembered what she had tried to forget, screamed and sank to her knees. She began to cry.

"That's better," he told her. "You're a great one for escape, aren't you? First suicide. Now this. What next?"

"*Go away.*"

"Probably religion. I can see you joining a cellar sect with passwords like *Pax Vobiscum*. Bible smuggling and martyrdom for the faith. Can't you ever face up to anything?"

"*Don't you ever run away?*"

"Never. Escape is for cripples. Neurotics."

"Neurotics. The favorite word of the Johnny-Come-Lately educated. You're so educated, aren't you? So poised. So balanced. You've been running away all your life."

"Me? Never. I've been hunting all my life."

"You've been running. Haven't you ever heard of Attack-Escape? To run away from reality by attacking it . . . denying it . . . destroying it? That's what you've been doing."

"Attack-Escape?" Foyle was brought up with a jolt. "You mean I've been running away from something?"

"Obviously."

"From what?"

"From reality. You can't accept life as it is. You refuse. You attack it . . . try to force it into your own pattern. You attack and destroy everything that stands in the way of your own insane pattern." She lifted her tear-stained face. "I can't stand it any more. I want you to let me go."

"Go? Where?"

"To live my own life."

"What about your family?"

"And find them my own way."

"Why? What now?"

"It's too much . . . you *and* the war . . . because you're as bad as the war. Worse. What happened to me tonight is what happens to me every moment I'm with you. I can stand one or the other; not both."

"No," he said. "I need you."

"I'm prepared to buy my way out."

"How?"

"You've lost all your leads to 'Vorga,' haven't you?"

"And?"

"I've found another."

"Where?"

"Never mind where. Will you agree to let me go if I turn it over to you?"

"I can take it from you."

"Go ahead. Take it." Her eyes flashed. "If you know what it is, you won't have any trouble."

"I can make you give it to me."

"Can you? After the bombing tonight? Try."

He was taken aback by her defiance. "How do I know you're not bluffing?"

"I'll give you one hint. Remember the man in Australia?"

"Forrest?"

"Yes. He tried to tell you the names of the crew. Do you remember the only name he got out?"

"Kemp."

"He died before he could finish it. The name is Kempsey."

"That's your lead?"

"Yes. Kempsey. Name and address. In return for your promise to let me go."

"It's a sale," he said. "You can go. Give it to me."

She went at once to the travel dress she had worn in Shanghai. From the pocket she took out a sheet of partially burned paper.

"I saw this on Sergei Orel's desk when I was trying to put the fire out . . . the fire the Burning Man started . . ."

She handed him the sheet of paper. It was a fragment of a begging letter. It read: . . . *do anything to get out of these bacteria fields. Why should a man just because he can't jaunte get treated like a dog? Please help me, Serg. Help an old shipmate off a ship we don't mention. You can spare ¢r 100. Remember all the favors I done you? Send ¢r 100 or even ¢r 50. Don't let me down.*

Rodg Kempsey
Barrack 3
Bacteria, Inc.
Mare Nubium
Moon

"By God!" Foyle exclaimed. "This *is* the lead. We can't fail this time. We'll know what to do. He'll spill everything . . . everything." He grinned at Robin. "We leave for the moon tomorrow night. Book passage. No, there'll be trouble on account of the attack. Buy a ship. They'll be unloading them cheap anyway."

"We?" Robin said. "You mean you."

"I mean we," Foyle answered. "We're going to the moon. Both of us."

"I'm leaving."

"You're not leaving. You're staying with me."

"But you swore you'd—"

"Grow up, girl. I had to swear to anything to get this. I need you more than ever now. Not for 'Vorga.' I'll handle 'Vorga' myself. For something much more important."

He looked at her incredulous face and smiled ruefully. "It's too bad, girl. If you'd given me this letter two hours ago I'd have kept my word. But it's too late now. I need a Romance Secretary. I'm in love with Olivia Presteign."

She leaped to her feet in a blaze of fury. "*You're in love with her? Olivia Presteign? In love with that white corpse!*" The bitter fury of her telesending was a startling revelation to him. "*Ah, now you have lost me. Forever. Now I'll destroy you!*"

She disappeared.

CHAPTER TWELVE

CAPTAIN PETER Y'ANG-YEOVIL was handling reports at Central Intelligence Hq. in London at the rate of six per minute. Information was phoned in, wired in, cabled in, jaunted in. The bombardment picture unfolded rapidly.

ATTACK SATURATED N & S AMERICA FROM 60° TO 120° WEST LONGITUDE . . . LABRADOR TO ALASKA IN N . . . RIO TO ECUADOR IN S . . . ESTIMATED TEN PER CENT (10%) MISSILES PENETRATED INTERCEPTION SCREEN . . . ESTIMATED POPULATION LOSS: TEN TO TWELVE MILLION . . .

"If it wasn't for jaunting," Y'ang-Yeovil said, "the losses would have been five times that. All the same, it's close to a knockout. One more punch like that and Terra's finished."

He addressed this to the assistants jaunting in and out of his office, appearing and disappearing, dropping reports on his desk and chalking results and equations on the glass blackboard that covered one entire wall. Informality was the rule, and Y'ang-Yeovil was surprised and suspicious when an assistant knocked on his door and entered with elaborate formality.

"What larceny now?" he asked.

"Lady to see you, Yeo."

"Is this the time for comedy?" Y'ang-Yeovil said in exasperated tones. He pointed to the Whitehead equations spelling disaster on the transparent blackboard. "Read that and weep on the way out."

"Very special lady, Yeo. Your Venus from the Spanish Stairs."

"Who? What Venus?"

"Your Congo Venus."

"Oh? That one?" Y'ang-Yeovil hesitated. "Send her in."

"You'll interview her in private, of course."

"Of course nothing. There's a war on. Keep those reports coming, but tip everybody to switch to Secret Speech if they have to talk to me."

Robin Wednesbury entered the office, still wearing the torn white evening gown. She had jaunted immediately from New York to London without bothering to change. Her face was strained, but lovely. Y'ang-Yeovil gave her a split-second inspection and realized that his first appreciation of her had not been mistaken. Robin returned the inspection and her eyes dilated. "But you're the cook from the Spanish Stairs! Angelo Poggi!"

As an Intelligence Officer, Y'ang-Yeovil was prepared to deal with this crisis. "Not a cook, madam. I haven't had time to change back to my usual fascinating self. Please sit here, Miss . . . ?"

"Wednesbury. Robin Wednesbury."

"Charmed. I'm Captain Y'ang-Yeovil. How nice of you to come and see me, Miss Wednesbury. You've saved me a long, hard search."

"B-But I don't understand. What were you doing on the Spanish Stairs? Why were you hunting—?"

Y'ang-Yeovil saw that her lips weren't moving. "Ah? You're a telepath, Miss Wednesbury? How is that possible? I thought I knew every telepath in the system."

"I'm not a full telepath. I'm a telesend. I can only send . . . not receive."

"Which, of course, makes you worthless to the world. I see." Y'ang-Yeovil cocked a sympathetic eye at her. "What a dirty trick, Miss Wednesbury . . . to be saddled with all the disadvantages of telepathy, and be deprived of all the advantages. I do sympathize. Believe me."

"Bless him! He's the first ever to realize that without being told."

"Careful, Miss Wednesbury, I'm receiving you. Now, about the Spanish Stairs?"

He paused, listening intently to her agitated telesending: *"Why was he hunting? Me? Alien Bellig— Oh God! Will they hurt me? Cut and— Information. I—"*

"My dear girl," Y'ang-Yeovil said gently. He took her hands and held them sympathetically. "Listen to me a moment. You're alarmed over nothing. Apparently you're an Alien Belligerent. Yes?"

She nodded.

"That's unfortunate, but we won't worry about it now. About Intelligence cutting and slicing information out of people . . . that's all propaganda."

"Propaganda?"

"We're not maladroits, Miss Wednesbury. We know how to extract information without being medieval. But we spread the legend to soften people up in advance, so to speak."

"Is that true? He's lying. It's a trick."

"It's true, Miss Wednesbury. I do finesse, but there's no need now. Not when you've evidently come of your own free will to offer information."

"He's too adroit . . . too quick . . . He—"

"You sound as though you've been badly tricked recently, Miss Wednesbury . . . Badly burned."

"I have. I have. *By myself, mostly. I'm a fool. A hateful fool."*

"Never a fool, Miss Wednesbury, and never hateful. I don't know what's happened to shatter your opinion of yourself, but I hope to restore it. So . . . you've been deceived, have you? By yourself, mostly? We all do that. But you've been helped by someone. Who?"

"I'm betraying him."

"Then don't tell me."

"But I've got to find my mother and sisters . . . I can't trust him any more . . . I've got to do it myself." Robin took a deep breath. "I want to tell you about a man named Gulliver Foyle."

Y'ang-Yeovil at once got down to business.

"Is it true he arrived by railroad?" Olivia Presteign asked. "In a locomotive and observation car? What wonderful audacity."

"Yes, he's a remarkable young man," Presteign answered. He stood, iron gray and iron hard, in the reception hall of his home, alone with his daughter. He was guarding honor and life while he waited for servants and staff to return from their panic-stricken jaunte to safety. He chatted imperturbably with Olivia, never once permitting her to realize their grave danger.

"Father, I'm exhausted."

"It's been a trying night, my dear. But please don't retire yet."

"Why not?"

Presteign refrained from telling her that she would be safer with him. "I'm lonely, Olivia. We'll talk for a few minutes."

"I did a daring thing, Father. I watched the attack from the garden."

"My dear! Alone?"

"No. With Fourmyle."

A heavy pounding began to shake the front door which Presteign had closed.

"What's that?"

"Looters," Presteign answered calmly. "Don't be alarmed, Olivia. They won't get in." He stepped to a table on which he had laid out an assortment of weapons as neatly as a game of patience. "There's no danger, my love." He tried to distract her. "You were telling me about Fourmyle. . . ."

"Oh, yes. We watched together . . . describing the bombing to each other."

"Unchaperoned? That wasn't discreet, Olivia."

"I know. I know. I behaved disgracefully. He seemed so big, so sure of himself, that I gave him the Lady Hauteur treatment. You remember Miss Post, my governess, who was so dignified and aloof that I called her Lady Hauteur? I acted like Miss Post. He was furious, father. That's why he came looking for me in the garden."

"And you permitted him to remain? I'm shocked, dear."

"I am too. I think I was half out of my mind with excitement. What's he like, father? Tell me. What's he look like to you?"

"He *is* big. Tall, very dark, rather enigmatic. Like a Borgia. He seems to alternate between assurance and savagery."

"Ah, he is savage, then? I could see it myself. He glows with danger. Most people just shimmer . . . he looks like a lightning bolt. It's terribly fascinating."

"My dear," Presteign remonstrated gently. "Unmarried females are too modest to talk like that. It would displease me, my love, if you were to form a romantic attachment for a parvenu like Fourmyle of Ceres."

The Presteign staff jaunted into the reception hall, cooks, waitresses, footmen, pages, coachmen, valets, maids. All were shaken and hang-dog after their flight from death.

"You have deserted your posts. It will be remembered," Presteign said coldly. "My safety and honor are again in your hands. Guard them. Lady Olivia and I will retire."

He took his daughter's arm and led her up the stairs, savagely protective of his ice-pure princess. "Blood and money," Presteign murmured.

"What, father?"

"I was thinking of a family vice, Olivia. I was thanking the Deity that you have not inherited it."

"What vice is that?"

"There's no need for you to know. It's one that Fourmyle shares."

"Ah, he's wicked? I knew it. Like a Borgia, you said. A wicked Borgia with black eyes and lines in his face. That must account for the pattern."

"Pattern, my dear?"

"Yes. I can see a strange pattern over his face . . . not the usual electricity of nerve and muscle. Something laid over that. It fascinated me from the beginning."

"What sort of pattern do you mean?"

"Fantastic . . . Wonderfully evil. I can't describe it. Give me something to write with. I'll show you."

They stopped before a six-hundred-year-old Chippendale cabinet. Presteign took out a silver-mounted slab of crystal and handed it to Olivia. She touched it with her fingertip; a black dot appeared. She moved her finger and the dot elongated into a line. With quick strokes she sketched the hideous swirls and blazons of a devil mask.

Saul Dagenham left the darkened bedroom. A moment later it was flooded with light as one wall illuminated. It seemed as though a giant mirror reflected Jisbella's bedroom, but with one odd quirk. Jisbella lay in the bed alone, but in the reflection Saul Dagenham sat on the edge of the bed alone. The mirror was, in fact, a sheet of lead glass separating identical rooms. Dagenham had just illuminated his.

"Love by the clock." Dagenham's voice came through a speaker. "Disgusting."

"No, Saul. Never."

"Frustrating."

"Not that, either."

"But unhappy."

"No. You're greedy. Be content with what you've got."

"It's more than I ever had. You're magnificent."

"You're extravagant. Now go to sleep, darling. We're skiing tomorrow."

"No, there's been a change of plan. I've got to work."

"Oh Saul . . . you promised me. No more working and fretting and running. Aren't you going to keep your promise?"

"I can't with a war on."

"To hell with the war. You sacrificed enough up at Tycho Sands. They can't ask any more of you."

"I've got one job to finish."

"I'll help you finish it."

"No. You'd best keep out of this, Jisbella."

"You don't trust me."

"I don't want you hurt."

"Nothing can hurt us."
"Foyle can."
"W-What?"
"Fourmyle is Foyle. You know that. I know you know."
"But I never—"
"No, you never told me. You're magnificent. Keep faith with me the same way, Jisbella."
"Then how did you find out?"
"Foyle slipped."
"How?"
"The name."
"Fourmyle of Ceres? He bought the Ceres company."
"But Geoffrey Fourmyle?"
"He invented it."
"He thinks he invented it. He remembered it. Geoffrey Fourmyle is the name they use in the megalomania test down in Combined Hospital in Mexico City. I used the Megal Mood on Foyle when I tried to open him up. The name must have stayed buried in his memory. He dredged it up and thought it was original. That tipped me."
"Poor Gully."
Dagenham smiled. "Yes, no matter how we defend ourselves against the outside we're always licked by something from the inside. There's no defense against betrayal, and we all betray ourselves."
"What are you going to do, Saul?"
"Do? Finish him, of course."
"For twenty pounds of PyrE?"
"No. To win a lost war."
"What?" Jisbella came to the glass wall separating the rooms. "You, Saul? Patriotic?"
He nodded, almost guiltily. "It's ridiculous. Grotesque. But I am. You've changed me completely. I'm a sane man again."
He pressed his face to the wall too, and they kissed through three inches of lead glass.

Mare Nubium was ideally suited to the growth of anaerobic bacteria, soil organisms, phage, rare moulds, and all those microscopic life forms, essential to medicine and industry, which required airless culture. Bacteria, Inc. was a huge mosaic of culture fields traversed by catwalks spread around a central clump of barracks, offices, and plant. Each field was a giant glass vat, one hundred feet in diameter, twelve inches high and no more than two molecules thick.

A day before the sunrise line, creeping across the face of the moon, reached Mare Nubium, the vats were filled with culture medium. At sunrise, abrupt and blinding on the airless moon, the vats were seeded, and for the next fourteen days of continuous sun they were tended, shielded, regulated, nurtured . . . the field workers trudging up and down the catwalks in spacesuits. As the sunset line crept toward Mare Nubium, the vats were harvested and then left to freeze and sterilize in the two week frost of the lunar night.

Jaunting was of no use in this tedious step-by-step cultivation. Hence Bacteria, Inc. hired unfortunates incapable of jaunting and paid them slave wages. This was the lowest form of labor, the dregs and scum of the Solar System; and the barracks of Bacteria, Inc. resembled an inferno during the two week lay-off period. Foyle discovered this when he entered Barrack 3.

He was met by an appalling spectacle. There were two hundred men in the giant room; there were whores and their hard-eyed pimps, professional gamblers and their portable tables, dope peddlers, money lenders. There was a haze of acrid smoke and the stench of alcohol and Analogue. Furniture, bedding, clothes, unconscious bodies, empty bottles, rotting food were scattered on the floor.

A roar challenged Foyle's appearance, but he was equipped to handle this situation. He spoke to the first hairy face thrust into his.

"Kempsey?" he asked quietly. He was answered outrageously. Nevertheless he grinned and handed the man a ¢r 100 note. "Kempsey?" he asked another. He was insulted. He paid again and continued his saunter down the barracks distributing ¢r 100 notes in calm thanks for insult and invective. In the center of the barracks he found his key man, the obvious barracks bully, a monster of a man, naked, hairless, fondling two bawds and being fed whiskey by sycophants.

"Kempsey?" Foyle asked in the old gutter tongue. "I'm diggin' Rodger Kempsey."

"I'm diggin' you for broke," the man answered, thrusting out a huge paw for Foyle's money. "Gimmie."

There was a delighted howl from the crowd. Foyle smiled and spat in his eye. There was an abject hush. The hairless man dumped the bawds and surged up to annihilate Foyle. Five seconds later he was groveling on the floor with Foyle's foot planted on his neck.

"Still diggin' Kempsey," Foyle said gently. "Diggin' hard, man. You better finger him, man, or you're gone, is all."

"Washroom!" the hairless man howled. "Holed up. Washroom."

"Now you broke me," Foyle said. He dumped the rest of his money on the floor before the hairless man and walked quickly to the washroom. Kempsey was cowering in the corner of a shower, face pressed to the wall, moaning in a dull rhythm that showed he had been at it for hours.

"Kempsey?"

The moaning answered him.

"What's a matter, you?"

"Clothes," Kempsey wept. "Clothes. All over, clothes. Like filth, like sick, like dirt. Clothes. All over, clothes."

"Up, man. Get up."

"Clothes. All over, clothes. Like filth, like sick, like dirt . . ."

"Kempsey, mind me, man. Orel sent me."

Kempsey stopped weeping and turned his sodden countenance to Foyle. "Who? Who?"

"Sergei Orel sent me. I've bought your release. You're free. We'll blow."

"When?"

"Now."

"Oh God! God bless him. Bless him!" Kempsey began to caper in weary exultation. The bruised and bloated face split into a facsimile of laughter. He laughed and capered and Foyle led him out of the washroom. But in the barracks he screamed and wept again, and as Foyle led him down the long room, the naked bawds swept up armfuls of dirty clothes and shook them before his eyes. Kempsey foamed and gibbered.

"What's a matter, him?" Foyle inquired of the hairless man in the gutter patois.

The hairless man was now a respectful neutral if not a friend. "Guesses for grabs," he answered. "Always like that, him. Show old clothes and he twitch. Man!"

"For why, already?"

"For why? Crazy, is all."

At the main-office airlock, Foyle got Kempsey and himself corked in suits and then led him out to the rocket field where a score of anti-grav beams pointed their pale fingers upward from pits to the gibbous earth hanging in the night sky. They entered a pit, entered Foyle's yawl and uncorked. Foyle took a bottle and a sting ampule from a cabinet. He poured a drink and handed it to Kempsey. He hefted the ampule in his palm, smiling.

Kempsey drank the whiskey, still dazed, still exulting. "Free," he muttered. "God bless him! Free. You don't know what I've been through." He drank again. "I still can't believe it. It's like a dream. Why don't you take off, man? I—" Kempsey choked and dropped the glass, staring at Foyle in horror. "Your face!" he exclaimed. "My God, your face! What happened to it?"

"You happened to it, you son of a bitch!" Foyle cried. He leaped up, his tiger face burning, and flung the ampule like a knife. It pierced Kempsey's neck and hung quivering. Kempsey toppled.

Foyle accelerated, blurred to the body, picked it up in mid-fall and carried it aft to the starboard stateroom. There were two main staterooms in the yawl, and Foyle had prepared both of them in advance. The starboard room had been stripped and turned into a surgery. Foyle strapped the body on the operating table, opened a case of surgical instruments, and began the delicate operation he had learned by hypno-training that morning . . . an operation made possible only by his five-to-one acceleration.

He cut through skin and fascia, sawed through the rib cage, exposed the heart, dissected it out and connected veins and arteries to the intricate blood pump alongside the table. He started the pump. Twenty seconds, objective time, had elapsed. He placed an oxygen mask over Kempsey's face and switched on the alternating suction and ructation of the oxygen pump.

Foyle decelerated, checked Kempsey's temperature, shot an anti-shock series into his veins and waited. Blood gurgled through the pump and Kempsey's body. After five minutes, Foyle removed the oxygen mask. The respiration reflex continued. Kempsey was without a heart, yet alive. Foyle sat down alongside the operating table and waited. The stigmata still showed on his face.

Kempsey remained unconscious.

Foyle waited.

Kempsey awoke, screaming.

Foyle leaped up, tightened the straps and leaned over the heartless man. "Hallo, Kempsey," he said.

Kempsey screamed.

"Look at yourself, Kempsey. You're dead."

Kempsey fainted. Foyle brought him to with the oxygen mask.

"Let me die, for God's sake!"

"What's the matter? Does it hurt? I died for six months, and I didn't whine."

"Let me die."

"In time, Kempsey. Your sympathetic block's been bypassed, but I'll let you die in time, if you behave. You were aboard 'Vorga' on September 16, 2436?"

"For Christ's sake, let me die."

"You were aboard 'Vorga'?"

"Yes."

"You passed a wreck out in space. Wreck of the 'Nomad.' She signalled for help and you passed her by. Yes?"

"Yes."

"Why?"

"Christ! Oh Christ help me!"

"Why?"

"Oh Jesus!"

"I was aboard 'Nomad,' Kempsey. Why did you leave me to rot?"

"Sweet Jesus help me! Christ, deliver me!"

"I'll deliver you, Kempsey, if you answer questions. Why did you leave me to rot?"

"Couldn't pick you up."

"Why not?"

"Reffs aboard."

"Oh? I guessed right, then. You were running refugees in from Callisto?"

"Yes."

"How many?"

"Six hundred."

"That's a lot, but you could have made room for one more. Why didn't you pick me up?"

"We were scuttling the reffs."

"What!" Foyle cried.

"Overboard . . . all of them . . . six hundred . . . Stripped 'em . . . took their clothes, money, jewels, baggage . . . Put 'em through the airlock in batches. Christ! The clothes all over the ship . . . The shrieking and the—Jesus! If I could only forget! The naked women . . . blue . . . busting wide open . . . spinning behind us . . . The clothes all over the ship . . . Six hundred . . . Scuttled!"

"You son of a bitch! It was a racket? You took their money and never intended bringing them to earth?"

"It was a racket."

"And that's why you didn't pick me up?"

"Would have had to scuttle you anyway."

"Who gave the order?"

"Captain."

"Name?"

"Joyce. Lindsey Joyce."

"Address?"

"Skoptsy Colony, Mars."

"What!" Foyle was thunderstruck. "He's a Skoptsy? You mean after hunting him for a year, I can't touch him . . . hurt him . . . make him feel what I felt?" He turned away from the tortured man on the table, equally tortured himself by frustration. "A Skoptsy! The one thing I never figured on . . . After preparing that port stateroom for him . . . What am I going to do? What, in God's name am I going to do?" he roared in fury, the stigmata showing livid on his face.

He was recalled by a desperate moan from Kempsey. He returned to the table and bent over the dissected body. "Let's get it straight for the last time. This Skoptsy, Lindsey Joyce, gave the order to scuttle the reffs?"

"Yes."

"And to let me rot?"

"Yes. Yes. Yes. That's enough. Let me die."

"Live, you pig-man . . . filthy heartless bastard! Live without a heart. Live and suffer. I'll keep you alive forever, you—"

A lurid flash of light caught Foyle's eye. He looked up. His burning image was peering through the large square porthole of the stateroom. As he leaped to the porthole, the burning man disappeared.

Foyle left the stateroom and darted forward to main controls where the observation bubble gave him two hundred and seventy degrees of vision. The Burning Man was nowhere in sight.

"It's not real," he muttered. "It couldn't be real. It's a sign, a good luck sign . . . a Guardian Angel. It saved me on the Spanish Stairs. It's telling me to go ahead and find Lindsey Joyce."

He strapped himself into the pilot chair, ignited the yawl's jets, and slammed into full acceleration.

"Lindsey Joyce, Skoptsy Colony, Mars," he thought as he was thrust back deep into the pneumatic chair. "A Skoptsy . . . Without senses, without pleasure, without pain. The ultimate in Stoic escape. How am I going to punish him? Torture him? Put him in the port stateroom and make him feel what I felt aboard 'Nomad'? Damnation! It's as though he's dead. He *is* dead. And I've got to figure how to beat a dead body and make it feel pain. To come so close to the end and have the door slammed in your face . . .

The damnable frustration of revenge. Revenge is for dreams . . . never for reality."

An hour later he released himself from the acceleration and his fury, unbuckled himself from the chair, and remembered Kempsey. He went aft to the surgery. The extreme acceleration of the take-off had choked the blood pump enough to kill Kempsey. Suddenly Foyle was overcome with a novel passionate revulsion for himself. He fought it helplessly.

"What's a matter, you?" he whispered. "Think of the six hundred, scuttled . . . Think of yourself . . . Are you turning into a white-livered Cellar Christian turning the other cheek and whining forgiveness? Olivia, what are you doing to me? Give me strength, not cowardice . . ."

Nevertheless he averted his eyes as he scuttled the body.

CHAPTER THIRTEEN

ALL PERSONS KNOWN TO BE IN THE EMPLOY OF FOURMYLE OF CERES OR ASSOCIATED WITH HIM IN ANY CAPACITY TO BE HELD FOR QUESTIONING. Y-Y: CENTRAL INTELLIGENCE.

ALL EMPLOYEES OF THIS COMPANY TO MAINTAIN STRICT WATCH FOR ONE FOURMYLE OF CERES, AND REPORT AT ONCE TO LOCAL MR. PRESTO. PRESTEIGN.

ALL COURIERS WILL ABANDON PRESENT ASSIGNMENTS AND REPORT FOR REASSIGNMENT TO FOYLE CASE. DAGENHAM.

A BANK HOLIDAY WILL BE DECLARED IMMEDIATELY IN THE NAME OF THE WAR CRISIS TO CUT FOURMYLE OFF FROM ALL FUNDS. Y-Y: CENTRAL INTELLIGENCE.

ANYONE MAKING INQUIRIES RE: S.S. "VORGA" TO BE TAKEN TO CASTLE PRESTEIGN FOR EXAMINATION. PRESTEIGN.

ALL PORTS AND FIELDS IN INNER PLANETS TO BE ALERTED FOR ARRIVAL OF FOURMYLE. QUARANTINE AND CUSTOMS TO CHECK ALL LANDINGS. Y-Y: CENTRAL INTELLIGENCE.

OLD ST. PATRICK'S TO BE SEARCHED AND WATCHED. DAGENHAM.

THE FILES OF BO'NESS & UIG TO BE CHECKED FOR NAMES OF OFFICERS AND MEN OF VORGA TO ANTICIPATE, IF POSSIBLE, FOYLE'S NEXT MOVE. PRESTEIGN.

WAR CRIMES COMMISSION TO MAKE UP LIST OF PUBLIC ENEMIES GIVING FOYLE NUMBER ONE SPOT. Y-Y: CENTRAL INTELLIGENCE.

₡r 1,000,000 REWARD OFFERED FOR INFORMATION LEADING TO APPREHENSION OF FOURMYLE OF CERES, ALIAS GULLIVER FOYLE, ALIAS GULLEY FOYLE, NOW AT LARGE IN THE INNER PLANETS. PRIORITY!

After two centuries of colonization, the air struggle on Mars was still so critical that the V-L Law, the Vegetative-Lynch Law, was still in effect. It was a killing offense to endanger or destroy any plant vital to the transformation of Mars' carbon dioxide atmosphere into an oxygen atmosphere. Even blades of grass were sacred. There was no need to erect KEEP OFF THE GRASS neons. The man who wandered off a path onto a lawn would be instantly shot. The woman who picked a flower would be killed without mercy. Two centuries of sudden death had inspired a reverence for green growing things that almost amounted to a religion.

Foyle remembered this as he raced up the center of the causeway leading to Mars St. Michele. He had jaunted direct from the Syrtis airport to the St. Michele stage at the foot of the causeway which stretched for a quarter of a mile through green fields to Mars St. Michele. The rest of the distance had to be traversed on foot.

Like the original Mont St. Michele on the French coast, Mars St. Michele was a majestic Gothic cathedral of spires and buttresses looming on a hill and yearning toward the sky. Ocean tides surrounded Mont St. Michele on earth. Green tides of grass surrounded Mars St. Michele. Both were fortresses. Mont St. Michele had been a fortress of faith before organized religion was abolished. Mars St. Michele was a fortress of telepathy. Within it lived Mars's sole full telepath, Sigurd Magsman.

"Now these are the defenses protecting Sigurd Magsman," Foyle chanted, halfway between hysteria and litany. "Firstly, the Solar System; secondly, martial law; thirdly, Dagenham-Presteign & Co.; fourthly, the fortress itself; fifthly, the uniformed guards, attendants, servants, and admirers of the bearded sage we all know so well, Sigurd Magsman, selling his awesome powers for awesome prices. . . ."

Foyle laughed immoderately: "But there's a Sixthly that I know: Sigurd Magsman's Achilles' Heel . . . For I've paid ¢r 1,000,000 to Sigurd III . . . or was he IV?"

He passed through the outer labyrinth of Mars St. Michele with his forged credentials and was tempted to bluff or proceed directly by commando action to an audience with the Great Man himself, but time was pressing and his enemies were closing in and he could not afford to satisfy his curiosity. Instead, he accelerated, blurred, and found a humble cottage set in a walled garden within the Mars St. Michele home farm. It had drab windows and a thatched roof and might have been mistaken for a stable. Foyle slipped inside.

The cottage was a nursery. Three pleasant nannies sat motionless in rocking chairs, knitting poised in their frozen hands. The blur that was Foyle came up behind them and quietly stung them with ampules. Then he decelerated. He looked at the ancient, ancient child; the wizened, shriveled boy who was seated on the floor playing with electronic trains.

"Hello, Sigurd," Foyle said.

The child began to cry.

"Crybaby! What are you afraid of? I'm not going to hurt you."

"You're a bad man with a bad face."

"I'm your friend, Sigurd."

"No, you're not. You want me to do b-bad things."

"I'm your friend. Look, I know all about those big hairy men who pretend to be you, but I won't tell. Read me and see."

"You're going to hurt him and y-you want me to tell him."

"Who?"

"The captain-man. The Skl— Skot—" The child fumbled with the word, wailing louder. *"Go away. You're bad. Badness in your head and burning mens and—"*

"Come here, Sigurd."

"No. NANNIE! NAN-N-I-E!"

"Shut up, you little bastard!"

Foyle grabbed the seventy-year-old child and shook it. "This is going to be a brand new experience for you, Sigurd. The first time you've ever been walloped into anything. Understand?"

The ancient child read him and howled.

"Shut up! We're going on a trip to the Skoptsy Colony. If you behave yourself and do what you're told, I'll bring you back safe and give you a lolly or whatever the hell they bribe you with. If you don't behave, I'll beat the living daylights out of you."

"No, you won't. . . . You won't. I'm Sigurd Magsman. I'm Sigurd the telepath. You wouldn't dare."

"Sonny, I'm Gully Foyle, Solar Enemy Number One. I'm just a step away from the finish of a year-long hunt . . . I'm risking my neck because I need you to settle accounts with a son of a bitch who— Sonny, I'm Gully Foyle. There isn't anything I wouldn't dare."

The telepath began broadcasting terror with such an uproar the alarms sounded all over Mars St. Michele. Foyle took a firm grip on the ancient child, accelerated and carried him out of the fortress. Then he jaunted.

URGENT. SIGURD MAGSMAN KIDNAPED BY MAN
TENTATIVELY IDENTIFIED AS GULLIVER FOYLE, ALIAS
FOURMYLE OF CERES, SOLAR ENEMY NUMBER ONE.
DESTINATION TENTATIVELY FIXED. ALERT COMMANDO
BRIGADE. INFORM CENTRAL INTELLIGENCE. URGENT!

The ancient Skoptsy sect of White Russia, believing that sex was the root of all evil, practiced an atrocious self-castration to extirpate the root. The modern Skoptsys, believing that sensation was the root of all evil, practiced an even more barbaric custom. Having entered the Skoptsy Colony and paid a fortune for the privilege, the initiates submitted joyously to an operation that severed the sensory nervous system, and lived out their days without sight, sound, speech, smell, taste, or touch.

When they first entered the monastery, the initiates were shown elegant ivory cells in which it was intimated they would spend the remainder of their lives in rapt contemplation, lovingly tended. In actuality, the senseless creatures were packed in catacombs where they sat on rough stone slabs and were fed and exercised once a day. For twenty-three out of twenty-four hours they sat alone in the dark, untended, unguarded, unloved.

"The living dead," Foyle muttered. He decelerated, put Sigurd Magsman down, and switched on the retinal light in his eyes, trying to pierce the wombgloom. It was midnight above ground. It was permanent midnight down in the catacombs. Sigurd Magsman was broadcasting terror and anguish with such a telepathic bray that Foyle was forced to shake the child again. "Shut up!" he whispered. "You can't wake these dead. Now find me Lindsey Joyce."

"They're sick . . . all sick . . . like worms in their heads . . . worms and sickness and—"

"Christ, don't I know it. Come on, let's get it over with. There's worse to come."

They went down the twisting labyrinth of the catacombs. The stone slabs shelved the walls from floor to ceiling. The Skoptsys, white as slugs, mute as corpses, motionless as Buddhas, filled the caverns with the odor of living death. The telepathic child wept and shrieked. Foyle never relaxed his relentless grip on him; he never relaxed the hunt.

"Johnson, Wright, Keeley, Graff, Nastro, Underwood . . . God, there's thousands here." Foyle read off the bronze identification plates attached to the slabs. "Reach out, Sigurd. Find Lindsey Joyce for me. We can't go over them name by name. Regal, Cone, Brady, Vincent— What in the—?"

Foyle started back. One of the bone-white figures had cuffed his brow. It was swaying and writhing, its face twitching. All the white slugs on their shelves were squirming and writhing. Sigurd Magsman's constant telepathic broadcast of anguish and terror was reaching them and torturing them. "Shut up!" Foyle snapped. "Stop it. Find Lindsey Joyce and we'll get out of here. Reach out and find him."

"Down there." Sigurd wept. *"Straight down there. Seven, eight, nine shelves down. I want to go home. I'm sick. I—"*

Foyle went pell-mell down the catacombs with Sigurd, reading off identification plates until at last he came to: "LINDSEY JOYCE. BOUGAINVILLE. VENUS."

This was his enemy, the instigator of his death and the deaths of the six hundred from Callisto. This was the enemy for whom he had planned vengeance and hunted for months. This was the enemy for whom he had prepared the agony of the port stateroom aboard his yawl. This was "Vorga." It was a woman.

Foyle was thunderstruck. In these days of the double standard, with women kept in purdah, there were many reported cases of women masquerading as men to enter the worlds closed to them, but he had never yet heard of a woman in the merchant marine . . . masquerading her way to top officer rank.

"This?" he exclaimed furiously. "This is Lindsey Joyce? Lindsey Joyce off the 'Vorga'? Ask her."

"I don't know what 'Vorga' is."

"Ask her!"

"But I don't— She was . . . She like gave orders."

"Captain?"

"I don't like what's inside her. It's all sick and dark. It hurts. I want to go home."

"Ask her. Was she captain of the 'Vorga'?"

"Yes. Please, please, please don't make me go inside her any more. It's twisty and hurts. I don't like her."

"Tell her I'm the man she wouldn't pick up on September 16, 2436. Tell her it's taken a long time but I've finally come to settle the account. Tell her I'm going to pay her back."

"I d-don't understand. Don't understand."

"Tell her I'm going to kill her, slow and hard. Tell her I've got a stateroom aboard my yawl, fitted up just like my locker aboard 'Nomad' where I rotted for six months . . . where she ordered 'Vorga' to leave me to die. Tell her she's going to rot and die just like me. Tell her!" Foyle shook the wizened child furiously. "Make her feel it. Don't let her get away by turning Skoptsy. Tell her I kill her filthy. Read me and tell her!"

"She . . . Sh-She didn't give that order."

"What!"

"I c-can't understand her."

"She didn't give the order to scuttle me?"

"I'm afraid to go in."

"Go in, you little son of a bitch, or I'll take you apart. What does she mean?"

The child wailed; the woman writhed; Foyle fumed. "Go in! Go in! Get it out of her. Jesus Christ, why does the only telepath on Mars have to be a child? Sigurd! Sigurd, listen to me. Ask her: Did she give the order to scuttle the reffs?"

"No. No!"

"No she didn't or no you won't?"

"She didn't."

"Did she give the order to pass 'Nomad' by?"

"She's twisty and sicky. Oh please! NAN-N-I-E! I want to go home. Want to go."

"Did she give the order to pass 'Nomad' by?"

"No."

"She didn't?"

"No. Take me home."

"Ask her who did."

"I want my Nannie."

"Ask her who could give her an order. She was captain aboard her own ship. Who could command her? Ask her!"

"I want my Nannie."

"Ask her!"

"No. No. No. I'm afraid. She's sick. She's dark and black. She's bad. I don't understand her. I want my Nannie. I want to go home."

The child was shrieking and shaking; Foyle was shouting. The echoes thundered. As Foyle reached for the child in a rage, his eyes were blinded by brilliant light. The entire catacomb was illuminated by the Burning Man. Foyle's image stood before him, face hideous, clothes on fire, the blazing eyes fixed on the convulsing Skoptsy that had been Lindsey Joyce.

The Burning Man opened his tiger mouth. A grating sound emerged. It was like flaming laughter.

"She hurts," he said.

"Who are you?" Foyle whispered.

The Burning Man winced. "Too bright," he said. "Less light."

Foyle took a step forward. The Burning Man clapped hands over his ears in agony. "Too loud," he cried. "Don't move so loud."

"Are you my guardian angel?"

"You're blinding me. Shhh!" Suddenly he laughed again "Listen to her. She's screaming. Begging. She doesn't want to die. She doesn't want to be hurt. Listen to her."

Foyle trembled.

"She's telling us who gave the order. Can't you hear? Listen with your eyes." The Burning Man pointed a talon finger at the writhing Skoptsy. "She says Olivia."

"What!"

"She says Olivia. Olivia Presteign. Olivia Presteign. Olivia Presteign."

The Burning Man vanished.

The catacombs were dark again.

Colored lights and cacophonies whirled around Foyle. He gasped and staggered. "Blue jaunte," he muttered. "Olivia. No. Not. Never. Olivia. I—"

He felt a hand reach for his. "Jiz?" he croaked.

He became aware that Sigurd Magsman was holding on to his hand and weeping. He picked the boy up.

"*I hurt,*" Sigurd whimpered.

"I hurt too, son."

"*Want to go home.*"

"I'll take you home."

Still holding the boy in his arms, he blundered through the catacombs.

"The living dead," he mumbled.

And then: "I've joined them."

He found the stone steps that led up from the depths to the monastery cloister above ground. He trudged up the steps, tasting death and desolation. There was bright light above him, and for a moment he imagined that dawn had come already. Then he realized that the cloister was brilliantly lit with artificial light. There was the tramp of shod feet and the low growl of commands. Halfway up the steps, Foyle stopped and mustered himself.

"Sigurd," he whispered. "Who's above us? Find out."

"*Sogers,*" the child answered.

"Soldiers? What soldiers?"

"Commando sogers." Sigurd's crumpled face brightened. *"They come for me. To take me home to Nannie. HERE I AM! HERE I AM!"*

The telepathic clamor brought a shout from overhead. Foyle accelerated and blurred up the rest of the steps to the cloister. It was a square of Romanesque arches surrounding a green lawn. In the center of the lawn was a giant cedar of Lebanon. The flagged walks swarmed with Commando search parties, and Foyle came face to face with his match; for an instant after they saw his blur whip up from the catacombs they accelerated too, and all were on even terms.

But Foyle had the boy. Shooting was impossible. Cradling Sigurd in his arms, he wove through the cloister like a broken-field runner hurtling toward a goal. No one dared block him, for at plus-five acceleration a head-on collision between two bodies would be instantly fatal to both. Objectively, this break-neck skirmish looked like a five second zigzag of lightning.

Foyle broke out of the cloister, went through the main hall of the monastery, passed through the labyrinth, and reached the public jaunte stage outside the main gate. There he stopped, decelerated and jaunted to the monastery airfield, half a mile distant. The field, too, was ablaze with lights and swarming with Commandos. Every anti-grav pit was occupied by a Brigade ship. His own yawl was under guard.

A fifth of a second after Foyle arrived at the field, the pursuers from the monastery jaunted in. He looked around desperately. He was surrounded by half a regiment of Commandos, all under acceleration, all geared for lethal-action, all his equal or better. The odds were impossible.

And then the Outer Satellites altered the odds. Exactly one week after the saturation raid on Terra, they struck at Mars.

Again the missiles came down on the midnight to dawn quadrant. Again the heavens twinkled with interceptions and detonations, and the horizon exploded great puffs of light while the ground shook. But this time there was a ghastly variation, for a brilliant nova burst overhead, flooding the nightside of the planet with garish light. A swarm of fission heads had struck Mars's tiny satellite, Phobos, instantly vaporizing it into a sunlet.

The recognition lag of the Commandos to this appalling attack gave Foyle his opportunity. He accelerated again and burst through them to his yawl. He stopped before the main hatch and saw the stunned guard party hesitate between a continuance of the old action and a response to the new. Foyle hurled Sigurd Magsman up into the air like an ancient Scotsman tossing the caber. As the guard party rushed to catch the boy, Foyle dove through them into his yawl, slammed the hatch, and dogged it.

Still under acceleration, never pausing to see if anyone was inside the yawl, he shot forward to controls, tripped the release lever, and as the yawl started to float up the anti-grav beam, threw on full 10-G propulsion. He was not strapped into the pilot chair. The effect of the 10-G drive on his accelerated and unprotected body was monstrous.

A creeping force took hold of him and spilled him out of the chair. He inched back toward the rear wall of the control chamber like a sleepwalker. The wall appeared, to his accelerated senses, to approach him. He thrust out both arms, palms flat against the wall to brace himself. The sluggish power thrusting him back split his arms apart and forced him against the wall, gently at first, then harder and harder until face, jaw, chest, and body were crushed against the metal.

The mounting pressure became agonizing. He tried to trip the switchboard in his mouth with his tongue, but the propulsion crushing him against the wall made it impossible for him to move his distorted mouth. A burst of explosions, so far down the sound spectrum that they sounded like sodden rock slides, told him that the Commando Brigade was bombarding him with shots from below. As the yawl tore up into the blue-black of outer space, he began to scream in a bat screech before he mercifully lost consciousness.

CHAPTER FOURTEEN

FOYLE AWOKE IN DARKNESS. He was decelerated, but the exhaustion of his body told him he had been under acceleration while he had been unconscious. Either his power pack had run out or . . . He inched a hand to the small of his back. The pack was gone. It had been removed.

He explored with trembling fingers. He was in a bed. He listened to the murmur of ventilators and air-conditioners and the click and buzz of servomechanisms. He was aboard a ship. He was strapped to the bed. The ship was in free fall.

Foyle unfastened himself, pressed his elbows against the mattress and floated up. He drifted through the darkness searching for a light switch or a call button. His hands brushed against a water carafe with raised letteres on the glass. He read them with his fingertips. SS, he felt. V, O, R, G, A. VORGA. He cried out.

The door of the stateroom opened. A figure drifted through the door, silhouetted against the light of a luxurious private lounge behind it.

"This time we picked you up," a voice said.

"Olivia?"

"Yes."

"Then it's true?"

"Yes, Gully."

Foyle began to cry.

"You're still weak," Olivia Presteign said gently. "Come and lie down."

She urged him into the lounge and strapped him into a chaise longue. It was still warm from her body. "You've been like this for six days. We never thought you'd live. Everything was drained out of you before the surgeon found that battery on your back."

"Where is it?" he croaked.

"You can have it whenever you want it. Don't fret, my dear."

He looked at her for a long moment, his Snow Maiden, his beloved Ice

Princess . . . the white satin skin, the blind coral eyes and exquisite coral mouth. She touched his moist eyelids with a scented handkerchief.

"I love you," he said.

"Shhh. I know, Gully."

"You've known all about me. For how long?"

"I knew Gully Foyle the spaceman off the 'Nomad,' was my enemy from the beginning. I never knew you were Fourmyle until we met. Ah, if only I'd known before. How much would have been saved."

"You knew and you've been laughing at me."

"No."

"Standing by and shaking with laughter."

"Standing by and loving you. No, don't interrupt. I'm trying to be rational and it's not easy." A flush cascaded across the marble face. "I'm not playing with you now. I . . . I betrayed you to my father. I did. Self-defense, I thought. Now that I've met him at last I can see he's too dangerous. An hour later I knew it was a mistake because I realized I was in love with you. I'm paying for it now. You need never have known."

"You expect me to believe that?"

"Then why am I here?" She trembled slightly. "Why did I follow you? That bombing was ghastly. You'd have been dead in another minute when we picked you up. Your yawl was a wreck. . . ."

"Where are we now?"

"What difference does it make?"

"I'm stalling for time."

"Time for what?"

"Not for time . . . I'm stalling for courage."

"We're orbiting earth."

"How did you follow me?"

"I knew you'd be after Lindsey Joyce. I took over one of my father's ships. It happened to be 'Vorga' again."

"Does he know?"

"He never knows. I live my own private life."

He could not take his eyes off her, and yet it hurt him to look at her. He was yearning and hating . . . yearning for the reality to be undone, hating the truth for what it was. He discovered that he was stroking her handkerchief with tremulous fingers.

"I love you, Olivia."

"I love you, Gully, my enemy."

"For God's sake!" he burst out. "Why did you do it? You were aboard 'Vorga' running the reff racket. You gave the order to scuttle them. You gave the order to pass me by. Why! Why!"

"What?" she lashed back. "Are you demanding apologies?"

"I'm demanding an explanation."

"You'll get none from me!"

"Blood and money, your father said. He was right. Oh . . . Bitch! Bitch! Bitch!"

"Blood and money, yes; and unashamed."

"I'm drowning, Olivia. Throw me a lifeline."

"Then drown. Nobody ever saved me. No— No . . . This is wrong, all wrong. Wait, my dear. Wait." She composed herself and began speaking very tenderly. "I could lie, Gully dear, and make you believe it, but I'm going to be honest. There's a simple explanation. I live my own private life. We all do. You do."

"What's yours?"

"No different from yours . . . from the rest of the world. I cheat, I lie, I destroy . . . like all of us. I'm criminal . . . like all of us."

"Why? For money? You don't need money."

"No."

"For control . . . power?"

"Not for power."

"Then why?"

She took a deep breath, as though this truth was the first truth and was crucifying her. "For hatred . . . To pay you back, all of you."

"For what?"

"For being blind," she said in a smoldering voice. "For being cheated. For being helpless . . . They should have killed me when I was born. Do you know what it's like to be blind . . . to receive life secondhand? To be dependent, begging, crippled? 'Bring them down to your level,' I told my secret life. 'If you're blind make them blinder. If you're helpless, cripple them. Pay them back . . . all of them.' "

"Olivia, you're insane."

"And you?"

"I'm in love with a monster."

"We're a pair of monsters."

"No!"

"No? Not you?" she flared. "What have you been doing but paying the world back, like me? What's your revenge but settling your own private account with bad luck? Who wouldn't call you a crazy monster? I tell you, we're a pair, Gully. We couldn't help falling in love."

He was stunned by the truth of what she said. He tried on the shroud of her revelation and it fit, clung tighter than the tiger mask tattooed on his face.

"It's true," he said slowly. "I'm no better than you. Worse. But before God I never murdered six hundred."

"You're murdering six million."

"What?"

"Perhaps more. You've got something they need to end the war, and you're holding out."

"You mean PyrE?"

"Yes."

"What is it, this bringer of peace, this twenty pounds of miracle that they're fighting for?"

"I don't know, but I know they need it, and I don't care. Yes, I'm being honest now. I don't care. Let millions be murdered. It makes no difference to us. Not to us, Gully, because we stand apart. We stand apart and shape our own world. We're the strong."

"We're the damned."

"We're the blessed. We've found each other." Suddenly she laughed and held out her arms. "I'm arguing when there's no need for words. Come to me, my love. . . . Wherever you are, come to me. . . ."

He touched her and then put his arms around her. He found her mouth and devoured her. But he was forced to release her.

"What is it, Gully darling?"

"I'm not a child any more," he said wearily. "I've learned to understand that nothing is simple. There's never a simple answer. You can love someone and loathe them."

"Can you, Gully?"

"And you're making me loathe myself."

"No, my dear."

"I've been a tiger all my life. I trained myself . . . educated myself . . . pulled myself up by my stripes to make me a stronger tiger with a longer claw and a sharper tooth . . . quick and deadly. . . ."

"And you are. You are. The deadliest."

"No. I'm not. I went too far. I went beyond simplicity. I turned myself into a thinking creature. I look through your blind eyes, my love whom I loathe, and I see myself. The tiger's gone."

"There's no place for the tiger to go. You're trapped, Gully; by Dagenham, Intelligence, my father, the world."

"I know."

"But you're safe with me. We're safe together, the pair of us. They'll never dream of looking for you near me. We can plan together, fight together, destroy them together. . . ."

"No. Not together."

"What is it?" she flared again. "Are you still hunting me? Is that what's wrong? Do you still want revenge? Then take it. Here I am. Go ahead . . . destroy me."

"No. Destruction's finished for me."

"Ah, I know what it is." She became tender again in an instant. "It's your face, poor darling. You're ashamed of your tiger face, but I love it. You burn so brightly for me. You burn through the blindness. Believe me . . ."

"My God! What a pair of loathsome freaks we are."

"What's happened to you?" she demanded. She broke away from him, her coral eyes glittering. "Where's the man who watched the raid with me? Where's the unashamed savage who—"

"Gone, Olivia. You've lost him. We both have."

"Gully!"

"He's lost."

"But why? What have I done?"

"You don't understand, Olivia."

"Where are you?" she reached out, touched him and then clung to him. "Listen to me, darling. You're tired. You're exhausted. That's all. Nothing is lost." The words tumbled out of her. "You're right. Of course you're right. We've been bad, both of us. Loathsome. But all that's gone now. Nothing is lost. We were wicked because we were alone and unhappy. But we've found each other; we can save each other. Be my love, darling. Always. Forever. I've looked for you so long, waited and hoped and prayed . . ."

"No. You're lying, Olivia, and you know it."

"For God's sake, Gully!"

"Put 'Vorga' down, Olivia."

"Land?"

"Yes."

"On Terra?"

"Yes."

"What are you going to do? You're insane. They're hunting you . . . waiting for you . . . watching. What are you going to do?"

"Do you think this is easy for me?" he said. "I'm doing what I have to do. I'm still driven. No man ever escapes from that. But there's a different compulsion in the saddle, and the spurs hurt, damn it. They hurt like hell."

He stifled his anger and controlled himself. He took her hands and kissed her palms.

"It's all finished, Olivia," he said gently. "But I love you. Always. Forever."

"I'll sum it up," Dagenham rapped. "We were bombed the night we found Foyle. We lost him on the Moon and found him a week later on Mars. We were bombed again. We lost him again. He's been lost for a week. Another bombing's due. Which one of the Inner Planets? Venus? The Moon? Terra again? Who knows. But we all know this: one more raid without retaliation and we're lost."

He glanced around the table. Against the ivory-and-gold background of the Star Chamber of Castle Presteign, his face, all three faces, looked strained. Y'ang-Yeovil slitted his eyes in a frown. Presteign compressed his thin lips.

"And we know this too," Dagenham continued. "We can't retaliate without PyrE and we can't locate the PyrE without Foyle."

"My instructions were," Presteign interposed, "that PyrE was not to be mentioned in public."

"In the first place, this is not public," Dagenham snapped. "It's a private information pool. In the second place, we've gone beyond property rights. We're discussing survival, and we've all got equal rights in that. Yes, Jiz?"

Jisbella McQueen had jaunted into the Star Chamber, looking intent and furious.

"Still no sign of Foyle."

"Old St. Pat's still being watched?"

"Yes."

"Commando Brigade's report in from Mars yet?"

"No."

"That's my business and Most Secret," Y'ang-Yeovil objected mildly.

"You've got as few secrets from me as I have from you." Dagenham grinned mirthlessly. "See if you can beat Central Intelligence back here with that report, Jiz. Go."

She disappeared.

"About property rights," Y'ang-Yeovil murmured. "May I suggest to Presteign that Central Intelligence will guarantee full payment to him for his right, title, and interest in PyrE?"

"Don't coddle him, Yeovil."

"This conference is being recorded," Presteign said, coldly. "The Captain's offer is now on file." He turned his basilisk face to Dagenham. "You are in my employ, Mr. Dagenham. Please control your references to myself."

"And to your property?" Dagenham inquired with a deadly smile. "You and your damned property. All of you and all of your damned property have put us in this hole. The system's on the edge of total annihilation for the sake of your property. I'm not exaggerating. It will be a shooting war to end all wars if we can't stop it."

"We can always surrender," Presteign answered.

"No," Y'ang-Yeovil said. "That's already been discussed and discarded at HQ. We know the post-victory plans of the Outer Satellites. They involve total exploitation of the Inner Planets. We're to be gutted and worked until nothing's left. Surrender would be as disastrous as defeat."

"But not for Presteign," Dagenham added.

"Shall we say . . . present company excluded?" Y'ang-Yeovil replied gracefully.

"All right, Presteign," Dagenham swiveled in his chair. "Give."

"I beg your pardon, sir?"

"Let's hear all about PyrE. I've got an idea how we can bring Foyle out into the open and locate the stuff, but I've got to know all about it first. Make your contribution."

"No," Presteign answered.

"No, what?"

"I have decided to withdraw from this information pool. I will reveal nothing about PyrE."

"For God's sake, Presteign! Are you insane? What's got into you? Are you fighting Regis Sheffield's Liberal party again?"

"It's quite simple, Dagenham," Y'ang-Yeovil interposed. "My information about the surrender-defeat situation has shown Presteign a way to better his position. No doubt he intends negotiating a sale to the enemy in return for . . . property advantages."

"Can nothing move you?" Dagenham asked Presteign scornfully. "Can nothing touch you? Are you all property and nothing else? Go away, Jiz! The whole thing's fallen apart."

Jisbella had jaunted into the Star Chamber again. "Commando Brigade's reported," she said. "We know what happened to Foyle."

"What?"

"Presteign's got him."

"What!" Both Dagenham and Y'ang-Yeovil started to their feet.

"He left Mars in a private yawl, was shot up, and was observed being picked up by the Presteign S.S. 'Vorga.'"

"Damn you, Presteign," Dagenham snapped. "So that's why you've been—"

"Wait," Y'ang-Yeovil commanded. "It's news to him too, Dagenham. Look at him."

Presteign's handsome face had gone the color of ashes. He tried to rise and fell back stiffly in his chair. "Olivia . . ." he whispered. "With him . . . That scum . . ."

"Presteign?"

"My daughter, gentlemen, has . . . for some time been engaged in . . . certain activities. The family vice. Blood and— I . . . have managed to close my eyes to it . . . Had almost convinced myself that I was mistaken. I . . . But Foyle! Dirt! Filth! He must be destroyed!" Presteign's voice soared alarmingly. His head twisted back like a hanged man's and his body began to shudder.

"What in the—?"

"Epilepsy," Y'ang-Yeovil said. He pulled Presteign out of the chair onto the floor. "A spoon, Miss McQueen. Quick!" He levered Presteign's teeth open and placed a spoon between them to protect the tongue. As suddenly as it had begun, the seizure was over. The shuddering stopped. Presteign opened his eyes.

"*Petit mal*," Y'ang-Yeovil murmured, withdrawing the spoon. "But he'll be dazed for a while."

Suddenly Presteign began speaking in a low monotone. "PyrE is a pyrophoric alloy. A pyrophore is a metal which emits sparks when scraped or struck. PyrE emits energy, which is why E, the energy symbol, was added to the prefix Pyr. PyrE is a solid solution of transplutonian isotopes, releasing thermonuclear energy on the order of stellar Phoenix action. It's discoverer was of the opinion that he had produced the equivalent of the primordial protomatter which exploded into the Universe."

"My God!" Jisbella exclaimed.

Dagenham silenced her with a gesture and bent over Presteign. "How is it brought to critical mass, Presteign? How is the energy released?"

"As the original energy was generated in the beginning of time," Presteign droned. "Through Will and Idea."

"I'm convinced he's a Cellar Christian," Dagenham muttered to Y'ang-Yeovil. He raised his voice. "Will you explain, Presteign?"

"Through Will and Idea," Presteign repeated. "PyrE can only be exploded by psychokinesis. Its energy can only be released by thought. It must be willed to explode and the thought directed at it. That is the only way."

"There's no key? No formula?"

"No. Only Will and Idea are necessary." The glazed eyes closed.

"God in heaven!" Dagenham mopped his brow. "Will this give the Outer Satellites pause, Yeovil?"

"It'll give us all pause."

"It's the road to hell," Jisbella said.

"Then let's find it and get off the road. Here's my idea, Yeovil. Foyle was tinkering with that hell brew in his lab in Old St. Pat's, trying to analyze it."

"I told you that in strict confidence," Jisbella said furiously.

"I'm sorry, dear. We're past honor and the decencies. Now look, Yeovil, there must be some fragments of the stuff lying about . . . as dust, in solution, in precipitates . . . We've got to detonate those fragments and blow the hell out of Foyle's circus."

"Why?"

"To bring him running. He must have the bulk of the PyrE hidden there somewhere. He'll come to salvage it."

"What if it blows up too?"

"It can't, not inside an Inert Lead Isotope safe."

"Maybe it's not all inside."

"Jiz says it is . . . at least so Foyle reported."

"Leave me out of this," Jisbella said.

"Anyway, we'll have to gamble."

"Gamble!" Y'ang-Yeovil exclaimed. "On a Phoenix action? You'll gamble the solar system into a brand new nova."

"What else can we do? Pick any other road . . . and it's the road to destruction too. Have we got any choice?"

"We can wait," Jisbella said.

"For what? For Foyle to blow us up himself with his tinkering?"

"We can warn him."

"We don't know where he is."

"We can find him."

"How soon? Won't that be a gamble too? And what about that stuff lying around waiting for someone to think it into energy? Suppose a Jack-jaunter gets in and cracks the safe, looking for goodies? And then we don't just have dust waiting for an accidental thought, but twenty pounds."

Jisbella turned pale. Dagenham turned to the Intelligence man. "You make the decision, Yeovil. Do we try it my way or do we wait?"

Y'ang-Yeovil sighed. "I was afraid of this," he said. "Damn all scientists. I'll have to make my decision for a reason you don't know, Dagenham. The Outer Satellites are on to this too. We've got reason to believe that they've got agents looking for Foyle in the worst way. If we wait they may pick him up before us. In fact, they may have him now."

"So your decision is . . . ?"

"The blow-up. Let's bring Foyle running if we can."

"No!" Jisbella cried.

"How?" Dagenham asked, ignoring her.

"Oh, I've got just the one for the job. A one-way telepath named Robin Wednesbury."

"When?"

"At once. We'll clear the entire neighborhood. We'll get full news coverage and do a full broadcast. If Foyle's anywhere in the Inner Planets, he'll hear about it."

"Not *about* it," Jisbella said in despair. "He'll *hear* it. It'll be the last thing any of us hear."

"Will and Idea," Presteign whispered.

As always, when he returned from a stormy civil court session in Leningrad, Regis Sheffield was pleased and complacent, rather like a cocky prizefighter who's won a tough fight. He stopped off at Blekmann's in Berlin for a drink and some war talk, had a second and more war talk in a legal hangout on the Quai D'Orsay, and a third session in the Skin & Bones opposite Temple Bar. By the time he arrived in his New York office he was pleasantly illuminated.

As he strode through the clattering corridors and outer rooms, he was greeted by his secretary with a handful of memo-beads.

"Knocked Djargo-Dantchenko for a loop," Sheffield reported triumphantly. "Judgment and full damages. Old DD's sore as a boil. This makes the score eleven to five, my favor." He took the beads, juggled them, and then began tossing them into unlikely receptacles all over the office, including the open mouth of a gaping clerk.

"Really, Mr. Sheffield! Have you been drinking?"

"No more work today. The war news is too damned gloomy. Have to do something to stay cheerful. What say we brawl in the streets?"

"Mr. Sheffield!"

"Anything waiting for me that can't wait another day?"

"There's a gentleman in your office."

"He made you let him get that far?" Sheffield looked impressed. "Who is he? God, or somebody?"

"He won't give his name. He gave me this."

The secretary handed Sheffield a sealed envelope. On it was scrawled: "URGENT." Sheffield tore it open, his blunt features crinkling with curiosity. Then his eyes widened. Inside the envelope were two ¢r 50,000 notes. Sheffield turned without a word and burst into his private office. Foyle arose from his chair.

"These are genuine," Sheffield blurted.

"To the best of my knowledge."

"Exactly twenty of these notes were minted last year. All are on deposit in Terran treasuries. How did you get hold of these two?"

"Mr. Sheffield?"

"Who else? How did you get hold of these notes?"

"Bribery."

"Why?"

"I thought at the time that it might be convenient to have them available."

"For what? More bribery?"

"If legal fees are bribery."

"I set my own fees," Sheffield said. He tossed the notes back to Foyle. "You can produce them again *if* I decide to take your case and *if* I decide I've been worth that to you. What's your problem?"

"Criminal."

"Don't be too specific yet. And . . . ?"

"I want to give myself up."

"To the police?"

"Yes."

"For what crime?"

"Crimes."

"Name two."

"Robbery and rape."

"Name two more."

"Blackmail and murder."

"Any other items?"

"Treason and genocide."

"Does that exhaust your catalogue?"

"I think so. We may be able to unveil a few more when we get specific."

"Been busy, haven't you? Either you're the Prince of Villains or insane."

"I've been both, Mr. Sheffield."

"Why do you want to give yourself up?"

"I've come to my senses," Foyle answered bitterly.

"I don't mean that. A criminal never surrenders while he's ahead. You're obviously ahead. What's the reason?"

"The most damnable thing that ever happened to a man. I picked up a rare disease called conscience."

Sheffield snorted. "That can often turn fatal."

"It is fatal. I've realized that I've been behaving like an animal."

"And now you want to purge yourself?"

"No, it isn't that simple," Foyle said grimly. "That's why I've come to you . . . for major surgery. The man who upsets the morphology of society is a cancer. The man who gives his own decisions priority over society is a criminal. But there are chain reactions. Purging yourself with punishment isn't enough. Everything's got to be set right. I wish to God everything could be cured just by sending me back to Gouffre Martel or shooting me . . ."

"Back?" Sheffield cut in keenly.

"Shall I be specific?"

"Not yet. Go on. You sound as though you've got ethical growing pains."

"That's it exactly." Foyle paced in agitation, crumpling the banknotes with nervous fingers. "This is one hell of a mess, Sheffield. There's a girl that's got to pay for a vicious, rotten crime. The fact that I love her— No, never mind that. She has a cancer that's got to be cut out . . . like me. Which means I'll have to add informing to my catalogue. The fact that I'm giving myself up too doesn't make any difference."

"What *is* all this mish-mash?"

Foyle turned on Sheffield. "One of the New Year's bombs has just walked into your office, and it's saying: 'Put it all right. Put me together again and send me home. Put together the city I flattened and the people I shattered.' That's what I want to hire you for. I don't know how most criminals feel, but—"

"Sensible, matter-of-fact, like good businessmen who've had bad luck," Sheffield answered promptly. "That's the usual attitude of the professional criminal. It's obvious you're an amateur, if you're a criminal at all. My dear sir, do be sensible. You come here, extravagantly accusing yourself of robbery, rape, murder, genocide, treason, and God knows what else. D'you expect me to take you seriously?"

Bunny, Sheffield's assistant, jaunted into the private office. "Chief!" he shouted in excitement. "Something brand new's turned up. A lech-jaunte! Two society kids bribed a C-class tart to— Ooop. Sorry. Didn't realize you had—" Bunny broke off and stared. "Fourmyle!" he exclaimed.

"What? Who?" Sheffield demanded.

"Don't you know him, Chief?" Bunny stammered. "That's Fourmyle of Ceres, Gully Foyle."

More than a year ago, Regis Sheffield had been hypnotically fulminated and triggered for this moment. His body had been prepared to respond without thought, and the response was lightning. Sheffield struck Foyle in half a second; temple, throat and groin. It had been decided not to depend on weapons since none might be available.

Foyle fell. Sheffield turned on Bunny and battered him back across the office. Then he spat into his palm. It had been decided not to depend on drugs since drugs might not be available. Sheffield's salivary glands had been prepared to respond with an anaphylaxis secretion to the stimulus. He ripped open Foyle's sleeve, dug a nail deep into the hollow of Foyle's elbow and slashed. He pressed his spittle into the ragged cut and pinched the skin together.

A strange cry was torn from Foyle's lips; the tattooing showed livid on his face. Before the stunned law assistant could make a move, Sheffield swung Foyle up to his shoulder and jaunted.

He arrived in the middle of the Four Mile Circus in Old St. Pat's. It was a daring but calculated move. This was the last place he would be expected to go, and the first place where he might expect to locate the PyrE. He was prepared to deal with anyone he might meet in the cathedral, but the interior of the circus was empty.

The vacant tents ballooning up in the nave looked tattered; they had already been looted. Sheffield plunged into the first he saw. It was Fourmyle's traveling library, filled with hundreds of books and thousands of glittering novel-beads. The Jack-jaunters were not interested in literature. Sheffield threw Foyle down on the floor. Only then did he take a gun from his pocket.

Foyle's eyelids fluttered; his eyes opened.

"You're drugged," Sheffield said rapidly. "Don't try to jaunte. And don't move. I'm warning you, I'm prepared for anything."

Dazedly, Foyle tried to rise. Sheffield instantly fired and seared his shoulder. Foyle was slammed back against the stone flooring. He was numbed and bewildered. There was a roaring in his ears and a poison coursing through his blood.

"I'm warning you," Sheffield repeated. "I'm prepared for anything."

"What do you want?" Foyle whispered.

"Two things. Twenty pounds of PyrE, and you. You most of all."

"You lunatic! You damned maniac! I came into your office to give it up . . . hand it over . . ."

"To the O.S.?"

"To the . . . what?"

"The Outer Satellites? Shall I spell it for you?"

"No . . ." Foyle muttered. "I might have known. The patriot, Sheffield, an O.S. agent. I should have known. I'm a fool."

"You're the most valuable fool in the world, Foyle. We want you even more than the PyrE. That's an unknown to us, but we know what you are."

"What are you talking about?"

"My God! You don't know, do you? You still don't know. You haven't an inkling."

"Of what?"

"Listen to me," Sheffield said in a pounding voice. "I'm taking you back two years to 'Nomad.' Understand? Back to the death of the 'Nomad.' One of our raiders finished her off and they found you aboard the wreck. The last man alive."

"So an O.S. ship did blast 'Nomad'?"

"Yes. You don't remember?"

"I don't remember anything about that. I never could."

"I'm telling you why. The raider got a clever idea. They'd turn you into a decoy . . . a sitting duck, understand? You were half dead, but they took you aboard and patched you up. They put you into a spacesuit and cast you adrift with your micro-wave on. You were broadcasting distress signals and mumbling for help on every wave band. The idea was, they'd lurk nearby and pick off the IP ships that came to rescue you."

Foyle began to laugh. "I'm getting up," he said recklessly. "Shoot again, you son of a bitch, but I'm getting up." He struggled to his feet, clutching his shoulder. "So 'Vorga' shouldn't have picked me up anyway," Foyle laughed. "I was a decoy. Nobody should have come near me. I was a shill, a lure, death bait . . . Isn't that the final irony? 'Nomad' didn't have any right to be rescued in the first place. I didn't have any right to revenge."

"You still don't understand," Sheffield pounded. "They were nowhere near 'Nomad' when they set you adrift. They were six hundred thousand miles from 'Nomad'."

"Six hundred thous—?"

" 'Nomad' was too far out of the shipping lanes. They wanted you to drift where ships would pass. They took you six hundred thousand miles sunward and set you adrift. They put you through the air lock and backed off, watching you drift. Your suit lights were blinking and you were moaning for help on the micro-wave. Then you disappeared."

"Disappeared?"

"You were gone. No more lights, no more broadcast. They came back to check. You were gone without a trace. And the next thing we learned . . . you got back aboard 'Nomad'."

"Impossible."

"Man, you space-jaunted!" Sheffield said savagely. "You were patched and delirious, but you space-jaunted. You space-jaunted six hundred thousand miles through the void back to the wreck of the 'Nomad.' You did something that's never been done before. God knows how. You don't even know yourself, but we're going to find out. I'm taking you out to the Satellites with me and we'll get that secret out of you if we have to tear it out."

He took Foyle's throat in his powerful hand and hefted the gun in the other. "But first I want the PyrE. You'll produce it, Foyle. Don't think you won't." He lashed Foyle across the forehead with the gun. "I'll do anything to get it. Don't think I won't." He smashed Foyle again, coldly, efficiently. "If you're looking for a purge, man, you've found it!"

Bunny leaped off the public jaunte stage at Five-Points and streaked into the main entrance of Central Intelligence's New York Office like a frightened rabbit. He shot past the outermost guard cordon, through the protective labyrinth, and into the inner offices. He acquired a train of excited pursuers and found himself face to face with the more seasoned guards who had calmly jaunted to positions ahead of him and were waiting.

Bunny began to shout: "Yeovil! Yeovil! Yeovil!"

Still running, he dodged around desks, kicked over chairs, and created an incredible uproar. He continued his yelling: "Yeovil! Yeovil! Yeovil!" Just before they were about to put him out of his misery, Y'ang-Yeovil appeared.

"What's all this?" he snapped. "I gave orders that Miss Wednesbury was to have absolute quiet."

"Yeovil!" Bunny shouted.

"Who's that?"

"Sheffield's assistant."

"What . . . Bunny?"

"Foyle!" Bunny howled. "Gully Foyle."

Y'ang-Yeovil covered the fifty feet between them in exactly one-point-six-six seconds. "What about Foyle?"

"Sheffield's got him," Bunny gasped.

"Sheffield? When?"

"Half an hour ago."

"Why didn't he bring him here?"

"He abducted him. I think Sheffield's an O.S. agent . . ."

"Why didn't you come at once?"

"Sheffield jaunted with Foyle. . . . Knocked him stiff and disappeared. I went looking. All over. Took a chance. Must have made fifty jauntes in twenty minutes. . . ."

"Amateur!" Y'ang-Yeovil exclaimed in exasperation. "Why didn't you leave that to the pros?"

"Found 'em."

"You found them? Where?"

"Old St. Pat's. Sheffield's after the—"

But Y'ang-Yeovil had turned on his heel and was tearing back up the corridor, shouting: "Robin! Robin! Stop! Stop!"

And then their ears were bruised by the bellow of thunder.

CHAPTER FIFTEEN

LIKE WIDENING RINGS IN A POND, the Will and the Idea spread, searching out, touching and tripping the delicate subatomic trigger of PyrE. The thought found particles, dust, smoke, vapor, motes, molecules. The Will and the Idea transformed them all.

In Sicily, where Dott. Franco Torre had worked for an exhausting month attempting to unlock the secret of one slug of PyrE, the residues and the precipitates had been dumped down a drain which led to the sea. For many months the Mediterranean currents had drifted these residues across the sea bottom. In an instant a hump-backed mound of water towering fifty feet high traced the courses, northeast to Sardinia and southwest to Tripoli. In a micro-second the surface of the Mediterranean was raised into the twisted casting of a giant earthworm that wound around the islands of Pantelleria, Lampedusa, Linosa, and Malta.

Some of the residues had been burned off; had gone up the chimney with smoke and vapor to drift for hundreds of miles before settling. These minute particles showed where they had finally settled in Morocco, Algeria, Libya, and Greece with blinding pin-point explosions of incredible minuteness and intensity. And some motes, still drifting in the stratosphere, revealed their presence with brilliant gleams like daylight stars.

In Texas, where Prof. John Mantley had had the same baffling experience with PyrE, most of the residues had gone down the shaft of an exhausted oil well which was also used to accommodate radioactive wastes. A deep water table had absorbed much of the matter and spread it slowly over an area of some ten square miles. Ten square miles of Texas flats shook themselves into corduroy. A vast untapped deposit of natural gas at last found a vent and came shrieking up to the surface where sparks from flying stones ignited it into a roaring torch, two hundred feet high.

A milligram of PyrE deposited on a disk of filter paper long since discarded, forgotten, rounded up in a waste paper drive and at last pulped into a mold for type metal, destroyed the entire late night edition of the *Glasgow Observer*. A fragment of PyrE spattered on a lab smock long since converted into rag paper, destroyed a Thank You note written by Lady Shrapnel, and destroyed an additional ton of first class mail in the process.

A shirt cuff, inadvertently dipped into an acid solution of PyrE, long abandoned along with the shirt, and now worn under his mink suit by a Jack-jaunter, blasted off the wrist and hand of the Jack-jaunter in one fiery amputation. A decimilligram of PyrE, still adhering to a former evaporation crystal now in use as an ash tray, kindled a fire that scorched the office of one Baker, dealer in freaks and purveyor of monsters.

Across the length and breadth of the planet were isolated explosions, chains of explosions, traceries of fire, pin points of fire, meteor flares in the sky, great craters and narrow channels plowed in the earth, exploded in the earth, vomited forth from the earth.

In Old St. Pat's nearly a tenth of a gram of PyrE was exposed in Fourmyle's laboratory. The rest was sealed in its Inert Lead Isotope safe, protected from accidental and intentional psychokinetic ignition. The blinding blast of energy generated from that tenth of a gram blew out the walls and split the floors as though an internal earthquake had convulsed the building. The buttresses held the pillars for a split second and then crumbled. Down came towers, spires, pillars, buttresses, and roof in a thundering avalanche to hesitate above the yawning crater of the floor in a tangled, precarious equilibrium. A breath of wind, a distant vibration, and the collapse would continue until the crater was filled solid with pulverized rubble.

The star-like heat of the explosion ignited a hundred fires and melted the ancient thick copper of the collapsed roof. If a milligram more of PyrE had been exposed to detonation, the heat would have been intense enough to vaporize the metal immediately. Instead, it glowed white and began to flow. It streamed off the wreckage of the crumbled roof and began searching its way downward through the jumbled stone, iron, wood, and glass, like some monstrous molten mold creeping through a tangled web.

Dagenham and Y'ang-Yeovil arrived almost simultaneously. A moment later Robin Wednesbury appeared and then Jisbella McQueen. A dozen Intelligence operatives and six Dagenham couriers arrived along with Presteign's Jaunte Watch and the police. They formed a cordon around the blazing block, but there were very few spectators. After the shock of the New Year's Eve raid, that single explosion had frightened half New York into another wild jaunte for safety.

The uproar of the fire was frightful, and the massive grind of tons of wreckage in uneasy balance was ominous. Everyone was forced to shout and yet was fearful of the vibrations. Y'ang-Yeovil bawled the news about Foyle and Sheffield into Dagenham's ear. Dagenham nodded and displayed his deadly smile.

"We'll have to go in," he shouted.

"Fire suits," Y'ang-Yeovil shouted.

He disappeared and reappeared with a pair of white Disaster Crew fire suits. At the sight of these, Robin and Jisbella began shouting hysterical objections. The two men ignored them, wriggled into the Inert Isomer armor and inched into the inferno.

Within Old St. Pat's it was as though a monstrous hand had churned a log jam of wood, stone, and metal. Through every interstice crawled tongues of molten copper, slowly working downward, igniting wood, crumbling stone, shattering glass. Where the copper flowed it merely glowed, but where it poured it spattered dazzling droplets of white hot metal.

Beneath the log jam yawned a black crater where formerly the floor of the cathedral had been. The explosion had split the flagstone asunder, revealing the cellars, subcellars, and vaults deep below the building. These too were filled with a snarl of stones, beams, pipes, wire, the remnants of the Four Mile circus tents; all fitfully lit small fires. Then the first of the copper dripped down into the crater and illuminated it with a brilliant molten splash.

Dagenham pounded Y'ang-Yeovil's shoulder to attract his attention and pointed. Halfway down the crater, in the midst of the tangle, lay the body of Regis Sheffield, drawn and quartered by the explosion. Y'ang-Yeovil pounded Dagenham's shoulder and pointed. Almost at the bottom of the crater lay Gully Foyle, and as the blazing spatter of molten copper illuminated him, they saw him move. The two men at once turned and crawled out of the cathedral for a conference.

"He's alive."

"How's it possible?"

"I can guess. Did you see the shreds of tent wadded near him? It must have been a freak explosion up at the other end of the cathedral and the tents in between cushioned Foyle. Then he dropped through the floor before anything else could hit him."

"I'll buy that. We've got to get him out. He's the only man who knows where the PyrE is."

"Could it still be here . . . unexploded?"

"If it's in the ILI safe, yes. That stuff is inert to anything. Never mind that now. How are we going to get him out?"

"Well we can't work down from above."

"Why not?"

"Isn't it obvious? One false step and the whole mess will collapse."

"Did you see that copper flowing down?"

"God, yes!"

"Well if we don't get him out in ten minutes, he'll be at the bottom of a pool of molten copper."

"What can we do?"

"I've got a long shot."

"What?"

"The cellars of the old RCA buildings across the street are as deep as St. Pat's."

"And?"

"We'll go down and try to hole through. Maybe we can pull Foyle out from the bottom."

A squad broke into the ancient RCA buildings, abandoned and sealed up for two generations. They went down into the cellar arcades, crumbling museums of the retail stores of centuries past. They located the ancient elevator shafts and dropped through them into the subcellars filled with electric installations, heat plants and refrigeration systems. They went down into the sump cellars, waist deep in water from the streams of prehistoric Manhattan Island, streams that still flowed beneath the streets that covered them.

As they waded through the sump cellars, bearing east-northeast to bring up opposite the St. Pat's vaults, they suddenly discovered that the pitch dark was illuminated by a fiery flickering up ahead. Dagenham shouted and flung himself forward. The explosion that had opened the subcellars of St. Pat's had split the septum between its vaults and those of the RCA buildings. Through a jagged rent in stone and earth they could peer into the bottom of the inferno.

Fifty feet inside was Foyle, trapped in a labyrinth of twisted beams, stones, pipe, metal, and wire. He was illuminated by a roaring glow from above him and fitful flames around him. His clothes were on fire and the tattooing was livid on his face. He moved feebly, like a bewildered animal in a maze.

"My God!" Y'ang-Yeovil exclaimed. "The Burning Man!"

"What?"

"The Burning Man I saw on the Spanish Stairs. Never mind that now. What can we do?"

"Go in, of course."

A brilliant white gob of copper suddenly oozed down close to Foyle and splashed ten feet below him. It was followed by a second, a third, a slow steady stream. A pool began to form. Dagenham and Y'ang-Yeovil sealed the face plates of their armor and crawled through the break in the septum. After three minutes of agonized struggling they realized that they could not get through the labyrinth to Foyle. It was locked to the outside but not from the inside. Dagenham and Y'ang-Yeovil backed up to confer.

"We can't get to him," Dagenham shouted, "But he can get out."

"How? He can't jaunte, obviously, or he wouldn't be there."

"No, he can climb. Look. He goes left, then up, reverses, makes a turn along that beam, slides under it and pushes through that tangle of wire. The wire can't be pushed in, which is why we can't get to him, but it can push out, which is how he can get out. It's a one-way door."

The pool of molten copper crept up toward Foyle.

"If he doesn't get out soon he'll be roasted alive."

"We'll have to talk him out . . . Tell him what to do."

The men began shouting: "Foyle! Foyle! Foyle!"

The Burning Man in the maze continued to move feebly. The downpour of sizzling copper increased.

"Foyle! Turn left. Can you hear me? Foyle! Turn left and climb up. You can get out if you'll listen to me. Turn left and climb up. Then— Foyle!"

"He's not listening. Foyle! Gully Foyle! Can you hear us?"

"Send for Jiz. Maybe he'll listen to her."

"No, Robin. She'll telesend. He'll have to listen.

"But will she do it? Save him of all people?"

"She'll have to. This is bigger than hatred. It's the biggest damned thing the world's ever encountered. I'll get her." Y'ang-Yeovil started to crawl out. Dagenham stopped him.

"Wait, Yeo. Look at him. He's flickering."

"Flickering?"

"Look! He's . . . blinking like a glow-worm. Watch! Now you see him and now you don't."

The figure of Foyle was appearing, disappearing, and reappearing in rapid succession, like a firefly caught in a flaming trap.

"What's he doing now? What's he trying to do? What's happening?"

He was trying to escape. Like a trapped firefly or some seabird caught in the blazing brazier of a naked beacon fire, he was beating about in a frenzy . . . a blackened, burning creature, dashing himself against the unknown.

Sound came as sight to him, as light in strange patterns. He saw the sound of his shouted name in vivid rhythms:

F OYL E F OYL E F OYL E
F OYL E F OYL E F OYL E
F OYL E F OYL E F OYL E
F OYL E F OYL E F OYL E
F OYL E F OYL E F OYL E

Motion came as sound to him. He heard the writhing of the flames, he heard the swirls of smoke, he heard the flickering, jeering shadows . . . all speaking deafeningly in strange tongues:

"BURUU GYARR?" the steam asked.

"Asha. Asha, rit-kit-dit-zit m'gid," the quick shadows answered.

"Ohhh. Ahhh. Heee. Teee," the heat ripples clamored.

Even the flames smoldering on his own clothes roared gibberish in his ears. "MANTERGEISTMANN!" they bellowed.

Color was pain to him . . . heat, cold, pressure; sensations of intolerable heights and plunging depths, of tremendous accelerations and crushing compressions:

RED RECEDED FROM HIM

GREEN LIGHT ATTACKED

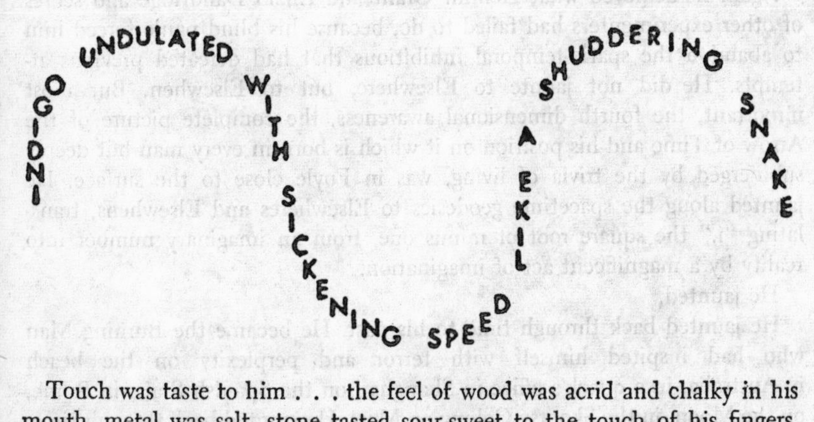

Touch was taste to him . . . the feel of wood was acrid and chalky in his mouth, metal was salt, stone tasted sour-sweet to the touch of his fingers, and the feel of glass cloyed his palate like over-rich pastry.

Smell was touch . . . Hot stone smelled like velvet caressing his cheek. Smoke and ash were harsh tweeds rasping his skin, almost the feel of wet canvas. Molten metal smelled like blow hammering his heart, and the ionization of the PyrE explosion filled the air with ozone that smelled like water trickling through his fingers.

He was not blind, not deaf, not senseless. Sensation came to him, but filtered through a nervous system twisted and short-circuited by the shock of the PyrE concussion. He was suffering from Synaesthesia, that rare condition in which perception receives messages from the objective world and relays these messages to the brain, but there in the brain the sensory perceptions are confused with one another. So, in Foyle, sound registered as sight, motion registered as sound, colors became pain sensations, touch became taste, and smell became touch. He was not only trapped within the labyrinth of the inferno under Old St. Pat's; he was trapped in the kaleidoscope of his own cross-senses.

Again desperate, on the ghastly verge of extinction, he abandoned all disciplines and habits of living; or, perhaps, they were stripped from him. He reverted from a conditioned product of environment and experience to an inchoate creature craving escape and survival and exercising every power it possessed. And again the miracle of two years ago took place. The undivided energy of an entire human organism, of every cell, fiber, nerve, and muscle empowered that craving, and again Foyle space-jaunted.

He went hurtling along the geodesical space lines of the curving universe at the speed of thought, far exceeding that of light. His spatial velocity was so frightful that his time axis was twisted from the vertical line drawn from the Past through Now to the Future. He went flickering along the new near-horizontal axis, this new space-time geodesic, driven by the miracle of a human mind no longer inhibited by concepts of the impossible.

Again he achieved what Helmut Grant and Enzio Dandridge and scores of other experimenters had failed to do, because his blind panic forced him to abandon the spatio-temporal inhibitions that had defeated previous attempts. He did not jaunte to Elsewhere, but to Elsewhen. But most important, the fourth dimensional awareness, the complete picture of the Arrow of Time and his position on it which is born in every man but deeply submerged by the trivia of living, was in Foyle close to the surface. He jaunted along the spacetime geodesics to Elsewheres and Elsewhens, translating "i," the square root of minus one, from an imaginary number into reality by a magnificent act of imagination.

He jaunted.

He jaunted back through time to his past. He became the Burning Man who had inspired himself with terror and perplexity on the beach in Australia, in a quack's office in Shanghai, on the Spanish Stairs in Rome, on the Moon, in the Skoptsy Colony on Mars. He jaunted back through time, revisiting the savage battles that he himself had fought in Gully Foyle's tiger hunt for vengeance. His flaming appearances were sometimes noted; other times not.

He jaunted.

He was aboard "Nomad," drifting in the empty frost of space.

He stood in the door to nowhere.

The cold was the taste of lemons and the vacuum was a rake of talons on his skin. The sun and the stars were a shaking ague that racked his bones.

"GLOMMHA FREDNIS!" motion roared in his ears.

It was a figure with its back to him vanishing down the corridor; a figure with a copper cauldron of provisions over its shoulder; a figure darting, floating, squirming through free fall. It was Gully Foyle.

"MEEHAT JESSROT," the sight of his motion bellowed.

"Aha! Oh-ho! M'git not to kak," the flicker of light and shade answered.

"Oooooooh? Soooooo?" the whirling raffle of debris in his wake murmured.

The lemon taste in his mouth became unbearable. The rake of talons on his skin was torture.

He jaunted.

He reappeared in the furnace beneath Old St. Pat's less then a second after he had disappeared from there. He was drawn, as the seabird is drawn, again and again to the flames from which it is struggling to escape. He endured the roaring torture for only another moment.

He jaunted.

He was in the depths of Gouffre Martel.

The velvet black darkness was bliss, paradise, euphoria.

"Ah!" he cried in relief.

"AH!" came the echo of his voice, and the sound was translated into a blinding pattern of light.

AHAHAHAHAHAHAHAHAH
HAHAHAHAHAHAHAHAHA
AHAHAHAHAHAHAHAHAH
HAHAHAHAHAHAHAHAHA
AHAHAHAHAHAHAHAHAH
HAHAHAHAHAHAHAHAHA

The Burning Man winced. "Stop!" he called, blinded by the noise. Again came the dazzling pattern of the echo:

StOpStOpStOp
OpStOpStOpStOp
StOpStOpStOpStOp
OpStOpStOpStOpStOp
OpStOpStOpStOpSt
OpStOpStOpStOp
OpStOpStOpSt

A distant clatter of steps came to his eyes in soft patterns of vertical borealis streamers:

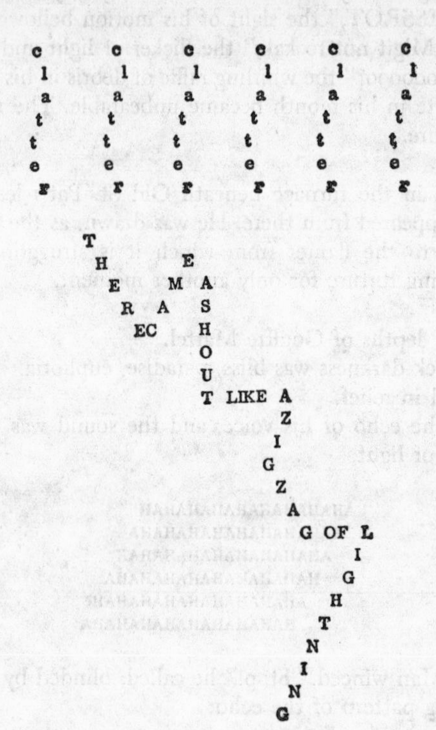

A BEAM OF LIGHT ATTACKED

It was the search party from the Gouffre Martel hospital, tracking Foyle and Jisbella McQueen by geophone. The Burning Man disappeared, but not before he had unwittingly decoyed the searchers from the trail of the vanished fugitives.

He was back under Old St. Pat's, reappearing only an instant after his last disappearance. His wild beatings into the unknown sent him stumbling up geodesic space-time lines that inevitably brought him back to the Now he was trying to escape, for in the inverted saddle curve of space-time, his Now was the deepest depression in the curve.

He could drive himself up, up, up the geodesic lines into the past or future, but inevitably he must fall back into his own Now, like a thrown ball hurled up the sloping walls of an infinite pit, to land, hang poised for a moment, and then roll back into the depths.

But still he beat into the unknown in his desperation.

Again he jaunted.

He was on Jervis beach on the Australian coast.

The motion of the surf was bawling: "LOGGERMIST CROTEHAVEN!"

The churning of the surf blinded him with the lights of batteries of footlights:

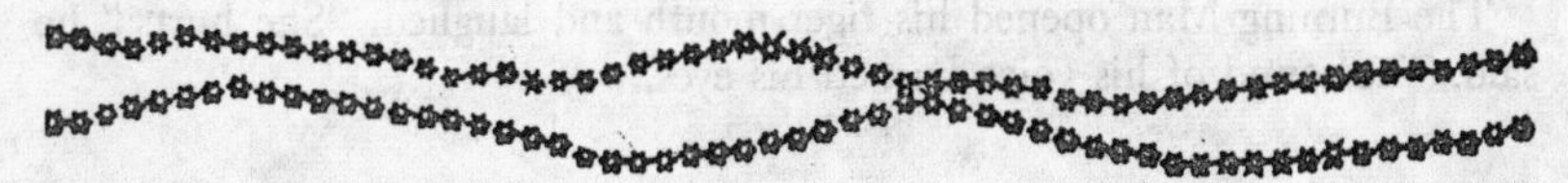

Gully Foyle and Robin Wednesbury stood before him. The body of a man lay on the sand which felt like vinegar in the Burning Man's mouth. The wind brushing his face tasted like brown paper.

Foyle opened his mouth and exclaimed. The sound came out in burning star-bubbles:

Foyle took a step. "GRASH?" the motion blared.

The Burning Man jaunted.

He was in the office of Dr. Sergei Orel in Shanghai.

Foyle was again before him, speaking light patterns:

W A Y   W A Y   W A Y
H R O   H R O   H R O
O E U   O E U   O E U

He flickered back to the agony of Old St. Pat's and jaunted again.

HE WAS ON THE BRAWLING SPANISH STAIRS. HE WAS ON THE BRAWLING SPANISH STAIRS. HE WAS ON THE BRAWLING SPANISH STAIRS. HE WAS ON THE BRAWLING SPANISH STAIRS. HE WAS ON THE BRAWLING SPANISH STAIRS. HE WAS ON THE BRAWLING SPANISH STAIRS. HE WAS ON THE BRAWLING SPANISH STAIRS. HE WAS ON THE BRAWLING SPANISH STAIRS.

The Burning Man jaunted.

It was cold again, with the taste of lemons, and vacuum raked his skin with unspeakable talons. He was peering through the porthole of a silvery yawl. The jagged mountains of the Moon towered in the background. Through the porthole he could see the jangling racket of blood pumps and oxygen pumps and hear the uproar of the motion Gully Foyle made toward him. The clawing of the vacuum caught his throat in an agonizing grip.

The geodesic lines of space-time rolled him back to Now under Old St. Pat's, where less than two seconds had elapsed since he first began his frenzied struggle. Once more, like a burning spear, he hurled himself into the unknown.

He was in the Skoptsy Catacomb on Mars. The white slug that was Lindsey Joyce was writhing before him.

"NO! NO! NO!" her motion screamed. "DON'T HURT ME. DON'T KILL ME. NO PLEASE . . . PLEASE . . ."

The Burning Man opened his tiger mouth and laughed. "She hurts," he said. The sound of his voice burned his eyes.

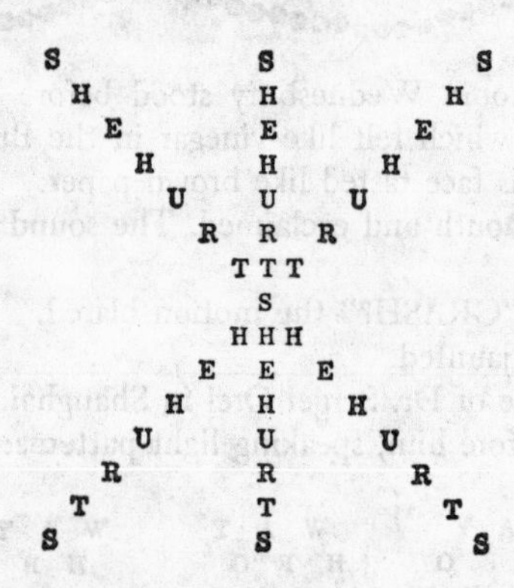

"Who are you?" Foyle whispered.

WWWWWWWWWWWWWWWWWWW
HHHHHHHHHHHHHHHHHHH
OOOOOOOOOOOOOOOOOOO
AREAREAREAREAREAREARE
AREAREAREAREAREAREARE
AREAREAREAREAREAREARE
YYYYYYYYYYYYYYYYYYY
OOOOOOOOOOOOOOOOOOO
UUUUUUUUUUUUUUUUUUU

The Burning Man winced. "Too bright," he said. "Less light."

Foyle took a step forward. "BLAA-GAA-DAA-MAWW!" the motion roared.

The Burning Man clapped his hands over his ears in agony. "Too loud," he cried. "Don't move so loud."

The writhing Skoptsy's motion was still screaming, beseeching: "DON'T HURT ME. DON'T HURT ME."

The Burning Man laughed again. She was mute to normal men, but to his freak-crossed senses her meaning was clear. "Listen to her. She's screaming. Begging. She doesn't want to die. She doesn't want to be hurt. Listen to her."

"IT WAS OLIVIA PRESTEIGN GAVE THE ORDER. OLIVIA PRESTEIGN. NOT ME. DON'T HURT ME. OLIVIA PRESTEIGN."

"She's telling who gave the order. Can't you hear? Listen with your eyes. She says Olivia."

WHAT? WHAT? WHAT?
WHAT? WHAT? WHAT?
WHAT? WHAT? WHAT?
WHAT? WHAT? WHAT?
WHAT? WHAT? WHAT?

The checkerboard glitter of Foyle's question was too much for him. The Burning Man interpreted the Skoptsy's agony again.

"She says Olivia. Olivia Presteign. Olivia Presteign. Olivia Presteign."

He jaunted.

He fell back into the pit under Old St. Pat's, and suddenly his confusion and despair told him he was dead. This was the finish of Gully Foyle. This was eternity, and hell was real. What he had seen was the past passing before his crumbling senses in the final moment of death. What he was enduring he must endure through all time. He was dead. He knew he was dead.

He refused to submit to eternity.

He beat again into the unknown.

The Burning Man jaunted.

He was in a scintillating mist a snowflake cluster of stars a shower of liquid

diamonds. There was the touch of butterfly wings on

his skin. There was the taste of a strand of cool pearls in his

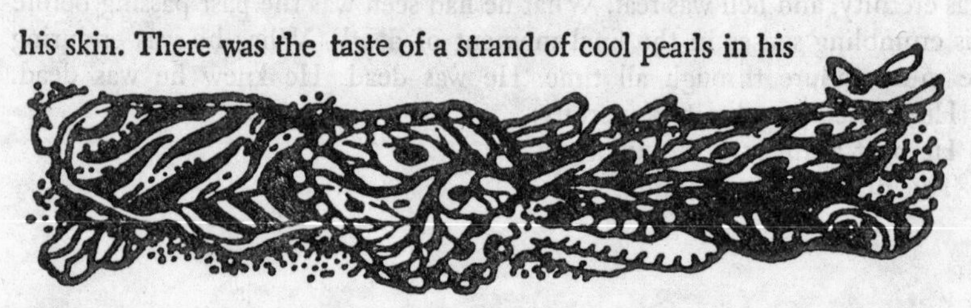

mouth. His crossed kaleidoscopic senses could not tell him where he was,

but he knew he wanted to remain in this Nowhere forever.

"Hello, Gully."

"Who's that?"

"*This is Robin.*"

"Robin?"

"*Robin Wednesbury that was.*"

"That was?"

"*Robin Yeovil that is.*"

"I don't understand. Am I dead?"

"*No, Gully.*"

"Where am I?"

"*A long, long way from Old St. Pat's.*"

"But where?"

"*I can't take the time to explain, Gully. You've only got a few moments here.*"

"Why?"

"Because you haven't learned how to jaunte through space-time yet. You've got to go back and learn."

"But I do know. I must know. Sheffield said I space-jaunted to 'Nomad' . . . six hundred thousand miles."

"That was an accident then, Gully, and you'll do it again . . . after you teach yourself . . . But you're not doing it now. You don't know how to hold on yet . . . how to turn any Now into reality. You'll tumble back into Old St. Pat's in a moment."

"Robin, I've just remembered. I have bad news for you."

"I know, Gully."

"Your mother and sisters are dead."

"I've known for a long time, Gully."

"How long?"

"For thirty years."

"That's impossible."

"No it isn't. This is a long, long way from Old St. Pat's. I've been waiting to tell you how to save yourself from the fire, Gully. Will you listen?"

"I'm not dead?"

"No."

"I'll listen."

"Your senses are all confused. It'll pass soon, but I won't give the directions in left and right or up and down. I'll tell you what you can understand now."

"Why are you helping me . . . after what I've done to you?"

"That's all forgiven and forgotten, Gully. Now listen to me. When you get back to Old St. Pat's, turn around until you're facing the loudest shadows. Got that?"

"Yes."

"Go toward the noise until you feel a deep prickling on your skin. Then stop."

"Then stop."

"Make a half turn into compression and a feeling of falling. Follow that."

"Follow that."

"You'll pass through a solid sheet of light and come to the taste of quinine. That's really a mass of wire. Push straight through the quinine until you see something that sounds like trip hammers. You'll be safe."

"How do you know all this, Robin?"

"I've been briefed by an expert, Gully." There was the sensation of laughter. *"You'll be falling back into the past any moment now. Peter and Saul are here. They say au revoir and good luck. And Jiz Dagenham too. Good luck, Gully dear . . ."*

"The past? This is the future?"

"Yes, Gully."

"Am I here? Is . . . Olivia—?"

And then he was tumbling down, down, down the space-time lines back into the dreadful pit of Now.

CHAPTER SIXTEEN

HIS SENSES UNCROSSED in the ivory-and-gold star chamber of Castle Presteign. Sight became sight and he saw the high mirrors and stained glass windows, the gold tooled library with android librarian on library ladder. Sound became sound and he heard the android secretary tapping the manual bead-recorder at the Louis Quinze desk. Taste became taste as he sipped the cognac that the robot bartender handed him.

He knew he was at bay, faced with the decision of his life. He ignored his enemies and examined the perpetual beam carved in the robot face of the bartender, the classic Irish grin.

"Thank you," Foyle said.

"My pleasure, sir," the robot replied and awaited its next cue.

"Nice day," Foyle remarked.

"Always a lovely day somewhere, sir," the robot beamed.

"Awful day," Foyle said.

"Always a lovely day somewhere, sir," the robot responded.

"Day," Foyle said.

"Always a lovely day somewhere, sir," the robot said.

Foyle turned to the others. "That's me," he said, motioning to the robot. "That's all of us. We prattle about free will, but we're nothing but response . . . mechanical reaction in prescribed grooves. So . . . here I am, here I am, waiting to respond. Press the buttons and I'll jump." He aped the canned voice of the robot. "My pleasure to serve, sir." Suddenly his tone lashed them. "What do you want?"

They stirred with uneasy purpose. Foyle was burned, beaten, chastened . . . and yet he was taking control of all of them.

"We'll stipulate the threats," Foyle said. "I'm to be hung, drawn, and quartered, tortured in hell if I don't . . . What? What do you want?"

"I want my property," Presteign said, smiling coldly.

"Eighteen and some odd pounds of PyrE. Yes. What do you offer?"

"I make no offer, sir. I demand what is mine."

Y'ang-Yeovil and Dagenham began to speak. Foyle silenced them. "One button at a time, gentlemen. Presteign is trying to make me jump at present." He turned to Presteign. "Press harder, blood and money, or find another button. Who are you to make demands at this moment?"

Presteign tightened his lips. "The law . . ." he began.

"What? Threats?" Foyle laughed. "Am I to be frightened into anything? Don't be imbecile. Speak to me the way you did New Year's Eve, Presteign . . . without mercy, without forgiveness, without hypocrisy."

Presteign bowed, took a breath, and ceased to smile. "I offer you power," he said. "Adoption as my heir, partnership in Presteign Enterprises, the chieftainship of clan and sept. Together we can own the world."

"With PyrE?"

"Yes."

"Your proposal is noted and declined. Will you offer your daughter?"

"Olivia?" Presteign choked and clenched his fists.

"Yes, Olivia. Where is she?"

"You scum!" Presteign cried. "Filth . . . Common thief . . . You dare to . . ."

"Will you offer your daughter for the PyrE?"

"Yes," Presteign answered, barely audible.

Foyle turned to Dagenham. "Press your button, death's-head," he said.

"If the discussion's to be conducted on this level . . ." Dagenham snapped.

"It is. Without mercy, without forgiveness, without hypocrisy. What do you offer?"

"Glory."

"Ah?"

"We can't offer money or power. We can offer honor. Gully Foyle, the man who saved the Inner Planets from annihilation. We can offer security. We'll wipe out your criminal record, give you an honored name, guarantee a niche in the hall of fame."

"No," Jisbella McQueen cut in sharply. "Don't accept. If you want to be a savior, destroy the secret. Don't give PyrE to anyone."

"What is PyrE?"

"Quiet!" Dagenham snapped.

"It's a thermonuclear explosive that's detonated by thought alone . . . by psychokinesis," Jisbella said.

"What thought?"

"The desire of anyone to detonate it, directed at it. That brings it to critical mass if it's not insulated by Inert Lead Isotope."

"I told you to be quiet," Dagenham growled.

"If we're all to have a chance at him, I want mine."

"This is bigger than idealism."

"Nothing's bigger than idealism."

"Foyle's secret is," Y'ang-Yeovil murmured. "I know how relatively unimportant PyrE is just now." He smiled at Foyle. "Sheffield's law assistant overheard part of your little discussion in Old St. Pat's. We know about the space-jaunting."

There was a sudden hush.

"Space-jaunting," Dagenham exclaimed. "Impossible. You don't mean it."

"I do mean it. Foyle's demonstrated that space-jaunting is not impossible. He jaunted six hundred thousand miles from an O.S. raider to the wreck of the 'Nomad.' As I said, this is far bigger than PyrE. I should like to discuss that matter first."

"Everyone's been telling what they want," Robin Wednesbury said slowly. "What do you want, Gully Foyle?"

"Thank you," Foyle answered. "I want to be punished."

"What?"

"I want to be purged," he said in a suffocated voice. The stigmata began to appear on his bandaged face. "I want to pay for what I've done and settle the account. I want to get rid of this damnable cross I'm carrying . . . this ache that's cracking my spine. I want to go back to Gouffre Martel. I want a lobo, if I deserve it . . . and I know I do. I want—"

"You want escape," Dagenham interrupted. "There's no escape."

"I want release!"

"Out of the question," Y'ang-Yeovil said. "There's too much of value locked up in your head to be lost by lobotomy."

"We're beyond easy childish things like crime and punishment," Dagenham added.

"No," Robin objected. "There must always be sin and forgiveness. We're never beyond that."

"Profit and loss, sin and forgiveness, idealism and realism," Foyle smiled. "You're all so sure, so simple, so single-minded. I'm the only one in doubt. Let's see how sure you really are. You'll give up Olivia, Presteign? To me, yes? Will you give her up to the law? She's a killer."

Presteign tried to rise, and then fell back in his chair.

"There must be forgiveness, Robin? Will you forgive Olivia Presteign? She murdered your mother and sisters."

Robin turned ashen. Y'ang-Yeovil tried to protest.

"The Outer Satellites don't have PyrE, Yeovil. Sheffield revealed that. Would you use it on them anyway? Will you turn my name into common anathema . . . like Lynch and Boycott?"

Foyle turned to Jisbella. "Will your idealism take you back to Gouffre Martel to serve out your sentence? And you, Dagenham, will you give her up? Let her go?"

He listened to the outcries and watched the confusion for a moment, bitter and constrained.

"Life is so simple," he said. "This decision is so simple, isn't it? Am I to respect Presteign's property rights? The welfare of the planets? Jisbella's ideals? Dagenham's realism? Robin's conscience? Press the button and watch the robot jump. But I'm not a robot. I'm a freak of the universe . . . a thinking animal . . . and I'm trying to see my way clear through this morass. Am I to turn PyrE over to the world and let it destroy itself? Am I to teach the world how to space-jaunte and let us spread our freak show from galaxy to galaxy through all the universe? What's the answer?"

The bartender robot hurled its mixing glass across the room with a resounding crash. In the amazed silence that followed, Dagenham grunted: "Damn! My radiation's disrupted your dolls again, Presteign."

"The answer is yes," the robot said, quite distinctly.

"What?" Foyle asked, taken aback.

"The answer to your question is yes."

"Thank you," Foyle said.

"My pleasure, sir," the robot responded. "A man is a member of society first, and an individual second. You must go along with society, whether it chooses destruction or not."

"Completely haywire," Dagenham said impatiently. "Switch it off, Presteign."

"Wait," Foyle commanded. He looked at the beaming grin engraved in the steel robot face. "But society can be so stupid. So confused. You've witnessed this conference."

"Yes, sir, but you must teach, not dictate. You must teach society."

"To space-jaunte? Why? Why reach out to the stars and galaxies? What for?"

"Because you're alive, sir. You might as well ask: Why is life? Don't ask about it. Live it."

"Quite mad," Dagenham muttered.

"But fascinating," Y'ang-Yeovil murmured.

"There's got to be more to life than just living," Foyle said to the robot.

"Then find it for yourself, sir. Don't ask the world to stop moving because you have doubts."

"Why can't we all move forward together?"

"Because you're all different. You're not lemmings. Some must lead, and hope that the rest will follow."

"Who leads?"

"The men who must . . . driven men, compelled men."

"Freak men."

"You're all freaks, sir. But you always have been freaks. Life is a freak. That's its hope and glory."

"Thank you very much."

"My pleasure, sir."

"You've saved the day."

"Always a lovely day somewhere, sir," the robot beamed. Then it fizzed, jangled, and collapsed.

Foyle turned on the others. "That thing's right," he said, "and you're wrong. Who are we, any of us, to make a decision for the world? Let the world make its own decisions. Who are we to keep secrets from the world? Let the world know and decide for itself. Come to Old St. Pat's."

He jaunted; they followed. The square block was still cordoned and by now an enormous crowd had gathered. So many of the rash and curious were jaunting into the smoking ruins that the police had set up a protective induction field to keep them out. Even so, urchins, curio seekers and irresponsibles attempted to jaunte into the wreckage, only to be burned by the induction field and depart, squawking.

At a signal from Y'ang-Yeovil, the field was turned off. Foyle went through the hot rubble to the east wall of the cathedral which stood to a height of fifteen feet. He felt the smoking stones, pressed, and levered. There came a grinding grumble and a three-by-five-foot section jarred open and then stuck. Foyle gripped it and pulled. The section trembled; then the roasted hinges collapsed and the stone panel crumbled.

Two centuries before, when organized religion had been abolished and orthodox worshippers of all faiths had been driven underground, some devout souls had constructed this secret niche in Old St. Pat's and turned it into an altar. The gold of the crucifix still shone with the brilliance of eternal faith. At the foot of the cross rested a small black box of Inert Lead Isotope.

"Is this a sign?" Foyle panted. "Is this the answer I want?"

He snatched the heavy safe before any could seize it. He jaunted a hundred yards to the remnants of the cathedral steps facing Fifth Avenue. There he opened the safe in full view of the gaping crowds. A shout of consternation went up from the Intelligence crews who knew the truth of its contents.

"Foyle!" Dagenham cried.

"For God's sake, Foyle!" Y'ang-Yeovil shouted.

Foyle withdrew a slug of PyrE, the color of iodine crystals, the size of a cigarette . . . one pound of transplutonian isotopes in solid solution.

"PyrE!" he roared to the mob. "Take it! Keep it! It's your future. PyrE!" He hurled the slug into the crowd and roared over his shoulder: "SanFran. Russian Hill stage."

He jaunted St. Louis-Denver to San Francisco, arriving at the Russian Hill stage where it was four in the afternoon and the streets were bustling with late-shopper jaunters.

"PyrE!" Foyle bellowed. His devil face glowed blood red. He was an appalling sight. "PyrE. It's danger! It's death! It's yours. Make them tell you what it is. Nome!" he called to his pursuit as it arrived, and jaunted.

It was lunch hour in Nome, and the lumberjacks jaunting down from the sawmills for their beefsteak and beer were startled by the tiger-faced man who hurled a one pound slug of iodine colored alloy in their midst and shouted in the gutter tongue: "PyrE! You hear me, man? You listen a me, you. PyrE is filthy death for us. Alla us! Grab no guesses, you. Make 'em tell you about PyrE, is all!"

To Dagenham, Y'ang-Yeovil and others jaunting in after him, as always, seconds too late, he shouted: "Tokyo. Imperial stage!" He disappeared a split second before their shots reached him.

It was nine o'clock of a crisp, winey morning in Tokyo, and the morning rush hour crowd milling around the Imperial stage alongside the carp ponds was paralyzed by a tiger-faced Samurai who appeared and hurled a slug of curious metal and unforgettable warnings and admonitions at them.

Foyle continued to Bangkok where it was pouring rain, and Delhi where a monsoon raged . . . always pursued in his mad-dog course. In Baghdad it was three in the morning and the night-club crowd and pub crawlers who stayed a perpetual half hour ahead of closing time around the world, cheered him alcoholically. In Paris and again in London it was midnight and the mobs on the Champs Élysées and in Piccadilly Circus were galvanized by Foyle's appearance and passionate exhortation.

Having led his pursuers three-quarters of the way around the world in fifty minutes, Foyle permitted them to overtake him in London. He permitted them to knock him down, take the ILI safe from his arms, count the remaining slugs of PyrE, and slam the safe shut.

"There's enough left for a war. Plenty left for destruction . . . annihilation

. . . if you dare." He was laughing and sobbing in hysterical triumph. "Millions for defense, but not one cent for survival."

"D'you realize what you've done, you damned killer?" Dagenham shouted.

"I know what I've done."

"Nine pounds of PyrE scattered around the world! One thought and we'll— How can we get it back without telling them the truth? For God's sake, Yeo, keep that crowd back. Don't let them hear this."

"Impossible."

"Then let's jaunte."

"No," Foyle roared. "Let them hear this. Let them hear everything."

"You're insane, man. You've handed a loaded gun to children."

"Stop treating them like children and they'll stop behaving like children. Who the hell are you to play monitor?"

"What are you talking about?"

"Stop treating them like children. Explain the loaded gun to them. Bring it all out into the open." Foyle laughed savagely. "I've ended the last star-chamber conference in the world. I've blown the last secret wide open. No more secrets from now on. . . . No more telling the children what's best for them to know. . . . Let 'em all grow up. It's about time."

"Christ, he *is* insane."

"Am I? I've handed life and death back to the people who do the living and dying. The common man's been whipped and led long enough by driven men like us. . . . Compulsive men . . . Tiger men who can't help lashing the world before them. We're all tigers, the three of us, but who the hell are we to make decisions for the world just because we're compulsive? Let the world make its own choice between life and death. Why should we be saddled with the responsibility?"

"We're not saddled," Y'ang-Yeovil said quietly. "We're driven. We're forced to seize the responsibility that the average man shirks."

"Then let him stop shirking it. Let him stop tossing his duty and guilt onto the shoulders of the first freak who comes along grabbing at it. Are we to be scapegoats for the world forever?"

"Damn you!" Dagenham raged. "Don't you realize that you can't trust people? They don't know enough for their own good."

"Then let them learn or die. We're all in this together. Let's live together or die together."

"D'you want to die in their ignorance? You've got to figure out how we can get those slugs back without blowing everything wide open."

"No. I believe in them. I was one of them before I turned tiger. They can all turn uncommon if they're kicked awake like I was."

Foyle shook himself and abruptly jaunted to the bronze head of Eros, fifty feet above the counter of Piccadilly Circus. He perched precariously and bawled: "Listen a me, all you! Listen, man! Gonna sermonize, me. Dig this, you!"

He was answered with a roar.

"You pigs, you. You goof like pigs, is all. You got the most in you, and you use the least. You hear me, you? Got a million in you and spend pennies.

Got a genius in you and think crazies. Got a heart in you and feel empties. All a you. Every you . . ."

He was jeered. He continued with the hysterical passion of the possessed.

"Take a war to make you spend. Take a jam to make you think. Take a challenge to make you great. Rest of the time you sit around lazy, you. Pigs, you! All right, God damn you! I challenge you, me. Die or live and be great. Blow yourselves to Christ gone or come and find me, Gully Foyle, and I make you men. I make you great. I give you the stars."

He disappeared.

He jaunted up the geodesic lines of space-time to an Elsewhere and an Elsewhen. He arrived in chaos. He hung in a precarious para-Now for a moment and then tumbled back into chaos.

"*It can be done,*" he thought. "*It must be done.*"

He jaunted again, a burning spear flung from unknown into unknown, and again he tumbled back into a chaos of para-space and para-time. He was lost in Nowhere.

"*I believe,*" he thought. "*I have faith.*"

He jaunted again and failed again.

"*Faith in what?*" he asked himself, adrift in limbo.

"*Faith in faith,*" he answered himself. "*It isn't necessary to have something to believe in. It's only necessary to believe that somewhere there's something worthy of belief.*"

He jaunted for the last time and the power of his willingness to believe transformed the para-Now of his random destination into a real . . .

NOW: Rigel in Orion, burning blue-white, five hundred and forty light years from earth, ten thousand times more luminous than the sun, a cauldron of energy circled by thirty-seven massive planets . . . Foyle hung, freezing and suffocating in space, face to face with the incredible destiny in which he believed, but which was still inconceivable. He hung in space for a blinding moment, as helpless, as amazed, and yet as inevitable as the first gilled creature to come out of the sea and hang gulping on a primeval beach in the dawn-history of life on earth.

He space-jaunted, turning para-Now into . . .

NOW: Vega in Lyra, an AO star twenty-six light years from earth, burning bluer than Rigel, planetless, but encircled by swarms of blazing comets whose gaseous tails scintillated across the blue-black firmament . . .

And again he turned now into NOW: Canopus, yellow as the sun, gigantic, thunderous in the silent wastes of space at last invaded by a creature that once was gilled. The creature hung, gulping on the beach of the universe, nearer death than life, nearer the future than the past, ten leagues beyond the wide world's end. It wondered at the masses of dust, meteors, and motes that girdled Canopus in a broad, flat ring like the rings of Saturn and of the breadth of Saturn's orbit . . .

NOW: Aldeberan in Taurus, a monstrous red star of a pair of stars whose sixteen planets wove high velocity ellipses around their gyrating parents. He was hurling himself through space-time with growing assurance . . .

NOW: Antares, an M1 red giant, paired like Aldeberan, two hundred and fifty light years from earth, encircled by two hundred and fifty planetoids of the size of Mercury, of the climate of Eden . . .

And lastly . . . NOW.

He was drawn to the womb of his birth. He returned to the "Nomad," now welded into the mass of the Sargasso asteroid, home of the lost Scientific People who scavenged the spaceways between Mars and Jupiter . . . home of Joseph who had tattooed Foyle's tiger face and mated him to the girl, Moira.

He was back aboard "Nomad."

Gully Foyle is my name
And Terra is my nation.
Deep space is my dwelling place,
The stars my destination.

The girl, Moira, found him in his tool locker aboard "Nomad," curled in a tight foetal ball, his face hollow, his eyes burning with divine revelation. Although the asteroid had long since been repaired and made airtight, Foyle still went through the motions of the perilous existence that had given birth to him years before.

But now he slept and meditated, digesting and encompassing the magnificence he had learned. He awoke from reverie to trance and drifted out of the locker, passing Moira with blind eyes, brushing past the awed girl who stepped aside and sank to her knees. He wandered through the empty passages and returned to the womb of the locker. He curled up again and was lost.

She touched him once; he made no move. She spoke the name that had been emblazoned on his face. He made no answer. She turned and fled to the interior of the asteroid, to the holy of holies in which Joseph reigned.

"My husband has returned to us," Moira said.

"Your husband?"

"The god-man who almost destroyed us."

Joseph's face darkened with anger.

"Where is he? Show me!"

"You will not hurt him?"

"All debts must be paid. Show me."

Joseph followed her to the locker aboard "Nomad" and gazed intently at Foyle. The anger in his face was replaced by wonder. He touched Foyle and spoke to him; there was still no response.

"You cannot punish him," Moira said. "He is dying."

"No," Joseph answered quietly. "He is dreaming. I, a priest, know these dreams. Presently he will awaken and read to us, his people, his thoughts."

"And then you will punish him."

"He has found it already in himself," Joseph said.

He settled down outside the locker. The girl, Moira, ran up the twisted corridors and returned a few moments later with a silver basin of warm water and a silver tray of food. She bathed Foyle gently and then set the tray before him as an offering. Then she settled down alongside Joseph . . . alongside the world . . . prepared to await the awakening.